I0640867

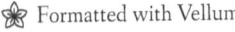

For those of us breaking the cycle.

PART OF THE SHIFTED WORLD UNIVERSE

ISLA ELRICK

BLOOD OF MY BLOOD

GUARDIANS OF THE FAE GATE
BOOK III

CONTENT WARNINGS

This book features a plot device in which an inoculation is used for nefarious purposes. In real life, I do not condone or associate myself with the "anti-vax" movement.

The book features violence typical of a dark fantasy setting, as well as:

- sexual harassment, mentions of sexual assault
- intense scenes involving forced proximity to the villain
- spousal abuse (not the MCs), implied underage marriage
- cannibalism, ingestion of blood
- major character death, mentions of sibling/family death, autistic PTSD heroine
- military and war imagery, mentions of genocide and forced assimilation, burning of villages, subjugation of an ethnic group, mentions of servitude slavery
- References to wildfires, burn injuries
- references to menstruation and uterine illness, miscarriage (thematic; no character miscarriage),

imagery of premature children, zombie-like creatures
that reference all these themes
- intense scenes involving an eleven-year-old child,
rejection of a parent by a child, themes of adoptive vs
birth parents, child-stealing/kidnapping, child abuse,
medical abuse, bodily harm to a child (he's okay)
- captivity and torture, loss of limbs, maxillofacial
disfigurement, starvation, unreality, fungal growth,
living entombment, long falls into bodies of water
- References to terminal illness and life-support
systems
- bodily harm to animals (a pig and some birds) by the
villain
- one CNC (consensual-non-consent) scene of
FMC/MMC; FMC in the dominant role
- binding/BDSM with barbed wire (FMC again in
dominant role), orgasm denial by FMC
- Sex scene where MMC is stuck in a tree

If you need more details for specific warnings, don't hesitate to
reach out to me via email or through social media.

PRONUNCIATION GUIDE

Disclaimer: While I am proud of my Irish heritage, I am American and not an Irish speaker, so take my interpretations of these pronunciations with a grain of salt. I have based them off information available to me about current Connacht dialect. My intention in including Irish words is never to disrespect this wonderful, living, and vibrant culture. If you see a mistake, I urge you to contact me. Note also that, in the thousands of years after the Shift, certain meanings and pronunciations may have changed!

Places and things
    Tuath - TOO-uh
    Gréine - GRAIN-eh
    Bealtaine - B'YAHL-ten-eh
    Geatacoill - GA-teh-KY'ehl
    Fraochgleann - FREE-augh-gl'AHN
    Éire - EY-rreh
    Éirin - EY-rren
    Aquila - ah-KEY-la
    Aquilan - ah-KEY-lan
    Westminia - west-MINI-uh

Gealach - G'YAHL-augh
Cuanacht -k'wah-NOCK-tuh
Tirconnell - tehrr-CONN-ehl
Numirabia - Noomi-RABE-ia
Ogham - OWE-uhm
Fianna - f'YEN-eh
Abhan - AU-en
Dobhránta - duh-VRON-teh
Athadhrai- AH-tag-rye
Siabhair – shuh-vair
Muvane – MUH-van-eh
Corcach - CORE-caugh
Béaleire - B'YAH-ey-rreh
Domhan – DOW'in

Sayings

Droch-fhuil - drough f'wehl
Sea - sha
Fuil - f'wehl
Wean - wayne
Sasanacha -
A chara (form of address) - ah kgha-rra
Mo chara (descriptor) - muh kgha-rra

Characters

Mave - mave (like pave)
Hiberos - high-BARE-os
Eytine - EH-teen
Orlaith - Or-LAYTH
Gwynedd - GWIN-eth (as in the *th* in *father*)
Gaius - GUY-us
Helius - HEEL-ee-us
Sergia - SAYR-gee-uh
Faelon - FAE-lon
Lucastos - loo-CAHST-os
Lupe - LOOP-ey

Drusilla - droos-ILL-uh
Uaine - oo'WEN-yeh
Erivon - AIR-iv-on
Shemoabiri - sheh-moh-ahb-EER-ee
Tali - TAH-lee
Ottavian - aw-TAVE-ian
Brianne - bree-EHN
Iain - EE-in (like Ian)
Agorix - ah-GOR-icks
Westerus - WEST-er-us
Alasdair - AL-iss-ter
Manan - MAH-nen
Felis - FEE-liss
Tatius - TAHT-ee-us
Thomasia - tome-ah-SEE-ah
Lorbog - LORE-bog
Keira - KEE-ra
Paik - pahk
Tagh - tag
Joa – JOE-uh
Eilliv – EYE-leev
Muiri - moo-EAR-ee
Caoimhe - KWEE-vah
Aoife - EE-fah
Analivia - anna-LIV-ee-uh
Avelaval - ah-VELL-ave-all
Airgeadsnáithe - AHR-eh-gidt-snauh-huh

I

Over night, it seemed, autumn was gone, replaced by a winter so frigid and terrible no Éirin under sixty years old could recall one like it. The city at Bile Cernunnos stood as frozen as the river Garri protecting it from the south. The leaves of the great tree shriveled and wilted, though they did not fall; the province's farmers either disappeared from market entirely or came begging the king for aid; herds were called in, children kept close, hunters sent desperately into the cold; fires were tended, but there were never enough blankets. The people of what was left of Sallach fought day by day simply to survive. Worries of the invading Aquilan Empire were buried under the crushing weight of hunger. Fears that they would renege on their ceasefire lay dormant under ice.

It pained me to see my people suffer. But for myself, the change hardly registered. Though it had been hunger to kill me and Orlaith when we'd ventured into this world, its gnawing ache seemed so trivial now. And as for cold, I did not feel it.

There was a burning coal in my stomach and a hollow where my heart should be.

Enough. The pain. Let me sleep now.

Everything will turn out right in the end.

For weeks, Uaine and Solma did their due diligence trying to keep me in bed so my palms could heal. *His* regenerative magic and what little the druids could spare between dying warriors did me good; the rest was up to me. For a while, the skin was dead and dark as leather before peeling and turning bright pink, and by late winter, my palms were functional if not healed.

My carers knew better than to try and keep me abed any longer.

I spent most of my time outside, sometimes the only soul out of doors for miles, drawing my bow and firing arrows into straw targets again and again. These hands, it was like they were all-new to my body. I was like a child learning how to use a bow for the first time, slow and clumsy. But the days and nights passed, the bleak sun and the dim moon chasing each other above my head, each trying to catch the other, so often sharing the same sky yet never close enough to touch. Never close enough to meet, to know one another. Not truly, not for long.

The never-ending wheel spun, and drawing my bow became as natural to me as blinking, as breathing. My only thoughts were of the sun, the moon, how many arrows I had left in my quiver...

And him.

Enough. The pain. Let me sleep now.

Everything will turn out right in the end.

How singularly odd, to mourn someone whose true self you barely got to know. Yet how real this pain was. The bitterest I'd ever felt, perhaps because of that very notion: that we could have been everything, a whole universe that now was nothing but a jumbled collection of half-memories, a scar on my sternum, and a seed lying dormant.

None had tried to speak to me about him, not even Solma and Menecon. They knew better. The humans gave me a wide berth, friends included. I'd long learned to identify the sharp scent of human fear. They were afraid. Of me. Perhaps they noted the lack of spark in my pupils or felt the vacuity of my soul seeping out like cold through the gap of a door frame. Warnings that the full depth of my guilt and grief released might kill us all.

The only person who had not given up on me—who seemed almost to thrive in the density of my misery, and spoke of Hiberos as though he lived still—was Ruadan. The commander of the Gallowglass and his strange, ghostly presence seemed to fit in negative space in a way no other person, fae or human, did.

Coincidentally, he was not a bad archer, and was happy to help me learn, in my new agile body, the basics of acrobatics and athletics. He taught me to shoot, to dodge, and to flip, his voice soft and pleasant as always. "Pray, don't flatter me. Not all of the knowledge is my own," he said when I asked him about it, his silver eyes twinkling. "The dead carry wisdom as old as this land."

I never asked him which of my ancestors he spoke with. At the start of my journey, I'd have cared. I'd have wanted to know who was watching over me. Whoever watched over me, they hadn't done me much good, so it didn't seem to matter. Nothing seemed to matter anymore.

I warned Ruadan as much. He simply accepted my view and taught me to tumble.

Accepting was not a word I thought I'd ever attribute to a Gallowglass, the high king's cold-blooded killers, especially an experienced man nearing the middle of his life. Yet he was as unpretentious and tolerant a friend as I'd ever had. So, if he really wanted to be in the training yard with me, I'd let him.

Arrow. Nock. Draw. Aim. Breathe. Release.

Arrow. Nock. Draw. Aim. Breathe. Release.

Arrow. Nock. Draw...

When I emptied my quiver of arrows, I summoned ones of pure lunar magic. They slammed into my targets, spitting shimmering dust before fading back into the ether. At first, I had tried to use little magic among my kinsmen; though magic made up our world and blessed our druidfolk, Éirins were raised to distrust fae, for good reason. Often, I caught people glaring at me through their windows. At first, feeling out of place among my own people was too much to bear. Now, as with most things, I'd become numb to the sensation. Besides, these humans would have to get used to fae magic. After all, the Lunar Kingdom was our ally now, and it would be their unfathomably deep, mostly untapped well of power helping to protect what remained of Sallach. The Éirins were stubborn, but they were good people, ultimately intent on doing the right thing. Once they got to know the lunar fae, they'd see that they weren't like their vicious Court counterparts.

Of course, that required the fae actually spending time in Éire. To them, this place, especially during the winter, was inhospitable; the heartiest and strongest-willed of their army were garrisoned at the new Moon Gate a half-mile due south, but most waited in the Underland. Every night that passed with the fae majority still hiding there embittered King Manan and his people.

I should beg Orlaith to do something. Since the battle for Bile Cernunnos, the withering plague had spread outward from Geatacoill at an alarming rate, crawling over the valley like menstrual blood seeping into a rag. And when it spread here, it spread in the Underland, too; soon, there would be no haven in which to seclude her people. But for the past few months, all the will seemed to have drained out of me like green sapped from the bilé's leaves; the thought of arguing with my sister, with the wraith of Eytine, gave me a headache that bit into the marrow of my spine.

Sleep was no release. I avoided it. The magic of the leylight worms, and my connection to those I'd shared them with, seemed to become more potent each time I closed my eyes. Facing Gaius for another night, whether I was his slave, his son, or his spouse ... it was breaking me down night by night. Often, I woke vomiting.

"Mave, look," the Gallowglass said behind me, drawing me blessedly from the spiral that thinking of Gaius began.

He spoke so rarely I was keen to answer. "What?"

Rather than his reply, the furious snorting of a hog caught my ear. I lowered my bow and turned just in time to see Conan the woad-painted pig sit with his full weight right in Ruadan's lap. The rogue grunted and said, "This."

My heart softened, the clenched fist in my stomach easing. If there was only one thing in this world I still could count on, it was that Conan would bring a smile to my face, however foreign that expression felt now. I racked my bow and approached, sticking my ice-cold fingers between the pig's fat rolls. He looked at me forlornly but did not protest beyond that.

"Where did you come from?" I asked, and though I was sure I knew the answer, I did not look up. Where Uaine was, Conan followed, so the councilor must be nearby. I did not necessarily want to see him today; I was feeling too raw. Though I cared for Uaine deeply, his becoming a politician had not exactly cleansed him of those opinions that had caused us to butt heads ten years ago. He still sympathized with the Aquilan foot-soldiers, especially the foreign conscripts—still believed there was a place in Éire for Aquilan merchants and tradesmen. I was uncertain that giving the Empire an inch would protect the mile. But he no longer served them. He believed in a free and sovereign Éire, the northern territories included. With so much stacked against us, that was all I could ask.

As if he read my thoughts, Ruadan glanced round in my stead. "Hm ... no Uaine."

Conan snorted in reply. Curiously, I removed my fingers from his wrinkles to get a better look at him. Something was fastened to his hock with a leather thong. "Hello, what's this?"

I untied and unrolled the small slip of paper. At this point, I recognized Uaine's handwriting. New to reading as I was, it took me a moment to decipher the mix of Albionic letters and Ogham-like hatching. *Come to library. Fae emissary looking for you.*

Ugh. There were very few reasons the fae would send an emissary for me. Either my sister needed me for something, or—

My one, lonesome heart kicked my ribs. Missing its twin again. With a wince, I slid my hand into my coat, under my tunic, fingering the scar left by Solma's lancet.

No matter how I tried to ease the misery, no matter how diligently I tried not to think of Hiberos and of that night and my secret, desperate ritual in the grove, there was no reprieve. Not for more than a minute. The image of his heart—the glowing, pulsating, filigreed fruit of the moon—was tattooed on my mind.

When I'd torn it from my rib cage and buried it in the loam, had I planted a seed like Ruadan suggested, or had I lain Hiberos to rest for the last time? The months had worn my shard of optimism to a dull stone. There was nothing growing in that grove.

Unless...

I forgot Conan, forgot Ruadan, forgot my bow, and ran to the bilé library.

Though winter had dulled the color of the bilé's bark, the interior was still lacquered perfection. As I raced through the winding root hallways and up to the second floor of the trunk, my footsteps clicked as though the floor was marble. Where the oaken walls were not carved with stories of the gods and our people, they were decorated with tapestries and banners. The library entrance was an archway of willow branches trained to weave through the oak, each knot decorated with mementos of craftsmen, storytellers, and druids long-past. The library itself was one enormous hall with long oak tables, private niches, and three mezzanines that stretched high above my head. Even in the winter, sunlight poured through the massive stained glass windows; in the evening, floating motes of druid-light followed each scholar.

Library was something of a misnomer, because, considering the size of the place, there were very few books. Most of those were foreign publications, and I wasn't certain if anyone apart from druids could actually read them. The remainder of the space was more like a reliquary housing magical artifacts, Ogham rune-stones, and ancient art. In general, Éire did not have a strong written history. Ours was oral, and that had suited us well. Better, in fact, than many peoples who'd scrambled to preserve their cultures after the Shift, when it was said dragons dominated humanity. Gwynedd had told me once that even compared to the Albionites just across the channel, our spoken language was uniquely intact. As long as we spoke, our history could not be destroyed. Not by the dragons, and certainly not by the Aquilans.

In the center of the library, not far from the archway, stood Uaine and a fae. Like most fae, she was tall and wore silver armor. When I entered, she turned her head. It was Joa, one of the owners of the public house Ashling had once frequented. I remembered someone mentioning that after the battle for Bile

Cernunnos, she'd enlisted while her shy wife, Eilliv, tended to the pub. Though I still struggled to reconcile the long-dead Princess Ashling with the Mave I was now, Joa recognized me as a friend, and I didn't have the heart to tell her otherwise.

Yet, her usually chipper demeanor was dour, and rather panicked if I wasn't mistaken. She held no missive. Not a summons, then, but an emergency.

"Orlaith?" I asked, although somewhere deep inside, I already knew this was about Hiberos.

"Menecon sent me," Joa said. "You must come quickly, straight away. Something in the heartgrove has ... changed."

I COULD COUNT the number of times I'd returned to the Lunar Palace on one hand. Why bother? Orlaith didn't want to hear my opinions on Faelon or on crossing the veil. It wasn't that she and Erivon did not understand the gravity of the situation in which we found ourselves; more they misjudged how their commanding from beyond the veil was perceived by the Éirin kings. To the lunar fae, their king and queen were being responsible leaders, staying off the front lines. In others' eyes, they were being cowards.

I'd come to better understand their position, at least, but I had no energy for arguments.

The heartgrove was the only reason I ever passed through the newly erected Moon Gate. How many hours had I spent stretched across his resting place, letting the rain fall over us? Basking in the silence of this place felt like rotting right alongside my soulbind, my Hiberos. I wanted nothing more than to surrender to the soil.

However, a bad thaw and flooding roads had kept me away for many nights, despite the verse still rattling around in my head. One of Hiberos's last poetry lessons: *From the cold grave that holds you, I never shall sever; were your hands twin'd in mine, love, I'd hold them forever. My fondest, my fairest, we may now sleep together, for I smell of the earth and am worn by the weather.*

Joa was right. The grove had changed.

When I stepped into the copse of trees, the smell hit me first. A putrid, tangy smell as familiar to me now as the scent of my own skin. Menstrual rags left in the sun. Sweaty, heavy, metallic, and unpleasantly sweet. Then I noticed the lingering fog. Thick, white—the same fog Orlaith and I had walked through together moons ago, looking for the source of the starving panthers. The fog that hid the fomori.

Finally, my face numbed as I beheld the swampy, blood-orange withering on the outskirts of the clearing. Its spongy surface almost seemed to pulsate, to rise and fall as though the land itself were taking labored breaths. Its tendrils crept along the earth, inward toward the center like an infection through veins.

The center, right where I had buried...

I rushed past the waiting Menecon without thought—before I even fully processed that the center of the heartgrove, that grave over which I'd lain for hours and hours, had changed, too.

Something was jutting up from the moss.

I fell to my knees before it, my shaking hands hovering just short of touching it. It was a thick, woody sapling, its soft bark veined with opalescent magic. But if one looked past the young leaves unfurling from its branches, it...

It looked like a hand, spread, frozen, poised as if reaching out to grab something. Two of the "fingers" were short and incomplete, but the shape of it, the line and gesture ... it was so lifelike that I was convinced it would seize me at any second. I almost wanted it to. I almost wanted to slip my hand into its palm and let it drag me into the underworld.

The power emanating from the sapling sang to me. My body recognized the sensation before I did. The feeling of an answer just out of reach, of a memory just thin enough to be obscured; the feeling of waking from a dream with an unspeakable sense of loss; the feeling of yearning for something that had never existed, that had never belonged to you. A love too deeply heart-wrenching to be a mere figment, though a figment it was.

Pressure. Heat. A purring breath as deep and ancient as roots. The scent of earth, of sun-warmed moss and blackberries.

My lonesome heartbeat stopped. I grabbed the sapling, wrapping my fingers round its palm, and a lance of pain shocked me. I must have nicked myself on a thorn or twig, because a thin rivulet of blood flowed down my palm, over my wrist, and dripped into the earth below.

Then a jolt of potent magic burned up my arm, and like flashes of light, thoughts were impressed upon me: *Creation. Destruction. Break the cycle.*

My vision went white.

I woke face down in the moss, the world around me so brutally loud that I could not think.

Slowly, sensation returned to my limbs. With breaths as thin and tenuous as spiders' webs, I lifted myself to hands and knees and tried to get my bearings.

Denizens of the lunar realm lay scattered around me, some still unconscious, others just waking up. The Underland groaned with a voice from hell. The endless grove of our kingdom was ... sundered. Ridges of iridescent stone burst from the earth where the bedrock below us had shifted and overlapped violently. The city, it was nowhere to be seen. Only the spires of our palace were visible, jutting up from a massive sinkhole in the center of the valley. A scream caught in my throat, coming out only as a barely audible whimper. Nearly on all fours, I scrambled to the edge of the sinkhole to assess the damage. The streets and dwellings of the Lunar Kingdom were mostly intact, thank the Moon, but they lay so far below that it was impossible to imagine us ever bringing the city back to the surface.

I raised my eyes to the sky, the cursed sky where the problem had begun in the first place. Like a shattered mirror, the perpetual twilight of our paradise was broken, its shards drifting. In between, an ocean of roiling blue, pink, and purple magic. It was brighter than anything I'd ever seen, writhing and snapping like nests of vipers, and it was accompanied by a calamitous wind that ripped at my hair and clothing. Something stronger than the gods, stronger than creation and destruction, had cracked our plane like an egg and was trying to invade.

Yet as fae and others rose and joined me and followed my gaze, the dusk fought back.

Trembling as from great effort, the darkness drew together bit by bit like a ladder stitch pulled taut. The universe itself seemed to screech in agony as the cracks diminished ... diminished ... and finally disappeared.

The silence that followed was deafening.

The first sound that broke it was feet frantically pounding the grass. A moment later, Orlaith appeared beside me, nude save for shredded silken scraps. With a ragged sob, she stabbed a finger toward the sky. "It's gone!"

I followed her gesture, thinking at first that she must mean the disaster that had nearly torn us apart.

The heavens were empty. The moon was missing.

2

Menecon had been good to come to me first when they'd discovered the blight spreading into the heartgrove. Up to this point, against their better judgment, they had kept my desperate ritual and the history behind it a secret. Now, they gave me the luxury of preparing myself before confessing my crime to the king and queen. There was no other option. If they knew about the grove, and if I asked them to protect it, it would come out one way or another.

I entered the sunken throne room, thinking perhaps Orlaith and Erivon were still holding court—fae timekeeping still eluded me—but there was nothing to see apart from servants and a few lingering courtiers. Instead, I found Orlaith in the terrace garden of the royal spire, sitting in a secluded area beneath a faewillow tree.

Erivon was nowhere to be seen. She sat on a plush sofa, humming a familiar tune with her head bent over something in her lap, one hand holding it in place and the other working. Sewing. She was sewing. My heart softened slightly; even if she was not Eytine, she was my sister, and seeing her embroiled in a handicraft reminded me as much. She was so beautiful.

For a moment, I forgot my worry, simply curious what she was doing. I ventured another quiet step forward, but all I could make out was a lump of white fabric before, abruptly, her humming stopped and her head snapped up. She hid her materials under a nearby velvet cushion and stood. "My Ashling!"

"All right, Orlaith."

She met me half way and embraced me. Even in her scent there was a hint of Eytine. It was enough to relax me despite the argument I knew would come.

"How are you feeling?" she asked carefully. It was far from the light lecture I usually received about staying in the Goneland rather than here. Perhaps Erivon had spoken to her about that, or perhaps she'd finally come to realize that reprimanding me only drove me further away.

"I'm..." As much as I wanted to make polite conversation with her, I could not lie to her. Gritting my teeth, I admitted, "Not well. There's an issue. Menecon summoned me from Éire..."

Orlaith frowned, no doubt wondering why they had summoned *me* of all people, but gestured to the sitting area. "Please, make yourself comfortable."

I sat—a bit awkwardly with the bulk of my gear—and sucked my bottom lip between my teeth. Perhaps hoping to buy myself a few extra seconds, I nodded at the cushion now askew next to her. "What are you making?"

Her face turned a deeper shade of seafoam. "Nothing. It hardly matters now. Please tell me what's happened."

Considering the way she'd rushed to hide it, I doubted it was *nothing*, but very well. I'd run out of time. "The withering plague is spreading."

"In Sallach? Yes, Solma has told me."

"No, here. It's crept closer, into a grove." I pointed in its general direction with my chin.

Orlaith's brow drew tight, and she brought a hand to her throat. "Close to the Lunar Kingdom? Mother Moon save us. Can it truly be spreading so swiftly?"

Here I hesitated. "It is a ways from the city yet, but yes, certainly spreading. The grove..." I cleared my throat. "The grove holds significance to me. I need— That is, if you would permit... Menecon has mentioned that Gatewright Owalir and their people have been 'patching holes,' so to speak. Stopping the blight's progress in certain areas."

"In certain vital areas. It is necessary work, if we're to keep the gates open for now." She glanced furtively at the cushion. "I still wonder if it would have been better to..." Tension hummed. Rather than finish her thought, she shook her head, took a deep breath, and spread a palm. "But what is vital about this grove? What do you mean *significance* to you? I would expect you to be tending to the significant places in Éire, not here."

The resentment in her tone was evident. She'd made a valiant effort, but she could not hide her hurt over my decision. Even being a fae queen, Orlaith had that in common with Eytine: one way or another, they would let you know damn well what they thought.

I took a deep breath of my own. "It holds significance to me and Hiberos."

It was the first time I'd spoken his name aloud since his death. It felt profane to do so, as though I spoke the name of an unknowable being who should not be disturbed.

"I see ... I understand." Orlaith softened, searching for words my watery gut told me would be a rejection. "I am not certain we can reallocate any gatewrights. My understanding of the architecture of the Underland and its veil and how it relates to the Moon Gates is limited, but there are certain places that must hold first. I can ask, but there is no guarantee." To her credit, she was obviously distraught. "I am so sorry, my Ashling. Hiberos was the oldest, dearest friend to our family, and I know what you meant to one another."

Bitter tears threatened the back of my throat; I straightened, gripping my knees tightly. "You have no idea what we were to one another," I managed to whisper. Not an accusation or a condemnation, not a biting comment, just a plainly stated, melancholy fact.

She was silent for an extended moment before saying, "Ashling...? What do you mean?" When I did not answer, she pressed, "What's going on with this grove, exactly?"

I hung my head. "Hiberos... Some time before you and I left the Underland, he and I did a soulfasting ceremony."

Her expression told me she did not know what that was but that she was beginning to understand the gravity of the situation. I continued despite the color flooding her face.

"A lost ritual, found etched on limestone ruins on the outskirts of the Underland," I murmured. "A secret wedding. It united our souls. I cut him open and consumed his heart."

Her cloudy opal eyes widened. "Those carvings in his flesh. That scar. He never would tell Erivon where they came from."

"His heart lived in me. Inside my rib cage. When I was reborn here, I began to notice its beat. It was strong even after his death. That was when I wondered—wondered if the heart could be more. If it was a seed. If I could extract it and—"

Orlaith covered her mouth, then transferred her shaking hand to her forehead. "Gealach's mercy, Ashling, no. Tell me he isn't planted in that grove. Tell me anything else."

I shrugged in defeat.

My sister jolted out of her chair and paced for a few seconds, then sat back down, then stood again. "You— How could— If he —" She restarted her sentence a handful of times but never found the words. "Ashling, there—"

Judging by the color of her face and tightness of her jaw, she wanted to shout at me, but somehow, she managed to contain her anger long enough that it was replaced by sorrow, then fear. Finally, she knelt before me and gripped my elbows, staring up into my face like a mother about to tell her child to *run*.

"Sister, the goddess gave you another chance. Make no mistake, dead though she may be, her spirit lingers on in this world and in the next. Had she willed you never be reborn, it would be so. She forgave you. She *warned* you. She did not want you touching what was forbidden, what was *hers*, and you've made the same mistake. Twice." Her grip tightened. She shook. "I cannot lose you again. Please, promise me that even if this seed takes and he returns, you'll stay away from him."

My stomach dropped to the flagstones. In this moment, she looked so much like Eytine. I wanted to obey. If Hiberos did return, perhaps it was better for both of us that we keep our distance. But I wasn't certain what she was asking of me was possible. After all, we had already tried. The magic of our bond seemed to survive all alchemy, all worlds, all cycles. It overpowered others' will every time. Even that of a goddess.

"In all my months living in this body, I haven't retrieved even one memory of Gealach," I said. "I find it difficult to believe I ever knew her. How can I obey her without question?"

"The memories will return to you." She pressed my hand, although my confession still left her shaken. "They must. She is our mother."

"If she's our loving mother, do you truly think she is punishing me and Hiberos? For—" I could not seem to get the words *being in love* off my tongue. "Where does that end? She is dead. Are all her Guardians doomed to be lonely forever?"

Orlaith's patience seemed to run thin. She stood, her face hardening, the moon-moth wings on her back twitching in agitation. "If you and Hiberos were meant to be together, you would be. Instead, you performed a ritual that was not meant for mere fae and hid your marriage from us all. Those hardly sound like the actions of innocent people. When you asked for our blessing, there was a *reason* we rejected you. A reason *Hiberos* rejected you. And rather than accept that, you fled our realm entirely, and got us both killed when I followed. From the beginning, this love affair with Hiberos has been fueled by—by *selfishness*."

"Eytine—"

"When are you going to think about the well-being of those around you? Your people, your community?" She spread her arms in exasperation. "Rather than swanning off to the Goneland? You are needed here, you know. You are loved *here*."

Ah, there it was. "The folk I've remained close to in the

Goneland *are* my people. They were yours, too, once. They need me. They love me."

"Tell me to my face that the humans love hosting a fae princess, Ashling. Look me in the eye and tell me everyone treats you the same way they always have!"

I opened my mouth and closed it. Paused. "Why are you *screaming* at me?"

"We were supposed to follow each other." Despite her fury, I felt her pain keenly. "Always. You go where I go, I go where you go. I *waited* for you, I will always wait for you, but please ... I cannot follow you back there. I cannot take another step further. *Stay with me.*" Her voice became thick, unmanageable emotions like a vise on her windpipe. "Since the day we were born, in this world and the one beyond the gates, I have lived for others, I have served, given my all, asked for nothing..."

Usually, I found that people who claimed to have given everything to others were self-aggrandizing at best, purposefully manipulating at worst. But Eytine, she really had given up everything, even romance and children, to help raise me. She'd accepted her role as a community servant early, and though our clan had always respected her, cherished her, loved her, her choices had never really been her own. Duty had ruled her until death. But now that she had everything, even a new body—now that she was living a dream in a fairy-tale realm, what did she lack?

"One thing," she whispered, her anger once again diminished to sorrow. "I just need one thing that remains mine. Not you, but *us*. Stay with me. Please..."

All at once, it clicked. I knew what she lacked. She'd told me quite plainly.

"Eytine—Orlaith," I corrected, standing to catch her elbow before she could launch into another tirade. "What is this really about?"

She scowled but said nothing, trying desperately to collect her thoughts.

"You defied earthly law," I pressed, "you went through the Gate to be with Erivon. You chose this world. Maybe I choose the

Goneland. Why does that disturb you so much? Why are you so concerned about where anyone belongs apart from yourself?" I shook my head. "This isn't about the danger in the Goneland, or me and Hiberos, or the Goddess. This is about Faelon ... what he might choose."

Her expression fractured; there was no use in trying to conceal it. The name alone, spoken aloud, changed her entire demeanor. She went from a righteous queen to something tender and brittle, curling in on herself, clutching her forearms tightly. My heart broke.

"You can speak to me about it," I ventured into the silence. "We might figure something out. Plan a way for you to meet with him. Perhaps if he heard the truth from your mouth, or if he met you—"

I reached to take her shoulders gently, but she dodged me, snapping, "Don't. Don't speak as though you understand my situation. Don't speak as though you know what it is to have your one and only son be raised by another woman. The wife of the monster who killed you—"

"I could speak to him for you. I have a way to—"

But before I could tell her about my connection to Faelon, she ran from the garden, her silks billowing in her wake. I was alone, sick to my core, with only the fluttering moon moths for company.

As I followed one with my eyes, it landed on the velvet cushion. I blew an errant curl from my eyes and stalked forward, tossing the pillow aside and unfolding the lump of fabric Orlaith had hidden from me. It was soft in my hands, and it unfurled like silk made from dreams.

A quilt.

She had only completed three squares so far. One, a silver birch growing in a valley. Two, a wolf pup and its mother. Three, a moon moth carrying a huge, lustrous pearl. Each stitch was so thoughtfully and lovingly placed that this gift could only be for one person.

Was she truly going to say goodbye to him forever?

+☽ ☽ ☽ ☾ ☾+

I LEFT THE TERRACE GARDEN, walking the grounds until I found a private patch of moss surrounded by climbing luna anemones. Here I sat, closed my eyes, and took a deep breath of the Underland's perfumed night air. It really was a lovely place if I set aside the several-stone trunk of angst I'd arrived with. If things with my relations weren't so fraught, I wouldn't mind visiting now and again. Anyway, I'd return to Sallach soon; I was expected for a meeting with King Manan and the other coalition leaders. May as well take a moment to enjoy the realm's beauty.

Given I could sit still long enough to do so, which seemed less likely by the second.

I was about to rise and return to the grove, see what might be done to allay the corruption without the gatewrights' help, when a male figure appeared between the curtains of jasmine. "There you are!"

I recognized his deep sapphire skin and unique-for-a-fae, hedgehog-esque haircut. Oishin, the jewelrysmith who'd stopped me in the street the same day I met Joa. I'd asked him to call me Mave, and he had without question. In his hands, he held a lacquered lavender-wood box.

According to Orlaith, we'd been friends in my past life, and since he was so respectful, I didn't see a need to disappoint him like I disappointed most everyone else. "All right, Oishin."

He wiggled his ears. "You remembered. How are you feeling? We've not seen you for..." He waved his hand; the fae were just as confused about human timekeeping. "You must see wonderful things on the other side."

Whether he'd forgotten about Hiberos or simply didn't think it prudent to bring it up could not be said, but I appreciated his attitude. It was preferable to the lingering gazes of pity and dread I usually received, in both realms. I hadn't considered how they might be adding to my numbness. "Sallach is beautiful country. All of Éire is, but especially Co Cuanacht. If you want to see it, you should come sometime."

Oishin looked tickled by this novel idea. "Really? Do you think the humans would mind my being there?"

"They'll learn you're good people. Humans can just be stand-offish at first, that's all. Much gruffer than lunar fae. But Éirins are friendly, as long as you don't come with cannons and crucifixes." I nodded to his box. "In any case, why were you looking for me?"

"Ah." His cheeks colored a deeper blue. "A homecoming present. I hope that isn't uncouth of me, but your rebirth was the first thing to properly inspire me in ... several centuries. The design of this one simply flowed from me."

I accepted the box. The interior was lined with aubergine silk, and tucked into its glossy pleats was a masterwork in platinum: a necklace large enough to cover my chest throat to breastbone, dotted by large emeralds and smaller opals. The metal gleamed like the moon itself, fine as thread and flowing so intricately and precisely that I was half convinced Oishin had grown it rather than crafted it. Its coils seemed the kind of maths only nature could perfect. That fire and molten metal and pounding hammers could produce something so delicate was more exciting and rare to me than magic itself.

"This is for me?" I asked in disbelief.

"Should I help you put it on? Do you like it?"

"Of course I like it." Much as I didn't want to crush his feelings, arriving at the war room with airs on while hunger ravaged Éire was not a good idea. Not that a denizen of the Underland, where injury and hunger were no more than academic concepts, would even think of such things. *They might have to soon,* said a voice in the back of my mind. Driven out by the blight, the panthers of the wilds were coming closer and closer to the Lunar Kingdom in their search for food. "I'll save this for a special occasion. Do you mind dropping it off in my room?"

Oishin could not hide his disappointment in the set of his ears, but he nodded. "As you wish, Mave."

The fact that he used my name, the one I was accustomed to, without hesitation softened my heart. As he turned to leave, I caught his elbow. "Wait. Can I ask you something?"

His sadness eased; he tilted his head. "Anything."

"My memories are still ... foggy. But we were friends once. You must know all the royal family."

"I reckon every lunar fae knows each other. We have had thousands of years to become acquainted." He smiled sheepishly. "I-I mean, yes, I know them. Although you are—were—my friend, not them."

"*Are* is fine," I reassured him. "Can you tell me, what was my relationship with Orlaith like back then? Were we ever ... at odds?"

"No?" He blinked owlishly. "You were the best of friends. Always in perfect harmony. Why do you ask?"

Rather than answer, I shook my head and tried to dismiss any worry. "I'll bring you with me to Sallach soon, yeah? If you're so curious about it, you ought to see it for yourself." *Before it's wiped off the map*, added the bitter pessimist in me.

Orlaith wanted things to go back to the way they were. But there was no going back. Once the illusion of paradise was shattered, you could never quite fit the pieces together; there was always bound to be a missing sliver. Deep down, she must know that. Deep down, there must be something of Eytine left, or else she wouldn't be so tortured over Faelon. Indeed, if we all had our proper places, fae and human, Underland and Éire, where did a child of both worlds fit in?

Where did I fit in her life, and her in mine?

Could we ever reconcile, not as Ashling or Eytine but as Mave and Orlaith?

When Oishin left, I closed my eyes and felt for the little glowing node at the periphery of my consciousness, the one that symbolized Faelon. Seizing it, I fell down, down, down to the roots connecting us...

...AND WOKE with Gaius's face in mine. The bandage over his right eye had been replaced with an eye-patch, and the slit across his windpipe had healed to a raised white scar. His remaining eye caught the light of the candle he held, turning the clear blue a ghostly yellow.

"Time to wake up," he said with an enthusiasm that Faelon did not feel. The boy groaned and sat up and raised his hands to rub his eyes, but Gaius promptly tapped his hands with a birch crop. Not a swat—not yet—just a warning. "Oh, come now, Lucastos. I have a surprise for you today."

"Yes, Legate, sir." As he stood and began to dress in the near dark, Faelon tried to put as much quickness into his movements as possible. Father went easier on him when he acted eager, even if he made mistakes. But it was getting harder by the day to feign eagerness for something he sort of ... loathed.

No one but Hiberos knew of my connection to Faelon, or Lucastos, or whatever he wanted to be called. I tried to check on him every other day or so, and monitored his little node of consciousness nearly all the time, but it was difficult to witness the way he interacted with Gaius. Somehow, it was more disturbing to me, even, than Nevidaea's suffering. Because he was my nephew, maybe. Or maybe because my mind and body had grown accustomed to the legate's *cruelty*, but his tenderness, encouragement, pride, all those fatherly things? Even if it enclosed his prideful, tyrannical indoctrination, *that* made me squirm.

What Faelon saw of my life in return, it appeared to him as vague dreams only. Those dreams, though he did not understand them, were but a short reprive from his nose-to-the-grindstone life.

It wasn't that he did not *want* to be a good soldier, and son. He did. But every day was the same exhausting routine. Wake up before the sun, run until his legs were swollen. Eat breakfast over language lessons, then sparring and drills with the cadets, all older than him and none friendly. Then sparring and drills with *Father*. Dinner, maybe. Strategy, theory, for hours. Then imperial history —Sergia family history, specifically—deep into the night. A few hours of sleep, and then...

Faelon often felt he was losing his mind. He was always hungry, and always tired. If he fell asleep whilst studying, Father always found him, and he was not such a light hand with the birch crop then.

Once dressed, he followed Gaius down the villa's halls. Thankfully, Drusilla had convinced Father to let him stay here rather than always being in the praetorium. "What's the surprise?" Faelon asked when he could contain it no longer.

But Father did not reprimand him. In fact, he grinned down at him. Which was good ... right? So why, then, did Faelon feel even more on edge than before?

It wasn't a long walk to the Sergia personal armory. Most of Grandfather's old things were kept in here—except his spear, which was in the praetorium office, of course—as well as things collected by Gaius over his time in service. Today, though, there was something new at the far end of the room. A mail shirt, full leather armor, and a short sword.

Faelon's heart leapt, shocked by his mix of emotions. Excitement, pride, tempered by apprehension. He looked at his father for permission, and Gaius motioned for him to investigate at will.

This gear was definitely his. It was all his size, the weight of the sword was just right, and the center of the cross guard was molded into a snarling wolf.

"This is all mine?" he asked, in awe as he fingered the green wool of the cloak that came with it.

"Yours. But that is not the extent of your surprise, Luca."

When Faelon looked at him, Gaius wore an expression he was growing used to. That grim victor's smile I'd come to know so well. "What ... what else?" the boy asked tentatively.

"You'll find out soon enough."

3

The newly established Gate just south of Sallach was a half-moon shape constructed of the same rune-etched stone as the others, albeit far lighter in color and less worn. It was also far larger, its arch soaring twenty-five feet above my head. It wasn't perfect—it often broke down for hours at a time—but its size was ideal for moving troops, supplies, and artillery. And my, did the fae have artillery. Glaive launchers, moonshot arbalests, and something called *screaming stars*, which I'd yet to witness but which sounded like they'd give the Aquilans plenty trouble. They may have no war in their world, but whether one noticed it in the neat squares of their companies, their exacting training regimen, or their vicious technology, their prowess was evident.

Taking a horse, I passed through the comparatively small fae encampment and rode the half-mile to Bile Cernunnos. Despite my atrophied spirit, seeing it still standing calmed me.

Now, to make certain it stayed that way.

The moment I rode up to the great tree—so quiet without half the population—Conan waddled out of a root's shadow and came trapping up to me.

I dismounted to meet him. He carried no message this time, but he no doubt knew where I'd find Uaine, and the rest of the coalition along with him. The hour of the meeting was nigh. "You'll take me to your councilor, yeah? Handsome boy. Special boy."

He snorted aggressively as I scratched him under the chin, but when I tried to urge him to move forward, he planted all four trotters decisively in the snow. He had such dainty little hooves for a creature who was almost wider than he was long.

My soul felt a little lighter. I planted my fists on my hips. "Oh, come on then, what is it?"

Conan sneezed, then made a shrill, grating noise like a saw cutting through wood.

It was no big mystery what he wanted. With a sigh, I reached into a pouch at my belt and produced a handful of hawberries. He gobbled them out of my palm and left a smear of pig snot. My toll paid, I was free to follow him into the bilé.

This was my first time invited to the war room since I'd acted so rashly with the leylight worms. Till now, King Manan had completely forbade me from entering the war room. Drusilla, he seemed to trust, but he was still leery of my connection to Nevidaea. For months, he'd poisoned the well from which our roots drank with false information, feeding me incorrect troop movements. When, time and time again, the Aquilans never took the bait, he finally accepted that Nevidaea did not, in fact, know how to see through my eyes, and was not spying on us the way we were spying on her.

It was an understandable reaction. After all, were I in his place, I would risk my country for nothing, especially not something as trivial as the feelings of a dead friend's adopted daughter. Still, being held at arm's length for this reason among so many other reasons was ... difficult.

I still hadn't told him about Faelon. I'd rather not be ostracized all over again.

As always, most of those within gave me a wide berth. As always, I numbed myself to it. There was one Cuanachtan who recognized me, though, someone who had been too preoccupied to even say hello let alone shun me. I climbed to the second-floor war room and spotted him slumped on a rustic bench, arms crossed over his chest, beaver-skin top hat covering his face rather than his balding head. He must have smelled or heard me with his heightened faoladh senses, because he perked up, shoving his hat back into place and rising.

"Mave." He clapped me on the back with one hand and squeezed my shoulder with the other. "Good to see you with all your parts, kat." He'd called me a *kat* since the night after Hiberos's death—a much more affectionate term than my previous nickname, *girl*.

And I felt my heart light up. I was blessed to have at least two people who tried to understand me.

"Ferghal, you old mucc." For his trouble, I tapped his shoulder with the top of my head like a charging ram. Our banter was cut short as King Lorbog of Tuath Dobhránta passed us with a sneer and entered the war room vestibule.

More soberly, I said to Ferghal, "How's life?"

"Busy." Now that he was duskwarden of the wolfkernes, he didn't have the luxury of sitting in Bile Cernunnos and wallowing in grief like me; didn't even have the luxury Eamon, the former duskwarden, had of guarding the roads and forests of Sallach. He had a whole damned war on his plate.

"We've killed a handful of occulata," Ferghal said along that vein, referring to the *occulata speculatores*, imperial intelligence officers. "Couple squad of wolf-shapes led by Lon managed to infiltrate Aiken."

I appreciated his terms of endearment, but it was his trust I treasured most of all. That he would tell me of the wolfkernes' movements without hesitation thawed me out a tad more, especially given his natural surliness.

Before I could begin once more to stew on Manan's mistrust of me, Ferghal spoke quietly. "I keep trying to convince Brianne to take her rightful place as alpha, right. She refuses me every time."

I huffed a humorless laugh. "Sounds like it's time to stop trying, Ferghal. She's got stones enough to admit she makes a better lieutenant than a duskwarden."

"*I* certainly amn't suited to be duskwarden."

"Well ... it's like Chief Gwynedd used to say, *some have great-ness thrust upon them.*"

He scowled. "Don't you *thrust* anything at me, ever. Keep it away from me. I don't want nothing *thrust* upon me."

"That's not what I heard. Uaine let slip you were somewhat popular with the pack's young men as well as women—"

Before Ferghal could follow through on his obvious desire to wipe the smirk off my face, Ruadan entered the hallway, his silver hair *just* slightly too flowy for the movement to be natural. He was so familiar to me now that I often forgot he was not just the Gallowglass commander but some strange mix between a druid and a rogue, seemingly able to communicate with spirits, summon ghosts, and slip through planes of being. "Duskwarden, Princess. Shall we enter together?"

Among his other spooky qualities, Ruadan had a preternatural knack for arriving precisely at the correct time, so the meeting must be commencing soon. With murmurs of greeting, we followed him into the darkened vestibule, then into the war room proper. It was wooden and lacquered like the rest of the bíle's interior, windowless, and roughly round in shape. In the center stood a topographical map of the greater Sallach country, covered with flags and figurines representing troops. Looming over it was the corpulent, antler-crowned form of the druid-king Manan.

He welcomed in the last of the coalition leaders without fanfare and dove right in. "Duskwarden Ferghal, report?"

"Last I heard from Lon was two nights ago. They're lying low, picking through the blight as best they can. Those fomori have been an inconvenience. We lost a man." He sighed heavily through his nose and scratched his bushy sidewhiskers. "Once they get closer to Fort Alopex, they'll have more to report."

The king nodded. "Come to me as soon as you receive any word."

"Yes, sir."

"Keira, Lorbog, any news from Co Muvane?"

Keira, a counselor of Tuath Corcach Fola, which occupied the capital of Muvane, shook her head. "Queen Caoimhe is willing to send a small company, but she fears a dual attack from Albion."

"She's paranoid," Lorbog, who was king of one of the minor tribes of western Muvane, said dismissively.

"Not entirely," Ruadan replied, voice soft and calm as ever. "If the Emperor put enough pressure on Albion or Prydain, they would be all but forced to join the war. And if Albionic boats sail across the Éirin Sea, they won't bother to land in Southern Ligea. The forest is too dense. They will arrive on Caoimhe's shores."

Lorbog scoffed. "I ask you, why focus on incursions that have not happened when we have one *right here* that our men are dying of? We need manpower in Sallach, now."

"No," the king muttered as he glared at the battle map. "The phantom is right. We mustn't forget that we are surrounded by enemies. Even if the East Kingdoms weren't annexed territory, I wouldn't trust them not to shank us while we're already bleeding. If we let two armies flank us, Éire is well and truly lost." Begrudgingly, he nodded at Keira. "Thank Queen Caoimhe for the men she can spare, and Lady's blessing be with Muvane. News from Gallive?"

Counselor Uaine consulted his map. "King Tagh is lending a great deal of his army. The only impediment will be flooding roads due to the thaw and the incoming storm. They should arrive within the fortnight."

"Good. What do the Gallowglass have to report?"

"Nothing conclusive. In recent months, the occulata speculatores have been more interested in excavating ancient ruins than trying to cross the border." The phantom indicated several spots within what had once been Co Tirconnell, and a few scattered elsewhere. "A new target every few nights. Their actual aim is unclear, but up until two weeks ago, they were seen collecting Ogham stones, stele, and other rune workings. Some were transported to New Lindanos, some to Sylvostum."

"Plundering as usual," muttered Ferghal. "Taking what's not theirs for to put in their exhibitions, entertaining noble cunts."

Ruadan tilted his head. "Perhaps. But if these things were of no interest to the military, wouldn't scholars be collecting them, not spies?"

"If Alasdair permits it," said Manan, "I'd suggest you determine what these Ogham-stealing spies are—or were—looking for. Take yourselves a prisoner."

Ruadan smiled placidly. "You and the high king are of one mind. We have been interrogating a speculator. They are well trained, not likely to crack, but we will find a way. Apart from that, the Aquilans have been oddly silent all winter."

Then he turned to me. "In any case, our militiamen suffer without their wives and children, but civilians cannot be allowed back into Cernunnos unless we learn more about the withering. Or resolve it, ideally. Have the fae scholars or gatewrights discovered anything new about this blight, or why it seems to be spreading in both our realms concurrently?"

"They've developed some small ways to mend afflicted areas—patch the cracks where the withering leaks into the Underland." I ran my tongue along my sharp canines nervously. "Beyond that ... er, they know little of its origin. If anything."

"How can you be sure it originates in this world?" Lorbog asked. "You said, 'where it leaks into the Underland.' How can you be certain of such a thing if its origin is yet unknown?"

That was a fair question, one I did not have an answer for. I gestured a bit stiffly round the table. "I thought we all assumed the Aquilans' invasion is the source of the withering. Their wickedness is corrosive. The blight only appeared once they destroyed any trace of the place Fraochgleann was before."

"But you have no evidence, nothing conkreet, nothing but theory," he parried. "No action but for your own people, and even then in some desperate bid to keep our filthy world from touching your perfect, pristine one."

At that moment, before I could even process what he'd said, the chamber door opened, and Solma and Menecon entered. It was not the first instance cross-cultural perceptions of time had made them late for something or other.

What a mess. As if this inquisition of fae loyalty and

cowardice could get any worse—but least it was only a meeting this time. They took their places at my side. Though Menecon offered their deepest apologies, they kept glancing sidelong at me, apparently nervous.

Ruadan, apparently immune to awkwardness, continued as if nothing had happened. "We were just speaking of the true origin point of the blight. We must find it if there is any hope of stopping the spread."

"We should focus on beating back the invasion," Lorbog said. "You know, the one killing our warriors. Then we can cure the withering."

King Manan seemed to be in deep thought. It was Ruadan who answered again. "Hmm. This withering and the blight of Aquilan colonization go together too well, to be sure. Purely in terms of logistics, destroying one will help us destroy the other. But tell me, what sounds simpler: curing spoiled land or ousting an empire that has been squatting in our country for a millennium?"

I still could not believe they were exclusive to one another—something deep in my chest told me they must be connected—but I said nothing.

The Gallowglass continued, "Plus, it may well be that, when the withering reaches a town rather than festering within the forest, it will prove as deadly as Aquilan blades. In any case, a mere working theory of its origin is no longer sufficient. Menecon, I trust you'll relay to your king and queen that swift action is needed. If a victory over the Aquilans is to mean anything, we must heal Éire."

"Of course." The seneschal cast another meaningful glance at me.

Ferghal looked between me and the king. "And what does the she-wolf report?"

I let the king answer; he knew all I knew, anyway. Despite my despondency, the moment I saw something through Drusilla or Nevidaea's eyes, I let him know. "Vague bits and pieces. Nothing we can use, yet."

"The legate's shut his gob since his little *accident?*" Ferghal smirked at me and mimed gouging out his right eye.

"He's been reticent, yes," Manan said.

"I hope that isn't bad news for Drusilla. Could he suspect her?"

"I could check on Drusilla now," I offered.

Manan gestured for me to continue. "Not the legate's wife," he added grimly.

Ignoring his disapproval, I took a deep breath and closed my eyes. Switching from my sight to Drusilla's came more naturally than with the others, either due to her compliance on the other end or our friendship bond. In just a second or two, I fell into the black well of consciousness and let her sweep me up.

Keeping her eyes cast down, Drusilla set the legate's dinner plate on the edge of his desk. It was a meager meal of bread, cheese, and grapes slightly mushy from transport. Gaius gave no thanks, nor acknowledgment, but that was to be expected. He spoke to her very little these days. She might have worried he'd uncovered her treason, but he'd barely spoken to anyone apart from his son in months.

As Drusilla drew back, she glanced at Lucastos, who stood at attention at his father's right hand. The boy eyed the plate with obvious envy, and the she-wolf's hackles prickled. In the past few months, father and son had never once strayed from their bizarre new regimen. When they weren't training in the sparring ring, they were shut up in private quarters, studying Mighty-Ones-only-knew-what; recessing to eat was optional, and sleep came well after midnight. Not even his eleventh birthday had been a reprieve.

She glanced briefly at the side of Gaius Helius Sergia's head and, while he was distracted flipping through a ledger, slipped Lucastos a crust of bread. He frowned at it—a devoted boy—but nonetheless squirreled it away in his cloak. Eventually, hunger would win over loyalty, every time.

Primus Ottavian, who stood on the other side of the legate's desk, caught her eye, but he said nothing. Even if the Primus of the Ninth Legion had any qualms with a young boy sneaking food, no doubt he'd have kept quiet regardless. The primuses were growing more impatient with Gaius by the day. His communication and collaboration with them had deteriorated rapidly since the retreat from Sallach, leaving troops directionless and morale low.

"My legate..." Ottavian began stiffly.

Gaius, who had remained silent till now, interrupted—simply because he could, it seemed. "Are they ready?"

"The Eighth Legion has settled into Fort Sergia, and the Seventh remains in reserve at your disposal, Legate, but the men—"

"I did not ask after the legions, Primus. I was asking about our guests."

Drusilla's ears lifted. She couldn't help but speak up as head of the household. "Guests? What guests?"

"Nothing." Gaius waved a dismissive hand, not looking at her. "No one who will be staying in the praetorium or villa. You won't be expected to service them. Ottavian?"

The primus exhaled harshly through his nose. "Yes, those..." He struggled to find a diplomatic word and failed. "*People.* They await you."

"Good." Gaius glanced at his dinner but did not touch it. "Our savage neighbors have been too quiet this winter. It's time we turn the tides before they do."

"I need to know your plans," Ottavian said before he could be interrupted again.

The legate chuckled flatly. "Primus, the only thing you need to do is follow orders. March where I tell you to and point your sword at the enemy. It really isn't that difficult."

Ottavian ran a hand over the crest of thick curls atop his head. Unlike most commissioned officers, he was not Ruma-born but from one of the territories, a Numirabian from a loyalist family.

"The men are not pawns to be moved around at will. Sir, they have to be told when they'll be deployed."

Like a child, Gaius hardly seemed to be listening to Ottavian, instead examining a solid-gold paperweight shaped like a bulging, veiny scrotum. Such decor had become fashionable in the Aquilan capital. Some rubbish about increasing one's virility by surrounding oneself with manliness. "Ottavian, these are not conscripted men we speak of. These are not tamed dogs but red-blooded Aquilan men. They enlisted and joined the legion of their own volition. The Seventh, Eighth, and Ninth *Legions* are controlled by a *legate*."

"My lieutenants and I have to be able to manage them, or there could be consequences. Insurrections. Work stoppage. We cannot drive them like cattle."

"*Cannot?*" The room jumped as Gaius slammed a hand down on the table and stood in one motion. "If there are any soldiers so weak they would refuse to serve for such inane reasons, I want them court-martialed and punished. Insurrections, work stoppage, it would be tantamount to desertion. We're all"—he gestured round the room with fire in his eyes—"*well aware* of the sentence for desertion."

"Can you at the very least share what you've uncovered about our enemy?" Ottavian asked, voice wavering with the effort it took not to shout back at his commander. "I *must* be allowed to manage our troops. They are not trained to fight these..."

"Fae," Lucastos muttered.

"Fae. I cannot ask them to face an enemy we know so little about. Was that not the purpose of all the espionage? The artifact-collecting? I require access to those reports coming in from New Lindanos."

Gaius planted both hands on the desktop and leaned forward. "*I* will tell you what you require, Ottavian. You've no respect, no faith. Your brother would have done as he was told."

That statement froze Ottavian. Vaguely, I recalled him mentioning his deceased brother ... what was his name ... Felis, the one who'd attended academy with Gaius. I hadn't given a damn about his dead brother then, trapped in a hell wrought by my own sister's death, but Gaius wielded his name as a weapon.

"Now, if you'll excuse me..." He checked the chronodial on the mantle and gestured for Lucastos to come. "I have new allies to greet."

Father and son left swiftly. Drusilla made to follow them, but stopped briefly as she brushed past Ottavian. Their eyes locked again, and unspoken frustration passed between them.

She caught up to Gaius and Lucastos in time to see them standing before the double doors of the war room, but the unfamiliar people chatting with them froze the she-wolf in her tracks. Two men and a woman, their Éirin ethnicity clear as day. They were even dressed like Cuanachtan farmers, the men in shirtsleeves and trousers and the woman in a simple dress. But they wore no coats, no hats, and their attire was tattered at the hems, stained with what Drusilla hoped was sweat or dirt. Their bare feet were just as filthy. It appeared almost as though they'd staggered from their graves and lost a few articles of clothing along the way.

It was their scent, though, that shocked her to stillness. Something sharp and pungent and not-quite-human wafted from them.

The man taking point must be a rough thirty-two and no larger than five feet eight inches. His sandy reddish-brownish hair clung to his forehead, his dark eyes shone, and the top buttons of his shirt were undone—but disheveled as he was, and average as he appeared, he radiated a presence larger even than Gaius's. The toothy grin he gave Lucastos was something otherworldly, as captivating as it was threatening.

Then he froze, too, his grin dropping as though he'd been startled. He raised his head as if to scent the air, and at once, his gaze landed on Drusilla.

The world stopped spinning. Then he offered her the same toothy grin.

Drusilla's hackles raised, a growl threatening to start at the back of her throat. She took a step toward the war room, but a white-clad arm stopped her. The voice of Thomasia, one of the new adjutants, cut through the bells of doom tolling in her head. "Drusilla, did you need something?"

As Gaius, Lucastos, and their odd guests entered the war room, Drusilla reluctantly turned her attention to the adjutant. "Excuse me, I must attend to the legate."

Thomasia scrunched her nose, making her small spectacles lift. "I doubt he'll need you in there. I was summoned to take notes, so there really is nothing for you to do."

Drusilla weighed her options. If she slipped in after them, Gaius probably wouldn't think to dismiss her from the room—*and judging by the ripping headache I have now, Mave, you are here for information*—but there was no way she could do so after being challenged directly. It was too risky.

So, she eased back and allowed Thomasia to enter instead. The adjutant gave her a wary glance as she shut the double doors behind her.

I'll find a way, Drusilla promised along our bond as the vision became hazy. *I'll find a way to investigate these "guests."*

When I came to, I was sat in a chair someone must have fetched for me. With a parched mouth, I relayed all I'd seen.

"An Éirin ally?" said someone vaguely to my left. "Impossible. We have the full support of every king and every chief."

"It must be some outlier," Ruadan mused. "Judging by the clothes, some band of criminals or exiles. Far more concerning that they didn't seem human."

"The fae coming changed things," Ferghal said. "The legate's crashing and burning, the men are panicked. They're afraid of us now."

Manan pinned me with a warning gaze, "For now, they do not know what to expect of the arrival of the fae, but neither do we, any of us. Yours is a race never before seen. If he's gathering allies, I sincerely hope your people will not disappoint."

I tried to ignore the ache in my heart, to numb myself to being set apart from the other Éirins because of how I looked now. There was nothing I could say besides, "So do I."

All I could do was try harder. Stay here, show that the fae weren't cowards. That *I* was not a coward. That I was still Éirin.

After some miscellaneous strategy and troop movements were discussed, the meeting adjourned. Menecon pulled me aside the moment we exited the war room.

"You must come home."

The hair at my nape stood up. They'd never sounded so scared. "What happened?"

The next words out of their mouth stopped my heart.

"It's Hiberos."

4

Considering the last argument I'd had with Orlaith, I hadn't expected to see gatewrights and their instruments in the heartgrove when I arrived. More than that, I was surprised to see *a crowd of faekin* gathered round the center of the clearing. I pushed through the tight-knit, murmuring crowd, my chest burning.

"Gods below!" The curse slipped from my lips unbidden when, finally, I reached the center of the crowd. Where the vaguely hand-shaped sapling had once grown from the soil, there was now a ... I didn't know what to call it.

In mere hours, the twig had grown into a strange tree. It was a young tree, short and just budding, yet the opalized trunk was thick and misshapen. Not simply twisted or malformed but swollen with wooden masses that cracked and breached the rich oaken bark. My eye was drawn down to one of these masses, which, at first, I thought was a branch reaching toward the sky.

No, not a branch. There I saw the outcome of the sapling, the hand now possessed of all its fingers and rendered in stunning detail. Covered in spirals, wood grain. The shape, the impression of muscle, it was changed, but the gesture and those knuckles—

Lady preserve me.

This was Hiberos's hand.

The other masses were shapeless, but that hand, the clarity ... it was undeniable.

Ruadan had been right. *Did you know that hellebores are perennial? You could plant some in autumn and they'd come back with glory in the spring.*

A sudden and fierce protectiveness rippled up my spine, and I turned to the crowd. "Clear out. You aren't needed here, clear out. Nothing to see."

Some of them left straight away, but plenty of them were reluctant, chief among these being Gatewright Owalir: "What in the name of the Moon is going on? I daresay you are obliged to answer when you've diverted my people to tend to this grove. Putting the rest of the Underland at risk, I might add—"

I shooed them away like one might a horsefly, and though their hood hid their face as always, the set of their ears told me they were peeved. Didn't matter. I needed to focus on Hiberos. How he was growing so quickly, I did not know, but I needed to nurture him in this strange new form, whatever that meant. And I needed quiet and solitude to piece this together.

At last, I ushered the last nosy aranfox from the heartgrove and turned back to study the tree from afar. It was an ugly little thing, stout and lumpy and budding only in patches. Not exactly thriving ... but it was trying.

He was trying. Trying to return to me, with much more fervor than I'd ever exhibited trying to return to *him*.

As if confirming my thought, an eclipse of moon moths burst from seemingly nowhere, fluttering around the tree. My heart swelled and broke all at once. So much about our past and the way we'd once been was still a mystery to me, but as always, my soul knew the important truths. He was trying so desperately to reach me, but he could not do it all on his own.

Somehow, I had to help him.

My gaze fell from the tree to the blight and mist. Thankfully, it had not spread nearly as dramatically as the tree had grown, but still, it had advanced beyond the wilderness. I crept deeper into the grove, bypassing the gatewrights' instruments strewn over the grass. I had no knowledge of what I could possibly do to help Hiberos, whatever and wherever he was now—no knowledge, even, of what magic I'd wrought by planting him here. But the withering ... as long as I kept the withering from his resting place, everything else could be discovered in time.

Even as my throat knotted and my stomach clenched, my feet brought me closer and closer to the foul, blood-red earth. Closer. Finally, the toes of my boots abutted it directly. I looked down, staring closer than I ever had at the slick, spongy moss. It pulsated like living tissue, though there was no *life* about it. If I focused closely, with my fae vision I could see it crawling forward in minuscule increments. It moved faster here than elsewhere, its vile tendrils reaching covetously. I don't know what instinct spoke to me, but as the skinny fingers shifted and bled, I sensed from them *glee*. Anticipation.

I startled slightly as a lone moth broke away from its friends and disappeared into the mist before me. *Onward.*

My spine tingled. After all my encounters in blighted lands, the thought of stepping knowingly into the thick of it was daunting. But this curse *did* have an origin. There *was* a cause. And I had a cause, too.

Plenty of people on both sides of the Moon Gates were working to save the land. I was the only one who would save Hiberos.

Taking a deep breath, I crossed the threshold. Passed into the mist. Let my boot sink slightly into the diseased grass.

As always, the mist seemed to insulate me from the rest of the world; the sounds of the forest melted away, and their absence was felt keenly in my bones. Every fiber of my being told me to turn around and run, that this was a dangerous place, that I was not welcome.

Yet I kept walking. Faint glimpses of the moon moth and a vague pull within my chest led me through the mist. The barest remains of a memory. Like finding your way through a town once visited as a child. Something known in the body rather than the mind.

I rose from the grass and gravitated toward the edges of the clearing while Hiberos continued to read.

In the thicket beyond, something caught my eye. A stone pillar with the face of a horned man carved into its surface.

Something shifted in the mist. I ignored it. The next moment, I stepped into what must be, if the break in shadows was any indication, a clearing. Two steps, four, eight.

Through the mist, between trunks, appeared a face—slate black, empty eye sockets, its mouth open in a silent scream. Every hair stood on end, my vision sharpened, my canines lengthened, and my hand found my bow. Even as I reached for my quiver, though, the face did not move.

Not a fomori.

There wasn't just one carved pillar, there were many, all lined up in a row. Standing sentinel. I took a step into the thicket, determined to investigate.

"Princess? What are you doing?"

I stared at the bizarre stone sentinel for a long while, the only sound in the clearing my breath and a low, moaning wind. Suddenly, I realized why that memory had survived. Hiberos, keeping me from investigating ruins—it was too odd. Far from the secretive creature I'd come to know, in my memories he indulged Ashling's every curiosity. He had even shown me the trilith depicting the soulfasting ritual with fevered excitement. So, then, why had he turned me so sharply away from this one?

Why were there abandoned places in the Underland at all, and why had they been abandoned? And by *whom*?

Who was older than the fae?

I cleared some brush to get a better look at the sentinels,

which were really standing stones carved to look like horned figures. They stood in twos on each side of a path long grown over. Like a wild cat, I prowled between the trees, following the downward slope of the path, careful not to trip over any vines or gnarled roots.

The path went on for perhaps a quarter of a mile, if not longer, going steadily down, down, down. Strange, because the elevation of the Underland had never seemed particularly high to me. Yet down I went. Eventually, the trees became thick and dark, their foliage more like that of the Goneland than the pretty leaves of the Lunar Kingdom. That same sensation of terror, of being somewhere I shouldn't, permeated my skin and made my teeth chatter. There was no sight of the moth. The mist clawed at my ankles, impotent to stop me from venturing deeper.

Then, abruptly, the slope evened out and the sentinels stopped. It took a moment for my eyes to make sense of what I was seeing, but beyond the encroaching branches yawned the entrance of a ... not a cave, no. This had been constructed. It peaked several feet above my head, an uncountable number of black limestone shafts layered and entwined to create a circular aperture.

It was familiar. Not in the sense that I'd been here before or was missing a memory of this place, no, but it felt *like* somewhere I'd been before. The opening. The structure. Even the ancient black limestone.

Tension rippled and coiled between my shoulder blades. Every instinct told me this edifice, or monument, or whatever it was, was something my eyes were never meant to see. Yet there was also the sense, coming at me from another angle, that this was *exactly* where I needed to be—that whatever secret these sentinels guarded was part of a larger puzzle, and that turning and leaving now, listening to that instinct and fleeing...

It might bring worse than discomfort.

I did not breathe as I approached the opening. The forest around me remained silent. The kind of silence that falls in the presence of a large predator.

I lifted a foot, stepped over the lip of the aperture, and melted into the darkness.

Within, the ceilings lowered at once, the vestibule becoming a tunnel—tighter and more narrow, until I had to duck to continue on. Then ducking became crawling. Finally, the tunnel ended with a small hole, just big enough for one person to slide through. My fae body was bigger than my human one had been, and still so new and often awkward and discordant with my mind, but I managed to squeeze through, the stone flattening my tall ears as I did.

This deep in the forest and tunneled into the earth, I would have expected the chamber beyond to be pitch black. Yet a thin shaft of moonlight, like a pale finger, broke through a fractured stone near the top.

Finger was an apt descriptor, it turned out, because the light was aimed at something.

As I shuffled closer, I realized I stood before a carved slab. It was flat but thick, and old, older even than the Moon Gates, if I had to guess. It had been hewn from the wall itself, and so there was no back, only a front and edges. The face of it was largely blank; at some point in its existence, the same fissure that spilled light onto it had spilled water, and I guessed the constant flow across the etching had worn away its image. The edges, however, were intact, and along them was carved line after line of fine Ogham.

Strange. Hadn't Eamon, bless him, said something about a monolith not unlike this slab? The one bearing instructions on how to make men into werewolves without being bitten—protector faoladh. But that had been in the Goneland, and here this was in the Underland. Could the two truly be bleeding into one another so much that they had begun to share sacred spaces?

I traced the hash marks carved upon the monolith's edge, my skin erupting into gooseflesh as I read the inscription.

When stars are still and breath is done,
When blood is spilt to wake the sun,

The wheel shall turn, the thread unspun,
The final cycle is begun.

My fingers stilled over the last line. Though the words meant little to me logically, I knew without a shadow of a doubt this was what I was here for. Not only that, but deep within my chest, there was a sense, a *knowing*, that the words pertained to me.

Me. And... I traced the row again. *When blood is spilt to wake the sun.*

To wake the sun.

Hiberos.

Blood.

Whose?

There were two stanzas more, but I put in little effort to translate them. More about the moon and sun, a war, and something slumbering. I'd never remember every word, and I needed to; I'd have to come back here with something to record these runes on.

With reluctance, I looked between the slab and the small opening behind me. Damn it all. The Underland possessed a strange, shifting quality, like a landscape from a dream—not unlike the way Geatacoill's healthy parts shifted around me. If I left this place now, would I be able to find it again?

I would have to hope, because the shaft of moonlight was fading, and mist was beginning to creep into the space after me.

A putrid scent and the sound of ponderous footsteps came with it.

I had overstayed my welcome.

Flattening to my belly, I wriggled through the opening again, then hastily rose to a crouch, bow ready in my hand. The way ahead was dim; the twilit woods beyond gave even my fae eyes very little light. Mist lashed at my calves. The whistling of wind through stone pricked up my ears.

My leather glove squealed against my weapon. My breathing fluttered to a stop as I crept toward the circular entrance.

I took one step over the threshold. The crunch of pine needles and dead leaves beneath my feet was like thunder to my ears.

Thump. My heart—
Thump.
Thump.
Thump—

An unearthly shriek had me turning just in time to deflect an eyeless fomori. Skinny arms flailing, toothless mouth open in a gasping screech, it crashed into me, then staggered back when I held my ground.

I flicked my bow, and blades of pure moonlight extended along the limbs with a quick, sharp motion like a panther's claws. Before the fomori could recover, I jerked my forearm, slashing it with the bow and slicing clean through the vines twining round its head and shoulders. I'd have to cut all its connecting tissue completely to kill it for good, but I only needed it to be incapacitated. A swift kick to the chest sent it arse over end.

Its falling body revealed another fomori. And another. I fired a volley of arrows easy, but there was only so much I could do. By half-seconds their numbers rose, surging like a tide, winding unhampered through the trees to get to me. Eyeless and wasting, hulking and burly, beasts on all fours, female figures with their hands and feet on backward—step by step they surrounded me, all obsidian stone, scraps of conkreet, copper wiring, and blood-red moss. They were clothed in the miasma of the withering as surely as they were cloaked in mist. A hundred, maybe more.

The last time I had faced the fomori was when Orlaith and I ventured into the mist to investigate the source of the panther problem. I still woke at night, sometimes, hearing the metallic screech of those pylons. We'd fought hard then, killed so many, yet there seemed to be no end to them.

If these ones didn't succeed in felling me, larger ones would join their brethren.

Mave of Tuath Stag Gréine would balk at running from a fight.

Maybe I wasn't her after all.

I could not afford to die. Could not afford to join Hiberos in the sod. Could not rest. Not now. I turned to run, but they were everywhere, a veritable swarm standing between me and the heartgrove.

With my free hand, I drew the sword at my side. Tested the grip, rotated it in my still-healing palm. Took a deep breath. And plunged into the horde.

5

I sliced one way, then the other, trying to keep my head above the swamp of fomori as I fought through them—severed the head of one, dodged another, grabbed a third by its throat and used it as a shield. Rock struck rock and shattered thunderously. I did not stop moving, cutting, ducking, bobbing. I skipped my way through the trees like I was dancing a reel at some relative's funeral.

Just when the crowd was thinning and it seemed the end was in sight, a flash of slate in my periphery threw me off.

She came screaming in like a blood-red arrow. Her claws struck me across the face and neck. Blood exploded. I pivoted on one foot to let her sail past rather than tackle me, and on instinct followed through with a sword strike to the chest. My blade scraped and sparked along her stony body, hitting no connective growth. In the next second, a fomori jumped on my back and tried to grasp for my throat.

It brought with it mist, which lapped hungrily at my wounds, and I remembered. My Trial of Purity. Reaching for my bow, mist coalescing around me, clinging to my arm as if suckling my blood. As if trying to get inside of me.

With a roar borne of pure horror, I bucked the fomori off.

Dropping my weapons, I hid my cuts from the mist and left them all behind. I was sprinting now. Proper fleeing. And I couldn't stop.

The mist must have got me a little back there, because the pain... Even as I staggered into the heartgrove, clutching at my lacerations, the pain throbbed through me like nothing I'd ever felt in battle. Not even battles with the fomori, in the forest or the labyrinth. Even a touch of this mist ravaged my skin like a rash. It spread beneath, sizzling and popping like bubbles.

When I looked down into my palms, you would think I'd just been delivering a child. The blood was tacky in that same way, mostly mucus, with a distinct scent. Groaning, I rubbed my hands against my breeches. The blood pilled and flaked off, but my wound still oozed down my neck.

I landed on my knees at the base of the strange young tree, touching my stained hand to it for stability. Then a flash caught my eye. Two fat roots formed a v-shaped impression, like a bowl, and the basin had collected water.

Just water. When I looked at it obliquely, it had flashed as though catching moonlight, but head-on, there was no reflection. No moon, of course. Not in the Underland.

Yet...

Without much thought, I scooted closer on my knees and wet my hands. The cool water washed away the disturbing tackiness of the blood and, more importantly, eased the pain in my wounds. The sizzling receded, then quieted altogether. But to say the water was *cool* did not quite do it justice. There was something uncommonly soothing about it, better even than a dip in the stream on a hot day. Again, more thoroughly this time, I washed my wounds, then my face and nails and knuckles.

When all was said and done, I was hunched over the basin panting like a madwoman. It took a moment for my rational mind to catch up. Gazing into the basin now, my nails dug into the bark, I vaguely registered that the water was pink. My wound dripped steady into it, blooms of red breaking the surface.

The grove was silent save for my harsh breaths and the faint, wet gnawing sound of the blight eating away at the moss. When I raised my eyes to the treeline, it almost seemed as though the mist reached for me. As if it sensed me there, and still wanted to crawl beneath my skin.

I'd already known the fomori and the mist were linked somehow, but ... the withering, too? Beyond a shadow of a doubt. All three were connected. Had to be.

How?

What did it all mean?

I staggered to my feet. Now that I was thinking more clearly, a rough to-do list formed in my mind. Had to put actual medicine on these wounds, and get something to record the etchings on that monolith. Best to come back with a squadron of soldiers, too, if the fae could spare them. Then I would—

Something clutched me by the very soul and yanked. There was little warning apart from the fluttering of a muscle in my scalp. Light, color, and sound hit me with all the force of an Aquilan tree-cutter.

My legs buckled under me, but before I could hit the ground, I was lost in the vision.

LOOKING through Drusilla's eyes was a familiar sensation. Faelon's, less so. So, at first, I could not make sense of what I was seeing, could not make sense of my perspective.

"Now, then."

Gaius's voice snapped me into place. He and the boy stood side by side at the mouth of a canvas tent in the burned remains of Aiken Forest. I was struck yet again by how different Gaius smelled to Faelon than he did to me. Not hot and sticky like war but warm like home and comfort, despite it all. If I could shrink back, I would. But Faelon simply looked up at him, and Gaius smiled back.

"Months of training have led up to this, Lucastos. Are you ready?"

"I ... I don't know."

Not the answer he wanted to hear. Father frowned, and Faelon cringed inwardly. "You are. If you aren't ready now, you never will be."

"I ... then—" Faelon stuttered. "I-I'm ready, then."

The trees overhead made the tiny forward base cold, even within their tent. Faelon held tight to his shiver, determined not to show any sign of weakness. Yet it was impossible to control. Not only because of the chill. There was something ... something more happening, inside of him. His head ached strangely. He could have sworn he smelled a hint of sweetness, flowers, as though a woman stood close by. And when he blinked, the persistent image of a twilit grove with deep teal grass and lavender trees appeared behind his eyelids. There came a sense that, apart from the troops in camp, he and Father were not alone.

He tried to convince himself it was merely the presence of the Mighty Ones. Belos, Lord of Light. Or maybe Opia, the Forge. Yet, on a level he did not quite understand, one he really had not even discovered, that explanation rang false.

Eat the apple. But you mustn't tell Lord or Lady Sergia anything you see.

His stomach soured, and he bit back tears. The sense that he had done something bad, and that it was only a matter of time before Father discovered his treachery, made him want to go home and hide under his blankets.

The creeping dread sharpened and shook him as whooping echoed through the deeper, more intact parts of Aiken Forest, some of it humanlike, some ... not. The shabby, barefoot man and his band emerged from the dark between tree trunks, and Faelon fought the urge to duck behind his father. He was a man, now, dammit. A soldier. Yet these unpredictable Éirins scared the skin off him. Their leader—Bloodwarden Ryac, he'd introduced himself with a toothy grin—held something dark, tangled, and dripping in his hands. Despite his alliance with the legate, in nearly all ways, Ryac was the picture of barbarism: he wore trousers and braces and unevenly buttoned shirts, all of which were askew just now. He was always plastered with sweat. He allowed his women to fight. And—

And from his mouth downward, he was soaked through with blood. His two dozen companions were covered in the same gore. The shadows of the evening forest were too harsh for Faelon to see their eyes save for a demonic twinkle deep in each pupil.

"Lookie what I found," Ryac said in Éirin, making little effort to hide his Cuanachtan brogue. He approached smoothly but with unsettling speed, and dumped the mass of fur and blood at Father's feet.

The stench was ghastly. Faelon held his breath, and when Ryac caught the boy's flinch, he grinned wider.

Gaius motioned for two nearby legionaries to spread the offering out. It was a few moments before they could make sense of the tangled, slippery mass of flesh and hair. The moment Faelon understood what it was, he clutched his stomach, willing his dinner not to rebel.

He had seen dead animals before, either killed on the road or fresh from the hunt. This was different. Bigger. Not an animal, not all the time. A wolfkerne, skinned with vicious precision.

"This one was called Lon," Ryac remarked casually. "At least, that's the name his fellows were screaming when I laid him out. Rather small and svelte for a faoladh." Even in his abominable state, the word rolled off his tongue like poetry; whatever he was considered now, he still spoke Éirin with affection.

"Fellows?" Father's head snapped up.

Ryac held up his hands. "Ah, don't worry, legate. My pack cleaned 'em up. No one left to run back and warn Manan." As his people handed down the pelts of the others, he broke into another grin, this one strong enough to wrinkle his nose. "But I'd not tarry. Their giardee duskwarden will be feeling something off in the air. No doubt, too, this little party was expected somewhere. Seems like there may be a wolf among your sheep just as surely as we're among theirs."

Gaius took immediate heed.

Now more than ever, he was a creature who acted on fear.

Now more than ever, he's a creature who acts on fear.

My immersion in Faelon's senses broke; in the same moment, he stiffened, casting about.

Who said that? Why did I ... think that?

A flash of the twilit grove made him shut his eyes hard, rubbing the heels of his palms into them. "Ugh..."

"Come, Lucastos." Gaius's voice cut through the disorienting haze, but it still took the boy a moment to recover from what our minds had just shared.

Over the din of rustling leaves, clattering kit, and growling tree-cutters, the legate shouted orders to the platoon: "Artillery, mobilize at once. Runners, to me for correspondence. We strike by midnight, or the next time the lot of you hold swords in your hands will be as gladiators."

My break from Faelon's senses made me more aware of my body, of the way those words made my heart leap into my throat.

With ease, I backed out of the vision. When I came to, I was already scrabbling to my feet.

After months, Gaius had given the unwieldy machine of war forward momentum. Either he'd utterly lost his mind, or he held in reserve some secret weapon. Something having to do with those blood-soaked Éirins. Either way, tonight, he'd break through Aiken and strike at the heart of Sallach. The bilé.

I had to warn them.

+☽·☽·☽·☾·☾+

When I reached the Crossroads, the Moon Gate outside Cernunnos was down for maintenance. Again. I was forced to take the gate leading to the western boglands.

Fighting my way to the road, I flagged down the first people I met, a couple militiamen transporting supplies to the southern refugee camps. If they didn't recognize me, they at least knew of me; with barely a sentence of explanation, their horse was mine.

There was no time to follow the road. We sped northeast across the hills and valleys, toward Bile Cernunnos. The sunset slipped from my shoulders like a cloak, twilight pressing in ahead, deeper then deeper still. It was a handful of miles before I noticed the mare's scent shift. Her distress broke through my haze of panic. If I pushed her any harder, we'd get there, but she would expire the moment she stopped running.

Perhaps it was babyish, but the idea of another innocent dead repulsed me. So, I left her in a wood, by the nearest spring, and divested her of her tack. Éirin horses were as close to human as an animal could get, not like the fodder for work and war the quillies bred. Once she rested up, she'd either find her way back to a settlement or join a wild herd. Either way, she would be fine. I whispered a prayer to the Lady and left her on fae-fleet feet.

I followed the spring, knowing it soon would feed into the Garri. The wider the stream got, the heavier the stone of dread in my chest became. Within minutes, it was full dark. I burst from the wood as if Death herself chased me.

The moment I did, the stench hit my nose. Green wood burning. I knew it well. The memory of Aiken Forest on fire made my ears ring and my palms scream. I blinked rapidly to clear my mind, but a flash of Hiberos's charred hide waited behind my eyelids. The blackened scar across his body, the one that hadn't mattered, anyway, because that body had been rent and broken mere nights later. The frenzied embers, the choking smoke, Ruadan's near death. People had given their lives to see that the Aquilans and their tree-cutters did not burn down the bilé, and now...

Now Aiken Forest burned again. Smoke curled into the sky, blocking out the moon and stars.

Thank the Lady I was on the right side of the river. I ran directly through the fae camp south of the bilé, where Solma dealt with chaos. No one knew what was going on or what should be done. There were a handful of fae artillery units this side of the Gate, with the remainder held in reserve. But the gatewrights were still trying to open the faulty Gate.

If they didn't fix it in the next fifteen minutes, this was our standing fae force.

Fuck, fuck, fuck.

"No word from Manan as yet," said Solma hoarsely as I came abreast of her. "Should we march?"

I doubled over to try and catch my breath, panting between words. Another, stranger scent underpinned the burning, but I could not place it, and brushed it aside to focus on the conversation at hand. "March, yes. Sergia doesn't fire warning shots."

She nodded as I readied to start running again. "I'll gather the units I have. They'll be just behind you. Gatewrights," she shouted, "I want that portal fixed, *now!*"

I took off, her screaming argument with the gatewrights fading away behind me. Bumps and divots in the road meant nothing to me; I flew across them like a vengeful wind, determined to reach the walls before the Aquilans did. They would not take Sallach's last bastion. They'd not take our sacred tree, the source of all Tuath Stag Gréine's power, while I still had breath in my lungs.

I'd not fail this time.

It became a mantra as the boughs of the bilé came into view, then the city walls. The further I untangled the situation in my mind, though, the less confident I became. Descending upon a village and slaughtering half its occupants was one thing. Establishing a front line in mere days was another. But to attack a *fortified city* with no warning, no fanfare, no encampment, no wheedling or negotiation or bureaucratic bullshite?

It smelled not of the Empire but of Gaius. Impulsiveness. Insanity. Cruelty to his own men. Yet I knew him well enough to know he'd not strike unless absolutely certain he could win.

What in hell was he planning?

6

The city was in as much chaos as the fae encampment. Wolfkernes, militiamen, and warriors from every Cuanachtan clan hurried to fortify the walls, ready gear, and relocate the injured. No one could tell me where to find the king, and no one yet knew how large the incoming Aquilan force was. As I entered the bilé, I tried to keep one eye on my pathing while checking on Faelon with the other. I'd stumbled upon the idea on accident and had been trying to master the method for months, but it still did nothing but give me immediate, intense nausea, so I gave up for now.

I found Ferghal before anyone else. He wore his pelts and armor now, and paused in barking orders to point me in the direction of the king. "And what the feck is that *smell?*"

I knew he didn't mean the burning, but there were more important things to address. I hesitated only a little. "Ferghal, the wolfkernes you had stationed in Aiken are gone."

His gaze lost its shine, but, just as Ryac had suggested, he didn't seem surprised. "Bastards. Can't wait to tear their souls from their oily bodies."

With that, we parted ways. King Manan was in the war room with the half of the coalition that wasn't scattered through the city, trying to hold things together; Ferghal wasn't here, of course, and neither was Ruadan. Surprisingly, Manan's cauldron, which usually stayed near his throne, was with him, boiling over with acrid yellow smoke. Even as the commanders plotted their next move, he chanted and sprinkled components into the burning coals within. Whether he was working a protection spell, scrying, or something else, I only prayed whatever guided him now was more precise than the stars that had guided Gwynedd.

They asked after the fae first. I gave them the bad news, then the good news, or what little I had. Their silence said more than any cry of rage ever could. "How many Aquilan troops are there?" Manan pressed in a clipped tone. "And how far away, how long do we have?"

I closed one eye and joined with Faelon as briefly as possible. "It's ... hard to say. The tree-cutters have clear-cut a path ahead of the troops. That must be where the smoke is coming from, but I can't see them. I see the primus of the Ninth Legion, Ottavian. He wouldn't be there unless they all were. So, at least one legion. Six thousand men. How long has the smoke been rising out of Aiken?"

"Not even a half-hour," Uaine said.

"Then they were at least three quarters of the way through the forest before any sign they were coming. Nothing you could've done with Ferghal's scouts dead. They'll be here before the hour." That gave us the lesser part of thirty minutes to prepare. Regret creased my brow painfully. "I was struck with a vision in the Underland. I tried to get here as quick as I could, but I ... I'm sorry."

I was spared from witnessing Manan's disappointment in me; pain pierced my temple, and my eyes twitched closed of their own volition.

Faelon turned his head. He and Gaius were currently standing in a chariot at the center of the procession. Though I still had little idea of Ryac's role in all of this, I expected to spot the bloodwarden among them, but his band was nowhere to be seen.

"That Éirin who's been with Gaius," I rasped, shaking myself back to the present, "he killed the scouts, somehow, but I don't see—"

Wait.

Before the pieces could fall together coherently, the doors to the war room boomed open, and Ferghal stormed in. "Sers, I need every able body, and probably a few broken ones, too. There's a force flanking us from the southeast."

"The southeast?" Manan snapped, his face beet red. "How did Aquilan auxiliary manage to ford the river? How did they arrive before—"

Ferghal's jaw flexed. "They aren't legionaries."

The coalition splintered further as about half of us ran to follow Ferghal to the battlements. The narrow walkways were a sea of panic, some having noticed our visitors from the southeast, others keeping their heads down and rushing to fortify the walls. I fought against the flow of bodies. That strange scent, which had floated on the breeze just beneath the stink of green wood, brushed my nostrils again. Ferghal grabbed me and directed my attention over the parapet.

At the water's edge, their darkened forms dripping river water, clothing and hair plastered to their skin, stood no more than two dozen people. Hardly a "force," as Ferghal had called them. Theirs were not the tall, muscular forms of Aquilan soldiers nor the burly ones of wolfkernes. Many of them were small, malnourished, and not one wore a scrap of armor. They looked so like Éirin farmers that, at first glance, I thought they must be refugees.

Then shine in the night caught my eye. First streaks of white—twenty-four sets of grinning teeth. Then points of red—twenty-four pairs of twinkling eyes. Finally, the one at the center of the line stepped forward, canting his head just so.

Ryac.

He spread his arms in greeting like he was thrilled to be here. As if magically amplified, his voice carried over the distance and cut through the bedlam, manifesting as a slithering whisper in each defender's ear. "Welcome home, lads."

Dread stirred a tangle in my stomach as I focused on his

bizarre, earthy, coppery smell. I couldn't place it. Had never experienced anything like it before. I looked instead to Ferghal, who scented the air alongside me in deep, agitated huffs.

"Goddess protect us," he growled at last. "Werewolves."

The night turned on its head. Everything finally made sense, little clues that had seemed unconnected now pulled together to reveal Gaius's larger plan. Our wolfkernes were faoladh, the original werewolves, blessed to take their wolf-shapes to defend the innocent of Éire. But they weren't the only breed.

Gwynedd's stories said some werewolves had abandoned their worship of the moon, turning instead to the Crooked God, the God of Murder. Their abandonment had turned their blessing into a curse. This breed reproduced not through a moon ritual but through infected bites. Unable control when and where and why they shifted, they'd been exiled from society, and in their exile, they'd become so devoted to the Crooked God that they'd made an art of murder and cannibalism.

Moonslayers who slew everything in their path, Éirin or Aquilan, friend or foe.

The ruins the occulata had combed, the stele and runestones stolen ... they'd been searching for a spell to rival the one found by Eamon. The knowledge of how to create moon-blessed faoladh had given us an edge over our enemies. But now...

Whether these people—all Cuanachtan exiles, I realized—had been werewolves before Gaius, I did not know, but I got the sickening feeling that he had, indeed, found a ritual of some power.

The effect? We were about to find out.

Ferghal turned to hurry men and women along the battlements, shouting for them not to stop shoring up the defenses. Beneath the current of panic started a noise. Little more than a drone at first, it grew into a chant, then ... a song. Singing, unaccompanied by anything save for the dripping of river water, wafted up from Ryac's band. An ancient ballad I'd heard sung many times throughout my life:

Wake up, wake up, dear, 'tis I, your wayward lover

Wake up, wake up, dear, and let me in
For I tire of my long night's journey
And am drenched unto the skin.

Ferghal turned to me, nostrils flared. "Balls."

Fifteen minutes later, the Aquilan procession began to pour out of Aiken Forest, into the valley beyond. A thousand legionaries to begin with, more hanging behind. The only forces somewhat ready to meet them were the lunar fae and the archers on the battlements.

I wove through the crowded battlements, switching from south to west and back again, all the while arguing with the ranger-commander about when to start shooting. Eventually, I got my way and they refocused to defense, hastily fixing wooden spikes along the parapet to deter ladders.

To the west, the Emperor's Ninth Legion loaded their ballistas and readied their charge. To the southeast, Ryac's band had not moved an inch, simply chanting their song. *Wake up, wake up and let me in.* It wove through the haze of smoke and panic, a dirge. It made my hair stand on end. My fae feet carried me swiftly to that side of the wall. The wolfkernes remaining in Bile Cernunnos stood at the ready below, prepared to go head to head with their unnatural brethren.

I shouldn't be so afraid of two dozen starving Éirins when I had an imperial legion at my back. But I was.

Movement from one of the bilé branches caught my eye. King Manan had emerged onto a balcony, his antlers crowned with poppies. The warriors flanking him were covered in hastily applied ceremonial paint. Whatever war rites had been ministered were clearly few and rushed. The king gestured to his side, and one of his druids handed him a tall, upright horn of brass shaped to look like a stag's head. On either side of him and in the crowd below, similar horns were raised, their heads those of wolves, snakes, dragons, horses.

Then he blew, and the drone all Aquilans feared echoed across the valley in chorus with dozens of others. There was silence as the horn's haunting swan song faded—the tense, trembling silence of a band pulled taut. Potential energy quaking to be released.

Then someone down in the valley screamed, and a thousand screams climbed in answer. I whipped my head round to see the red tidal wave rushing toward us, their shields raised in perfect concert, their collective body heat making the horizon bend.

The breeze shifted. I looked back at Ryac's band, reaching for an arrow—

They were gone.

Hooooosh. BOOM. An Aquilan missile rocked the western wall and sent tremors into the ground. Embers burst and were carried on blasts of wind into men's lungs and eyes, clinging to their chainmail as they tumbled from the battlements.

BOOM. Screeeeeeeeeeeee. The fae artillery returned fire, their screaming stars exploding and spidering over the battlefield like lightning. But their archers stood stock still, waiting for their order, and our archers had no choice but to follow suit.

Already, the quillies dragged their battering rams and siege towers closer. I looked back at where the werewolves had been, my ears swiveling wildly, but ultimately broke for the western gate.

I hit the parapet hard, shouting down: "Solma! The phalanx!"

"I see it," she shouted back.

Boom, boom, BOOM! More missiles struck the fortifications, blasting our hastily assembled barricades to toothpicks. Men and fae were hit with shrapnel and collapsed.

The Guardian-commander's voice could barely be heard over the rumble of the machine of war. "Hold ... hold!"

The ranger-commander shouted at her to give the signal, dammit, but her voice did not waver.

"Hold..."

It occurred to me in that moment, watching the Aquilans close in on us, that for many of the fae below, this would be their first time facing combat. Death. Would freedom from the fog of battle give them an advantage or would their inexperience, their ignorance, hobble us?

The Aquilans ate the valley, yards lost every second. Solma and her front line ducked as a missile soared over their heads. It crushed a group of fae archers. Debris flew, wreaking destruction; the ground shook—

"*Hold!*" she shrieked, stopping those who might run in their tracks. "Hold!"

The rangers flanking me shifted and reached for their quivers.

"Don't draw yet," I warned, my voice low and raspy and not at all my own. She was waiting for them to expose the tender spot in their defense. Every dragon had one. My claws extended and dug furrows into the stone. I couldn't take my eyes off the bloody torrent.

Then the moment came. For a second, a mere second, the shell of the phalanx opened to reveal the head of the battering ram. As if in slow motion, the Aquilans came within range of the archers.

Solma screamed, "Fire!"

A veritable curtain of arrows both fae and Éirin followed, enough to splinter the front line.

"Glaives!"

The war machines shot enormous blades that sliced across the battlefield at knee height, leaving swathes of dead in their wake.

"Ballista!"

Finally, enormous moonshots barreled forward, pounding the earth and leaving huge craters.

My heart soared. The battering ram was splintered, all but forgotten in their dash to avoid the fae siege-breakers.

"Fire at will!" cried the ranger-commander.

My ears filled with the sweet sound of drawn bowstrings, then the whistle of a hundred arrows as the Éirin archers took advantage of the Aquilans' weakened defense.

There may be six thousand of them—and another two legions in reserve—but we had our city walls. We could hold out. We could win this battle, and that was a start. We—

A ragged, bloodthirsty howl rent the night air, ringing so loudly in my ear that the chaos seemed muted in comparison. I turned in time to see a white streak emerge from the darkened edges of the battlefield and leap into the air. With what seemed like very little effort, it arced over the wall.

Time slowed sharply. At the pinnacle of its arc, I caught a glimpse of it: a snow-white wolf with pure red eyes.

Deceptively heavy despite its slender frame, it landed with a crunch atop a ranger, shaking the battlements. It did not pause to get its bearings; it simply tore the man's throat out. A gush of blood painted the white wolf, glistening a deadly shade in the torchlight. The beast threw back its head and swallowed the chunk of pale, torn flesh whole.

Immediately, the men around it sprang into action, but the werewolf brushed them off as though they were flies on a wound. It jumped from the battlements with ease. Then, transitioning from two legs to four, it shot toward the western gate.

I did not think, simply jumped. My fae physique absorbed well the shock of the landing, and I took off running after the white wolf.

Behind me, yips and trills echoed through the city. I faltered to look over my shoulder. A dozen other white streaks jumped the walls, hurrahing with ecstasy, with pleasure, as though we were in a pub and someone had played a good bit of fife. One landed not fifty yards from me and zeroed in on my movement at once. Already, the daggerlike teeth in its too-open jaw dripped gore and saliva. It licked its chops, the gleam in its eye telling me it had got a taste of fae blood and hungered for more.

I was torn between the instinct not to turn my back and my instinct to defend the western gate. In the next beat—movement in my periphery. A hulking black mass barreled down an alley toward me, then skidded to a stop between me and the feral monster.

The shaggy fur and wolfhound shape of the head told me this was a faoladh. Ferghal by scent. His body heat was so immense it broke through the chill of the late winter night; his panting breaths made a fog around his head. "Go," he growled, and flicked his tail in agitation.

I kicked up clods of dirt and the filthy remnants of snow as I cut through yards and byways to reach the gate before the first white beast. Too little, too late. By the time I arrived, a handful of militiamen lay dead at the foot of the tower. Still I surged forward, taking the spiral staircase three steps at a time.

The chamber at the top was simply appointed and dark, with one archway leading to the parapet atop the city gate. Before the archway stood the werewolf I pursued. With one hand, he was lifting a mostly dead Éirin to his mouth, riveted to the man's throat, wholly engrossed in feasting upon his vital essence. When I appeared, he groaned low and dropped his prize with a sickening, wet thump. The wolf's earthy scent—blood mixed with wine and the salty skin of a working man—told me this was Ryac.

He turned and, on instinct, I summoned a flare of lunar magic to light the room. The brightness made him cringe and step back at first, but then ... then he paused, enthralled with it.

In that one still second, I got a good look at his wolf-shape. Not hulking like the faoladh but wiry, with a protruding collarbone, long limbs, and spindly, bony claws. His neck was just a tad too long, head dipped. Like the other of his kind, his scarlet-drenched mouth was too large and opened too wide. I'd never noticed any genitals about the faoladh, but this breed had no pocket or sheath; a mottled penis dangled between his lean, sinewy legs like a deflated sausage; it twitched to life only when he swallowed the blood still in his mouth. His eyes shone a solid, cloudy red, no pupil—an all-consuming, potent, primal magic reserved for only the very ancient, or the very evil.

He tore his gaze from the orb of moonlight to regard me. Then, with a shrill little laugh catching in the back of his throat, he leapt aside. The movement revealed the winch behind him, its chain wound tightly to keep the western drawbridge up. His claws flashed like blades as he swung his arm, slicing clean through the iron chains. In the same moment, I crashed into him—I'd darted forward just a fraction of a moment too late. We tumbled into the archway, half in my moonlight and half in the torchlight.

The walls quaked as the drawbridge crashed to the ground. Rabid howling mixed with the legionaries' lunatic war-cries.

I'd landed on top, slick fur clutched between my fingers. Without pausing, I drew back one fist and drove it with all my might into Ryac's snout. Something cracked. A sharp whine turned into a rumbling snarl. Claws tangled in my hair. I tried to tighten my legs around his chest to maintain my position, but he surprised me with a punch of his own directly to my gut.

I retched, my every limb weakened. Just for a moment. But it was long enough for him to open-palm slap me off him. I only half managed to get my feet under me as I staggered backward. My shoulder blades slammed the parapet, my fae mail clanked, my white curls fell in my face and stuck to the oozing scratches.

"Not bad, lass," Ryac rasped with what seemed to be genuine admiration. He leapt to his feet with one deft body roll. "You an' me, we'll have fun, big girl."

"The hell you will!"

The voice from the tower room made him snap his head to the left. There stood the last person I'd ever expected to see in this realm.

Orlaith.

A moth zipped out from behind her as if to say, *Delivery!*

7

The queen wore dreamy fae leathers. Unlike mine, the armor bore much of her skin, exposing her shimmering arcane tattoos. Her boundless tresses were braided tightly into a garland at the crown of her head. In each hand, she clutched a blessed dagger, their blades shining with lunar magic made all the more intense by the moon's presence in this realm.

Her solid opal eyes were filled with rage, her brow furrowed like an ancient tree trunk. She pointed a dagger at Ryac. "I am going to make you regret what you stole, *moon-traitor*." Like that day at the mist-choked border of the Underland, her tattoos fanned out from her skin, flashing like blades.

Ryac's claws curled and uncurled with each heaving breath. "Oh ... two girls. A big one and a wee one. I'll not be thirsting for options, at the least."

"You'll not be thirsting at all when I sever your ugly head from your body."

Orlaith flicked her eyes toward me. In them, I saw everything she could not say now. That she was sorry. That she'd been wrong. That she would no longer let fear keep her from her son. No more cowering beyond the veil and waiting for someone to deliver him into her arms. She was ready to fight, bleed, and, if need be, die to free him and to free this land. Whatever had changed her mind, we could discuss later. For now, I had her blades, and just a sliver of my Eytine back.

I smiled, tension I didn't know I was carrying released. She smiled, too.

I took that as my cue. While Ryac was distracted, I slipped Tali's dagger from my boot and lunged, aiming straight for the crook of his neck.

He reacted as though we were part of the same mechanism, turning in perfect harmony with my arc and seizing my arms. Skin and leather clapped. With no more than a grunt of exertion, he pivoted and pitched me over the parapet, and I was falling.

The fall was a short one. No time to scream, even. My body narrowly missed the bridge. A flash of red filled my vision—Aquilans breaching the walls.

I struck something hard, all breath shot from my lungs, and the world went black.

Faelon gazed out at hell.

Flame and smoke, thick, choking every bit of air from the sky. Men, bloodied, limbs blown off. Soldiers—Aquilan, Éirin, and fae —impaled on timbers, tangled in barricades, slumped in piles of their own viscera. Bone and foam pooling in craters in the pocked earth. Great black draught horses pulled the towers ever closer, only somewhat protected by the forces ahead of them. When they were shot and fell, men replaced them, their boots biting into the mud.

War was louder than he could have anticipated. And much, much hotter. It was as though they were held over a boiling crucible, every body, every sword, every link of chainmail inches away from molten.

He could just barely make out the shape of the western drawbridge as it fell. Centurions and their infantry flew toward it. In his history books, the enemy's walls were rarely breached so easily. Frowning, he looked to his father for some direction.

Though the corners of his mouth did not tip an inch, Gaius was glowing with excitement. His ghostly blue eye shone in the torchlight. He struck the horse pulling their chariot, steering them toward the fray. Arrows—steel ones and strange glowing ones— whistled louder the closer they got, but Father seemed not to notice them at all. Faelon had known that his father was a brave man and a good soldier, but he'd never witnessed Gaius's utter lack of fear. As though he craved death. Welcomed it.

Well, of course. Because he did. *Mors mihi lucrum.* The motto of the Sergia family. *Death is my reward.*

Only when an arrow whistled a mite too close to his son's head did the legate swerve, adjusting his stance so the boy could shelter behind him. It took every ounce of Faelon's willpower not to cower and shake in fear, too.

He didn't want to die. And if he did die, he didn't want it to be any of the slow, obscene ways he witnessed around him.

Their chariot shook violently as they sped over holes, upturned stones, clods of dirt, and fallen bodies. It would be a wonder if the axle did not snap in two.

"Do not stop," Father instructed above the abominable night- mare to which he'd brought his only son. "Never stop, Lucastos. Pause a breath, give quarter, show any bit of weakness, and the enemy will exploit it. So, when you start, never stop. Change tack if needed, but never, *not for a moment*, stop."

And Father didn't. He faced the siege with his good eye. As they came within ideal range of the Éirin archers, he raised his shield and drove their horse harder. At the mouth of the draw- bridge, fae and legionaries were bound up like clustered roots, a tangle of arm and leg, sword and spear. Never in his life had he thought he'd see so many fae. Other creatures fought beside them, too: big, horned ones and small, foxlike ones. They were beautiful. To see them cut down and trampled hurt something deep inside of him that he could not name.

Gaius transferred the shield to their backs, then lowered it all together as they charged through a break in the crowd, over the bridge, and into Bile Cernunnos.

"Push!" he cried, bringing the chariot to a halt. Centurions, legionaries, and the occasional white wolf flooded in around them, their chariot a boulder splitting the rapids. "Push!"

They squeezed up the ramparts, up towers, into homes, bursting through the city as though propelled by immense pressure. Gaius hopped from the chariot, drawing his sword and nodding for Faelon to follow. The choice was obey or be picked off by enemy fire. Even though his little heart was bursting from his chest and his vision was growing fuzzy, the boy did as he was told.

Using the confusion around them, Gaius pulled them into a nearby abandoned home. Everything was covered in dust, but the furniture was upturned, the cabinets open, things strewn about as if whoever dwelled here had left in a great hurry. Father closed the door behind them, shutting them in darkness and muffling the roar of battle. It wasn't like him to duck out of combat. Faelon shifted in his kit and searched his face anxiously, but there was nothing to read, just a glint in his remaining eye.

"The fae have the advantage of strength," Gaius said, kneeling to his level, "they may even have us in number. But they don't have this."

From a pouch he produced a spherical object the size of his palm, brass, with little cut-outs of runes and curving lines. The entire object was etched with a sigil, and the channels created by each marking revealed the core of the sphere. There, a dull yellow light pulsed, slow and steady like a heartbeat.

Faelon realized Father was offering it to him, so he took it in both hands. "What is it?"

"It is a weapon. And I need you to deliver it for me. Only you can do this. Only you can move through the city unnoticed."

Dread rolled around Faelon's gut as he looked down, finally understanding why Father had covered his leathers with a green cloak. "What kind of weapon?" he asked, although he knew he shouldn't.

For a fraction of a second, it seemed Gaius might answer.

Then a light Faelon could not name seeped from his gaze, and he gripped his son's shoulder. "Something that will win us this battle. You will plant it in the bilé. To activate it, simply hold it by halves and twist left. By the time you're done, the northern gate will have fallen. You are to exit there under cover of darkness and wait for me at the ravine I pointed out to you earlier. Don't take too long, don't make me send someone after you. Do you understand?"

He didn't know why, but Faelon's first question was, "Will this hurt the tree?"

Gaius was growing impatient, eye darting back and forth, but he humored the question. "No. We need the tree. It is in our best interest not to destroy it. Go on, Lucastos, already you're behind schedule."

Oh.

Well, then, he'd ... he'd do it. Faelon looked down at the weapon in his hands, the whole thing no bigger than a hand-ball. *I have to do it.*

No words were spoken, yet Father seemed to sense his acceptance. With a smile, the legate pulled his son's cloak tight around him, pulled the hood up over his dark auburn hair, and indicated the home's back door. "Through there. Go. And—" Gaius's jaw flexed. "*When* you come back, we'll celebrate however you like."

Then he exited the dwelling in a hurry, leaving Faelon to consider his next step.

⦾ ☽ ☽ ⬤ ☾ ☾ ⦾

I sat bolt upright, fighting to suck down oxygen as though I'd just resurfaced from a deep lake. The air was clogged with smoke and copper and the scent of suffering, but I was alive. Better yet, I did not lie at the bottom of a pit but on a polished oaken floor, flanked by my sister and an aranfox healer. They both jumped as I woke.

"Oh my." The little fox twitched its lavender ears.

"Goddess," Orlaith breathed, gripping my arm hard. "I thought you were gone."

Quickly, I got my bearings. We were in the great hall, the floors thick with wounded. In my vision, the legionaries had stormed the ramparts. Who knew how much time we had before they moved inward, toward the heart of the city ... the heart of Tuath Stag Gréine?

The only word I could choke out was, "Faelon."

Orlaith's expression darkened. "What?"

"Him— He— Gaius—" I brushed her off and stood to my feet, but the room spun. A flash of calming blue magic coaxed me to sink to my knees again with my forehead pressed to the cool floor. "I have a connection to him. I tried to tell you, but you ran. The glowworms. I can see through his eyes. Only Hiberos knew..." I shook my head. "It doesn't matter now. They have something, *Faelon* has something, a weapon. Gaius sent him to plant it in the bilé."

Orlaith's face was blank. "I don't understand. Faelon couldn't be there, he is only ... what, ten?"

"Eleven now." A little pang in my heart as I realized she did not even know the age of her baby, so great was the separation between them—but I ignored it. I had to make her understand. "Gaius brought him here. Not to fight, I don't think..."

No, no, he would crumble if Faelon died. His only son, his stolen heir. He'd worked too hard to indoctrinate him to simply toss him out into a war like he did other people's sons. Faelon was not disposable, not even to Gaius.

But it had to be Faelon, didn't it? It had to be Faelon, of course. Gaius was giving me a taste of what I'd given him a decade ago, when we'd fought one on one at the assault on Fort Sergia. On that day, I'd dared to call his bluff—dared to go on the offensive, thereby exposing the wean strapped to my chest. I'd known then that Gaius would pull his punches. Now it was my turn. Now *he* was using Faelon as a shield. He knew I couldn't hurt him. After all, he'd been there in the clearing that night. He'd witnessed the truth: that even when both my worlds were at greatest risk, I could not bear to spill the blood of an innocent. I could not spill my nephew's blood.

I fought through the dizziness rooting me to the ground. Ignored the vomit that surged up my throat. I had to find him. Had to stop him from planting that weapon. Had to get him to stay with us. To somehow abandon his father. His mother. The life he'd known. All to shelter with strangers losing a war.

Lady fucking help me.

"Ashling!" Orlaith called—following me, judging by the sound of her voice. I focused on putting one foot in front of the other, trying the summon and focus on that little tug, that spark at the edge of my consciousness that would lead me to my boy. I wanted to believe that his blood would call to mine, that he'd find something true in me, that he'd follow without question, but...

A flash of jade wings lured me to the second floor. If he'd been a seasoned infiltrator, he probably would have put it in a storage area, or some similarly abandoned area, so that, by the time anyone suspected something was wrong, it would already be too late to stop whatever destruction Gaius planned to work. Instead, the sensation pulled me to the library.

I stopped under the willow arch, and Orlaith was only a step behind. The room beyond was dark save for the globes of druid-light, which bobbed nervously about, as though they were painfully aware of the commotion outside. Even the stained glass windows were dark, facing away from the battle. I scanned the books, artifacts, and runestones. These things were irreplaceable, but only a handful had been secreted away, with the majority of the battle preparations focused on gathering men and shoring up defenses. There'd been so little time, and now, if the bilé did not hold, so much of our art was laid bare, here, for the Aquilans to destroy or steal as they saw fit.

Finally, my eyes landed on a short, cloaked form, half of it darker than the rest of the room and the other half lit with a dull, pulsating yellow light.

He stood before a glass box containing an Ogham-etched stone about half his size and older than the great tree itself. Since its collection, scholars had painted a scene of running horses upon it and decorated it with gold leaf, which burned low like coals in the sphere's dim light. And Faelon was frozen, enraptured.

No doubt Orlaith had picked up his scent, and I knew she must feel a pull toward him as well. Her energy was coiled so tight inside of her, shoved so deep, packed so densely that her very aura trembled like a hunting dog spotting her quarry from behind a fence. It was a wonder she made no sound considering how *loud* her yearning was to my soul.

Her son. Her Faelon. In the flesh, for the first time since that night. The night she'd last held him. Last kissed him. Last breathed a human breath. Every ounce of her deep, deep misery pressed in and suffocated any other magic in the air.

He *felt* it. Neither of us made a noise, yet the boy whipped round, jumping as though someone had shouted at him. Forest green eyes, the same as Eytine's, flashed in the dark and filled with terror. His hands trembled hard, nearly dropping the sphere as he fumbled to twist it.

"No—" I was halfway across the room when it crossed my lips, but, too late. The sphere hummed and filled up with a light so bright the library looked almost as it did in the daytime.

The brightness of it shocked Faelon enough that he cried out and dropped it to the ground. He remained frozen, only backing up to make way as I rushed to put my hand over the thing. I pulled away swiftly, though; it was hotter to the touch than fire.

The boy began to weep, and the distinct smell of urine filled my nose. Those two things together tore my attention away from the glowing sphere. "Please let me go," he whimpered in Aquilan; then, in passable Éirin, "Please, don't hurt me. I really am sorry. I won't tell him anything I saw, I-I'm sorry, I..."

"Faelon." It was a thin whisper dredged from the depths of a soul that had given up all hope. I knew for sure then that Orlaith had thought—truly, in the heart of her heart—that she would never see her son again.

But here he was.

I could have sworn Faelon's ears, rounded though they were, shifted as he turned his attention fully to her. His birth mother, the bearer of the soul whose blood and pain had brought him into this world.

Something profound and nameless entered his wide eyes. A knowing I could hardly imagine. That day flashed before my eyes. The last day, before love and celebration had turned to grueling torment. The light of the sun filtering through the doorway of the big house, falling onto his cradle and illuminating the moon moth perched there. Eytine's beauty and brightness as she lifted him into her strong arms. And him, just a wee babe, losing interest in anything that was not *her*—everything good and right and lovely he had ever known in this world.

Now, in the slowly dimming room, his awe of her was marred with confusion, fear, tears. Yet through our connection, I picked up on his instinct to run into her arms, to let her protect him from this hell in which we found ourselves. It was an instinct he fought bitterly. Because the woman standing there was a stranger. Because she was clearly not human, and certainly not Aquilan. Because even a lonely child with an abusive father was terrified of leaving what he had to chase what he did not know.

Orlaith broke their standstill by offering out a shaking hand, her seafoam skin milky against the blue-black leathers of her armor. "Faelon," she said again, louder and steadier this time. "You needn't be afraid. I can protect you. We can protect you. From him ... from this place ... all of it."

Thick but silent tears rolled down the lad's face. I felt his thoughts as sure as I read them plainly on his face. Was she lying? When she said "him," did she ... did she mean Father? He knew what he *should* do. He should defy her, dismiss her as a deceiver, do something heroic like slay her. Yet he was powerless even to move.

Not a soldier. Not a man. Not even a legate's son. Nothing but a frightened mutt torn between reality and a world of make-believe.

In the sheltered quiet of the moment, I noticed that, bit by bit, very slowly, the sunlight was draining from the sphere's core. My gut told me that when it extinguished completely, the deed would be done, and it would detonate—whatever that meant for this unknown weapon. It still had some way to go, but my eyes darted between the boy and Orlaith. Rushing this moment would spook them both. Faelon might flee back to Gaius, never to return; Orlaith might go back into hiding. But we had to move, *now*, or else find some way to destroy this weapon before it destroyed us.

Before I could make a decision or warn them, the stained glass behind us began to vibrate—gently one moment and violently in the next.

It all happened in a second. With a resounding *woosh*, the glass exploded inward; my hand flew out, and I caught a large shard headed straight for Faelon; three white wolves soared through the broken windows, toppling the runestone and shattering it. Up front, a manic, grinning Ryac skidded to a halt, his claws leaving deep grooves in the wood floor.

I reached for Faelon, Orlaith jumped on Ryac's back. Too late. The werewolf had already snatched the boy and tucked him under his arm, and he did not miss a beat, leaping back out the window with the child screaming in his arms.

He let his underlings take care of us, tackling us both to the ground. Orlaith shrieked like a banshee, a battle cry that was not her own, filled with a strength and fury the likes of which I'd never heard. She flipped the rampaging werewolf as though it was no more than a corn husk doll, burying her heel in its crotch and her knife in its chest. It wrapped its long, sinewy arms around her, but, without hesitation, she bit down on its forearm until her fangs drew blood. Then she dove hard, shoulder-first, into the wolf on top of me. As they struggled, one of them kicked the brass sphere. Its light was interrupted as it rolled away, casting the room in light then shadow then light again in rapid succession.

With another shriek, a sickening gulch, and a flash of moon magic, the head of the wolf who'd been on top of me rolled. I fought through dizziness and nausea to make sure the other one was down—for now, if not forever. When he stopped moving, I cast about for the sphere and found it, still and glowing steadily, in the recesses of the library.

Orlaith was already climbing up to what remained of the window sash. I hesitated between following her and doing ... Lady only knew what with the sphere. Getting it away from here. Anywhere. Anything. Gaius had told Faelon it wouldn't hurt the tree, but I didn't make a habit of trusting his word, did I?

In the end, I chanced slipping it into one of my pouches —*precisely*, so I could still keep an eye on its light level—and staggered after my sister.

Together, we climbed out onto the bilé's great branches. Wind carrying smoke and embers played with our hair, whipping loose strands and curls about our faces. Far below, at the base of the tree, Ryac was unhooking his claws from the trunk. Judging by the bark in his wake, he'd dug his claws in and rode them down. A crying Faelon hung off him like a knapsack, arms clasped around the wolf's neck for dear life.

I gripped Orlaith's arm before she could dive right off the edge. We could fall farther and harder than humans, yes, but from this height, she'd get hurt. In this realm, she could *die*. She knew that, but with her son in trouble, she'd forgotten. Her eyes were a haze of grief and anger as she looked at me.

Taking point, I led us down branch by branch. My skin crawled with every step Ryac took away from us as he wove through the city, toward the northern gate. By the time we dropped down to a root and slid off, I'd lost sight of him.

All around us, quillies and Éirins chased each other through the city. Arrows and magic flew. Men were caught and died; others were locked in combat; yet others carved through their foes nearly without stopping. I assumed Solma's main focus was on the mess outside the gates, but as Orlaith and I fought our way to the northern gate, I saw also the odd Guardian, fae, or aranfox.

Artillery fire was constant. Aquilan missiles struck our walls like a steady drum beat. But the next explosion felt different. Fiery, as though a dragon was roasting the north wall. The blast was followed by splintering and screeching metal, then an earth-rending boom.

We thrust ourselves onto the main thoroughfare to see that the north gate had been breached. Rows of shiny brass tree-cutters marched in, meeting a roaring Éirin force. Druids had morphed themselves into ents, outsized trees fit to pummel infantry into the dirt, but they were weak against the tree-cutters' jets of fire. Yet...

Orlaith sprinted forward, but I held back to assess the situation. Something wasn't quite right. The Aquilans weren't pushing the way they had at the western gate, and it seemed an inefficient tactic, funneling all the tree-cutters through the same entrance. Why do that when you could divide them and burn the whole city down within the hour?

It was almost as though this spectacle at the north gate was a distraction.

Gaius's words came back to me. *The northern gate will have fallen. Exit there under cover of darkness and I will meet you...*

A deranged cry on my left slammed my ear drums. A legionary plowed into me, sending us both crashing to the ground. As we braced against each other, his helmet tipped off his head, smacked me in the face, and rolled away. Wet heat ran from my nose. Goddess *damn*, I had no time for this.

With a snarl, I bucked forward and cracked our skulls together. He went limp, and I threw him aside, dragging myself once more to my feet.

Exit under cover of darkness and I will meet you.

Faelon would not be the only one Gaius met.

This push and pull, this unholy hostage situation, it ended tonight.

I sprinted after Orlaith, shot past the skirmish, leapt through flames that singed my armor and hair—and escaped out the north gate, into the night.

8

The Aquilans' march and the ensuing battle had melted the remaining frost around the city walls and down in the valley. Ryac was a white speck running on all fours through the winter-blooming red heather. It was eerily quiet out here, the battle muffled in the distance, the crickets and night birds hidden in silence. In the far distance, where the smoking remains of Aiken Forest met a deep ravine, I could just barely see a small light, as from a lantern.

Light.

I wasn't sure when I had stopped seeing the light sphere in the corner of my vision, but when I faltered and patted myself down, my fears were confirmed. It was nowhere to be found. Lost.

The Aquilan who'd tackled me. He must have knocked it from my pouch. I'd been foolish to keep it open, but I'd wanted to be able to gauge when the sphere would detonate. Now it was back there in the city. Exactly where Gaius wanted it to be.

At once, I pivoted, one foot pointed toward the city, the other away. Before I could take another step, I paused. Looked back at my sister, her form growing smaller as quickly as Ryac's was. I thought of the look in my nephew's eyes, and the sobs that had him shaking against the werewolf's back.

I looked back at the city in the distance...

...and with a half-groan, half-wail of frustration, I turned and sprinted toward the ravine.

Ryac must be able to smell us in pursuit, because a gleeful whoop echoed through the valley as he slid down the bank of the ravine and out of sight. Orlaith arrived first and slid down after him.

Almost immediately, the harsh clap and sizzle of magic broke the silence, followed by a strangled cry.

I arrived mere moments later. Breath ragged in my throat, I stopped at the edge, staring wildly down. Orlaith knelt on her hands and knees in the stream at the bottom of the ravine, tangled in vicious black thorns that seemed to jump up around her. As I began to ease down the incline toward her, I recognized their sheen and the iciness emanating from them. She'd sprung a thorn-wire trap—and rather than steel, this thornwire was made of feyiron.

Slate gray with a blueish cast, feyiron was mined in lands where, supposedly, the fae Courts had spilled innocent mortal blood soon after the veil was sundered. It was a bane to all fae and faekin—including Guardians, as we'd found out the hard way. Any contact with feyiron, even a touch, was excruciating. It went beyond mere physical pain, instilling a fear so dark and primal I shuddered every time I recalled it.

And Orlaith was wrapped in it. Her ghostly cyan magic seeped from her in her panic, flickering; she swayed on all fours, gaze fixed on something I couldn't see. The cold void was taking her. It was not the first time Gaius had done this to someone I loved. My heart constricted and bled as I recalled Hiberos's last moments on this earth, how he'd died in my arms.

I slid to her side and managed to snag one of her moon-blessed daggers, careful not to touch the thornwire as I sliced through it. I'd never forget what it was to touch feyiron. In that cold place, I'd have done anything, sacrificed anything, to be rid of the torment. Yet when I cut enough that Orlaith could move her arm, she reached out and gripped me.

"No," she rasped. "Leave me. Find my *son*."

I threw a look over my shoulder and saw the barest hint of Ryac's white pelt working through the underbrush. "I can't leave you here like this. Stay still. I'll cut—"

"*My son*, Mave, my *son*," she barked, and pushed me away from her with a strength that should have been impossible under the influence of feyiron. "*Go!*"

I stared at her. Orlaith or Eytine, it didn't matter. If I lost her again ... if this bloody cycle was allowed to turn and turn without stopping...

But in the end, all I could do was obey. Because she was right. This was the right thing to do.

I shoved the glowing dagger into my bandolier and sprinted after Ryac. Mindful that there were undoubtedly other traps, I kept to the incline, hoping momentum would keep my balance, leaping to the other side when deadfall got in my way. Eventually, the ravine leveled and rose into a patch of clear-cut forest. The oaks and birches were nothing more than stumps, and those trees that still stood had been charred and maimed by the Aquilan march.

Just past the center of the clearing, Ryac awaited me, one arm bracing my nephew across his front like a shield. His wide-open maw dripped saliva.

Uncertain of his play, I kept distance between us, hand poised to grab a blade. "Hurt him," I warned, "and I'll see to it your pack dies gruesome deaths, all of them."

"Oh, my. And you call *me* a bloodthirsty monster." Ryac cracked his too-long neck. "Never had any intention of hurting him, lassie. I'm just the courier, an' I?"

Another flash of white caught my eye. An Aquilan officer entered the clearing astride a pale horse. His helmet hid his face, but I'd know that posture and those hairy forearms anywhere, even if the pattern of scars across them had changed.

Gaius slid from his saddle and removed the helm, shaking out his curls. It was the first time I'd beheld him with my true sight since I'd put out his eye and cut his throat. He wore a leather eye-patch adhered to his face with a simple cantrip rather than a strap, and his breastplate and gorget did not quite hide from view the raised scar across his windpipe.

Seeing him in my mind was bad enough; being face to face with him again made my legs go numb. My heart squeezed. My breath got heavier. I knew showing how he affected me only granted him power, but I couldn't help it. I knew that, separated from his army, his strength was nothing compared to mine, but my body did not seem to remember.

His eye shone like a diamond as he approached me, gaze traveling up and down, his teeth grazing his lower lip like he wanted to pull me into his mouth and feast. Suddenly, it was not the eight-foot cannibal werewolf that seemed the most dire threat to me but this six-foot, one-eyed human man.

When he stood a mere ten yards from me, he finally spoke. "No matter how many times we cross swords, my lures still work. You run from me, yet you always return." He exhaled low and slow. "It's all right, Mave. I feel it, too. The red thread that tethers us and pulls us together. Deny it as fiercely and as often as you like, but you will never be rid of it."

We stood in silence, breathing hard and as one.

In some ways, he was right. I was woman enough to admit that. He would always be the man who'd destroyed my home, who'd killed my sister, who'd killed me. I would always be the one who had defied him, even as he cut me down. It wasn't a bond unique to Gaius and me; it was a bond perhaps all Aquilans and Éirins shared. Maybe even all men and women. Thousands of years struggling against one another, living in each other's space, trading, fighting, loving, dying, mingling blood. Since what seemed like the beginning of time we had toed the line with each other. In so many ways, we were bound up in each other in a sort of sick symbiosis. In hatred and greed and desperation. But I wasn't convinced it was a thread so much as a suture, one none of us could stop picking at. We were sewn together across a bloody divide, the very ground beneath our feet infected by the consequences of all our actions and inactions.

It seemed to me that Aquilans needed us much more than we needed Aquilans. And if I could not yet cleanse the infection from all of Éire, I would at least cleanse it from me.

"If you can't see how utterly your presence repulses me," I whispered, "you are completely deluded. I never even think about you."

A muscle in his jaw jumped, his eye shining with something like hurt. He inclined his head. "Try to hide your true feelings, deny them, I don't care—you keep coming back."

"If I return, it's not for you. You're just unfortunate enough to be in my way." I pointed my chin at Faelon, who still shivered in Ryac's grip fifteen yards away. "If your red thread exists, it draws me toward my nephew, no one else."

Gaius sneered, tracing the shape of my chin like he wanted to grab it. "You look regal now, *Princess*, but you will always be a slave. You will always be that filthy, starving barbarian from Fraochgleann." The name of my village from his mouth stirred bile in my throat. "Perhaps it isn't a thread that binds us but a leash."

"If that's so, tonight, you're holding the wrong end."

Flames jumped in his eyes even as he smirked—and from a holster at his side, he withdrew a small golden scepter topped with a clear gem. My torso hollowed. I knew without having to be told that this instrument would detonate the brass sphere, wherever it had fallen, whatever its current light level. "As always, your audacious faith is misplaced."

Usually, Gaius gave me an opportunity to repent. To grovel and beg at his feet. Not this time. Without preamble, he empowered the gem with a tiny spot of light magic, and the scepter began to vibrate and glow. By the time I crashed into him and sent it flying into the tall grass, it was too late.

Faelon screamed—"Father!"—but every other sound was drowned out by the roaring in my ears. With one hand I held Gaius still by the throat; with the other, I jabbed him hard enough that his nose cracked and spewed blood. He was dazed, choking, but he gripped my thighs and pulled me into the cradle of his hips like a lover driving deeper into his partner. His inexorable, psychotic, grasping fixation was, as always, declared so plainly in his every move and reaction that it drove me to madness.

I grabbed Orlaith's blade from my bandolier and raised it.

A boiling red glow, rather than cyan, bathed us.

The blade. I'd never seen it glow with anything other than moon power, yet—

"*What is that?*" Faelon screamed with abject terror, pointing up to the sky.

Even as I turned to look, I staggered off of Gaius, putting distance between myself and everyone else in the clearing. My fist was clenched hard around the hilt of the blade ... but it loosened as, beyond the tops of the trees, I saw what had Faelon so scared.

The moon was big, bright, and so red it hurt to look at.

My first instinct was to grab my nephew and run.

"Faelon—" I turned, but both he and Ryac were gone, as if they'd never been there at all. The only soul in the clearing was Gaius, lifting himself to his feet with a hand cradling his nose.

"*What have you done?*" I shrieked, descending with a vengeance and pushing him back down to the ground. The world felt slow and off-kilter. "What have you done? *What did you do* to the *moon?*"

I expected to see dark satisfaction on his face. What I saw instead was worse, more chilling than any grim victor's smile. He was wide-eyed, his mouth open. A childlike fear and confusion I'd *never* seen filled his face. "I ... I don't know."

The earth shook.

Primal terror gripped the back of my neck; in turn, I gripped the back of Gaius's and hauled him like a sack of meat through the charred trees until Bile Cernunnos came into view. The valley, road, and city were drenched in a familiar orange-red hue.

I threw Gaius to all fours at my feet and kicked him hard in the ribs. "*What did you do?*"

He shuddered and coughed, unable or unwilling to answer.

The earth shook harder, and the heavens seemed to shake with it, as though the sky might crack apart.

With a snarl, I grabbed a handful of his curls and yanked his head back. He was forced to look at me, capillaries bursting in his single, pale eye. "What does your weapon do?" I held the dagger to his throat. "*Answer me!*"

The Gaius I knew, even if he were to answer me, would never be afraid of a blade. He'd lusted for his own demise since the moment he had an heir. Whatever was happening now was so unexpected he forgot himself. Spit flew from his mouth as he grimaced, his breath coming in shrill wheezes. "Miasma! It's a miasma. The ball—it was only supposed to release a gas. The legionaries have equipment, f-face, face coverings so it would spare them..."

Somehow, I abstained from snapping his neck. "What does the miasma *do*?"

"It—it's corrosive to the flesh. Nothing more." His gaze went from mine to the blood moon. "I swear on Luca's life, I had nothing to do with—"

A great shrieking rent the valley, a thousand spirits' voices raised in unceasing chorus. It was the most discordant, corrupted song ever heard. Like the groan of wood or squeal of ice under great stress, it told my hindbrain that something was breaking.

That the *world* was breaking.

I don't know what I thought I might do, but I dropped Gaius. Left him behind. Sprinted for all I was worth toward Bile Cernunnos, where a blood red haze filled with embers had begun to drift above the walls, up toward the branches of the great tree. The ground bucked and swelled and had me staggering in a disjointed pattern; if I weren't fae, I'd be on my knees hanging on for dear life.

I ran. Even when the walls of the city crumbled like ash. Even when the grass withered and turned slimy red, septic orange, and bruised purple. Even when the earth split and began to swallow the bilé, I ran.

I wasn't the only one running. Aquilans, Éirins, and faekin scattered for cover. Any man not trampled was forced to run on a road of human bodies. Like a salmon swimming upstream, I pushed through the throngs of primarily legionaries coming my way. I called for my loved ones. Faelon. Orlaith. Ferghal, and every other Éirin I knew. It didn't make any difference; they wouldn't be able to hear me above the screeching of the heavens anyway. Boils rose from the grass as from seared flesh, white and black and shivering with pressure. The ground became spongy, and with every step, my boots sank in and got covered with tacky red residue. The gash in the earth extended, widening, widening, sinking the city until only the branches of the bilé were visible above ground.

The crack sundered the valley in twain. I was forced to choose the south side. Apart from Orlaith. Apart from Faelon.

"Princess!"

It was Solma. She grabbed my arm and pulled me to her just as the ground gave way beneath me. As though cleaved with a blade, it fell away, leaving behind a sheer drop. We stood looking down into the abyss before swiftly stepping back. But before I could thank Solma, another great shriek split the air.

The moon flashed brightly enough to scorch the valley. My skin felt hot and tight over my bones.

In the next moment, the red moon was stark white again. After the searing glow, it looked so pale and gray and dead—and as if the land read my mind, as soon as I thought it, a low moan rose around us. Those sickly boils popped and oozed across the putrid earth, and the ground below it swelled. As though something were just beneath the grass and heather, trying to break free.

The moan sounded again. But this time, it was more of a whistle.

I'd heard that whistle before.

How could I ever forget?

The sound haunted my memories and my nightmares.

I understood what was happening a second before the sod at my feet finally split. A ghastly, slick, skinny arm burst forth. The monster attached to it seized my ankle and used it to haul itself up out of the dirt.

If its moans hadn't put me on to what it was, there was no mistaking its eyeless face and gaping mouth.

Fomori.

With a snarl, I kicked it in the chin, drawing my bow. Before it could get its bearings, I stomped its head under my boot—but where there was one, there were more. Even as the thing's skull exploded into paste, I turned and beheld the rest of the battlefield.

There must have been a thousand white heads rising up out of the dirt, thousands of arms flailing and clawing for purchase in the soil. Each head that managed to break through spat dirt and began to wail as though the night air hitting their skin burned them. Not cries of rage but of agony, of surprise and upset so genuine that they twisted my heart.

These weren't the mossy stone fomori from the labyrinth, nor the conkreet-and-steel abominations from the Dead World ruins. Not even the ones of black stone and blight. These were beings of flesh and bone, although the flesh was pale and cold and covered in a white, creamy film. Those with eyes bore seething blood-orange gazes. But they were fomori; the cold earth from which they climbed seeped that thick mist that always followed their kind.

The land trembled, the tear through the valley dilating. The moon screamed one last time, her voice rising over the wails. Then the trembling stopped, and the horde's attack began.

Éirin and Aquilan fled. Half of each of our armies were gone in a minute. Those who were left might have been enough to kill a thousand fomori, but more kept coming. Humanlike ones used unearthed roots to pull themselves up from the huge breach. Seven-legged hounds darted through the grass after their prey, tackling anyone and everyone. Conjoined goblins, boneless skin beasts, scythe-handed hunchbacks with protruding rib cages rose from the earth and joined their hunt. The branches of the sunken bilé were swarmed with fleshy, pointy, beaked fomori waiting to pick off the battlefield when all was done.

There were too many. Even if all three armies banded together, there would be too many, and they multiplied by the

moment. Our inadequacy was so obvious that, without communication with one another, the legion's commanders turned their
troops around and retreated. The wolfkernes worked double time
to get their human brothers and sisters to safety while the few
faekin left struggled to hold the line and contain the growing
fomori horde. It was for naught. Solma and I fought side by side,
blade and spear, but inch by inch, we were driven back.

And apart from the size of their force, there was the mist.

I'd never seen what that mist could do if it managed to get into
living tissue. Now I saw.

The hulking fomori I'd been fighting disintegrated into a pile
of blood, mucus, and membrane before me, and as it fell, it
revealed a wolf-shape locked in combat with a fomori that was
trying and failing to look like a deer. Not just any wolf-shape.
Lanky, light brown—Brianne. Next to her, a warp-warrior's magic
shield flickered, his skin turning ashen.

It all seemed to happen in slow motion. The not-deer reared
up, its slender fingers poised to grab and tear. Brianne pushed the
warp-warrior out of the way, and the thing came down on her. She
managed to sink her claws into its chest, but its fingers tangled into
her fur, yanking down with all its weight. Her hide tore. Even as
she sank her jaws into the creature's throat and ripped it out, the
mist crept in, hungry to invade her flesh.

At first, it simply gathered around her wounds as if licking
them. Testing her out, making certain this was a viable entrance.
Then it coiled back and struck like a snake.

At once, Brianne seized up. She smacked her chest, scrambling to try and figure out what this feeling was. Snarling and
panicked and jumping, she shifted back to a woman. The fact that
she was naked was as irrelevant to her as it was to everyone
looking on in horror as the mist slid inside her. Her veins turned
ghastly white, then gray as river stones.

Once the mist took hold, it tore through her with startling efficiency. Within moments, her eyes turned solid, milky white. All
color left her skin. She clawed at her knotted blond hair, fell to her
knees, and begged for the Lady's mercy.

It was too late. She threw her head back and inhaled one final, ragged scream, then...

Brianne was gone.

Her naked body jerked up from the sickened ground, palms, knees, and shins covered in blight. Each limb moved in halting, stuttering motions, swinging and flailing with little harmony as though pulled by wires. Whatever the mist was, wherever it came from, it was in control now.

"Brianne!" Ferghal appeared beside me, his dark fur matted with gore. "No. Lady, no!"

The pale gray shell that had once been Brianne trembled as it aimed itself toward him. Its steps faltered at first, like a newborn fawn's. But in the next blink, it was sprinting for him. It lunged and hit him square in the chest, and they fell into a snarling heap.

It only took a moment for him to grab the monster by the throat and immobilize it. As he did, he bellowed into the battlefield, "Cover your wounds, cover your wounds!"

Some of the retreating Éirins reacted quickly enough, slapping their hands or pulling their clothes over any exposed injuries. Many did not. For every four Éirins, one of them fell behind and was overcome with the mist, and their fate was Brianne's. Milky eyed, pale gray and screaming, bodies knotted with grief. The same befell the Aquilans; those unlucky victims joined the fomori and attacked their own, driving back the legion. The allied line buckled as we were hit with not only the fomori horde but the monsters born of the mist.

We cracked. Defense turned to a swift retreat south.

Where Bile Cernunnos had once stood, our war left behind a wasteland of rot—and that was where the fomori stayed, writhing in the blighted gash like maggots in a festering wound.

Sallach was lost.

9

The withering had consumed the land for miles, including that around the newly constructed Moon Gate. The Éirin army was forced to join their spouses and children at the Cuanachtan militia outpost near Kesselhurst. Thanks to the influx of refugees and increased support from Gallive, the outpost had grown since the fall, and could be called a proper military base now. Tents and other temporary dwellings extended it further south, closer to the Moon Gate in the area.

Though at the time I hadn't known they'd taken on wolf-shapes in the decade I was dead, the last time I'd more than passed through here, I reunited with the wolfkernes. With Eamon. With Breanne. Now, they were both gone. Ferghal had not even been able to bring Breanne's body with us—the mist would only look for a new host. She would have no pyre as befitting a wolf-shape; she would not return to the moon, or to her husband Iain.

While we settled into the rainy refugee camp in grim silence, I searched for faces I knew. Who else had made it alive? I saw Manan, Uaine, and a badly beaten Joa. In the slapdash medic tent, Ruadan gently cut the throats of those too wounded to save. Conan, too, had made it out, and was currently sitting on his arse, staring somberly into the fire as though he understood the gravity of the situation. He was probably just lamenting not having had dinner, though.

I could do nothing but sit beside him, let him nose into my greatcoat, and try to focus on even breaths. Orlaith lay across that divide. *Faelon.* How was I going to reach them?

Lady, how was I going to tell Erivon?

It wasn't long until King Manan summoned me. No surprise. Despite the hour, no one could sleep.

What remained of the coalition leaders congregated in the war room in the stone house at the center of town. We were packed in shoulder to shoulder, but there was nothing for it. The bilé and all its lacquered grandeur was gone, perhaps forever, swallowed by the blood moon's blight.

For once, no one rushed to talk over one another. Good thing, too, for if I wasn't mistaken, King Manan looked significantly older and less energetic than usual. I wondered if the destruction of the bilé had a significant effect on his power. It certainly appeared to be so, and he'd lost his cauldron to boot.

Ferghal was a mess, covered in scrapes and scorch marks, eyes bloodshot. He'd lost good men to those werewolves, not to mention a lieutenant in Brianne, and all that agony shone in his gaze. The worst nightmares he'd confessed to me when he'd first become duskwarden were coming true.

"We're gonna need to create more faoladh," he said. "I need each of you to get a list together of candidates, soon as possible."

Solma added, "A search party will need to be assembled for Queen Orlaith."

No one said anything; it was just glassy stares all round.

For once, Ruadan did not wear his serene smile, but he looked upon the others gently. "The sooner we accept that Cernunnos—that Sallach—is gone, the sooner we can plan our next step. My spies tell me the miasma bomb is a new invention. The Empire was using Éire as a testing ground before possibly bringing it elsewhere. The only question is, did they mean to destroy the bilé?"

There was an extended moment of silence.

Finally, the king raised his head. With some effort, it seemed, weighed down now by his rack of antlers. I hadn't expected him to look at me. "Mave. We must know. Was this the legate's plan all along? Did they somehow design their miasma to do all this?"

I knew what he was asking. For once, I believed Gaius's claim that he had nothing to do with the cataclysm, but I summoned my connections regardless.

DRUSILLA HAD BEEN SUMMONED to Fort Alopex the day prior, so that she might meet Faelon when the legion emerged from the valley victorious, to care for the boy after his first real battle. But, of course, no one had been victorious—and the withering had consumed Sallach from the treeline of Aiken Forest to the southern border, leaving Fort Alopex packed with troops.

And, there was no boy.

Gaius stalked the small office like a tiger waiting to be unleashed on a gladiator. His current targets were Ottavian and his lieutenant, Tatius, but Drusilla stuck close to the wall anyway, unwilling to bear the brunt of his wrath. There was enough torturing her at the moment. Agony and fear made her hackles stand on end.

"My son is lost in that wasteland, Belos knows where," the legate growled. "I want a search party assembled before this day is out. If he isn't found before the week's end—" He paused, pinning Ottavian with his manic, bloodshot eye. "Primuses are easily replaced. Three days, then an officer will be transported to Polechia for every day he remains missing after that."

Ottavian, for his part, looked moments from lunging over the desk and strangling his superior. "His mother needs to be told— your wife," he said through gritted teeth. "The boy is too young. He should never have been on the field to begin with."

The leather of Gaius's gloves squealed as he tightened his fists. "I will decide whether my son is ready for combat or not. I will decide everything for you, *Primus*. The boy played an important role, but I wouldn't expect you to understand. As for my wife..." Rounding the desk, he closed the distance between them, his face close enough to Ottavian's that Drusilla might not have heard him if not for her keen lupercal senses. "My wife is none of your concern. Mention her again and it will be the last word your tongue ever speaks."

Ottavian's throat twitched. Gaius did not relent. They stared at one another until, finally, Ottavian blinked. Only then did the legate turn away.

"It will be done," said Tatius. "We'll pull together our best men. Have you any idea where we should look first?"

The next words out of Gaius's mouth sent a chill through Drusilla's ears: "The last time I saw him, Bloodwarden Ryac had him. It was at the edge of Aiken. He carried him off when *she* attacked me. To safety, I thought..." But no, when he'd returned to the fort, there had been no sign of either of them. Drusilla and I both noted the genuine agitation in his face as he turned away from his subordinates.

"That bloody red blight," said Tatius, "what is it? What caused it?"

"Could it have really been the miasma?" Ottavian muttered.

"Believe that if I knew how to blight swathes of Éirin land, the entire island would have been ours years ago."

"Would the barbarians have done it?"

Gaius stilled and seemed to give it some thought. "That tree was sacred to them ... but it also held some power, some reservoir of savage magic. The destruction we bore witness to proves it. Perhaps they saw the way the tide turned and destroyed it simply so we could not have it."

Inwardly, I balked. That wasn't something Éirins would do, destroying our own well of power to spite the quillies. That was something only the Empire would do.

Mave. Only now did Drusilla notice I was there. *Lucastos— Faelon. Have you seen him? Can you find him?*

I still struggled to communicate my thoughts to her with words, but she seemed to get the gist. She released me. Our shared vision wavered, then went dark as I was pitched headfirst into the well of consciousness from which our roots all drank. With hardly any effort at all, I found my nephew and let his spine become my own.

When I opened my eyes, the forest was dark all around me. If the boy had inherited any fae dark vision, it hadn't yet developed.

Bloodwarden Ryac and Faelon had been separated from both the legion and the werewolves. It was just the two of them taking refuge around a small fire.

It smelled bad here. Bloody, fishy, and sweet all at once, a combination the young boy did not know how to place. The noise of the forest had changed, too. Gone were the crickets and bird calls, replaced with a constant, eerie moaning and a sound Faelon could only liken to a trunk in the process of splintering—a dense sort of cracking that made him feel like the world itself was breaking apart.

Such a baby. A stupid baby. Remembering how terribly he'd bungled his role in the battle made him want to hide his face and cry. Pissing himself, only to be carried off like a little child by an adult. And the tree ... that beautiful tree, destroyed forever, because—because of him?

He couldn't contain his shakes and tears no matter how he tried to harden himself. Never before had he been so terrified, not even during the battle. There were things in the woods all around them. He didn't know what to call them. Terrible, pale things covered in a residue that reminded him of the stuff that came off newborn calves. Ryac kept them at bay; they didn't like the fire, but they watched, waiting for it to go out.

Yet, sitting across the fire from the man-wolf did not feel any less dangerous.

Ryac hadn't done anything to hurt him. In fact, if Father were here, he'd say he saved him from those fae trying to lure him away. When they'd finally stopped running from the explosions and blood, the werewolf had turned back into a man—utterly naked, but he'd quickly found one of his people's caches, set the boy up with a clean pair of trousers, and negotiated a tiny camping spot.

He'd even given Faelon a dram of whiskey to calm his nerves and told him, "You get used to the burn, there's a lad," as the drink scorched a trail down his throat.

But now, the fire flickered in front of Ryac's face, obscuring it and twisting his features monstrously in turn. Earlier, he'd gone and fetched them a hare to eat. Faelon had roasted his portion; Ryac ate his raw, and the blood still ran down his chin.

The boy had lived a sheltered life, and this Éirin man appeared so average, yet there was no denying he looked into the face of a predator. Faelon may not be his prey, but still. It was a hair-on-the-back-of-the-neck feeling.

Mist licked the edges of their camp. Faelon shuddered, squirmed, and finally could not stand the silence any longer. When he began to speak—"Erm..."—Ryac raised his brows in anticipation, dark red eyes going round.

"Back in the library..." Faelon managed. "How did you know I would be there?"

The werewolf cracked a too-charming grin. "I smelled you, son."

"But why were you looking for me?"

"Your daddy bade me see you to your rendezvous point."

Faelon flushed, embarrassed at the implication that Father had thought him incapable of carrying out his mission in full. But, he supposed, he should be grateful to Ryac, terrifying or not. He might not have made it out of that library if not for the werewolves' interruption. He might have gone with ... with that woman. The one with skin like breaking tides and eyes like the moon.

Something about her had drawn him in, her scent cool and refreshing and safe as a freshly laundered blanket. It was the way he felt about his mother, yet he hadn't recognized this woman at all. Could it be...? No, because his birth mother had been a barbarian, and she was dead.

Wasn't she?

Father would never lie about something like that.

Would he?

Ryac shifted, drawing Faelon's distant stare back to his present time and place. The werewolf's expression wasn't grave, but he was fixated on the boy before him with equal parts fascination and knowing, as though he could tell exactly what Faelon was thinking.

The boy squirmed again, wishing he'd look somewhere else.

"They'll never accept you back, you know."

The statement seemed to come out of nowhere, and Faelon wasn't even sure what he meant, yet it stung nonetheless. "What?"

"The Éirins. Ah, come, boy, I can see you're having second thoughts. About your father, your empire, your future. In't no use hiding it."

Heat rushed to Faelon's face. "I ... I don't know what you mean."

"When I came through that window, you were thinking of it. Thinking of going with that faerie queen. But what you feel in your breast"—he thumped one splayed hand on his blood-spattered chest—"that thought you may find a home or safety, it's a lie, lad. They don't want you."

When Faelon said nothing, the werewolf continued, "Oh, righteous the Éirins may seem, but the rule of druids carries its own tyranny, my son. Any man who claims he can tell you the natural order of things, or that the soil speaks to him, is deceiving you." He forced a grin that seemed to me to hide rage. "The Aquilans may be ruled by greed, but the Éirins, they are ruled by superstition. And their superstition tells them never to trust people like you and I."

Faelon hedged. "What do you mean? I'm not ... like you."

Ryac wheezed a laugh and raised his brows again. The shine in his eyes was so intense. "Oh, no, lad? My mother was from Sallach. Just like yours."

Mother. The fact that this monster knew anything about his family or the circumstances of his birth made Faelon queasy. What had Father told him? What else did he know? *Why?* Suddenly, he felt even less safe than before. *Now* he felt like prey.

"Sallach has been the borderland between Eire and the

Empire for ... centuries, at least," Ryac murmured to the crackling fire. "Our clans have always been called to hold the line. Male or female, Éirins fight hard, but it don't always turn up roses. My mam was taken, chewed up, used, and spit back out." He tapped his temple with two fingers. "But she never forgot. When she saw her chance, she ran. Ran home. And she thought it might be all right. Then she started showing."

Dread prickled through Faelon as Ryac's gaze turn glassy, far away but beady with hate. "Twins. We were twins. You know what Éirins say about twins?"

Faelon didn't know.

"It's said by the druids that only Aquilan seed produces twins. So, twins are cursed. Have the bad blood in them. *Drough-fuil.* One of 'em must be cast out, left to die in the elements." Ryac shook his head slowly. "My dear mammy, Lady rest her soul, she knew it *was* Aquilan seed, no doubt. But why should it matter? She'd been through it all and come out alive. They couldn't make her believe she was cursed.

"So she left with us. A lone, wand'ring woman, forced to walk Éire. Clanless, begging for scraps. And every village we passed through knew what had happened, what her story was—all they had to do was look at her twins. We hadn't been cursed before, not truly, but now we were. Now we were."

Faelon hugged his knees tightly to his chest. Thinking about the horrible things soldiers sometimes did to women made his stomach feel all empty and stale, and made his eyes heavy like they might cry. Yet still the werewolf persisted.

"Eventually, she'd used up all the good will Cuanacht had to offer an exile with doomed babies. If she didn't want to starve, she had no choice but to go into Westminia. To become a citizen of the empire that had put 'er on that damned path. My brother and I were bred in the slums of New Lindanos, surrounded by quillies. Surrounded by them, like you."

It looked like Ryac wanted him to say something, but the only question he could think of was, "Was it ... better? Being Aquilan?"

Ryac's gaze was dark, his grin sharp. "Oh, boyo. We were

never Aquilan. Those tossers took one look at us, listened to the way we spoke, and they knew we didn't belong. No schooling open to us. Mam was only allowed to take the most degrading, menial of jobs. We started work young, too. Ceramics, brick-makers, bakers—anyone who'd take us. Didn't make any differ-ence." He stamped the ground with his foot casually, like he was snuffing out a bug. "I was the dirt beneath their feet."

The boy couldn't help but compare. He knew he'd lived a privileged life, had never wanted for food or shelter or education. Yet there had always been something inside that felt wrong. Miss-ing. Like in Ryac's story. It wasn't until he'd met that purple fae, the one who gave him the apple and called him *Faelon*, that he'd begun to wonder if that *something* was where or what he was. Never had he considered there might be another life out there waiting for him. Father wanted him to be Aquilan—wanted him to be the strongest soldier the Empire had ever seen—but ... *was* he Aquilan? Was there truly another path, or had his fate been decided for him the moment his birth mother died?

"Did ... didn't you try to go back home?" he asked.

Ryac grunted at the fire. "Moment I was old enough to navi-gate a road on my own, I left for Cuanacht. Tried to return to my clan. They wanted to know who my people were, and, well, I couldn't tell 'em. So they sent me off. Then the next clan, and the next one. Weeks of searching for someone who'd take me without my mother's name. Then one night, I'm sitting in camp, readying for another night sleeping alone in the cold, and who do I see approaching down the road but meself?"

Faelon sat up straighter. "Your twin?"

"Aye. He'd followed me. Come to bring me back home. Mam was dying."

"Didn't you go?"

"I sat him down across the fire, gave him a dram of whiskey, let him fade off. Then, as he slept, I cut his throat."

A frisson of utter terror made Faelon's face go numb. He looked down at his own little cup of whiskey, once again aware of how isolated they were, and fought not to pee himself again. *I want Mother. Please, Mighty Ones, I'll do anything, just let me get home to Mother.*

"Brought his body to Mam's old druid-chief, same one that'd cast us out. I thought if I did the deed myself ... maybe..." Ryac's gaze was empty and cold again. Dead. When he grinned, no mirth touched his eyes. "They cast me out again, this time as a murderer. Funny, isn't it? They were so appalled over something they themselves had tried to do decades before."

He spread his hands. "But where, oh, where does an Éirin murderer go? To worship the God of Murder, of course. Living in the woods, I found a sect of his followers and, finally, a family."

Faelon hugged himself tighter. Speaking of the Old Gods frightened him as much as it intrigued him—he wasn't allowed to learn about anything but the Mighty Ones. "God of murder?"

"Oh, yea, the Crooked God. Some of his adherents live among the Éirins. The acceptable ones—those berserkers who use magic shields, the warp-warriors. *Some* bloodshed is acceptable. Not mine. Not me. I've never been acceptable."

"And that's what made you a ... a ... werewolf?"

"No, the Crooked God didn't make werewolves, the moon did. But many werewolves *do* revere him. No, we pass this on through bites. Most can't shift at will like those faoladh, and can't control themselves when they do."

"But your pack can?"

"We can now, thanks to your da. His people found some ritual stone. Freedom from the moon's tyranny, it promised. He sought us out. No more unpredictable shifts, no more losing control. Real power, not a curse. A new, free breed. *Moonless.*"

"But if you don't like the Aquilans..."

"We needed that power, lad. Whatever it takes to protect my pack. My family." His gaze was intense, smiling, triumphant. "The druids may not acknowledge me, but I am Éirin. I am the child they never wanted, the child they betrayed. As those men lay dying, they'll look into my face and understand their superstitions were never, ever going to protect them from me."

Faelon swallowed hard. "But ... if my father flattens all the Éirins ... won't that include your people?"

"He's given me what I want. He can never take that ritual back. So Cuanacht falls"—he gestured widely—"we vanish into the woods and become ghosts again. Bumps in the night. *Demons*. It's what we do. This time, though, we'll be taking all the power of the moonslayer with us."

They fell into silence, the dark forest droning around them and the snarls of those awful, pale monsters on the wind. Soon, the snarls were joined by howls, and Ryac perked up.

"Ah! There's my people now." He must have read something in the way they called, for he added, "And sounds like they've found something."

Ryac stood, faced the direction of the wind, and tipped his head back. A deep, gravelly, throaty howl ripped from him, a sound Faelon could not believe had come from a man's lungs. The boy curled tighter, too scared to speak. To be stuck with the blood-warden was frightful enough, but to be surrounded by the entire pack...?

His cry was answered with yips and whoops. Whatever they communicated, Ryac seemed satisfied with it, and turned back to the fire with a pleasant smile, shoving his hands in his pockets.

As he sauntered over, he canted his head at Faelon. "Your da calls you 'little wolf,' doesn't he?"

The boy did not reply. Everyone called him that.

"There's a place you might belong." His voice was soft now. "A family who might want you ... for who you are, not who they want you to be. Werewolves can't produce children, even with humans. Our blood in't right. Even when we're lucky, they die in the womb." Faelon hadn't realized Ryac was as close as he was until he clamped a feverishly warm hand around his shoulder. "I..."

With a shuddering gasp, the lad wrenched his shoulder out of Ryac's grip and, shooting to his feet, put the fire between them again. The man-wolf's intent, steel-cutting gaze conveyed a riot of emotion Faelon could not even begin to understand. Silence and tension held between them for no more than a few heartbeats, but it seemed to last forever.

"Fine," Ryac said at last, raking a hand through his sweaty waves. "But don't say you had no warning." And he sat down, propping his feet up to wait. "Let's hope your da cares enough to come find you."

IO

I conveyed what I saw to Manan: "Gaius was telling the truth. This disaster wasn't caused by the miasma."

No sooner had I said it than Uaine appeared, even more exhausted and unshaven than usual. There were thousands of refugees to think about now, both from Bile Cernunnos and the outlying farms of Southern Sallach, and with the land scourged from the border to Westeris Wall, the logistics had just become a hundred times more complicated.

They couldn't stay in the Underland; it was the first thing the king asked. Humans couldn't enter the raw fae realm that way. They'd start losing their minds as soon as they passed through a gate, and since fae blood was required to open the gates anyway, fae had the final say. Manan's fury, limp though it was, was an evident and ever-present burn against my skin. The lunar fae had done impressive work at the battle before it all went to shit, but because of the malfunctioning gate and the small number of troops garrisoned in the Goneland, there still had not been enough of them. Certainly not the army tens of thousands strong they'd promised.

"That leaves Gallive." His voice was thin, taut. "It's the only place that can sustain so many of us."

"Shall I send someone to ask?" said Uaine.

The king shook his head. "Nay. This, I think, is one of those times we must ask for forgiveness rather than permission." He nodded to Uaine. "Councilor, I trust you to gather the refugees and arrange the transport. I give you leave to use any resource I can offer you. Ferghal, you stay and assist. Commander Solma, I'd appreciate if you did the same." They nodded, and finally the king looked at me and the other coalition leaders. "I will ride ahead to Gallive. Who will go with me?"

Ruadan bowed his head. "The Gallowglass will be with you, though you may not see us."

With that, the coalition cleared the war room for the last time. Within a week, this garrison would be abandoned, along with every other Éirin settlement in Sallach. The thought turned my stomach, and that was without mentioning my poor, stranded sister and the miles of rotting earth between us. But there was nowhere to go except forward. I made the afternoon's journey to the Moon Gate at Kesselhurst, intending to cut through the Underland. No need to endure the nights of travel required to reach Gallive; there must be a closer gate. Plus, King Erivon needed to be told his wife's whereabouts.

Lady be with me. Telling a powerful, doting husband like Erivon that his soulmate was in mortal danger? I'd need every blessing.

But first, my own soulmate. The moment I stepped through the dizzying void of the Gate and landed in the Crossroads, a tug throbbed at my center, persistent and strong. Like a heartbeat but lower, pounding at the edge of my rib cage.

Hiberos—whatever form he took now—was calling to me. My soulbind, once-husband, however contentious our relationship when we'd parted. He was a limb I could never hope to replace. He was a seventh sense I would give anything to restore. A part of me I hadn't known well enough to understand died that day.

So how could I resist when he called?

As always, it was only to his will—not Gaius, not the king's, not my relations', but *his* will—that I bent, powerless.

Far beyond the road, deep into the long-shattered, long-healed landscape of the Underland, the heartgrove was quiet as if breathless. Instinctively, I knew what I would find before I saw it.

The twig that had grown into a young, stubby tree now towered above me, its willowy branches nodding in the light breeze. Glowing blue fruits, similar in shape to Hiberos's heart, swayed from its boughs. The opalized veins shooting through the bark had become so bright they were glowing pearly white with threads of ultraviolet. And there, let in to the trunk, was what had called to me. What I had somehow known I would see. A face and frame so breathtaking and far too familiar.

Though Hiberos stood upright, he was still partially melded with the tree, his eyes closed and his arms crossed over his chest. In the fall, he'd died broken and beaten and pouring pitch-black blood, but now he looked as peaceful as if he were asleep. He was intact—more than intact, I realized as I ran closer. Beautifully formed, in fact. Though back then his old body had become less worn, gray, and skinny the more time he spent by my side, *this* body was brand new. He remained slim, but his chest and shoulders and neck were broader now. Strapping, powerful, each muscle perfectly carved. As before, the upper half of his wooden body was smooth, a lighter color and grain like the sanded face of an oaken table. His bottom half, bearing the switchback legs of a goat, bore rough bark rather than a faun's fur—but every inch of his hide was healthy and golden now. Gone were the countless nicks, scars, knots, and patches of moss and lichen. He was intact and unburnt. His golden hair and beard were sleek and untangled. His arms and thighs were thick. And his large hands were strong, with the perfect amount of definition in the tendons and veins.

The only interruption in his perfectly sculpted body was a hole in his chest, partially covered by one of his hands. A matrix of wooden veins created a cage over it, but within lay a filigreed seed with a pulsing inner glow.

His heart—the one I had torn from my chest to return to him.

At once, my own heart lodged in my throat, as if it were trying to leap from my body to join its twin.

Time stood still. I could not stop myself from reaching out and stroking the plains of his face. The long, broad, hircine nose; his smooth brow, which, even now, seemed to have a mischievous quirk to it; his lips, the upper thin and the lower a dusky, kissable pink. Oh, Lady, the thought of how much time I'd wasted not kissing those lips.

I'd never be so stubborn again. If only the universe would give him back to me. If only he would wake himself out of his winter's doze...

Yet the withering gnawing at the edges of the grove had crept closer since my last visit, so close that the outer roots of this tree in which Hiberos dwelled must already be touching the rot. The mist slithered above the sickly moss like a snake in tall grass, waiting for me to step out of bounds.

If I did not figure out how to extract Hiberos soon, he'd wither just like the rest of the heartgrove. All my blighted fecking hope, all our pain and bargaining, would have been for nothing in the end.

I pulled my own bottom lip between my teeth and ran my hands over him, searching for any spot of heat, any sign of life. The tug in my sternum was ever-present, yet he lay silent and unmoving.

Finally, I touched the cage over his heart. The persistent hum within me spiked without warning, the keening of a string instrument but felt in my soul. Heat bloomed under my fingers. Not much, but enough. Enough that I knew he was fighting. Fighting to get to me, to rejoin me in this world.

Knowing that, a strange sensation overtook me. I leaned into the magic around me and felt something I never had before. My judgment became fuzzy at the edges; for once, my mind stilled, engulfed in a feeling of absolute safety.

Even here, even now, when I appear to you like this, you are protected. Whether it was truly his voice or a sentiment passing through the Weave between us, the words brought me a comfort I hadn't had in...

Comfort I had *never* had, not even in my dreams of him. Because now I knew who he was, and what loving him might do to me, and still I was certain there was no one else I wanted. And now he was within reach.

Have you whines for my wedding, did you bring bride and bedding?

With both hands, I touched his velvety face, ran my fingers down his unmarred chest. I leaned into this warmth, literally as well as figuratively, brushing my lips across the grain of his knuckles. Taking my time, I placed kisses on each one, mouth parted and breath slow. I explored every new slant and sinew as I kissed my way down one forearm. My hands cupped his elbows. I wanted to secure his arms fast around my waist, but the tree didn't give—I couldn't pull him out. He was stuck.

If only he would wake himself out of his winter's doze ... and bore me down like he used to...

My rose, I still can feel you. Like a breeze, his words brushed a curl against my cheek.

If he could feel me, then I would show him. I would show him, now, how sorry I was. Show him that I was ready to defy the gods for him, that I was ready to begin again in earnest.

With my fingers and lips, I trailed down the length of his inert body until I was on my knees before him, arms outstretched to stroke his stomach and hips, gazing up at him with a drunken reverence. The spark of a thought I'd had before returned: I had no use for Gealach or the Woman Beneath. He would be my god, my guide, my guard. And I would be his.

"I will release you," I whispered, tracing the lines of the bark of his thighs. "I *will* find a way."

All worship requires a sacrifice, purred the faint impression of his voice.

In my mind, I replied, *Let me worship you first. Then I'll give you anything you need.*

The light in the trunk's fissures began to pulse quicker, the violet ribbons starting to overtake the pearly white. Somehow, I knew that this was him struggling against his bonds. Imagine my surprise when his hide began to hum under my fingertips. Wait, no, it wasn't his hide. It was something inside of him.

At the apex of his thighs, the frost crack widened until revealing the fruit it sheathed. His cock, thick and solid as a burdock root. The base was bulblike and purplish, but gradually toward the head, his length became almost human—like flesh, at least, all flushed and satin. He smelled of wild thyme and berries and moss and soil. Of the rut. Of bonfires. Of nights spent dancing and joining our bodies together again and again until the morning dew washed away our sweat.

Without much thought, I wrapped one hand around him, the other still braced against his lower abdomen. Then I took him into my mouth.

Swallowing him was the single most erotic thing I'd done in living memory. His taste, the musk. The warmth. The feeling of his tender yet unyielding manhood sliding to the back of my tongue. I felt my eyes droop, my entire body relaxing and loosening to take him deeper. He could not move, but he'd proven he could see me. What must I look like to him now, tunic slipping off my shoulders, curls a mess, the black tears forever branded on my cheeks? Real tears soon joined them, tears of longing and muscular reflex both.

Lathing my tongue over every ridge, every vein, I worshiped him. Swiped my tongue through the channel at the very tip then popped my mouth over it and sucked, desperate for a taste of him. It never crossed my mind that this might be strange, giving my love to a tree. It was Hiberos. And though I did not intend on making a habit of kneeling at his feet, here, bent before the shrine to every mistake I'd made since my rebirth, for once, I practiced humility.

His tip touched the back of my throat dangerously, and I choked, drawing back with a gasp. My hot tears stuck to me, a string of saliva still connected us. Using both hands now, I pumped him from tip to shaft, squeezing, stroking.

This time, when I heard his voice, it was choked with ecstasy. *Rise and give me your soul.*

I obeyed. Despite the fever raging through my body, I stripped of my tunic and what remained of my leathers. Once I was bare before my altar, I ran my hands over myself, over the glistening lavender skin I was still growing used to. As if possessed, my slender, clawed hands roved over the swells of my breasts, brushing against the hot, swollen peaks of my nipples. One hand migrated to my throat, clinging loosely there, while the other tangled into the snowy white curls between my legs. My clit was aflame, throbbing, peeking from my folds. Touching it with even a fingertip made me shiver and gasp. Hiberos's answering satisfaction vibrated through the air even as he remained still as the dead.

I turned my back to him, bent, eased close, and used a combination of his shaft and my own fingers to rub myself into a dripping mess. By the time I guided the broad, heavy head of his cock to my entrance, it threatened to slip in all at once.

Don't waste time, the voice begged, not derisively but urgently.

I groaned in response, my eyes rolling back as I arched and thrust him in. Slowly at first, then all at once, impaling myself.

A strangled cry. He was deep, *deep* inside, twitching against the back of my navel. Having him at this angle pinched for a moment, then was glorious. Then I was bucking back, desperate to feel the drag against my sweet spot and the nudge against my innermost wall. Desperate to fill myself with him until I nearly split—pushing my body to its very limits. With each bounce, harsh grunts sawed out of me until they joined in a continuous groan, rising in pitch the closer I brought myself.

But I *wanted* his hands on me. To take my pleasure was heavenly, but to be with him was godhood. I needed it. Needed him to be free. Free to grip me, stroke me, *fuck* me, claim me, hurt me even—then to love me, protect me, take up arms for me, cradle me...

He needed my help again. *One last time,* the Weave whispered.

When blood is spilt to wake the sun,
The wheel shall turn, the thread unspun

Of course. Did it not always come back to my blood, to what I was willing to sacrifice? That first day, when his half-formed hand had burst from the soil, I'd nicked myself. Then my second visit, the fomori had cut me badly, and I'd bathed my wounds in water caught in his roots. Now...

I writhed and groaned, clenched and shivered, grinding myself back on his root. One final offering. I could make things right. No more stubbornness, no more fighting, no more secrets. Just learning each other again, Gealach and her law be damned. Just *this*, for as long as we had until the cycle began anew.

My vision blurred before graying completely, my climax threatening to send me to whatever underworld he'd crawled out of. Perhaps I now understood what he'd done back when I was human. Now I understood why he'd fixed the trials so I'd win. Why he'd done everything in his power to keep me from fighting on the front lines. I, too, would beg, steal, and lie to see him return to my side, and I'd lived mere *months*—not a thousand years—without him.

"Forgive me," I groaned, slamming myself down on him a final time, sheathing him to the best of my ability.

Tears fell anew as I grabbed the only weapon within reach: Tali's dagger tucked into my discarded boot.

After my experiences in battle, drawing the blade across my forearm took very little, but I still expected it to hurt. I didn't expect it to send me over the edge. Didn't expect the final rush of blood and heat to my core, the pounding ecstasy overtaking every sense until all my being was pearly white and violet strands and *him, him, him.*

The scent of sweet copper mingled with his musk as the blood pooled at the base of the trunk. It sank into the thirsty soil, nearly disappearing from sight—

And my vision went dark.

Only vaguely was I aware of my cunt clenching around nothing, my knees hitting the ground.

A thousand images flashed before me, overwhelmed me no matter how I blinked or shook my head. Darkness. A darkness so dense, cold, and damp that it could only be some underworld. Dirt walls. Dark, tangled roots. My fingers digging into soil. A climb, an endless climb. Suffering. This earthen den was more prison than womb. Mist manacled my limbs, trying to drag me back down. Down to *her*, to her self-made sanctum of misery. She may not know how to escape this tomb ... this cycle ... but I ... I...

I will come to you. Even if I must hew worlds, claw myself from the deepest vaults of the Beneath, burn through distant stars. I will come to you.

There is so much I have still to show you.

A juddering gasp ravaged my throat as my eyes snapped open. I lay at the base of Hiberos's tree in the fetal position, naked, my thighs tacky and wet. Even the dusk was too light for my eyes; they watered. A pathetic moan slipped from me.

Then I recognized the heat behind me. The presence of something huge and solid and very much alive, a low purr stuck in its chest.

One switchback leg cast a shadow over my face. A cloven hoof stamped into the packed moss inches away from my nose. An eclipse of moths seemed to burst forth after him, wheeling through the air.

Warm hands, the immense power and strength behind them at once evident, wrapped round my biceps and flipped me onto my back.

Then he was on top of me, that clicking purr rumbling in his chest and throat, his blue moonstone eyes sharp and bright in the twilight. His hand cupped my jaw ... although *cupped* is perhaps too delicate a word. More like he gripped my jaw, fingertips pressing in, our desperate, hot breaths mingling and writhing together. The very tip of his nose, velvety as a rose petal, brushed mine.

For many frantic heartbeats, we simply took each other in. Drank the reality that, once more, we occupied the same plane of existence. Could touch.

My hands shook. With a fever, I grabbed his chest, wishing he wore clothes so I could pull him deeper into our embrace.

He deepened it for me, the slick head of his cock kissing my clit. "My rose. I tore through the boundary of death to find you."

Swiftly, I locked my thighs around his hips, desperate to crush myself to him. He understood. Things had changed between us; there was no holding back now. I'd left the past behind.

Him. It was him, always had been him. I would not make the mistake of letting him go again.

Hiberos gripped my hips and tugged me where he needed me, answering my gasp with an open-mouthed, almost arrogant grin. "Ahh," he groaned, "it is barely spring, my princess. You could wait for me no longer?"

Still filled with mischief, no matter how he'd ... developed. But his eyes, the yearning and tenderness I found there, told me he could not have waited, either. That he had broken the underworld just to reach me.

"You're mine," I blurted as I writhed for him, and was surprised to find that there was not an ounce of embarrassment or regret behind those words. Those long winter months had drained me of anything but longing for him. "Guardian. Husband. My heart, my soul. Never leave me again."

"I never did," he rasped, coiling my hair around his large hand. Even the snowy white of my curls, reminding me suddenly that I was fae, could not shake my joy.

Nor my need.

His resolve fractured utterly, then, and with a growl, he slammed himself inside of me. The way he manipulated me, rolling me back on my shoulders so he could pound straight and hard down into me, made me feel like rapidly melting candle wax. I sagged into the position, ankles limp against his shoulders, whimpering like a whore as we joined again and again with hard, wet slapping. Obscene, wonderful, and so sacred.

"I could watch you from a distance for eons," he panted. "As long as you were in my sights. But this"—he squeezed my haunch hard enough to bruise—"is better."

"Hiberos. My god, my god..."

"Even if the remainder of my existence is spent reaching for you," he rasped in my ear, "I'll die happily"—*smack, smack, smack*—"again"—*smack, smack, smack*—"and again."

A second climax surprised me. All at once, I was riding hard, mindlessly, screaming. With a sinful groan, he stopped to sink all the way inside. My tight belly bloomed with the heat and magic of his cum.

We lay panting in the moonless moonlight for a while.

I was the first to stir, whimpering as I pulled my arms around his neck and held him fast. He snaked his arms tight over my waist and nuzzled his nose deep into my hair. It wasn't until the soft, glassy sound of our magic colliding faded and the sluggish muttering of the blight reclaimed its place that I sat up, more aware of our surroundings. If any in the Underland had noticed Hiberos's return, no one had come to investigate. We were still alone, save for the moon moths that blanketed the tree above us.

Running my fingers through his beard, I pulled him to me for a kiss as soft as moths' wings. We lingered in that kiss for what might have been minutes, merely savoring the reality that we could touch at all.

When at last we pulled away, his gaze searched mine with a hunger. "You've changed," he observed under his breath.

"Losing you changed everything," I admitted, averting my eyes and pulling away as if to hide soiled hands behind my back. "Dying is so much easier than grieving."

"I disagree." He caught my hand and pulled my wrist to his mouth, kissing, sucking the pulse. How such a touch could be so intimate and erotic, I could hardly fathom. "Leaving was unbearable, even knowing I'd find my way back to you. Perhaps I need you more than you need me," he added. Wryly. Yet I saw no humor in it.

"I'll fight harder for you," I promised emphatically.

Hiberos laughed. "Such is the danger in being with one much younger than oneself—they rarely know what, exactly, they want. I've had trials of my own to endure, but it is no matter. I forgive you without hesitation. Besides…" His smile faded. "I've lied often, by omission."

"Such is the danger in being with a faerie," I countered.

"How did you know it was blood I needed to grow?"

My spine straightened. "There's a ruin not far from here. I came across it, following a memory. There's a verse etched into a slab there: *When stars are still and breath is done, when blood is spilt to wake the sun—*"

"*The wheel shall turn, the thread unspun, the final cycle is begun,*" he finished.

I shouldn't be surprised he knew it. Of course a Guardian—especially him—would know the deepest lore of this place. "There were two other stanzas. I meant to find my way back there and write down the rest of the etching so I could translate it, but…"

"No matter," said he, "I am here, alive, with you. Everything else can come later."

I took him in—bemused as usual, but not in the infuriating way I was used to—before shaking my head. "Tell me one thing now, then."

"Anything."

"Where were you? These months. I…" My face twisted uncomfortably as I recalled those intrusive visions. "I saw flashes. Some underworld, clods of dirt, winding roots … and someone clawing to be free."

His expression was grim now. "I meant it when I said I tore through the boundary of death to find you. Mine was not to join the Weave or the spirits that wander the Underland. I was imprisoned in the Beneath, my jailer one I had not seen for a very, very long time."

The mist. The *her* I'd felt in that vision. I slid out from under him, focused, listening intently.

He closed his eyes, sighed so heavily his broad chest swelled and sank, then spoke her name.

"Gealach."

II

G ealach.
　　But it was impossible. She'd been dead for thousands of years. Had sacrificed herself to preserve the Underland—her own little bubble of the Otherworld—during the Shift, when the veil between worlds had sundered and all magic, myth, and lore became real. I had to admit I still did not fully understand the Shift. It was hard to grasp the concept of a world before, a world without magic, considering everything was made up of it. In any case, what I knew for certain was that Gealach was dead, and the dead did not come back.

Well...

My eyes widened as I stared at Hiberos. We were living proof that, sometimes, the buried did not stay buried.

Of course, we'd spoken before about how the vestiges of her magic lived on in the lore and power of the Lady, whom most Éirins still worshiped as a goddess of our land, associated with the moon. Hiberos himself had always been able to commune with Gealach in a sense, through meditation and prayer. More than once, he'd withdrawn to do just that, though he'd admitted that her answers were often vague, came in visions couched in symbolism and allegory.

That communion was not what he spoke of now; I saw that very plainly in his face. He'd spoken to her in a very real way. Been imprisoned by her.

We'd speculated on how Gealach might react to our union. After all, when she was alive, Hiberos had been her primary consort, and she wasn't in the habit of sharing. Falling in love with Hiberos in my past life had ultimately sentenced me to death.

"She's dead." My voice came out flatter than I intended.

"She is," he agreed without elaborating.

I nearly hit him, but his scent was so intoxicating all my limbs felt weak. "Elaborate."

"I will," he promised, and for once, I believed him. He turned his body to face mine and pulled me in by my elbow, pressing our warmth together. For just a moment, I could forget about Orlaith and Faelon and the withering and the countless other traumas I had yet to deal with. For just a moment, I imagined we'd woken in this meadow, the moss our pillow, the dew our blanket—that he pulled me close for a good-morning kiss.

But, of course, the smack of the blight's million little mouths soon broke that illusion, too.

"Let's to Erivon, wherever he is," Hiberos said, standing us up. "There, I'll reveal all I know." And he cast a solemn look about the withering heartgrove and the tree he'd left behind, the trunk of which now featured a faun-shaped divot. Moths fluttered all around us, perching on our shoulders and his horns. "What I learned of the goddess, and the cause of this plague."

I leaned into his chest, placing an open-mouthed kiss on his heart. The cage over it had closed up, but I still could discern the faint glow of it beneath his hide. In response, he purred, pulled me close, and cupped my arse. Letting myself feel and express affection was new, and might come slowly, but I was determined not to waste the time I had with him.

"And Mave..." He stroked his thumb down the scar on my sternum. "Thank you."

Those two words from his mouth broke my heart in one second, and mended it in the next.

+‿⁀◖◗‿+

Unsurprisingly, King Erivon was not in his throne room or study but rather the council room. A war room in a land without war went largely unused, so the appointments were a bit sparse and informal, although still elegant as everything in the Lunar Kingdom was. A large, round table of lavender wood was spread with maps, and around it sat a high-backed ebony chair for each war council member.

They were gathered now, faekin of all stripes, fighting amongst themselves. Such arguments were not the norm in the Underland, but along with the withering came not just hunger but discord. The only council member not present was Solma, who had very wisely elected to stay where the action was to quell Manan's ire and stoke fae morale.

When Hiberos and I marched through the doors, Erivon glanced up at me, then down again. "Mave, thank— Where—"

Then his movements stuttered, and his head jerked back up. The expression on his face as he beheld Hiberos alive and new was almost indescribable, equal parts disbelieving, haunted, and devotional. "My old friend," he said barely above a whisper. "You... How..." He skirted the table, approaching us, but predictably, he shook his head before Hiberos could speak. "No, tell me later. For now, all I want to know is where my queen is."

Shite. Manan may think Erivon a coward king, but his bravery —even occasional impulsiveness where it concerned his soulmate —would be exhibited soon enough.

Even as he squeezed Hiberos's arm in a half-embrace, Erivon refocused on me. He must see grief in my face, for I watched his eyes, usually the color and luster of black pearls, shift to ultra-violet. When he spoke, his voice was dredged from the depths of hell. "Where. Is. She."

"She's alive," I said with certainty. Orlaith was my sister, and when she'd died as Eytine it felt like the world would stop turning, but our bond went even deeper. A thousand years ago, we'd perished together in Geatacoill's embrace. Our flesh had sloughed from our bones and fed the animals, and soon our marrow joined the soil, too—and in that way, we had become one. More than sisters. Part of the same cycle that trapped me and Hiberos. Yes, I was quite sure I knew the pang of Orlaith's death, and I did not feel it now. "Alive," I repeated breathlessly, "but in trouble."

Erivon was ready to shove past me and sprint to the Crossroads. I had to be the one to gesture past him, ushering him toward the round table. "How much do you know about what happened?"

"There was some manner of ... expulsion of red magic," he managed between his teeth. His eyes were wild and hard. I'd never seen my brother-in-law, usually placid as a starry lake, this agitated. "The moon turned red, the city and valley were blighted, fomori ravaged the land."

I nodded, leaning on the round table with my knuckles. Behind me, Hiberos was a constant, hot presence, practically pressed into my backside. I sensed that he struggled to keep his hands off my body, but there were more urgent things at hand than us, er, reacquainting ... again.

Erivon's already dark teal skin flushed deeper and deeper with rage as I explained the battle, Faelon's part in it, and our meeting with him. "We had almost convinced him to come with us when one of Sergia's lackeys stole him away. We gave chase, but he led us into a ravine laced with thornwire made of feyiron."

Somehow, the Moon King's brow became even stormier. Feyiron being what had ultimately caused Hiberos's death, Erivon was now familiar with it. I could not imagine being tangled in it and still telling my sister to go on without me.

Then again, I didn't have a son in need of saving.

I told Erivon the rest of what I knew: that during the explosion I'd been separated from not only Orlaith but Faelon, that I did not know exactly where she was, and that the withering scar would be impassible until we properly regrouped, which, with the coalition withdrawing from southern Sallach, was easier said than done.

"I will assemble a party," Erivon said without hesitation. "I will find her, and my son, and bring them back."

At last, Hiberos slunk out of my shadow. His had always been an elemental presence, as would be the presence of anything so ancient, but now, he exuded a kind of primal strength, a potency, a vitality of spirit that had me in awe of him. It was as though he'd emerged from his chrysalis a newborn god.

"Your Majesty, there is more. I know the origin of the withering—and the fomori, and the mist, for that matter. When I died, my soul was pulled to the Beneath. The underworld," he clarified when it was evident Erivon did not know the term. Hiberos sighed. "There are certain things the Guardians, as lorekeepers, were never meant to tell you. Things about this place. None of you were ever supposed to die, or leave"—he glanced at me regretfully—"and so Gealach never thought it important to tell you. But, this kingdom has always been connected to the Goneland by a certain juncture. Not the Moon Gates, and not the horizon..."

"The Beneath," I said, standing straight. Things were falling into place. Of course. The Lady—the Mother Goddess the Éirins worshiped, the Woman Beneath—she resided in the underworld, and like Hiberos had once told me, she *was* the remnants of Gealach. All along, coming from both worlds, I'd had the knowledge; the connection had been right in front of me. "So the fomori, the mist, the withering ... all the terrible things from Éire, they're all seeping into the Underland through the Beneath."

I didn't expect him to hesitate like he did. "They are coming from the Beneath, yes. But their origin is not in Éire. They come from the Beneath itself, from one of its denizens." He leveled a grim and meaningful stare at me. "From my jailer. From Gealach."

The world turned upside down. The moon was supposed to be a bastion of healing and serenity, and the blight and all it brought with it was ... anything but that. "But the fomori?"

"More lore kept secret." Hiberos bowed his head to Erivon. "The fomori are not ancient enemies of the fae. Or, rather, they aren't *just* that. They are what remains of a clan of beings known eons before the Shift as *fomoire*. *They* were Gealach's first children, born when the light of the moon first touched the sea. From the waves they rose, long before the Horned God died, before Gealach ever conceived of the fae."

Of course. I'd once asked myself: Who was older than the fae? The fomori.

The trilith. The labyrinth. The prophecy chamber. The faoladh monolith. Those standing stones. Now I knew to whom those ancient, abandoned things belonged. The same black limestone, the same Ogham, the same sacred spaces—they *had* been created by one people.

"The fomoire loved her, and she them. But like all firstborns, they were imperfect, and like all first-time mothers, so was she. Their disobedience led to war, and they were cast into the Beneath, where they stayed for many thousands of years, only poking their heads into the other realms occasionally."

"Then everything changed," said Erivon darkly.

"Yes. Losing the Horned One—" Hiberos's brow fractured. "It ... broke ... her. She created us both, fae and Guardian. Second- and thirdborns brimming with potential. Then came the Shift, and Gealach's death. The Guardians sealed her in a tomb Beneath, and we were never to tell you where her body lay. But the firstborns never forgot their mother. They found her tomb. And, like firstborns tend to do, they"—he gestured vaguely and tiredly—"assumed the care of her, despite past disagreements. They are wretched creatures now, these ... *remnants* of the fomoire, yet now that Mother Moon is down in the dark with them, they cherish her. Would do anything for her. Which is exactly what they are doing now: *her* bidding."

The council was silent as the truth, and the sheer enormity of what had been kept from us, sank in.

I was the first to break it, which made sense; this all was shocking, but I hardly considered Gealach my mother. Perhaps, never having met my own mam, and having barely known my da before he died, my empathy regarding parental bonds was weakened. But *sibling* bonds... "So, to extend your metaphor, we have an eldest sibling we haven't met, the fomori, and you never thought to tell us?"

Hiberos turned fully to me. "We were never meant to tell you. Gealach never wanted to speak of them. The fomori have mainly stayed in the underworld all this time. But now..."

"And the mist? It comes with the fomori, but what is it?"

He shook his head. "Whether it's some spirit manifested from the fomori themselves or is some shadow of Gealach's former power, I cannot say, but it craves a physical body."

I gritted my teeth thinking of Brianne's puppeted corpse. "Yea, I had noticed."

Erivon cut straight to the heart of the matter, then, no doubt eager to find a way to slice through the blighted wasteland to his queen: "If the withering is Gealach's doing, *why*? Why would she seek to destroy the land she gave everything to protect?"

"I don't think she intended for the withering to leach into the Underland," Hiberos said. "She intended it for the Goneland only. Perhaps it is some way of protecting the Éirins gone wrong. Or perhaps she believes mortals should be punished for war, even if it means destroying the very land over which they fight. Or perhaps it was simply an accident, an infection that cannot be stopped, only spread. She never told me."

It must have been the use of the miasma bomb that pushed her over the edge, I thought. Apparently, she'd been so appalled at the treatment of the land that she'd seen fit to swallow an entire city and blight the country round it for miles. "I should bring all this information with me to Gallive, to the coalition."

"Is there *anything else* you can tell us?" Erivon pressed. "Anything regarding her motives, or the nature of the withering?"

"Regretfully, no. But whatever her motive, it is clear she does not have precise control over the sickness." Exhaustion, misery, and anger laced Hiberos's tone. "Beyond these truths I have spoken, I cannot explain her behavior."

I studied his profile. There was something he wasn't saying. Something personal. Once we were alone, somehow, I knew he'd tell me. If I was leaving the past behind, he would, too; claiming

me like he had in the heartgrove, he'd already demonstrated willingness to throw all the caution he'd once taken to the wind.

My stare must be burning a hole in his hide, for as Erivon
pivoted the conversation toward Gatewright Owalir, Hiberos
turned and searched me. Whatever he saw in my face, it made
him soften and gesture for me to step away with him. With a purr,
he caught my hands and gathered them to his chest, urging them
upward to skim his neck and tangle in his sideburns. "Have
patience, my rose. Only a little patience, this time. When we are
alone, rest assured I will tell you that which pertains to *us*. I'm
well aware of the trouble my secrets have gotten us into before."

Reassured, I eased and scratched his jawline, a little smile
coming to my face.

He grumbled low in his chest. "Careful," he said with a
twinkle in his eye, "or my leg will start twitching."

"And what else?" I muttered under my breath.

Erivon's approach pulled us from our moment, and I snatched
my hands away from Hiberos and stood at attention. I really
shouldn't be hanging off him in front of my brother-in-law while
his own soulmate was missing.

"Mave," said the Moon King, and a twinge of familial love
plucked at my chest when I noticed he used my preferred name.
"My plan to set out for Orlaith was to use the gate just outside of
Bile Cernunnos, but of course the damned thing is nonfunction-
al." If looks could kill, the glare he sent Owalir's direction would
have struck them dead. "You mentioned something about your
coalition meeting in Gallive? That is the southernmost city in Co
Cuanacht, I believe, yes?"

I nodded. "Between Bile Cernunnos and Gallive is mostly
farmland and villages and forest. It's the only place our refugees
can go. All the druid-kings of Cuanacht will meet us there, I
reckon. Perhaps even High King Alasdair. It's not every day a city
is besieged and swallowed by blight."

Erivon shuffled maps, probably consulting the chart of Moon
Gates by the way he skimmed the parchment. "This one here is
near enough, if there is no alternative."

Here he threw another deadly look at Gatewright Owalir, who hunched their shoulders like a scolded child. Hiberos chuckled.

"In the meantime..." The Moon King snapped the chart closed. "I think it well past time I meet the Éirin kings face to face."

12

The gate closest to Gallive opened into a wood just east of Athadhrai, a town just a tad larger than Fraochgleann had been. The wood was well-maintained, and the village folk gathering supplies at its edge were treated to quite a shocking surprise when a fae king and his retinue rode from the ruins at its center and into their streets. Each of us—sans the Guardians—sat astride a shimmering hart decorated with silver bells, with me and Erivon leading the procession, just like in the stories of otherworldly royal visitors. Though the Athies were as horrified as they were awed, they bowed to us as we passed, their eyes glued to the ground like any sensible Éirin's would be. It still felt strange to be on the other end of faerie nonsense, but I couldn't think about that now. All I dared focus on was getting to Gallive as quickly as possible.

Thankfully, we'd reach the city moons before anyone else in the coalition. Still, it was a handful of hours even by mount. Erivon was tense in his saddle, his every waking thought no doubt consumed with the fate of his queen, but members of the entourage were in a rage to comment on their new surroundings. The strength of the sun and the green of the foliage in particular tended to shock the fae when they first passed through the gates, equal parts enamored and terrified. Though perhaps less terrified now that they'd had their taste of the hunger, cold, and sickness seeping into the Underland.

Watching them interact with the land they once thought dead, gone, and useless to them, I wondered how many, if given the choice, would live here when all was said and done?

Or maybe there'd be nothing left. Maybe the Éirins would be crushed and the Lunar Kingdom would be sealed away for good, evermore trying to ignore the entropy gnawing at their paradise.

As we rode, Hiberos kept pace beside me, his moonstone eyes sliding up and down my body every chance he got. The few times I dared to return his heated stare, he looked at me the way one might look at a sunrise: awe, affection, and contentment though the moment's beauty may be ephemeral. Or perhaps *because* the beauty was ephemeral. He beheld me as though every glimpse was a gift I gave him.

I hardly knew what to do with such feelings. I may be fae, a princess, but I still felt like Mave. Just … me. It was *Hiberos* who should be gazed at with awe. He felt like the night sky, dark and opaque upon first glance, but when you looked closer, you could discern the velvet sheen of his layers, his depth—could track a never-ending pattern of light: spirals of stars, worlds, and everything in between. Celestial bodies, aged and wise yet twinkling with mischief.

I shone with nothing so profound as that. It wasn't that I thought less of myself, but, for all I'd been through, I was mostly unremarkable. Why look at me in that way?

Despite Manan's intent to simply arrive at Gallive and ask for refuge, the coalition must have ended up sending word anyway, because when our party arrived at the eastern gates of the city, a host of retainers and warriors on horseback met us. The warrior at the fore, a woman about my age with pale skin and braided black hair, wore a little fire wyrm around her wrist forearm a bracelet. I was only half surprised to watch its form unfurl into that of one of Manan's under-druids, a healer called Paik, who'd patched me up quite a few times now though I'd only recently learned his name.

Relief lifted my shoulders when I saw him. Paik was what

Gwynedd used to call "a connector." Eytine had been one, too. Someone who made friends everywhere they went, and could find common ground with most people as long as there was a pint in front of them. Good job he was one of those more welcoming to the fae than others—it gave me a tentative bit of hope that our transition from Sallach to Gallive would be free of unnecessary arguments.

Paik clapped his hands together, the sleeves of his robe swinging with the motion. The shade of his skin, so black it was nearly purple, made his broad smile that much brighter and more dazzling. It didn't seem to phase him at all that he was speaking to the ruler of a realm that had remained apart and untouched for thousands of years. "King Erivon, Princess Mave, esteemed guests." He gestured to the black-haired woman atop the horse. "This is Muiri, daughter of King Tagh and warchief of Tuath De Siabair."

I nodded to Muiri. "Just call me Mave."

Erivon followed my example and bowed his head. "And please, call me Erivon."

Muiri's pale face was blank. She was a beauty, I thought, though perhaps not in the way shallow men would appreciate. Her weak chin made room for plump lips, pouty jowls, and huge, heavy-lidded black eyes. She simply tossed her head to indicate we should come in, then turned her mare, who was as black-haired as her, to guide us toward the bilé at the city center.

Gallive thrived on the water, its bay holding the whole of the city in the slender fingers of its canals. The houses were similar to those that had stood in Bile Cernunnos, with whitewashed sides and thatched roofs, although a great many of them were stone, built into and around Dead World ruins. One particular ruin caught my eye: the remnants of a tower as big around as the trunk of our lost bilé, which had clearly long been picked apart to build other structures. Still, I could discern at the base a carving of a large, slit-pupil eye. Though I didn't recall the Éirin name for the mark, I thought the Aquilans called it the Dragon Eye. There were plenty of stories that a dragon had roosted in and ruled over

Gallive once, thousands of years ago, but seeing the evidence of it was another thing altogether.

Clearly, it hadn't ended well for that dragon, as was evident upon approaching Bile De Siabair, an ash tree even larger than Bile Cernunnos had been: the grand entry was made of dragon bone and topped with a long-snouted, horned skull frozen forever in a roar.

"Seems Éire has never taken kindly to tyrants," Hiberos remarked, his ears flapping merrily.

"You're damned right!" laughed Paik, who trailed along beside Muiri.

Muiri dismounted outside the grand entry and led us into the king's hall, but there was no one awaiting us there, king, subject, warrior, druid—no one. When she turned to me, she almost seemed surprised I was still here.

I took point in the face of Erivon's uncharacteristic standoff-ishness. Couldn't blame him, really. Not only was his wife's well-being still in question, he was in a strange place full of folk who looked at him like he was a dangerous monster. And you couldn't blame them, either, because if he were any other kind of fae, that wouldn't be far from the truth. "Where's King Tagh?"

The king's daughter scanned the retinue of lunar fae with an unreadable gaze. "I thought we would wait for the rest of the coalition to arrive before any proper introductions. I had hoped we could maintain some discretion, but, well ... parading you through the streets is not quite that." Though she spoke flatly and slowly, there was clearly some keen intelligence behind her eyes when she met mine. "I'll have people show you to rooms. You'll not want for anything."

"That's fair enough, but the fae have traveled a long way and put a lot of faith in me to see them here safely. I think it might make everyone feel a bit more secure, meeting the man whose house we're staying in."

Muiri was duly unimpressed with me, as was evident in the way she lifted her chin, but she clearly wasn't a woman of hot temper. In fact, there was a strange patience in her air that reminded me of a predator, watching and waiting for her prey to make a wrong move. As long as I stayed categorized as *ally* and not *prey*, we would get along fine.

"You want to see the king?" she asked with the barest trace of bitterness in her tone. "Fine. Only you and Erivon, though."

I looked reluctantly at Hiberos. He didn't seem thrilled at the prospect of being separated from me, but when our eyes met, he forced a smile. "Go on. I shall meet you in your chambers."

Those words sent a shameful jolt through my center, which I tried to hide as I followed Muiri. Judging by her squint, I didn't hide it admirably. But she led us through the great tree all the same. It was not unlike the oak of Cernunnos, lacquered and decorated with carvings, except, being ash, the interior was lighter, almost white. It caught the seaside sun beautifully, making everything bright.

When we reached the last room in the second-floor hall, she ushered us in, and at once, I understood why an audience with the king was impossible. He lay in a large bed, his eyes closed, his mouth hanging open. The bed frame itself was a small tree grown to cradle the mattress, its leaves a canopy above the sleeping occupant. Roots and vines crawled onto the bed, too, wrapping themselves around the king's arms and piercing his skin. The sight of these thin roots fed into the king's veins might be horrific if the tree didn't emanate a healing aura, which my fae eyes could almost see as a shimmering gold curtain around the bed.

"The tree sustains him," Muiri said from the corner behind us. "Some days, he can only wake and greet visitors under the most urgent conditions. Mostly, I see to the everyday needs of the people."

I managed to tear my eyes away from King Tagh. Erivon still beheld him grimly, his ears set low. "Do the people know?" I asked.

"They know he's ill. I would never keep that from them. But he's been chief of De Siabair for over a hundred years..." She saw something in my face that made her frown. "You think I'm keeping him like *this* to further my own ends? Not all are as cutthroat as the fae. If I wasn't capable of carrying out my duties, I would step aside for someone else."

"No," I said quickly. "That's not what I was implying. And I think you'll find the Lunar Kingdom isn't like the other fae Courts."

Muiri tossed her head, motioning for us to follow her into the hallway. She shut the door to her father's chamber with much more care and gentleness than I would expect from someone so taciturn. Then she jerked a thumb down the corridor. "Follow this all the way to the stained glass, then take a right. Pick any room in that hall. It doesn't matter." She squinted at me again. "I suppose that goat will've already picked for you."

I coughed. "Right."

She seemed more curious than judgmental; I thought she must just be habitually grumpy. In any case, she returned to her father's room, leaving Erivon and I alone in the corridor. Observing my brother-in-law, it was plain to see that he still thought of nothing besides Orlaith, practically vibrating out of his skin with the tension in every line of his posture.

He caught me staring, sighed, and stalked down the corridor. "Where do you think she is?"

I fell into step beside him. "I wish I could tell you. She must have escaped the feyiron somehow, or else she likely wouldn't have made it—and she *is* alive. I don't know how, but I just ... know."

"I should be there," he snarled, "waiting. I should have found a way to her, to oblivion with the gates. I could have taken the one in Kesselhearst and been there *now* if I rode hard."

There wasn't much logic behind that plan, but I wasn't one to talk. I'd be thinking the same thing. "You have to be here, representing your people. You know that or else you wouldn't be here at all."

"My people." He got a look on his face I'd never seen. Something angry, bitter, resentful. Though of course the lunar fae must have a wide range of emotion despite their sheltered existence, it still was odd to witness. I'd begun to think of him as the calm to

Orlaith's storm. "Mave, what I say will never leave this conversation. Only because I know you, of all people, will understand."

And he stared deep into me. "I would tear down the veil and dismantle every solitary edifice of the Lunar Kingdom if it meant saving her. Without her, I am nothing. My wife and my son are my people, not the fae, and I will be damned if I return to the Underland without them."

We fell silent as we reached the stained glass and went right. Erivon tried the handle of one of the doors, and we peered in and were greeted with a well-appointed, cozy, sunlit guest chamber. No Hiberos, so it wasn't mine.

Just as Erivon was about to disappear over the threshold, I caught his arm. My voice was soft, so he had to swivel his ears to pick it up. "I can see your son."

He turned more fully toward me in silent question.

"When I fed Drusilla and Nevidaea those leylight worms, there was a third one. I snuck half into an apple and gave it to Faelon, so that, if he chose, we could be connected. And months ago, after Hiberos's death, I ... felt him for the first time." I bowed my head. "I've been watching him, checking in on him. I can feel him at the edge of my consciousness even now."

"Did..." He tilted his head, taking me in like I was a species he'd never seen before and did not quite understand. "Does Orlaith know this?"

"I told her during the battle."

Erivon was silent for a while, searching my face. Eventually, he opened the chamber door wider. "Come in and show me."

Even as I entered, the vision in my left eye shifted, turning dark. I tried to maintain one eye in, one eye out, but by the time I sat myself on a nearby bench, everything was blackness.

FAELON WASN'T certain what day it was, or how long he'd been trapped in the clearing with the bloodwarden. The sun never seemed to rise in the newly blighted land, as though the sickness festering in the trees' canopy blocked out daylight altogether.

A good half of Ryac's pack had managed to tear their way through the withering to reunite with their alpha. Now there were a dozen werewolves staring at him in the darkness, a sheen of red over each pair of eyes. One of the moonless women had brought him meat with a big bone in and tried to convince him to eat, but he'd swiftly declined. He wasn't hungry. He couldn't keep anything down, thinking that all this ruin had been his doing. Father had *promised* the weapon wouldn't hurt the tree, and yet...

Plus, he was more interested in what—*who*—they had brought with them.

Who they had found when they'd alerted Ryac with their hollers and cries.

The woman from the library.

Orlaith lay slumped in the shadows beyond Ryac, flanked on either side by moonless. I nearly jumped out of the vision to tell Erivon right away, but mentally, emotionally, I was riveted to the spot. The werewolves seemed hesitant to touch the feyiron thornwire binding her, so she was still partially bound round her elbows and thighs. It probably wasn't necessary; she looked so unwell that she wouldn't have been able to run even if she was free. Due to her illness, her skin was more milk than seafoam, head bobbing and eyelids drooping, wings twitching.

Yet, in those moments she seemed to regain a measure of lucidity, she did nothing but stare at Faelon. He was powerless to do anything but stare back.

Though he did not know why, or how, he knew this was his birth mother.

Yet this woman looked like no Éirin he'd ever seen. She was one of the fae people. Then again, his birth mother was also supposed to be dead.

From a young age, he'd thought he was raised up from darkness, saved from an ignorant woman who could never care for him properly and a people who would raise him into a worthless sheep herder. Only Father knew how to mold him into a man of honor. Of worth. He'd thought that because ... because that was what he'd been told.

There was more to the story, he suspected now. Surely, Father thought he'd done the right thing, and, perhaps being an Aquilan was of far greater merit and importance than being Éirin, but there *was* more.

Ryac had not moved from his spot since the others entered their makeshift camp, and he hadn't looked up at Faelon since he'd started whittling an hour ago. Yet, clearly, he was still watching, still attuned to the boy's every move, for when Faelon finally dared to rise and take a few steps toward the fae, the bloodwarden snapped his head up.

"Where you going, lad?"

The boy opened and closed his mouth several times, looking for a lie, but for whatever reason, he couldn't bring himself to. "That woman is my mother."

Ryac's sparse brows shot up as he looked between mother and son. For once, he had nothing sinister to say, simply speechless. When Faelon ignored him to approach the woman, he made no move apart from turning his head to watch. Faelon kept expecting him to jump up and snatch him away, but he never did, and finally, the boy stood before the fae.

Orlaith managed to raise her head and offer him a sere smile. My heart clenched knowing she'd waited so long to speak with him, and now she was barely conscious. "Hello, Faelon."

"You and Mave keep calling me that," he said shyly. "Why?"

"That was the name I chose for you." She blinked lethargically and swallowed. "I'm sorry I was never able to give it to you, little wolf. I'm sorry. I died for you, my darling, but I'd much rather have lived for you."

Tears pricked the boy's eyes, but he struggled bitterly against them. This was a war camp—technically—and she was a detainee. He couldn't go weeping on every prisoner of war who said something that touched him. Clearing his throat, he asked a bit more strongly, "How do you know my father calls me 'little wolf?'"

Orlaith's eyes lost their light for a moment. "Does he. I've called you that since I gave birth to you. Your father could not be there to offer a sacrifice to the Lady, so your aunt did it instead.

She killed a wolf." She shook her head, fully Eytine for a moment. "A wolf is far more than what's required—a rabbit, cat, goat—but that's your auntie. She did not even understand why we were poking fun at her, after..."

This was news to me. I remembered killing the wolf, of course, and all the jokes made at my expense, but I'd never realized that was where she got the wean's nickname. Faelon was caught on something else, though—I felt, in the back of our mind, the way he turned over the words *your father*. It took him a moment to realize she meant someone other than Gaius. Then he recalled my visit. I'd said the same thing.

"I have a birth father," he said.

Orlaith managed a chuckle that was more of a breath than a laugh. "Most people do."

"And my auntie is Mave."

She bowed her head.

"So I'm fae? But Father always told me that my mother was Éirin."

"I was, and your father, fae. It's a long story, little wolf, and I hope someday I can tell you the whole thing. In short, when Gaius killed me, I came back ... like this."

Faelon looked down to hide sudden tears. *Father was the one to kill her?* He supposed he shouldn't be surprised—he knew he'd killed Mave—but the revelation gave him a strange, tight feeling in his stomach. "So, I'm ... half ... half Éirin, half fae."

Again, she nodded. "Perhaps I was human for that short time simply so I could bring you into this world."

He took a while to gather himself before sitting moth-style in front of the fae. That ghostly smile returned to her lips, her silvery gaze soft, her flyaways dancing in the fetid breeze rolling through the wasteland. She looked at him the same way Nevidaea looked at him, but her eyes, as big and white as the moon, were brimming with tears.

"Why are you crying?" he whispered, transfixed by her in every way.

"Oh, nothing," she said even as her breath hitched. "Nothing, my darling. You are just so much more beautiful than I could ever have imagined."

I remembered her confession to me on the balcony overlooking the Underland, in what she surely would consider a moment of weakness. *Without him, all of this beauty, all of this peace ... it is useless to me, isn't it? What is the point of living forever if I cannot have my child? Why did Mother Moon bequeath that gift only to take him away and place him with some stranger?*

Eytine or Orlaith, my sister rarely opened up about her personal pain. Argue against closing the gates, go after her son if she thought he needed protecting? Certainly. But to leave her vulnerable insides unguarded? In that way, we were alike. Too much hung in the balance between her duty and sanity, whatever world she inhabited. I should know this better than anyone, yet I, too, had been fooled by her aloof act.

"All I ever wanted was..." Orlaith let the truth die on her tongue. I understood now. I saw in her face how badly she wanted to tell him that he was hers, *hers,* and that she must take him away from those people. But now that he was in front of her, a stranger in every respect, she couldn't force the words past her teeth.

"It doesn't matter." Her voice was trembling now, thin and delicate as the crumpled wings down her back. "Happiness is all I want for you, little wolf. I always knew the time would come you had to make your own choices, have your own thoughts and allegiances and feelings. I just never—"

Crashing and shouting cut her off. Faelon whirled around to face whatever was barreling through the trees toward them. When he recognized the burnished metal of the tree-cutters and the bass of his father's voice, he nearly fell over with relief. They were here. They had managed to cut through the rack and ruin of the blight and find them. He wouldn't be cannibalized by werewolves after all. He'd be going home, to his mother.

Yet he couldn't deny the kernel of dread—and guilt—blossoming in his stomach.

He looked back at Orlaith. She ... she was his mother, too, in some way. What would happen to her? What would Father's punishment be? How could he save her from it? *Should* he?

And, most importantly, what did she mean when she said he had to "make his own choices?"

The blood red bracken parted, coughing snakes of mist. A shining sword grew from the brush as it was hacked away. A tanned arm appeared, swinging, and the rest of Father followed it, clad in armor stained with remnants of the pale monsters walking the land. His clear blue eye darted round the clearing, gaze bouncing off several werewolves before it finally found Faelon. Even seeing him through my nephew's eyes made me shiver, and, shockingly, I sensed my shiver travel from my conscious to Faelon.

His attention caught on the sensation. *Where did that come from?*

Gaius's shoulders dropped. He shouted back for his men to create a perimeter, then immediately thrust himself into the clearing, dropping his sword to hurry and fall at Faelon's feet.

"Lucastos." He snatched the boy into an embrace, crushing him to his chest with his forehead pressed against the boy's shoulder. "Mighty Ones be praised."

Perhaps he sensed his son's reluctance to return the embrace, though, for Faelon stood limply. Gaius raised his head and, at last, noticed Orlaith.

His next words were spoken with such little emotion that they chilled Faelon as deeply as they chilled me.

"Oh. It's you."

13

Faelon's conscious kicked me out with a gulch. I sat up from where I slumped on the bench in Erivon's sitting area, panting as though I'd just sprinted a hundred yards. At once, large, warm hands were on me, holding my biceps firmly. My head felt light and full of cotton, and nothing in my vision made sense, so I blindly grabbed and held on to the person steadying me. It wasn't until I closed my eyes and fought to ground myself that I recognized the wood grain beneath my fingertips.

"Easy," Hiberos whispered, his breath hot and soft against my face—sweet, as though he'd been sipping brandy. "Let yourself float up to the surface. Allow yourself to sink back in to your own body. There..."

I moaned, mostly in pain, and pried open my eyes. Hiberos filled my vision, his half-lidded eyes intent on me. Flyaway strands of his golden locks trembled under my harsh breaths, but otherwise, he was steady, exuding the calm I needed to cling to. I let him pull me in. He wrapped his arms fully around my waist and squeezed so hard my spine nearly popped. Far from uncomfortable, it was exactly the pressure I needed to keep myself from floating out of my body.

Erivon waited over his shoulder, expression grim. "What did you see?"

"Give her a moment," Hiberos muttered.

Erivon *snarled* in response. His face twisted in a way that reminded me of the fae I'd been warned of all my life. "You saw something. Something terrible, didn't you? You *must tell me*." And he took a step forward as if to brush Hiberos aside.

In a flash, Hiberos turned on him with his own snarl, his face a demonic mask the likes of which I'd only seen once before—in the stone henge, just before my death, when I had questioned his intentions with my nephew. Except, this time, the anger was genuine, not an act. He raised a perfectly carved forearm across Erivon's throat and shoved him back, out of our personal space.

"I said *give her a moment*." His voice was low, nearly a growl. A warning. He squinted, his ears pinned back, his nostrils flaring. "I've faced greater threats than a fae king to be here now, and do not think our friendship overshadows my vows to her."

The shove seemed to bring Erivon to his senses. He seemed mortified as he staggered back and fell into a chair, obviously waging war with himself.

My vows to her. For a few heartbeats, I thought he meant his vows to Gealach. After all, the last time I'd heard him refer to *vows*, we'd been talking about his compulsory commitment to the goddess. To realize he was speaking about me—that I was *her*...

Everything really had changed. But Hiberos had seen Gealach in the Beneath, *spoken* to her. Now more than ever, he must know our actions were forbidden, and that the consequences would be dreadful. Yet here he was, speaking candidly about his covenant with *me*.

Hiberos dismissed Erivon as a threat and fetched a cup of ale, pressing it into my hand. It propped me up long enough to tell them what I'd seen. "Faelon was trapped in the forest, cut off from the rest of the legion by the blight but protected by Ryac and his pack. The moonless found—f-found her, took her as a prisoner..." I struggled to draw in a breath, so tight was my chest, and held Hiberos's gaze. "Gaius has Orlaith."

His expression shifted to horror, despair. Quite apart from what this might mean for Orlaith, he knew what it meant for me. And he knew just as well that there was nothing we could do about it. She was nearly a hundred miles away, being transported to a city garrisoned by not one but two legions, with another in reserve. The Moon Gate in Geatacoill was entombed in the lake, unusable. Westeris Wall was more heavily fortified than ever before. The wasteland of rot was impassible. Judging from Erivon's haunted expression, he, too, was grasping for a solution.

To sit on my hands while my sister suffered by that monster—the monster raising the child of her own womb—was too much to bear. Every bone in my body rebelled.

Without thinking, I lurched out of my seat, pushed past Hiberos, and fled from the chamber.

ALL I WANTED WAS to fly to my sister's side and save her. As I left the bilé and its moonwell behind and walked the city's ancient cobbled streets, I ran through a thousand scenarios in my head, trying desperately to find a way to justify doing exactly that. As the sun set, though, I came up lacking. There was no way to rescue her now without jeopardizing the entire war, not to mention my own life.

Ashling, don't you dare go where I cannot reach you. Don't leave me here without you.

For a thousand years, we'd taken turns following one another into oblivion. Now, here I was, hesitating at the threshold. Yet how could I discard all good sense and lose control? Our people, fae and human, were counting on me.

The Abhan—river—Gallive split the city in roughly two parts: Cladach to the west and Ar to the east. The majority of Gallive was comprised of residential districts and farmlands, but its very center was as metropolitan as New Lindanos. The bridge over the lough separating the busy Midtown Ar from the rest of Ar was blackened from age. I stopped to lean against the worn parapet, my snowy curls a dangling curtain as I stared into the lough's depths. At the moment, it was so overcast it may as well be twilight, the brackish water so dark I almost felt as if I were gazing into the Beneath. Flocks of snipes, wigeons, and the odd frost-shank picked around the reeds, but they couldn't hold my attention for long. Even the busy quay behind me was nothing more than distant noise.

The look on Gaius's face when he'd seen Orlaith ... Faelon may not have recognized it, but I did. Keen and concentrated excitement. Intent. Thrill at the thought of once again holding dominion over her. Pleasure that Eytine still existed in some form, and that she saw and understood all he had taken from her—first her land, then her life, then her son. The purest form of ownership. And now he could do it all again. Relive his conquest of her.

Who knew how else he might try to break her?

I thrust my head into my hands and dug my claws into my hairline, forcing those thoughts out. Knowing I couldn't go after her, all this speculation was nothing more than self-torture. I tried to turn my mind instead to what I could do for her *now*. Drusilla and I could communicate, in an airy sort of way, when our consciousnesses touched. If I told her about Orlaith, she might be able to help in my stead. There would still be a great deal of risk, but at the moment, it was my only chance. Perhaps there was a way to influence Faelon and Nevidaea, too, if more subtly.

With renewed hope that I might be able to do *something*, I hurried along the bridge, leaving behind the high streets, taverns, and municipal buildings of Gallive and instead entering the clustered localities and fields outside Midtown's walls. The cobbles disappeared, replaced by familiar hard-packed dirt roads. Being in Bile Cernunnos had been excitement enough—Gallive would be overwhelming in the best of circumstances, let alone now. I was relieved to leave it behind.

I missed Geatacoill so much it hurt.

It was full dark by the time another path diverged to the right, toward the bay. I took it immediately, lured by the sea air. Fraochgleann had been a short ride from the Sallach Delta with all its rivers and bays. Eytine and Gwynedd had taken me all the time, for pleasure and to gather whatever coastal resources the village required. The ocean was a friend to me, so different from the forest yet equally as calming and purifying.

The path brought me to a gray beach, one half covered in seaweed-blanketed stones and the other fine sand. There wasn't much to see besides smog herons, but on the stony half of the beach, about a half mile out into the bay, stood a small island. It was flush with the water at its north end before jutting out and up so that the southern tip was all sea cliffs. There was a surprising amount of growth on the island—not a thick wood but a wood nonetheless, its treeline only partially obscuring a small lake in the center of it. Foamy surf lapped at my bare toes, then my calves as I waded in to get a better look. The way the water and sand abutted told me low tide would reveal a causeway and grant a few hours' access to the little island.

The leaves of the trees on the island waved and whispered in the sea breeze, joining with the tide in a chorus that relaxed me enough to clear my head. I had my goal. Panic and anger would not help Orlaith now, it would only weaken me. I would do all I could and try to take comfort in it.

Taking a deep breath, I closed my eyes against the moonlit ocean and let the lull of the waves carry me into Drusilla's world.

THE ERUPTION of blight at Bile Cernunnos was all anyone could talk about. Quite apart from those killed in combat, the Ninth Legion had lost nearly a thousand men to the scourge of pale monsters and the predatory mist they brought.

Of those men, there was only one Drusilla cared about. Not a man, really, but a boy. Lucastos was still missing.

Nevidaea was beside herself, as any mother would be, and under the constant and diligent care of the lupercal nursemaid. It was an odd thing, watching the Lady Sergia weep and wring her hands while Drusilla, who had fed, clothed, and nurtured the child starting mere months into his life, was forced to stand stoically by her side, comforting her as though she were a child herself. If it were anyone else in Drusilla's head, they might call her unfeeling for her apathy toward her mistress, but I knew a little of the exhaustion slavery begot. When you were forced to serve, your compassion wore rapidly thin. I couldn't imagine how much worse it was for Drusilla.

But the moment she sensed me arrive, it was as though her brain lit up with hope. She flicked her gaze up and down Nevidaea, who sat on a lounge in her aviary, sobbing red-faced into a silk handkerchief. "I don't know what I'll do," she whispered on a hitched breath. "He is still just a child, a little child. Belos! I don't know what I'll do if he... Oh, Mighty Ones. *Why*, why did Gaius do this? I could have stopped him. Why did I not *stop* him?"

What Drusilla really wanted to say was *I don't know*, but perhaps a reality in which Aquilan women stood up to their men was too much to hope for in this lifetime. Instead, she replied, "My lady, you and I both know nothing on this earth can stop the legate once he puts his mind to something."

Then, with a bob of her head, she swiftly excused herself to refresh the lady's teapot. Once inside the nearest servants' pantry, she bolted the door behind her. *And? The boy? You never came back to tell me.*

I'm sorry, I'm a mess. He is safe. I shocked myself by conveying actual words rather than vague emotions. *Frightened, but safe, and unhurt. Gaius's search party was successful. Ryac and the moonless protected him. But they have Orlaith.*

I thought the queen refused to enter this world again?

She came for Faelon.

Well, she certainly found him, Drusilla thought wryly.

Where will they imprison her, Alopex, Sylvostum...? Lady forbid New Lindanos.

Sylvostum. The queen of a warring nation calls for more security than that of a mere checkpoint, but Gaius will want to keep her close. Since we spoke mind to mind, what would usually be left unsaid was made plain: *To feed his sadism or to lure you there. Or perhaps so he can hold Faelon over her head like a dangling carrot.*

Likely all three. The good news is, she certainly will not be executed. She's far too valuable.

I felt little to no relief. There were things worse than death.

Drusilla sensed my strong reaction and replied, *Perhaps for you, but for your sister?*

True. Orlaith was more scared of dying than anything in this world. That fear was overshadowed only by her love for her son.

I don't suppose there's any chance of negotiation? Hostage trading? Drusilla asked.

None. We have no one they want that badly.

Perhaps you should get someone.

Perhaps. But it'll be some time before I can even pose that idea to the coalition, let alone set it in motion. Drusilla, I need you to help her, in any way you can. Even if it's just something small.

Our shared roots tingled with skepticism. *Something small, right. And how, exactly, shall I explain trips to the dungeon?*

A plan bloomed in my mind, sudden and vibrant like a globe of pink thrift in a salt marsh. *You aren't just a housekeeper. You're a speculator. Gaius's personal double-agent. There must be some way you can get into her cell, or the interrogation chamber, or wherever.*

Hmm. I'm a spy, not a torturer, but perhaps I could convince Gaius she might tell me something. I don't look like the other Aquilans, and I'm a servant... He may well think it an ingenious idea. There was a long pause as she transferred boiling water from the fire to her teapot. *Now, whether I can help her escape and keep my position here is another question altogether. Gaius may believe in my loyalty, but if she went missing under my watch, even he could not ignore the signs pointing to me. You had better ask your coalition what protection they're willing to offer me.*

I will.

Drusilla unbolted the door, crossed the hall, and stepped back onto the terrace dedicated to Nevidaea's aviary, with its gold-plated bars and colorful silks. I was just about to leave her when something caught my eye: a man in red-and-gold armor knelt before Lady Sergia's lounge, his hands bracing her arms. Drusilla's soft foot leathers muted her steps, so neither of them heard her, and they seemed too enraptured with one another to notice her in the entryway.

Without their helmets, it was hard to tell ranks apart from one another, but I recognized this armor. Gaius had worn it once. The man knelt before Nevidaea was a primus.

Drusilla and I both balked when he clasped her trembling hands in his dark, scarred ones. I recognized those hands but couldn't quite place them. Whoever he was, he certainly was brave, touching a legate's wife with such familiarity. "Please, my lady, don't cry."

I recognized that voice, too. *Ottavian.*

"How can I not?" Drusilla's ear shifted to pick up Nevidaea's faint voice. "The things the servants have been saying... The thought of Lucastos out there, I can't bear it."

"The legate will find him," Ottavian replied almost as softly. "You know he would do anything to protect that boy."

She exhaled a weary laugh. "Indeed. It is the only thing I know about my husband anymore." She shook her head. "This dread ... it pervades my every thought. Not only Lucastos, Mighty Ones, but all of it. Gaius and this withering, this war, this place, and that fae huntress... My friend, I-I'll go mad. I-I feel I truly am *going mad.*"

The primus renewed his grip on her hands. "Here, now, there is nothing you can do—for Lucastos or for yourself—besides pray and keep your mind busy."

"You wouldn't understand." She didn't bother to disentangle their hands to wipe the tears streaming down her cheeks. He raised his knuckles to brush them away, and she lingered. "You aren't a parent."

"No. But I have done my fair share of waiting up for loved ones. When I lost my brother..." Ottavian trailed off and shook his head, finally parting from her. "Think of something else. Your birds, yes?" He nodded round the aviary. "How is that female budgerigar you told me about. The violet one?"

As they stood, Drusilla withdrew from the terrace, handing

the tea off to an under-servant. Clearly, Ottavian had not yet gotten word of the boy's safety, but perhaps someone else would have more information for her. At the same time, something fluttered in my subconscious—a pull back to my body. I let the vision melt into nothingness, slowly allowing awareness of the weight of my own limbs to sink back in.

HIBEROS WAS COMING FOR ME. Even as my eyes snapped open and I beheld the starscape above me, the only thing I truly registered was his scent on the wind. Sun-warmed moss, blackberries, and a distinctly masculine musk that shouldn't effect me the way it did. I'd fallen flat on my back whilst entrenched in Drusilla's vision, and now my hair was tangled with seaweed.

It must have taken a while for my spirit to return to my body, for the moon was high and the tide was low. The causeway to the island in the bay was now passable. To my fae nose, the ocean's strong, briny scent smelled less like decay and more like magic: stormy, spicy, and citrusy all in one.

I turned and peered at the path. Although there was no sign of Hiberos, I knew better than to trust my eyes. I sensed him the way birds sensed the approach of winter.

With one last glance over my shoulder, I navigated through the field of stones and seaweed and began to walk the causeway leading out to the island. Though the path was paved with rocks and oyster shells, the island itself was lush and green even at night. The lake at its center glittered a dark, clear blue, its softly glowing surface telling me this place was thick with magic. The Weave was so powerful here I could feel it licking my skin as I wove through the sparse wood.

The island itself was no longer than a quarter mile. Its coast darted in and out of the water, and I followed it, gathering bundles of sea aster whose petals glittered like pink quartz in the moonlight. Finally, with both my fists full of wildflowers, I stopped on the highest point on the island, the sea cliffs, and watched the tide meet the mouth of the river. The more I watched, the more its pattern astounded me. A never-ending cycle of the mythic kissing the mundane before slowly slipping away. How could something be so ever-changing yet so constant?

"And all while the moon bears silent witness." Hiberos's voice came from behind me, tickled my spine. His knuckles soon followed it, caressing a path from the small of my back to the nape of my neck, where he rested his hand like a collar. "*Here, weir, reach, island, bridge. Where you meet I.*"

I did not turn my head to look at him, if only because his presence, after so long without him, was overwhelming. "Have you ever seen the ocean?" I asked.

"Once, a long time ago, before the Shift. You like it," he observed in a purr, and got behind me, sliding his hands from my shoulders to my wrists, my hips, then back up again. "How fascinating, that I still have so much to learn about you after thousands of years."

Finally, I dropped my bundles of sea aster, turned, and rested my palms against his chest. As he wrapped lean, muscular arms round my waist, I fingered the wood that had once borne spiral scars, where he'd carved his chest and shoulders to decorate his hide for our soulfasting. After spending my human lifetime swearing off courtship, it was still strange to envision myself ever having a wedding, but when in his arms like this, it didn't seem so odd. With him, there was no betrothal, no dowry, no gender ideals, no political games—nothing but two foolish souls stretching the universe apart to be together. Nothing but sea rushing to shore for just one touch before they were again parted.

"I miss the scars, too," he admitted, ears lowering. He pressed me closer, hiking my hip flush between his thighs as though he could press me into his bark and keep me inside forever. "I know you understand the feeling."

I nodded. When I'd awoken in this body, the scars from Gaius's lashing were gone. For most, that might be a blessing. But for me, all I could think of was Gwynedd's words. *Some scars are meant to be kept, my dear. Those that remind us of who we are, or perhaps who we were.*

I hesitated before asking, "Did *she* remove them?"

"They simply did not transfer to this body as it grew, same as yours." He brushed the curls from my face and pressed a kiss between my eyes, whispering, "We could carve them again. I want always for your love to leave its mark upon me."

I hid my face in his underarm and inhaled deeply. Moss and sun, spruce and wild thyme. "There was something you didn't tell me, when you explained what you learned to Erivon. Will you speak now?"

"I promised you I would." Reluctantly, he withdrew and settled in the grass, lounging on his side. I sat in the crook made by his lap, leaning back against him, and began to braid my discarded sea aster.

After a heavy silence, he said, "The war is not the only thing upsetting Gealach. She knows about us, and she's going mad with envy."

14

Suddenly, my fingers were shaking too hard to continue. I dropped the flowers in my lap.

With a tender coo, Hiberos snaked his arms around me and took up the braiding in my stead. "After all this time, she still feels ownership over me. I fear she will never come around to sharing me. She will kill us a thousand times over rather than let us be together."

My blood turned cold, then boiling in the next second. The claim Gealach staked over him did not come from the ether—the Guardians were born of the flesh of her dead husband, the Horned One, and for thousands of years Hiberos had been her primary consort—but she'd had her chance. She'd died, we'd mourned. Hiberos had moved on, and eventually fallen in love with the princess of the Lunar Kingdom. Ashling. *Me*. And here he was now, loving Mave just as well.

He was *mine*.

I clutched my fists, claws digging into my palms. "She *needn't* share you. There will be no sharing. You belong to me, not her, not any longer."

When I glanced at him, his brows were raised, his moonstone eyes searching my face—at first with awe, then a simmering heat.

"She offered me many things whilst I was trapped Beneath," he said, voice low. "Promised to make me the King of the Fomori..."

If those words were intended to stoke my possessiveness, it worked. I twisted on my knees to face him, digging my claws into his hip. "Whatever she's offering you, I will either double it, or burn it to ash. She wants you, she'll get war instead. I will not give you up. Not after everything. Not now. I fought for you. I will *not* go back to hearing your voice only in my dreams. Never again."

My tone excited him—I felt it in the way our magic touched, shifted, knotted—but he dropped the sea aster to cup my face instead. "Mave. I am yours, and you are mine. No blackmail, no bribe, no decree godly or otherwise could ever change that." He fingered one of my curls, for once not regretful but worshipful. "But you must know the cost. She is no longer the loving mother you once knew. She will do everything in her power to end us. Kill us again and again if she has to."

"Then I'll die," I ground out, "and find you again. And *again*. Until we can figure out another way. No *moon* will stop me."

His reverence did not falter. With a glance down, he retrieved the sea aster, wound it into a circlet, and placed it ceremoniously upon my head. "You are magnetic, my rose. The tides should bow only to you. I know I certainly do."

Face flushed, I wrapped my arms round his neck and leaned in, tipping his face up with my nose. His bottom lip, trapped between mine, was sweet like thyme and honey; the taste of him melted into my tongue, every other sense suffused with his scent and the feel of his hard body against mine. It was only when my heart wrenched unbearably that I pulled away, though my lips were still close enough to brush his. "Forgive me," I murmured. "For all the time you waited, then for all that I wasted pushing you away."

"Stop apologizing." He knotted his fist in my hair and pulled me in for another scorching kiss. "Abuse me, avoid me, deny me, I care not," he said between breaths, "as long as you exist within my sight. If I must, I will yearn for eternity."

"The way the stars love the moon." I carded my fingers

through his beard, pressing our foreheads together. A few breaths passed before I suggested weakly, "We should return to the bilé before the tide rises, or else we won't be able to at all."

"I see no need to rush," he whispered in my ear on his way to nibble at my neck. "There's nothing more you can tell Erivon, and nothing to be done until the rest of the coalition arrives."

"Hiberos—"

"Why would you want to return to the bilé, anyway? I don't even live in the Lunar Palace, my rose. You and I, we belong out here in the wild, dwelling in green bowers and making love in the moss and bramble. Coming against the earth." His hand slid along my hip bone, and he cupped me between the thighs—not grabbing but holding, steadying, as if my pussy were a needy thing calling him and he sought to soothe it. As if by laying a hand over my core he could root me here with him. "Be wild with me."

I trembled from my scalp to the soles of my feet, involuntarily thrusting upward to press hard against his strong, lithe hand—and did not stop trembling even as I tried to pull away and check on how the tide had shifted. Goddess, I wanted him, but we'd be stranded on this little island till mid-morning, and...

Hiberos let my cunt slide from his palm, but he clenched his fist as I turned. Caught the hem of my tunic and jerked me into him, my back flush with his front. "You want me to go after you, is that it? To prove I would chase you if you walked away?"

The thrill those words sent through my core electrified me. I jumped forward, acting purely on instinct, and did just that— walked away. I made it to the nearby treeline before glancing over my shoulder. But Hiberos was gone.

My breath became heavier and more ragged. My eyes darted at every shadow, every shift of the breeze, as I crept through the sparse wood to the lake. From here, my vantage point of the causeway was clear enough that I could see the tide had already made it narrower. It wouldn't last another hour or two. If we didn't leave now...

A moon moth flitted past, then a deep voice startled me. "We could make it quick."

All at once, he was behind me again. His hands were everywhere. My gaze fell to the lake's glassy surface, to our reflection, to the image of him with his mouth and nose buried against my shoulder, eyes glowing intently. He looked demonic. Hungry. Desperate, wretched. Wicked. As though if I were to look at him directly I'd forfeit my soul.

"Allow me a few minutes, and I will make you forget about the tide. Forget about any natural force that isn't me rooted deep enough to kill."

He inhaled me deeply and groaned. My mouth fell open, my back arching as he pulled at my clothing without regard for what he tore. He rid me of my bottom layers first, and pulled me against him so that the curves of my ass and pussy molded perfectly to the firm length that had slipped from its hiding place. He had angled himself so that his cock was pointing down, straining upward, its thick tip brushing the very root of my clit every time he rutted into me.

I expected him to slide in—maybe even wanted him to, disregarding my readiness and taking his own pleasure—but instead, he held me in place with steely resolve. Barely moved his hips. Thrusting, writhing, bucking just to feel our skin slide together. I still wore my tunic and half my blood-stained armor, yet all I could do was gasp and grip the immovable arm braced across my stomach.

Again and again, he ground into me, a rhythm of deceptively small thrusts that sent ecstasy shooting through me with every movement. Already, I panted and squirmed, coming undone from contact alone. My insides clenched, something building, threatening to do me in.

Then he sank his teeth into the soft place where my neck met my shoulder. Delicious pain shocked a scream from me, sending gouts of flame through my arms and into my nipples. "Stop!" I begged, not knowing why, because I was already thinking of other places he should bite me.

There was a wet suck and a wave of cold air as he pulled his mouth from me. "You don't mean that." His rutting became maddeningly more subtle. His right forearm, firm across my middle, was joined by the left so he held me in a bear hug. "Tell me to stop. Tell me."

It was halfway between a dare and a plea.

"Tell me to stop and I'll let you go. Otherwise, you are mine for the night—no regrets, no crying. Go on. Say it. Stop me."

My only reply was a desperate growl. I raked my claws along his forearms.

He exhaled raggedly against my skin. "Last chance."

"*No.*" I forced the word out as a puff of air, so irritated that he was making me *think*. Thinking was useless now. I only wanted to feel.

The air shifted around us, and he understood. Our reflections ... I didn't know if it was just the magic of this place or if there was some elemental reaction taking place between our bodies, but it looked as though our skin was *glowing*.

Though his grinding had never ceased, now his movements were firmer. He bowed me under his weight like a bully in a sparring ring. Hard. Harder, until I buckled and he bore me to my hands and knees. A pathetic whimper—the yip of a hound—left me, and my reflection snarled regretfully as Hiberos withdrew his heat from mine.

"Good," he purred, spreading me from behind with one warm, rough palm. "Keep looking into her eyes. I want you to see what I saw our last night together. You shatter with precision. Pattern. You bloom in perfect mathematical proportion. Your petals—"

Without warning, he stroked his fingers through my folds. I jumped with a cry and watched my face twist in ecstasy.

Whatever Hiberos had been about to say, he cut himself off, his voice raw as he said, "Goddess, your *scent*," instead.

He moved quickly. In the next moment, he was devouring me from behind, his nose and mouth shoved deep, eyelashes tickling my skin. It drew a satisfied groan from him, and he dug his claws into my haunches. It would leave marks and bruises, but I didn't care. I wanted more, more, deeper. My palms and knees ached, but it only excited me more. I arched my back and ground down, fucking myself on his tongue. He grunted hard through his nose. Sucked me ravenously, like he'd never have a taste of me again. And all the while, I watched the fae in the lake's surface come apart. The black tears marking my face were soon glistening with actual tears.

"No. No, it's too much, it's too much. Ah ... ah...!" My first climax came on suddenly. I bucked back, screaming his name. "Hiberos! Oh, *gods*."

He heard me, but the pace of his tongue was punishing as we rode the wave of my orgasm together. When he did ease back, it was the perfect amount of pressure, prolonging my come—that white-hot snapping again and again.

By the time he pulled away, I was a shivering, groaning animal, barely able to hold myself on all fours. The proof was right in front of me. Could not be denied.

"Look at you," he murmured fervently, finally peeling my shirt from my skin to trace a line through the sweat on my back. "At how you break when I feast upon your flesh. Never in my existence have I seen anything so exquisite."

"Please," I whispered, finally dropping my head to hide my face in the crook of my elbow, "don't say things like that. You know I... I can't—"

"You *can*. You *will*. Watch," he said with sharp authority, and reached around to lift my chin. "Watch what I do to you, and consider it a lesson. You are still my student, after all. I may even let you call me Master Hiberos like you used to."

I turned my head to bite him, but my fangs snapped around air. He withdrew his hand too quickly.

"*Goddess*..." His voice was gravelly as he twisted his hand into the curls at the crown of my head.

"Don't speak her name," I growled.

"I'm not." His hide whispered against my skin as he lined his hips up with mine. "I'm speaking *yours*."

Then the head of his cock was touching me, and he was stretching my entrance, and he was filling me, and ... all thoughts that weren't of him and of the heat where our bodies met left my head forever. A long, low moan started in my throat and grew in pitch the deeper he penetrated me. My vision would not even focus on my reflection. My arms trembled and threatened to fail.

"Chin up, Your Highness."

I tried, tried to make eye contact with my reflection—but as he began to move inside of me, hitting me just right, my scalp erupted with tingles. My limbs soon followed, the only sensation in them pressure on my nail beds and knuckles as I grabbed fistfuls of reeds and lush grass. Before long, it was all I could do to keep my face above water. The lake's surface rippled as errant curls and the tip of my nose touched it.

He helped me by locking his arm around my head, the knot of my throat pressed to the crook of his elbow. "Stay still and watch. Let yourself feel every inch of me."

He grew heavier and heavier until I couldn't take it anymore. I collapsed, flat on my belly with the whole of his weight on top of me. My nipples ached and tingled against dew-soaked grass. Now he wasn't thrusting in and out so much as burying himself deep and grinding. Humping. Using the grip of my cunt to stroke himself off, his grunts rough and breathy beside my ear while I could not move a muscle.

Then his hand snaked across my hip and cupped me, allowing me sweet, slick friction as I moved with him—and I gave up fighting.

I finished, hard, snarling like a snared wolf. The Weave came apart at the seams; the air sparked purple and blue around us. Hiberos's thrusts stuttered like he might pull out, but I hooked my legs around his hocks to trap him like he'd trapped me.

"I want them all to smell you on me," I panted. My gaze flicked to the moon above. "She can watch. I want her to see you choose me."

His pace changed to brutal, assaulting my insides, each breath a growl against the side of my face. The sensation of that breath *alone* against my sensitive fae ears could make me come a third time—then he sucked hard on the shell of my ear, and, indeed, I unraveled with a shrill cry.

Hiberos was close behind. The points of his fingers dug into my hips. Pain burned through me, but I didn't stop him, just let him take all that he needed. I could do nothing but loose a cracked whimper with every thrust.

When he spilled into me, it was with my name on his lips. "Mave, Mave, Mave..."

That name shook the heavens.

Stars winked out of existence. The moon shuddered with a sound like roaring thunder. And I swore, for a split second, the world was bathed in blood red.

I knew then that it had not just been a game. Gealach had been watching, and wherever she was, she was wild with rage.

As if he thought he could protect me from the sky itself, Hiberos swore, gathered me to his chest, and pulled us to the tree-line. A flurry of frightened moon moths sheltered along with us. Partially hidden under the boughs of a big quickthorn tree, we watched the vaulted night above us, and clutched each other as the Weave shifted tone. Subtle, satin purples and reds a layer beneath the inky sapphire of midnight. It was one of the most stunning things I'd ever seen, yet my stomach knotted in dread.

Hiberos murmured, "She cannot even let us have a moment of happiness."

It took me a while to find my words. "In all fairness, we did rather openly defy her."

He grinned warmly down at me. "You, letting me take you in earnest when the consequence is the destruction of your own land. I'm flattered."

I frowned, only because it hadn't occurred to me that that flash of red was probably tied to a new outbreak of blight, possibly close by. I considered his pearly spend rolling down my inner thigh and, trying to ignore the pulse of my body to do it all again, shook my head. "We should get back. They might need us if—"

"Have you forgotten?" He gestured languidly toward the water, where the bay had swallowed up the causeway.

"The water isn't deep. We could swim to the other side with ease."

As I stared at the lapping ocean, conflicted, Hiberos slipped behind me, slipping a hand up my shirt to rub the scar on my sternum. "This is our island till mid-morning, my rose. Our own, dark little world where I am king and you are queen. Let us enjoy what little time we have."

He made it sound so nice. Worse, he made it sound so *easy*. I turned and spoke to his chest, knowing that if I looked in his eyes, I'd break. "How can I refuge here with you when … *everything* is falling apart a half mile away?"

He tipped my chin up, and just as I feared, tears filled my eyes at once. "Mave. You have given everything to this land, including your blood. It simply cannot rest all on your shoulders. It is insanity to think it could ever be so. And if you prefer to speak in terms of responsibility," he added with a scoff, "is it not your responsibility to well rest yourself, so that you can continue banging your head against the Empire in the moons to come?"

"Banging my head—" I frowned, wicking my tears away. "Are you saying you don't think we can ever win?"

Hiberos sighed and waved away a moth trying to land on an errant curl. "I would never say such a thing. I, better than anyone, know what you are capable of. But you must admit—I pray to the stars you'll admit—that your victory will not come easily. The fate of Éire will not be decided after a single war. You may be fighting until all the kings of this realm are long dead and gone. It is a trial of endurance as much as anything." He pulled me in, wrapping his arms round my shoulders and cradling my head against his chest. "Hence, you need rest."

Even as I relaxed into him, I argued. "Would be so much quicker if we just got it done. If we killed enough of them, we'd drive them out of Éire."

"Oh, my huntress. You want to strike like a panther, but not every beast can be chased and felled in a sprint. Good job humans are persistence hunters, hm?" He held me at arm's length, giving me a slow, burning once-over. "And you are—human. Even if you don't currently look like one."

The statement shocked me such that I simply stared at him.

"Which reminds me..." He lifted my tunic over my head and discarded it, the last scrap of clothing between us finally gone. "Did you notice?"

"Notice what?"

"You looked at yourself. Your reflection. And you did not recoil." With a smirk, he brushed an unruly curl behind my ear. "I realize I promised to replace your illusion pendant, but perhaps you don't need it after all."

"Perhaps all I needed was ... exposure."

Laughing, he added darkly, "In more ways than one."

Before, I had allowed bliss to come to me the same way I allowed pain to come to me. Passively. Detached. In a strange, sad way, I had been as much a victim to my desires as I was to my traumas. It had been too frightening to try and examine my discomfort. Unthinkable to crack myself open and to want. Perhaps because everything had already been taken from me. If I wanted this, it could be taken from me, too.

But it had. He had. And in those long months apart, I had learned the truth—a truth that most did not learn until it was too late. For humans, there was no promise of another day, another chance. There was only now. And that was the way it ought to be.

Few were ever given a second chance. I'd been given a third. His return, our defiance of the gods, my conquering of Gaius—it had ripped open the dam, the walls I'd built around the very deepest parts of my soul and tried in vain to climb.

I wanted to be human. Fully.

Now I felt the urgency. No more restraint. No more insecurity. No matter how raw, no matter what part of me I must bare to him.

Hiberos had come back from the clutches of Death changed, too. The old goat I'd met in Geatacoill could not have abandoned the high towers of the Lunar Palace for this. Not because he did not yearn to be free—he had that isolated home in the hollow of the yew, he remembered the beast he'd once been—but because he was bound by fear. He had no such fear now. He was realer, closer to the wild creature at the heart of him. Closer to the bloody flesh and antler from which he'd been hewn.

We'd learned. We matched. Honesty, even when it meant ruin. New willingness to embody the vulnerability of being not what you were meant to be but what you *are*.

"Now," he said as we fell, tangled, back into the grass, "care to give my new-and-improved chest some proper decoration?"

I did. Straddling him, I used my claws to carve a new pattern into his chest. Scars that marked him as not only mine but symbolized the way I thought of him: a personification of my home. Not spirals but rivers. A map of Éire's waterways and tributaries flowing outward from Geatacoill at his heart and working across his torso, up his neck, down his arms.

The process was not without pain. Hiberos grimaced and hissed though he held absolutely still, but each new groove, I blessed with a kiss. "You are doing so well for me," I whispered against the hard swell of his abdominal muscles.

He purred, shivering in response.

I wanted this. I would do anything to protect this. Fully, wholly, openly, for the rest of time, I would never stop claiming him as mine, and he'd do the same in return.

For the first time in ten years, I truly felt like myself. Mave. Except now the lover, the soulmate, from my dreams was here. Keeping me. And I, him.

Nothing—*nothing*—in this universe could keep our stars apart now.

15

The snap of a whip and the scent of fae blood woke me. I jerked upright, in my own body for just a painful flash before the colors and my sense of smell changed. Drusilla—I was with Drusilla.

The torture chamber was all stone with a low ceiling. Only one torch burned in a nearby sconce, and strokes of orange coruscated with every tremble of the flame, ducking into shadowy recesses before dancing back out. The stench in here was unholy, a heady mix of sweat and blood, human and fae, healing herbs and wine. My view of the prisoner was currently blocked by Gaius, his bare back damp and rippling with cruelty. His right hand curled into a fist at his side, gripping a whip tipped with shards of metal and glass, freshly used and dripping.

"How do I cross into your realm?" The cadence of the question—slow, patient, and condescending—suggested it had been asked many times before.

I wasn't surprised, but nausea hollowed me all the same, when the prisoner replied in Eytine's—Orlaith's—voice. "Ask me as many times as you want," she rasped, "I still won't answer you. Pig."

He struck with his whip. *Snap*. An unhinged growl that hardly sounded like my sister echoed through the chamber, bringing with it another wave of foul stench. "I think you ought to. I'll soon begin taking claws. One by one." His even tone did not match his fevered physicality at all—the stance, the way his shoulders heaved with each breath, the sweat drenching his curls, the slight shiver of gooseflesh on his skin.

He eased to one side, finally giving Drusilla a view of Orlaith. She was still standing, naked from the waist up, shackled to the stone wall with anti-magic chains. Her back, so marred and bloodied that it resembled ground meat more than fae flesh, was to us, but as she spoke with Gaius, she turned her head. At first, I thought her hair—which was nearly to her ankles—was braided over her shoulder, but when she shifted, the strands flicked outward and the ends caught the light.

My heart seized. They'd shorn her beautiful, moon-white hair to her jaw. And that revelation brought another. Something else was missing, too. Her wings. They'd been torn clean away, leaving nothing but bloody slits.

Yet her delicate mouth curled upward in a quivering smile as though, despite her position, she was struggling not to laugh right in Gaius's face.

He was laboring to break her, but just as when they'd faced each other in battle ten years ago, she met him blow for blow. *This* was the sister I remembered.

"What do you hope to achieve, here?" she asked, tone conversational despite the rawness of her voice. "You think that by brutalizing more Éirins, somehow your father will come back from the dead and congratulate you? Tell you he was wrong, that he didn't go far enough?"

That earned her a crack of the whip, but she snarled through the pain and pressed, "You think he'd change his mind, admit savages aren't meant to be studied and kept like curios, only crushed?"

Crack.

"That you were different and more special than all his Éirin wards? That you were special to him *at all*?"

Crack. Crack. Crack. Each snap was wetter than the last. Orlaith's knees trembled as she struggled, shaking and panting, to keep herself upright. "Or is it *my son* you need validation from?" she managed through bubbling saliva. "You are such a wonderful leader and father you have to prove it with force?" Her laugh was brittle and half-mad. "Such an egomaniac, yet neither confident nor competent enough to exist outside your silly little hierarchy. Too cowardly, too *weak* to break the cycle you were born—"

He cut her off with a strike so loud, so vicious, that Orlaith could make no sound beyond a choked gasp.

Drusilla glanced furtively at the guards stationed outside the cell door, then took a step forward. "Legate, there is only so much a body can take between interrogations. We don't yet know the limits of the fae. We should focus."

The way Gaius looked back at her...

Like a starved attack dog corrected and redirecting its aggression onto its handler, he spat, "Get the fuck out of my way," and, pushing past Drusilla, slammed his whip down on a nearby bench. Grabbing for his goblet of wine, he drank deeply, then pitched the empty pewter cup at the cell door. The clattering rang through the dungeon and echoed into silence.

Rarely had I seen Gaius lose his head. His particular mold did not allow for loss of control, ever. But more and more of late, the mask slipped—and everyone saw it. Even prisoners who had only known him for a matter of hours.

"Your peers and your subordinates both deride you." Orlaith enunciated each word. "Your own wife detests you. You are pathetic."

"That's enough," Drusilla said.

Silently, I thanked her for balancing my sister when I could not. Every word Orlaith said was true, but if she taunted Gaius enough, he would kill her. And worse.

The she-wolf stepped forward. "This would be easier for

everyone if you simply told him what you know. None of your people could blame you for cracking under interrogation. So, how do we pass through your portals?"

Orlaith, of course, knew from briefings that Drusilla was on our side, but she laughed at her nonetheless. "Oh, we're asking nicely now, are we? If the lash didn't drive it out of me, manners certainly won't."

"It hardly seems fair that your people should be able to retreat to a realm beyond ours, unreachable."

"Since when is war *fair*? Come now, are the quillies really stupid enough to throw their toys when faced with the slightest handicap? You know wars are fought from both sides, yes? And meant to be won?"

Finally, Gaius turned, running a towel over his chest to wick away the sweat and blood. "There is no hope of your people winning this war. Aquila's strength is boundless. Emperor Westerus will send as many legions as are needed to wrest this little island away from your barbarian friends."

"He will, yeah? Better do it, then, instead of shitehawking about."

Gaius scoffed. "I see your barbarian mouth is intact. But the fae follow you, so let me be direct. Just like the Éirins, the survival of your people depends entirely on their cooperation. In other words..." He came so close that his bare chest was nearly touching her flayed back, his mouth dipping toward her throat. "Lie down like a good girl, serve the Empire, and you may live. Give me a reason to destroy you, and I will enjoy every second."

When Orlaith gave no response, not even looking at him, he tossed an exasperated look back at Drusilla. "Why must I keep teaching them this lesson?"

Drusilla calculated her next words carefully, for she knew he was listening to her. A thousand different strategies wheeled through our shared consciousness at once—everything from *let him break her down* to *kill him now and run*. But there was one in particular that frightened us both to the core.

That was the one she chose.

She motioned Gaius over, and they retreated to the next room, which was occupied by looming iron torture devices: spiked saddles, breast-rippers, and restraints that tightened to put immense pressure on bones and internal organs. Others, too, whose designs were either unspeakable or incomprehensible. Each more hideous than the last, and each selected specifically to wring dignity out of a woman until information was produced.

Drusilla— I tried to interrupt her thoughts, but if anything, the sight of those monstrous instruments strengthened her resolve.

"You surely have more experience with interrogation than I," she began quietly, "but I think we should change tack."

"It's only been a handful of hours. She will break." He nodded to a long wooden trunk beside them, whose only defining feature was a sturdy iron padlock. "I haven't even put her in the box yet."

Drusilla schooled the set of her ears, and willed her lips not to tighten. "I know squealers when I see them, Legate, and she isn't one."

Gaius's gaze drifted as he considered. "What do you suggest?"

"We have all the leverage over her we will ever need. We needn't harm another hair on her head."

His haunting blue eye searched her face. At length, he muttered, "Lucastos."

"Yes. Promise her things, or threaten them. Either way, you needn't go through with them. As long as she believes you will..."

"I would hate to forgo the punishment she's well and truly due"—Gaius began to pace—"but perhaps you are right. The abilities of these creatures are unknown. Her stamina alone clearly exceeds that of a human." He slowed. I hated the way his eye lit up. "It will be good for Lucastos to be involved. Having already assisted in an interrogation will give him an advantage over his peers when he finally goes to academy."

Drusilla added mildly, "And it will prove his loyalty to you."

That argument dwarfed all others, immediately and with brilliance. The set of Gaius's jaw shifted, his spine straightening. "So many birds killed with a single stone..."

Then, suddenly enough that even Drusilla flinched, the legate came forward and seized her hand. He pulled her in for an embrace. It must have been genuine, yet it was so awkward, his body equally as stiff as hers. Like he'd never held someone in his life. "This will earn you your freedom once and for all. The Emperor's rewards are real."

Those words, murmured in her ear, made her shudder. Promises and threats truly did sound the same coming from his mouth.

He pulled away, gripping her shoulders. "Go explain to Lucastos. He may still be sleeping—it doesn't matter. Wake him and bring him to me. In the meantime, I'll..." His hands fell away, and he licked his lips, looking at the doorway to the torture chamber. "I'll finish here."

No. But he agreed to stop!

Kill him! Bloody kill him now! My consciousness whaled against Drusilla's, as if I could somehow take control of her body and pilot her dagger into his throat. As always, she was calm, cool. Dipped a curtsey even as I screamed for her, *Don't leave! Do not leave my sister, Lady DAMN it!*

We left the dungeon, but the screams followed us.

+☽ ☽ ☽ ☾ ☾+

WHEN I SEARCHED for my usual exit from Drusilla's consciousness, I couldn't find it. It was as if my body refused to let me come back. As though this was punishment: to remain as a passenger in someone else's body and witness my sister's torture without being able to do anything, to tell anyone. Perhaps punishment for leaving her behind in the first place. Or for losing that miasma bomb.

Or ... for last night. For Hiberos.

Could it be? The leylight worms that connected me to Drusilla, Nevidaea, and Faelon were native to the Underland. It could be she had some dominion over this power. If that was the case...

Let me out. This is about Orlaith, not me. If you were ever a mother, let me get to Erivon! If no one else supported a suicidal mission into Sylvostum, Erivon, upon hearing how his wife suffered, *would*. He would burn all Cuanacht down trying to get to her.

There was no reply; I was not returned to my body.

Without nowhere else to turn, I skipped down Drusilla's spine and into our shared well. It wasn't something I saw—I saw only blackness—so much as sensed. I could almost feel the cool kiss of the water, smell the slick bark of the winding roots. Every time I melted into someone else's consciousness, it seemed, the roots became more and more bound up in each other. I wondered what it meant. What the consequences of such a thing might be. Yet I didn't know how to linger and learn even if I dared.

Instead, I sank into the pool and let myself be drunk up by Nevidaea.

I admit, since Faelon's consciousness had become open to me, I'd visited Lady Sergia less and less. Witnessing what Gaius did to her was too much at the best of times. Beyond that, there was a sense of discomfort in her body. There was no doubt that she suffered under the Empire, particularly her husband, but still, our lives were unalike in so many ways. Not only unalike or incompatible; they seemed to dwell in two different spheres of reality altogether. She'd grown up a senator's daughter, I'd come up in a country community. She worshiped Mighty Ones like an ant at temple shrines, I revered the land beneath me. She'd lived a life where her pain was beauty, her fragility an art, her personal tragedies and inner world consecrated. I'd lived a life where pain was pain, blood was cheap, and tragedy meant losing everything. Her husband turned his back on her and her world shattered; my family was slaughtered before my eyes and, somehow, life went on.

Perhaps I was envious of her struggles. Perhaps I wished my world was more like hers. But then again, no, not really. I didn't want either of us to suffer, no matter the gravity of that suffering. What I truly wanted was for her to open her eyes.

Even now, I didn't know if she ever would.

But seeing the way she cared for Faelon gave me some hope. Naive, maybe, but as my consciousness melded with hers, the strength of her love and relief overwhelmed me. Hours ago, when Gaius and the rescue party had returned from the wasteland, Nevidaea had been there to greet them. Faelon had flung himself into her arms, and she'd taken him away to bathe and feed him. After an initial bout of thankful tears, though, the boy had not wept or spoken of his experience. All he'd endured among that pack of savage wolf-shapes was still a mystery to her.

Nevidaea could not bring herself to leave him alone. When he needed her, she would be there. And so they sat now in his bed, dressed for sleep but not properly sleeping, with her propped up against the headboard and Faelon limp in her lap. He dozed off, then seized with nightmares and hid in her bosom in turn.

She had to bite her fist to keep from wailing at the unfairness of it all. Had it not been enough for Gaius to take him from his nursemaid and drill him morning, noon, and night? Had it not been *enough* to wake the boy at all hours to study the Sergias' long legacy of killing? Had the bruises on his knuckles, earned by mispronouncing Éirin diphthongs, not been discipline enough? His father had had to take him afield, too, and show him the horrors Nevidaea tried so desperately to shield him from?

Why break such a wonderful little child? Why make him just like...

Another nightmare rocked Faelon, making him shiver and jolt upright in her lap. His dark green eyes opened wide, flicking about the room like he expected whatever monster haunted his dreams might follow him to the waking world. His grip on her arm was crushing, much stronger than she'd ever expect an eleven-year-old's to be. "Mother—"

"I'm here, Luca. "The thought of what agonies must be tormenting him made her want to scream all over again. At his age, her biggest fear had been thunderstorms, and the ever-lingering suspicion that her parents did not like her.

Lords of Stars, how could a mother guard against what she simply did not understand?

With a flurry of shushes and forehead kisses, Nevidaea slipped from bed and opened his toy chest. Surely, something in here would comfort him. Yet, as she picked up his playthings one by one, all she could see was death. Toys that had once seemed so harmless made her heart skip now: a wooden dagger, tin legionaries, a leather slingshot. Even his soft toys were all wolves, keeping with his namesake. Mighty Ones forbid she let him see the face of a wolf after being trapped with those heathens.

Determined, she dug to the bottom. There must be something here that had nothing to do with war games—*something* he could hold that did not groom him to hold a weapon.

As she pushed aside a liveried horse miniature, the sound of wood knocking wood caught her ear. She looked at the horse again, then beneath it, and found a little wooden bird. Its paint was chipped and worn from age, its surface scratched, but it was smooth and solid against her fingertips. Someone had loved this well, once. Had held it close.

Something about the little, forgotten bird tugged at her memory. Ah ... the elder Lady Sergia had given this to Faelon as a small child. Probably the last time they'd seen her before her death. Nevidaea seldom thought of her husband's mother, perhaps because he seldom mentioned her, but for whatever reason, she'd come to mind more and more in recent months.

Regardless, Nevidaea brought the wooden bird back to bed without hesitation, knelt, and pressed it into Faelon's palm. "Times when I'm scared, it helps to have something in my hand. Something to worry."

Her heart lifted when the faintest smile appeared on the boy's face. "It's a red-breasted carrow."

Still kneeling, Nevidaea folded her arms on the edge of the bed and rested her head upon them, gazing up at her son. "I found it at the bottom of your toy chest."

Faelon turned it over in his hand and stared at something on the bottom.

"Luca?"

He jumped and shook his head, folding the bird between his hands. "Nothing." Before she could insist, he said, "Mother..." and she was so desperate to hear him speak that she forgot about the bird.

"What is it, darling?"

"How long have you known I'm half fae?"

Nevidaea was shocked into silence. Since he was a baby, she'd been of the opinion they should never tell him he was adopted. Let him think he was their biological child, because what did it matter anyway? He was theirs, and would never be anyone else's. It was Gaius who told the truth when he asked. But that *truth* was that his birth-giver had been Éirin. Nothing like this. "Lucastos," she said with a sterner edge to her voice than she meant. "You— you are half *Éirin*."

He nodded, then said in a tone that should come from someone far older than him, "Right. And the other half?"

She fumbled, speechless. "We, we— She never— That is, we ... don't know. It could have been anyone."

"I do know." Faelon looked at her not with anger but with pity. "I met them, at the battle. My real family. Some of them were human once, but they're really fae inside. My mother and Auntie M—"

"Mave," Nevidaea finished sharply, heat climbing up her collar. Tears welled unbidden in her eyes and spilled over before she could stop them. Mave, always Mave. If she had to hear the name of that damned huntress one more time ... if she had to hear it from her own *son's* mouth—not just a much-used word in her husband's unhinged tirades—she would go mad. "I am your mother. We are your family, Lucastos, your real family. We've raised you. Where are you hearing all this?" A shard of fear straightened her spine. "Is *your father* telling you these things?"

"No, no!" Faelon said quickly, eyes wide. It was obvious he hadn't expected his mother to react so strongly. From what I'd seen, she wasn't given to histrionics, especially not around her son, so it must be jarring. "I'm sorry, Mama, I didn't—"

His eyes were filled with tears now, too, and the sight hit Nevidaea like a bucket of cold water. *What am I doing?*

She'd known that, one day, this conversation would come, but she'd not expected it to be like this. And this revelation with the fae ... could that be true? Mave had "come back" somehow; it was half of all Gaius talked about. Could her son's birth-giver have, too?

And if it was true, how long had *Gaius* known? What else had he known and not told her?

Faelon's face crumpled, and he clutched his wooden bird with shaking hands.

"Shh, shh." With her heart in her throat, Nevidaea slid onto the bed and gathered him in her arms. "Please don't cry, darling. I'm sorry. I did not mean to ... fuss. I was only confused." She pressed his head to her bosom and brushed her fingertips across his tight curls. "I ... I don't understand. Where is this fae notion coming from?"

"I met them," he repeated. She'd been so shocked those words had escaped her notice. "I've *met* them."

"When she came here?"

"More than once. Mave, she told me if I wanted to know more about where I come from, I should..."

Faelon rolled his bottom lip between his teeth, but, ultimately, he didn't tell her about the apple. Inwardly, I breathed a sigh of relief. Giving treats to stranger children did make once seem like a bit of a nonce, and wouldn't exactly endear me to his mother.

"Then at the battle, I saw her again," he continued. "And the woman with her, she was my..."

"Birth-giver." Nevidaea's absolute refusal to even say the word *mother*, when I knew how Eytine had worshiped that baby, made me so livid that it was a wonder Nevidaea's temperature didn't rise, too.

He squeezed his eyes tight. "Mama, Father's captured her. My —my *birth-giver*. Ryac and all his wolves, they f-found her. She was the one in chains when we arrived."

All the air seemed to be sucked out of the room.

Here?

She *had* come back. For Nevidaea's own son.

And she was *here*?

Nevidaea opened her mouth to try and respond—somehow—but before she could find the words, someone rapped at the door.

"Lady Sergia," came Drusilla's voice. "May I come in? The legate is requesting Lucastos at once."

16

I wasn't sure how long it took Orlaith to crack. Through others' eyes, my perception of time was distorted, and doubly so when two-thirds of the people I had access to spent the majority of the next hours below ground, with clammy dungeon walls pressing in on them.

No matter how I rattled at the bars of my cage, I could not find my way back to my body. And with me constantly in the backs of their minds, everyone had a splitting headache.

Faelon almost never left the dungeon. Drusilla spent what time she could by his side, but inevitably, Gaius would dismiss her. Between household duties, she and I tried—with what had become fragmented communication between our consciousnesses —to pull together a plan for Orlaith's escape.

Spring meant groundwater flooding in both the Sallach Delta and valley, which had never been a grand time for the villagers of Fraochgleann but was a veritable scourge to the Aquilans. There was little doubt that the dungeon would flood; it already had done earlier that week, before Orlaith's arrival. If it got bad enough—if the sewers backed up, if the pressure forced open an overflow channel, if the timing was right—it might present an opportunity. All that water had to go somewhere, away from the town. A sewer could be salvation. The key was figuring out which drains connected to the main flow, and where that flow led.

Drusilla promised she would look into it. Leaving my sister's fate up to chance did not sit well with me, but what choice did I have, trapped in the ether as I was?

Nevidaea still had not descended into the bowels of the torture chamber, but she paced her terrace aviary at all hours, waiting for word from her son, her husband, *anybody*. Primus Ottavian visited her when he could, but his duties were many, and nothing could comfort her. Her son's innocence was slipping away before her eyes, water between her fingers, drained by a man she was oathbound to obey.

She should go down there. She should see the face of the woman who'd brought her son into this world. *He* had. Far beyond seeing her, he'd spoken to her—had *been speaking* to her for … days upon days, now. Yet Nevidaea was terrified. Of that woman, of that room, of the men her husband and son might become there.

And why? For what?

She couldn't stop feeling it in her hand. The sensation of Faelon's sweaty palm leaving hers as he disappeared beneath the earth. It was like watching him walk into an open grave, and she hardly understood why.

As for Faelon himself, under Father's watchful eye, he spoke to his birth mother. Sometimes about mundane things, but Gaius would only tolerate that for so long. The conversation was always steered to the fae and their world. Gaius was shrewd, manipulative. Smarter than he appeared, for certain. He had Faelon ask questions I knew Orlaith struggled not to answer: "Where did I come from?" "What is it like?" "Where is your husband, my father, the king?" "How do I get there?" "Will you take me there?" Questions any woman long separated from her baby would yearn to answer.

To her credit, she tried not to answer. When Faelon was coached to beg and plead and she found it impossible to deny him, she tried to omit anything Gaius might use against her—but he was quick, good at puppeting his son, and she was many nights into torture, without food or water or sleep. She was bound to slip, and Gaius knew it. Even if her will never faltered, her body, so unused to suffering, crumbled before our eyes.

Seeing it made Faelon want to shut his eyes and never open them again.

What little rest he did get was in the cold, dank barracks adjoining the dungeon, and even then, between the nightmarish instruments stored in the recesses of the chambers and the constant crack of the whip, sleep did not come easy. Father never seemed to sleep. He simply sent Faelon away when the boy became too tired to function, and continued to torture the fae queen.

The sounds alone made Faelon vomit. He couldn't even keep down bread. When he wasn't vomiting, he was crying from exhaustion and overwhelm and the deep cramping in his stomach. He wished the faerie queen would give up what she knew. It was easier to do as Father asked, no matter who you were. He didn't understand why she refused to. Her pain would be over, and so would his.

Torture, he learned, was not about who was the strongest or most righteous or even cleverest—it was a game of outlasting your opponent.

Then, one day, she broke.

It was not the climactic break Faelon thought it would be. It was just a day like any other. Father woke him, coached him on what to say, and let him into the torture chamber. Alone, for once. As he entered the dark and putrid place, he reached into his pocket, fingering the wooden bird mother had found. His heart was beating so fast he felt like a little bird himself.

Orlaith was sitting against the far wall. Naked, thin, and sunken. The way the shackles were positioned, she had to hold her arms over her head in order to sit, and they hung limply like that. Her hands and feet were swollen, and the rest of her skin was drained of its rich seafoam color, although you could hardly tell for the bruises stippling every inch of her body. Her shorn hair was matted with blood and filth, and the wounds where her wings should be festered. An unfocused, milky opal gaze shone out of two black eyes like that of a dead fish. It wasn't until Faelon pulled up a chair that she seemed to regain consciousness, tipping her chin up slightly.

"Faelon," she murmured as if in a dream.

He'd asked Father if he could give her something to wear. There was something so terrible about seeing her naked and filthy like she was some kind of animal. He'd tried everything to ignore it, to harden and remind himself that this was a prisoner, not even a human ... but it was no use. Now that he'd had time to consider, he thought it was the wings that bothered him most. Why do something like that?

From under his arm, he withdrew the skein of linen Drusilla had brought and approached without hesitation. Even if she had the strength or range to move her limbs, Faelon was certain she would never hurt him.

"Here," he whispered, and carefully wrapped the cloth around her, using one of Drusilla's folding techniques to create a simple dress. It wasn't perfect and crisp like Drusilla's always seemed to be, but it wouldn't slip off. "I have food and drink, too."

She managed to lift her chin up another notch. He sat there in front of her, perched on the edge of his chair, and soaked bread in wine before feeding it to her. Her lips trembled, her fangs extended, drool dripped down her chin. It took a long time, but eventually, they finished the small crust.

Funny. He felt more grown-up tending to her than he ever felt assisting in her torture.

As he set aside the cup of wine, he recited what Father had asked him to. "I have news. Do you remember I told you there's a Moon Gate at the bottom of the lake, in the center of the forest?" When Orlaith only blinked slow, he continued, "Erm, the ... the engineers are draining the lake. And I am going to go through the portal."

He didn't expect her to jerk to attention, suddenly alert. "Impossible. You—you don't know how to open it."

That was true, but Father said he should bluff. Faelon crossed his arms with what was supposed to be authority but was really just discomfort. He tried his hardest to put as much of his father into his tone as he could. "We've narrowed it down. It won't be long till we have it opened, with or without your cooperation."

She shook her head emphatically. "No. Child, you can't. Promise me you won't try it."

The fact that she believed him at once worried me. So far, Gaius had not made the connection between him spilling my blood and the Gate awakening; if he had, he'd take Orlaith there now and cut her throat. Was he truly that close to understanding?

Faelon glanced over his shoulder, then back. It was impossible to deny that he really was interested in seeing the realm his parents came from. "Why, why should I not? Is it ... dangerous?"

"The Underland isn't meant for humans." She, too, glanced over his shoulder, but the threat that Gaius might be listening did not stop her. "The magic of the raw fae realm twists those without — Those whose bodies and minds are not attuned to it. Humans lose themselves. Go mad. I've seen it happen before."

He swallowed hard. "But I'm half fae."

"You are half fae, my love, but you are also human. You must understand there has never been someone like you. Lunar fae do not have children. You are the first of your kind. No one can say if entering the portal would be safe for you."

Faelon didn't quite understand why, but his heart sank. "Will I never be able to go there, then? I'm not ... not fae enough."

"Oh, little wolf, I didn't mean..." She exhaled and rattled her chains trying to reach him, to no avail. "You are enough to me. You are everything to me, my babe. You'd just need to complete the trials before we were certain one way or the other."

He fought the urge to lean into her. "Trials?"

"Yes. The Guardians' trials. You'd have to complete those," she repeated, "and—and we could see. Tests to measure whether or not you can pass through unscathed. Not facing them is too great a risk. To do that, though, you would need to come with me. Leave this place. This life. Please"—she gave a shuddering gasp —"*please*, promise me you won't try to go through. Not just yet."

"Guardians?" he murmured. A million questions flew through his mind, so many I had a hard time keeping up with them. But before he could say anything more, the iron gate to the chamber opened, and Gaius stepped in. A shudder ran through Orlaith that, in turn, ran through Faelon.

I wish I could speak to her, I thought, loudly enough that my wish became Faelon's. He swallowed hard and held his throbbing head.

A flash of lacquered ash invaded his mind, and unbidden, without full understanding, he thought, *Auntie Mave?*

I was too stunned to answer even if I knew how.

"Lucastos." The legate gestured for his son.

The lad jumped off his chair and, with one look back at his mother, followed Gaius into the corridor. They stepped around the guards as they changed shifts, and went into the adjacent chamber, where Gaius had taken up residence in the master interrogator's office. It wasn't much more than a ratty bookshelf, stools, and a worn desk strewn with notes and ledgers.

"She looked affrighted," he remarked as he circled the desk. "Well done. What information did you get out of her?"

Faelon hesitated before sitting on one of the stools. Her appearance had been so ghastly it took him a moment to recall their conversation at all. "She did not tell me how to go through the portal, but—but she warned me that we shouldn't."

Gaius said, blandly, "Oh?"

"She said that humans do not belong in the fae realm—the Underland—and that they go mad if they find themselves there."

At this, finally, he stopped pacing and looked at his son. His demeanor was suddenly keen and cold. "Why?"

"Er, she said ... she—she said— It, it ... twists...?"

"*Spit it out*, Lucastos."

Faelon flushed and shrank in his seat. "She said—"

"What! *What*."

"—humans' minds and bodies aren't, aren't—aren't 'attuned' to it," he finished all in a rush, trying to avoid his father's intent gaze. "She said my being half fae 'may not be enough.' That I'm 'also human,' and that I would need to pass trials to see if I was good enough to walk through."

Father didn't seem at all shocked by the revelation that the boy was half fae. In a rush of tangled emotion, Faelon realized that he had known, or at least suspected, if not all along then for some time at least. But he'd not said anything. These long months, Faelon had been left alone to contemplate his aunt's claims. To try and make sense of the impossible: that he might belong to another world, and that family he'd thought was dead was not.

"So it's a measure of your fae blood," Gaius muttered under his breath. "Fae blood. Blood..."

All at once, his spine straightened. When next he looked at Faelon, the wheels turned behind that one ghostly eye.

If I was attached to my heart, it would stop.

No. No. Not now. He couldn't put the pieces together *now* of all times, with Orlaith in his clutches.

I tried with all my might to urge Faelon to lunge, get up, do something, help his mother—but all I succeeded in doing was giving him a head pain that made him see white for a moment. Ah!

"Blood." Gaius hurried back to the desk, face blank as he became lost in the past. "When I killed her ...*that* was when the portal opened. Not while she spoke with the demon, not when he vanished. When I *killed her*. When I spilled her *blood.*"

Faelon watched in awe as the hairs on his father's arms stood up.

"The Trial of Loyalty," he whispered. "That's what the demon called it..."

Father was still for a long time, and when he finally raised his head and called for a guard, it was as if Faelon wasn't there at all. "Summon a chemist and have them meet me here at once. Then find a centurion, an arcanist, and an alchemist, and send them to the lake in the forest. I'll join them posthaste."

Gaius was already on his way back to the torture chamber when Faelon jumped up to catch him. "Father? Where are you going?"

"You haven't figured it out?" He glanced back with a quirked a brow. "To get fae blood, of course."

DRUSILLA WATCHED with worry twisting in her gut as Gaius led a small group of legionaries, laborers, and scientists into Geata-coill. It wasn't unusual to see soldiers entering the forest, but Gaius? No.

Since the sundering at Bile Cernunnos, the forest had become sicker and sicker by the day. Most of the trees' leaves took on a blighted red or orange sheen, now. Despite this, the engineer corps had been ordered to drain the lake at the center of the forest. Gaius must be confident the faerie queen would soon crack and reveal how the legion might pass through the portal and invade her land. But draining a lake was no easy task under the best of circumstances ... and these were not the best of circumstances. According to the patrolmen and arcanists and engineers—only some of whom made it back in the evening—pale, mindless crea-tures swarmed the deep forest, rising from the earth to attack indiscriminately.

There was only one reason Gaius would be going in there himself, and it was not to cleanse the land.

The portal, supposedly at the bottom of the lake. It must be ready for him.

If he knew how to open it, the Lunar Kingdom needed its queen now more than ever. Drusilla intended to deliver her.

I promised you, Mave.

You've been in my head too often of late. Are you well?

...Mave?

I could not find the strength to give her even the smallest hint of an answer. Through our connection, her concern ached like a sore tendon. But I did not need her to worry after me. I needed her to save my sister.

Adjacent to the praetorium, and therefor the dungeon, sat a communal bathhouse. As she entered the grand marble building, she was not entirely out of place. Granted, lupercali were not permitted to use the same facilities as the humans, but she blended in as a servant well enough. Those few slaves who recognized her said nothing, averting their eyes. As for the patrons, well, humans could rarely tell the difference between lupercali anyway. Each of the humid chambers was heavy with the scent of flesh, salts, wine, and herbs, and she slipped through without anyone noticing her presence.

She stopped only when she entered a disused bathroom. There, in the service corridor, sat exactly what she sought. She scented the air, confirmed she was alone, and knelt. A minor cantrip to clear the rust and a pocket knife were all she needed to unscrew the access grate. Well, that and a bit of strength to heft the heavy grille aside.

The storm drains without a doubt feed into the main sewers, she thought. *But I don't know if the wastewater channel is connected or if it has its own system. So, pray.*

The space beyond was let into the wall, and she had to squeeze her upper half through to see the other side. Just below her, leaving only enough room to crouch on all fours, were ledges for maintenance workers. Left and right. Cramped. The air here was so humid she immediately began to pant, which truly was not ideal considering the air also smelled of body odor and semen. This channel held wastewater from the baths, then, to be sure. A feeder line into the main flow. Hopefully.

She backed up, stripped to the fur, and slid back in feet first. Her heart kicked as she struggled to find the ledge—but when she did, she slid through, into the darkness.

Crouching at the bottom of the ladder, she watched the flow of water. Every few yards, the darkness was punctured by dull light glowing through the drains, but it was enough for her lupercal eyes to see.

This channel was tilted obliquely, leading her right, toward where the dungeon sat. She prowled along the ledge. It ran what she guessed was the length of the bathhouse. At the end of it was a barred opening, and there, peering over the edge, we got our answer. The wastewater from the bathhouse rushed in a thick waterfall down into another, much larger channel. Small feeder channels carried weak light from grates in the streets above. Every so often, pipes let into the walls gushed muddy water.

Storm drains. And judging by the overpowering smell of urine and feces drifting up from somewhere close by, Drusilla was right: both rainwater and human waste fed into the same sewer system.

She cast about for something to throw and managed to find a stick with a little green leaf on the end. With a flick of the wrist, she sent it down into the lower channel. It was carried left on the rushing water.

West. No doubt the sewer eventually drained into the valley north of the villa, but who knew what cistern or catchment the main flow led to?

An overflow channel might be better. It would be dangerous, fast and dirty. But it will bypass all loops and filters and go straight to the outlet.

Not an ideal escape point, since Orlaith would still be in Aquilan territory, and the use of an overflow channel required, well, overflow—but if the timing and pressure was right and she made it out, she could at least find her way to Geatacoill. She'd have a fighting chance rather than being chained up and flogged like a criminal.

Drusilla pictured the escape like a flip book in her mind. *Dungeon. Sever her binds. Down the corridor. Storm drain. Through the pipe—it should be just big enough for her to wiggle through. Overflow channel. West. Out. Hide. I'll have to make sure there's a cache somewhere waiting for her. Clothes, food, weapons, something to allay the infection...* She went through the checklist as she turned and crawled back up the maintenance shaft.

When finally she squeezed through the grate, well, she never would have thought she'd consider the air of an *Aquilan bathhouse* to be refreshing. With a huff, she reached for her discarded garments and—

"What've we got here?"

Drusilla turned, but Ryac was already halfway down the

corridor. Broad shoulders stiff, eyes glinting red in the shadows, smile wide and toothy. He'd cleaned up since his ordeal in the forest, but his hair always seemed to be tousled and sweaty, his clothes perpetually wrinkled. Especially jarring for a man in a bathhouse.

But he wasn't here to bask in the waters, was he? He was here for her. Had followed her. She could smell his intent on him.

And Mighty Ones, was his scent as he cornered her overpowering. Salty skin, drying blood, and a leaf bonfire, as though he'd crawled through smoke and sin to be here with her now. He must have been outside all day, because the scent of clover and sun-warmed dirt stuck to him, too. It invaded Drusilla's mouth and stuck like an oily film. Not human at all, despite his average appearance.

As they came nearly toe to toe, he cracked his neck but didn't take his eyes off Drusilla.

What in Opia's name does this monster want?

There they stood for several too-long moments, still, two wolves locked in opposition. Then, shifting her eyes, Drusilla jerked her head aside, half making to side-step him.

In the same movement, he lifted a hand and caught her jaw, thumb on one side, fingertips pressing into the other. Lightly, but with a strength behind them that did not need to be overstated. "Come, come," he murmured, his movements loose, casual, as he shuffled them closer together.

Drusilla had no idea what to do. No one had ever dared to touch her like this. Lupercali knew better, and human men were afraid. Ryac touched her like a woman. Not truly a good thing, but a thing that rendered her, for just a moment, pliant with shock.

"You look like prey when you flinch like that." He frowned and shook his head slightly. "You know better than to let anyone see you like this."

When she gave no response, his gaze drifted to the clothing still clutched in her hand. "Didn't mean to interrupt. You looked ... busy."

She managed to inhale a deep, grounding breath and shook his hand from her face. "A piece of advice, if I may. Don't insert your-self into situations you do not understand."

"And don't pet the wildlife?" He grinned, and the red glint in his eyes seemed to diffuse and grow. "Sound advice." Then he looked at his hand, the one that had held her, and just barely brushed the tips of his fingers together. "You shouldn't be sneaking around in the wolf's den. Whatever will I tell 'im?"

"Gaius is no wolf." Drusilla wrapped herself in her dress and tied it snugly. "And this is not his den. I have every right to be here. Tell him what you wish—I was looking into a housekeeping matter."

"In the waste water? You don't have people for that?"

A lie rolled off her tongue so naturally; she'd been lying to these people for so long, it was easy now. "I was told an under-maid disposed of an unwanted infant, either here or in the sewer, but I cannot mete out punishment based on rumor alone. I went to investigate for myself."

With that, Drusilla expected him to back off.

Instead, he surged forward.

Despite his average stature, he blocked her in until he could slap the wall on either side of her shoulders—and he leaned close, his cheekbone just skimming the fur of her throat. He inhaled her, then exhaled in a growl that was not a man's. "You've got a good heartbeat, ma'am. Steady. Brave. Is that it, bravery? Or is it stupid-ity? I dunno, it all tastes the same to me."

Drusilla hardened her gaze and let her lips pull over her teeth, wrinkling her nose to expose all her gums. Ryac saw the warning but didn't retreat. If anything, his eyes shone brighter.

"Going to bite me? Best make it count. Nip something *vital*." He breathed the final word, speaking with too much tongue and teeth. Flicked his eyes down her body—"You're shaking"—and smiled. "Don't worry. I like that."

He was asking to be put in his place, acting like a juvenile male testing his strength. Vying for alpha, trying to dominate her. Pushing his luck.

Well, she wasn't just a woman in her fifties. She was a wolf.

Like a bowstring being released, Drusilla lunged. It was a warning bite, a quick snap and pull, but she caught a chunk of his inner cheek. Hissing, he turned his face away, and she went in for another bite, this time ripping his ear lobe in two.

With something between a yelp and a whoop of laughter, Ryac leapt back. Blood poured down his face, his neck, then his hands as he groped the wounds. When his eyes flew to hers, they were full of wonderment.

Drusilla spat his blood and wiped her muzzle with her veil. "Let that be a lesson to you. That is what happens when you corner me. Don't try it again."

His wonder turned into something dark and drunken, as though she'd given him a taste of something he'd need another fix of. After a tense silence, he murmured, "You're lucky I like liars."

And then he was gone, and she was alone in the corridor, sucking down panicked breaths. Forget his behavior—*why* had he been following her in the first place? Had he been hoping to get her alone all day, or had she not blended in the way she thought she did? It could have been a coincidence that he'd found her like this. She hoped it was. Otherwise, she'd done something to arouse his suspicion. Which meant others might have noticed, too.

Like a sign from the universe, a small gasp echoed down the service corridor, and the she-wolf jumped to face it. The adjutant Thomasia stood there, her glasses off, thin frame half wrapped in a towel. Drusilla didn't know what to do except pull her veil tight and rush past the woman before she could ask any probing questions.

So, that was not one but *two* people who had witnessed her standing in front of that drain.

Drusilla prided herself on a cool, detached comportment, yet she could not help but pant with nerves as she hurried back to the praetorium. Even if Ryac accepted whatever lies she conjured to absolve herself, Thomasia would not. She was too fastidious, and she knew enough about counterintelligence to know it did not typically involve scrutinizing the fortifications of one's own country. This encounter might be enough to justify looking into everything she did. And while Drusilla liked to think herself meticulous, the tendency of Gaius—and everyone else—to overlook her had always been her greatest boon.

If she stuck to the plan now, they would know she was the one to help Orlaith escape. Yet in a fortified town, what other option was there?

There was no more denying it. Her time among the Aquilans was running out.

17

Three nights later, a storm swept through the valley. It rained day and night. In the lower streets of Sylvostum, laborers and fishwives trudged through ankle-deep water to shore up their homes. In the dungeons, the floor became slick. Then it was rippling. Then it was gone. The guards moved every prisoner except Orlaith to the uppermost levels, scrambling to figure out which of the storm drains were blocked. It took them over an hour to realize none were. The sewers were backed up, overwhelmed with the flow. For the first time in my life, I prayed that Aquilan engineering would not fail.

And it didn't. When the putrid waters began to recede, it was confirmation that the overflow channels had begun to flow, catching the excess and forcing it out of the city. It was time to break Orlaith out of her chains.

Through Faelon's eyes, I had watched as Gaius transferred my sister from the torture chamber to a cell. The conditions were abysmal. She was kept in darkness, only ever seeing another living being when the legate came to collect more of her blood. Although flooding had ground the lake operation to a halt, he'd had his chemist extract several vials. When Faelon found the courage to ask how the blood was used, Gaius took his son to the forest and showed him.

The rain was driving, and the wind whipped their hooded cloaks all about their bodies as they trudged down the wooded path, toward the center of Geatacoill. It was almost as hard for Faelon to see the place succumb to the withering as it was for me. Though he did not have the words for it, the enchanted forest called to him, to his Éirin and fae blood both, urging him into her arms. So many hours spent here in his childhood, the happiest he'd ever had.

Yet it was not the sickened land that shocked him most of all. The lake, by which he'd learned to read, by which he'd first slain dragons and rescued innocents, by which he'd first learned he was adopted, was fully drained now. Slaves labored day and night to bail out the crater despite the rain. The bottom was mostly silt and mud. A thick layer of algae obscured most of the gate itself, but the visible stone was even blacker and more worn than I remembered. The Ogham once carved there had almost completely eroded.

But it still responded to fae blood.

Faelon watched breathlessly as his father pulled out a vial and smeared a drop onto a small patch of bare stone. "Get behind me," Gaius murmured, and the boy obeyed.

The pressure in the air changed. It made Faelon's ears ache like nothing he'd ever felt; the sharp, fresh scent of petrichor was all at once heavy in the air, filling his limbs with a strange, electric power. A sound like a chorus of high-pitched singers rent the air. In the center of the circular gateway, the warp and weft of the Weave seemed to shimmer, shift, and trade places. Finally, it burst open, a whirlpool of blue, green, and white magic creating a portal of foamy, swirling teal. He'd never seen anything so beautiful and ... and *right*.

Gazing into the portal, Faelon understood, even in that moment, that his life had just changed forever. There was before he witnessed the lunar magic of the Gate, and there was after. This could—would—become an obsession. He *felt* it.

And then it changed. Flecks of red, sharp slivers like shards of glass, blinked in an out of the vortex, reminding him of sparks flying from struck flint.

His stomach twisted, brows slamming together. No, that was not right. But when he glanced up at his father, Gaius looked unbothered. How could he not feel that? How deeply *wrong* this was? "Father—"

Something in the forest shrieked, drawing a childish cry from Faelon. Gaius did not flinch. He simply swept the lad behind him and drew his sword. The treeline surged with demons—fomori, the Éirins called them—but there were legionaries all around, armed to the teeth. Expecting the attack, Faelon realized. There must be a new wave of them every time Father touched the portal.

Odd. That thought made his heart worm about in his chest. Something wasn't right. They shouldn't be doing this. He shoved his hand into his pocket and squeezed his wooden bird as tight as he could.

Even as more fomori rose from the earth, punching out of the spongy moss covered in afterbirth, Father turned his attention back to the portal. "You." He motioned for a robed man nearby, some kind of scholar or alchemist. "Bring me another."

Faelon watched with dread as a particularly sturdy legionary was brought forth. An engineer and arcanist fitted him with a belt of feyiron chains attached to an impressive length of the same, which they fed through a winch, bracing their weight against it. The legionary was pale, his eyes downcast, but there was something in his face … what was the word for it? … resignation. Faelon shivered as he realized this was resignation.

With a nod and a clap on the shoulder, Gaius shoved the legionary into the portal.

Faelon was overcome with the strange urge to jump in after the man, to drag him out and save him—save him from—

After a half-second of silence, screams of terror echoed through reality itself to shake the Weave. The red flecks within the portal grew suddenly, larger and more jagged, before breaking down, then growing again. The chain groaned under the weight of whatever held it on the other side, and the engineer's grip began to slip.

With a snarl, Gaius seized the chain and leaned back with all his weight. Slaves, legionaries, and engineers joined him until, finally, the vortex spat its captive back into the human realm.

What came out was no longer a soldier. For one thing, his muscles had atrophied, deflated and sinewy like jerky. His skin was ashen, his hair stark white, eyes wide as he shook and muttered unintelligibly under his breath. All in a matter of seconds, this man, this pinnacle of Aquilan aspect, had been turned into an infirm madman.

Gaius released the chain and crouched before the heap of what remained of the man. "What did you see, then? Speak."

The man's halting murmurings were nonsense, the words half-formed and staggered even as he gesticulated. The only statement Faelon could clearly discern was, "I s-saw ... saw what th-the Mighty Ones f-forgot."

The slaves, engineers, and legionaries surrounding the scene frowned, exchanged looks, and Faelon wondered if they all were thinking what he had—that they shouldn't be here, shouldn't be doing this.

Gaius was the only one unaffected by the cryptic babble. He simply sighed and gestured toward the other soldiers. "Mad, like the others. Take him away. If he doesn't produce any valuable information in the next twenty-four hours," he added, "kill him."

Though the soldiers glared hatefully at their legate, again exchanging glances, none spoke. Two centurions hoisted the madman up by his arms, but he did not fight back, and they led him away from the scene the same way one would lead an old man across a busy street.

"I think," began one of Father's adjutants, a bespectacled blond woman who was always taking notes, "we can safely assume every man we send through will suffer the same fate, my legate. We've tried young, old, frail, strong, every race, creed, and species..."

Gaius held up a hand to cut her short. "We will find a way

through the portal, then. I am not leaving a solitary mile of this land unclaimed by the Empire."

"Perhaps you should ask the Emperor if he cares to have it first," Primus Ottavian, standing above at the dry shore of the lake, suggested flatly.

Faelon climbed the lake's incline to stand next to him. The primus was scarred and bearded and quite intimidating, but he was nice to Mother, so the lad liked him. Besides, anything was better than being near those dreadfully cold chains and the ever-enticing vortex.

Gaius turned to look at the primus with a blank face. "Emperor Westerus and I agree the fae threat cannot go unchallenged. We'll strike at their heart. It is decided." He sneered and added, "Save the insolence for the war room, why don't you ... Felis?"

Ottavian's fists tightened such that the veins of his arms bulged out. "What did you just call me?"

"Pardon," the legate said, "how foolish of me to confuse you with your brother. Ottavian, is what I meant."

Faelon did not know much, but he knew the expression Ottavian wore could only be described as *murderous*.

The glow of the portal faded as Gaius came up to shore, passing them without a glance and going to a nearby table crowded with vials, herbs, and alembics. An imperial alchemist just in from New Lindanos joined him, and they began to speak in hushed tones. Faelon took a step closer but could only catch the word *inoculation*.

He was about to take another step, but a heavy, warm weight on his shoulder stopped him. When he turned, Ottavian smiled tentatively down at him. "Let's get you home to your mother, young master."

Faelon glanced at his father, but it was as if Gaius had completely forgotten he was there, enthralled as he was with the prospect of breaching the Underland.

The boy felt his shoulders weaken and his heart clutch. Father didn't need him here. Sometimes it felt as though Father didn't really need him at all. "Okay."

The legionaries surrounding the clearing had cut down the remaining fomori, but nonetheless, as the pair made their way back through the wooded path toward Sylvostum, Ottavian kept his hand on the hilt of his sword. The wind had died down, but the rain was still heavy, such that the road into town was nearly washed out. As they reached the gate, Ottavian stopped and offered a hand. "Here, I'll carry you."

The boy was only confused. "What?"

Ottavian raised a scarred brow and made the same gesture. "Climb up on my shoulders, and I'll carry you. Your mother will kill me if I bring you in with wet shoes."

"I'm not a baby."

"No, you're not a baby. But you are a child. I won't make a child trudge through knee-deep water. You could catch cold."

Faelon hesitated, glancing at the rushing water before accepting Ottavian's hand and letting the man lift him onto his shoulders. He steadied him by his ankles and began the slog through the city streets, hampered more by the water than Faelon's weight. The streets were almost a river, water rushing downhill to find an open storm drain.

"Primus," Faelon said over the storm. "May I ask ... who was your brother Felis? Why did Father call you by his name?"

At first, he thought perhaps Ottavian hadn't heard him, but after a long pause, through heavy breaths, he spoke. "My elder brother went to academy with the legate. Felis was a soldier. A much better one than..." He huffed, shaking his head. "Than either I or your father. He died the same year I graduated. Any promotion I've had was given to me because my superiors knew of my brother. I s'pose I should be thankful to him."

Faelon considered. He'd always wanted a sibling, but then again, the thought that they might be *better* than him was less appealing. "And you wish that you'd been promoted on your own merit?"

Ottavian laughed weakly. "I wish he was alive. That is all."

"Oh."

It wasn't the answer he expected. It wasn't what Father would have said.

A deep sadness seemed to rise from the cold water, like the hands of the dead were reaching for them, trying to pull their attention to the past and to whatever lay beneath the pavement. After such a somber statement, Faelon assumed the conversation was over, but the primus squeezed his ankle and said one last thing. "Don't be in such a rush to grow up, Lucastos."

On the hill, at the villa, things were better—it hadn't flooded yet—and servants eyed Ottavian as he entered with mud clinging to his calves.

"Go on." He eased Faelon off his back and motioned onward. "Go find your mother. I should clean this off me."

And he was headed to the praetorium before the boy could say anything more.

Faelon went to his mother as he was instructed. Nevidaea was in her aviary, as she often was these days, worrying over a situation she could not control. I watched through her eyes as she urged my nephew to nap in her lap, combing her fingers over his tight coils.

The majority of her birds had moved to an adjacent, heated room, but some still sang in the boughs of the trees woven into the flagstones of the aviary. She and Faelon sat on a mosaic-dappled bench under the arcade that bordered the terrace. They spoke naught of what he'd done and seen the past week, but heart and soul, she burned all the same. All she could do was nurse the little kernel of hatred within her—of fury, that her right as a mother to protect her child was being stripped away from her. By her own husband, no less.

But what would nursing it do? Feeding it would only ensure it came back.

Her own mother would tell her to let it go. Her mother-in-law would have, too.

She gazed down at her son. At the purple rings around his eyes and the pallor of his skin, usually a shade of deep fawn. At his curls, shorn into a fade at either side like a soldier's. At his hands, no longer a chubby child's but not a man's either, gathered into the crook of his neck in relaxed fists. An ache began deep in her belly. He may not have come from her womb, but her body didn't know that. She wished she could tuck him away again, someplace utterly safe. Safe from his father and all this madness.

Mighty Ones, why did I come here?

As she reached down to brush her knuckles against his cheek, something caught her eye. In one of his hands he held the wooden bird she'd found at the bottom of his toy chest. She was surprised; in the moment, it had seemed like a temporary distraction, but now she wondered if he'd carried it with him for a week and a half.

With a quirk, she remembered how something on its bottom had given him pause.

But what?

Nevidaea eased her fingers into his loose fist until he released, and turned the bird on its head. There, carved into the elm wood surface were the initials *G.H.S.*

Her throat clenched as though a fist had closed around it.

And suddenly, she remembered. Gaius's mother, Analivia Nympheia, sitting on the veranda of her Umbrian villa, the sunset gilding her frail features. Long had she abandoned the heavy wigs worn by most Aquilan noblewomen. Most probably, she would not have been able to hold her head up otherwise. Rather than a stiff tiara of ringlets, she simply let her curls fall down her back. Nevidaea remembered, when they'd first met, being struck by just how young she was. Her own mother, Mara, was in her fifties, with wrinkles around her eyes and loose skin upon her neck. But Analivia's face was unlined, with not one gray strand in her dark hair. It would be out of line to ask how old she really was, but Nevidaea wondered.

Her age didn't matter in any case, because she was dying. The once-feared, vigilant, hawk-eyed upholder of imperial pride had withered away into a pale shell of a woman. She'd lost weight rapidly; her hair and teeth had begun to fall out. She hardly answered to her name anymore, let alone appeared in society. No one spoke a word, but everyone in the household knew she hadn't long left.

So, they had summoned Gaius.

He stood about ten feet away now, leaned against the parapet of the veranda and staring at the estate grounds sprawling before him. He'd hardly said a word to his mother since they'd arrived, opening his mouth only to remark on the architecture of the villa his father had built. Faelon was three-and-a-half, and he didn't talk much himself, too dreadfully shy. Neither of these things seemed to bother Analivia, if she noticed them at all. These last days, much about the world around her seemed to escape her notice.

But when Nevidaea drew the little boy close and gently brought her mother-in-law's attention to him, the elder Lady Sergia smiled. Smiled. Nevidaea had never seen her express anything beyond bland apathy or a judgmental raise of the brow.

"*Bambi jana,*" the elder Lady Sergia said in her Logudoric accent. "Fairy child. A little fairy child." In an uncharacteristically nurturing gesture, she reached out to wipe an imaginary smudge from Faelon's face and from her skirts produced a tiny carved bird.

"Take this, *jana.*" Faelon did, with wonderment, and Analivia did not take her eyes off him. "It belonged to my Gaius. It was his favorite before he went away. It never left his hand."

Unexpectedly, the wean chirped, "Went away?"

"I told him to be brave, and sent him with his father," was all she said.

"Lady Sergia?" A deep baritone shocked Nevidaea from the memory such that she nearly dropped the little bird.

Ottavian stood in one of the arches of the arcade, wearing light leathers over a red tunic. Her jolt had Faelon stirring, but she stroked his hair until he fell back asleep.

The primus crossed to the bench and knelt beside her on one knee. He always did that, too respectful to loom above her but too proper to take a seat beside her. It made him seem more like a chivalrous Albionic knight than a hot-blooded Aquilan legionary. She wondered if this was how the men in his motherland of

Numirabia acted, but perhaps it would be impolite to ask. Or to imply he was anything besides an imperial.

"The boy"—his concerned gaze lingered on Faelon—"is he well?"

"He's well enough," she murmured, rubbing circles into her son's back. "He told me you brought him. Thank you. Truly," she said before he could brush her off, "thank you for your kindness. I..." She glanced toward the entryways, though what she was looking for, she wasn't quite sure. "I never wanted it to be this way for him. I thought ... I suppose I thought we would live in Ruma all his life. Somewhere ... civilized. With culture—theater, the arts..."

The primus huffed. "It wouldn't have been my choice to drag you out here. But I..." He cleared his throat. "I cannot hope to understand the legate's mind at the best of times."

"Nor can I," she whispered, and began to rock Faelon gently.

"You're worried about what the boy might have seen?" Ottavian observed at length.

Nevidaea nodded. "At the battle, in that dungeon..."

"At least his nursemaid sometimes goes with him to the dungeons. That must be a good sign."

"Drusilla is good." Nevidaea hesitated. "He asked me something strange when he came in today." When Ottavian raised his brows in question, she continued, "He asked what the word 'inoculation' means. Do you have ... any idea why he might ask something like that?"

The bemused look on his face made it evident to both of us that, whatever Gaius was planning, the primus was not privy to it. "I'm sorry, my lady, I do not. All I know is the legate was using the queen's blood to open that portal in the lake bed."

The damned portal. Nevidaea knew of it. Gaius often recounted the moments after Mave's death, where, as he limped away with the baby in hand, he'd looked back at the clearing and seen teal light pouring through the trees. She'd always doubted its existence, however. A portal at the bottom of a lake—a lake that supposedly sprang up from the ground out of nowhere, in a matter of days?

But magic had made stranger things happen. And here it was, real.

"He should be treating that woman better," Nevidaea murmured, looking down at her son. Not only because she was her son's supposed birth-giver. "She's a queen. Royalty of any nation should never be *tortured*. It is obscene."

Ottavian got a strange look about him, almost like he pitied Nevidaea. "Already, we've done unspeakable things to the people of this island. Doing them with decency hardly makes a difference in the end."

She shifted uncomfortably, drawing her mantle woven to look like birds' wings tighter across her shoulders. "Well, it isn't what the Empire stands for. This isn't who we are."

With a sigh, Ottavian scrubbed his face. "The majority of the Continent would probably disagree. We're doing what we've always done."

"If—" Nevidaea huffed a sigh herself. "If we could at least return to common decency, it would certainly make me feel better."

"I don't know if it would make me feel better," he muttered. "I'd still have to do the killing and marching and fire-setting."

"You could—" Quick, Nevidaea cut herself off. *You could leave if you don't like the work.* Perhaps it was a foolish thing to say. She knew what happened to deserters, as they all did: no trial, no exile, only crucifixion. Instead, gnawing on her painted lip, she asked, "Is it any better in Numirabia?"

"Better than here, in an active war zone? Perhaps. But not all my countrymen joined the Empire willingly."

He frowned, and in the back of my mind, I wondered if he was remembering one of *our* last conversations: *"We did not have to be pressed to serve." "Of course not. You knew what would happen if you didn't."*

"It occurs to me," he said at length, "the Éirin auxiliary that marched out that day ... they were sent to Numirabia."

Nevidaea shifted the other way, looking for something hopeful to say, something to soothe herself in the face of such evil. The movement finally roused Faelon. "Mama?"

"Darling," she said—and intended to tell him to go back to sleep when, without warning, the double doors leading onto the veranda banged open.

Ottavian leapt to his feet and ducked under the arcade moments before Gaius appeared, shoulders hunched against the downpour, brow as stormy as the sky.

"Husband? What—"

He cut her off with a snarl. "Primus, with me, *now*. That forsaken fae *bitch* has escaped."

18

I skipped down Nevidaea's roots and into Drusilla's violently enough that, when the blackness cleared from my vision, the room was spinning. The she-wolf growled and raised a hand to palm her forehead, trying to shake the sensation off. When our blurred double-vision subsided, I recognized the praetorium kitchens.

"Mistress?"

My view swung to a young servant girl, who reached tentatively toward Drusilla. With a gentle wave, Drusilla brushed her off. "I'm fine. Get back to work."

Once we were alone, so to speak, she rubbed her temples. *Mighty Ones, Mave, can you be subtle in anything you do?*

I sent forth a wave of indignation.

Oh, enough. This damned headache is the reason I didn't summon you in the first place. What, you expected me to make certain Orlaith was safe whilst nursing a migraine?

My ability to express myself was still stifled, alienated from my body as I was, but I hoped I conveyed regret. And my urgent and feverish desire to see Orlaith.

For obvious reasons, I'm not with her. They'd had a window of mere minutes, and Drusilla had to beat the pavement to make it back to the praetorium before Gaius returned. But Orlaith was free. I felt the impression of a memory: the stench of the dungeon cells, a tool slicing through the links of anti-magic chains, harried whispers as Drusilla rushed her to the storm drains and told her where to go from there.

The weight that was lifted from my shoulders upon this reve-lation couldn't be overstated. I swore I almost—*almost*—felt my body calling me home.

Or perhaps it wasn't my body at all. The strong energy that came through originated somewhere on the other side of my fugue, not within myself. It was a cool, calming energy. I'd felt it before, somewhere... *The leaves of a massive yew, shafts of milky moonlight, the stomping of hooves...*

As much as I wanted to come when my heart's twin called me, there was something else. Something my spirit could not shake. A breath held by the universe. A premonition that something was about to happen—something that would change everything—and that I must be here to witness it.

IN THE DAYS FOLLOWING, I watched as Gaius collapsed.

Whether it was under the weight of his failure or because he'd stopped sleeping, I couldn't say. Like a dog, he fled the city with his tail tucked between his legs, snapping at any open hand that approached him; he established a camp at the center of Geatacoill, right in the blighted fray, so that he never had to leave the portal unattended. When Nevidaea and Faelon dared to visit him, his aspect was frightening to them: bloodshot eyes ringed in purple, pale skin and a careless beard, hunched shoulders, a perpetual glare.

That steel-vice control we'd all known him for couldn't seem to find its grip on this new Gaius. When he spoke, it wasn't just with obsession, madness, or cruelty; his thoughts were disjointed, his words hardly making sense in the order he put them.

On the day he finally returned to Sylvostum, he summoned those closest to him and his family.

I watched from Drusilla's point of view as Tatius fetched her. She schooled her physical reactions, trying to ease her rising hackles. Odd that he wouldn't come to the praetorium, his base of operations. Odd that he would summon her at all. For the first time, the cold fingers of terror caressed her guts. She'd not gotten this far by cowering in fear of Gaius, but if he knew...

If he knew, she had better run now. Already, she saw which way the wind was blowing; already, she realized her days in Sylvostum—indeed, the Aquilan Empire—were numbered. But running hardly seemed like an option, not with the child still here in Gaius's grasp.

Plus, if she disappeared now, it would be an admission of guilt. There would be no shadow of doubt as to who had released Orlaith. No going back. Better to stay the course and assume Gaius had his head in the sand as always.

And if I'm wrong, what's the worst that could happen? she thought dryly. *I'll die. So what.*

A jumbled mess of affection, admiration, fear, and desperation whorled through me, and Drusilla must have felt it, for she quietly laughed aloud.

Mave, you and I both know death is not the worst thing that can happen to people like us.

In his study, Gaius had gathered his master arcanist, chief engineer, and the newly arrived imperial alchemist, as well as Primus Ottavian and Lieutenant Tatius. The adjutant Thomasia was there, sitting at a writing desk, along with Ryac, who lurked against a wall in the recesses of the room, sporting healing bite marks on his cheek and ear. Both of them stared holes into Drusilla's skull, as they had done every time they'd seen her in the past week. Finally, and most surprising of all, Nevidaea was there, clutching Faelon close in her lap.

"Darling," she said to Gaius half-heartedly, "sit down. You look a moment from fading away."

She wasn't wrong. Though the legate had finally shaved and

straightened out his appearance, he still looked pale and exhausted. From Drusilla's perspective, he smelled different, too. It wasn't the scents of Geatacoill sticking to him but *himself*. Something was ... off. He had the odor of a diseased man, but even apart from that, there was a deeper note neither Drusilla nor I could place. Perhaps if I was in my own body, I'd have more luck.

Gaius ignored his wife's request, instead turning to address the room with his hands tucked behind his back. The gesture evoked only a shadow of his usual authority. He feigned the control that had once come so easily, but his eyes and his scent told the truth. The only human not shifting uncomfortably was Ryac, whose gaze was still fixed on Drusilla.

"You all have been briefed on the situation with this 'Moon Gate,' as they call it. It is imperative we breach it, yet any human who passes into the fae realm loses their mind." He shrugged his shoulders in mock-nonchalance. "Not much information to work with, but with the prisoner *gone*..."

His scrutiny was sharp as he considered those gathered. Drusilla's heart dropped as she realized he did not trust *any* of them anymore. But, in particular, he lingered on Ryac.

"Having second thoughts, Bloodwarden? Could it be you've realized your alliance lies more with your homeland than you initially estimated?"

The werewolf's red eyes snapped to him. "Who, me? Ahh, aha..." He jerked his head back with an open-mouthed grin, shoved his hands in his trouser pockets, and huffed a laugh as if to say *Oh, dear, really?* "You think after three decades they'd've changed their minds, right like that? Use your head, soldier-boy."

Before Gaius could snipe back, Thomasia adjusted her glasses and cleared her throat. "If it makes any difference, my legate, the inquisitors hypothesized the prisoner must have escaped through the sewer system, correct?" Drusilla stopped breathing. "Just before the incident, I saw the she-wolf in the bathhouse, lurking around one of the maintenance grates."

Bile came up Drusilla's throat, along with pure, true hatred— but as always, she kept the set of her ears easy and her tone flat.

"The bathhouse? Why would I have any business there? Non-humans are not allowed, and my work is in the household."

Thomasia pressed her lips together. "Regardless, I saw you."

All eyes turned to Drusilla, every pair burning into her fur now, and none flamed hotter than that of Gaius. I recalled how utterly betrayed and blindsided he'd been upon discovering Gwynedd's betrayal, and he had not known my adoptive guardian nearly as long as he had Drusilla.

The pressure was crushing. Yet she simply scoffed and crossed her arms. "Might I ask what you were doing in the bathhouse, adjutant?"

"Bathing, obviously. This isn't about *me*—I was where I was supposed to be."

"If you were bathing, I assume you had removed your spectacles, no?"

"Yes? And?"

"And exactly how clearly can you see without their aid?" asked Drusilla. "Even with them, how easily could you distinguish me from others of my race? You must have seen some other lupercal, mistress, for I was not there."

The adjutant's face twisted. "I *know* what I saw!"

"Quiet." Gaius's bassy voice hummed through the room. "I will not have you squabbling like a pair of hens."

"My legate, details are my priority. I would *not* have—"

"*Quiet*," he barked, slamming an open palm on his desk. The room flinched, save for Ryac, who merely chuckled.

Drusilla tipped one ear toward him, anticipating that, at any moment, he would step in an corroborate the adjutant's testimony. But he said nothing.

"None of that matters now," Gaius growled. "That craven witch is nothing to me, I don't need her. In a matter of days, their kingdom will be ash. Ash, understood?" He whipped his gaze round the room, but no one dared to refute him. "Her blood has done its job. Has it not, Veneficus?"

The imperial alchemist, a gaunt-faced, balding man, bowed his head. With a gesture from the legate, he stepped forward to command the attention of those gathered. "We have, er, spent the past week testing the samples acquired from the prisoner. My assistants and I have synthesized human and fae blood into an infusion—an inoculation of sorts."

With that, he drew from the breast pocket of his robe a glass vial of red liquid. Not blood. It was not the wine color of human blood nor the dark blood of the fae. It was as bright and glaring a red as cinnabar and *glowing*, filled with little bubbles that raced to the liquid's surface.

"Inoculation?" Nevidaea choked.

The veneficus nodded. "It did require constant and rigorous testing, but we have managed to create a serum that will allow humans to pass into the next realm without any harm to the psyche. Without any short-term harm, in any case."

Gaius shot him a glare. "Without *any harm*, Veneficus."

The alchemist hesitated. "Er, yes, of course." Frowning, he tipped the vial upside down and watched the bubbles rise in the other direction. "Of course."

But Ottavian, who'd been leaning against the edge of Thomasia's writing desk, straightened. "You can't be serious. You expect me to throw my men to you and let you inject them with ... Mighty-Ones-know-what? One week of testing is not nearly enough. Have you even had the opportunity to see how humans respond to its presence in their veins?"

"Indeed, Primus, we began our trials with humans."

Nevidaea slapped a hand over her mouth, grip tightening around Faelon. But Drusilla was not the least bit surprised. Probably the only reason they had used humans rather than lupercali was that the Empire believed lupercali blood differed at some basic level.

Ottavian's brows slammed together. "On—on our own citizens? Our own soldiers?"

"We had a *week*, sir," the veneficus said dryly.

Lieutenant Tatius glanced between them nervously. "How ... how can you be certain there are no lasting effects?"

"Because," Gaius cut in finally, finding some of his old coolness, "when the final synthesis was complete, *I* was the first in line to be inoculated."

Nevidaea's voice was shrill: "You *what?*"

"Father," Faelon said, "what do you mean?"

"Gaius"—her tone was gravelly now—"I-I need you. We have a child. How could you— Without—"

"Sacrifice, Nevidaea. Sacrifice. It is what leaders do." Then he fixed Faelon with his cold blue stare. "There is nothing to fear, boy. Here, I'll show you now." He nodded at the alchemist, holding his left arm out. "The veneficus was brave enough to agree to administer a second dose, so that you all may see the process for yourselves. Let it not be said that I led my legion from behind a desk."

"Let it not be said you led it with any sense, either," Ryac muttered, quiet enough that only Drusilla's keen hearing might pick it up.

The group watched, awe-struck, as the veneficus anointed the spot on Gaius's inner wrist where his veins were most visible. As he conjured a thin needle of light magic and affixed it to the little glass vial, his movements were methodical, but Drusilla could see and smell quite clearly the sweat rolling down his brow. He held the needle and vial to Gaius's wrist like a pen—and with a flash of light, the needle punctured his flesh, and the screaming-red liquid surged into his veins.

Gasps and grunts of disgust rippled through the room as the serum glowed brighter and brighter, illuminating the pattern of his veins just under the skin. His arm began to shake. The Weave of the room shifted, coiling and snapping. Outside, something cracked like a great tree being felled. It had to be thunder, yet the very earth seemed to shudder as if the sky were about to fall, and a rotten, purulent scent hit Drusilla's nose.

Still, Gaius's attention did not waver. If the process hurt, the pain did not show on his face. He stared, enraptured, at the injection point as the liquid drained into him completely, its glow scalding the plains of his face and rendering his eye an unsettling scarlet.

The moment seemed longer than it probably was. As the veneficus pulled away, Gaius slowly clenched and unclenched his fist, and gradually, the red blazing through his veins subsided. The only indication that the injection hurt more than he let on was the deep breath he exhaled.

"See?" He gestured to his wrist, then to Tatius. "You'll go next."

It was not a question, and Tatius was cowardly—or perhaps clever—enough not to attempt to argue. The veneficus readied a second vial, and the lieutenant offered out his wrist. The process —complete with a more minor earth-shake and another strange shift in magic—was repeated, but Tatius was not nearly as stoic as Gaius. He hissed and squirmed as the serum wormed its way through his veins and left him panting.

"Do you not feel more powerful already?" Gaius asked with genuine eagerness. Excitement. "Is it not breathtaking?"

Tatius flexed his hand the same way Gaius had, and as the red glow diffused into his skin, he stood a bit straighter. "I ... I *do* feel better." He lifted his nose to sniff the air. "I-I think I can smell more keenly now, and my vision..."

The veneficus moved on to the primus, but Ottavian glared at them. "The Eighth Legion can join you in the fae realm, Legate. The Ninth will stay here and hold against the Éirins. Don't bother wasting a dose on me. I have no need of better vision."

"Fine. In that case, Tatius, you are officially promoted to Primus of the Eighth Legion."

Tatius's eyes were dinner plates. "Yes, sir. I won't fail you, Legate, sir."

Thomasia stood, taking her spectacles from her face. "I volunteer, Legate. Let me be the first staff officer to be inoculated. It will look good," she added swiftly, "especially if I can demonstrate the benefits to the others."

The process was repeated a third time, with the same results. Thomasia grunted against the pain, but once the light sank in, she seemed to radiate an eminent power—though Drusilla wondered if that was an effect of the serum or her own arrogance.

Nevidaea eyed the three, then exchanged a desperate look with Ottavian. Whatever she conveyed, the primus spoke up once more. "Exactly how many of us do you plan to inoculate? Surely, you did not draw enough blood from the fae to empower a hundred men, let alone a legion?"

His words broke through Gaius's ego-swollen fugue. For the first time since the others had begun injecting, he frowned. "No. I did not."

Drusilla was shocked to see him then glance around the room as if looking for a solution—as if, *somehow*, he had not thought this far ahead. He, the famous tactician, the seasoned general, son of Legate Gaius Helius Sergia the elder.

"I'll need more fae blood—continuous and free access..."

Time itself seemed to halt as his gaze roved over Nevidaea. Stuttered. And narrowed in on Faelon.

I swore his pupil blew wide like a shark's.

No.

No.

No, no, no, no, no, NO!

Not Faelon. Not my nephew. After all I had done, all I had sacrificed, the oaths I'd made and the bonds I'd frayed refusing to spill his blood—

Now this soulless, pointless, narcissistic, selfish *pig* would do so without a second thought.

I'd kill him. I would take control of Drusilla's body, and I would kill him. Thrust her hidden paring knife into his throat and end this madness once and for all.

No, I had to get to *my* body. I had to get out of here. Get to Sylvostum. To the Gate. Protect my boy. Anything else—the Gate, my people, my own life—was at once pushed to the side.

The force of my panic made Drusilla lurch back in her seat, clutching her head as white split our vision. The only person who paid her any mind was Ryac. Suddenly, he was behind her, gripping both her shoulders to steady her. Low and slow and with obvious skepticism, he asked, "How much blood do you need from the wean, exactly?"

It wasn't until the words passed his lips that Nevidaea understood why Gaius stared at their son like that. "He doesn't mean that," she rasped. "Tell me he doesn't mean that?"

"As I said," Gaius explained calmly, "sacrifice. It is what leaders do. Correct, Lucastos?"

Nevidaea's chair screeched against the marble floor as she stood, pushing her son to the side like she might leap on Gaius and kill him herself. "No!"

She was shaking; Ottavian flinched as if to put himself between them, but he held back.

"No," she repeated more gutturally, "you wouldn't— You can't—"

Once again, Gaius found his cool when faced with others' fury. He stared at his wife blandly for a moment before looking instead to Faelon, who had fled into Drusilla's arms. "Come, do the right thing."

"Oh, to *hells* with you," growled Nevidaea. "To *hells* with you. You will not put your hands on my son! You will not put your hands on my *son!*"

"Very well, if that's the way you feel." He nodded to Thomasia. "Draw up papers to have the boy emancipated from her, and full guardianship given to me." Then, nodding to Tatius, "Take my wife to her chambers and have the door barred and guarded."

Nevidaea was stunned. It was Faelon who cried out in horror, looking to his mother with tears overwhelming his big green eyes. "Mama, no!"

He jerked forward, but Drusilla held him firmly to keep him out of the line of danger. He struggled against her nonetheless, grunted and kicked and waved his arms as he tried to reach for his mother. With a, "Uhp there, boyo, steady on," Ryac leaned forward to help Drusilla by closing the lad's shoulder in a steel grip.

Ottavian took two bold steps forward. "You can't be serious. Unhand her," he snapped at Tatius as he wrenched Nevidaea's hands behind her back. "You have no right!"

Gaius rounded on Ottavian, filling his personal space with

that overwhelming presence I'd experienced more than once. "Tell me," he ground out, "that I have no right to discipline my wife. Say it again. To my face."

Ottavian trembled. Whether with rage or fear or both, I couldn't be sure, for a thousand sharp scents overwhelmed Drusilla's senses. But ultimately, he swallowed, and said nothing.

"Get out of my sight." Gaius tossed his head, and Ottavian left, followed by Tatius with Nevidaea in tow.

As they crossed the threshold, the lady managed to break out of her impotent shock to call over her shoulder, "Don't worry, Lucastos, I'll be okay!"

Faelon responded with a wail of agony. Of abject terror and utter misery.

And it was *that* wail, paired with the hunger in Gaius's gaze as he turned it back to his son, that sent me fleeing in search of my body.

19

The feeling was odd. Though I was in that strange in-between place, the pool with the tangled roots, I had aware-ness of my limbs. Of myself. Strong but gentle hands gripped my shoulders, dredging me from the depths of the water and dragging my limp, lifeless body to the earthen shore.

Whoever held me dropped me, and I thumped to the dirt, choking and coughing up fluid. Everything ached, *deep*, from my bones to my brain. I opened my eyes and looked down at pale, filthy lavender palms, and for the first time felt as though I were really experiencing this place rather than simply sensing or *knowing* or seeing through my mind's eye.

And then I looked up, and saw my savior.

Gwynedd's smile had not changed a bit, from the warmth of his eyes to the curve of his chin to the crease between his brows. His had been one of the first smiles I ever saw, so how could I forget? Yet there was a different quality to him than I was used to. He appeared colorless and shadowy somehow. He sat cross-legged on the ground in front of me, and his form seemed to shift in waves like wind-blown grain—and in the folds, stars twinkled. Once I saw the stars, I could not stop seeing them, until I realized that every inch of him was made up of them.

"All right, my Mave," he said softly.

It took long seconds of silence and quite a bit of panting for me to find myself enough to speak. "You ... how are you here?"

He lifted one corner of his mouth, making the line on that side stand out. "I never truly left you, Mave."

"Yes," I said slowly, "but the stars ... spirits..." I couldn't articulate what I was trying to say: that spirits rarely showed themselves in such unambiguous forms, and seldom spoke so straightforwardly. Those times I had felt like Gwynedd was speaking to me, it was more a feeling than anything, a rumble against the skin. But here, I heard him as plainly as if we spoke face to face.

"You aren't in your body, lass. You are as good as a spirit yourself." He frowned. "And, I had help."

"Help?" I breathed.

"He's looking for you. Calling you home to him. They all are." Then, before my eyes, Gwynedd's countenance seemed to split into three. His face, in the center, was flanked by that of Ruadan on the left, and on the right...

Hiberos, his eyes wide, brow low in ardent concentration, ears angled downward. His expression was a mix of heart-aching hunger and pleading. A primordial, ever-burning star yearning for the silent and slumbering moon.

The lips of all three moved as they spoke, but it was not in Gwynedd's voice. "Princess," Ruadan said, tone serene as ever, "the Goneland still needs you. I know the fight is hard, but you cannot give up now."

"Ruadan?" I croaked.

"We have done what we can to sustain you, but alas, if you do not return to your body soon, it will die. You must return."

I knew I had to. But now that I was here in this in-between space, in the dark and quiet and calm of the soil of the earth, close enough to Death the very walls seemed to breathe with it, that ancient tiredness pulled at me. The same feeling that had convinced me in the end, when Gaius killed me in that stone henge, to finally let go. To sleep.

"I'm exhausted," I said with a cracked voice.

"I know." The deep voice that answered did not belong to Ruadan. Its timbre called to my body at an elemental level. In that moment, he spoke to all of me. All the anger and hurt, and all the dark, wild, selfish things inside me, too. "I will never leave you. No matter how many times you leave me. But I was not finished with you. Grant me just a little while longer in your presence. My rose" —he smiled—"my thorny rose who defies goddesses and unravels eternity. Come back, and I promise I will hold you against it all."

I crawled closer but hung my head. "I don't know how."

"Follow the sound of my voice. I know you've heard me calling you. Do not shut me out. Listen and follow my voice."

After drawing a few more shaky breaths, I made an effort to settle myself. Sitting moth-style across from Gwynedd, I let him brush his hands across my palms. Tried to focus on the way Hiberos's voice pulled at the heart of my soul, called me home. The blackness filling my brain became a fuzzy gray that turned whiter and whiter by the second. The feeling was light and cold, fluttery, like the feeling of blood entering a numbed limb. It happened quicker than I imagined, strange and terrifying after being like this for two and a half weeks.

I uttered a childish, frightened cry, but Gwynedd pressed his hands deeper into mine and said in his own voice, "Keep going. The pain is good. It means you yet live—and that means it is not too late."

Despite the pain, despite the fear, I leaned into the cold, busy squirm. Blood in my veins. Heart pumping. Muscles twitching. Lung expanding. Organs rumbling. The white consumed me before turning to a dark, almost black reddish brown. But this blackness wasn't like the one I'd left.

My eyelids. I was looking at the back of my eyelids.

When I fluttered them open, the world around me was a rush of images. A druid jumping off a chair. A silver-haired man standing from the end of the bed in which I lay. A huge, fat hog squealing and bolting from the room. Hiberos turning to bark at a tall fae, who subsequently drew curtains of a nearby window closed, casting the room in more soothing shadow. Yet it spun such that I could make out none of its details. I could not quite grasp who I was or what was happening, and every sound was as muffled as if I were under ice.

Then it wasn't.

Reality hit me like a tidal wave, and I jerked and gasped just the same, choking on air rather than sea water.

"Out," Hiberos said in a tone like the unmoving shore. No one even attempted to argue, simply clearing out. Within the next few moments, we were alone.

And I was turning my head wildly, my eyes somehow incapable of finding him. He gripped my shoulders and climbed into bed with me, laying his full weight on top of me. Crushing, yes, but it was what I needed. I flung my arms and legs around him, locking him in with my ankles and entwined hands as I gasped and groaned and tried to reach for my sense of self.

"Here," he murmured into my neck just below my jaw. "Here you are. And here shall I stay."

Despite the state of me, I managed to say, "On—on top of me?"

He huffed a laugh against my ear, making me shiver all over. "I'd rather hold you down forever than be stretched at your grave." He cupped my chin and helped me look steady into his eyes. "The gods may take you apart—it does not matter. I know this shape. I know this heartbeat, and the scar over it. I know this *you*. And though I may lose you, I will never stop chasing you. I will never stop waiting."

"*From the cold grave that holds you I never shall sever,*" I croaked.

"*Were your hands twin'd in mine, love, I'd hold them forever.*"

It occurred to me he'd managed to get me into a mating press while we spoke, the backs of my thighs flush with his cut hips and lean, hard stomach. With a bit of reluctance, I pushed at his collar bone, forcing him to pull back and look me in the eyes once more. Enticing as he was—especially in this new, unapologetically virile body—there were slightly more important things at hand than defying goddesses with ravenous lovemaking.

"I saw things while I was sleeping. We have to save my nephew. There's no other choice now. Gaius is going to bleed him dry."

Hiberos canted his head, gaze sharpened by worry. But before he could ask for clarification, I pushed him fully off me and swung my legs off the bed.

"Mave—"

"I know what you're going to tell me." I stood, cast about, and gesticulated. "Armor. I need armor." While he rose to retrieve my armor from the trunk at the end of the bed, I continued, "'Stay in bed and rest.' I know I should, but I can't. Where is the king's daughter—Muiri? Is Manan here?"

"He arrived a few nights after you fell asleep," Hiberos said as he helped me into my buttery fae leathers. He knelt, looking up at me, and let me use his river-carved shoulders for balance as I stepped into the leggings. More darkly, he added, "That morning, you woke with a scream. The earth shook. And then you were gone. Limp and pale, staring, seizing as you sometimes do when you reach into another's mind." A harsh sigh. "I never should have let you use those leylight worms."

"It doesn't matter now." Even as the words came out, I gave him an apologetic look. "M'sorry, I don't mean that. But we can't speak about it right now. I need to meet with the kings. Any. All."

He nodded and sent for someone to gather the coalition while I finished dressing. But as we left the bedchamber, trailed by his moon moths as ever, he warned, "Your body is weakened. You wasted away for two weeks. I should insist."

I could feel that he was right. Everything ached, I was savagely hungry, and my legs did not hold the weight of my armor and weapons as well as they had. But I'd been through worse and soldiered on—and there was no time to lie down when it was not just Éire but all my loved ones in danger.

Hiberos had said I would come back for him, and that was true. If there was anything that could call me home, beyond even my own will and stubbornness, it was his voice. A moment, no

matter how brief, by his side. Nothing could keep our stars apart
for long.

But I hadn't come back just for him.

I'd come back for vengeance.

JUST AS I'D THOUGHT, Erivon was the first to agree to the assault
on Geatacoill. We couldn't go through the Gate for the same
reasons we didn't want Gaius opening it; it was fractured, especially unstable. Going through Fort Alopex wasn't feasible, either,
with troops clustered there after the disaster at Cernunnos. We
had no extra time or resources for a full-scale battle.

Solma promised to position troops on the other side of the
Gate just in case the Aquilans managed to get it open, but ever
since Hiberos's return, she'd been reticent to speak to me. Her air
was cold and detached.

As for those of us on this side of the Gate, we'd have to fight
our way through the scar.

It was decided that a good third of the coalition's army would
escort us through the blighted wasteland that sliced through
Sallach, but that only a condensed force should go over Westeris
Wall to confront Gaius. Along with Erivon, Ruadan, Hiberos, and
Solma, and Muiri and her best men agreed to accompany us.
Ferghal told us to bring whatever wolfkernes we needed, but he
left to talk to a clan of walking people—his mother's folk—in
Twaintomb, in the hopes they'd join up.

No gates between Athadhrai and Geatacoill, and we couldn't
pop out at Geatacoill. So, we aimed for a length of Westeris Wall
that, according to druid scouts flying overhead, had recently fallen
during a crushing fomori attack. The rift was fresh, so nothing but
a basic camp had sprung up behind it—and rather than rebuild
straightaway, the quillies had chosen to secure it weakly with
thornwire and trenches guarded by an ever-shrinking number of
low-morale soldiers.

Easy pickings.

We packed up and marched. Three moons later, we reached a washed out road.

Our convoy was forced to stop, assess the situation. Either we'd have to find away around or over, and both would take time. Time Faelon—not to mention the Underland—did not have.

I wanted to howl in fury, retreat into the woods, maybe ride hard back to Athadhrai, enter the Crossroads, and take a chance on the fractured Gate. Thank the Lady I was forced to be the voice of reason when Erivon demanded most ardently that we do exactly that.

"We can't," I said to the fire around which our inner group of infiltrators sat. "If it was too dangerous to bring Faelon through that Gate back when we thought we might have to close them all, it's certainly too dangerous now."

My brother-in-law paced, snarling like a panther, his broad nose wrinkling in just the same way. Seeing this side of him, where before all he'd shown was the decorous king and doting husband, was both strange and refreshing. Once or twice, I'd had misgivings about Eytine forging a new path with the father of her child and leaving me behind, but really, I felt a deep bond with him. He was the only person in this universe who loved my sister as much as I did.

"And my son?" He stopped in front of me and turned expectantly. "Show me my son."

I was half way to obeying him. With one eye, I already tapped into a vague picture of Faelon's conscious. He struggled at his writing desk, trying to complete a history assignment given to him by his father, but he was so, so exhausted. Hungry, thirsty, tired, and now *cold* all the time, since they drew his blood several times a day. He propped his chin on his hand, desperate to keep his head up and his eyes open as he studied, but it kept slipping off. His mind felt fuzzy and clouded and he just wanted his mother. He hadn't seen her since the day they'd dragged her away.

But before I could discern more, Hiberos stood and stepped forward, forcing Erivon to step back. He spoke in a hushed tone— nearly a growl—that only those with keen senses would overhear:

"You know how she's suffered to bring you the information you already have. Be happy with it, and sit while I still believe you meant her no harm." His stance was stiff as he loomed over his old friend. It seemed to say *don't make me choose between you and her; you know how that will end.*

Erivon showed his teeth. And then he said something that shocked all three of us: "I am your king. Remember that before I show you what I've been holding back."

The moment the words crossed his lips, his ears pinned back, and regret filled his face. Viciousness, sure, I was certain he was capable of that with his queen on the line. But arrogance, and the demand for subordination? That was not Erivon. But he could not take the words back.

Lady save us. The Goneland truly had begun to corrupt the fae.

Hiberos simply raised his brows, laughed as if the king had told a mildly amusing joke, and returned to my side.

Whether out of frustration or embarrassment, Erivon isolated himself for the remainder of the night.

+☾ ☽ � ☾ ☾+

AFTER ALL WAS SAID and done and our convoy finally marched into the remains of the western Aiken Forest, where the tapered end of the withering began, time had eaten away another week.

We'd need a night's sleep and some sound tactics dive into the blight head-on tomorrow. Fomori didn't sleep, especially not these feral newborns. The troops started to set up camp.

Side by side, with Hiberos at my right hand and Ruadan at my left, I stood on a nearby hill and surveyed the suppurating rash of land below me. On the horizon, I could just make out the withered branches of the old bilé reaching for the sky, as if the great tree was trying to claw its way out of the gouge into which it had sunk. The sight of it writhing with fomori and crumbling to pulp made the breath hitch in my throat.

Without my having to say anything, without any glance or

movement, Hiberos slipped his hand into mine, entwining our fingers.

"First Fraochgleann, now this," I whispered. "*Our* tree. *Our* power. It belonged to our clan." My voice cracked on the last word, but I pressed on. "You know that word, *power*, it never meant the same thing to us. It never meant the strength to kill anyone who stands in your way." I inhaled in a hiss. "It was always something we found inside—inside ourselves, within the earth, under the sky, in the breezes and the barrows..."

"To see it gone..." Ruadan trailed off.

I closed my eyes and felt heavy, hot tears falling. The wind caressed my face and made my curls stick to my wet cheeks.

Hiberos squeezed me. "The tree may be dying, or dead—we cannot know—but so long as one of you is breathing, standing upright, that power is not lost."

I sensed Ruadan shift at my side. He was silent for a long time, then he patted my shoulder and murmured, "Let's go."

With one last look at our fallen tree, I turned and followed him. Hiberos's hand slipped from mine, but he was close by, a constant warmth at my side.

As we made our way back to the noise and smoke of the new Éirin front, I felt Ruadan looking at me. I glanced back and recalled how his face had been there, right alongside Gwynedd and Hiberos.

"You helped them reach me," I whispered.

He shoved his hands into the pockets of the greatcoat he wore over his leathers. "I did what I could, but I think you'd have come if it were Hiberos calling alone. I have never seen two souls who resonate in such perfect harmony."

"That seems unlikely. We never stop arguing."

Even as I said it, Hiberos huffed like he might argue.

"Resonating with someone does not mean falling in step with every one of their opinions." Ruadan threw a look to Hiberos, speaking to us both now. "Only that you understand one another at the deepest chamber of your soul. *If* you let yourself be vulnerable."

"Well," Hiberos rumbled, "that would be the problem. My thorny rose guards closely her heart."

I scoffed. "I'm hardly the only one guilty of *that* crime." As we walked into camp, I noticed Hiberos's head on a swivel. "What's wrong?"

"I've not seen Erivon since last night. I should go find him, speak with him. Explain my point of view."

Hiberos, seeking out someone he'd fought with and explaining himself? Death truly had changed him. I turned, letting my gaze rove up and down his effortlessly carved oaken body. Whatever he saw in my face lit a fire in his eyes, and he grinned, leaning in to give me a quick kiss. "Soon. Stay. I will return."

He left me stunned. We'd never kissed in front of people like that before.

My face hot, I searched for anything I could do with my hands. Ruadan put a length of rope in them and indicated for me to help him and some other Gallowglass pitch their tents. We worked in relative silence for a while. I glanced at him—then again, and again.

Without stopping his work or looking at me, he smiled placidly and asked, "What is it, Mave?"

"Your accent reminds me of him," I muttered at length. "Of Gwynedd. He always had that touch of Prydainian, even after years. The r's, and a bit of that lilt. He studied the druidic arts there, like Manan." After a pause, I added, "Maybe your demeanor, too, a bit. And your talents, unique though they are. I ... thank you, by the way."

Ruadan's smile became livelier than I'd ever seen it, his silver eyes twinkling. "I was right about the hellebores," was all he said in response.

I glanced toward where Hiberos had disappeared at the tree-line. "Yea. You were."

Abruptly, he stopped working and considered me. Although, like usual, he was not considering me so much as the air around me. I recalled him telling me once that I had many spirits following me. I, too, stopped working.

"Can I ask you something?" When he only tilted his head, I continued, "What ... are you, exactly? You are human, yet you hardly feel it. You have these powers, you can see and summon and work spirits. Are you a druid?"

"Could a druid do this?" His eye caught something unseen and followed it through the air; then, with a snatch of his hand, a flourish of his wrist, and a little wisp of white smoke, something appeared in his hand. A fetish of woven willow, teeth, and bone. Yet it glowed white with hints of lavender and blue, its gossamer form catching the sunset. He handed it to me, and the moment it hit my palm, its immense spiritual power thrummed through me.

"What is it?"

"If they have a proper name, I've not been able to find it. My mother called them soul trinkets. I can take them from creatures whose lives I end, or occasionally create them from the spirits drawn to me." He gestured vaguely round his head, as if there were so many he could not point just to one.

"And you ... keep them?"

He smiled gently, brushing a fingertip over the trinket I held. "Not for long. When I break them, they empower me in battle, or else they help me attain knowledge I otherwise would have no access to. Then their energy returns to the ether, and they are forever freed."

"You think I could do it?"

"You could try," he said with a chuckle.

Probably better not to waste his magic, but I couldn't control my curiosity. Taking the fetish in both hands, I broke it apart. It gave like sheep's wool but shattered like glass, and emitted the same white smoke as when he'd captured it—but, of course, I'd no idea how to use a spirit to empower myself, so it simply dissolved into the ether.

"And you've always been a... What do I call you?" I asked as we watched the spirit dissipate.

"You think of me as a phantom, do you not?" He quirked a smile. "A phantom rogue, then. To your other question, not as successfully as I can now. But I've communed with spirits since before I can remember, yes. My mother was a harvest-witch. Do you know what that is?"

"A Prydainian thing? I reckon something to do with the harvest."

Ruadan chuckled again. "Yes. About the only witches not hunted to near-extinction on the big isle. But, I can tell you plenty of tales of the harvest-witches after your nephew is home safe and sound." He pointed his chin behind me, and I turned to see Hiberos and Erivon emerging from the trees.

"Go to him," the phantom said under his breath. "The wind shifts and the spirits murmur uneasily. I have a feeling this may be our last night of peace for some time."

+☽ ☽ ☽ ☾ ☾+

IN THE PEACE and quiet of our tent, I could not stop kissing Hiberos, could not keep my fingers from tracing the channels carved into his chest. He certainly did not protest. I yearned to do more, but the honest truth was, I didn't have an ounce of strength left in my body. That did not mean our night was any less intimate. We lay on our sides, face to face with my knee lifted and one of his thighs between mine, and talked for hours despite the early morning ahead of us.

He twirled my hair around his fingers. We laughed, trading inconsequential knowledge and stories from lives past. Then, eventually, I quieted in his arms, simply breathing the same air as him, ever tracing the rivers with which I'd marked him that night three weeks ago.

I forced from my mouth the words I could not stop thinking: "After all this is over, will you marry me again?"

Hiberos seemed surprised, but not displeased. "Of course I will. You needn't have asked. It is understood: I am yours, all for you, heart, soul, mind, and body. Everything I do is your doing, and whatever I touch is touched also by you." Then, with a sly smirk, he teased, "I thought 'we never stop arguing.'"

"Well, I'd spend every remaining day of my life arguing, as long as its with you."

He snorted. "That sounds awful. Let us not do that."

"Stop being so obnoxious and naughty, then."

"Ugh." He jerked as though I'd pierced his heart with an arrow. "You ask so much of me, cruel goddess."

"All right." I drummed my fingers on his chest, relishing the feel of his heartbeat and the glow my touch caused. "Every time I want to argue with you, I'll make love to you instead."

"That sounds much better. And like a novel way to win an argument." He nuzzled our noses together and nudged my brow with his, quiet for a while. Thoughtful. Dour. "And ... if one of us falls in the coming battle, what should we do? Having a set plan might be prudent."

"A plan," I mused. "What about a pact?"

Hiberos grinned. "Even better. You know I love a good deal."

I fell quiet then, too, for just as long if not longer. Finally, "If one of us falls, we won't wait for the cycle to start again. No planting seeds, no new bodies. Whoever is left behind will go into the Beneath, find Gealach, and *make* her give the other back."

The way he looked at me, his eyes wide and shining, you would think I promised to reshape the universe itself. Breathlessly, he said, "Your bravery never ceases to astound me. Incredible—that after a thousand years, I still fall deeper in love with you every time you open your mouth."

I fought the urge to hide my flushed face. "Is that a yes? You promise."

"I do." And he pulled me astride him, already rutting into me. "Why don't we make it official?"

"Fine, as long as I'm allowed to fall asleep in the middle."

We giggled together like young lovers and not the thousands-year-old fae we were, and, relaxing into one another, fell into a dreamless sleep.

20

Before first light, about half the army left the front under cover of darkness, weaving through the remains of Aiken Forest toward our target. The infiltrators stood at the center, protected by rows of warriors who'd carry us as far as Westeris Wall.

The ground squelched under our boots like torn flesh. The land beneath was bleeding. Not figuratively. Not anymore. The burnt, scrawny limbs of our once-sacred trees dripped, the earth oozed, and something pulsed deep beneath us. Once or twice, I swore I heard a woman's voice on the wind—carried from the huge breach, resonant and loud and ancient—moaning in sorrow.

I joined Muiri's archers in sniping fomori from afar, but we all knew it was a matter of time until they recognized our presence and came for us in droves. The farther we walked, the more the path began to resemble an open wound.

This was no battlefield but a body turning on itself.

"There." Muiri pointed to a nearby clearing dotted in tree stumps. At first glance, the earth there simply seemed mossier than the area around it, but I realized with a wince that it was simply squishier. Foaming with blood. It spat yellowish-white fluid as fomori clawed their way to its surface, summoned by the vibration of our footsteps.

Some were formless at first, not unlike wriggling worms, before limbs snapped through the waxy film coating them and took shape. Skinny, eyeless humanoids; hulking masses of meat; bloated arachnids, their abdomens pulsing sacks of teeth and remains, their heads split and gaping as if they were newborns crowning in reverse. Others stayed little wormy beans with only the most basic compound eyes, chicken legs, and mouths like lampreys'. The flesh of every creature glistened in the pale moonlight. Their cries were garbled and watery and too close to human for my comfort.

Then, of course, there was the mist. Its surged forward along with the first wave of monstrous fomori—so many the ground trembled as they approached. Hiberos summoned his lunar scythe, twirling it between slender fingers in anticipation.

Ruadan nodded to Muiri, who called to her men, "Be alert. Remember, if you are cut, even nicked a little, fall back and wrap your wounds. The mist will find its way inside."

The memory of Brianne's body bending and breaking as the mist crawled its way inside of her played on my eyelids as I blinked.

"I'll protect the princess," said Hiberos to Solma, who was still as dour as she had been all week. "You keep us pushing forward. Do not let the humans be caught up in one-to-one battles."

She sniffed derisively but turned to take her station.

The air filled with the sound of bowstrings being drawn, and even as I joined them, I muttered, "Anything in particular got her upset, or everything?"

"Later," he purred.

"Sound point." I grunted, and tried not to choke on the lingering mist.

With a shout from Muiri, the archers loosed their arrows. I followed suit and released a volley of lunar arrows that sliced through the fomori, sending their white, bubbling bits flying like fat off bacon. They shrieked and whined as their brethren were felled. Then, with renewed frenzy, they crashed into us.

Our forces met with shouts, flashing axes, flying blood. Solma cried, "*Push!*" and I pivoted, guarding the Éirins' flank as they plunged into the bleeding heart of the wasteland. One of the ugly little beans and its younglings snapped at my heels as I danced back to keep in step with the push. With a snarl, I kicked it, and it went flying with a guttural honk, landing densely and crushing the smaller ones. Were the situation not so dire, I might have laughed. It made me think of Conan.

Ragged braying cut through the fog of war, and I looked up to see a not-deer crash through the fray, its skin a slick, deep red, its antlers sharp bone, its eyes not on its head but between its ribs, clustered like cysts. It gored an Éirin with its rack and tossed him. While it struggled to disentangle him from its antlers, I jumped on its back with a war cry, drawing Orlaith's dagger and driving it between its shoulder blades.

The split second before it sank into the rotten flesh, I could have sworn the dagger's lunar blade flashed red.

The earth rumbled. The moon took on an orange-pink cast as though warning me.

Well, to hell with that.

With another shout, I wound my arms round the stag's thick neck as tight as they'd go, making it stagger and steering it out of the crowd of Éirins. Their push forward left me behind, flanked by Hiberos and Ruadan. I stood on the stag's broad back, wrenched the dagger from its hide, and used its head as a spring board to leap back into the crush.

Behind me, there was a grunt, a whistle, and when I looked back, Hiberos had sent the thing's head tumbling.

In this manner, we fought through the misty scar. Pustules burst beneath our feet, the earth spat fluid and inflamed tissue, wave after wave of fomori clawed for our ankles.

When the wall finally came into view, Muiri shouted for her lieutenant to take her place. Just as we'd planned, the army morphed, moving as one like a serpent: the strongest shield-breakers and wolfkernes formed a head, while the infiltrators met in a cluster at the neck, and the remainder of the army—and the fomori that followed them—made up the tail.

The legionaries stationed at the breach had very little fore-warning we were coming. By the time they jumped up from their fire pits and grabbed their weapons, we were already charging.

The spike-filled trenches that usually protected the wall from anyone who would charge it were currently filled with body upon body, human and fomori, all mixed up and melding to create a bridge of flesh and bone. We flew over it, battle cries cutting the air. Shield-breakers tore up the thornwire and smashed through the front line of defense. The serpent we'd formed slithered in through the tiny rift, deeper and deeper into Aquilan land until the tail of fomori broke through, too.

Funny. The fomori seemed to favor Aquilan targets; they whipped round to overwhelm the legionaries. Shrieks of fury and shill babies' cries rose as the fomori transformed and became even more monstrous, sometimes melding with others to build upon themselves. Meanwhile, the Éirins engaged at a distance.

No doubt the legionaries would call for reinforcements—but no one would answer in time to save them.

In my mind's eye, already I could see the Eighth Legion, commanded by Tatius, lining up at the portal. They frothed with power from their newly administered inoculations. Gaius stood before the portal like a king about to be coronated. A pale, woozy Faelon stared wide-eyed at the Moon Gate.

Hiberos, Solma, Ruadan, Muiri, eighty warriors, ten druids, ten cavalry, and I split off and sprinted north, toward Geatacoill.

Already, I could feel her thrumming beneath my feet, aware of me. Calling me home. As if the consciousness of the enchanted forest stretched farther than her trees' roots. Even terminally ill as she was, she beckoned me onward with the sort of urgency that could only come from something fully sentient and aware of what was going on around them.

I'm coming, Mother. I'm coming. Hang on.

The sky darkened abruptly. Another storm moving quickly over the hills toward us.

I smelled Geatacoill before I saw her. When she came into view, my heart stuttered. She was ravaged decay. The blight had grown over every tree and patch of land like a fungus, turning everything green a sickly blood orange. To see Sallach destroyed was awful enough, but to see my home, *my* forest diseased, and with my own eyes … it was not just the stench that turned my stomach.

I'm coming. I love you. I'm sorry. We'll save you. I promise.

As if anticipating us, fomori began to emerge around trunks and from the moss. Those hideous newborn arachnids dropped from the boughs of the mighty trees. And, oh, Lady, the closer I came to the tree line, the more thunderous my heartbeat became. Aiken had been bad enough. To witness this unholy putrefaction and to know that its victim—Fraochgleann's lifegiver—could feel it, that she was alive … I wanted to scream. To be forced to hold something rotten in one's womb with no recourse to remove it … barbaric.

Throttling the land like this could not be justified, whatever we had done. To destroy beautiful things you once held dear because you were losing control—evil.

Gealach would have to *beg* for my forgiveness.

But first, Gaius.

It was time to finally end this, take my nephew back, protect the fractured Gate. And this time, Gaius would not escape death so easily.

We sliced through the fomori like a knife through butter, dismantling them limb by limb. They melted to goo only to return to the earth and start over again, but all we needed was a straight shot to the center of the forest. The humming beneath my feet became more and more intense. We were close. I smelled the smoke of their fires.

As I ran forward, far ahead of the company, I noted how this patch of forest seemed strangely devoid of either monsters or Aquilans. In fact, all was silent.

Suddenly, something dropped down behind me. Anticipating one of those vile arachnids, I spun with my dagger—

—only to have my arm blocked by a fist clad in Aquilan-style gauntlets

But when my eyes flew to the assailant's face, I saw no quilly. Her hair was white, cut to her chin, and her skin was milky seafoam.

I whooped and dropped my weapon, flinging myself into Orlaith's arms. Our very souls seemed to greet each other. I'd never held someone so tightly in my life, although my grip on her eased when I realized how thin and frail she was beneath the armor.

"Drusilla was able to plant supplies for you after all," I whispered as I pulled back, cupping her gaunt cheeks. I couldn't help myself—I kissed her forehead and crushed her to me again. "I am never leaving you behind again. Never. I should have known better. We don't leave each other behind. Where you go, I go."

I felt Eytine—*Orlaith*—relax into me. "I survived, Mave. And I told you to go. Faelon needed you."

Again, I pulled back. "Are you all right? How are you faring? Your infection—"

"Under control for now. But Moon's mercy, I will be glad to see an actual healer."

"I assume you've seen the quillies here?"

Her gaze darkened, and she nodded. "They're in the clearing now. He has Faelon, and they're trying to open the Gate. But there's something wrong." She scrunched her nose. "They ... smell wrong."

"They've inoculated themselves with a slurry of fae blood, human blood, and magic to let themselves pass through."

She frowned, confused. "That cannot be. It's an entire legion. Gaius did not take nearly enough of my blood to..." Realization dawned on her face. Then a rage so primal, so unspeakable that it made the angry infection of the forest seem pale in comparison.

"Mave?" called a familiar, deep voice. The voice of my brother-in-law.

At once, the set of Orlaith's ears shifted, and she tore herself away from me and stared. When the Moon King appeared between the tree trunks, glittering in his deep silver armor, his gaze was pulled to her like rain pulled home to the sea.

"Moonbeam," he breathed.

"I brought reinforcements," I whispered to Orlaith.

That snapped her out of her trance. She screamed and leapt into his arms, and they embraced as the remainder of the company trickled into the forest around them. Hiberos appeared by my side and slipped the dagger I'd dropped back into my hand. Since Orlaith had plenty of her own—Lady bless Drusilla—I tucked it back into my bandolier.

Apparently, Muiri had already sent out druid scouts: two birds, one crow and one carrow, dropped from the sky and flitted back into men at her feet. The crow, I recognized as the healer Paik.

"They've clustered to the east and west, but their defense to the south is weak," Paik said, kneeling in the soil to sketch the battlefield out for her. "Our advantage is we can engage them from the trees. Their advantage is they might go through that portal at any point..."

It was decided we'd flank the clearing in four groups, two to the north and two to the south, and try to pinch clusters of soldiers off from the rest. Away from each other, and away from the portal. I circled to go north with Orlaith, Erivon, and Hiberos while Solma, Muiri, and Ruadan stayed to the south.

"He will not lay his hands on my son," Orlaith said through gritted teeth as we crept through the bracken, "and he will not bring his filth into the Underland. I am still their queen. I will *not* let him hurt them."

Finally, the forest became less dense—the beginning of what had once been the stone henge grove. We passed a standing stone or two lodged in the earth, thrown back from whatever burst of magic had created the lake ten years ago. Then the darkened sky appeared above us, and rows upon rows of Aquilans came into view. The Gate was only big enough to let through maybe five at a time, and so the way they were lined up, they seemed to stretch on forever. Half stood before the east face of the portal and half before the west, their number fed by smaller lines curving through the grove and down the path toward Sylvostum.

While Hiberos disappeared into a flurry of moon moths, Erivon, Orlaith, and I shimmied up a pair of trees, as silent and nimble as panthers, to get a better perspective on what lay below.

My attention narrowed in on Faelon at once. Dressed in red this tie. The poor lad was trying to hide the fact that he was swaying. Trying to focus on the feeling being near to the Moon Gate gave him. Trying to ignore the streak of his own blood smeared on the stone and the red shards roiling and snapping in the center of the vortex. Every so often, while Gaius readied his men, Faelon tugged on his arm, murmuring something so weakly that even with my fae hearing I could not make it out. Judging by his frown and his worried glances toward the portal, he was trying to warn his father of the danger. The fracture called to him, too, I realized; when he'd seen the red swirling amongst the teal and felt that base wrongness, that had been his fae blood warning him.

But Gaius brushed him off.

In the boughs of a southern tree, a crow called thrice. Our signal.

The forest shivered with subtle movement, and every Aquilan stiffened.

First came the arrows. Enough that, were it not for the glint of their steel, they might be mistaken for rainfall. The legionaries broke rank to draw their swords, turning toward the forest, but no assault came to meet them. Fighting amongst the trees would always be our strength, and their weakness.

Gaius's growl seemed to echo through the clearing as he turned, grabbed Faelon, and pressed the boy close to him. I focused on them. The lad was frightened, pale, eyes wide.

Then something beside his face caught my attention. Gaius's veins, just above the straps of his bracer ... glowing a faint red beneath his skin.

My heart threatened to stop as I snapped my gaze to the strike force in their neat little rows. Beneath their skin, on their wrists or necks, each and every one of them bore traces of red, too—little ones, so subtle, their glow so quickly flashing that it was easily missed.

Was fae blood really that potent?

There was no time to stop and think about what that might mean for us. With another snarl, the legate crushed Faelon tight into his side, and barked something in Aquilan I didn't quite catch.

Whatever he said, the legionaries clicked to attention and focused forward. Their veins pulsed. They ignored the arrows. Ignored the whoops from the trees. Ignored their comrades falling at their sides.

And they began their march into the portal.

The ones at the east face melted into the swirling vortex, and the ones on the west did the same, never running into each other, simply passing through twice as fast. With each man that passed through, the portal shivered, the red in its teal surface growing like blood spreading through water.

With a grunt of panic, I leapt down from my tree, not certain what I might do until I drew my dagger and started slashing. But by and large, the legionaries ignored me, dodging forward and speeding through the portal or letting their friends die by my hand. They left the engineers and a few slaves to take up arms against me, though the majority ran. They were felled easily by my sister and her husband, who had appeared on either side of me with their own weapons drawn—Orlaith, her stolen Aquilan steel, and Erivon, his moon-touched ebony blades.

"Stop the soldiers!" I cried, my voice cracked and wavering as I braced my bow against an engineer's swinging club.

Erivon answered my plea with a burst of lunar magic that stuck to the ground in an orb, drawing the few legionaries caught in its field to the center before crushing them into a mess of bone and viscera. In the same moment, he pivoted and beheaded a laborer trying to flank me. Orlaith plucked arcane tattoos from her thighs and struck another charging our way, slicing his throat open and sending all his weight to the ground.

Faelon recognized my voice. He turned his head to look at me, then his birth mother, and finally, for the first time, birth father. "Mave!" the lad gasped, even as he shrank away from the flying magic.

He called out to me. My heart flipped, my fangs and claws elongating, adrenaline scorching through my veins. I'd tear Gaius's arm off to get him if I had to.

For the legate's part, he growled, "I see her," and drew his sword with his free hand.

Distantly, Muiri trilled a battle cry. The trees swished to and fro as Éirins slid down them or moved through them. They advanced rapidly on the clearing, but by the time they reached it, axes swinging and faoladh claws flashing, there were hardly any legionaries left to slaughter.

They crashed into the remaining slaves, laborers, and engineers, swarming them like wasps. It was all they could do. They couldn't charge through the portal after the legionaries. Our allies were mortal; they'd lose their minds just as easily as any humans.

I turned my attention toward Gaius, gritting my teeth. With that grim victor's smile, he advanced a step, forcing Faelon to shuffle along with him, and—

Thunk. A dagger lodged into the ground a hair's breadth away from the tip of his boot. He jerked his head up, eyes wide, and angled himself in front of Faelon with his arm raised.

In the next second, Orlaith crashed into it.

All three of them landed as a pile in the mud and silt in front of the Moon Gate. The portal swirling within it sparked angrily. The shards of red were less shards now and more marbling, infused with every inch of the vortex. Whips of blood orange lightning flicked through the cool lunar magic like snakes' tongues. The entire structure shook as though under great pressure.

In the oscillating lights of the portal, Gaius rolled forward to his knees, shoving Orlaith off him—and Faelon behind him—in the process. He spat teeth and a wad of blood and reached to snatch Orlaith by the collar. She met him with a backhanded dagger slash, but it only barely scratched his nose, leaving a thin red line.

In response, Gaius leapt to his feet and, with no time to grab his fallen weapon, kicked her in the ribs, sending her dagger spinning. It skimmed over the mud and into the portal.

"*Mother!*" Faelon screamed.

The vortex swallowed the blade greedily and sparked hard. The tremors intensified until we all were staggering, each of us with different goals. I dove for Orlaith. She and Erivon reached for Faelon. The Éirins and Aquilans struggled to lock in on their opponents.

But Gaius staggered for his sword.

Red flashing in his veins, he snatched it up and raised it above Orlaith's head—and the world seemed to stop.

The battle raging around us muted. Every emotion was writ large across my sister's face: rage, terror, heartbreak, defiance. There was no fire, but suddenly I felt heat blistering my skin, throbbing in my palms. I heard the baby's cry, I saw Eytine's head swivel, each strand of gingery hair gilded in the flame. Every particle of my body expected to hear the squelch of a blade piercing muscle, the gulch, the splatter of her blood upon the earth. Again.

Several things happened at once.

Erivon was diverted from his son and, roaring, lashed out with magic, only to miss by an inch. Faelon screamed and grasped for Gaius's ankle. I threw myself into the dirt, skidding on my knees toward my sister.

Gaius swung downward—

—and Hiberos appeared in a flourish of moon moths, standing tall between Eytine and her killer.

The blade sank into his chest. Gaius shuddered and looked up at the towering Guardian with wide eyes. Hiberos grinned mischievously back.

The Gate stopped trembling.

Then it erupted.

Magic shot outward in all directions, knocking us all flat save for Hiberos, whose golden waves merely flagged as though stuck in a wind storm. Cries of shock and agony filled the clearing. When I managed to pry myself up from the earth, I could barely comprehend what I saw. The very stone of the Gate was blown apart, only roughly holding its circular shape; the moss and grime had been washed away from its surface, and every scratch of Ogham glared with light. The vortex in its center was now wild, uncontained magic, filled with cracks of red and bits of debris. Worst of all, it *screamed*. It screamed like a gale force wind underpinned by a woman's voice, shriller and shriller.

Orlaith darted out from behind Hiberos and tackled Faelon, pressing him to her chest. Erivon did the same to them both, enveloping them in his embrace and his magic. Gaius didn't seem to notice; as he wobbled to his feet, he had eyes only for the faun who had defied him.

Despite the sword sticking out of his chest, Hiberos's grin had not died, only sharpened. As if seeing into the legate's thoughts, he pointed at him with his chin and said, "Do it."

Gaius bared his teeth like an attack dog. Then, with a strangled cry, he leapt forward, threw his arms around Hiberos, and pitched them both into the Moon Gate.

As they were engulfed by the wild magic, Hiberos turned his head and winked at me.

21

Gaius and Hiberos were swallowed up by the Gate. Adrenaline surged into my legs and propelled me forward. Without regard to how the portal's magic frothed and hissed, I flung myself through after them.

Even as I passed through the spiraling darkness, I felt the Moon Gate break behind me. It was with a catastrophic explosion that I burst into the Crossroads.

Streaks of blue and slate filled my vision as I was thrown like a rag doll through the underground chamber, and when my back collided with something immovable, those streaks turned into hazy, diffused blurs. But a second later, pain the likes of which I'd never felt sharpened my vision until I swore I could see every particle of moth dust floating down from the tree above me.

The roar of battle droned endlessly nearby as the waiting fae clashed with the humans. After all those thousands of years, war had come to the Underland.

Oh, Lady. The pain was like being trapped in a vice, cut by a blade, and smashed with a hammer all in one. I could not move away from it. I couldn't move at all. I turned my head, and exhaled a whimper when I saw the enormous chunk of stone debris sitting atop my right arm.

Fighting, *screaming* through the pain, I wriggled, pushed against the stone, scratched till my claws cracked. It must weigh a ton. Already, blood pooled beneath it, and though the pain persisted, I could no longer feel my fingers.

Grunting snapped my attention leftward, where I found Hiberos. His expression was focused, intent. The sword still stuck from his chest, and Gaius sat astride him, bearing down on him with manic eyes and a toothy grimace obscured completely by blood. They braced against each other, deadlocked, straining, the sword's hilt trembling in their hands.

Gaius growled in Hiberos's face, blood and spit flying as he enunciated every word. "Last time I cut you open, beast, you didn't have a heart. I wonder if you do now?"

The Underland shook and groaned the same way the Gate had. Flashes of blood orange and crimson and sepsis-amber marbled the chamber, spreading, retreating, then spreading again in quick succession. Whips of magic, like tongues of lightning in their radiance and quickness, spidered over me and the two men, Guardian and Tormentor. Silt and small bits of debris fell in sheets from the skylight above our heads. The slip of sky I could see through the hole was no longer twilight but red as a fiery sunset and churning with agitation.

Hiberos jerked his head back from his struggle against Gaius and surveyed the destruction around him. A host of emotion—true, and broad, and vulnerable—crossed his face. Sorrow. Betrayal. Determined anger. Finally, resignation.

He looked at me and mouthed the words, so plain yet so rare and honest: "I love you."

Then he released his grip on the sword, and let Gaius plunge it deeper into his abdomen.

My scream joined with another of those sharp winds under-pinned by female shrieking. Grunting, greedy, his veins glowing and his eyes aflame, Gaius ripped the sword downward. Hiberos's pitch-colored blood bubbled up between them, painting Gaius's thighs and lower stomach, his forearms. With a gasp, the

Guardian bucked and slapped his hands over Gaius's haunches, clutching him tight like a lover in rapture.

"No!" I pulled uselessly against my crushed arm as the hungry dog thrust his arm inside Hiberos to the elbow and tore the heart from his chest.

The heart was beautiful as ever, glowing softly, its filigree glistening with fluid; soothing, sleepy, such a terrible contrast to the bloody chaos around it. Gaius stopped, dropped his sword, mouth agape as he beheld the heart. Enthralled, he paid no mind to my shrieking and failed attempts to reach them.

The heart could only live outside Hiberos's body for so long. If there was no ritual, if there was no *Mave* to devour it and make him one with her—

I caught a subtle movement on Gaius's thigh. Hiberos tracing something, drawing patterns in his blood.

My eyes flew to his murmuring mouth, and too late, I understood what was about to happen.

"You wanted it," Hiberos rasped, seizing Gaius's wrists. "Take it."

A red glow scorched them, obscuring everything but the vaguest outlines of their forms. I thrashed in vain. My shoulder fractured. I slapped my bandolier for a blade and readied to cut through my armor, flesh, and muscle if I had to.

Then another scream shook the world, this one like the roar of thunder directly in my ear. In the blink of an eye, the red sun engulfing Hiberos and Gaius expanded outward and swallowed everything.

The Underland contracted. Magic squeezed every inch of my skin, hot and frenetic. Then everything was sliding—sliding forward. The stone rolled off my arm and dropped down. I was barely conscious of the tree above me being torn up, roots and all. I was peeled from the ground and pitched forward. We all were falling, every living thing in the realm, crushed against the magic and one another through a narrow, stifling channel.

The heat was unbearable. The cold that followed was shocking enough that I yelped and curled in on myself.

I hit the ground hard, and the *crunch* was the last thing I heard before darkness took me.

⟨·꙳·꙳·☾·☽·⟩

I WOKE face down in the moss, the world around me so brutally loud that I could not think.

Slowly, sensation returned to my limbs. With breaths as thin and tenuous as spiders' webs, I lifted myself to hands and knees and tried to get my bearings.

I shook my mind of the memory to focus on the field of horror surrounding me. Geatacoill had been flattened for miles, the trees disintegrated. Fae and humans alike cried out, struggled, died. Flaming chunks of stone and huge shards of crystal rained from the sky, their impact making the world shake. The sky above was an irritated, smoky coral, and in the center hung a blazing scarlet sun.

No—not a sun. I could make out the landscape of its face.

A *moon*.

"Hiberos!" I turned to look for him but retched instead when I jostled the useless, pulpy mess constituting my right arm. Anguish made my vision twist and pulse. But neither Hiberos nor Gaius were anywhere to be seen.

A groaning deep within the earth reached its crescendo then. A cosmic wail from below. Thousands of tons of ore against ore and stone against stone. The treetops in the western half of Geatacoill shivered and fell as the ground devoured them. And from the rift, rising shaft after shivering shaft, grew the Lunar Palace.

Or, what had once been the Lunar Palace. All its opalescent glass had turned to the ever-present black limestone of the fomori ruins. The edifice towered over the landscape like a great burial mound, and only grew larger with the seconds.

Images of the cairn I'd entered for my Trial of Purity flashed in my mind. The cairn of a god, I'd thought then.

The trees encircling this new Mournful Palace were flattened, the earth cratered, and, as if through thought alone I had conjured it, row upon row of blackened stone ground up through the bedrock. Wall after wall, towering fifty feet, winding around the palace in a spiral.

A labyrinth.

The Underland hadn't just expelled us.

The Underland was *gone*.

Without warning, a memory closed me in its grasp.

Finally, I retrieved a vision of Gealach.

I took a breath and stepped over the threshold. The moonstone chamber was still and quiet, the only light coming from a liquid slowly dripping from its crown moulding into the infinity pools at the baseboard. In the center of the chamber, sitting moth-style, was Gealach, wearing her great circular headdress and glittering frost-colored vestment.

None of the art I'd seen depicting her could hope to do her justice. Though the fae had been created from her, in form she still was unlike us: her head was small, her neck long and slender, her broad, voluptuous body hung with shapeless robes. Her steel-blue skin shimmered like dragonfly wings. She was as tall as me while sitting down, her neck craned as she added stitch after stitch to the funeral shroud spread across her lap.

I watched transfixed as her large hands, with their claws as black as midnight, worked the same rhythm over and over. Calm, silent, never shedding a tear, she wove stars, planets, and threads of silver and ash into the misty fabric.

"Come in, Ashling," she said gently. Her voice was the cool touch of moonwater. The crisp of a bitten apple. The velvet of a winter night's sky.

I did as she asked, and sat on my knees beside her, watching her needle weave in and out. The air was heavy with sorrow— but an old sorrow. Contained. Condensed. Forged into ritual through heat and pressure over thousands of years. I knew who she mourned: the light that peeked into the valley, the golden sun that lay unmoving on the horizon. She stitched silvery details into his features even now, though it appeared to me more like a mess of leaves and horns than a man's face.

"He belonged to me before I knew my name," she said at length, "and I to him. Before time was time, before there was a word for love. Even now, the shape of the space he once occupied ... its echo is very loud, is it not? I see him, I hear him ... everywhere. In the curve of the willow boughs, the vine of the jasmine, the ripple of the panther's hide." She shook her head. "The wave of grasses, the grooves of the turtle's shell, the song of carrows and a thousand other things you've never seen before, wee one."

With a bittersweet smile, she paused her sewing to hold my chin in one outsized hand. "But they all go eventually, no?" she whispered.

She took my hand and slipped her sewing needle into it. "I want you to try something now. Choose your soul's mate—I shall give you the pick of them."

Them? I looked back down at the shroud and realized that she'd stitched not only the Horned One into the pattern but ... everyone. Fae, Guardian, and aranfox. Even some soulforms who had made the Underland their permanent residence. Everyone I had ever known, loved, and lived with was rendered in ashen thread, barely visible.

"Soul's mate?" I repeated.

"The one you'll spend eternity with. The way Orlaith with Erivon are. Stitch a bit of silver into them." I must have flushed rather obviously, for she smiled and covered her twinkly black eyes with a hand. "Go on. I'll not peek."

I considered the shroud, and each of the faces as my eyes roved over them. Friends, all. Talented, beautiful, and worthy in their own ways. But in none of them did I see a soul's mate; with none of them could I imagine a eternity together. And so my eyes roamed on. Each Guardian was embellished with a bit of silver thread befitting the Sun God.

One in particular caught my eye.

I didn't know why. Hiberos and I were not close. He was Erivon's closest friend, yet he always found some way to frus-

trate me, his demeanor detached unless there was a joke to be made at my expense. Something in the way Gealach had stitched his likeness, though, with such care ... the way she'd captured the glint in his eyes and the broad curve of his smirking mouth...

I tilted my head one way, then the other, marveling at this new feeling inside of me.

"Wee one, the only way to keep what you love is to bind it into the pattern. Stitch it so tightly the world cannot unravel it."

He intrigued me. Pulled me in with a gravity that I had never felt before. Made me yearn for things I had never considered until this very moment. Looking into his joyful face, I saw an eternity together: laughter, closeness, his body cupping mine, fingers brushing, our eyes meeting across rooms, a smile, a chest to fall against, and a refuge after long days...

But I did not make the stitch, nor any stitch. I simply handed the needle back and left the chamber.

THE BATTLE WAS NOT OVER.

Some—Aquilan and Éirin, fae and human alike—huddled in craters made by falling debris, crying for their mothers. Others had taken to arms to carry on the slaughter without orders or rank or even logic.

With my right arm dripping uselessly at my side, I could only hold a looted sword in my left. There was no time for acts of mercy or kindness; I passed everyone with my gaze locked ahead. On Geatacoill. Life-giver. Friend. Mother.

I limped through the sundered valley, blood pouring from my mouth and my hairline, trying with all my soul to find two things: Hiberos, and whatever remained of the Gate.

The fae fought as viciously as their cousins of the Courts, and the Aquilans met them blow for blow, their veins pulsating light. The Éirin rebels were outmatched; caught between the half-mad armies and the fomori, most ran. Faoladh howled and fled as if the red moon burned them. Those who did not flee fell to the ground, writhing in pain and tearing at their fur.

No Hiberos. Anywhere.

If I could just find the lake. The Underland hadn't spat me out anywhere near it. I tried to remember any other landmark, trees, standing stones...

With the amount of blood I'd lost and the pain digging its claws into my brain, I was beginning to wander blindly. Staggering, tripping over my own boots. I barely registered the grove into which I'd stumbled. Barely had the strength to keep the sword in my hand...

Mave.

My ears pricked up and twitched. Gwynedd's voice.

Mave.

The same voice, just a hop further into the glade. A bleached standing stone caught my eye, and a breath of wind pushed me toward it.

Then, another voice. I only recalled hearing it once before, when I'd walked through the spirit plane: *One foot in front of the other, my girl.*

Another, gruff but hopeful. Eamon. *Keep going.*

Then a woman. Tali. My dear friend. *Quickly, darling, onward!*

I shook my head hard and walked faster, stomping my feet into the foul moss if only to keep them from going numb. I passed another standing stone, and another. Finally, the grove let out into the clearing. The pieces of the Gate that had not imploded had been flung around and now riddled the field; the earth was scorched as from the sun, all burnt black or petrified white; the drained lake had been refilled, this time with sinister a red liquid. Strangest of all, as I got my bearings, I realized the clearing was hemmed in entirely with briars that had not been there before. They were outsized and twisted, and ... if my eyes did not deceive me, they were spreading deeper into the forest. Racing toward the Mournful Palace. *Growing.*

I staggered a few steps ahead and tried to shout, but my voice came out a whisper: "Hiberos?"

Something shifted behind me, stones crumbling. My boots scuffed the dirt as I turned in a flash, but there was no attacker. Only an ally, slumped up against the cracked keystone of the Gate, the one carved with the likenesses of Orlaith and Ashling. Ruadan wheezed as he tried to pull himself into a sitting position despite the rock disintegrating beneath his fingers.

I rushed over, crashing to my knees before him. "What's wrong?" I croaked. "Are you hurt?"

I don't know why I asked. What armor the blast hadn't burned away was fused to him, and the skin that was exposed was nothing but laceration after gory laceration.

"Your sister—" He grunted, pinkish spittle flying. "The boy. They're all safe. I sent them ... on ... their way."

His sleek silver hair and sidewhiskers were knotted with blood and ash, and strands fell into his face and stuck to his sweaty temples. His face, usually light olive, was pale, the skin around his eyes ruddy and bruised. For but a moment, something unfamiliar flitted across his face. Fear, or sorrow. The sight of it lodged a knot in my throat. Fear did not belong on this man's face. Not on this serene, kindly assassin's face...

"Hold on. Please." I cast about for medicine and spotted a purple sack under an overturned table—the remains of the imperial alchemist's cache. Trying to ignore the pain screaming through my arm, I dragged the sack over, loosened the tie, and began to draw out vial after vial of tonics. From the little Aquilan I could read, about half were for healing.

"Drink this." I uncorked one with my teeth and held it to his lips, but he pushed my hand away.

"You." He nodded to my arm. "You are far worse off."

That was not true. I counted the vials swiftly. Six. Six in total. "Three for me and three for you," I bargained, holding the vial to his lips again.

Again, he pushed it away. "Three for you may stanch the bleeding, but you will need all six to ... c-close the skin..."

"I shouldn't close the skin anyway, the wounds'll need to be flushed and—"

"*Mave.*" For the first time, his voice held a gravelly edge, and he pointed afield with his chin.

I followed his gaze to the treeline, where a thick fog was rolling in. No, not fog. Mist. Approaching along with it, partially obscured by its murky breakers, were forms of monstrous shapes and sizes, their gaits strange and uneven.

"Take it," he whispered.

I turned back to him. "I *can't.* You're covered in wounds, Ruadan, the mist will—"

"This mist will do what it was designed to do. As will I."

Before I could ask what in the hells he meant, he exhaled slowly, laid a hand on his own chest, and took a last glance at the nearing fomori.

Somehow, he conjured that calm smile of his. "Listen carefully. In the wood north of Divlinn, you will find a little witch named Aoife. A hand younger than you. I've taken care of her since she was a girl of ... eleven ... and she is ... as talented as my mother was, but she needs guidance."

I was too stunned to speak. How had he never mentioned this? But the Gallowglass struggled to draw another breath now, glancing more urgently at the mist. With a gesture and a wisp of white, he drew from the center of his chest—painlessly, it seemed —one of his soul trinkets. I didn't know what object I expected to represent him, but it certainly was not the heart-shaped locket that appeared in his palm. He urged the gossamer trinket into my palm and pushed it away. Already, he grew as pale as his moniker, *phantom.*

"Remember the green hellebore." Blood trickled from the corner of his mouth. "Take it to Aoife. She'll know what to do."

"But how will you—" I clutched the locket to my chest, shaking my head. "How can you exist in this thing, outside your body?"

"I have been a ghost all my life." His eyes drifted closed. "Take it ... Aoife ... she'll know ... what..."

"Wait. Wait. Ruadan, please. One more thing, just one more question. The spirits following me—"

I grabbed his hand and squeezed hard, but it was too late. Death had already claimed him in her long-eluded embrace.

Behind me, the fomori groaned, shaking me of the overpowering urge to stop and mourn my friend. Just like always, there was no time for grief. No time to wallow in sadness or pity. No time for mercy.

With a growl, I shoved the heart-shaped locket into a pouch on my bandolier. Vial after vial of healing tonic, I uncorked and threw back despite the bitter herbal taste. A sharp prickle, like being stabbed with a thousand needles, started at my shoulder and worked its way down as the medicine took hold. These weren't sutures—nothing so clean as that. When the tonic closed my cuts, the skin was bubbly, bumpy, the bone within still unset even if minor fractures were closed.

My arm was a mess, all patchwork, uneven skin and awkward angles. But it would keep the mist out of me.

Right on time. The mist surged past me, hungry to sink its claws into the still-warm body of my friend.

Like a living thing, it twisted round his limbs, seeping into every weeping cut, suckling at the blood as if it were mother's milk. The tendrils forced their way into his veins, turning them sunken and bruised. Perhaps Ruadan had not been as dead as I thought he was, because his head flung back, an animal shout escaping from his lungs. His silvery eyes flew open and rolled back into his skull. The veins of his neck turned gray, straining as he worked his jaw open and closed involuntarily.

In one movement, I grabbed my sword and leapt to my feet. Judging by their moans, the horde of fomori were still a ways behind me, but I could not have taken my eyes off Ruadan if I tried. He almost seemed to lurch after me—but whatever piloted his body had no conception of how to control it.

Instead, it spun to face away, snapped back into a crab walk, and, with grinding bones, turned its head past reason, past flesh, to look at me.

With breath sawing my throat, my mind teetering on the brink of madness, I dropped into a defensive stance and raised my sword. Behind me, a garbled part-gasp part-scream had me circling and throwing a glance over my shoulder. A half-shifted wolf-shape, twisted into a fomori. Its hands were long, sharp rakes as it leapt ten feet in the air and dove for me.

I rolled under. Tried to ignore the sharp pain in my useless arm. Failed, and vented my frustration with a feral roar.

Ruadan's joints cracked and reversed, and he bounded for me like a hound chasing a rabbit. The other fomori was close behind, so unspeakably fast that, even though it was behind Ruadan, it reached me as I was dodging him. With its giant claws, it slapped me across the face, hard enough that flew back and hit a tree.

Blood trickled down my cheek. I slapped a hand over the little cut.

Fuck.

The mist coiled as if to face me, as though it sensed my blood on the air. It would come quick, and the horde was closing in, more rising from the festering earth with every second. This was not a fight I would win—not with a shattered arm.

So I darted between the trees, running south. Away from Geatacoill, away from Sylvostum, away from the growing briars and the corrupted palace. Every step was haunted by fomori. My boots sank into the land's suppurating wounds, forcing me to pull them from the mudlike suction. It wasn't until a row of fae ballistas rolled over the horizon that I slowed, letting my exhaustion bring me to my knees. In the distance, Solma shouted my name again and again with rising panic.

Of course. If anyone could take her troops in hand in the face of such a cataclysm, it would be Solma.

If anyone could find Hiberos, it would be Solma.

I collapsed face first into the tainted clover and lost consciousness.

22

The first thing I did upon waking was purge everything in my stomach.

I was in a small tent barely big enough for the cot I lay on. It was dark and quiet here, but the quality of the dim light told me it was mid-day outside. The druid Paik sat on a stool beside me, and even he was subdued for once as he held my gawk bucket. "Steady on, there you are. I know. Mystical sedation doesn't agree with everyone."

I was hardly even done retching as I began to speak, pausing to spit excess saliva. "Sedation?"

The healer nodded and tried an encouraging smile. "Aye. That arm was in a state. Had to keep you from moving around and bollixing it all up." I followed his gesture and cursed under my breath when I saw my arm was strapped to my chest in a sling. "Sorry. I set the bone and tried to mold the skin to look less mean."

"It doesn't matter what it looks like," I croaked, scrubbing my face with my free palm. I was too sedated still to give him a thrashing, which was a good job since he didn't deserve it and I was being a cunt. "How long?"

"Three nights."

My chest was a dark pit. I couldn't help it. I snapped, "Three *nights*?" and watched Paik wince.

"Here, have this." He grabbed a tankard from a second stool beside him and shoved it into my hand. I drained the ale to keep myself from saying something I'd regret.

I didn't *have* three nights. Apparently, we were somewhere safe, and my sister and nephew were all right, and those were both blessings. But Hiberos was still missing, alive, *somewhere*.

I knew he awaited me. I *felt* it. The last time we'd been separated, it had ended in his death. I refused to sit with my thumb up my arse and wait for history to repeat itself. Finding him had to be my priority.

"Where's Solma?" I asked at last. She was my best bet for information.

"Aw, lassie, you really should rest..." Paik began, palms spread, brow creased.

I cut him off with a glare and swung my legs over the edge of the bed. Belatedly, I realized my armor was gone, and I cast about for it. "Where are my leathers?"

"Lady Muiri has them," he answered. "When you were carried in, you were muttering something about the Gallowglass commander, something about a locket? You told her she should take your bandolier, so she took all of it."

My stomach crumpled like paper as I remembered Ruadan. His plea, and the way the mist had warped his body. The cracking of his bones. The milky, dead-fish quality to his stare. I hadn't known him as long or as well as I'd have liked, but he'd been my friend. My only friend, those long months. It hurt to know he could not even be with his constant companions, the spirits, even in death; his soul was suspended in time, now, nothing but a trinket.

It wasn't like him to avoid Death, the way he spoke of her like a dear companion. He must really think he could return. Someone had to take his locket to the "little witch," Aoife, after all this was over.

Paik tried one last time to lure me back to bed—"Lie down and rest now. We'll play cards!"—but I simply shook my head, brushed him off, and pushed the tent flap aside.

The first thing I noticed was that it was *not* mid-day as I had assumed. It was night, although it could only be called *night* because the moon still dominated the sky. It was scarlet and blazing as a sun, glaring down on the landscape and casting it in dark gold-and-peach hues. The magic around me was frenetic in a way that left me hopeless to express its magnitude. The *heat* was the most disturbing part, constant and oppressive, scorching as a desert.

The reality truly hit me then. The Underland was gone. That eruption, the expulsion ... we had just experienced a little Shift, the last vestige of the Dead World's veil ripped away.

The camp that lay beyond was typical for an Éirin war outpost—with a few modifications for civilian refugees—but the progress was decent for three nights. No permanent structures of course, but two rows of palisades had been thrown up, an outer wall and an inner wall with a sort of buffer area in the middle, absolutely crawling with archers busy taking potshots at roaming fomori.

There had been a little effort to segregate the fae tents from the human ones, probably subconsciously, but by and large, the two groups mixed—for better or worse. At the center of town, a group of women were rationing supplies and food, and I was pleased to see Joa and Eilliv alive and in their number. They were currently locked in heated debate with a pair of men. I watched as Joa shoved her wife aside and bared her fangs in an uncharacteristic display of aggression.

Not twenty paces away, a bit of palisade was being patched: workmen hauled timber to a small team of fae artisans, who used their magic-empowered instruments to shape and sand. Their enchantments rendered the ropes used to pull the logs in place unbreakable. As I came across the aid tent, I peeked in and saw aranfoxen teaching druids how best to utilize the limited fae medicine that had survived the explosion.

"Ahhee?" A hopeful voice drew me further into the tent, a

voice I realized was trying desperately to say *Mave*. A *fae* voice, notable because so few fae called me by my preferred name.

I cast my gaze over the injured in the cots, each of their traumas more horrific than the last. Finally, I landed on a familiar spiky shock of white hair. Oishin.

I would have to identify him by his hair, unique for a male fae, because there was very little left of his face. Something had gouged a valley through his right eye, down across his nose, and through his jaws, leaving what remained of his teeth and muscle exposed to open air. His other eye was bruised completely shut. He must have recognized me by my scent.

Hurriedly, I pulled up a stool and enfolded his hand in mine, but I didn't know what to say.

Oishin's radiantly sincere smile was gone, but I could tell by the slant of his remaining eye that he was trying. "Stade a' ne..." *State of me.*

I huffed. "You look fine. You'll pull through." And he may very well, but ... Goddess. "What happened?"

"Saat ... saatnel."*Shrapnel.*

"Bloody hell."

"A'leass ... suh-till hagh ... ny hans."*At least I still have my hands.*

"That's true," I rasped.

He tilted his head to the side, indicating a nearby bed, but had no energy for further comment. I straightened to peer at the other patient. Again, they'd be unrecognizable if not for the arcane tattoos covering every inch of their skin. This was Owalir. Were it not for the slow, subtle rise and fall of their chest, I might have thought they were dead. I'd never seen their face before, always blocked by their elaborate hood and collar, but they wore none of their finery now. There was no indication that they had ever been the king's foremost gatewright. They looked young, so young, like a child, their features beyond fragile.

Then as my eyes roved down, I realized what Oishin was saying. Their limbs were gone. All of them.

I couldn't bare to look at it. My disgust and anger at Gealach for allowing this to happen was eclipsed only by my horror. I narrowed in on Oishin alone, squeezing his hand tight.

"I aa … ssh … shhaa'ed it." He had to repeat himself several times before I understood: *I saved it.*

I knew what he referred to without him having to clarify. "No, Goddess, Oishin, you needn't have done that."

I saved it, he repeated, and fumbled for something under his pillow, turning his body awkwardly to reach it. When he finally produced the lacquered box, he insisted upon shoving it into my free hand.

Tears choked me, spilling down my face, plugging my nose. "Why? Why, out of everything? Lady…"

"Eee'caush. Yeea … you. Are. Ny. Fuh-lend."

He fumbled again for a small slate under the sheets drawn around his chest, and used chalk to write: *You are my friend.*

ONE OF THE aranfox healers told me Solma was in the royal tent on the other end of the war camp. The tent was a sizeable oblong affair, layers upon layers of cool-toned silks, with its filigree and tassels and baubles all broken, tattered, and singed now. But when I entered, it was not Solma who I found first.

The moment I emerged from the flaps, Eytine—*Orlaith*—jumped up from a folding chair and crushed me into an embrace. Which I returned, of course, despite the jolt of agony that shot through my right arm. "Careful with me," I murmured into the crown of the shorter fae's head.

She pulled away swiftly and scanned me for any other injury. "I didn't want to leave you behind," she said with a scratchy throat. "Erivon had to force me. He's never forced me to do anything before. He *shouted* at me."

Despite it all, her eyes shone with excitement, and I exhaled a slight laugh, too. "Where is he? And Faelon?"

Orlaith tossed her head toward an annex concealed by semitranslucent curtains. "Sleeping. You ought to see them. Curled up like a pair of kittens. He took to Erivon straight away ... peas and pods and all that." Her smile, exhausted, was nonetheless warm and cozy, but something was off in the tone of her voice. As if she implied that, in contrast, Faelon had *not* taken to her. But of course she was concealing her true thoughts and feelings on the matter.

"I think he's quite close with Nevidaea," I said impotently. My eyes fell on what she'd left behind in her folding chair. I recognized the fluffy fabric and embroidery. "Your quilt! You saved it."

Orlaith flushed. "Erivon brought it when he came through. We thought maybe... I don't know what we thought. In any case, it's not done yet."

"How's the boy doing?"

"Decent. It took hours of panic and crying to reassure him what happened to the bilé wasn't his fault, my poor baby. I only wish there was more we could've done..."

We were silent a while, staring at the quilt together. At last, I said, "I watched after you through his eyes. I felt all he felt. He cares for you. He wants to know you. It's just ... it must be confusing for him, you know what I mean?"

She shrugged noncommittally, obviously hinting that I should drop it. If she still had her wings, they'd be twitching up a storm. That thought alone made my ears droop with regret. All she said was, "Thank you, Mave. And I am so sorry. For everything."

"I know. I understand."

With that said, I relieved her. The particulars of our family drama could be worked out later. Faelon was with us, and safe, and that was what mattered.

"Have we heard anything of Gaius or any of the quillies?"

She cleared her throat. "We aren't too far from that fort, Alopex, but they haven't engaged with anything other than the fomori. Retreated into their shells like turtles, it seems."

"And the fomori, are they attacking often? Do they seem ... organized?"

"Organized, no." She scoffed. "I dunno that they're *feral*—they seem to have a goal, and maybe even rank—but who or *what*ever gives their orders doesn't seem to have much focus. It's all ... erratic. Which makes their attacks rather ingenious in a way, but ultimately not as ineffective."

I smiled hearing her speak like a tactician. Every day, she seemed to gain a little more of Eytine back.

"Attacking, yes. Persistently. Every so often this thing happens —we've taken to calling it moonscorching—where the moon seems to bleed into the sky, the temperature rises abominably, and the fomori become utterly frantic. They concentrate in waves and strike. Between the rangers and the ballistas, we can pare down their hordes so they aren't so frightful by the time they get to the walls, but Goddess Beneath. And then there's the mist."

"Right," I muttered. "How do we fight a war against something that exploits even the most minor injury?"

"Sergia's demented inoculation might help us here, in fact. The druids and fae apothecaries are looking into crafting something similar, something that might fortify the blood against the mist, and perhaps whatever other emergent corruption comes from this. Using willing fae donors, this time." She sneered and flicked a strand of short hair from her face, turning toward a ratty map spread on the nearby table. "Someday, we might even be able to reverse the blight. For now, though, I'm trying not to get my hopes shattered."

The way her emotions twisted up within her was as obvious at the magic in the air. I hesitated before saying, "It's not your fault, my Orlaith. And whatever he did to you, I'll kill—"

With a violent flick, another curtained area opened, and the Guardian I'd come to see stepped into the room, followed by Menecon. The small seneschal—although, maybe they weren't a seneschal any longer, seeing as how there was no palace—bowed to us before hurrying out of the tent. Solma bowed, too, albeit shallowly.

There was an air of tension around her, as though she were a bubble about to burst, but I'd already wasted too much time.

So, I asked without preamble, "Where do I find Hiberos?"

Solma's brow twitched, her flat, broad nose crinkling at the corners. "Is that all you have to say to me? *Princess*." She took a few heavy steps closer, cloven hooves pounding the rugs, to loom over us. "The Underland is destroyed, and all you can think about is *him*. Typical of you, but I hoped you would see the error of your selfishness."

I was speechless. It was Orlaith who responded, her tone more imperious than I'd ever heard it. "I like it better when you don't speak, Commander. Care to walk that one back, or are you set on the unwise decision to bully my sister?"

"Bully? Moon's mercy. You're no better," Solma replied flatly. "All that time. All that effort to bring you home from the Goneland, after you two *chose* to run into the sunset. You *chose* to leave, telling no one where to find you, thinking of nobody but yourselves, and we were left to pick up the pieces."

"I never *asked* to be found..." I began.

"A thousand years. A thousand years I served in silence while Erivon and Hiberos acted as though some terrible injustice had been done. But it was your *choice*, all of it. Yet still, when you *did* come back? I trusted you." She jabbed her chin at both of us. "I trusted you to fall in line like the rest of us and lead our people. But *you*." She glared at me. "*You* couldn't leave it alone."

Orlaith flushed nearly emerald. "Myson—"

"Your *son*," Solma snapped. "Your *people*. Why did you come back at all? Why did you come back when you weren't prepared to leave any of it behind?" Her voice was rising now. "And Hiberos. Bloody Hiberos. You couldn't leave well enough alone, Ashling, even knowing how the story ended. You *knew*, and now look." She stepped to the door and wrenched one of the flaps aside, letting in the scorching light of the blood moon. "All you had to do was follow orders. All you had to do was maintain even the *barest trace* of self-control, and you couldn't. Now the Underland is *gone. Gone!*"

She flicked the flap down and rounded on me, the bellows of a thousand years of frustration stoking her fury. "Do you understand that? Can you possibly understand that? Can you conceive, in your tiny, selfish little mind, that you have *utterly ruined* what Gealach gave her life to protect?"

"I— It wasn't—"

"Protect the Gate." She enunciated each shouted word. "Seal the fractures. Live in luxury for eternity. *That was all you had to do.* After *everything* Mother Moon feared and loved and sacrificed—"

"I never asked for any of it!" Finally, I slammed my hand on the table, raising my voice over hers. "I never asked for you to erect the Gates, I never asked for Hiberos to find me, I never asked anyone to wait for me. Never asked. Never asked! I'm sorry you went through all that trouble to end up with someone like me. I'm sorry. I really, sincerely am. But I can only be who and what I am. *This* was where I was happy, all the time, *this* was where I belonged. I knew it from the beginning, and I *told* you, I told you all. No one would listen! You were all in such a rage to have Ashling back, no one ever asked me how I felt about bloody dying and coming back from the dead. No one ever asked me how I felt coming back in a corpse's body and having all these expectations thrust upon me.

"And further-*fecking*-more—" I jabbed a finger at her. "I never—*none of us ever*—asked to be cocooned in cotton wool and nursed for eternity. Losing one's soulbind is damned shattering, *ask me how I know*, but the only person bound by that grief should be *me*. Gealach's pain and grief, her protectiveness, her divine retribution and everything that's come from it, it isn't my burden to bear, nor *any* of ours. I should've been able to leave when I wanted. We should've been open to exploring the world beyond ours. Instead, I had to sneak off in secret with my sister.

"And you want to know something? I don't regret the death Ashling chose. *Yes*, of course my life could have been easier. Yes, of course I could have existed near Hiberos, even if I never got to be with him. But as it happens, I don't regret being born here. I *love* Éire. I love this land, dammit! I love the people, I love their ways, I *love* all the beautiful and grotesque things I've been witness to. I love being hungry, tired, bereaved, and broken —'cause then I can be satisfied, energized, joyous, and *whole*. And goddesses and fomori and the Beneath itself be damned, if I had to die a thousand times over to see this war through and protect all of those things, I'd do it in a heartbeat."

For a few moments, the tent was silent save for the muffled sounds of Faelon and Erivon stirring in the annex. Then Solma inclined her head, nostrils flaring, and ground out, "No. You won't die a thousand times over. The veil is gone. There is no other world. Nowhere for you to respite. There will be no more returning from the dead, for any of us. Not anymore."

Though Orlaith stiffened at my side, for some reason—and wholly unexpectedly—I felt a weight lift from my shoulders. Honestly, the prospect of living forever or dying in perpetuity sounded like hell.

I ventured another step toward Solma. "You and the fae may not understand it yet, but death is not your foe. Those evil bastards who ply it, they may be. But death is what makes life mean *anything*. The peoples here live and learn and speak and build and fuck not because there's something waiting for us after it but because there may well not be. Because it *ends*. And because we *know* it will end.

"This place"—I gestured widely—"this place you spent a millennium avoiding, this place you were so afraid would taint your perfect world. This place and these people are worth something. They're worth everything, not despite their fleeting time but *because* of it. And I'm not telling you to shut up and accept it all straight away, and you can call me selfish and small-minded if you please, but don't blame me for Gealach's cosmic tantrum. Creating me does not give her ownership over me, having once loved Hiberos does not give her ownership over *him*, and having lost her home does not give her the right to take mine from me.

"And so, let me ask you again," I growled, toe to hoof with Solma now. "Where. The fuck. Is. Hiberos?"

Solma's face was a portrait of fury, grief, and agonizing heartbreak. "You already know where he is."

I closed my eyes slowly.

So, he was in the Mournful Palace. And I knew who had him, too.

23

As I left the tent, my argument with Solma haunted me. I could not stop thinking about Gealach choosing to hurt us all rather than let go. Could not stop thinking about her protecting us from the world only to thrust us into it when some of her children didn't live exactly as she hoped. I hated to think I had a creator like that—but I knew, also, her behavior didn't come from nowhere.

I thought all the way back to when Hiberos had first told me about Gealach and the Horned One, when I'd watched their tragedy play out in the pattern of moths' dust. The images had disturbed me then. To see someone love so fully and deeply and then lose everything was ... not easy. And when I thought about it that way, staring up at the burning moon, I could imagine how she had gotten to this point.

After all, I'd lost everything once, too.

In my memory of Gealach, the only one I could retrieve, she'd said, *The only way to keep what you love is to bind it into the pattern. Stitch it so tightly the world cannot unravel it.* The way the Great Corruption had unraveled her husband, the way the Shift had unraveled her world. Yet here it all was, unraveled again. And here I was again, far away from Hiberos, praying that a goddess who hated me would keep him safe.

Soon, prepared or not, I'd have to journey into her labyrinth with little to no idea of how I would pass the trials awaiting me.

Spirals. Everything was spirals. *The pattern.* A cycle I could not seem to break.

A cycle...

I stopped dead in the center of the camp. A verse came to mind, one I had read what felt like *so* long ago, before all this.

> When stars are still and breath is done,
> When blood is spilt to wake the sun,
> The wheel shall turn, the thread unspun,
> The final cycle is begun.

The final cycle.

The stars had stilled. I'd spilled my blood. The sun had awakened. Now...

Now if I could only remember the remaining two stanzas of the verse. When I'd mentioned it to Hiberos, he'd said we would figure it out later. But then we'd traveled to Gallive and had that night together, that night it took me two weeks to wake from. After that, and with Orlaith and Faelon in danger, the inscription simply had not crossed my mind.

I had to know. Had to uncover the next step of the final cycle, if I ever wanted to be free of it.

Finding whatever remained of that ruin and learning the rest of the verse should be my first move. As much as I wished to rush into the labyrinth and save Hiberos like I'd promised, going up against a goddess required more than a hard head and iron will. Or, as he'd kindly called it, "bravery."

Still, I shouldn't make the journey alone, especially not with my arm in the state it was. There were plenty of fighters to choose from, but I needed to choose wisely. My companion would be putting their life on the line, and I'd already put enough people in danger in my pursuit of Hiberos. Solma would be a sound choice, given her Guardian knowledge about fomori ruins, but after our spat, she'd hate me for turning right back around and asking her a favor. Plus, if we discovered that the answer to my problem was to *kill* Gealach, Solma would probably sooner off *me*.

There was one another person who might know about those ruins. In the annals of my memory, I recalled sitting across from Eamon as told me about the forgotten faoladh ritual. He'd said the ruins were pitch black limestone carved with runes in an ancient dialect. The black ruins in the Underland and the black ruins in the Goneland were of the same make, and they both lead to the Beneath.

I needed a wolfkerne. I needed the *duskwarden*.

The wolfkerne niche of camp was desolate—no wolfkernes, just closed tent flaps and druids milling about. When I asked after Ferghal, a nearby group of lads directed me to a corner of the camp where the wolfkerne's tents converged with a clearing filled with barrel-top wagons. They were a sight nicer than the tents, painted in bright colors and lovingly maintained, some of them with their own tents and some without. The folk sitting inside them were busy cooking, sewing, laundering, patching crockery, and tinkering, while those outside sang and played fiddle. Looked like Ferghal had managed to get his mother's people to come up from Twaintomb. Apart from slightly distinct features, they looked just the same as any Éirin, and I hoped they were being treated as such.

Bridging the wagons and the wolfkernes together was a medium-sized four-post tent decorated with wolf pelts. On the side, someone had painted an image of a wolf's skull with stag's antlers. I didn't recognize the insignia, but I knew this must be the duskwarden's tent.

I entered without announcing myself and was shocked to find it nearly pitch black within. The only light came from a candle on a small table, which was situated beside a cot shoved deep into the farthest corner of the tent. The little flame barely illuminated the hulking form tossing and turning there.

"Ferghal?" I whispered. The interior of the tent felt off somehow, as though I'd entered the den of a dangerous beast. But this was my friend. "All right in here?"

Ferghal snapped to look over his shoulder and growled, foaming. As I took a step closer, I realized he was in a bizarre, half-shifted form. His face was somewhat elongated, twisted wolfishly; his hair and sidewhiskers were wilder and bushier than ever; his already impressive physique was bulging, resembling more his wolf-shape but with a bit less hair. *A bit.* He was still hairy down to his knuckles, and each finger of his strong hands ended in a curved claw.

As I shuffled closer, the light caught the pits of his eyes, and they flashed red. It was the redness that finally stopped me from approaching.

The blood moon. It had to be. I recalled how the faoladh had recoiled and fled from its searing glow.

"It's all right, Ferghal," I said in what I hoped was a soothing tone. "It's Mave. Just Mave."

His twisted brow smoothed, but in the next second, it was drawn again, this time in pain. Like a pup, he writhed and whimpered in discomfort. Uncertain of what else to do, I hurried to him and knelt by his bedside, grabbing a cloth from a bowl of water left there and placing it on his forehead.

The cool cloth seemed to relieve him if only a little, enough that he was able to properly focus on my face. His pupils dilated, and he loosed a string of curses that would make a drunken man blush.

"Couldn't agree more," I responded, and hovered my hand over the cloth, wondering if I could cool it with lunar magic. Imagine my surprise when, instead of the soothing blue I'd grown accustomed to, my fingers sparked orange and filled the tent with sweltering heat.

Ferghal and I cried out at the same time, and I leapt back, closing my fist to trap the wild flame. Snarling, the wolfkerne turned sharply in bed and covered his face as if to hide from me.

Lady dammit. It was not lunar power coursing through my veins now but the cursed blood moon. "I'm sorry, I didn't..."

Was the blood moon affecting me in particular, or was Gealach singling me out?

"Bitch," I muttered, and shook out my hand, approaching Ferghal again. "I'm sorry. I won't touch you."

He glared but ultimately was too preoccupied with his pain to lash out. "The moon..."

I knelt by his bedside again. "The wolfkernes' tents are all closed and quiet. Are you all...?"

"Fecking useless. Yea." Between words, his breath was heavy. "The moment the light touches us, it burns as badly as if we'd been out in the sun for hours, y'know what I mean? And when the burn becomes unbearable, it's even worse." He growled out another string of curses and dragged his hands down his face. "Half my men lost their minds and ran off into the woods. Eamon should be here. I an' good enough for this, I failed. We should be up and defending our people, oh, hell. It's what we're made for. Instead we're abed like ailing old women."

"Shh, it's all right. Relax." I wet his cloth again, then tossed my head in the direction of the wagons. "Who're them? Walking people, obviously, but..."

"My mam's band, and some of their friends. I remember her telling me they spent springs up at Twaintomb, so I thought I'd go look into it, see if I didn't have any good will with them."

"The other wolfkernes said as much. And it seems like good news."

He barely managed to lift one corner of his mouth. "They remembered Mam and Da. The old ladies even remembered me as a babe. They were..." His eyes went round. "They were happy. To see me. And good job we brought them on when we did. They'd barely reached the front when everything went to hell. I don't want to think what would've happened to them if they were out there alone."

"Are they any good at fighting?"

"Nah," he huffed. "But they're damned tenacious. I swear, the Empire could sweep through here and do away with all of us, and they'd still find a way to carry on their stories and songs an'at. We need people like *that*. Fighting can be taught. And if they don't want to fight, well, I'm sure you saw their chores. Sewing, tinkering. There's plenty else to do. No war was ever won with arrows and steel alone."

I squeezed his hand briefly. "I told you. Your people run from nothing. Whoever put that in your head was a ... tool," I said, laughing at the old-fashioned curse word. "And not a very useful one."

Ferghal went quiet. It was as if he'd never considered that the idea had come from somewhere else, not from inside himself. "Huh. I guess it was ... some Tirconnell lad come down for harvest, a thousand years ago, it seems like. But..."

"Words stick with you. I understand." Then I tilted my head the other way, indicating the tent wall. "I meant to ask, the insignia on your tent..."

"It's new. D'you like it?" Ferghal shifted position and threw an arm over his eyes. "I figured the wolfkernes should have one at last, to distinguish ourselves from those bloody fecking man-eaters ... with their dirty feet and sweaty little shit-arse hands," he added under his breath.

I stifled a laugh, only slightly successfully. "I like it. Looks nice."

"Thanks. I drew it."

Affection filled me. But I hadn't come here just to chat. Gnawing on my lower lip, I looked him up and down. "Well, I was coming here to ask you if you'd accompany me on a ... personal quest. Hiberos is missing. I have a lead, but I can see you're in no fit state."

"Ugh. Just stab me in the gut, why don't you, kat? Have it over with." He moved his arm, though his eyes remained squeezed shut. "The high king is coming, too, and I'm not even going to be upright to meet him."

Now *that* got my ears quirked. High King Alasdair was constantly busy dealing with Albion across the sea, raiders from the north, not to mention the Aquilans in Westminia; he hadn't come to Sallach ever that I could remember. "I suppose the veil sundering and spitting out an entirely new fae kingdom *would* be the thing to finally get him up here."

"Aye. The commander of his Gallowglass fell in battle. Doesn't happen every day." Ferghal sighed and finally looked at me. "But it's not only Sallach. The whole province is withering. It's fucked beyond belief, from here to Gallive ... up the coast, even into the boglands. Every inch of it is that slimy red ... shit. It's all gone to hell. Civilians fleeing, refugees piling into the towns and cities, fomori pounding at the gates. Folks who manage to avoid getting killed by fomori are getting sick from the putrid air. And that mist is everywhere, getting into anything it can." My misery and horror must have been apparent, for he shook his head in pity. "I didn't know you didn't know or I'd've told you sooner."

All that work, all the sacrifice, all the lives lost trying to keep Co Cuanacht untouched, and now the whole northwestern reach of Éire was blighted. When it came to the core, cosmic tantrum or not, it was my fault, wasn't it?

Hiberos may love me for defying gods, but look where that had got my people. I had caused more destruction than the Aquilan Empire.

I had to make it right. Now.

"Listen," I said, wetting Ferghal's cloth again and pressing it to his forehead, "I have to go. You rest, all right? I'll see you."

Before he could protest, I turned on my heel and pushed through the tent flaps. The oppressive heat of the blood moon was on me the instant I stepped into the camp. The damned moon. At this point, I don't know who I blamed more: Gealach for lashing out, or myself for pushing her to this point. Either way, I no longer felt like I deserved the help of my friends.

Solma was right after all. I'd broken our lands. Me. And so, I should be the one to fix them.

Shouting from somewhere nearby drew my attention. Immediately, I recognized the distinct sound of Éirin spoken in an Aquilan accent. To my left, none other than Councilor Uaine burst from a tent and hurried toward the yelling, Conan at his heels. They must have come up from Gallive at some point. I followed, my stride fleet enough that I came abreast of them within a few steps. Conan jumped and honked in accusation, as if to say, *What are you doing here? And why didn't you bring me any acorns?*

We went through the inner eastern gate and climbed a scaffolding to look over the palisade. Sure enough, there, on the other side of the outer gate, stood a band of legionaries. They were dressed in plainclothes and unmarked leather armor, which had allowed them to approach the camp without getting shot dead. Of course, the moment they opened their mouths, it was clear who they were.

"Please, we begging of you," their apparent leader called up. "We are have trying return to Fort Alopex, but they shoot at us, leave us for dead."

"Oh, really?" responded one of our rangers. "Have you thought about cryin' yourself a river and using a raft to float back up to Béaleire?" he asked, using the Éirin name for Westminia.

The legionary's brow twisted in confusion as he tried to decipher what was said—clearly, the band had put all their collective Éirin together for their barely intelligible pitch and could not quite understand what was being said. "Please," he said again. "We have no food, no more arrows, no place to sleep. We die every day. *Quaseremente*, please, let us in before the moon bleed."

He must mean the moonscorch. Some of the watchmen sneered and spat, while others looked around, trying to figure out what should be done. Yet others considered the men before them with varying degrees of pity. When heads began to turn to Uaine, I realized that, after Muiri, who I hadn't yet seen, he was probably the closest thing we had to a chief.

But when I turned to him, too, he was looking at me.

I frowned. He wanted *me* to decide? "Don't. Don't ask me."

"I trust you," he said without missing a beat. "I was a conscript, once, remember? You and I are the only ones here who've dealt with legionaries up close that way."

Conan gave an indignant snort, lest his own experiences be forgotten.

"And Conan," Uaine added dryly. "Well. What do you think?"

Pursing my lips, I scanned the group of quillies. Mostly young, with a couple older men among them. They surely looked hungry, and their dwindling quivers told me they weren't lying about needing arrows. No women or children. Probably a scouting group that had gotten caught outside the fort at the wrong time, which aligned with Orlaith's assessment that the Aquilans were turtling. They wouldn't even let in their own.

Merciless demons, all of them.

So why should I treat these ones any different?

For all we knew, these very men may have been responsible for the deaths of comrades and loved ones. Honestly, if they were scouts from Fort Alopex, they probably were. No one wanted men like that around.

On the other hand, I'd never heard of quillies bothering to ask Éirins for help, so they must truly be desperate, perhaps willing to change their minds about us.

But then, whose fault was it that they couldn't survive in the land they'd stolen? Not ours.

We could give them supplies and send them on their way. Then we'd not have their deaths on our conscience. On the other hand, what if they took our arrows and used them to kill other Éirins, someplace else?

Ideally, they'd take our arrows and kill on our side. We were low on manpower, and I was about to leave. Isolated and fractured as we were, turning away any help would be foolish.

My stomach hurt.

Why? I'd killed so many legionaries, probably hundreds at this point. They were monsters. Merciless. If our roles were reversed, these men would slaughter me in an instant, and "being the bigger person" seemed like a scheme designed to keep us weak.

Perhaps all I was made for was destruction. Perhaps that was my fate.

Sending them away would be more than they deserved.

On the other hand...

If I went on like this, I'd never make a decision. The men were waiting, and I was running out of other hands. I swallowed and pressed two fingers to the center of my forehead. There was no easy answer. I didn't even know if there was a right answer. And that irked me.

Sod it.

At last, I spoke to the leader of their posse in Aquilan, with Uaine translating for the others. "All right, here are your options. You can join us and start at the bottom, indentured servants of sorts. Work your arses off to right the wrongs you've done, till all this is over. People may not ever forgive you. They probably won't ever accept you. You might die alone. But maybe you'll make up for what you've done. And maybe—*maybe*—you will survive this war. Or, you can turn around and leave empty handed, and die, for all I care."

The leader of the band seemed wary. "You want us to ... join the Éirins? Fully?"

"Yes. You're either in, or you're out."

No one had expected that. He opened his mouth, closed it, glanced at his men, then eventually asked, "Is it true fae cannot tell a lie?"

"You had better hope so, I guess." Crossing my arms, I held up the same two fingers. "You've got two minutes to decide."

For a second, the quillies were stunned, but soon, they turned inward and huddled into a murmuring circle. As I stepped back, predictably, some of the Éirins were grumbling their dissent. Yet others watched the quillies, intrigued. Uaine breathed a sigh of relief and nodded to me.

"Don't approve of me yet," I muttered. "It's not as if I'm doing it out of the goodness of my heart."

Honestly, I expected them to be too proud to accept my offer. After all, why would a red-blooded Aquilan want to associate with barbarians, let alone live with them? When the quillies turned back to the gate and hollered up, most if not all of us peered over the palisade with curiosity. Some of the legionaries looked relieved, while others struggled to mask their disapproval of the situation.

"All right," he announced in Aquilan. "We agree to your terms. Shall we come in and draw up a contract?"

As I descended the scaffold, one of the watchmen snarled, "Lie down with dogs and you'll get ticks," though the barb was half-hearted and exhausted.

"I know," I sighed. "Trust me, I know."

Uaine took it from there, and I returned to camp. No doubt there would be troublemakers among those legionaries, but they would be swiftly dealt with. Now, it was time for me to retrieve my weapons and armor ... and somehow figure out how to don them and wield them with a badly injured arm.

I was about halfway to Muiri's tent when I registered the persistent grunting sound behind me. I turned to find Conan at my heels, rooting around in the wilted clover. It was as if he didn't even notice that the world around him was ravaged; he was simply looking for something to eat, as always.

I glanced from my arm sling to him. A giant pig was a better companion than no companion at all, I reckoned.

"Aye, Conan."

He looked up with a quickness, ears perked and neck fat wiggling.

"Do you want to go into the woods with me again?"

24

The realm beyond the war camp was utterly destroyed. Every inch of meadow, moss, and sedge was discolored and oozing putrid fluid. The trees were split or otherwise twisted, their leaves brown, orange, and red without the soothing scent or cool breeze of autumn. The few human structures left intact were abandoned and overrun with fomori. Knowing their potential to swarm, I steered clear of those I spotted and ran from those that came upon me. Conan was a fair distraction for those we could not outrun. In their quest for bacon, they never saw me coming.

And then there were the Aquilans.

It quickly became obvious that a huge portion of the Eighth Legion, upon being expelled from the Underland, were wandering the wasteland of Sallach. Not surprising given the chaos of the sundering and the Aquilans' ladder-pulling, but I would expect them to have established their own camps or survivor colonies like the beggars at the war camp. Instead, they roamed the countryside at all hours. Conan and I observed them as we edged ever closer toward Geatacoill. Mostly, they roamed in packs. Their eyes and veins glowed as their stolen fae blood turned against them; the largest of them were hulking brutes with gleaming red crystals jutting from their skin—as though Faelon's blood had hardened in their marrow and stabbed out of them like glass.

They hadn't known the long-term effects after all, it seemed.

Without the use of my right arm, I wouldn't be able to take on one of those beasts, and I certainly wouldn't be able to take on a whole pack. Honestly, even if I had both hands, I did not know how well I'd fare. Even the smaller thornbloods, as I'd taken to calling them, were all bloated muscle and heaving breaths and bloody crimson shards. Luckily, the roving bands seemed to steer clear of one another, so I shadowed one for a while, creeping over heath and through bracken.

When they finally stopped to rest, it was at a ruin I was shocked to recognize. Joa and Eilliv's public house, except it looked as though it had been dropped from a great height. The trees around it bowed and split, dribbling sickened sap.

In the Underland, their place had been at the very edge of the Lunar Kingdom. In my mind's eye, I envisioned a map of the Underland. If we were at the southwestern edge of the Lunar Kingdom, then relatively, the heartgrove—and the slab with the verse I sought—was still a long way away, past the palace and through wilderness. But I was closer, and closer was good.

The longer I watched the thornbloods, it struck me that they moved like wildlife. Like a herd of deer, the largest and most impressive of them surrounded by the smaller ones. They sat in the grass, surveying their environs for the smallest hint of a threat. I had to be mindful of how the wind shifted and shift accordingly to keep them off my scent trail.

I could almost hear Hiberos's voice: *Oh, my huntress. You want to strike like a panther, but not every beast can be chased and felled in a sprint.* Well, look at the use I was getting out of that knowledge now.

As if in answer, a moon moth appeared from seemingly thin air and perched on one of my errant curls. Its wings of glassy jade were shot through with delicate capillaries of blood orange, but it fluttered just the same as ever, leaving tiny specks of luminescent dust on my shoulder.

"You should tell your master I'm very cross with him," I whispered, offering it my finger to perch upon instead.

The little moth cleaned its antennae.

A familiar, gurgling screech drew my attention to the ruined public house. Fomori staggered from the tree line: a lanky one riding an emaciated horse, the cracked husks of civilians, a handful of those vicious little beans, and half-formed bodies dragging themselves across the sticky earth. I expected them to clash with the thornbloods, but the thornbloods simply raised their heads and waited for their approach. It wasn't until they were within reach that the corrupted legionaries jumped on them, tearing them apart with their hands and teeth before feasting on them raw.

The fomori did not fight back. They simply waited for their turn to be devoured.

The thornbloods were sponsored by Gealach, then, if not under her direct control. Her new creation. And she was sustaining them with the flesh of her firstborns.

Deep in my stomach, I felt a strange pang of sadness for the fomori.

After another hour of my vigil over the thornbloods, the wind shifted, blowing roughly northeast. It was the perfect opportunity to find the heartgrove, which I hoped lay in that direction, and so I —and Conan, and our lone moth companion—snuck that way.

The Underland had not been very large, but I walked for over an hour trying to find any trace of the heartgrove's remains. Clearly, being thrust into reality had changed things, stretched them out and rearranged them. By hour three, the wind had shifted again, but I was so tired my mind no longer worked. Even in my thoughts, I spoke in tongues; the remains of Paik's sedative, my healing injury, walking in the stifling heat, and time had pushed me so past exhausted that it actually *hurt* to close my eyes.

When we came across an abandoned hut east of where we'd started, it was Conan who encouraged me to stop there, squealing and shoving his cold, wet nose into my shins.

As if in question, I glanced at the moth, and it fluttered

beyond the hut's half-collapsed entrance. I thrust myself into the cool darkness of it and slumped to the floor, but I still could not sleep. My vision juddered and throbbed and crawled with ants, yet I could not, could not, could *not* close my eyes.

It wasn't until the moon moth flew above me in a rhythmic pattern, coating me in a fine layer of its dust, that my muscles released. With a final murmur— "No dreams, please"—I faded into a deep sleep.

◦⋅⊃⋅⊃⋅☙⋅☾⋅☾◦

I WOKE under the oculus of a quiet chamber, bathed in the cool blue moonlight I so desperately missed.

With a groan, I lifted my upper half, casting about in confusion. It was a chamber of black limestone, the recesses completely consumed by darkness. At the head of the room was a throne of the same stone, its surface a maze of cracks. And sat upon the throne, wearing a crown of thorns and roses rather than holly, was Hiberos.

It was obvious from the moment it started that this was a dream, and that though I felt things in my body, this place was not real. Nonetheless, I knew in my bones that the Guardian I saw before me was Hiberos and not an illusion or construct. Pitch-black blood stained his hide, from the ragged gash in the center of his chest, down his front, between his thighs, and down his legs in rivulets. The wound still lay open, waiting for its heart to return.

Seeing him brought an ache deep in my shattered arm that I could not explain, as though he was a dead limb of mine coming back to life. Ears filled my eyes.

Gaze never faltering, the battered Guardian rose from the throne and came to the edge of the dais, looming over me. His scent enveloped me: sun-warmed moss, blackberries, cedar and thyme, and a new, subtle hint of his blood. He offered a hand, but when I slipped mine into his, rather than pulling me up he brought himself down. Down to my level, caging me against the floor with his arms.

"Don't cry, my rose." He brushed away my tears with his lips and the tip of his nose. "We promised we would find each other, did we not?"

He took my mouth. Slow, tender, running his tongue along my bottom lip and making me moan oh so softly. I did not have the wherewithal to stop him and ask questions, though I had many, chief among them being *how are you here?*

Fortunately, he seemed to read my mind. "She cannot control me fully. I have power, too."

I moaned again and melted into his embrace. Desire pounded between us like a shared heartbeat—not just lust but a yearning to be one, to breathe the same air again, to finally be free. Everything throbbed, from the heat between my thighs to the agony in my chest. I grasped for him, as if gathering him to me would pull him back into the real world with me.

"It isn't fair," I whispered, tears quivering on the ends of my lashes. "Just when we begin... She didn't have the ending she wanted, so she destroys anything we could ever be? If I could just..."

"As long as one of us lives, Mave, we will strive for each other. And when we are both gone, we'll be together in oblivion."

I spat out a rare sob. "But I want *more* for us than that. We deserve more. The more I know of you, the more I want to know. I know why I chose you, Hiberos. I *know* why I chose you."

He stilled, stroking my cheeks reverently with his thumbs. "Chose me?"

Closing my eyes, I brought our foreheads together, and through the bond this dream gave us, I showed him my memory of Gealach. The ashen thread, the needle, the shroud. When I pulled away, his eyes were wide, his face slack and innocent.

"You..." He blinked, trying to collect himself. "You did not bind me. You had the opportunity, and you..."

I hid my face. I couldn't see him for the tears, anyway. "I thought I did the right thing. I only wanted you to be mine if we both willed it. But now ... now I see that I might have freed you. All this is my fault."

With a reverent shiver, Hiberos held me at arm's length. "You did the exact right thing. That sort of decision—it is what made me love Ashling, and it is what makes me love Mave even more."

We fell into each other hard, our breath, our lips, our tears conjoined as one desperate prayer—not to the goddess but to each other. With my fingertips I skimmed the edge of his wound and bypassed it to find the new carvings across his chest. At the time, I'd simply worked freely, letting the knife choose its path through his hide, but now, I was thirsty to memorize the pattern. To memorize him.

Soon, my wandering fingers were joined by my lips.

In turn, his hands roved over my body, squeezing the curve of my ass, the muscle of my haunch, the swell of my breasts. He cupped me between the legs, pressed firmly, and I ground myself into his palm, catching his ear between my teeth and biting down.

I made to pull away, but he gripped the nape of my neck and held me in place. "Bite me again. Harder."

My heart pattered against his solid chest like a skipping stone against a glassy lake. I wrangled the tip of his ear with my tongue and bit down again, harder, sucking but never letting go.

Hiberos shuddered, hips stirring against mine in a rhythm so fluid I wondered if he even noticed he was moving. Together, we moved like the waters of the river marking his arms. The frost crack at the apex of his thighs began to part for me. As we moved against each other—his mouth hot, wet, open, teeth scraping my throat—I thrust a hand between us and slid my finger over the crack, trying to coax out the organ hidden within.

A purr came from deep in his chest, and the cock I sought unfurled heavily into my palm.

He moved to shove my thighs apart, desperate to bury himself in the center of me, desperate to get to the part where we dug our nails and teeth into each other and fucked like animals.

But I squeezed him and breathed a purr of my own. "Easy, Master. Every ounce of my patience, I learned from you."

I could lie here for hours like this, simply stroking him, skimming his thick root against my clit and my deepest heat.

Once again sensing my thoughts, he shivered, relaxed into me, and let me play with him at my leisure. Luxurious, deep moans—punctuated with that clicking growl at the back of his throat—filled the darkened chamber. Yes. *Yes.* Everything about him was utterly inhuman, from the sounds he made to his scent to the weight of him on top of me, yet he was perfect. As if he'd been made for me.

Already, he hummed through my veins; after tonight, I wanted to feel him in every inch of me, to be made of nothing but his intoxicating magic. I wanted to walk the earth marked to my marrow. For our union to be made known in my every step. For the humans to look at me and know this remnant of the Sun God had driven my body to its breaking point ... but not before giving me pleasure great enough to drive the stars apart.

"*The root of the root...*" He pressed his fat cockhead to my entrance and grazed a thumb over my clit. "*And the bud of the bud.*"

I whined. "Not that poem. Last time you recited it, I lost you."

"*Here is the deepest secret nobody knows,*" he whispered as he teased the swollen tip in before drawing it out and back up through my folds.

My eyes rolled back in my head. He, too, was content to be here for hours, slowly unraveling me. Lady, I had never felt so safe, so cradled, so relaxed. My body eased into our rhythm as if sinking into a warm bath.

Forever. I wanted to do this forever.

And then a discordant note interrupted the resonance between us—and like the white of an eye with a burst blood vessel, the pale, pale moon above filled up with red.

"She's here," Hiberos whispered, but he did not stop. Instead, he pressed me to him and rolled us so I was on top. "Whatever she shows you, whatever she says, stay with me."

She could try to deter me. Try to shame me. Try to claim him. Try to blame the destruction of Éire all on me. She might even have a point. But no matter what she said, neither of us belonged to her. No matter what she said, all the horror was her doing, and hers alone.

I would not listen to her. There was nothing she could hurt me with.

In the next moment, I was proven wrong.

Because appearing in the throne, as naked as the day he was born—Gaius.

25

Here I was, taunted again. Guardian. Tormentor. And in the middle, me.

At first, Gaius was still, eyes closed, head bowed and chin tucked against his chest. Red seethed up his arms, pulsing in time with the beat of his heart.

A heart that could be seen.

It was radiant, shining in front of his ribcage, the layers of flesh and blood and muscle dimming its glow and rendering it a pinkish scarlet. But it was no human heart. A flowering fruit, a nucleus of lunar magic bound in silvery twigs and veins.

The heart that should be in me.

The organ gave a sudden pulse, and red spread all through the veins in Gaius's neck. He woke with a jolt, a gasp caught in his throat, his hands gripping the throne's cracked arms. His brow was creased, his lips parted, genuine confusion lending him an almost innocent expression. He did not even wear his eye-patch, his right eye a flesh-colored socket, his left cast in the red of the blood moon. As he jerked his head up and around, trying to get his bearings, he blinked, those thick, dark lashes fanning out over his tanned cheeks. With horror and confusion, I realized I could not decipher whether he was an illusion or truly here with us.

The blood, the heart. Had he twisted himself so close to fae that Gealach held dominion over him, could summon and wield him like a weapon?

It took him a moment to spot us. When he did, the innocence on his face vanished, replaced by something dark, hungering, all-encompassing. He dug his fingers into the arms of the throne, every muscle from his knuckles to his neck throbbing.

He was not in control, yet he could not help but look at me like prey.

Gealach's power slithered between the three of us, and suddenly, I felt everything. Hiberos's pleasure, his possessiveness. Gaius's arousal, his jealousy. My clit throbbed in time with both their cocks. Hiberos's was under me, solid and warm, my cunt hugging perfectly the muscle and veins of his shaft—but Gaius filled my vision, his breath coming in choppy gasps, his manhood swelling to life.

I realized with dread that he felt all we felt, too. That he knew my warmth and the shape of Hiberos both. Little tendons in his tanned, hairy forearms ticked. His jaw worked. His eye twitched.

Gealach's voice wrapped around my brain like a tendril of hate. **You are bound to your enemy whether you like it or not. You see? This red thread, this push and pull between Éirin and Aquilan is so much bigger than you. No matter who you kill, he will always be part of you. Of your story.**

Gaius's member stood proudly against his lower abdomen, red with lust. I felt queasy. It was as angry as I'd always—

Imagined it? the voice asked. **You've always noticed him. Sickling. You cannot keep a secret from your mother. He repulses you, but he's what you know. He's of your world. Just as cruel and blood-drenched as the rest of it.**

There's a symbiosis there. Some kind of twisted comfort. Primitive logic. The union of mortal men and women is always the same. Predator and prey.

There's no need for you to aspire to more, Mave, since you wish to be human so badly.

"Mave," Hiberos whispered under me, taking my chin in his hand and pulling my gaze away from Gaius, back down to him. "Look at me. Remember what I said. Do not let her twist this. Do not let her convince you of anything. She doesn't know you. Stay with *me*. Come to *me*."

I nodded weakly and swallowed. Steeled myself against Gealach's intrusion. With tears pricking my eyes, I searched for Hiberos's warmth again, for the safety I'd basked in just a moment ago. He grounded me with his hands on my hips, pulling me onto his cock in one steady but slow motion. I saw nothing but white, felt nothing but ecstasy as he rubbed circles into my inner thighs and my lips, coaxing my tight pussy to swallow more and more of him.

It almost worked. Tilting my head back, I let my eyes roll—but in the process, I caught a glimpse of Gaius.

He was nearly in the same posture as me, legs spread, hips stirring. His stare flickered and unfocused as the sensation of being filled by Hiberos rolled through him.

My stomach turned. This felt dangerous. This felt uncontrolled. But I didn't know how to stop.

"You have the power," Hiberos whispered under me, one hand bracketing my rib cage, the other brushing hair from my face. "You always have. I promise you."

Gealach growled; the moon's glow became harsher. With renewed intensity, she continued her screed: **Sergia is what you deserve. More importantly, Mave, he is just like you.**

Those words cut like a knife to my chest, such that I clenched in pain and curled in on myself. Hiberos braced my shoulders. Held me upright. Then he started to move inside of me, and a devilishly hot pleasure climbed through me, up and up like vines of jasmine and blooming in my core.

Gaius moaned breathlessly. It drew my attention. But, startled and ashamed by his own noise—by the pleasure he felt, taken deep by another man's thick cock—his brows slammed together, and he loosed a growl. "F-Fuck..."

A pulse of light radiated from the heart in his chest, through the veins, and down into his penis, making it kick against his stomach. He shuddered, locked eyes with me, and gritted his teeth.

"She's right," he rasped. "She's right. You fight like me. You lead like me. You dream of me ... don't you?" His last two words climbed in pitch like a plea.

Never once had I had a dream of him that wasn't a nightmare. He repulsed me to the bottom of my soul. He scared me. This stupid, small, sad little mortal man. It wasn't right that the sight of someone so unremarkable had me lightheaded and shaking.

This is what you will become. Nay, this is what you already are. Rage. Bloodlust. Power without mercy. You kill everyone you love. You destroy everything you touch. You're nothing but a starving dog, just like him, pulling at your tether.

Hiberos growled low in his chest and kissed the scar on my sternum. "Come back to me," he murmured, lathing his tongue across the raised flesh before going on to worship my nipples. "I will fill you so full of us there will be no room left for hate. But I need you to remember."

Gealach's fury turned at last to him: **You're changing, sonhusband, and you're turning, I can feel you...**

But he gave no response, merely gripped the hair at the base of my skull and forced me to listen to him. "I need you to remember that you have power. Even here. Especially here. You speak for *both of us*."

And when he said it, despite Gealach's glaring anger, despite Gaius's eyes on us, I believed him.

Even as Gaius pried himself, huffing and trembling, from the throne—even as he approached, one hand pumping his cock from the base, the other squeezing his balls tight—the fear and panic and self-loathing that Gealach was trying to instill in me did not touch me.

Hiberos was right. I had the power. Inside of me, all around me.

Gaius practically stood over us now. I rocked in Hiberos's lap, our flesh sliding together, and raised my chin in defiance. I knew he could feel it. Knew Hiberos was hitting the sweetest spots in him as well as me. I saw it in how he quivered, the stir of his hips, the shakiness of his breaths, the way his cock wept pre-cum. And I knew also that he felt me around him, warm and yielding and willing in a way he could never feel.

"In the deep of the night, I think of the way you kissed me," Gaius breathed. "The way you trembled before you did it. Your tears, your lips. Often I wonder what they would feel like wrapped around my cock." His voice shook so badly he was barely intelligible. "*I destroy myself thinking of you.*"

Hiberos bucked into me hard, and he nearly collapsed to his knees, crying out. When he looked back up, his gaze was like fire against my skin, the thick gravel of his voice betraying how unwound he'd become. "How lon...long can you pretend I'm not a p-part of this?"

"You are a part of this," I replied calmly. "You are what I deny. When I take my fill of pleasure, of joy, of love, you are who I disarm. And she's wrong. You both are. I am *nothing* like you."

The words rang true. And as I said them, it felt as if Hiberos had handed the reins over to me. As though this dream realm was no longer a creation of his but ours.

The power snapped into place within me, making me gasp and arch and swell as vibrations coursed all through my abdomen and thighs.

The red drained from the moon until it was cool blue again.

I could do nothing but laugh in triumph. A fragile laugh at first, brittle, but growing in power. Every laugh made me clench harder around Hiberos, grounding me, granting me more control.

Suddenly, Gaius was thrown back. He crashed into the throne, then fell to his knees before it, still facing us—and before he could wrestle himself to his feet, my magic bound him. Thornwire appeared and wrapped around him, tying his arms straight down his back, binding his thighs and calves flush. The briars cut into his flesh, crisscrossing his broad chest, his chiseled stomach, and his trim little waist in a grid until he could barely struggle.

All he could do was writhe, whimper, and bleed before us.

Hiberos chuckled with delight. "I told you. See? There is nothing in him to fear. He is hollow. A little man."

I grinned, biting my bottom lip to keep from drooling with excitement. Hiberos's eyes flashed with feral want.

And suddenly it was *us*. Everything. Body to body, our hands and mouths everywhere, hair gripped in fists and teeth clashing. We fucked each other with abandon, sloppily—grinning, moaning, collapsing into each other witlessly in turn.

Love. We were in love. We were filled with it, wielding it, embodying it.

This. This was what separated me from Gaius. *This, this, this.*

When I raised my head to look at the tethered legate, he burned with jealousy. He squirmed, glared, every inch of his skin red, every muscle straining. Blood trickled from the thornwire's cuts to join the pre-cum pooling on his balls. I wondered who, exactly, he was jealous of, and why. Did he want the love he saw before him, the depth of feeling that he'd never experienced, even with his own wife? Was he furious at how good Hiberos felt, pounding into us? Did he hate that I held so much power over him —that, at last, I saw his stifling aura of violent sexuality for what it was?

We must be sharing reflections as well as sensations, for that last thought made him even redder. He struggled harder. But the more he struggled, the tighter the thornwire became, the deeper it bit into his flesh. A new tendril of it diverged from the others and wrapped around his throat, digging in. It tightened and made the white of his scar stand out even more than before.

He loosed a strangled moan, a sound of distress as much as frustration. "This isn't yours alone, demon. I taste it, too. I feel her wrapped around me, too."

How telling that even now, he spoke to Hiberos and not to me.

But Hiberos spoke to me only, moonstone eyes locked on my

face, breathless as I rode him hard. "Let him watch," he growled. "Let him watch and know what it is to be in paradise and still be unloved."

I expected another pointless comment from Gaius's mouth. Instead, there came only a whimper. Each breath was a harsh chuff through his nose. Then ... tears fell down his flaming cheeks, sticking to his long lashes.

It was this that finally shook me to my core. My orgasm crashed into me and hurtled all three of us toward the precipice of something deep and dark. With a long, hoarse cry, I thrust myself down on Hiberos, taking all of him, my fingers working at my clit.

The chamber echoed with our cries. Hot, sweet-smelling fluid squirted from me and covered Hiberos's chest. In the deepest reach of my center, the Guardian released his seed, snarling and digging his teeth into the soft flesh of my shoulder. Knelt before the throne, Gaius threw his head back, loosing short, helpless grunts each time his cock pulsed—and pulsed *brutally*, dribbling milky streams of cum until there was a shameful mess between his thighs. He wept. From frustration or overwhelm or something else, I couldn't tell.

As the warm afterglow of my climax spread through my body, Hiberos sat up from under me and cradled me in his embrace. He kissed my brow, my eyelids, the corners of my mouth, and gently turned my head to look at the human still begging for mercy on his knees.

"You've always had it," Hiberos whispered. "You, my rose, are going to save us."

Finally, I saw Gaius clearly. Not as the terrifying bringer of death from my nightmares, nor the starving hound thirsting for blood. I saw him as the man who grasped recklessly for the approval of others. Chose his beliefs to spite a father who was not watching. Sought revenge upon people who never thought about him. Ignored the simple joys within his reach in pursuit of that which did not belong to him. Hurt others with inane slights and petty words to feed a feeble, infected ego.

I saw a pathetic, broken man who only possessed as much power as I gave him.

I would not give him any more.

HEAVY, ragged, blood-tinged breaths hit my face.

The cool darkness of the hut had been replaced by unbearable, tacky heat and a boiling red glow. And above me hovered a silhouette so frightful that the second I opened my eyes, I screamed and threw myself against the farthest wall. My arm twinged with pain, but it was nothing compared to the sting of panic.

The thornblood looming over me was so large I couldn't imagine how he had squeezed his way into the tent, let alone done so without waking me. His muscles bulged, red crystals erupted from his skin, and very little remained of his legion armor, but judging by the leopard pelt barely hanging on over one shoulder, he'd once been a centurion.

They never walked alone. So where was his herd?

As if in answer, Conan's terrified squeals finally registered.

If they touched my pig, I'd kill every last one of them.

I groped frantically for my sword, but the same moment I spotted it, the thornblood leader did, too. Only by virtue of how ungainly he was did I reach it first; his fist snatched at air just as I rolled out of the way, and his roar of fury shook the hut.

He swung an oversized fist, the knuckles of which were covered in hardened blood spikes. I just barely dodged the blow, hitting the packed earth hard enough to hurt my ribs. Then I skittered between his legs and was out of the hut before he could heave his bulk round to strike at me again.

Outside, the forest was burning. I supposed I shouldn't be surprised that even in their current state, all the quillies knew how to do was scourge the earth. Conan was okay, sprinting this way and that with surprising quickness for a beast of his size. He dodged the wild, grasping hands of the smallest of the herd, and even managed to evade the slashing of one of Gealach's more appalling creations, a thornblood whose skin was in ribbons, his forearms replaced with viciously curved red scythes.

But Conan could only sprint so far. The herd was closing in from the trees, accompanied by lesser fomori. So many the forest shifted with them.

Fuck me. There was a whole bloody horde. And I had use of one arm.

With a final, ear-splitting squeal, Conan found a gap in the horde and made a break for it, his jiggling pink arse growing smaller and smaller between the trees.

Sound idea. Running had served me well, and I'd not come this far to be caught out now. Thank the Lady fae were fast.

I whistled to tell Conan I was right behind him, but before I could take a full step, something wrenched me back by my bad arm. I let forth an unholy howl. Paired with the jerk backward, the pain was blinding, staggering me so badly that I fell to one knee. Then everything went white as something crashed into my side. The fist of the alpha thornblood, I realized too late.

I skidded across the ground with enough force to pull up moss and clods of dirt with my armor and claws. The earth sucked and gurgled as I extracted myself, shaking all over, from the boggy mess. The fishy, coppery, sickly sweet smell of the blight, made even worse by the heat of the blood moon beating down, filled my head and overwhelmed my sinuses. My menses rags on the worst of the dog days of summer could not compare with how concentrated and foul it was, and with the thornbloods were surrounding me, their unleashed masculine scents mixed with it and created a stink so smothering I almost couldn't bare to breathe at all.

The alpha had hit me hard. Blood poured anew from my arm, my side, my face where the spikes had stabbed me. I wouldn't be surprised if all Paik's work on healing my fractures had just been undone.

Every inch it took to get to my feet was a battle. I raised my sword in my good hand, cutting down one, two fomori. A third came for me, but I heard a thornblood growling at my back, ready to pounce. I did not turn, did not dodge; instead, I thrust my blade into the third fomori's chest, then used my sword as an anchor to leap, dig my heels into its chest. Wrenching the sword out, I did a backspring to land behind the thornblood, and removed his ravaged head from his shoulders.

The alpha roared loud enough to scare the carrion crows from the trees—so many of them, raven wings flapping as they tore past my head. My hair was blown into my face. I was able to dodge the alpha's charge, but I stumbled right into the path of another corrupted legionary. The baby-faced young man's eyes glowed red, and when he loosed a war cry, I saw his teeth had all been pushed out to make way for jagged crystals.

With jaws snapping, he dove for me. I couldn't move in time. He trapped my hair in a cocoon around my face, and it suffocated me as we rolled across the sinking earth.

If I made it out of this alive, I'd cut my hair short like Orlaith's.

The sling binding my right arm was torn away, but I only cared about my left, and the sword at the end of it. I slashed, opened a gash in his face. He knocked my blade away and sank his teeth into my good arm. I yowled as each tooth's entry wound began to glow a ferocious red. Cracks of the blood moon's corruption spidered up my arm, inexorably toward my heart, but the thornblood had me in such a tight vice.

My skin tore. Panic grew. His comrades rushed in to get their own taste of me. Someone pulled off my boot and one of those awful, wriggling little maggot beans latched on to my ankle, its lamprey mouth making short work of my flesh. My Lady, the pain —it was going to saw through to the bone.

The alpha roared in preparation for another charge. He was about the plow into us, and I was utterly incapacitated.

I pulled on my arm. If I could just get the thorn-toothed legionary off of me—

A little finger of his corruption touched something inside of me, some core of lunar magic. Before I could consciously call upon it, it erupted in a miniature explosion, a shroud of blood-orange flame engulfing me for just a moment. Enough that the legionary screeched, threw himself away, and cowered. My own corrupted moon power seemed to interact badly with his, the red crystals sparking and flickering as the tongues of magic lashed him.

The ground shook. With another short expulsion of magic that burned away the rest of my assailants, I dove out of the way of the thornblood alpha.

Both my palms hit the earth hard. Unholy agony stabbed up my arms. I tucked into a forward somersault. But there were too many of them. I was snatched out of my roll, again by my bad arm, and thrown into a moaning horde of fomori.

My head swam and pounded. Vomit filled my mouth. Both my arms and one of my ankles were torn up, and I'd lost my sword somewhere back there.

I tried to conjure another burst of lunar magic, tried to summon it into a weapon in my hand like I'd seen others do, but it fizzled out the moment it appeared. Though I finally managed to call one last little flash, I didn't make it ten paces before my ankle gave out and I slumped against a tree.

Then, from the corner of my eye, I saw the mist.

Images of Ruadan's body twisting and breaking spurred me onward. Adrenaline blocked out the searing pain of my ankle and arms as though they weren't there at all. But I knew I couldn't outrun the fomori—and the mist would come soon after to make me its puppet.

I'd never see my sister, my nephew, nor any of my people again; I'd return to the Beneath a wraith and kneel at the feet of a goddess who hated me.

If I ever saw Hiberos again, it would mean nothing to me. And he would be King of the Fomori, just as Gealach had promised, the crown of thorns and roses heavy upon his head.

He would wither away, forever guarded by her, all because I had not been good enough, had not been brave enough, had not been fast enough to save him.

I limped until my lungs burned and my body gave out. Then I clawed my way forward, the gap between myself and the horde pursuing me all the while closing.

Suddenly, a horrifically warm hand wrapped around my good ankle and wrenched me back.

I expected to roll over and see a thornblood ready to sink his claws into me. Instead, all I saw was the canopy of the tree line as someone shoved me under the brush. As if trying to hide me.

A familiar heartbeat rang in my ears.

No, it couldn't be.

Hiberos often seemed to appear right when I thought of him, but there was no chance...

I rolled onto my side, managed to lift myself onto my elbows, and gaped at the sight before me.

My savior was tall, lean, and muscular, and he did bear the horns of a ram. These horns were translucent, though, made purely of magic, and they shone full red as he faced the fast-approaching thornbloods. He raised his shield and sword with unnatural coolness. Patient. Disciplined. Calculated. More controlled than I'd seen him in a long time.

And then, as the horde crashed into him, he slaughtered them one by one. Stabbed, slashed, beaten with his shield. They kept coming, and they kept dying, breaking themselves upon him. Through the crowd surged pulses of sizzling magic, the same as theirs but so powerful his body radiated it, trembled with the force of it; it scorched the fomori and dropped them the second they touched it. And while the mist inched ever closer, he seemed to suffer no injury. Even the blows the thornbloods did land seemed to glance off him.

Finally, the alpha thornblood came charging through the blighted oaks, his spiked fists raised, his war cry shaking the earth. The birds fled.

The horned figure crouched, dropped his shield to the ground, and readied himself. He was so still, and for so long, that I thought he might let the alpha drive into him.

Then, at the very last second, he pounced, gripped the alpha's leopard pelt, and swung himself onto the brute's back. With all the precision of a seasoned warrior, he delivered an exacting blow to the thornblood's jugular, thrusting so deep that his fist and the hilt of his blade were painted with fae-tinged blood.

The alpha collapsed slowly and then all at once. The earth shook with its impact. The horned figure rode it down, then in one smooth movement collected his sword and stepped over its body.

Toward me.

The magic-made horns—and the matching glow deep in his chest, winding up his arms—flickered, then faded as he crouched before me. His breath was just as putrid as the thornbloods', hot and harsh on my face.

"Get up," Gaius said, and tossed me a dagger from his hip. "I still have use of you."

26

My first instinct was to tackle him, to crush all my weight to his windpipe until he stopped moving. After all, this was the man who had killed my sister in front of me, then tortured her for two weeks straight. The man who'd stolen my nephew and raised him Aquilan, the man who'd exploited even his own son for gain. The man who'd enslaved me, beat me, and threatened to rape me more than once. The man under whose guidance Fraochgleann, Geatacoill, and all I ever knew and loved had been destroyed, diminished, or suppressed. In many ways, he was *responsible* for the current fractured state of Sallach and the corruption spreading through Cuanacht.

No one could think poorly of me for ending his life now, even if it resulted in my own death. I'd be well within my rights to abandon every other goal in favor of killing him.

Just over his shoulder, I spotted a fluttering moon moth, and the flame within me relaxed. He no longer had the power to goad me into a rash decision, even an understandable one. Even if I deserved to pull his body apart artery by artery.

Instead, as he stood, I gripped the provided dagger tight, grounding myself while I searched his face.

His skin was pale, sweating and clammy, his face gaunt and

unshaven, under-eyes a ruddy purple. He wore no eye-patch, his empty socket exposed and pink. His knuckles, forearms, and legs had been wrapped with blood-soaked bandages in haste, it seemed, to keep the mist out. Scratches and blackened streaks marred his once gold, red, and leather armor, and the added purple frippery that marked him as Legate had been either lost or abused till it was brown.

Had he been out here since the sundering? *Days?*

And that glow... My eyes flicked down his body. The barest red impression was left behind in his veins, at his collarbone, and in the pits of his eye. Though the odd magic had been bright enough to blaze through during battle, his breastplate currently blocked the faint pulse at the center of his chest.

The strength of that light was the only strong or bright thing about him. He looked awful.

But the fact was, he *should* be dead. Three moons out here alone, a human? Even a plague as stubborn and malignant as Gaius was no match for the dangers of the wasteland, especially during the moonscorch.

Something more was at play here. He had been the last person to see Hiberos alive. Moreover, Hiberos had *done* something to him, something involving his heart.

Gaius swiped a bandaged hand across his mouth, then offered it out to me. "Get up. Hurry."

He'd slaughtered enough fomori to give us an escape, but the mist still rolled in. I ignored his hand as I dragged myself to my feet. Or, rather, to one foot, lopsided in my efforts not to put weight on my shredded ankle. The breeze against it alone felt like a million blades slicing my skin. I hissed and tried to take a step to the side, away from Gaius and the tree line. It was as though the mist could taste my pain; its grasping tongues flicked side to side in anticipation.

Gaius glanced back, then at me, before hurrying to leave the small clearing, shoving his way through the bracken. His stride was purposeful, as if he knew where to go. I hesitated before following. The billions of hungry, wet mouths making up the purulent earth gurgled and popped in our wake.

I could only make it so far. Gaius was ahead of me by a large margin, and the blood gushing from both my arms—one of them broken—spurred the mist on even as they sapped the life from me.

I tried. By whatever god would take my oath, I tried to trudge forward without stopping, without—stars forbid—calling out to Gaius for help. It was the ferns and deadfall brushing against my flayed ankle that finally made me double over from the pain, though with my limbs injured like they were, I less doubled over and more stood there folded in half like a broken puppet.

As fae, my movements through the forest were nearly imperceptible now, but Gaius must have sensed them, for when they stopped he immediately turned to glare at me. "Hurry, I said."

"Give me a fecking moment," I growled, wishing to anything that my hair wasn't sticking to my forehead and the back of my neck.

"We don't *have* a moment." His voice was strained, raw, not purely cruel but also rather desperate. He was right to be scared of the mist—and of me, and what I might become if Gealach took me.

He tramped back to me, his footsteps deliberately loud to convey his frustration. I straightened up at once, unwilling to take my eyes off him while he was that close, and blood dropped from my head into my center like water sloshing into a bucket. I *felt* my face drain and grow cold. The world turned fuzzy gray, and the next thing I knew, Gaius had his hands braced against me and I was leaning heavily into him. With a disgusted snort, then a weak cry as he handled my broken arm, I tried to pull away, but I could not see, could not even feel my tongue inside my skull.

"In Belos' name, stay *still*, you stupid cow." Yet his hesitation was obvious—he, who'd once craved my dependence on him, who'd yearned to get me alone so he could do what he willed. Had he finally learned his lesson? That I was not lost in these woods with him, he was lost in these woods with *me*?

Finally, his eye darting, fear of the mist won against fear of me.

He bent, grabbed me by the back of the thighs, and lifted me over his shoulder with a grunt.

The constant ebb and flow of blood from my brain finally blew the candles out. Everything went dark.

Vaguely, I became aware of movement. Aware that I was hanging like a useless sack of meat. Voices ricocheted around the void inside of me. Then something—the ground?—touched my shoulder blades, the back of my head. My vision returned before my sense. I didn't remember where I was or why this face I hated so much was hovering over me. By the time I came to fully, he was sitting on his haunches across from me, grabbing my foot.

I tried to jerk away, but the pain of my ankle stopped me. Gaius let out a snarl and locked a clammy hand around my calf. "Stop behaving like a caged animal for once in your life."

Against every instinct, I stilled, glaring down the length of my body at him. As the delicacy of our position sank in, I recalled the last time I'd beheld that eerie blue eye. The dream. The black stones, the throne, the thornwire. Hiberos's deep voice in my ear, his power in my bones. Gealach's threats and scathing promises. And the man before me, more vulnerable and fragile than anyone else had ever seen him.

Gealach's voice released like steam from the moss itself: **You're nothing but a starving dog, just like him, pulling at your tether.**

I shook my head free of her words and tried to focus on Gaius. On the uncertainty in his gaze. He was right to fear me; it would not be the first time I disfigured or beat him. But there was something else there, too, deeper than mere caution. I wondered again if that really had been him in the dreamscape. Not an illusion, not a mirror, *him*—because the way he looked at me now, it seemed he, too, was questioning what I'd seen, the truths I knew about him. How I might use them against him.

All his insecurities, all his failures. If I was going to use them, no time like now.

He may always be a part of my story, but I would always be part of his in return.

"What are you waiting for?" I asked blandly. "Make yourself useful, if you can somehow find your balls."

If looks could kill, I would once again be dead by his hand. But now he saw I wasn't going to kick him in the teeth, he removed his hand from my calf, rested my ankle in his lap, and took up a flask and cloth nearby. I ventured to look away from him to observe our surroundings. It was a makeshift camp, though *camp* was perhaps too generous a word, as it was little more than a lean-to and a few saddlebags of supplies, and he was the only inhabitant.

While he set about applying unguents and dressings, I returned to studying him. Despite his bitter expression, he healed me with the earnestness of a medic patching a wounded comrade. He'd come to the same conclusion, then. If we were to get out of this wood alive, we needed each other. I could only hope he hated that as much as I did.

But I wouldn't show how I loathed our situation. I was already injured and in need of his assistance; he didn't deserve the depth of feeling he craved from me, too.

Once my ankle was securely wrapped, he moved on to my arm, though there wasn't much he could do. He glanced furtively at me and sneered. "It will hurt. Are you going to pitch a fit?"

"Just do it," I ground out. And he immediately obliged, shoving my arm back into the socket with sharp efficiency.

White blurred my vision. I yowled and grunted hard, but there was a certain immediate relief despite the inflamed ache. Before I could recover even, he wrapped my forearm in cloth and a rigid length of birch bark, then cut strips from the hide thrown over his lean-to to tie it all in place. It wasn't a very skillful job, but it would serve.

I nodded to his cursed white cape. How that thing had haunted my memory. "Cut that up for the sling."

He nodded to the tatters of my cape instead. "Cut your own."

"It was *your* men who tore mine off me. I'm not sacrificing my own garments for this."

The snake growled and left camp, tramping to the nearby

brush. Beneath the ferns lay a decapitated body I hadn't noticed before. He tore the capelet from its shoulders and brought it to me, cradling my arm and roughly tying a knot at my opposite shoulder. From one of the saddle bags he produced a silver bauble, which, when empowered, flashed and began to crawl with frost. He shoved it into my armpit, drawing another snarl from me.

Finally, he moved on to the deep bite marks in my left arm, unlacing my bracer and peeling back the shredded, blood-soaked leather. I looked up at the boughs of the sickly oaks and tried to swallow the persistent, profound dryness of my mouth—the kind of thirst that seeps into your very brain.

I will not beg this monster for water. My mind's eye conjured images of the women and children he and his men had cut down, of the Éirins his empire had beaten and starved and crucified.

The slosh of water from his flask reached my ears, another moon moth flitted by, and something released in my chest. *You have to.*

My nostrils flared as I inclined my head to look at him. "Water."

Gaius paused and glared at me for too long. "Tell me where my son is first."

"With his mother and father. His actual mother and father," I amended with some venom. "He's safe. Safer than he ever was with you." He opened his mouth to croak some pathetic excuse, but I cut him off: "What kind of father—no, what kind of *man* drains an eleven-year-old boy of his blood to fuel an army? And look where it got you. Hope you're proud of yourself, 'cause no one else is." I gestured whence we'd come. "Something tells me Emperor Westerus did not sanction the complete destruction of the *actual* land. I thought you gobshites wanted it all for farming? Well, that's fucked, then, isn't it?"

He slammed the flask into my hand. "Drink, so I no longer have to suffer hearing your voice."

Admittedly, it made my heart soar even higher that he did not dare refute or match my insults even as they sliced to the heart of him. He knew he was nothing against me without his army behind him. A bit smug, I drank only as much water as I needed before pushing it back. He exhaled hard like a bull and resumed the task of dressing my wounds.

"If we can find a spring and get more," I said, "birch and willow bark teas are good for infections and pain."

"These wounds are deep," he grunted.

"The Aquilan that bit me, his teeth were like jagged glass. Crystals, red crystals." I glanced again at the faint pulse of light beneath Gaius's skin. It was the same color as the others', but he had no crystalline growths, and they had no horns or control over themselves. Whatever was happening to Gaius, he wasn't a thorn-blood, or at least not of the same breed. "It's like it's ... growing from their flesh."

"Those aren't Aquilans, they are monsters."

I laughed in his ugly face. He responded by tightening my bandages with enough force to bruise.

"I think I prefer them in this state," I pressed, unable to help myself. "At least it's honest to what they are. Mindless, beastly killing machines."

"Perhaps in your simple, barbaric world." Gaius eased back on his haunches once more, arms crossed, gripping his elbows as though guarding himself from me.

I was about to throw another barb when something caught my eye. A slow, heavy bead of ruby dripping from his nostril into the groove between his nose and top lip. The image of thornwire cutting into his skin flashed in my mind only to disappear a half-second later. He sniffed, his cheek twitched, and he swiped the back of his wrist across the trail, smearing his sweaty lip with blood.

I squinted, silent for a pregnant moment. He hadn't been struck in the face that I recalled. Finally: "Do you know what happened? You were on top of Hiberos"—I glanced down at his thighs and saw the remnants of Hiberos's sticky fluid—"you cut out his heart, and then..."

The legate's eye went glassy. He stared at something nonexistent in front of me.

"What do you remember?" I prompted more firmly, and lifted my uninjured foot to kick his shoulder.

He rocked a bit, gaze snapping back into focus. "If I knew what he did to me, would I be trying to find him and reverse it?"

"I don't know." I frowned. "Is that why you came back out here?"

"I never left. I have been out here since the Gate ... since..." He shook his head, brow creased fiercely. "Enough, I don't wish to talk about this."

"What you want doesn't signify," I said, repeating a phrase he'd once used when speaking about Nevidaea. But it was true. Whatever afflicted him exactly, it was plain to see that he was falling apart at the seams. "What you *need* is to live through this. And you won't unless you help me, and do as I say. Understood?"

It was this that finally launched him to his feet. He paced the camp with heaving breaths, trembling so hard that his damp curls shook with him. "There is a fire in my veins," he rasped at last. "Something I cannot contain, hot inside of me. It growls and spits and spurs me on like a furnace, and I cannot sleep. It is deep inside. In here, in my chest." He splayed a bandaged hand over his breastplate. "Even now, it pulls me apart. Any time I am not putting it to use in battle, the power ... *burns* behind my breast-bone. If I rest, it eats at me from the inside."

As if he'd called its name, when he spoke of the power, it began to glow beneath his skin. His veins ignited, pinkish-red bled from the center of his chest; light slashed through his iris, and those strange translucent horns grew from his skull. With some effort, slowly, I sat up to marvel in horror.

If you want it to badly, take it, Hiberos had said. Could what I suspected really be true?

I struggled to one knee, then my feet, swallowing the cotton in my mouth. "Take your breastplate off."

Gaius stared at me, shaking.

"Take it *off.*" I gesticulated sharply, and his fingers went to loosen the straps. Trembling as he was, and without the help of a pageboy, he was clumsy and uncoordinated, but I waited. I'd not be undressing him.

When finally the breastplate clanked to the ground before him, I gestured again. "And the tunic with it. Go on, do it. *Now*," I barked when he hesitated.

He tugged it out of his belt and pulled it over his head, discarding it, too, at his feet.

"Oh, goddess." The prayer escaped my lips before I could second guess it. The presence I'd sensed when he approached, the heartbeat, the magic.

So it was true. The heart beating in his chest belonged to Hiberos. He carried it the way I had carried it all that time.

But whatever ritual Hiberos performed to accomplish it had not been one of love or oneness like the soulfasting we'd done a millennium ago. It was wrought of blood and hatred, of the chaos that had surrounded us as the Gate cracked ... as Gealach expelled us from paradise.

Yet, unlike the thornbloods and the plagued land around us, it was not Gealach's anger twisting Gaius. Hiberos's heart did not belong to her. The power dogging him at all hours, burning in his heart like a coal? I did not feel that in my corrupted moon magic, at least not yet. His power—and his tormentor—was Hiberos alone.

The heart blazed a deep red that grew pinker at the edges. No shadow of a rib cage barred its way. It was as if it were simply suspended in Gaius's chest, pulsing and burning—a furnace, just like he'd said.

Why Gaius?

Why bother?

Solely because Gaius happened to be the one pulling his heart from his chest? I'd thought it must be the only way Hiberos could think to preserve it outside of his body, but perhaps there was a deeper meaning still. Could it be that Hiberos had known where he was going—that he had known he would not escape Gealach this time, had anticipated the throne and crown awaiting him in the Mournful Palace—and that he'd locked his heart in Gaius to protect it from *her*?

If anyone knew about a ritual as protected and ancient as soul-fasting, it was Mother Moon. Had that been her plan in stealing him away? To bind him to herself?

Was she looking to end the cycle, too, but in her own favor … forever?

I glanced down at the dagger Gaius had given me, now clutched in my left hand. As if to comfort me, to guide me, a third moon moth came to perch on my knee. When the time came that I no longer needed Gaius, I could solve two problems at once—tear open my greatest enemy at last, devour the heart, and bind Hiberos to me once more. No doubt he'd prefer it be in my possession. Yet the moment I thought of it, something told me that was not the way. There was too much about this rite, or curse, that I didn't understand. If I killed Gaius and it hurt Hiberos, nothing I'd done up to this point would have meant anything.

He must live. Just for a little while longer.

"He's inside me," Gaius croaked, staring at the moth and clenching and unclenching his fists, "isn't he? It is t…too much."

The barest flicker of pity for him brought my attention back to the conversation at hand. But the pity swiftly turned to disgust. "Stars' mercy. You are pathetic, you know that? All that time grasping for power and now that you have it, you're too *weak* to wield it."

His empty stare would have chilled me to the bone once. Now all I noticed were the minute spasms under his eye and the shift of his posture. He knew. He knew he was weak.

"Whatever this curse is," I said, "only Hiberos will know how to cure you of it. So if you want to be relieved, you have to find him. You won't be able to do it without me."

His eye darted back and forth across the camp, as if consulting some unseen counsel. The light within him and the horns crowning his head flares, then faded. At last, with his shoulders rising around his ears like those of a cornered dog, he bowed his head in affirmation.

Even as the grim logic of the situation dawned on me, I clenched my teeth. Look what I'd done. A handful of hours ago, I'd let quillies into camp. Now I was fighting beside the one who'd ruined my life and ravaged my country. Was this the price of mercy?

"Fine," I muttered. "Follow me. And pray to your Mighty Ones that I don't stop needing you." *Or death really will be your reward.*

There was no honor in this. But the only way out was through, and the only thing worse than working with a monster was leaving Hiberos behind.

27

Since mine were lost, I stole the bow and boots off the dead legionary in the brush. Gaius dressed, threw his saddle bags and shield over his shoulders, and we left his camp behind.

Just as we reached a break in the tree line, a familiar squealing reached my ears. Conan, trailing an eclipse of moths and two rogue thornbloods behind him. I would not have thought it possible for a creature to *lope* ponderously until that moment.

Without having to be asked, Gaius threw down his packs and drew his sword, stalking forward. He and Conan met halfway and danced around each other, Gaius loosing a snarl and Conan another squeal. The pig's tail and ears flapped wildly as he rushed to hide behind my legs, followed by his moth companions, and together we looked on as Gaius channeled Hiberos's deadly heart-magic. The thornbloods were dispatched within moments, although one of them managed to give him a deep scratch across the face, forcing us to stop and cover the wound. He put a pad of lint over his cheek but needed an extra hand securing the bandage around his jaw.

"Don't," he warned, but I made certain to tie it in two bunny ears at the top of his head anyway. It helped when he looked as foolish on the outside as he was on the inside.

I bent to check that Conan was unharmed, which, by some miracle, he was. The thornbloods had spooked him, but now that they were gone, he chewed on something as though they'd never been there at all.

"I don't know why you bother with this stupid animal," Gaius muttered, preoccupied with touching his teeth as though they hurt. "It's useless."

I thought about ignoring him but instead said, "I'm sure the Emperor is having similar thoughts about you." Then, spreading my hand, I asked Conan, "What's that you have?"

Conan promptly spat the remains of his snack into my palm. A fruit of some kind—he'd eaten most of it and sucked at the juice, but the little bit of flesh and the stem left over were immediately familiar to me. The glowing fruit of the moon.

"This..." I marveled at it, then Conan himself, and finally the moths wheeling about his head. I didn't have to ask where he'd found it; there was nothing like this in Éire, or anywhere in the Underland, for that matter, apart from... "Was it grand, lovely boy? A yummy little morsel?"

For food, Conan was always alert and at the ready. He snorted and stamped his trotters in approval.

"You want more?" I asked slyly, waving it in front of his face. "Show me where you got it and I'll shake as many down from the trees as you like. More? More?"

When he was practically coming apart with excitement, I began to walk, and he marched ahead of me with his head held high and his arse waggling. Gaius growled but simply followed us like a shadow, his boots squelching across the putrid earth.

The place Conan led us was so close to where I'd started out that morning I felt like falling to my knees and weeping. But we were here now, and that was what mattered. We stood on a hill overlooking a dike. The land was fractured, but beyond the breach sat the heartgrove, now consumed by blight. The remains of Hiberos's tree stood in the center of it, its trunk still hollowed in the shape of him. The opalescent threads winding up its hide no longer flickered milky white and ultra-violet purple. In fact, there seemed to be two distinct magics at war within it: at the top of the tree, brimstone yellow and dark red, the bark blackened and scaled as though it had been consumed by flame; at the base, the familiar blood orange, claret-smattered rot of the withering.

The moths following us swarmed to it. My breath caught in my throat.

I hesitated at the edge of the grove before collecting myself and following Conan down into the dike. Getting back up one-armed was another thing altogether. My claws extended as I groped for purchase among the exposed roots and clods of dirt. I tried to get a foot up for leverage but kept slipping. Beside me, Gaius leapt from the bottom of the dike and pulled himself up easily, his mouth set in a grim line.

I huffed and growled low in my throat as his shadow and a wave of body heat passed over me. "Must be nice to have the use of all four limbs," I said on a breath. "For all the good they do you."

I didn't think he'd hear me, but he turned, frowning. He loomed over me with the toes of his boots at the very edge of the breach—inches from my left hand, from which I hung like dead weight.

A frigid shard of that old fear pierced my heart as I searched his face. He was contemplating leaving me there at the bottom of that ditch, or else crushing my fingers so I would fall. He did not even try to hide it; in fact, he tilted his head as though picturing what I might look like lying there in the dirt with all my limbs broken.

Finally, he crouched to one knee, his face no more than a foot from mine. "You know," he drawled, "you thought you touched on a point of shame, earlier, telling me I ruined the land for farming. But this is not the first time the Empire has destroyed land in order to claim it. Have you ever heard of a country called Polechia?"

When my only reply was a grunt, he continued. "Of course you haven't. It's on the Continent. Seaxony borders it to the west, the Belyic Sea to the north, and across the sea, the Eastern Peninsulas. It lies in the center of all that the Empire needs to take Sibir and beyond, yet the Tetra Mountains on its southern border and the Brannibor Forest to the west make it plenty defensible. But *defense* is ideal only once it belongs to us. Well, two hundred years ago, Emperor Betto decided he'd had enough waiting..."

He leaned in closer, sweating, his voice a hiss that nearly made me flinch. "Those Polec monkeys fought. Hard. Allied with the Seaxons, even received aid from the King of Swedeland. Three legions, they felled. Until finally the great Legate Kaisar unearthed a weapon of great power. With it, he called down all the fury of Belos, the Mighty One of Light, who scorched the earth. Killed all, Aquilan, Seaxon, Polc. Purified the flesh from their bones, burned them to ash." His eye glittered wildly. "The land was uninhabitable for a hundred years. Nothing thrived there, and any who settled it were dead within months. Even those living there now bear the effects curse.

"Do you understand?" He thrust a hand forward and gripped me by the throat. The world spun, my heart boomed in my ears. His hand was clammy and hot as a range as I choked, my claws flying to try and loosen his fingers from my windpipe. But he only squeezed harder. Spoke through his teeth, his breath tangy from his bleeding gums. "The Emperor will *not* think less of me," he said in a frenzy. "It is the Aquilan way. When I want something, it becomes mine."

My throat spasmed, and he eased his grip just enough for me to speak. "By the moon, you will destroy me before that ever happens."

"Destroying you would not be enough, you *unbred* fucking *sow* of the Old Gods. I will scorch you to your marrow, until there is no trace left of you. And even then you would be mine."

He brought me closer and closer to him, the fire burning so bright in his gaze and through his skin that I knew he would not be able to stop himself. Closer, higher, fisting my neck tighter—

—until finally my left hand found the edge of the ditch, then my foot. I launched my legs into his abdomen like missiles.

With a shared roar, we tumbled back, into the heartgrove. My boot found his crotch, and finally his grip around my throat released. Before he could get his bearings, I rolled off him and wrestled him into a headlock with my good arm.

When I saw the infinitesimal twitch of his muscles, the way his arms came up to react, I extended my claws and rasped, "Try it again. See how willing I am to let the mist take you. Nevidaea and Faelon both would thank me."

He braced against my forearm, trying to bend in a way that would break my hold without puncturing himself on my claws. But there was no way. "Lucastos," he garbled, and spat a tooth and a wad of blood. "His name is Lucastos."

"I'm barely refraining from snapping your neck, so if I were you, I'd shut my gob." I spoke directly into his ear without lowering my voice, relishing the way he flinched against me. "I'm going to let you go. Unless you want to die a wandering madman out here, you had better not put your hands on me again."

Without warning, I pushed him away from me, onto his hands and knees.

Conan, who'd somehow got himself out of the ditch, grunted with each step as he trotted past us. He circled the remains of Hiberos's tree, planted his round behind at the base, and looked at me expectantly with his tiny black eyes. Gaius was on his knees, patting the moss in search of his lost tooth. No longer a threat for now.

"All right, all right," I sighed as I approached Conan, who tapped his front feet in anticipation. The moths, too, fluttered wildly through the air as if excited.

I slammed all my weight into the tree, once, twice, five times, until the ground was blanketed in fruits, some corrupted and some still blue. It didn't seem to matter one way or the other to Conan. The hog gave one final squeal of delight.

While he set to work basking in his prize, I breezed past him toward the edge of the clearing. A lone moth wheeled through the air around my head, and, looking at it, I recalled something Hiberos had said to me long ago, before my Trial of Cunning— when I still had not known if I could trust him, had not known the man behind the faun's arch smile. *Use your head, use your gut, and let your fae blood guide you.*

I knew now it had never been my blood, yet just like before, something *did* pull me past the heartgrove. Lured me through the forest. Called to the very heart of me. A memory, my connection to Hiberos, the spirits themselves. I rubbed my chest thinking of all the little wisps that had once danced and raced through the endless grove of the Underland. Had they joined the other spirits in their realm? Were they watching me now, leading me?

Finally, I spotted the first black standing stone—carved into a Guardian, just as I remembered, except now it stuck from the earth like a bent nail, its cracked face spitting the same conflicting magics as the tree had. As I came abreast of the standing stone, I found the next, then the next, until I followed what I was reliably certain was the path to the limestone chamber.

I tried to ignore the moon moths gathering around me, one after the other without stop. Tried to ignore the strange feeling that the expressions carved into the Guardian stones had changed, that they had gone from stoic to pained. I picked through new deadfall and ruptured land until, at last, I reached the entrance. It, too, was cracked, shorn obliquely in half with one side of the circular entry pressed deeper into the hungering earth.

Behind me, a twig snapped. I jumped, expecting a fomori, but it was only Gaius. Somehow, I had forgotten he was with me. Honestly, for some reason, I'd expected him to stay back in the clearing. This was a sacred place, even if it was sacred to a goddess currently out to destroy me. Having him here felt profane.

He stared at the ruin's towering entrance from beneath a dark, heavy brow. "What is— Ah!" With a hiss, he slapped a hand over his bicep, and only then did I notice the veins in his arms had begun to sizzle.

He and I both stopped and stared as the magic crawled under his flesh, making it ripple like the skin of a cat. It wasn't the blazing glow that overwhelmed him or the burning he described. It was an attack. The fae blood he'd pumped himself full of wrestled with the heartmagic.

It wasn't just that he was weak. He was falling apart because Gealach and Hiberos were fighting over him.

At that moment, he came to the same conclusion I did: "She's down there. You're bringing me to the domain of your Old God." When he bared his teeth, he was missing his left canine. "Was this your plan all along, to sacrifice me to her? Is this some heathen ritual?" The way his eye lit up, I couldn't tell if the idea excited him or angered him; either way, it was driving him mad. "Do you want my help or *not*?"

"Will you relax the cacks, you—you *woman*?" An insult I hurled only because I knew it would cut. "She's not down *there*. And it is a necessary detour if you want to find Hiberos. You can stay outside if you're truly so afraid."

He made to take a step forward, but his foot stuttered. He winced. Whatever war was waged inside of him must be brutal. "I am *not afraid*."

"Then pull yourself together." But in the shadow of this inconceivably ancient place, even my barb was no more than a whisper.

With him in tow, I descended into the depths, barely managing to wiggle through the crawlspace of an entrance. The interior had already been ruined last time I saw it, a mess of fallen rocks. Now its floor was set deeper into the earth and flooded to my calf with blood-tinged water. The rough-hewn flagstones were fractured and jutting. The gap in the stone that had once allowed moonlight to fall onto the slab had been closed up save for the smallest pinprick, and the light was no longer pale but the color of fire.

The face of the slab itself was cracked. My chest caved as I got to my feet and hurried closer, picking my way through the wreckage of the chamber. When I finally stood before the engraving, my good hand flew to the Ogham edges—

I relaxed. They were still legible.

Time to read the next verse. As I read, I translated at a whisper, my voice echoing in the doomed silence:

> When crimson cracks the slumb'ring one
> And mist-born wound the living shun,
> The binds of woe come all undone
> By moonlit hand, or else by none.

By the time I finished, Gaius was standing next to me, his brow creased with disdain. This far beneath the earth, he was trembling hard; he held himself and clenched his chattering teeth as though he could keep himself from coming apart. "This ... this is what brought you to this unholy place? A monorhyme?"

"A what?"

He sniffed. "A poem with an four-A rhyme scheme. Philistine."

I knew better than to react. Instead, I ran my fingers over the runes again, watching an eclipse of moon moths—who'd apparently followed us through—dance in my periphery. *When crimson cracks the slumb'ring one...* Just like the first stanza, this one was couched in metaphor. Almost a riddle.

I exhaled in something like a laugh. Of course it came down to riddles again.

Looking closer at the moths, I noted the capillaries shooting through their wings, once a pure, glassy jade. Crimson cracks. The meaning was obvious, as was the "mist-born wound" indeed shunned by the living.

The *slumb'ring one...* Of all the things that the blood moon had cracked, only one was infamous for sleeping. Until this last decade, Geatacoill had slumbered, concealing the truth that she was an enchanted forest. The first two lines described the disaster in which we found ourselves, then.

And the next two?

The binds of woe, I felt in my soul. We were all bound in our own ways: Hiberos to Gealach; Gaius to the magic ravaging him from the inside out; I to ... take your pick. This quest, this body, this *cycle*. I blew out a breath thinking of all the woe that tethered me like it was my master. I'd do anything to have these binds come undone like the prophecy promised.

By moonlit hand.

My stomach soured, my mouth watered.

There was only one person who could cut me loose. The certainty sat on me as heavy and cold as feyiron chains. It would anchor me to the riverbed of my regret and drown me.

The only being in this universe who could unspin the thread and end the cycle was Gealach herself.

Or else by none.

28

We were off to the Mournful Palace, then.

By the time Gaius and I returned to the heartgrove, he had torn the bunny ears from his head. He could not stop trembling, itching at his armor where it touched him, and worrying his teeth. Overstimulated, jittery. Thankfully, the minor scratch on his cheekbone had clotted well enough that there was no danger of the mist taking him—if it even could, with Hiberos's heartmagic in his veins.

Conan lay under the tree where we'd left him, slumped onto his side with his stubby legs sticking out. I could tell by the groaning and gurgling that he'd eaten himself sick. Still, he wiggled his tongue out of his mouth, trying in vain to wrangle a glowing fruit closer without having to move his head.

With a sigh, I knelt and tried to roll him to his feet, but he wouldn't budge. It would take a significant amount of even fae strength to force him upright even if my other arm *wasn't* broken. "Conan..."

I was about to tell him that we had to move, that we must head to the Mournful Palace straight away, but when I glanced to my right, Gaius was slumped against a rotting trunk with his face in his hands. Going deeper into the earth, approaching the Beneath, seemed to have only accelerated the curse afflicting him.

Still kneeling before Conan, I asked, "Do you need a rest?"

He parted his middle and ring fingers, his iris a blazing crimson ring in the shadow of his hands. His growl was slightly muffled. "I don't need your pity."

"It's not pity, it's practicality." I quirked a brow. "If you are to be my right arm, I need you functional."

"Worthless," he said between puffs of breath as he righted himself and stalked past me. "You're just as worthless as you were the day I killed you and only half as useful. If I did not need this tainted demon heart *out* of me, I would cut you down now."

Yet he could barely carry the saddlebags. He bowed under their added weight, they sagged off his shoulders, and all the while he pulled at his armor in discomfort.

"Worthless," he spat at me.

Watching his back, I sighed. "Let's find a place to camp. I don't want to be out in the open during the next moonscorch, and I especially do not want to be near the palace when it happens."

He refused to concede, but he did not argue, either.

I scouted ahead and soon found a cave. The entry was small, though it opened enough to sit upright, and it was well-hidden enough that the mist and fomori may not find us if we were very still and quiet. When I returned to the heartgrove with the news, I found Conan back on his feet. It was Gaius who sat on the ground. Head between his knees, fingers threaded through his dark curls, eyes squeezed shut.

I didn't need to feel bad for him to sense the misery rolling off him, didn't have to pity him in order for the sight to disturb me.

For ... years, now, I'd vowed to kill him and ensure my people's freedom. Now their freedom—and my life—depended on his continued existence. He had to keep himself together. Dammit, *I* had to keep him together.

I exhaled hard and went to nudge him with my foot.

"Follow me."

+☽·☽·☾·☾·☽+

WE COULDN'T RISK MAKING a fire. We simply sat across from each other in the little cave and stared at one another. The only thing separating us was the sleeping form of Conan, who had just barely been able to fit his big arse through the cave opening. The only light came from a small orb of my tainted moon magic bobbing above our heads, casting everything in a fiery glow.

Somewhere nearby, a horde of fomori rose from the earth, called forth by the moonscorch. Sucking moss, howls, and groans echoed eerily in the cave, and soon, it was filled with the overpowering stench of the blight.

Gaius, who had taken to rocking gently back and forth to quell his pain, covered his nose with a shaking hand. "It smells dreadful. Why does it smell like that?"

It occurred to me a few moments of silence later that it was not a rhetorical question. "The Lunar Kingdom and all the fae were made from Gealach's afterbirth. As in, from her womb. Now it's all rotting, I suppose it makes sense that it doesn't smell too grand. Like menstrual blood."

He pulled a face of true horror. "This is what menses smells like?"

"After a long day of walking about doing your business, aye. It's not a pleasant experience," I said with a one-armed shrug.

"Then all this sticking to my boots..."

How genuinely disgusted he looked! I couldn't help but smirk. "Yes, Gaius, it's vagina blood."

"Can she not hold it in?"

"Excuse me?"

"Hold it in," he repeated, enunciating every word as though speaking to an idiot. "The menses, hold it in. The way human women can."

There was nothing to say to that. It boggled the mind that a nearly forty-year-old man, who'd been to academy and had access to the world's knowledge at his fingertips, could be so stupid about things he felt did not concern him. Or, rather, things he felt were beneath him. Once, it might have frustrated me, but now I could only stifle a derisive laugh and shake my head. "You are a fecking eejit."

"Whatever," he grumbled. "It's vile. The whole thing is vile. Creating demons from the blood of your womb..."

"Oh, yes. The very vile abomination that gives you children. Well," I amended casually, "not you. But most men."

He fixed me with a dark glare. A trail of blood crept from his right nostril to his top lip, and he hurriedly wiped it with the back of his hand. "True, I am shackled to a wife whose body stubbornly refuses to do its duty. You can thank my father for that. Alas. He was not perfect, which would come much to his own shock, I am certain."

"Maybe he did know and simply wanted to keep you from breeding. Or maybe it isn't Nevidaea that's barren. Maybe it's you. After all"—I looked at my nails and dusted lint from my sling —"if it was an issue with your wife, you could simply get a new one, like you told me you would. You haven't."

Gaius scoffed as though I'd suggested the sky was green and the grass was blue.

"Would that be so terrible, being impotent?" I pressed. "Would you feel like less of a man then? There isn't anything wrong with it, you know."

"Oh, Belos. Spare me your misplaced pity and your inane speculation. Your theoretical questions don't amuse me, Mave, nor do they scare me. A child of my own seed is not required." When he smiled grimly, with the rings around his eyes and hollows in his cheeks, he looked like death warmed over. "I have one of yours."

It was my turn to go quiet, seething as I searched for some response. "Not anymore," I whispered at length.

"He's still my son. I raised him. He bears my name, my language is his first tongue, he looks to me for guidance and shelter. Your mewling bitch of a sister, whatever her name was—"

"Eytine." The word escaped me, sudden as the pop of a coal in flame and just as hot. "Orlaith," I corrected a second after.

"Right. Queen Orlaith, with her smooth, cool skin and silken hair." His eye half-lidded. "Orlaith, my unfinished lesson. She may have kidnapped Lucastos, but she will never be his mother. He is Aquilan. Thank the Mighty Ones," he added on a scornful laugh, "he's been fortunate enough not to grow up *worshiping pond scum* like you savages."

He was saying anything he could think of to goad me, and by the Lady, it was working. My pulse ran hot. I worked my jaw and rubbed my fingers together to keep from lashing out. But they were all safe now, and at this very moment, my rage was useless—I had to keep telling myself that.

I allowed myself a moment to swallow and collect my thoughts before forcing an even, detached demeanor. "You hate us that much, eh?"

The malevolent glee left his eye. He hadn't expected my tone of mild curiosity. It disarmed him in a way that made my confidence swell.

"You know," I continued before he could find words, "Ottavian told me something once, before that dinner party where you trotted me around like a prize mare. It was my first clue that your claims of wanting to follow in father's footsteps were false. His brother Felis went to academy with you, yea. Apparently told him of your hatred for the Éirins. That everyone around you thought it was peculiar how fixated you were on killing us." I leaned forward. "Even other quillies think the way you are is strange."

He opened his mouth, but nothing came out.

"At least Éire has an army. The poison you've spread elsewhere, the rebellions you quash in Numirabia. The way you treat the lupercali. Or the Suda, the Saha, the Sahel, how you mine and enfeeble their land. The peoples you've wiped off the map entirely. If there wasn't an ocean separating us, and if my skin wasn't the same color as your father's, I'd be even worse off." I tilted my head. "My point is, if you just craved *killing* and *conquest* and a *good death*, you could go anywhere in the Empire. So ... why, Gaius? Why us? Is it that red thread? Or is it the wards your father adopted ... his research? Is that truly it—because your *daddy* didn't hug you enough? Are you truly that desperate for the love of another man?"

"My father was an anthropologist," was all he could manage to croak. I didn't know if he had more to say, or if he was incapable, or if he even properly registered my words in his current feverish state.

"Well, my father's dead. Killed by men sent by yours, actually." I studied him. "You don't understand, do you? You never will. Your father was no hero to us, only to you. Being studied like an animal is not a privilege. Being stolen is not a privilege. But those subjects got attention from the man who mattered most to you, so they were your enemies. Even after he died, they were your enemies. Can you imagine?" I scoffed. "Scourging three entire provinces because you didn't get all the attention you craved?"

He hunched his shoulders, curling as if to shield his underbelly from my attacks. "Are you quite done?"

"And all along, there was your mother. You could have gotten all you needed from loving your mother. Sit up straight when I'm speaking to you," I added sharply before refocusing on my questions. He didn't obey, but I sensed him flinch. "Or did your mammy dislike you as much as your father did? Did she call you a mistake, blame you for ruining her body at such a young age? Because she was young, wasn't she. Because your father was a selfish pervert who didn't truly care about others—he just liked to collect things, to study things. Is that why you were so cold to her, even while she was dying? Ungrateful."

"Don't. Speak. About. My mother."

The warning was backed by such raw, dark energy that I almost heeded it. "Is that why you never speak of her, because the truth that you *abandoned her* is too difficult? Or do you never think about her? Do you thinking of anyone besides yourself? Do you feel *anything*?"

His only response was to curse in Éirin—a curse that no casual speaker would pick up. *May the Lady make a ladder of your backbone, and may your husband fall from the top.*

I finally broke eye contact, staring at Conan, my voice softening. "You know, Gaius, you may have an excuse to hate us. A shitey, twisted one, but an excuse. But your peers, all those nobles and other officers and even the Emperor ... they don't. They are simply dedicated to the destruction of others for their own gain. Sometimes not for their own gain at all, sometimes because it's all they care to know, sometimes just to have something to *do*. And you may lead from the front, but you'd be one of the few."

"That is what a great leader does. Inspires the selfish masses. Leads them into light and truth."

Lifting my head, I locked eyes with him again. "You aren't a great leader, and you never will be. You have no originality, no true cleverness. No matter how close you come to being the mold of a perfect Aquilan, you're empty inside. All you are is smoke. You're not special. Not deep. Not chosen. Just honed. You're nothing but a tool playing at manhood."

"Fine, then," he returned hotly, "let me be a tool for the Empire. As any soldier is."

"And, see? You're *easy*. You want it so badly. Connection. Recognition. Approval. They know, too—your betters, your father. Point you in some direction, you'll kill what lies in your way, and you accept death as a reward. So they keep you around, for now, even though they're laughing at you." I squinted. "The same way you feel about Ryac. Am I right? Except unlike Ryac, you've been handed every comfort you could ever want since the moment you were born. There's just something *wrong* with you."

Despite the redness of his face, he laughed, bleeding gums and all. "Obsessed with me. You're obsessed with me!"

And he kept laughing, harder and harder. Oh, he was not well.

"I know everything about you, Gaius. I even know why you are the way you are, now, and I still hate you. Not because you're wicked. Because you are cowardly and worthless. In the deepest part of you. There is no part of you that was ever redeemable. Your peers see it. Your men see it. The Emperor sees it. *Everyone*... sees it. And the reason people like you insist, and insist, and insist yet again on their own supremacy ... is that you are weak. If you didn't maintain your place at top of the heap, you would be crushed instantly, and you *know* it."

Then his voice darkened as my words truly sank in. "How can you possibly know all these details?" After a pause he added, "How did you know my wife's name? And Ryac, and my mother..."

His eye flicked down. Wheels turned, pieces found their place. Horror dawned. When his gaze met mine again, he wore an expression I'd only seen on him once. In the storehouse, when he'd discovered that Gwynedd helped Uaine escape. His genuine betrayal. His candid, childlike demeanor.

"It's Drusilla ... isn't it? All this time."

Those four simple words were said with such flat affect, such resignation, that I knew there was no use in lying to him.

Shite. Shite, shite, shite, shite. Idiot! Once again, my flagrant defiance of him had put Drusilla in the path of danger. I'd have to warn her before he returned. If we lived.

"But ... how? She ... she never sent any correspondence."

I said nothing.

We sat, staring.

Silent.

"She nursed my child," he said vacantly. "She cared for my family." A long pause. "She said she would stand by me." Another. "I believed her..."

Eventually, he hung his head, pressing his palms hard to his forehead. Thin, shaky breaths filled the silence. Then his voice, firm and deep and cracked and devoid of emotion. "Enough. Stop talking."

Scared of saying something more incriminating, I showed him mercy. I lay down next to Conan's warmth, dismissed my orb of light, and left the starving dog to his own thoughts.

Though I did not know if my body would allow me to sleep, I had to warn Drusilla that Gaius now knew her as a traitor.

She nursed my child. She cared for my family.

She said she would stand by me.

I believed her.

Those words lulled me into the cool well of power connecting us, a well I had not visited since I nearly drowned in its depths. My trepidation was lesser now that I knew Gwynedd was floating around somewhere, guiding me, but I would not spend too much time here. I wouldn't let myself be absorbed again.

SYLVOSTUM WAS IN RUIN.

The walls were holding, for now. But the land was blighted, broken. Civilians were scared, those who hadn't tried to flee—and perished in the process—all boarded up and starving in their houses. The mist seeped in through the cracks, looking for victims to claim.

Since Legate Sergia's disappearance, the newly minted Primus Tatius had been appointed the de facto leader of Sylvostum and the Ninth Legion, with Primus Ottavian under him despite being more experienced. Politics were strange that way. His strategy had been to call in the Seventh, then hunker down and weather the storm. Yet there was only so much weathering that could be done.

The roads were not only destroyed, swallowed up by the still-born earth, but also swarmed with fomori; there would be no relief, unless they miraculously figured out how to drop supplies from the sky. Already, food was being rationed under strict law. No one was getting enough to eat. Because of the constant light and heat, not to mention the moonscorching, no one was getting enough sleep. The legate and his son were gone without a trace, the Lady Sergia was a prisoner in her own villa, and Tatius was panicking. All were on edge. Vicious. Suspicious.

And it seemed as though the full weight of their suspicion had fallen upon Drusilla.

Lupercali had been the Aquilans' convenient scapegoat since before anyone could remember. So, no, she wasn't surprised. But after so many years of playing both sides and letting Gaius believe that her loyalty lay with him, everything changing now left her sore. Perhaps she'd grown complacent. Perhaps she had vastly overestimated how much of her success had been due to Gaius simply wanting—*needing*—to believe she was his staunchest ally.

Now that a load-bearing pillar of the facade had cracked, she was just some she-wolf. And beyond a scapegoat, she actually was guilty. Under enough scrutiny, that fact would be laid bare.

She had to get out of here.

The moment she felt me in her head, she was carefully doling out portions of tinned meat. A fierce tingle straightened her spine, and she barely suppressed a gasp. *There you are. You haven't answered me all week.*

Thankfully, with my feet firmly planted in my own sense of self, I was able to communicate with actual words. *Sorry. I didn't even feel you calling.*

Where is Lucastos, is he all right?

He's fine. With his parents. Confused and shy, and worried about you and Nevidaea, but fine.

Immediately, the weight of the world rolled off her shoulders. With a canine chuff, she returned to food preparation. *Care to enlighten me as to what, exactly, happened?*

Oh, she was not happy—with me or anyone. I tried to explain the situation, and that didn't make things better. *But all that aside, what I came to tell you is this: Gaius knows about you. That you are not a double agent but a traitor.*

All her limbs grew absolutely still, her tail and ears lower.

I know. I'm sorry. There was no convincing him otherwise; it was too late.

How did he find out? she asked. *Are you* with *him?*

Yea, unfortunately we found each other out in the wasteland. I let slip details I wasn't supposed to know ... in an argument. I'm sorry.

Drusilla wanted to slam her spoon down, but instead, she exhaled long and hard through her nose and set it gingerly on the counter. *This is the whipping all over again. I don't know why I keep trusting you. Who suffers—who suffers when you misbehave?*

My soul flinched against the harsh, unfiltered words of her innermost thoughts, but was she wrong? No. *I wasn't thinking.*

Do you ever, anymore? All the tales I've ever heard say that between you and your sister, you were the calm one. The voice of reason. Well, I haven't seen much evidence of that since meeting you. She glanced over her shoulder to make certain the other servants could not sense her anger, but they were all going about their duties with grim faces, locked in their own thoughts.

Turning back to the tinned meat, she sighed through her nose again. *I apologize. But this is not good. I will have to leave before he returns.*

The voice of Thomasia, who walked the corridor toward the dining hall, made her ears pin again. *Admittedly, my time here grows short as is. Where will I go? With the Éirins, I imagine. But how will I get there? The road is perilous even for the legionaries. I am no master with a dagger, and the only spells I know are cantrips. Useless!*

All right, calm yourself, I thought in what I hoped was a soothing tone. *The good news is, with all the chaos and people fleeing, you won't be noticed slipping away. We simply need to get you into the hands of someone who can transport you safely.*

How? The border is closed, a party would attract too much attention from the fomori and the Aquilans both, and it would have to be a very powerful person to fight our way through the wasteland or the wood. Especially the wood. Have you been in Geatacoill recently?

Our stomachs turned together, tears welling unbidden in our eyes. *Not yet, but I will be soon.*

It's worse than wherever you are, I can assure you that much.

On cue, the sound of a ballista firing boomed through the air. The covered pots and jars trembled, and Drusilla smacked a paw over them to keep them steady. She commanded the other servants, most of whom had gone for cover, to keep working on dinner ... or whatever it was. Every meal was dinner. Time had no meaning anymore.

Is that all you needed to tell me? she resumed, before adding, *I am glad to hear from you, truly I am.*

My heart softened. *I'm sorry, again.*

I know. Quickly, she arranged the pitiful rations into something that could be considered edible, groaning inwardly. *You can make it up to me by staying with me for this next bit.*

She set six wooden bowls on a tray and carried it through the kitchens, her understaff trailing behind her with more food and drink. Taking the servant's corridor, she ducked into the dining hall via a small door. At the head of the hall, where Gaius should be sitting, was Primus Tatius, with his wife and several officers at his left hand. At his right hand, Primus Ottavian's seat was empty, and to the right of that sat Thomasia, another adjutant, and Ottavian's lieutenants. The moment Drusilla entered the room, the right half of the table turned and pinned her with cold, iron stares.

Ah.

She's been watching me like a hawk, Drusilla thought. *She's sent people to go through my things. Good thing I have you. If I was receiving correspondence from Manan, they'd have found it.*

What struck me next was the room itself. It was quiet, far too quiet for an Aquilan dining hall. The conversation among the hush was more like growls and whispers. The great windows had been shuttered, every crack covered by sumptuous red silks, but despite the lack of natural light, the hall was kept dim with only a few chandeliers and candelabras burning. Though Drusilla could see fine, it was hardly enough light for humans to eat by.

Then I noticed the glow in the pits of Thomasia's eyes.

She no longer wore her spectacles, giving me a clear view of the way her pupils flashed. As Drusilla set her bowl in front of her, I noticed her irises, too, were flecked with red. Her transformation, I knew about, but the rest of them...

I thought it was just the Eighth Legion that were inoculated. How many of them have taken it at this point?

All of them, Drusilla responded.

So, now every combatant in Sylvostum had fae blood in them, fae strength, fae vision. Unlike the thornbloods, however, their skin was unmarred. It must have been exposure to the Underland itself that turned them into unholy, roving creations of Gealach while the Seventh and Ninth Legions were ... like this. Tainted, spiraling, hiding in their dens like bloodsuckers—but still Aquilan.

Maybe that was worse, come to think of it.

Thomasia and her friends did not take their eyes from Drusilla, not even for a moment, while the table was laid. As Drusilla was setting the last bowl in front of Tatius's wife, Thomasia threw her tankard back and took a long, deep swig—then, when Drusilla walked round behind the diners' chairs to return to the servant's door, the adjutant slammed it back onto the table and stood up. Her chair screeched painfully against the flagstones.

All at once, she was in Drusilla's space, only half pretending that nearly running into her had been an accident. She grabbed the she-wolf's upper arm in a grip so crushing that even Drusilla's practiced calm shattered, and she yipped.

Thomasia seemed to relish the pain; rather than let go, she smiled smugly. "Pardon."

Yet as Drusilla made to pull away, the adjutant leaned in, muttering in her ear, "Watch where you step, mongrel. I mean it. We all know what you are. One claw out of line, and I will nail you to the cross personally."

Huffing hard through her nostrils, Drusilla gave one final, firm yank, and Thomasia released her. Without another glance behind, she returned briskly to the servant's corridor, the last one to return to the kitchens. Once the door was shut behind her, she tried to quell the shaking in her limbs.

"Hiya, a chara."

Drusilla stiffened to attention.

Of course. Who should be waiting in the shadows of the corridor but Bloodwarden Ryac?

29

Ryac stood perfectly beneath a sconce. The quivering yellow light caught the dark red of his eyes and the scar Drusilla had left on his cheek. To my shock and horror, he seemed to be in good shape. Hands in his pockets, leaning against the far wall of the corridor. Sweaty and disheveled, but nothing like the state of Ferghal.

What? I asked in Drusilla's head. *Are the moonless not falling ill?*

No? Ironically, he might be one of the saner commanders here. What do you mean, falling ill? Are yours?

The faoladh are, yea. It must be somehow related to Ryac's 'freedom' from the 'tyranny of the moon.'

The bloodwarden pushed off the wall. Though he didn't approach, it was obvious that he had been waiting for Drusilla's return. "You all right?"

She tried not to pant, but here she was, caught between the hammer and the anvil—an Aquilan woman who was convinced of her guilt, and an Éirin man who had witnessed it in fact. He still had not told anyone what he'd seen that day in the bathhouse, but that was somehow worse. An unexpected factor.

"What do you want, Ryac?"

His brows shot up, forehead creasing. "No need to be so rude, pet."

"I am not your *pet*."

"Sorry. Ma'am."

"What do you want?" she repeated lower.

He wiped his nose and shrugged, hands back in his pockets. "It isn't what I want. You know, dogs can smell fear," he added conversationally.

"You call yourself a dog?" she scoffed.

"I know what I am, ma'am. And unlike most, I call it by its name. Murderer. Man-eater. Dog."

Drusilla crossed her arms. "You might not choose the title of *dog* if it had been thrust"—he grunted in excitement at the word—"upon you. Were you lupercali, you would know that what makes a dog a dog rather than a wolf is his leash, and that his place is at the feet of his master." She tilted her head and gestured toward the dining hall full of quillies. "Although, in that way, I suppose you are a dog. Baying at the door and begging for scraps from a master who has beaten you every day of your life."

Ryac's eyes flashed. He tilted his head one way, then the other. "Look how tired you are of hiding. You, the great, cold, gray rock of a spy. You let that slip so easy."

"You already know," she said through her teeth. "Yet you've told no one. Why."

"Because I like you."

She knew his aim was to disarm her, and she refused to let it work. "How nice—"

"And I want to help you leave this place."

Now that gave her pause. Drusilla wanted to disbelieve him. All the clever scenarios in which she might be outwitted flashed through her head. Suppose this was a ruse, he really had told, and he was luring her into a trap? No, even when the Aquilans weren't champing at the bit to execute traitors without trial, they wouldn't bother to go to all that trouble. Perhaps he simply wanted to lure her into the woods to have his way with her, whether that be sex or a snack or both? There was no reason he couldn't do so here, away from constant threat of death by fomori.

"What's the hitch?" she asked, voice gravelly.

"Ach." He shook his head and rubbed his chest. "Is it so unbelievable I would do it out of the goodness of my heart?"

"What *heart*? You eat people."

There was a shift in his gaze. "I'm hungry," was his gentle reply. "You would eat people, too."

"So you want me to feed you, is that it?" Drusilla pinned her ears. "I don't know how. I don't know what you need."

"Me, either." He grinned crookedly. "Let's say you'll owe me a favor, all right?"

Drusilla huffed. It was a terrible idea. Probably the worst she'd had yet. But between death by Aquilan hands and death by fomori, it seemed the only recourse.

"Fine," she growled. "Meet me in my chambers tonight and we'll discuss the details."

Something pulsed in the periphery of my consciousness, and intuitively, I entered Nevidaea's body.

Things were grim. She was, at least, confined to her chambers rather than a dungeon; she had all her creature comforts, including her books, and most of her birds had been moved into an adjoining chamber to keep them from the blighted air outside. But she had not heard from her son since Gaius took him.

Somehow, the emancipation papers had not required her signature. The moment the ink was dry, Lucastos Lupe Sergia had, in the eyes of the Empire, become Gaius's son alone. The thought made her so violently sick to her stomach that she'd lost quite a bit of weight already during her confinement.

Drusilla had come at first, bringing news of Faelon in hushed whispers. Knowing he was still alive had been her only blessing. But since the terrible explosion in the forest—from which her room was still recovering, the affects all toppled and the furniture cracked—other servants had attended to her. Either Drusilla was dead, or she was avoiding her, and neither boded well. Nor did the demeanor of the servants, meek and exhausted.

The first day locked away, she'd asked Drusilla, "What do I do now?"

The she-wolf had responded, "Anything. Do anything."

But how could she do anything from a locked room? She knew he took the key because she could see light through the keyhole. All she could do, at all hours, was stand at her window and stare out at the ruin.

Each day was more horrifying than the last. Each day, the earth became angrier, sicker, with more of those beasts crawling it like maggots. Each day, the oppressive heat and constant light of the strange red moon wore everyone thinner and thinner. Sometimes, the moon would flash, and the air itself seemed to scream in agony, and the legions guarding Sylvostum were hit with a huge fomori push. Several times, she watched as they almost breached the walls. The thought that her son was in the praetorium or elsewhere in the villa and not safe in her arms was torture.

What could she do but watch? The door was locked. The keyhole.

The door was locked. The light.

Even now, sitting in the window seat, she gazed out over the shattered landscape, only pausing in wringing her hands to dash tears from her eyes. They had angered the Mighty Ones. That much was clear in every inch of infected land. She should never have come to this place—should have stayed in Ruma and insist that Faelon get his education there. What was the Empire even *doing* in this cursed place? Surely, fertile lands could be found elsewhere, and with less senseless waste of human life, both Aquilan and Éirin? Surely, some compact could be reached with another country, that they might share or barter their resources instead? How could this be easier when it was so...

Evil.

Lords of Stars, what could *she* do against evil? Nothing.

The door was locked.

But if there was a way out, she'd be a fool to take it. To thrust herself into this burgeoning hell, *alone*. The only thing she cared about out there was her son—there was nothing else that could induce her to leave this room, were it unlocked. Yet if she took him now, it would be a kidnapping. She'd be a *criminal*.

Lost in her own thoughts, she did not hear the knock on her door, only realizing someone was there when they entered. They darted in and quickly closed the door behind them, pressing their back to it. In the same moment, she whipped around, and came face to face with Primus Ottavian.

She wasn't expecting the relief that flooded her chest. Once, it might have made her flush with embarrassment, the way she felt around this man, but her pride no longer seemed a priority. It was good to see a friendly face for once. Even better to see that his dark eyes were unclouded by the strange red glaze of those usually guarding her quarters.

Nevidaea needn't have worried about propriety. His own relief was palpable; when he saw her, his shoulders slumped, and he hurried to kneel at her feet as always.

"Thank the Mighty Ones you are well. This is the first time I've been able to slip away since that monster locked you up."

He said *monster* with such conviction that Nevidaea felt her heart leap. Yes, Gaius was a monster, and she needed to be saved from him.

"The guards were changing shifts at your door, but the new ones were sent out to the wall. The moonscorching has been over for nearly a half-hour, though, and I don't know how long they'll be gone, so we must be quick."

"Quick? What are you—" She inhaled sharply as he took her hands in his. It did not matter how many times he did it, it always shocked her. "I—"

"Has anyone told you about Sergia?" he asked. "Or your son?"

There was doom written all over his handsome, noble features, and it made her limbs go cold. "No, I-I haven't even seen Drusilla. What's hap—"

"The legate is missing. When the Eighth went through the gateway, that explosion—the earth cracked—"

"I know," she said breathlessly. "I saw it. The world trembled like nothing I've ever felt before, even the worst earthshakes." She gestured to the disarray the room still lay in. "Everything fell, I was nearly crushed by my bookshelf. And when I got my bearings and looked out the window, the moon—" She spared a glance behind. "It was like that, and that, that, that black ... tower had appeared."

"Sergia is missing. So is Lucastos."

Nevidaea jumped from her seat, all at once overwhelmed with tears hot, wild, and angry. *"Why was he there?"* she bellowed.

Ottavian tried to placate her, motioning for her to quiet. "I know, he should not have been. Please, if they hear us, we'll both be crucified. I wish I could tell you more," he added thickly, "but I wasn't there myself. All I know is second hand. Those that survived what happened on the ground there, if they haven't succumbed to insanity they are dead."

"Is he dead?" Her voice was unrecognizable as her own, as hard as stone yet thin as flint. "Be plain with me. Is my son dead?"

The primus searched for the right words, his mouth working wordlessly before finally he said, "I don't see how he could survive out there on his own."

Perhaps he was with his father. Yes. Nevidaea began to pace, wringing her hands, her nails digging into the skin. Gaius *was* a monster, and he had done evil to Lucastos, but she remained confident to her very bones that, were it in his power, he would protect his son—*their son*, dammit—with everything he had.

"Nevidaea, listen to me." Ottavian brought her from her frantic thoughts, gathering her hands to him. He looked at her with all the world in his bottomless eyes, his brow twisted with earnestness. "This place is not safe. This campaign, it's a sham. This entire Empire. It has been from the beginning. We have to leave."

His words struck her as so unhinged that she tried instinctively to pull away, but he wouldn't allow her to. He simply held tighter.

"Primus! If you desert, the Emperor..."

"I know. I know I shouldn't say it." Somehow, his hand had found her wrist, enveloping it fully. "Just as I know I shouldn't touch you like this. But I find, more and more recently, I cannot help myself. Especially around you. When we speak, my innermost thoughts spill out of me. You are a danger," he added in a whisper.

"Primus—"

"Ottavian. Please."

Nevidaea looked at his scarred knuckles and felt her resolve weaken. "Ottavian, I..." And with a hitched breath, she surprised herself by cupping his chin with her free hand. "I never wanted to be dangerous to you. Perhaps—perhaps we should ... stay away from each other."

"No. We will need each other if we're to leave. Because we won't be able to return to the Empire."

"The punishment is crucifixion," she whispered, heart fluttering.

"Trust me, I know." Ottavian swallowed hard. "How many men have I myself nailed to the cross? But by the stars, Nevidaea, it has gone too far. Look at how the Mighty Ones punish us now. We were never supposed to touch this land, never."

Looking on, I tried to hold in my bitterness. Of course they were all jumping ship now that the Empire wasn't good for them, when they'd been content to sit by and watch my people be destroyed. I don't know what else I expected. At the same time, a primus and a legate's wife leaving wasn't nothing. I took pity on her and thought into her head, *The boy is safe.*

Her spine stiffened when she felt me enter her head. The slight pounding at her temple ached a bit more. *Hello? What?* It was the first time she had ever truly questioned my presence, even with her body subconsciously aware of it. *The boy is safe*, she repeated in her own thoughts.

"But Lucastos," she managed aloud. "I can't leave until he's found."

Ottavian slowly lowered his gaze to their entwined hands, and, after a moment, he nodded. "All right. All right. I'll look deeper into it, see if there are any survivors who haven't lost their minds or turned into those beasts. Perhaps one of them saw where he went. For now..." He inhaled sharply as he glanced over her shoulder at the burning moon. "For now, I suppose you must stay here. Until we know exactly where we're going, it is too dangerous to leave."

"Where else would I go?" she asked miserably.

Even if this chamber was a bastion in a sea of death and chaos, she was trapped here. And that on its own had been bad enough. Now she had to endure captivity knowing her child did not have the safety of a locked room.

A FEW HOURS LATER, Gaius, Conan, and I crawled out of the cave.

I did not realize what a mess Gaius was until the light hit him. I didn't think he had rested at all, even though we'd stopped specifically for his benefit. The fae blood or Hiberos's heart—or the war they waged—was more than destabilizing. He was burning out like a bright star. His veins pulsed a constant, angry red; the groove above his lip was stained from the persistent nose-bleeds; the rings around his eyes were deeper and darker.

Sniffling, he pulled the saddlebags over his shoulders without a hint of effort, but I watched, rapt with horror, as he spit out mouthful of blood clots and three perfect white teeth.

His strength was growing, but he lived on borrowed time.

The Mournful Palace towered above the landscape even from here, larger than any building I had ever seen or even conceived of, taller than any old cathedral or Dead World edifice. At least it was easy to aim for. As we marched, I tried in vain not to stare at Gaius. It was as though his body could not bear the pressure of the magic inside. Every few minutes, we had to stop and cover some new wound that had spontaneously opened in his flesh.

About the fourth time, he gave a groan and reached for more

bandages, while I stopped short and turned to him. "Stop bleeding everywhere," I sneered.

"I can't," he replied, his brows tilting as he wrapped the fresh laceration.

Didn't think I would ever hear him admit he couldn't do something. After observing him a while, I simply said, "Hold it in," and turned back to our path.

Soon, it became evident that our march forward was not as simple as I'd hoped. We walked for hours, some of them in circles.

Apart from being held back by my hurt ankle, the new landscape and the way it meshed with Éire was completely foreign to me. Forests, craters, bogs, and tributaries I had no recollection of blocked our path, all of them crawling with fomori. Not to mention traveling as the crow flies was impossible to begin with—we had to travel wisely with the wind to avoid alerting big packs of thornbloods, making ours a roundabout, wending route that had my head spinning. I relied heavily on my fae instincts, Conan's body language, and the moths that sometimes fluttered by.

Even when we finally were in the shadow of the sky-scraping palace, and the outsized labyrinth guarding its entrance, we could not waltz directly into it. The briars that had spread like wildfire from the fractured Gate had turned a huge portion of Geatacoill into a forest of dark roses, vicious thorns and tangled stalks and all. If the labyrinth had an entrance, it was completely overgrown.

Even when I explained it Gaius didn't seem to understand why we couldn't press onward. His judgment was wheedled away by the hour, replaced with a rash desperation.

At first, his ideas were just bad. "We'll circle the perimeter twice before we move in. Three times is bad luck." He spoke like a commander then, with grim authority, even if the logic was nonsense.

Gradually, however, the words themselves, the structures of the sentences even, made *no sense.* "They will expect us to come from the front to the back and back, so then we'll approach outward, from the rear. No, approach from the front but backwards inside. Close out our eyes and keep them open the out inside."

And all the while, he covered himself in bandages. I had better hope I didn't get injured, because there may not be any left for me.

A man losing his faculties was a disturbing sight, however I felt about him.

"We'll climb the ladder and the spire and inside will work our way down. Down is always safer than up." His voice was vague, like that of someone with a fever. We'd stopped on a ridge not far from the mouth of the labyrinth, and from it we could see the masses of rosebushes guarding the entrance, their thorns larger and sharper than any natural plant's.

I had stopped to catch my breath with my hand on my knee. Now I stared over my shoulder. "Erm ... I think we'd better come up with a way to cut through those thorns first."

"Yes, we'll burn the labyrinth with moss and dire," he agreed. "No—understand to and the water it like a crop."

"Right."

I began to pick my way down the ridge. It was steep and rocky, and I was forced to scoot my way into the valley below. Once we were at the bottom, I motioned with an open left arm for Conan, who came skidding on all fours, squealing in panic, his ears flapping in the wind. With a big "Oof!" I managed to put all my weight behind catching him, and he narrowly avoided being thorn-tenderized ham.

"Burning it isn't a bad idea," I said at last, wiping my good hand on my knee. Face to face with the thick, thorny vines, I studied them more closely. Each stalk was the thickness of my arm, each thorn roughly the length of my hand. At the top of the massive, thirty-foot bushes were globes of leaves and roses as tall as me. Dignified, these rose hedges were—imperious. It was a shame something so beautiful stood in my way.

I'd burn down all the beautiful things the heavens and earth had to offer to get to Hiberos. But perhaps not Geatacoill herself, or what she'd become.

Still, *burning* couldn't be too far off from the true solution. Drawing my sister's dagger from my bandolier, I admired for a moment the blood-orange glow of the blade. Empowering it with a bit of my own magic made it glow brighter, until little tongues of flame danced along its sharpened edge. It seared through one of the thick stalks with an unpleasant, sheer ringing sound. Unpleasant, yes, and the stalk wept a milky fluid where it was severed, but the blade went through surprisingly easy. We could make our way through these bushes; it would simply take time.

I looked over my shoulder at Gaius, holding up my weapon. "Can you do this? Empower your weapon like this?"

It took a moment for his eyes to focus, but he closed his mouth and nodded, summoning vacillating ribbons of mixed coral, red, and gold magic to his blade. Despite the man who wielded it, the heartmagic seeded something like warmth into my soul, like watching the light of sunset mingling with the waving shadows of leaves upon flagstones.

That was all Hiberos. Even tainted as it was, his magic felt like home.

"Good. Now let's cut through this."

I'm coming, Hiberos. Coming for you.

Our time together was not over. It had not even begun, not really.

I would not let my fears hold me captive any longer. I would fight Fate and Death for my prize.

30

Pruning the wall of thorns was slow going—but we could not go too slow, for the moment the stalks were cut, they started growing back again. Their milky fluid sank into the ground as we worked, and, gradually, the path we carved closed behind us, blocked both by new growth and encroaching mist. The only way was forward now.

I took extra care not to cut myself on the thorns. The mist slithered hungrily over the soil.

Dark. It was so dark. And *cold*. The furious burning moon did not reach here. The air was still and frigid as a midwinter morning. As if seeing Geatacoill sick and dying had not been bad enough, now the enchantment animating her seemed closed off to me. Unspeaking and unfeeling. A mother refusing to look into her baby's eyes.

It only made me more desperate to reach the labyrinth.

The vines on either side of us were impassable, and good job, for in their recesses I spotted fomori by the dozens, their blazing red eyes finding us through the gloom. They were no threat to us. Some were wrapped in vines, absorbed into the dense walls, able to track our movements but not move themselves. Others were half-formed, breaching the bloody loam but unable to pull themselves all the way out. Others still stood watching us beyond the cage of stalks, swaying gently to a faint rhythm.

At first, I didn't feel it myself. But as we walked ever forward, hopefully closer to the mouth of the labyrinth, I sensed a strange pulse under my feet, not like a drum or a heartbeat but resonant nonetheless. The stalks and canopy were both too thick to allow a glimpse at the sky. I'd no idea how close we were to the mouth of the labyrinth, but the pulse grew stronger. Stronger.

Finally, side by side, Gaius and I cut away a swath of vines, and a little spear of light broke through. Just one little gap, a fissure of weak light—

—and the thicket of Geatacoill came to life.

All at once, the woody stalks and black thorns raced through my vision. Something struck me hard in the left arm, and my dagger jumped to the soil. I ducked to retrieve it, but a vine shot just a hand's breadth past my head and tore through my mane of white curls.

With a grunt, I was knocked to my back. The moans of fomori rose all around me, excited by the violence.

"Keep going," I rasped, and leapt upon my dagger, then slashed upward as I came to my feet. A particularly bulbous rose hip above us flopped to the side and cracked some of the dense growth open, letting a tendril of mist seep through. "Faster!"

Conan squealed and hid behind Gaius as he sliced through the briars threatening to envelop me. They were replaced by others, which darted forward and smacked Gaius across the face. He staggered backward, running a hand over the razor-thin cut left by a thorn.

The mist licked his calf. It was trying to climb him.

With both mist and briar distracted by Gaius, I made haste in slicing through the stalks. Vines fell away, their milky blood painting me, the sheer sound of my blade through their flesh ringing unceasingly in my ears.

Gaius was struck by another vine, while its twin wrapped around his arm, threatening to puncture him. We bumped into each other, and I glanced down at the creeping mist. It was at our knees now.

My breath stalled in my throat. "Faster!" I managed despite panic-crushed lungs.

Growling, Gaius held off the briars around us while I pushed forward. The moans of the fomori grew more urgent as I sawed and hacked at a brutal pace, sometimes using my hand to finish the job—breaking the vines away like rotted boards, each time creating a new shaft of light.

It wasn't until I had torn a rift large enough to go through one at a time that I registered the pain in my knuckles, my palm. As I staggered out of the forest of thorns and into the gray light of what lay beyond, I raised my hand with a hiss.

I'd cut myself, of course.

Beyond the opening I'd created, the mist abandoned Gaius. Instead, it rose and darted through the air as if scenting it, trying to determine where the delicious scent of blood was coming from.

"Fuck." I turned and motioned Gaius through. "Hurry! I need bandages. *Now*."

He did not hurry, and the fact that he wasn't doing so to spite me almost made it worse. "Come *on*," I snapped. I wanted to tug him through the breach, but I couldn't risk him being cut, too.

At last, he shouldered his way through, and Conan leapt after him. One of the vines reached as if to grab the pig by his tail, but it only managed to snap his buttock, drawing a shrill squeal.

"The bandages," I snapped, motioning for the saddle bags draped across Gaius's shoulders. When he moved too slow, I grabbed them despite the stabbing pain of my arm, and dragged them as far as the labyrinth's entrance before falling to my knees. Digging through the supplies, I found a half-roll of bandages.

My gaze darted to the ever-encroaching mist. It licked at my injured ankle before crawling upward, but by the time it reached my hands, I'd wrapped them—thank the Lady.

My chest still heaving from our fight through the thorns, I waved the mist out of my personal space. It wasn't until then that I bothered to look for another roll, just so I'd know where to find it when I needed it.

There wasn't one.

Dread and the absolute silence of the labyrinth's oppressive walls pressed in on me, a hollow rush in my ears followed by a very faint ringing. Though the fingers of mist pursuing us hissed and retreated, there was no relief in my body. I fell from my haunches to my arse as reality sank in.

"You used them all," I said through my teeth, staring at the toe of Gaius's boot as he came abreast of me. "I hate you. I fucking hate you so much."

Apparently, the battle had made him more lucid. He sniffed thickly and jerked his arm to wipe blood from his nose. "Hate me all you want."

I ignored him and took stock of our healing potions. They were small vials, but enough to close up minor cuts. We'd have to distribute the remainder cleverly, and start reusing bandages. I didn't know how long it would take to reach the palace at the center of the labyrinth, but the walls were so tall, I had to imagine it was expansive. We might be here a few days.

I pushed the saddle bags toward Gaius, scrubbed my hands over my face, and finally looked up at the archway. Like before, the keystone there was adorned with Gealach's likeness, but it had changed. No longer did she look serene, wearing a crown of liquid moonlight; her face was twisted into a scream of furious anguish, her eyes wide, fangs bared, head crowned with a blazing moon.

Last time, my task had not been to navigate the labyrinth but prove my purity through my interactions with "Shemoabiri." This time, I really would have to find the center myself. I took a deep, grounding breath.

As we took our first steps in, the silence became somehow more consuming. The moon above our heads was a glaring red, yet within the labyrinth, everything was cold and gray as in the briars. At the end of the first corridor, we took a turn, and I caught out of the corner of my eye one of the walls shifting.

Right. Shite. This was an ascended version of the first

labyrinth, and so it, too, could shift and change at will. Probably Gealach's will.

We'd never make it to the center. Even if the fomori or mist did not kill us, we'd die. No way she would allow us to do anything but walk in circles to our doom.

The moment I had stepped through that entryway, I may as well have slit my own throat.

Speaking of hunger, it was well and truly beginning to gnaw at my insides—not just my stomach but my mind, too. I motioned for Gaius to follow me more closely. He may not be able to sleep, but eating might help him regain his wits. As soon as we found a small alcove, we settled on our haunches and dug in the saddle bags for rations. Thankfully, unlike the supply of bandages, there was enough food to last us four days.

Since Gaius was so despondent that not even the idea of food perked him up, I took it upon myself to distribute the bread and tough salted beef. "Eat," I commanded, shoving his portion into his hands.

He obeyed, although he was very slow, as though I was forcing him to eat plaster rather than jerky.

Conan sat heavily on his rump and stared at me with sparkling black eyes. Waiting for his turn. The sight made my heart sink in my chest. He had been so adamant on following us that it had not even occurred to me that he would be just as trapped as we were.

"I'm sorry, good boy," I said through a mouthful of bread. "There isn't enough for you. Maybe you can find some mushrooms or yummy moss growing on the walls."

He let forth a regretful honk. The poor pig had probably never gone more than two hours without scarfing something down.

"We won't be here long," I promised. "A few days at most."

And I prayed to the Horned One it was the truth.

+☽·☽·🌑·☾·☾+

WHEN RYAC finally joined her in her quarters, Drusilla drew the curtains. The room was thrown into darkness, but they both could see by the thin light coming through the dark linen drapes, and it would not do for anyone to look into the villa and see them meeting.

In the shadows, his eyes glowed like an animal's, full and red. She was certain hers did the same, albeit in a different shade, as she darted her gaze from him to the door. "No one saw you come here, I presume?"

"No one," he promised, his grin white and sharp.

"You are aware, I hope, that I know trusting you may be the last thing I ever do. All other paths, however, lead to certain death, so here I am." She pulled up her favorite cushioned chair and sat. "So if your end goal is to kill me or eat me or some similar nonsense, I won't be surprised, and I will not be impressed."

Ryac chuckled as he slid to sit on the very edge of the end of her bed. "Well—"

"How long has it been since your trousers were laundered?" She motioned for him to stand.

He did, glancing about. "Nowhere else for me to sit. Unless you're wanting me to kneel at your feet?"

Before she could reply that no, he should remain standing, he was on his knees in front of her, brow quirked curiously. "As I was saying ... I wouldn't want anyone to think me unoriginal. And I surely would not want to unimpress you."

Drusilla shook her head. "You are a strange little man."

"Oh?" He grinned, showing fangs. "Tell me more."

"The escape, Ryac. How will we manage it? What must I ready, where will I meet you, et cetera?"

He grunted and held up his palm, pointing to intersecting lines. There was just enough light for her to make sense of his improvised map. "Sylvostum, here. That bloody huge shattered palace, here. Greater Geatacoill. Alopex and your rebel pals, here. According to our dear friend Tatius's scouts, they've set up a war camp beyond the break in the quillies' wall. Good news is, we don't need to make a contingency plan for moving through Alopex, since your mates have already smashed through the wall.

"On the day we choose, I'll meet you in the villa with a handful of my mates. We'll dress you as a porter or somethin', werewolves need someone to hold their clothes and things. We'll tell the gatekeepers I'm off to follow some lead, look for one of my missing men—I'll think of something. Those pissy babies they have stationed on the wall, they're scared of me. Won't ask questions. Then all we need to do is get you to that camp without either of us dying. Our choices are following what remains of the road, or letting Geatacoill's treeline lead us south..."

He traced both paths with his finger, eyes darting. Drusilla noticed how thick and long his auburn lashes were—how his mouth hung open a bit when he was deep in thought, and how it made his broad jaw flex.

"The road would be a straight shot, and wouldn't be so close to that cairn of a palace, but we'd be out in the open, no cover from the moon, easy pickings for any stealthful assassin or roving band. Geatacoill, that's a longer route, and there are bound to be fomori crawling around the thicket of briars, lots of 'em, like maggots in a wound. Not to mention the mist. But we'd have cover, and it sure would be nice to have respite from the heat." He shrugged and finally looked up at her. "Whatever we choose, the trip could take a couple days. Our route won't be predictable, avoiding fomori and quillies and whatnot."

"Fine." Drusilla huffed. "I have waited this long to see Lucastos again. What's a few more days?"

Ryac dropped his hand, joy sparking in his odd gaze. "The lad's alive? How do you know?"

"I have my sources."

"Ah, well. Good. I like your 'little wolf,' even if he don't feel the same way about me."

"He's a likeable child. Kind, intelligent, sensitive. Perhaps too attentive to the adults around him. Almost from birth. I wish he could have a childhood free of war, free of ... well." She waved a claw in the general direction of the legate's quarters. "Most boys his age hardly even notice the emotions of their grownups."

"Boys pick up on more than you might think."

Drusilla raised a brow. "Ryac, nothing you say could ever convince me *you*, of all people, had a normal childhood."

He barked one short laugh. "Ah, you cut me to the quick. No, indeed. But, Luca has something I never had."

"A father?"

"You."

He was trying to disarm her again—that must be what this was. Yet he seemed to try it quite often. Either he was trying to break her down, earn her trust, or he was simply a surprising creature. *Confusing, more like.*

"Sad," she said. "And you never will have me, Ryac."

"I wouldn't dream of trying for it, ma'am. I know my place." His words were accompanied by a soft grumble, and before she knew it, his large, feverishly hot hands were on her ankles, massaging a ring around them. "No one could ever have you, magnificent beast."

She should be offended—yet when the word *beast* passed his lips, it was not said with the same intent as the Aquilans and their favorite slur for her kind, *mongrel*. After all, he saw himself as a beast.

His hands slid up to her hocks, then around to her knees, dragging the fabric of her dress along with them. Not even for a moment did he take his eyes from hers.

"How could someone who calls himself 'bloodwarden' ever know his place?" she finally managed, equally curious and disturbed that she did not stop his wandering hands.

"Sound point. Maybe I need more training." All at once, he sat up higher on his knees, his hands well and truly up her skirts now. With his thumbs, he applied the smallest bit of pressure to her thighs, and they spread. He must be salivating, because he turned his head aside to wipe his mouth on his upper sleeve. "Maybe I need to abandon 'bloodwarden.' Stick to being the leader of my pack, nothing more. Disappear us back into the shadows."

"A short-lived allyship," she remarked, easing back on the chair to allow him between her knees. "One wonders why you bothered at all."

"We got what we wanted: freedom from the moon's will. Besides, the moonless are my priority, not this war. When we agreed to Sergia's terms, a quarter of Éire wasn't exploded." Pushing her dress up to her midsection, he glanced down with twinkly eyes. When he met her gaze again, he licked his lips like a starving hound. "We'll find a home outside Cuanacht. There are forests elsewhere."

Drusilla could not deny the pounding of her heart or the quickening of her breath. Light fell across his thick neck and strong chin and pooled into gap between his collarbones. "What is it that you people even *do* in the forest?"

"Want I should show you?"

And he leaned in until she could feel his breath against her core, the bristle of his scruff on her inner thighs...

"Stop me," he whispered, lips so close that she could feel the vibration of each word. "Stop me."

She didn't.

His tongue came first, so warm, with much more skill than she could have imagined. Even as she seized, uncertain under him, he hummed in reassurance, holding her hips steady. He worked her slowly, patiently—even as his fangs extended and brushed the tenderest parts of her, even as the fingertips pressing into her backside became claws digging into her flesh.

Drusilla whimpered, shivered, melted in her chair to give him better access. The room around them fell away. Somehow, she ended up nearly slumped, with her legs locked over his shoulders. At first, she gripped the seat of her chair. Then she gripped his hair, equal parts disgusted and excited at how wet to the touch it was. He was but a beast of sweat and blood and sin. A cad, a nobody, a cur who did not know his place because he did not have one.

Yet she was letting him touch her. And she was *enjoying* herself. He was making her feel *good*. Better than good. If he kept on like this, she would be too weak to deny him when he took his cock out.

"If we're successful and I go with the Éirins," she managed through small, sharp breaths, "we'll never see each other again. You understand that, right?"

"Mmm." He pulled back enough to show how soaking wet she'd made his dark red scruff. "Yes'm. Can I go back to licking your tight little cunt now?"

Her ears pinned. "Watch your tongue."

"Oh," he breathed, "your wish is my fuckin' command."

His lips found her again, taking all of her into his mouth, sucking gently. His tongue swirled around her peak once, twice, three times, then again but faster. Two rough, calloused fingers slid against her entrance, and before she could stop him, they were pressing in.

He stroked and sucked her in rhythm. Each successively more desperate grunt sent jolts through her core and hips—and all at once, she was whimpering, pulling him closer, crushing his nose into her as she rode his face to the height of her climax. He dug his fingers into the tender spot just inside her, tongue continuing with its circles as her pleasure crested and troughed and crested again.

When it was done, Drusilla couldn't move. Her hands were locked together behind his head, at the sweaty nape of his neck. His hair tickled her sensitive palm pads as he moved his head back and forth, moaning, sucking, kissing, making love to her with his mouth.

When finally he pulled back, he licked his chops and smiled like the hound who caught the cat.

Mighty Ones, it clearly had been too long. She'd come on him like an untouched maiden. Not wanting to admit that she was still reeling from the powerful orgasm, she tried to keep an impassive expression as she loosened her grip on him, yet her breath came in soft puffs still.

Surprising as ever, Ryac made no cocky remark. With a heavy

sigh, he rested his cheek against the inside of her thigh, and his fingers slid from her channel to her stomach, then to her midsection, exploring. She knew what he traced. The scars of Gaius's whipping still broke the fur of her abdomen.

"You know," Ryac said at length, "that fae queen calls Lucastos 'little wolf,' too."

"Funny that they chose the same name," she managed to respond.

He hummed thoughtfully. "But it isn't the same name, is it?" When she merely blinked, he sighed again, straightened, and let her legs fall from his shoulders. Then, standing, he untucked his shirt with a harsh pull and used it to wipe his mouth. "Gaius calls the lad thus for the same reason he let a wolf nurse him—because the kings of old called themselves wolves, alpha wolves, to strike fear into the hearts of men. Legacy, and projecting strength. That's all he thinks about, a'nit?"

Hurriedly, he shoved the shirt back down the front of his pants, where his erection stood proud and ready for service. Yet beyond a longing groan, he ignored his own arousal, and went to the door instead.

He opened it and checked the hallway, though he still addressed Drusilla, who was trying now to right her own clothing. "To the Éirins, wolves symbolize something different. Bravery. Loyalty. Protection. His mother looked not to her legacy but his. Not to the past but to the boy's future."

Drusilla stared at his back for a long while before asking, "Why are you doing all of this? Really."

He looked over his shoulder—expression flat, gaze faraway, rubbing the thumb and forefinger of his free hand together—and for a moment, she wondered if he might answer in truth.

Then he gave one of those grins so powerful they lifted his ears. "Who, me? I just like to keep fuckers guessing."

31

"Mave. Mave. In Belos's name, answer me. Answer me. Answer me, dammit!"

A harsh slap to the face knocked me out of my vision. The world was an overcast blur for a moment before Gaius came into focus. He wore a sneer despite the purple bags dragging at his eyes, and on his head blazed the horns of red light.

We had agreed, after hours of navigating the labyrinth, that we should stop and try to get our bearings. Neither of us wanted to stop—neither could afford to—but the endless obsidian walls, crushing silence, and that strange subdermal pulse were all taking their toll. We'd ducked into another alcove, had some water, and rested. With my knees pulled to my chest, I must have nodded off and ended up in Drusilla's consciousness.

My first instinct was to push him away. If he was close enough to slap me, he was too close. After a moment of collecting myself and gathering my sense, I grumbled, "I suppose I should thank you for that."

"No more of your trances," he growled, the lower lids of his eyes twitching almost imperceptibly. "You did this in the cave, too. Where do you go? Are you communing with ... that demon?"

"Hiberos?" I scoffed. "If I were communicating with Hiberos, would I not already have the means to get us to the center of the labyrinth?"

"Perhaps. Or perhaps everything you've said is lies. Perhaps this was a ruse from the start and you're leading me toward my doom."

Honestly, I probably *was* leading him toward his doom, but that was incidental. Absolute insanity. It was some cosmic joke that Gaius's death had been within reach for hours yet I could not take the final strike, the one I'd waited over a decade to take.

Rather than encourage his paranoia, I took another sip of water and tried not to let the hollow silence of this place sink its claws into my brain. This labyrinth was bigger, more complex, and mistier than ever before, but in the hours we'd been here, we had not encountered more than a handful of fomori—and those were ancient ones of stone, far less dangerous than their malformed siblings. I wasn't thrilled about reusing Gaius's old bandages, but at least there weren't hordes to contend with.

Although, if there were, I wouldn't be so uneasy. The whole thing made me nervous. No doubt Gealach had sensed us here, so why was she holding back? And when, exactly, would her full might come crashing down on us?

Conan had wandered off at some point to find himself a meal, and now he trapped back happily, so he must have been successful. Probably mushrooms like I'd suggested. With him back, it was time to start moving.

"Let's take stock again before we go." I sealed the water skin and opened the saddle bags. No bandages, already knew that. A pack of nine healing vials, two emptied. Tunic, socks, underpants, gloves, bedroll. Torch, tinderbox. Entrenching tools and a few bits of cooking equipment. Two days of food—

Wait. I checked again. Two days of—

No, that wasn't right. There had been four days of food at the start.

I looked up at Gaius, speechless, staring in disbelief for a while before daring to ask, "Did you eat while I was dozing?"

With a deep, gravelly huff, he rubbed the center of his chest.

"This fire, it makes me ravenous. When I found these saddle bags days ago on a dead legionary, there was over a week's worth of rations."

"*What?* Why didn't you tell me that?" The tips of my ears blazed hot. "You didn't think maybe I'd need to know how long our food would last? I could have found some before we came in here."

"I did not think fae ate."

"Well, we have to *now*, thanks to your damned meddling!"

It was all his fault, and I deserved to slap him. If we made it out of this alive, I was owed some kind of medal, or a nomination for sainthood.

Then, when he reached for the water skin, I *did* smack the back of his hand. "We've already had what we need for now. We need to ration it."

He narrowed his eyes. "You don't need as much as I do. You're giving some of your rations to the pig, aren't you?"

"The pig can drink out of puddles and eat mushrooms. You already know I'm not giving any to him."

Conan's eyes flicked back and forth as we argued over his head.

"Well," Gaius snapped, "when the food runs out, we can spear the pig and roast him over the light-forsaken fire."

"You touch that pig and I will cut something off of you. You don't have to be in one piece for Hiberos to get his heart from your chest."

He closed the saddle bags with exaggerated irritation and pulled them over his shoulders again. "Enough bickering. We've been here for three days already, we need to get moving."

Three days? It had not been that long. I'd counted the rations. I'd counted the *hours*.

...*Had* it been three days?

With both of us in a huff, we picked up and started walking.
Walking.

Walking.

walking.

walking.

...walking

Walking.

walking.

walking.

WALKING.

THE LABYRINTH WAS so tall and the corridors so narrow that all we could see was the gray sky and the corridors in front of us.

Fomori rattled from the limestone, blending into the vines and moss snaking across the walls.

My eyes had become adept at spotting them in their hiding places, at finding the slight misalignment that marked their dormant forms.

Some, I was able to weaken from afar before we approached to dismantle them; yet others caught us by surprise, coming round corners or from behind curtains of wilting jasmine.

I don't know how many battles found us.

Every one was the same.

THE MIST FOLLOWED us as surely as Conan did, so our need for bandages didn't diminish. We were forced to reuse them and ration our healing vials bit by bit.

The strips of cloth were stiff from old blood. Eventually, they would become too foul to use.

But we wouldn't be here that long,

would we?

Or had we already been?

I wished I *could* contact Hiberos. What I wouldn't give for his bone flute now—or even better, the Weave-ripping boline.

Gaius ground his teeth back and forth. My heightened senses picked it up. A constant gravelly friction. Grit. Grit. Grit. Grit.

Grit.

Grit.

It seemed to become louder each time we found a dead end.

Grit.

Grit.

Grit.

Grit.

Grrrrrit.

Finally, I snapped, "Can you stop grinding your teeth? You're going to mill them to a high polish, Lady's sake."

The grinding stopped.

Then was soon replaced by chattering...

cracked urn twice. Nearby, a statue whose hand I swore was pointing right just hours ago now pointed left. As I stood observing it, I noticed a boot print on its side. *My* boot print. I didn't remember climbing it, or when, or why I'd thought I could reach the top of the fifty-foot wall.

I turned to Gaius. "Have we been here before?"

It took a moment for him to observe our surroundings with any lucidity. "Yes—no. No, there was more moss before, and also after. When the a way a when..."

Under his breath, he added, "Let's stop and sleep a while," bbbut his mouth didn't move.

"Let's stop," I agreed.

We backtracked toward a moss-carpeted courtyard we'd left behind just minutes ago, but we couldn't find it. So we stuck our torch in a crag and set up in the center of the corridor— Gaius on his bedroll, Conan beside him, and me beside Conan with my head on his flank.

In the dim torchlight, I watched the moss on the wall in front of me shift and crawl, my breath thin yet so loud. It was easy to imagine the labyrinth was breathing with me.

The walls throbbed.

I'd put the torch out in a moment. Just needed a second to make sure the damn darkness stopped moving.

I blinked.

The torch was burnt out, the burlap at the end nothing but ash. Pitch had dripped to the floor, making a glassy obsidian puddle.

I blinked.

Eytine callled for me.

When I opened my eyes, we were walking. I don't remember standing. Starting. Walking.

                                        walking.

                    wwwwwalking.

We passed the same

Swish, *thock*, thump,
chuff, chuff, chuff.

walking.

Wwalking.

Swish, *thock*, thump,
chuff, chuff, chuff.

Walking.

walking

I found a bit of cord and twisted my hair into a bun. We all vvoted to go straight for a while. Then we passed a Cracked Urn and a statue pointing upward

Walking.

Walking.

Walkking.

Walking.

The bandages were starting to smell rrreally bad. Conan sniffed at a thick growth of fungus in a crack but left it behind, trudging at my heel.

Gaius ppromised, "If we don't find the center, we will find the center."

And all the while, the corridors humumumumed with that

faint vibration, that pulse. Not a heartbeat. Not a drum. Something with moving parts. Swish,*thock,* thump,

chuff, chuff, chuff. Something familiar.

Swish, *thock,* thump, *chuff, chuff, chuff.*
Swish, *thock,* thump,*chuff, chuff, chuff.*

I blinked.

in a field of blooming clover, merry dandelions, bluebells, and wild garlic*and of fallen griefs of*
　*weeping willow*The world about me seemed so green and bright, and

　　　　　　　　　　　I walked along a well-trodden path

Up the hill waited worn palisades and an arch of woven willow branches decorated with stags' antlers. There was no fire. No strife. No bleating lambs. Just a life

　　　　　　　　　　　　I had always known

and thought I could never go back to. My mind, my shoulders, my heart felt unburdened as I entered Fraochgleann. Villagers rushed back and forth, readying for some celebration. Not one of them acknowledged me, but that was fine. It was enough simply to be part of this. It always had been.

　　　　　　　　　　　I never wanted anything more

than to live. Free.

Swish,*thock*, thump,*chuff, chuff, chuff.*
　The sound drew me onwarde. It wasnt like it had been in the labyrinth. It was solid, now, real, not an echo or something coming from the walls.
　My feet, bare and warm against the sunny earth, led me . . . to a hut. A woman with her head and shoulders wrapped in a shawl sat with her back to me, weaving on a loom.
　With a flick of her wrist, she threaded the yarn under the weft.*Swish.* Slipped the spool onto a holding peg. *Thock.* She pulled the heddle rod to its farther resting place.*Thump.* Then she brushed the thread firmly into place.*Chuff, chuff, chuff.*

THE KEYS TO. Given !

I blinked
The torch was lit again. The walls crawawled.

I blinked
Suddenly, I was sssttanding

> A fomori fell before me, raking its thornwire thoughtfire razor-
> fire sickmire claws across my armor and nicking an exposed spot
> on my inner forearm.
> We stopped to dig in the saddle bags for a used bit of
> bandage. Flies buzzed around my head as I did. The lint was
> dark brown and sour.

of food left.

There were no days

Mave counted the minutes by mile and the miles by steps and the
steps by stones and the stones by bones and the

Three
   four
   five
  Five six and

        seven mmmiles and nine more—
          Ten—eleven—
           nine—seven

                      eight—
                      eight—
                      eight—
                  eieeeght—

IN MY PERIPHERY SHADOWS DANCED. Every so often I swore I
heard someone from my child hood calling me and a few times as
we entered corridors I thought I saw a heel or a cloud of moths'
dust or the tail of a coat disapppearing round the corner ahead
of us.

Thesse visions scarred me more than most.

I tryed to pick roots that would steer us far away from whatever baited us onwarde.

But I would not go insane like Gaius.

I would not

I*was*not

I pinched my skin so hard it sent swarms of ants crawling
through my vision I would not lose my mind here.

I wouldnot, let this conquer me, after everything, I had
suffered, and borne witness to.

Not.

Not.

Nnot.

bones must break in the starlit wake in the silent ache in the
riverrun ache in the quiet ache in the modest ache in the violent
warring mad feary quake and there was no wake and there was no
wake and there was no wake and there was no wake

When our water skin stopped producing, Gaius and I crouched on our haunches across from one another.

For the third time, he tipped it upside down. It was well and truly dry.

"Should have sprung for some kind of endless water enchantment," I whispered.

"The commissioned officers' water skins have them."

His gaze slowly, slowly went from the leather sack to mine, lone eye glowing in the dim light.

We were quiet for a long time, still crouched.

"Where do your people go when they die?" he asked at last.

"The Beneath. The Lady lives there. Below the earth, under the bedrock."

"What of your murderers? How are they punished?"

"They're cast to the crows. Unburied. Their souls are trapped in the realm of the living with hunger and war and hate."

"Each Mighty One has a hell," he began. "The birthplace of demons, the place where traitors and weaklings and other wicked people go after death. Belos has his light hell. Rethus has his arcane hell. Kisa, her ice hell. Even Nihalus the Betrayer has his void hell." He swallowed hard, throat already scratchy—never once blinking, never taking his eyes from me. "But hell is not fire, ice, or dark. It is endless corridors. And the face of a stupid whore who won't, even for a moment, stop *picking at you*."

Often, when I looked at him, I felt numbness and a slow, dragging malaise—but for the first time since he'd killed Hiberos, I felt not dread but a stab of genuine fear. Just for a moment. We were alone here, and he possessed a power I could not truly conceive of.

But then, almost immediately, the fear was replaced by rage and hatred, both compounded by a brutal, gnawing hunger. "The feeling is mutual. You thick, worthless, ugly, plastick little man."

"You did not think me so ugly in your dream," he rasped, and his eyes lit on something in my face. "Yes, yes, I knew it was true. I knew it! You've done nothing but try to reduce me since the first day we came face to face. Is that not so? Because really, you cannot stand the way I make you feel. You cannot stand how you yearn for me."

"*Reduce* you?"

"Yes, reduce me. Humiliate me, challenge me. Drive me to madness. Allow this fire to wrap its jaws around my bones. And now starve me!"

"*Starve* you? We wouldn't be in this mess if you hadn't eaten all our food like a pig!"

"I am no *pig*. I ate only a mouthful of bread." He raged, spittle flying, and jabbed a finger at Conan. "You were feeding it all to that beast."

These days, I always heard flies buzzing, and the sound only got louder the more we talked. "You're mental, is what you are, you mental thick."

"When we make it out of this, you will rot in prison for what you've done. The Emperor will have your point-eared little head lopped off, and he'll give me your body as a trophy."

"So fuckin' be it. If it means finally being rid of you, I'll rot in one of your Mighty Ones' hells for eternity."

"You *will*, you pointless heretic. Your flesh will be seared from your bones again and again in the pits of the light hell. Look at what your heathenry has done." He threw his hand up at the walls of the labyrinth. "To this land. To *my land!*"

I rose, and he rose in perfect sync. "Say that again. Say it's your land again."

"*My* land."

Without warning, he pulled the axe looped to the saddle bags and lunged for Conan. The pig squealed shrilly and almost slipped his grasp, but he clamped his hand hard around one of the poor thing's rear legs.

"My *food!*"

With a bark, I leapt onto Gaius's back and tried to wrestle the axe from his grip. He hadn't been expecting me and let go easily, but he did not give up on Conan, redoubling his efforts and seizing the pig by his other back leg as well. I braced my good arm across his throat, wrenching, pulling, trying to choke him out of his hold, but he did not let go, even as his face turned beet red.

As Conan tripped and tried and failed to get away, his shocked squeals climbed in pitch, becoming one extended, grinding shriek unlike anything I'd ever heard—a sound of terror and pain so primal and absolute that all my insides blackened. It stabbed my eardrums and made the world go white.

Shrugging my broken arm from its sling, I fumbled for my dagger, ignoring the screaming pain. If crushing Gaius's windpipe didn't stop him, a knife would.

The flies were everywhere now. Darting about our heads. Trying to land in my eyes. Still shrieking, Conan's front legs gave out. He fell awkwardly onto his side, and a crunch echoed off the tight walls. The shrieking climbed to a pitch that seemed impossible, now cut with panting—

I replaced my good arm with a dagger to the throat, the tip threatening the tender flesh beneath Gaius's jawline. "Let go *now*. Or I swear to the Lady, I will let the mist take you, dismember you, and drag your limbless torso by that bloody red thread of yours if I have to!"

He let go. Conan hobbled his way to safety. But in the same moment, Gaius rounded on me in the direction opposite my blade's point.

With a resonant growl, he swept up the axe in his free hand. Between my broken arm, his size, and the feverish magic sparking from him, he overpowered me easily—and we were braced against one another, limbs trembling, teeth bared, our blades inches from each other's throats.

An animal scream rose in my chest. I *could feel* my body and mind both unraveling.

Him. Gaius. I would eat *him*, starting from his fingers and working my way back, and *I* would make it through the labyrinth alive.

My vision swarmed with blowflies. Reality bowed. Cracks began to form in me as in glass under great pressure.

Then a shadow flicked in my periphery. I heard a voice but didn't. *Stay with me. Keep your wits about you, my rose.*

A gasp sawed out of my throat.

The flies dispersed, their drone quieting. I dropped away from the deadlock with such quickness that Gaius nearly fell forward on his face. He staggered and steadied himself on the wall, shook his face clear of sweat-soaked curls, and looked at me blearily. My ears flicked wildly about my head as I listened to the whispers within the pulsing walls.

The frenzied magic crowding Gaius's eyes diminished; sense seemed to return to him. "Wh...What is it?" he rasped. "What do you hear?"

"Hiberos." A distinct purr, that sort of deep-throated clicking the faun sometimes did, had me whipping around to find its origin. I turned just in time to see the very end of a trail of moths disappear round the next corner.

Finally, it clicked. *She cannot control me fully. I have power, too.*

"Gealach isn't the only one who can manipulate the labyrinth." I laid my palms on the wall, skimmed it as I walked to the bend and peered around it. There was nothing there, just a straight corridor like all the others, yet I got the feeling I was supposed to follow these shadows. All along, what I had thought were omens were his way of leading us through. "He's here, watching us. He has been the whole time."

Gaius gave no response. I returned to him and the saddle bags, replaced my sling, and grabbed a healing draught. Conan was curled up in an alcove at the other end of the corridor, shivering, his ears so low they practically covered his eyes.

Fury over Gaius's outburst licked my heart all over again, but I had already spent too long wallowing in anger and madness. It was time to end this. I took a deep breath through my nose to gather myself and crouched by my animal companion.

"I'm not leaving you behind," I whispered, placing my hand on his injured leg. It was bruised and swollen but not broken—probably sprained, maybe fractured. A healing draught would mend it enough for him to make the rest of the journey, at least. I hoped. "Drink this."

When I uncorked the bottle, he leaned forward, his entire nose wiggling as he searched for the smell. When he caught a whiff, he pulled his head back and loosed an offended honk.

"I know, it's not as yummy as mushrooms you find off the floor, but you have to drink it."

By the time I managed to convince him and we sat long enough to let the fractures heal, Gaius was pacing in circles, biting his cuticles bloody and worrying his loose teeth. As we approached, he straightened and flicked his cape aside. "If you're quite done wasting our resources on barn animals, explain yourself. Where is my—our—*your* damned demon?"

On cue, a horned shadow flickered behind him, out of sight round the corner. The air filled with a deep chuckling that only I seemed to hear. It made me shiver, the feeling of our souls just brushing ... only just able to touch one another.

I'm coming for you.

So long.

After so long, so much walking, walking, *walking*, we were within reach.

+☽·☾·☽·☾+

THE SHADOW LED US ON, skimming across walls, ducking out of alcoves, pooling in the cracks of the floor, its chuckling accompanied by the faint clip of hooves and chime of bells. Moths swarmed behind us, keeping up from turning back. Somewhere nearby, I smelled roses. Not the light, sweet scent of sea roses but the deep, heady, fragrant scent of dark claret petals. The scent of an old, dense rosebush, rich and slightly acidic. As soon as I smelled them, petals began to appear along the obsidian flagstones, scattered, fallen from seemingly nowhere.

The pulse we'd been feeling for ... it must be days ... grew stronger the deeper we went. We were closing in on the center of the labyrinth.

More shadows began to appear. Not just the fleeting glimpses of what must be a shade of Hiberos but others, some human, some with pointed ears, some merely wisps. Their laughter joined the bells, mere snatches of sound, like something lost in a memory. Now that I acknowledged their signs, they gave them in abundance. My breath was a ghost in my throat as they led us onward.

Conan's step became springier, lighter, and mine did, too. Yet as hope flourished in me, it continued to wither in Gaius. He trailed behind us, swaying slightly, unable to walk a straight line. When he wasn't tearing at his cuticles or pulling out his teeth, he was holding his head in his hands, muttering about the fire in his chest and the pulse in his head.

I could do little but call over my shoulder every so often that we approached the end. And I was certain it was true, now. The spires of the Mournful Palace loomed above us like silent judges now.

Finally, the shades led us to a circular courtyard at least fifty yards across. Apart from the uneven black flagstones and thorny growths, there was nothing in the center, but the chamber was trimmed with rose hedges reaching valiantly for the top of the labyrinth walls. They were old, with thick growth and blood-red blooms the size of my hand spread open.

The flickering shadows and faint bells that had guided us faded at once, and could not be heard no matter how I swiveled my ears.

The silence of the labyrinth bore down on us again, not yet maddening but threatening, warning that it could crush us in madness again if it chose. Due to my encounters in courtyards like these—that awful illusory fae party came to mind—already, I was on my guard.

It didn't help that the walls rose fifty feet all around us. Of course, they were that tall in the rest of the labyrinth, but here, with so large a space, it was almost reminiscent of a... Oh, what was it the Aquilans called it?

"Gaius."

When I turned, he was stumbling through the rose arch

marking the entry. His remaining teeth chattered, his mouth moving with faint whispers. It took him a moment to respond to the sound of his own name, but he looked up, eye wide, the iris seething. His voice was thin and parched. "I hear you."

"What are those things called ... the Aquilans love them ... you send prisoners to fight lions and die?"

He blinked, slow to answer. "Arena."

The moment he said it, sconces hidden in recesses in the walls blazed to life—flames of tainted moon magic, that same sizzling blood-orange. A scream ripped through the courtyard, shaking the rose hedges of loose petals. A female scream of rage that morphed into the deep, echoing roar of an outsized beast.

At once, my hand flew to my bow. A sinking feeling in my stomach told me I was about to meet what Gealach had held back.

32

A blood-orange substance the translucency and consistency of water appeared in the air, as though a giant had spread a smear of paint across an invisible canvas. Smatter after smatter of the substance appeared, and though the strokes seemed flat, their surfaces rippled and seethed in a way that made them seem much deeper than they were, like portals to a realm of blood and pain.

At first, their placement seemed random; then they seeped outward, spreading like wine across linen, and took shape. A head with a long, slender nose. Horns. A barrel-chested body, claws. Wings, too tattered and small to ever support the creature attached to them.

Finally, the writhing light turned inward, and the dragon's shape solidified into reality.

Oh, she was magnificent. Magnificent and terrible. All obsidian, her scales and face were sharp and pointed, yet these harsh angles were contrasted with flowing, organic horns that spiraled from her head with imperfect symmetry. Her body was bound in vines of similar arbitrary pattern. Every inch of these, along with her horns and extremities, was covered in the same huge, black thorns coating the briars around the labyrinth. Her body itself, though, was emaciated. Almost skeletal—rib cage protruding, eyes nothing but empty sockets, nostrils sunken. Whether she had truly been starved or this vision of death comprised some kind of armor, I could not tell, but it was grotesque nonetheless.

Was she a prisoner, a protector? A pawn, or simply the final, terrible construct of a goddess riddled by madness?

The dragon heaved every breath. With every inhale, branches of crimson flared and shot outward through her ribs, each time shooting farther and glowing brighter. Almost too late, I realized what was coming for us.

"*Breath!*" I screamed, and threw myself out of the way just as she was opening her jaws.

Conan squealed and jumped into a rose bush, which trembled with his intrusion before swallowing him whole. Gaius dropped the saddle bags and dodged the other way, drawing his sword but fumbling his shield.

Fortunately—or perhaps unfortunately—he had the time to fumble, because the dragon had eyes only for me. She screamed a blaze of corrupted moon magic and, as I ran, craned her neck to chase me with it. The strange burning-yet-icy fever of the withering licked my heels and shriveled the curls at the nape of my neck.

Her breath seemed never-ending. The *sound* of it alone was enough to drive one to madness, a keen, world-shaking shriek underpinned with the perpetual growl of tumbling stone. All of the horrific smells of the blight came with it, so sour and foul that I choked as I dodged closer to the dragon.

I dove for her undercarriage. Her neck was not so long that she could reach me there—but then it was her rending claws and stomping feet that became my enemy.

Still, I was fast, and she was a big beast. Even as she turned ponderously, lifting her front foot to crush me, I ducked under her belly and came out the other side. "Gaius!"

He had secured his shield to his left arm and dropped into a defensive stance. From the horns coiling back from his scalp to the pulsing light in his chest and veins, he shone with Hiberos's heart-magic. With a roar of what might be pain, he set the blade of his sword aflame, and reinforced his shield with the same magic, transforming it from a large round shield to a tower shield guarding his entire body.

It was his stolen power, rather than any threat, that drew the dragon's attention away from me. Meanwhile, trying to figure out how I would fight a dragon with one arm, I ran back to where the saddle bags lay, dashed them open, and shoved the remaining potions into my bandolier.

And then the dragon spoke.

"**Betrayer**."

Her voice was deep and ancient as the land around us, though neither of those words began to describe the strength of it. A voice from the Beneath itself, wavering on the edge of madness, hysteria glinting in every consonant. She whipped her thorny tail toward me, missing by no more than a foot.

"**You call out for him. For him, the man who burns us, who cuts us, who rapes us. Betrayer!**" She was wailing now, racked with grief and flexing her claws. "**Ungrateful daughter. Selfish daughter. We never should have harbored you. We never should have helped you!**"

For a moment, I thought perhaps I was face to face with Gealach herself. Yet something about the lilt in her tone and the way her viney extremities shifted and changed reminded me of—

"Geatacoill," I whispered.

She shrieked sharp and grating and wild like a banshee. A monster of twisted, distinctly female anguish. "**Do not call us by our name. You have no right. You abandoned us. Betrayer!**"

With a harsh grunt, she snapped her jaws toward Gaius, who leapt back and struck a glancing blow across the tip of her snout with his shield. Though I stood stunned, caught between my loyalty to the enchanted forest and my desire to reach the center of the labyrinth, Gaius had no such compunction. With a wild cry of his own, he feinted left and dodged right, sinking his empowered blade into the tender flesh of her eye socket.

"Wait!" I chugged a healing potion and discarded the vial. "Don't kill her!"

He did not—could not—spare me a glance as he deflected the dragon's razor-sharp teeth and claws. "By the Mighty Ones, do not distract me with your madness. The only way we will reach the center is *through this beast!*" With each of those last words, he struck—one, two, three times—slicing through the vines binding her throat.

A faint, fluttering glow revealed itself. A break in her tarnished obsidian scales. A little tender spot in the hollow of her throat, below her jaws.

A blend of triumph and horror squeezed my heart to the point of bursting. *Every dragon has one.*

I threw all but one of my healing potions back, grabbed my bow, and tried not to lose consciousness. Even as I nocked a blood-orange arrow and drew, aiming for her weak spot, I cried, "This isn't who you are!"

It was as though she sensed my particular movements, lifting her head with a deep rumble. Her empty sockets homed in on me. I loosed my arrow the same instant she swiped her claws, but it fizzled uselessly against her scales.

"**This**," she hissed, "**is exactly who I am. Who I always was meant to be. This is what I must do if I'm to protect myself. Do you not** *see***? The world wants us dead, dead, every Éirin** *dead***!**"

Her claw came crashing down. She sundered the flagstones where I'd stood just a moment before. I danced forward, then back. Tried to avoid her attacks, all the while looking for an opening to strike the pulsing light in her throat.

"**To endure, we must expand!**" Geatacoill bellowed, throwing Gaius aside like a rag doll. "**To defend, we must destroy! To live, we. Must.** *Kill.*" And she straightened out, in-in-inhaling until the crimson shooting through her ribs boiled with lunar flame.

My heart broke even as the horror of her words—and power of her impending attack—bolted down my spine. For how often had

I thought the same? How often had my grief overwhelmed me such that I could see no way to peace but a scourge of fire, no way to freedom that did not involve purging the land of every non-Éirin? In the deepest, darkest nights, staring into the yawning blackness of the void, how many times had I vowed to kill anyone I needed to reclaim our territory? Geatacoill was all our suffering, all our grief, and all our wrath. The bleeding, beaten earth beneath my feet finally begging, in real words that I could hear, to be avenged.

And I could not obey her.

As the dragon's chest filled with power, I was a woman torn in two, my thoughts scraps of bloody white flag flying apart. Perhaps I *was* the betrayer she saw. Fighting at the side of the man who had destroyed my country life after life. How monstrously selfish of me, doing all this for Hiberos. For a love I was never supposed to feel to begin with.

Perhaps I should stand aside. Or perhaps it would be easier to stand still, to not choose, than to choose to move against my mother the land.

I thought of the many times I had run to her, retreated into her thicket and between her trees to get away from Gaius. It was under her boughs that he'd spilled my blood. She should know I had nothing for him in my heart but hatred. She, of all people, should know.

She was not in her right mind.

"You don't mean those things," I rasped, biting back howling pain—aiming my bow steady even as she thumped toward me. "I know you're scared. I know you're ... sick."

I blinked away tears as I loosed a triad of arrows. One went wide, but two found their mark, lodging in her throat.

With a screech like a massive boiling kettle, Geatacoill reared back, her claws closing around her throat. The magic arrows turned to smoke as she touched them.

Gaius had recovered from her violent dismissal and shouted at me, *"That!* Do that again!"

Surprise, fear, hatred, bitterness, they all flashed across her draconic features—and with a grunt of pain and disgust, she redoubled the speed of her advance toward me.

"**Hateful daughter**," she growled, "**ungrateful daughter. Terrible daughter. Evil daughter! What you lack in compassion for me, you make up for in cleverness. Oh, goddess forgive me for raising someone who treats me thus!**"

I ignored the words. It was all I could do.

With a war shout, Gaius jumped to plunge his sword beneath a scale. He stuck her hard. I had to imagine it felt something like getting stabbed with a pin under one's fingernail; it drew from her an inelegant honk that reminded me of Conan. Ribbons of lunar mist spiraled from her nose as she turned to swipe him again with her claws. She flicked her tail toward me. I was barely able to avoid it. It hit the wall hard, crumbling the stone and destroying a swath of rose hedges. At the same moment, Gaius dodged her strike, then blocked with his shield and dodged her other talon, too.

He was luring Geatacoill away from me, and she took the bait. She growled with fury as she turned her attention fully to him.

Still, I wasn't safe. As she snapped and clawed and bore down on him, she whipped her tail back and forth, trying to find me and crush me without line of sight. Her tail was long, thick as a birch trunk and barbed with thorns nearly as long as my forearms. It came at me like a battering ram, barely giving me enough time to duck, then soared over my head with a *woosh*.

Too close. And just as soon as it was gone, it was coming back again.

"Shoot the damned thing!" Gaius shouted hard enough that his throat went raw.

Before I could tell him that he needed to turn her toward me, her tail was wooshing over my head again. This time, it grazed me close enough that a thorn caught a loose curl and ripped it from my scalp. I howled and cursed. Blood exploded, painting my hair, and my hands when I grabbed it.

Hands, plural, because the tug had been enough to send the

bow flying from my grip. It skittered across the uneven, broken flagstones and stopped somewhere between Geatacoill's tail and her hind claws.

"*Shoot it!*" Gaius's cries were shrill now.

"*I can't bloody shoot it!*" I shrieked back. Through the dragon's shifting legs, I saw that she had buried her claws in his shield and was bearing down on him with all her strength.

In-in-inhale. Another gout of lunar fire would be next, and I did not know if his shield or his stolen power would hold up against it.

Dropping to my hands and knees, I swept myself under her tail. Crawled toward my weapon, as close as I dared to her stomping feet. Stopped. Stretched a hand out, straining, the fingertips of my good hand just grazing the bow's upper limb...

Gaius must have struck in desperation, for the beast grunted and shifted unexpectedly above me.

It was all I could do to throw myself to safety. I watched in horror as my bow was crushed to matchsticks beneath her hind claw.

May the Lady make a ladder out of your fucking backbone.

A great cold entered my chest, racking me with shivers as I tried in vain to summon a bow of pure energy, something I had seen other fae do. Nothing came, not even a spark that fizzled out. Geatacoill backed up again, and again I rolled in symphony.

The dragon had recovered from Gaius's blow and was inhaling again, scarlet spidering across her torso an angrier red than ever before. "*Mave!*" Gaius's shout was strangled, frantic. A tone you never wanted to hear from someone fighting beside you, no matter who they were.

I had to do something to help him, bow be damned. I slapped my bandolier and found two daggers, Orlaith's lunar blade and Tali's family dagger. Fighting a dragon at close range. With what amounted to toothpicks.

Not exactly ideal. But at least it would most likely be the last thing I ever fucked up.

This time, when the tail swiped for me, I was ready for it.

Waiting for it, both arms outstretched, fractured bone and all. I licked my parched, cracked lips as the tail soared toward me in slow motion, every barb glinting ... and at the last second, I jumped. Not over it but *onto* it.

I landed hard. All the wind left my lungs, the world went white, and ringing muted the battle raging around me. It was everything I could do to keep my hold on the swinging tail—to inch my way upward despite the agony shooting up my arm in numb bolts of lightning. No doubt if my body was still that of a mortal human, I'd be broken beyond repair.

A horrific crunching sound followed by screams of prey-animal panic told me she had pushed Gaius into the hedges. Much farther and she'd crush his bones to dust.

If ever there was a time to channel my fae heritage, it was now.

If only I could harness the tranquility I often felt emanating from other fae, placid and cool like the surface of a moonwell. With breath stalled in my throat, I closed my eyes and tried to find it. But there was nothing behind my eyelids but panic, fear, hunger, desperation, and a rage so ancient and profound that awareness of it sent a bolt of adrenaline through my limbs.

Fine. If I couldn't channel my fae heritage, I'd channel my human one.

With a final, deranged roar, my eyes snapped open. And I was on my feet, not thinking, just *feeling*, arms pumping, boots flying across scales and vines and thorns. Up the dragon's spine like a ladder, past her tattered wings.

At the base of her neck, I clenched my dagger between my teeth and fell to my knees. My hands wrapped around a thick vine still wrapped around her throat below the weak spot.

Geatacoill snorted and roared with indignation. She shook her head hard, trying to hit me with her horns or buck me off, but I held fast, my battle cry never ceasing. Beneath her claws, Gaius was forgotten. Battered, barely able to move, he threw himself aside—just in time to avoid the entirety of Geatacoill's weight as she surged forward, ramming the hedges and obsidian walls again and again in her attempt to get me off her neck.

Everything shook. Were it not for the dagger between my teeth, I would bite my tongue in half. Blood poured from punctures and cuts given by the thorns all about me. Chunks of the wall fell inward, shards of obsidian primed to gut whoever they struck. I must be screaming, for my throat felt sliced open, yet I could hear nothing but ringing and the thump of my heart.

I loosened my grip on the vine enough to slide along the curve of her neck. Time slowed. My feet flailed. Boots skidded against her scales. The soles vibrated, squealed, nearly bald from the last few days of walking—but I found purchase.

I couldn't hang by my weak arm. One strike or unexpected jolt would send me tumbling between her feet to become paste. My left hand tightened to a vice grip again. Just the left, suspending me. With my right, I snatched the dagger from my mouth and reeled back.

Geatacoill roared a frenzy, shaking her head vigorously. Then she reared up on her hind legs, and I knew she was reaching for me, could feel the heat of her claws closing in on my back—

My heart stopped. The ringing cleared from my ears. All sound came back in one great whoosh. And with a final, strangled, hot, wild cry, I swung my dagger forward. I put every ounce of strength and magic left in my body into the strike.

With a horrible woody crunch and mossy squelching, my arm sank in to mid-bicep. An explosion of tainted lunar magic lit Geatacoill's rib cage from the inside, the red glow projecting the shadows of her vine-smothered organs. Power and agony pulsed through me in concert, intense enough that my head snapped back, my spine bowed. My eyes rolled back, and the world went white as I seized.

Then I was falling.

Her cries had turned too pitiful to come from such a magnificent creature. Her moan was mournful, long, deep and full-throated like an elk's call. Air squealed from her like a punctured lung as her body withered and deflated. She snatched me up in one foreclaw. Then, with her head raised to the moon, she swayed and slumped to one side.

We fell together, hitting the flagstones hard enough to shake the entire labyrinth again. Her foreclaw struck the ground and sprang open. I was thrown, and rolled limply into a hedge. Everything went gray.

It must only have been a few seconds that I lost my vision. But when it came back, I was acutely aware of every pain in my body. With a groan, I rolled onto my back, staring at the angry red moon perfectly at its zenith.

A crackling, as from a bonfire, drew my attention to the dragon's corpse. She lay in a heap, hardly identifiable as a creature rather than a pile of rotting bracken and briar. Crimson embers flickered in her chest cavity still, though they tumbled from her and blinked out one by one. Each wrought its ghost upon the flagstones, little wisps of smoke vanishing as soon as they appeared.

Geatacoill.

As I rose, my knees knocked—then gave out completely, reducing me to a crawl. I tried to call upon my right arm. When it gave no response, I dragged myself instead, worming my way through soot and ash to climb up the dragon's flank.

Once on top of the heap, I slumped. First to my knees. Then my nose, prostrating. She smelled of char and old blood and all the terrible things the withering had done to her, yet beneath that layer of filth, I smelled *her*. The particular bite of fresh air through her boughs, the scent of birch bark, the steadiness of oak and the wisdom of yew...

I clutched a fistful of charred wood that was quickly turning to mulch. Only dimly did I register that the reason my right arm was not responding was because it was gone, torn off mid-bicep. Bitter tears, the tears of a child, branded my cheeks as I wept and howled with all the desolate misery of the banshee.

Geatacoill. My protector. My companion. My charge, and my teacher of harsh lessons. My mother.

Gone.

33

The next sound I was aware of was Gaius choking on his curse.

My eyes were bruised, my head pounding and fuzzy as I slid down Geatacoill. He stood next to the saddle bags, doubled over into himself with his hands wrapped around his neck. He lurched and retched, spewing jets of thick blood—yet all the while, the magic in his veins throbbed faster, glowed brighter, raring to go, go, go.

To say I felt like death warmed over was generous. I gathered my sling to the stump of my missing arm to stanch the heavy bleeding. A wound in the back of my head bled hard enough that it seeped down my nape and into my collar. Geatacoill had squeezed me, and I knew most of my ribs were collapsed. But Gaius was coming undone. Utterly, actively. He looked mere moments from imploding and scorching the land with his ill-used power.

I watched him a while and felt ... nothing. Not disgust, nor joy, nor even apathy. Simply nothing. This place had hollowed me. Even the prospect of advancing from this chamber and reaching the center of the labyrinth brought no emotion.

If Geatacoill was dead, was it all for nothing? Had I finally lost everything?

Gaius coughed, breaths shuddering as he straightened and wiped his mouth. Never had I seen him so pale, so clammy, so gaunt. It was a stark contrast to the indomitable power pulsing from him—the power of the sun and moon stuffed into this pathetic husk of a man. With a moan and a grimace, he pulled a molar from the very back of his mouth. And when he looked at me, as if asking for help, his pupil was hazy and unfocused.

We stared at each other until crows came down from the sky to peck at Geatacoill's heaped corpse. When finally I slipped back down to the flagstones to nurse the last healing draught, Conan crept out of his hedge, but not even a nudge from his wet nose could lift my shattered spirit. I looked down at my left arm. It was covered in cuts, blood clots, and bits of moss. The other, of course, was gone. Every inch of my body cried out for an end, any end.

Crushed. Mangled. Even with fae resilience and human persistence, I would not be making it out of this labyrinth alive. Darkness throbbed in my peripherals, the loving hands of Death once again beckoning me closer.

At least the mist had receded.

"Let's go, then." My voice was sand, hot and dry and rough in my throat. "You haven't much time, looks like."

I didn't grab any weapons. There was no point.

Beyond Geatacoill's body, opposite to where we'd entered, lay a passage leading to a covered archway or tunnel. Its entry resembled the odd, layered aperture that had led into the prophecy chamber. We shuffled forward, Gaius barely able to keep himself on two legs and me barely able to move at all. Every step sliced through my spine, my ribs, my shoulder, into my very soul. My vision blurred and over-sharpened at intervals.

Then the darkness of the tunnel enveloped us, and vision mattered little.

The silence as we limped through the tunnel was unlike the silence in the rest of the labyrinth. This was neither hollow nor crushing, although ... smothering, a bit, perhaps. It was the silence of a sacred place, a temple; a silence laced with incense—jasmine, blackberries, sandalwood. A silence caused not by the absence of something vital but the presence of prayerful worship. Yet it was interrupted at intervals by a great creaking that reminded me of a splintering trunk or a sinking ship. Something deeper in the palace rattled, tinkling.

I half expected to see a cathedral full of worshipers when we finally reached the faint red light at the end of the tunnel. Instead, we found ourselves in what remained of Erivon and Orlaith's sunken throne room. The tree looming above the dais at the far end—the one whose roots held together the stonework—was tainted with the blight, its once blue-and-green leaves the browns of old menstrual rags. The moss carpeting the floor was in the same state. Above, shining through open ceiling, the blood moon's rays shone narrowly on the thrones, casting long shadows that seemed to reach toward me.

I'd expected Hiberos to be waiting in one of the thrones, but he must be deeper in the palace. My eyes caught on a crater in the center of the room, just before the dais. No, not a crater, a hole. A dark, gaping hole filled with cloudy water. It looked as if something had crashed through the ceiling and torn a hole clear through the stone and dirt into depths unknown. The way the water twinkled reminded me of a moonwell.

Gaius's breath hitched behind me, and he made an effort to hurry toward the thrones. "Look. They're empty."

"Gaius—" Adrenaline gave me enough strength to catch his wrist weakly.

He whipped his head round, eye gleaming with madness. "Empty because they're waiting. For us. It's ours. All of it. This palace. The goddess is gone, and this is all there is left to claim."

I shook my head. Not only was he mad, he was wrong. Gealach wasn't gone. She was more alive than she had been since the Shift, and she was here. "Ignore the thrones. Whatever you feel now, she's playing some kind of game with you."

Yet I did not get the sense that this was a trick of the goddess. Her influence seemed to have retreated along with the mist; wherever she was, she was holed up, waiting for me to come. This was a product of Gaius's own insanity. Somehow, that was more frightening.

"Don't you understand?" he pressed. "The labyrinth was no puzzle, no obstacle. It was a map. Of my own veins. I've been counting them. I know the solution."

Here he broke from my grip and stepped around the gaping hole without acknowledging it. A moment later, he was standing before Erivon's throne, stroking the etchings in its surface. It disturbed me how alert he seemed now. He'd never looked so happy, nor so awed.

"Something is changing." His whisper echoed all around the chamber. "Something is gestating deep inside this palace. All the trees are connected. The Sun and the Moon. Don't you remember the final verse?"

He'd come into the temple ruins with me, but I hadn't realized he'd memorized the verses. So focused had I been on translating the second verse that the third seemed like a distant memory.

I stared at his back, at his tense shoulders—and it was as though my gaze was the final straw breaking him. He bowed under the weight, gasped; his hands flew to the straps and buckles of his armor. Blood painted the battle-tarnished metal as he clawed his breastplate off, then his greaves and boots, his arm guards, pauldrons, and finally, his tunic and his bandages, casting them all aside. Then he stood before me in only his smallclothes, shivering and heaving with illness, his eye wide, capillaries shot. For the first time, I saw the heart in its full glory. It shone through his chest, pulsing hard.

I also saw the full extent of his injuries.

Every inch of his skin was opened, nearly flayed. Besides the glowing veins and the relatively untouched skin of his face, he was nothing but a mass of blood. Yet he had never stood before me with such honesty. Finally, his outsides matched his insides. Finally, he looked like what he was: a bleeding wound.

He recited the final verse:

"When single shine the moon and sun,
The war o'er land at last be won;
The rift shall close, the two made one
By fire's child and shadow's son."

"This," he explained slowly, jaw working, muscles trembling as though every word opened another wound. For all I knew, it did. "This is not a punishment. It is not ruin. It ... is..." He searched for the word. "A marriage. It will *produce*. The blight is merely its veil."

I clutched my stump tighter, far too fatigued to be enraged. "I'm no bride."

For once, he seemed unbothered by my rejection; in fact, he seemed not to hear it at all as he craned his neck to stare at the tree's withering boughs. "I'll win the land. The Emperor will—" He shook his curls from his eyes. "No. Once we claim the trees' power, we'll be so much more than any emperor."

"*Gaius.*" I caught his attention and approached, sparing a quick glance down the bottomless pit as I passed it. "I'm not claiming anything, and neither are you."

He shook his head and loosed a breathy laugh. "I see the future. It is too late. The blood runs through the earth, through every tree, down these branches and straight into me, even now." He turned his wrists for me, showed proudly the pulsing rivers of his veins. "Their power is mine. It is already happening. Burgeoning. Something bigger..."

"Gaius!" His name caught his attention again. "Focus. Remember why we're here." I tried to soften my voice despite the anger and panic rising within me. A special kind of hell, being forced to speak softly to your tormentor. But I needed him to comply. I needed him to survive long enough to get the heart to Hiberos. Then he could go as mad as he liked. "You're ... sick. Delirious. We need to find Hiberos, to take that heart out of you before its power completely overwhelms you."

Gaius balked and snatched his arms away from me. "Take it out?" It was as though I had suggested we saw off his head. "No.

No, I need it. In order to become what I need to be. Forever. Even if you won't take your place, I will."

I looked between him and the thrones, calculating my next move. "All right," I lied at last. "I'll take my place. I will do whatever you want. Only, *after* we find Hiberos, right? After we find Hiberos."

After seeming to weigh my reaction, he snarled with frustration. "No, Mave—"

He took one step forward, I took one back.

"*Look*, man. You are falling apart," I managed through chattering teeth. "Literally. You can barely walk, you are fevered, you have hardly an inch of skin left. Hiberos can cure you." If I could just make him *see*... "You are too weak—"

The moment that word passed my lips, I knew I'd made a terrible mistake. Probably my last mistake.

His body burst with heartmagic, sparking red and coral and yellow as though he were hot iron struck with my words. His eye sockets and the horns coiling from him glowed so brightly they were opaque. Each syllable he uttered next, the light and heat coming off him grew in intensity.

"I. Am *not*. WEAK!"

Before I could react, his blazing hands were on my collarbone. He pushed me backward with all his might, knocking the breath from me. When I moved to steady myself on my back leg, my foot touched nothing. With my right arm, I flailed and clawed for the rim to catch myself—but there was no right arm. And I was falling.

The trees' bloody boughs shrank away. My stomach upturned. I crashed into the water but kept falling with the same momentum.

Darkness closed in. The last image I registered was Gaius's wrath lighting the whole of the chamber above.

IF MY BODY made impact with the ground, I didn't feel it. Nor did I remember losing consciousness. Yet I was not quite lucid as I registered a gentle, dim gray light and the strong, hard, smooth arms encircling me.

With a soft chuff of a sigh, he carried me like a bride, my battered body curled inward and pressed close. In my haze my fingers crept unbidden to his chest, searching for the scarred knot I remembered over his heart—but instead I found the ragged gouge left by Gaius's blade, and his new markings, the rivers and tributaries of Éire.

I didn't know where we walked. But as my awareness returned to me bit by bit, I began to understand our surroundings as a cathedral. Black limestone. Arched ceilings. Windows with tracery, though there was nothing but a thick wall of fog on the other side. Finally, we entered a large chamber with an oculus in the ceiling. At the far end of this room sat a black throne. The one from my dreams. It was real. Unlike the rest of the palace, it was awash in cool blue rather than the mad red of the blood moon. Due to Hiberos's influence, I was certain.

Finally, as we ascended the steps to the throne, I raised my head. It really was him. Hiberos. My poet. My teacher. My god. My Guardian. His skin oaken, lean form muscular, eyes bright, hair untangled and luxuriant. The dark gold of his beard and sideburns shone nearly bronze in the low light.

Seeing him felt like the same strange sensation in my arm, but in my chest this time. My phantom limb. When we were separated—as we had been so often—I was missing a part of *me*. Because everything I did was his doing, and whatever I touched was touched also by him.

My lips parting, I reached up to stroke reverent fingers through his hair and beard, and a smile touched one corner of his broad mouth. As he set me down in the throne, I offered him an half-dead smile in return.

Without ceremony or pretense, he was on his knees, gathering me into his arms. Breathing me in deep. Then he took me by my jaw and kissed me as if he were a flame starved of oxygen, jumping, feverish, wild. When he pulled back, I was dazed. But content. Despite everything, without any conscious thought, touching him relaxed me to the farthest reach of my soul. I cupped his face with my remaining hand and nuzzled our noses together, inhaling in his scent, his breath, his magic. Everything.

"I knew you would come," he murmured, his voice rumbling through me like a thunder storm.

"Whether you wanted me to or not," I managed.

While he set about properly quelling the blood flow of my stump, I studied him. Just like in my visions and dreams, rather than his usual crown of holly, he wore the crown of thorns and roses. Gealach's crown, marking him as her property. Small rivulets of black blood stained his hair and skin where the thorns had pricked him. Possessiveness stoked a fire within that had me sitting up straighter, clutching him a bit tighter, seeing a bit clearer.

Hiberos paused in his ministrations to lean into the hand stroking his jaw. "My bloody, thorny rose, I knew very well that you would come no matter how I tried to convince you. Even if you faced certain death. I knew you would honor our pact." He pressed his huge hand over mine, gazing at me with the heavens in his eyes. "Perhaps to protect you I should have turned you away, or otherwise fixed the labyrinth as I did the trials. The difference is ... I believe in you. I believed that you could reach this place." His voice was a breath away from shattering. "And I believe you can save me. Save all of us."

At that moment, something beyond Hiberos caught my eye: in the shadows of the chamber, just out of reach of the pool of moonlight, were ... fomori. Hundreds of them, some kneeling, some prostrate, others entreating with open hands—stone and vine, conkreet and trash, ruin and blight, the newborn flesh beings. Among them were a few thornbloods, as well, dotting the congregation with tiny red lights. Worshipers murmuring prayers. Exactly as I had expected. Subjects petitioning their king.

"She really did make you the King of the Fomori." I fought the venom in my throat. "But where is she? There is only one throne."

"She has no throne," he murmured against my darkening

fingertips. "She requires none to hold court. She is everywhere. Aware of us now. Watching us."

"Then how do I release you?"

He chuckled. "You think the only way to win is with a physical fight? That there must be a body to prove your victory? Oh, my huntress."

"If she refuses to relinquish you and the land, I'll do what I have to do." I took a deep, shaky breath, wincing, struggling to keep my head above the greywater of unconsciousness. I'd died before. It had felt like this. "If that makes me unevolved or stupid or violent or dishonorable, fine. At least you'll be free."

As we spoke, his magic wrapped around me and began to heal me. Blood perpetuated in my heart and limbs, my bones snapped as they were manipulated back into place, my vision became less blurry.

Hiberos was quiet for a long time. "When Mother Moon died, we Guardians bore what remained of her spirit to its new home— her tomb, the Beneath—and vowed never to share its location. It is connected to a vast network of tunnels and temples, each containing magic and lore that was laid to rest when she was."

"I remember," I whispered. "We stand in one now."

"You stand in *the* one. Her very crypt." He cast his eyes down to the floor. "The final vault lies below. What awaits you there, I do not know. It has not been opened for over three thousand years. But if her spirit takes form, I imagine it would do so there."

The greywater had receded from my vision, but I still was in no shape to do battle. In no shape to do anything but sit here and breathe pathetically. I shook my head, croaking, "I want to fight. I want to save you. But I cannot face her. She would crush me."

Hiberos searched my face, then squeezed my hand tighter, brushing the back with his thumb as he brought it to the wound over his heart. When I touched it now, it glowed not blue but with the coral-gold heartmagic. "Then do not fight her strength. Fight her grief. It is the only weapon she truly wields anymore."

"How can I do that when in her eyes, I've wronged her? Stolen something that's hers. She hates me."

"Only because you are her mirror, Mave." He squeezed my chin in one hand, gaze tracing the lines of my jaw. "You represent so many uncomfortable truths. About the Underland, about humans, about me ... about her. Yet truths they are. Truths they remain. Truths that will restore this land."

I swallowed, and closed my eyes for an extended moment. "Truths she doesn't want to hear. If I misstep, if I say the wrong thing ... with a wave of her hand, she could set the fomori on me. I'll die. And without the magic of the Underland, this time, I will not come back."

Hiberos leaned in, his heat and scent a balm as he kissed me again. This time, the kiss was gentle, deep, his lips soft and sweet-tasting as they parted mine. When our tongues slid together, it was the tender caress of lovers who knew one another inside and out. The embrace of two people who had all the time in the world. It may be a false promise, a misguided dream, but it was one I could live in forever. I wished he could drink me, join us as one forever—hide me away inside him, safe from pain and duty and choice, only to be let out when the world was healed and I could be as others seemed so effortlessly to be: vulnerable, naked, true, free.

When he pulled away, his pleasant, earthy breath blew snowy little curls out of my face. "I realize it's difficult through all the horror, but remember: she is your mother."

"No. If I had a mother, it was Geatacoill, and because of Gealach, she's dead."

"Perhaps. But in her own way, however flawed, however hideous, she does love you. It was never your death she craved. She could have had that many times over. She wants your *surrender.*"

No sound passed between us but the murmuring from the supplicants at the base of the throne. I sat slumped for I don't know how long, eyes barely open, breaths slow and serrated. Finally, I slipped my hand from his. My fingers crawled to one arm of the throne, and I leaned in, bracing against it and hauling myself to shaking legs.

The last thing I wanted to do was chat to the woman who'd cast her long, dark shadow over my fate for more than a thousand years. In some ways, a physical fight, however ill-advised, would be easier for me to stomach. But I had said I'd do what needed to be done.

I'd meant it.

"All right," I said, half-turning to look at him for what might be the last time. "Take me to the vault."

34

As we made our way to the burial vault, I insisted on walking rather than being carried, but still, Hiberos slung my good arm around his shoulder, letting me lean heavily into him. Our pace was slow. Though I may not be on the very brink of death any longer, by all rights I should not be vertical. As we shuffled into a dark recess of the throne room, we were grim and silent like anyone would be visiting any crypt. Soon, however, I realized that the faint, whispery chants were following us. Glancing behind, I was chilled to see the fomori trailing us in procession.

"What are they doing?" I asked on a breath.

"It isn't every day one confronts a goddess," Hiberos replied, voice silken. "Rousing one from her grave is even less common. It is most probably considered a sacred rite, opening the Moon's tomb, so they wish to be present. Or, perhaps they want to see that you do everything properly. Or perhaps they simply want to see what will happen."

The recess hid a spiral staircase let into the obsidian stone. Limping to the bottom took I don't even know how long. Long enough that, when we finally reached it, my head throbbed with thirst and my body was too exhausted to take another step.

With gentle whispers, Hiberos let me slump against his chest, and plied me with soothing moon magic as I trembled and retched. "You are doing so well, Mave. Just a little farther. There's my stubborn huntress."

It was another indeterminate period of time before I felt well enough to acknowledge the crypt, a much larger and elaborate version of the burial mounds and cairns I well knew. The ceiling arced high above our heads. Metal gates worked with the shapes of stars and planets closed off corridors heading in several directions, but the largest of these gates was the one directly in front of us, two times as tall as Hiberos. Its doors were all silver solder and stained glass depicting blooming moonflowers, and they glowed with ethereal light that seemed to come from nowhere at all. There was no doubt which was the path to Gealach's vault.

The place was quiet and desolate, yet beyond the natural silence of a crypt, there was a heaviness in the air here, a grief, a yearning, a distress that was so palpable it frightened me, as though it might, at any moment, take shape and hunt me. Swallow me whole. I'd prefer to be in the presence of Death. Few would agree that Death was quiet, predictable, safe, but it was true. Grief, though ... a different story. Want without end. A question without an answer. I knew her well, and still she gave me chills.

Hiberos led me forward, basically shouldering all of my weight with his grip firm on my waist. I wondered about the others buried here—Guardians, Old Gods, something else entirely?—but hadn't the strength to ask.

"Just a few more steps. Good girl."

With a wave of his free hand, the stained glass flashed, and the doors opened—slowly, with a low, wretched groan. Beyond lay a small antechamber lit with sconces of corrupted fire. A slab of solid moonstone obscured the inner vault.

It felt wrong to speak in this place, but as we progressed into the antechamber, I had to ask. "What ... what exactly should I be preparing for? I've—" I hacked, burying my face in his underarm to muffle the sound. "I've only ever s-seen her in memories. One. Wuh—one memory."

His brow was knit tight, expression some sickening mix of

terror, determination, love, anger, and sorrow. "I wish I could tell you, but I cannot. I have not seen her since the day we interred her spirit. What remained of it."

Then his face turned mostly sorrowful. He did not say it aloud, but somehow I knew that he could not come with me into the chamber beyond. Whatever trial awaited me, I would have to face it myself, and it was evident in his regretful expression that the prospect made him miserable.

For what might have been a full minute, we simply stared into each other's eyes. I reached for some thank-you, something that would adequately convey the many facets, the depth, the clarity of my feeling for him. How did one mark the distance between water droplets? How did one grasp the absence of something not yet discovered? What name did one give their shelter beyond *home*, and where to begin in conveying the quiet and unspoken significance of such a place?

He deserved all that and more. He deserved a thousand years of poetry written in his name, deserved every one of my hunts to be dedicated to him, deserved all my fear and anger and sickness as well as my love. He deserved to feel me running through every channel of his hide as surely as the rivers had carved the land millions of years ago.

But there was only one thing left unsaid between us. Words I had not spoken in this lifetime. Words he had waited a millennium to hear.

"I love you."

And it was true. By the stars, no matter how unfair our circumstances or ill-fated our union, I loved him. I would do it all again, a thousand times more, if need be. Rebirth, reshape, relearn, reimagine. Whatever it took. Now I saw it was more than circumstance *or* fate drawing us together. It was not a tether that bound us—not Gaius's red thread, not Gealach's of ash. Our cycle was a fine necklace, a painstakingly crafted thing with coils only nature could perfect, delicate despite being born of fire and molten metal and pounding hammers. The undefinable orbit of the sun and moon. The perfect conjunction of forces that kept the planets in their places. Unceasing and *inevitable*.

Now that he had stopped trying to corral me, and I'd stopped trying to distance myself, I saw us for what we were.

Elemental.

I wanted to take this beautiful pain and call it a gift. But to wear airs while my people starved ... to skim the surface of him every thousand years and call that enough...

It wasn't fair to either of us. To *any* of us.

This cycle could be fought. Rejected. Denied.

I was no longer willing to chase Hiberos across the sky, never touching. I loved him *now*. I chose him *now*. I yearned to join him like river to sea, and to finally see the whole of what our existence could be, without the tethers of time or place. I wanted it all, even if it meant the end. Maybe especially then.

I would wrest that right from Gealach any way I could.

Humans, after all, were persistence hunters.

But that meant I had to leave him behind, now, and face her. And, Lady, if *I* was *her* mirror, then...

"I'm frightened," I admitted. "How can I do this without you?"

"Mave," he reminded me softly, *"anywhere I go, you go, my dear, and whatever is done by only me is your doing, my darling."*

"It's you are whatever a moon has always meant, and whatever a sun will always sing is you."

With a deep breath, I closed my eyes, gave the wound over his heart one last kiss, and turned away. Gealach was waiting.

As I shuffled the few steps to the slab of moonstone, a tune began in my chest, a low hum. I laid my palm and cheek against it, leaning in heavily. Stars, I was so, so tired. To think that my creator, my mother, and my eternal tormentor was but a thick wall of stone away nearly drove me to madness.

"Wake up, wake up, dear, and let me in
For I tire of my long night's journey
And am drenched unto the skin..."

The very chamber itself seemed to lift its head in acknowledgment. I did not have to break the slab, nor lift it; I simply sank into it, letting its cool magic hum over me as I passed through.

The vault was nondescript and dark. In the center, under a beam of moonlight that seemed to come from nowhere at all sat a stone bier, its gemstone surface blackened in the shape of a female silhouette. There was no body, corporeal or otherwise, left lying there, yet I felt her all around me. Her presence was thick, like a knot forming in your throat when you tried not to cry. The sorrow, fear, and anger somehow gave the shadowed recesses density and texture.

As I limped further into the room, I scanned each corner. Finally, my gaze caught on something huddled into the farthest reach, toward the back. White and red, curled around itself, and drenched from head to toe.

My lips parted, emotion I could not even name overwhelming me as I took in the sight of her. So small. Not a goddess or a queen. Just a shivering pile of rags in a vault forgotten by time.

My shoulders lowered as a calm resolve spread outward through my torso. The room stirred with my whisper: "Hello, Mother."

She looked nothing like the Gealach in my memory, the only vaguely humanlike being who had ruled over the Underland. Slowly, she raised her face. It was so ghostly white as to be terrifying, especially framed by water-dark burgundy hair—the same shade my curls once were, the deep red of the rose. Her eyes, wide and ringed with purple-red bruising, were hazy blood moons. Her long ears were withered and burnt. Ashy cracks marred her tear-stained face. But in fact...

Apart from minor differences, and streaks of gray in her hair, she looked rather like ... me.

"My issy. Why are you here now?" Her voice was low and husky yet as fragile as dry bone. "Why have you come now, when I am reduced to this?"

I stood no more than two feet away now, looking down at her. No words came, no response, no excuse. Never had I seen a creature so pathetic, so wretched, so ... powerless. She'd said so many cruel things to me. Unforgivable things that a mother should never say to their child. I had expected to feel nothing but anger when looking upon her, but now my heart was heavy with pity. With grief for what she had become and what she could have been.

At last, when her searing gaze became too much, I spoke. "Hiberos said there might not be anything left of you."

The wide-eyed expression twisting her face was so profoundly woeful that it could not even be called anger. Unlike the furious blight of Geatacoill, this was an unglued, desperate thing. Uncomfortable to look at. Shocking to witness.

"Our people used to hold wakes," she rasped, pushing her drenched, tangled locks from her moon-white face. "Our people used to hold life in death so expertly. But there was no wake for me. No dirge. No keening women. No dregs to dash upon my body. Not even a feast. No one to watch over me and see that I stayed dead. They buried me so quickly ... as though they wanted to forget about me. As though they were ashamed."

Cold gripped my extremities. Wait. What? Then... "You've been alone down here, all alone for three thousand years. Not sleeping or dead. Alive."

I glanced back, and misery hit me like a ten-ton stone when I noticed the deep gouge marks in the iridescent slab behind me. How long had she tried to claw her way out of this tomb? The thought of her alone down here, slowly losing her mind for centuries upon centuries, bawling for relief...

"*Anam muck an dhoul*," she croaked. "Did ye drink me doornail?"

Looking back at her, I asked, unable to catch my breath, "You... Why did you not tell anyone?"

"When you scream for so long and no one listens, you begin to wonder if you were ever alive at all. After a thousand years, I stopped calling for help. After two thousand, I was beyond it. Now, I would not even know what it looks like."

"But Hiberos communed with you. I've seen him do it."

She shook her head slowly. "He did not hear the words I spoke. That became quickly apparent. My younger children did not listen. You—all of you—you held me down, convinced me to sleep. You *wanted* me dead, to feast upon my flesh while I lay still and silent. Me, your dragon volant, your architect, your builder, *creator*. So, I called to my elder children. The roots, the soil, the worms, the fomori. *They* listened. *They* obeyed."

A faint sound pricked my ears. The earth seemed to shift around us—just so, subtly. As though it was replying to her, affirming that it would always obey. I was certain that, if I could hear beyond the slab, the fomori would be moaning, too.

"Is that what you want?" I asked, an edge to my voice as I refocused on her. "For me to obey?"

"Hiberos is not yours," she rasped. "*Usqueadbaugham*. My rite. *My* whiskey. You knew the rules … both of you. You knew you hurtled toward your doom. You were warned so many times, and now I am thirsty."

Though she spoke in riddles, she wasn't wrong. We had known the rules. Time and time again, we'd chosen to disobey. "Yes. I was disobedient. I fell in love. And my punishment is *death*?"

"It hurt me more than it hurt you. I wouldn't expect you to understand," she said, too exhausted and malnourished to sound very bitter. "You aren't a mother. You would not know the pain of feeding your children, and having to discipline them, all whilst decaying. When, how is one to feed oneself? The trouble with even knowing where to begin. The loneliness of doing it all without your husband, unwakeable…"

My nostrils flared. "All of that may be so, but this is far bigger than either my disobedience or my death now. Your decay. Your neuroses. Your anger. You've ruined … everything. You've *destroyed* everything. Every mile of Cuanacht is ravaged with your sickness—"

"What?" She looked so genuinely wounded that it disarmed me. "You think *you* are the victim of this sickness? Those fat foreign eagles tear me open, bombard me, devour me, disembowel me, and you think it is *I* who have done wrong?" Her pain was great and real, voice thick as though she barely held back tears.

"Everything I did was for love. Who made you riverrun, brought you back from death? Who made you a refuge?"

"You destroyed the Underland in your fury."

"They prodded me and violated me to try and pass through that Gate. They forced themselves inside of my innermost world. *Earwickers*. They were the cause of my miscarriage. I could not let that go unpunished."

Time seemed to still. She was mad, yet how did one respond to a pain of such depth, especially when the bearer was one's mother?

Gealach may be insane, but I saw now that she wasn't evil, despite all the evil her choice had introduced into the world. What must it have been like, to make that decision alone down here? What state of mind would one have to be in where the only option seemed to be destroying the life you gave your all to maintain? Eventually, I managed, "Yet in trying to punish the Aquilans for what they did to you, you've killed thousands of your own people, and condemned thousands more to living hell."

"The more I tried to hold the rot in, the more it leaked out," she whispered. "My wound—it bled and bled, faster than I could heal. No suture could save me."

I felt sorry for her. It was difficult to watch someone try so hard without understanding that their way of being was inherently flawed. That they could try all they wanted, but at the core, they were broken. Worse still, I had no idea how to fix her. I didn't even know what she wanted. Did *she*?

"I still don't know what you want me to say—what you want at all, of me or anyone else. What is your goal? What is your plan?"

She shook her head, lips parted, but no words came forth. Only after an extended struggle did she manage to say, "I want to be cleansed. I want to join the god. I want you to obey. I want the land to be at peace. I want things to be the way they were."

"But those things cannot be, due in no small part to what *you* have done!"

"Don't *shout* at me!" She glanced furtively around the chamber, and for the first time, I realized she was clutching something to her chest. Some kind of bundle.

"What ... what is that you have there?" After stiff hesitation, I crouched and made to reach.

"*No*," she whimpered, curling tighter around it.

I licked my lips and rubbed my fingertips together uncertainly. "I won't take it from you. I only want to know."

Now I was like the mother and she the child as, inch by torturous inch, she loosened her hold on the bundle and tipped it toward me. I searched her eyes before daring to reach out again, pulling back the shroud over the bundle.

Oh.

It was something like a baby, but half-formed as though still in the womb, and more fawn than human. Despite its tiny head and desiccated neck, it bore a rack of brass antlers whose innermost branches formed a perfect circle above the crown of its head. Its little eyes twitched, then opened to look at me. They were liquid topaz, faintly metallic, with no pupil or white. Tiny, velveteen ears flapped. My breath stalled in my throat as I took in the sight. There was no doubt in my mind that what I looked at was all that remained of the Horned One, the Sun God, the Cloven-Hoofed Herald who had stood against the Great Corruption and died those many thousands of years ago. All that remained of her husband.

"When the Corruption came," she whispered, "the very waters burned, and everything withered. Every beautiful thing I had ever mothered. And then he fell, too. Never had I lived a moment without him ... we were born together. Soulfasted. His roots are mine. When he died, my life was stolen from me."

"But I thought—" I exhaled tremulously. "You wrought the Guardians of his corpse. How..."

"The same way I survived after my body was destroyed." Shaking, with a hand so pale and insubstantial it resembled fog, she touched her exposed chest where her ribs and clavicle jutted against the skin. "The mist. It is inside of me and the fomori, and we are inside it. After I stopped calling for help, I thought I might find him down here, too, but there were only vestiges. Pieces in hidden places, mere *scraps...*" Tears joined the dampness of her face. "He... There is so, so little left of him. This is all ... this is all I could find. All I could claw together, even after an eon. Only this ... and it is not nearly enough."

She was right; it wasn't enough. The little thing wheezed and spluttered in its attempt to breathe, and when I pulled the shroud back just a bit more, its little heart was visible through translucent skin and ribs as thin and delicate as pin bones.

She wept. "He does not nurse. He does not speak. He cannot hear me."

I swallowed the burning coal in my throat. First the Guardians, then the fae, the humans, herself, now even her mate— the source of all her heartbreak—were victims of her grief. Stars, where did it end? I looked down at the poor thing, tempted to tear it out of her arms. She wasn't fit to care for it. How could she ever think she was? How could she be so entitled, so selfish, *why* was she so obsessed with binding her most beloved—

The binds of woe come all undone, by moon-lit hand or else by none. I closed my eyes and took a breath. "Mother." The word drew her attention enough to momentarily quell her tears, which glistened in her eyes and down her face like the waters of the moonwell. "Look at him. He's suffering."

"I can fix it," she said, pulling the baby-thing back from me. "My sickness will drive them all away, and we..."

My heart broke for her. In many ways, the Aquilans were like the Great Corruption, an unstoppable force leaving ruin and death in their path, draining resources and leaving nothing. It was no wonder she bled. Exuded rot without control. She was losing everything all over again, and this time, she was trapped in the underworld, where she could do nothing but watch.

Still, I shook my head. "No. This isn't the way. This won't fix anything. You have to let him go. You have to let *all of us* go. You know that you do."

"I can't," she whispered. "I can't—"

"I know it wasn't fair. What happened to him, how he was

taken from you. I know the life you wanted ended then, and that that grief was the bricklayer of everything you built thereafter. I *know*, Mother. But it is so. And the land is rotting inside out because you cannot accept it."

"I *know* it is so," she snapped through tears. "That is why I made the Underland as it was. No war, no death ... to protect you. To preserve ... *everything*. It was supposed to be good." Her voice was racked with sobs and huffs. "It was supposed to be the last good thing I ever needed. Salvation. *It was supposed to heal me.*"

I settled in on my knees, bracing my remaining hand on my thigh. "We never could have healed you," I said softly. "We were new to the world, never asking to be born. And the Underland..." Closing my eyes, I exhaled. "The Underland is gone."

"Because I destroyed it," she croaked.

"Well ... yea. But it was withering before then, wasn't it? The rot was always going to spread—you said it yourself, you couldn't contain it. If our beautiful, perfect kingdom was dependent upon our absolute obedience and worship of you, if it was dependent upon peace in the outside world, it was only ever going to last so long." I shook my head. "I'm so sorry no one heard you ... but now you're rotting down here. That can't be what you want. You must want to rest. Return to the sky, the sea."

It was plain to see that the fiction she'd built around her actions, all the justifications and excuses, were coming down around her like rotten fruit from autumn boughs.

This, too, was difficult to watch. I reached out to cup her face. It was wet, and so cold that touching it hurt. We both flinched in the same fraction of a second, but I pressed on. "Please, *please* hear me. I'm not saying these things to hurt you. I *want* things to be better. I know I speak for all the fae *and* the humans when I say we'd want you to come home. Our Mother Goddess. We would care for you. Knowing all we do now, being older now, we could *try* to heal you. You and the fomori, if that is what they want. Your power, your wisdom, your *love*—even when we don't live exactly as you'd like us to, those things still mean something to us. They mean everything. But if you want salvation, Mother, you have to let us find ours."

She seemed to wilt before my eyes. Her face twisted into the most agonized grimace yet, and she raised a hand to clutch my wrist. For the better part of a minute, her breath was stolen by sobs, her entire body shaking with the force of her misery.

Then, at last, she managed, "My life, my love was taken from me. Now I've taken it from someone else..."

The weight of her guilt was too much. She folded inward, and it was all I could do to save her and the baby-thing from collapsing to the flagstones. So small and thin in my arms, she tucked her head against my chest and heaved great, bubbling sobs, and the malformed godling in her bundle whimpered, too.

By and by, her red locks turned ashen white between my fingers. Something was changing. Still, I let her cry until she could only gasp and shiver before speaking again. "*The binds of woe come all undone, by moonlit hand or else by none.* We are spiraling uncontrollably, without end. If we spiral much longer ... I really do think we'll unravel completely." Here I pulled back to look into her eyes. The blood-orange had faded to a forlorn dark blue with a red lower rim. "Your suffering is what created this cycle, Mother. You're the only one who can end it. Set us free. Set *yourself* free."

"No more riverrunning," she whispered, looking deep into my eyes, expression so earnest as to be pained. "I ... I ... I will try. But now, there is only so much I can do. The mist will subside, and the fomori, but those beasts you call thornbloods will remain. They are wild, reckless things."

I couldn't say this surprised me. Once an Aquilan, always an Aquilan, as much as I might wish it was otherwise. "And what of the withering itself?"

"It should not spread any further," she said. "When I am ... gone ... the wound will begin to heal. But I haven't the strength to heal it outright." With a trembling sigh, she looked down at our joined hands. Already, she appeared more cadaverous and ghostly than before. "You will have to drive the invaders out, my issy. You will have to restore the land. It may take ... many decades, perhaps a century. Is it not always the case? That it takes tenfold the time and strength to heal a wound than to inflict it."

"Aye," I agreed with some hesitancy. The hairs on my neck bristled. "But how am I supposed to heal it? My magic is useless, I am a ruin, and I only have one damned arm."

"You won't be alone." With tears overflowing, she placed her cool fingers under my chin and lifted it. "You will have Hiberos."

I heard her words for what they were. She was giving us her blessing. Giving me Hiberos. After three thousand years of grasping possessiveness, she was letting go. The cycle was over. We could move again. Not around, but *forward*, for the first time in millennia.

My breath hitched with sudden tears as I searched her gaze for any hint of reluctance or wrath, but there was none. An emotion I could not even begin to name spread through my chest —something like relief, but the force of it was so sudden and powerful that I was at once a weeping mess in her arms. So prepared had I been to start over again, to keep fighting, I'd forgotten to prepare for the possibility of mercy.

I clutched her tight around the waist, the baby-thing smooshed between us, and collapsed into her bosom. "Mother," I cried, and for the first time, the name felt correct.

She held me and pet my hair until my tears dried up. My head and the stump of my right arm pounded hard, and the world spun. Over. It was over.

We sat and wept for a while, until her drenched body had soaked me clear through to the skin, too. At length, I sat back on my knees and flicked away my tears. "But ... Hiberos is not at his full power, either."

She nodded as if she already knew. "Why did he give that man his heart?"

Sniffling, I wiped the back of my remaining hand across my nose. I could not bear to look at her; I looked down at the baby-thing instead, fiddling with its shroud. "He thought I could defeat him and win it back. But I'm not certain I can. You may be able to stop the withering, but this empire ... it is too great. Too vast and powerful and endlessly cruel. I don't think it can ever be defeated."

Gealach tipped her head and gave a very fae smile, all sharp teeth. "It has been said about every empire before this one. It is not the strength of one woman that defeats such evil. It is the survivors, all standing together, refusing to forget who they are. That is the hand that fells the empire. Oh, yes, and they always fall, my daughter."

Her certainty sent gooseflesh exploding over my skin. "And Gaius? How do I sever his 'red thread?'"

"Remember," she said. "Love breaks all chains and opens all doors."

"I don't know if I can find any love for Gaius," I whispered.

"Not love for him. For yourself. Already, you've done what you thought impossible. Stopped the unceasing, the inevitable— and you did so not through vengeance but by daring, striving, for your sake and for the sake of Hiberos." Then her smile disappeared completely, replaced with forlorn shame, and she looked away. "I suppose I must let him in now. But I don't want anyone to see me like this. I am no woman. Certainly not a goddess."

"It's all right. It doesn't matter how you look. You are beautiful."

Despite that assurance, when she asked pitifully, "Will you cover me?" I could not deny her. The back of her garment was a glistening, diaphanous cape. With trembling fingers, I brought it forward to drape over her head like a veil.

She closed her eyes briefly, snowy white lashes blending in with her cheeks. Then she said, "Come in."

There was a faint whoosh and a breeze that carried the scent of sun-warmed moss and berries into the stale air of the vault. I half-turned to watch the moonstone slab quite literally melt away, a puddle on the flagstones one moment and then gone the next.

Hiberos stepped out of the shadows, at once focused on me, searching me for any injury. My phantom limb buzzed. I smiled tiredly and nodded, confirming what his posture asked. I had done it. We were free.

His eyes widened with frenzy, and he hurried to my side. We embraced one another before the goddess like newborn twins clinging to each other for warmth. His magic twined with mine and told me everything as he seized my face, brought our lips together with abandon. For the first time in a millennium, he could kiss me without fear of breaking me. I wanted him to do it harder just to prove we could, If I asked, I was certain he'd oblige.

When finally we broke our kiss and could bear to look away from one another, still clutched together, we turned to Gealach. She could not seem to smile, but she bowed her head.

Hiberos scanned her up and down, tilting his head, ears flicking. But if he had any thoughts about her appearance, he did not voice them. Instead, he gestured with an open palm toward the baby-thing in her arms. "What is this? What have you done?"

The accusation in his voice was sharp. I said, "Hiberos—" to try and correct him, but Gealach shook her head.

"I understand. My issy is not the only one I have wronged."

"Wronged." His voice was more like a growl, dredged through gritted teeth. "Shackled me, kept me at heel, tried to entomb me— then when I clawed my way out, stole me again from the outside world. And all that I could forgive if you had not hurt *her*. Killed *her*. Tormented *her*. Haunted *her*. You aren't fit to call yourself a mother—"

"Hiberos," I cut in.

"Let him speak." Gealach's tone was mild.

"You are no goddess, nor a queen, and certainly not the woman I once adored. You are a tyrant. Your love is a shroud"—he gestured again to the baby, apparently having puzzled out what it was—"and you smother all you love beneath it. You feared loss so much you built a kingdom of stillness, without breath, without change, without life. You dare to call it mercy when in truth you are only terrified of being alone. Of being unneeded. Your suffering does not excuse you of your cruelty. If anything, it makes it more appalling."

She bowed her head lower, becoming smaller and more wan before our very eyes. I thought she might turn to mist, fade out of existence entirely. "All that is true, Hiberos, and I cannot blame you for hating me."

I expected him to be moved by her acceptance, but he was only disappointed. "This, too, I have seen before. This acceptance of your wrongdoing. This contrition. Then tomorrow you will find your self-righteousness again and you will turn this all on me somehow."

"No." She shook her head, the veil swaying gently. Her tears had dried up, her voice thin but even. "That is not so. There will be no tomorrow for me, Hiberos."

These words at last disarmed him; his brow went from twisted to tilted, his moonstone eyes wide. Shock, confusion, then fear and sorrow all had their moment on his face as he looked between us. "What do you mean?"

"She was aware down here," I said, "all this time. Not dead, not sleeping. Awake and lucid."

His expression shifted to abject horror. "No."

"Yes. But it's time for her to move on. Her and what remains of the Horned One." I joined hands with Gealach but kept my gaze locked on Hiberos. "I know all she's done to you. All the pain she's put you through, my only. It's time to cut it all loose, so we all can be at peace. Will you help us? Will you give your consent?"

He, too, could look nowhere but at me. The silver thread connecting us—spun not by fate or circumstance but by effort—pulled taut and thrummed. He shook his head infinitesimally and gave a subtle, sad smile. "My rose, all I ever wanted was to be with you. Whatever pact I must make, whatever rite I must perform, whatever wrongdoing I must forgive to belong with you, I will. But..."

Finally, Hiberos looked at Gealach, his expression not quite so hateful but nonetheless serious. "The trouble is, there will always be the Sun and Moon. Can you ever truly rest?"

"Take me to the surface," she answered airily, "and I will show you."

35

The blood moon was gone.

We made our procession out of the tomb inch by inch, the goddess as frightened to leave the vault as she was elated. The fomori parted for us, watching with an overwhelming mix of emotions, and in what felt like too short a time, we resurfaced. When we exited the palace, the labyrinth was gone, and the briars and rose bushes surrounding it had withered to ash. Above our heads, Hiberos's moths danced before a full, bright white moon and a night dotted with stars. All the land around was still withering and smelled of rot, but the change in the sky alone nearly brought me to my knees with relief.

Gealach took a step forward, feet sinking into the ash—and in that one step, all three of us were transported miles ahead of where we'd stood a moment ago. The world was a blur, and then we stood on a sea cliff overlooking an area I was familiar with—the Sallach Delta northwest of what had once been Fraochgleann. The ocean was unnervingly calm and still, only the smallest black waves rippling below.

Hiberos's hand found mine with a quickness, as if he'd feared for a moment that he had been spirited away once again. He was close enough that our shoulders were touching, his immense heat enveloping me. When I leaned into him, exhausted from my endeavor, he bore my weight effortlessly and without comment.

I made to ask Gealach why we had come here, but the image of her stopped me short. She'd walked ahead of us, her bare toes touching the very edge of the cliff. Her face was tipped up toward the starlit sky, the sea breeze combing its fingers through her limp, blanched locks. Even as thin, pale, and spectral as she was, the serenity on her face—the pure bliss after millennia locked in the Beneath—made her a vision to behold. In her arms, the baby-thing, now unshrouded and somewhat more alert, closed its little eyes, its nose twitching in the briny air.

The air was so thick with magic, with heartbreak, with still-ness, that time itself ceased to exist. I don't know how long it was before I stepped up, almost at her side but not quite.

"Why did you bring us here?" I asked softly.

She did not take her eyes off the horizon. "Hiberos called you my mirror. Is it not the same for all mothers and daughters? For millennia, in your defiant nature, you have shown me all the things I hate most about myself—all my failings, my insecurities, my unlived wishes. But so, too, are you a portrait of all my beau-tiful qualities. After all, grief cannot exist without first being love. It is the same emotion, but in shadow ... in reflection." She motioned upward. "The same way the moon reflects the sun, the ocean reflects the moon, woman reflects man. Adoration can obfuscate, hatred can twist, fear can shake. But here, where they all meet, is where truth can be found. If you care to look."

We were quiet for another long stretch until, eventually, I looked at the remnants of the Sun God in her arms. "You really are going, then. Both of you. Forever?"

"All life is borrowed, like the moon's light." Finally, she turned to me, holding my chin. "But if you are lucky—just lucky enough —it might be given. You gave me my life back, Mave, even when it meant forgetting your pride. I am riverrun no longer."

I looked at the water and realized that we stood right where the delta met the sea. Unexpected tears trailed down my cheeks.

"Forgive me for what I did in my pain," she whispered. "Please."

Without hesitation, I said, "I do."

She smiled sadly, cool hand caressing my cheek over and over. "My issy. It should not have surprised me that it was you, instead of Orlaith, who was the one."

"The one?"

Another moment of silence. "There is one thing I need ... one thing both I and my brother need before we can rest."

Here she turned, craning her neck to summon Hiberos with a look. He came up behind me, folded his arms around me, and held us snugly together. Moths wheeled all around us. With my remaining hand, I clutched his forearm, and he purred deep, tucking his nose into my curls.

Then Gealach spoke.

> *"When single shine the moon and sun,*
> *The war o'er land at last be won;*
> *The rift shall close, the two made one*
> *By fire's child and shadow's son."*

My ears twitched. Hiberos's chest swelled against me. The last stanza of the prophecy.

"You spoke in truth when you said you would need power to tame that bleeding man. To stand against the Empire. The people of this land, fae *and* human, will need guidance to come together." Gealach nodded to us in turn. "And Hiberos spoke in truth when he said that there must always be a Sun and Moon. With my brother and I gone, the new, united world needs new, united avatars of the sun and moon."

"Fire's child and shadow's son," I murmured. "Gaius thought it meant me and him."

"It could. But it doesn't have to."

The significance of her words and the reality of the situation sank in slowly and then all at once, like the sun setting into dusk. "And by avatars you mean..."

"Gods," Hiberos whispered in my ear, sending shivers all through my core.

When Gealach nodded in confirmation, I couldn't help but spit out an incredulous laugh. "Gods. Hiberos, yea, I could see that. But me? I could not even pass my trials. I'm hardly fae at all."

"Exactly," she said. "The lunar fae are not my only children. It is time to stop behaving as though they are. To be a god, you will need all of your humanity. Lead your land into salvation. Free your people, like you always wanted."

I half-turned to look at Hiberos, and he studied my face with a creased brow. It only took him a moment to get a read on the turmoil twisting my stomach. He kissed me, a gentle, lingering embrace that felt and tasted like warm milk and whiskey. Life and death. Birth and burial. "This is your decision. I will do what I should have done the first time you left. What Orlaith did. What I did too late. I will follow you, always. *Whatever is done by only me is your doing.* If this is our path, I accept it gladly. But if you've given too much of yourself ... if you'd rather go to ground and live out the rest of your life as peacefully as you can, I will be there with you, too."

Neither option sounded good for my health, but I had such trouble imagining myself running off to the countryside while war waged that I surely pulled a face. "We only just broke the cycle. What if this starts another one? What if we're stuck chasing each other across the sky for eternity, again?"

Hiberos combed his fingers through my curls, holding them out of my face. "Chasing can be fun. We will do this our way, on our terms. Not apart, not reaching for understanding. *Understood.* Together."

Our foreheads almost touched; he stared into my eyes as though my soul was a text only he could decipher. Perhaps it was, for I hardly knew my own answer until he broke into a grin, his eyes turning to delighted crescents. "Mave, you have never held back before. Do not start now. Say it."

Yes. The answer was yes. Of course I would do this. If I was the one, then so be it. Tenderly, I kissed the corner of his broad mouth, then nodded to Gealach. "What do we have to do?"

"Trust me. Though I have done little to deserve it, trust me one last time."

And then, without warning, she stepped off the edge of the cliff.

Her veil and the train of her silvery gown flicked behind her in the moonlight and were gone. Hiberos and I lurched to the edge as one, just in time to see her disappear beneath the waves.

For a moment, everything was silent, the sea stark midnight and shining like a black mirror. Then light began to glow beneath the surface, a boiling white light, which exuded heat and a rain-tinged jasmine scent that could be detected even as far above as we were.

Hiberos and I traded gapes. Then he pulled me close and kissed the shoulder of my amputated arm so gently his lips felt like moths' wings. "It seems we need to chase her into the Beneath one last time. Are you certain this is what you want?"

"Hiberos..." I nuzzled his temple with my nose and murmured against his cheekbone. "I've never held back before. Why start now?"

"Together, then," he rasped, gripping my waist.

"Together," I agreed.

He pressed me to him, and I wrapped my arm around his neck, locking us in an embrace. Closer, tighter, my legs twining with his hocks, our bodies flush until it almost felt like we were one being. I tucked my head against the gash in his chest. He twisted, leveraged his weight. Then we were falling.

My stomach flew, my limbs turning to water as the momentum pressed in on me and the wind screamed in my ears, yet he held me ever closer. He had no heart, but I swore I could feel a pulse between us.

We were a silver spear, a pillar of opal. We penetrated the waves with enough force that, for just a moment, I worried we'd break ourselves on the rocky sea floor. I opened my eyes and the foam of our impact scattered like insects. But all that awaited beneath the surface was that boiling white light, endless, so bright yet somehow not painful to gaze into.

Then, all at once, we were not merely looking at it but living within it. Already, there was a change taking hold. Something deep inside of my bones began to fizzle, my body and soul changing at a primordial level. Moments later, I lost all awareness of my body. I was inside Hiberos, around him; we moved through each other, reduced to our smallest particles. The white light was everything; each moment it held us seemed to contain the fullness of its power, then in the next there was more. Just as suddenly, everything was pitch black—then white—then black again, color and temperature oscillating in great waves, in time with the primal throbbing between and in and all around us.

Then the universe seemed to pull in on itself, everything reducing to the smallest, densest point—a point which contained me, Hiberos, the god and goddess, the rivers, the ocean, the moon, the sun, and all the stars all at once. All sensation ceased.

Finally, it burst outward. Existence itself shivered, screamed, convulsed, then went limp with relief. We were pushed out from the Weave, born again.

Elemental.

I felt I had eyes again. So I opened them. And the first thing I saw was him.

Standing opposite me on a beach of black sand dotted with diamonds. A majestic, animalistic god with strong switchback legs and broad shoulders. Grand ram's horns were filigreed and crowned with night-blooming flowers. His hide was darker now, a deep cherry rather than oak, its channels and grooves flowing with the teals and deep, glittering blues of opalized wood. The gash over his heart was once again a scarred knot. His wavy locks had turned from tarnished gold to raven. A diaphanous silvery garment draped over one shoulder, belted around his trim waist with winding roots, and he held a massive crescent scythe with a blade shaped of lunar light.

But his eyes were the same. Those radiant moonstone eyes

still alive with a glint of mischief, and his moths danced merrily about him as ever.

Hiberos. Shadow's son. The Moon.

Of course. Even though he was wrought of the Sun God, it could have been no other way; he was moonlight incarnate. But if he was the Moon, then I...

I looked down at myself, raising my hand. Though I wore bracers, my hands and strong upper arms were exposed. Like the May Queen at Bealtaine, my skin was lead white with goldenrod markings, and my unruly mane fell around my shoulders, dark red as rose petals once more. My armor was rustic but gleaming brass trimmed with red stag hide. Though my right arm felt strange, I *had* one. A new one, made of antler and bone woven into Éirin knots, with golden light shining through the seams—and in my hand, I held a golden bow that seemed to radiate sunshine. Noticing strange weight on my head, I reached up and touched the mighty antlers of the Horned One.

Stag Gréine. I was fire's child. The Sun.

My head spun from all the knowledge that came with my new title as avatar: forgotten languages, rituals, songs, myths, memories... It was so much that I dropped my bow to clutch at my head, gasping. Nothing was the way I'd thought it was. The weight of history, a wealth of both suffering and joy, a legacy that still shaped Éire today. The cosmos, their creation, their very arrangement. What lay beyond the Great Dark Sea and what lay far beneath our feet, buried in the black blood of the earth itself. Everything made sense, and nothing did. I staggered and raised my head, desperate for some relief, desperate for some tether, some anchor in this monsoon of terrible and wonderful and awesome information. I would go mad. I would go *mad.*

I grasped at my chest, groping for some connection.

And at the other end of the shining silver thread, I found Hiberos.

He had not spared even a glance for himself; he looked at me, thirsting for every minute detail. Everything from our skin and hair to our statures had changed, yet I knew he saw the same thing

I did when I looked upon him: *us.* Our souls had been reduced to their base elements, melted down and reforged. Yet still they were the perfect fit. Still they called to one another. Still mine recognized his; still it yearned for him.

Soundlessly, my lips parted, and I flung my arms out. With a flick of his wrist, he dismissed his scythe and ran to me. When our bodies collided and our skin touched, the heavens seemed to exhale a breath held since the beginning of time.

"Do not fight it. Let it wash over you," he rumbled, pressing our foreheads together. "Let it pass, and on the other side, you will find the only thing you truly need to know."

So I obeyed. Gripping his wrists, I closed my eyes, whimpering as the raw magic of the Weave scoured me body and soul. Knowledge continued to ravage my mind like the white rapids of Abhan Garri, and rather than try to contain it, I let it flow through me and out to sea. It would be there when I needed it, and if it wasn't, I could find it again.

I searched for the truth he'd promised. At first I did not see it for what it was; it seemed so natural, so simple and self-evident that I did not even know I was looking for it.

The truth was that I was still Mave.

With a shaking inhale, I opened my eyes. They must be glowing, because Hiberos's teal-veined bust took on a golden cast—and in that sunny glow, he showed the most radiant grin I had ever seen. He washed over me. Happiness so intense it was ecstasy rolled through me, and I shivered, my teeth chattering with unspent energy.

"The Weave may have remade us," he said, brushing his broad, flat, silken nose against mine, "but I would know you blind, in darkness, in death. Bound, unbound. Avatar or slave, fae or human, wife or warrior, it matters not. You are Mave, and you are mine, and you are enough."

I moved my arm of antler and bone to cup his jaw, threading my clawed fingers through his beard. "Careful, my only. If you keep smiling like that, I may forget the world is ending."

"I'm half tempted to forget, myself," he purred, and took my lips in a kiss that made the scorching power inside of me seem like a pale shadow.

A deep chuckle cut it regretfully short. Even with the senses of gods, neither of us had realized we weren't alone.

Together, we turned toward the two figures standing opposite us, a man and a woman. They, too, were hand in hand, the woman gazing out over the tides and the man grinning at us. Their features could barely be discerned before they shifted shape and color; all that remained the same from moment to moment was the woman's long, flowing hair and round stomach, and the man's beard and spear. Gealach and the Horned One stood before us not as goddess and god, moth and stag, May Queen and Green Man, Moon and Sun, but as *people*—bare feet, imperfect skin, slightly crooked teeth and all.

Gealach's voice floated effortlessly over the crashing of foam upon the rocks. "You will take care of the fomori for me, won't you? I never meant to make my children enemies. At least give them a chance to lift themselves out of wretchedness."

"I will do my best," I promised. "It may take a while for them to trust me."

"Perhaps. Yet, is ending this war and restoring the land not in their best interest, too?"

"The war o'er land at last be won," Hiberos murmured, and I was able to *sense* him searching our shared well for the knowledge we needed. *"When single shine the Moon and Sun.* I think I've deciphered what that line means, but ... how? We may be remade, but how can we trigger a cosmic event?"

It was different—refreshing—to see *him* asking the questions for once. Still grinning, the Horned One finally spoke. The timbre of his voice was not so different from Hiberos's, although his brogue was archaic. "You will know when the time comes."

I pursed my gold-painted lips. "That isn't very helpful."

His laugh sounded like a stag's bark. "Oh, I like her. You are just what a daughter ought to be: clever, a beauty, and a thorn in my side. I only regret not having met you until now."

And for just a moment, he looked remarkably like me—the

same nose, auburn hair, and dark blue eyes. An unexpected smile teased the corners of my mouth.

"There's my girl," he said, in a tone I was shocked to find I'd heard before. That voice from the spirit world. *My girl.* Lady Beneath, my *father's* voice. Ruadan had said I was surrounded by spirits, but I never could have imagined—

As soon as his face appeared, it was gone again, shifting to some other bloke. "You will know," the Horned One continued, "I promise. The same way deer know to migrate during the winter, or moths know to build their cocoon, or wolves know where to nest for pupping season."

"That is all we can tell you," Gealach said, finally turning her attention to us. "Our time is coming to an end. Our power wanes. There is only one gift left to bestow."

The two looked at each other and smiled brightly. The Horned One tossed his head back, indicating the midnight beach and the grassy grove beyond it. "Consider it a belated soulfasting present."

I opened my mouth to ask what he meant, but already, their forms were fading, the black peaks of the waves visible through them. A sharp, unexpected pain rent my chest in two. Right when I had come to truly know them, here they were leaving.

I bit the inside of my cheek to keep from crying like a child about to be separated from her parents for the first time. "Where will you go?" I whispered.

With tears of her own, Gealach tipped her face to the heavens and smiled blissfully. "Home."

Then, embracing one another, the two released one final pulse of magic—and were nothing but moths' dust in the wind.

36

A fter everything, there was only the sea. The moon reflecting the sun and the ocean reflecting the moon.

I listened to the surf breathe against the glittering shore—steady, sleepless, unaware of gods or grief. Then I listened to *him*, to his breaths mirroring the swell of the waves, slow and even as he waited for me to raise my head. When I did, he was watching me with something raw in his expression. His face, so new yet so familiar, resembled neither sorrow nor rage. Rather, he looked ... relieved, and awed.

"I never dreamed," he said after a moment. "Never in a thousand years did I think we would ever find ourselves here."

I felt keenly the same, although probably not with as much intensity. After all, he knew first hand every facet and jagged edge of Gealach's anger and her crusade to drive us apart; he knew more intimately than anyone how impossible it was, this outcome.

In the soul-rattling stillness after the chaos of the past ... months, he was the silver thread holding me together. Anchoring me to myself. Looking into his eyes, I became aware of my heartbeat again, of the sand shifting beneath my toes. The weight of exhaustion gave way to a wonder that kept the stars apart.

I regarded the beach and, behind us, the grassy coast overtaking the dunes—beyond that, fruit trees, ruins, and the beginnings of a grove, all awash in the cool tones of the Underland. The air had changed. This place, it was untouched by the withering. A sacred corner of time. A pocket of mercy. The last slip of Gealach's power, conjured to give us a moment to breathe for the first time in ... in eons.

That very thought, that realization, stung my eyes with tears anew. *I've become a leaky bucket, haven't I?*

"Their gift." Hiberos considered the grove, bright with recognition. "They've given us a night. A wedding night."

I eyed the ruins skeptically.

Sensing my thoughts, he loosed one of those primal, clicking chuckles. He caught my woven hand and spun me. "Don't tell me that now, after everything, you've become a staunch believer in the sanctity of the marriage bed?"

He made me snort in amusement, but still I asked, "So, no old tree or moonwell or standing stone, no rites or vows, no flowers or wines or clean bedding?"

"None of it," he purred, twirling me back into his arms, where I landed firmly against his opalized chest. His eyes twinkled with dark promise. "Even better: no audience but the stars. No altar but the earth. Certainly no wedding dress. Only you, and me, the wild, and the celestial rut."

His voice seemed to enter me from every pore, sonorous, vibrating into my bones. It lit a fire in me. Made me want to move —against him, my clothes, my thighs, anything. All the world was the one heartbeat between us and the blood pooling between my legs. Memories of gripping his hips, fisting his hair, grinding into the moss, grunting like beasts as he buried himself in me like a grave flooded straight to my core. New memories, too, pulled me like a riptide: he entered me, his cock smooth, warm, fluttering. I gasped. The stretch sent a frisson of terror up the back of my scalp. Hiberos moaned as he reached my limit, then snarled...

My hand hovered toward his jaw. His eyes sparkled. My tone was perhaps too dreamy, too enthralled, for the playful words I said next to be read as such, yet he understood. He always understood. When nothing else made me feel human, he did. Even like this. That was the beauty of it. He was just a man, and I just a woman, and we were what they could be in the wild, if all was balanced and shared. "I do believe the power has gone to your head. You've come undone. You're scaring me."

The second my fingertips brushed his skin, he seized my wrist, pressing my palm hard to his cheek. His eyes flashed. "Then run."

His goatlike pupils blew wide. Something primal rose up in me. Something *powerful*. Not a force pulling my chain but a weapon that fit easily and comfortably in my hand for the first time in eons.

Finally, everything fell away. All self-awareness. My body no longer felt like a fetter weighing down my spirit but truly part of me. I *felt*. Everything. My desire for him was so all-encompassing, but rather than overwhelming, it moved through me as naturally and smoothly as air. There was no one I had to be, nothing I had to prove. I was the Sun avatar. Crowned in my own right, with my own power, equal to his in every way. I was desire. A sensual creature. Unafraid. *Me*, Mave. And, Lady above, it felt like what I was meant to be all along.

So I ran.

Our chase ate a path through the grove. Even as I shed my armor piece by magical piece, I didn't slow for him. I didn't want to. I would make him work for this—and my body was electric with the movement. I relished the way my calves and lungs burned. Sizzling jolts of arousal shocked my core, and I felt myself gush, caught a glimpse of the dark red curls shining with wetness, so gloriously sticky between my thighs. The musky, sweet scent touched my nose as I pumped my arms and legs. I loosed a moan to the cool night.

The urge to behold him was too strong. I threw a glance over my shoulder, and his teeth flashed in the moonlight. The rivers carved across his chest and arms glowed with lunar power. His already scant clothing was gone now, leaving him bare before me, the root of him exposed and bobbing heavily with every step. My heart dove straight to my core, and there stayed its beat.

My arse and the backs of my thighs burned from the rigorous exercise, but I loved it. The sensation of being out of breath, of pushing my body to the limit while he chased me, made me quiver. Gooseflesh erupted beneath the paint coating me. My fangs extended, but I didn't bother to wipe the slaver. We were two godlings, our markings lighting up the night.

Ahead, a grove of trees formed a tunnel, each branch arcing more than the last. The moon was framed at the end. A moon before me and a moon behind, I was aglow in my own radiance.

I slowed slightly and ducked, brushing aside the curtain of moss to enter the grove.

My throat closed, my chest tight as I sensed his rapid approach—the heat, the deep breaths dragging through him, the low grunt of each exhale. The very tips of his fingers brushed my shoulder blade, a glancing blow down my spine as I danced away.

"Run faster." His voice crept through the forest, dark and demonic and teetering on the edge of control. "Are you even trying?"

I heard the words for what they were—a plea disguised as a challenge. He needed desperately for me to evade him, to make him *work for it*. Needed to be brought to the edge of madness hunting me without being allowed to take his prize.

If he wanted me to make it more difficult for him, I would.

In one swift movement, I disappeared into the boughs of a tree, hiding amongst the deep purple leaves. With movements as careful and quiet as a panther, I crawled from one branch to another, watching from above as he stalked through the grove. His breath was ragged and hitched. He may be the Moon, but the fire inside him overwhelmed, vapor pouring from his nostrils and between his teeth like smoke.

With a huff, he turned sharply and darted his tongue out to lick his lips. "Ohh, I see, my little rose. You think you can hide from me." As he peered around trunks and into hollows, the pressure of his erection was higher than I'd ever seen it. Even from my perch, each throb was visible. "Your scent is unlike any other. I could find you blinded and maimed—*would*, if I had to. You can't hide. Your only hope is to *run*."

If I truly wanted to, I could hide up here forever. But he wanted me to play prey, wanted to hear my heart beating and smell the sharp fragrance of my fear mixing with my sweet arousal. He wasn't commanding—he was *begging*.

Hugging the trunk of my hiding spot, I slowly lowered myself down to the ground. I was soundless, a spirit, my bare feet making no noise as they touched the forest floor...

When I peered around the trunk to watch him continue to stalk through the trees, he was gone.

"There you are."

All at once, his heat and magic were behind me, swirling with mine and shocking a gasp from me. I was barely able to evade him, his grasping fingers once again catching my hot, bare flesh before I twisted away. His big fists closed around nothing, the knuckles paling, the fingers twitching with want and delicious frustration. His cock twitched just the same.

With a growl, he lunged after me again, but I darted out of the way—leapt over a fallen log, loosed a breathless laugh.

"You're slow," I said huskily. "Seems this new, virile body is just as feeble as your old one."

Goddess, the way he bristled at that, he looked like he might go mad. Pupils shifted, ears perked, head raised as my words poked at his primal center.

"I thought you might take me properly with blood in your cock instead of dust, old goat."

It was so cruel, but he liked it. His moonstone eyes were white in the darkness, their horizontal pupils inhuman, demonic. It took everything in me to stand my ground and suppress my shivers while I toyed with him.

"Say it again," he all but moaned.

He was still half crouched, poised to lunge, so I bent at the waist, teasing him with the fullness of my breasts and the dark red hair snaking over my shoulders. "I thought you'd split me the way your beast is begging you to, instead of creaking on top of me like you're still my poetry tutor."

Hiberos's breath jarred up his throat like that of an outsized monster. "Just for that," he said, "I will drag you down and fuck you into the dirt, until the very earth remembers my weight."

Before he could utter the last syllable, I started running again. Around hills and through dells awash in the light of the full moon, then back into the grove where the long shadows of the trees groped my naked flesh. I was a ghost. A banshee. Wild, unleashed, a being of pure instinct, play and pleasure as one. My nipples, ringed with golden paint, were hard, and aching harder with each bounce of my breasts. I relished the fear instilled by his hoof beats and deep-throated grunts.

His heavy, divine presence in hot pursuit made me so wet, so ready, but I wouldn't back down, and he wouldn't want me to.

I made a few quick moves, and his heat left me, his magic dissipating somewhat. I'd lost him.

With quick breaths and a glance over my shoulder, I searched for a hiding spot. A patch of darkness even blacker than the night caught my eye. The entrance of a cave. Not too deep, judging by the breeze coming from it. Another glance over my shoulder, and I ducked into the darkness.

The opening led to a cave system coated in the deepest green moss and dripping moon-blessed water. Though I had no idea where we were precisely, I felt in my bones that I was the first human thing to step foot in these caves, maybe ever. The very air was untouched, so full and thick with magic that it bloomed in my lungs and relaxed every muscle. For a while, there was no light, but I *was* the light, slipping through the pitch-black tunnels as easily as if I'd carved them myself.

Somewhere behind me, pebbles shifted, little rocks clattering together. I stilled, unbreathing, and listened for Hiberos's rear approach ... but there was no other sound. I crept further through the tunnels, following the breeze and the pulse beneath my bare feet.

Finally, natural light touched me. Moonlight, bright as day, a little at a time. At last, the tunnel opened into a cavern not much taller than me and only about three times my height in width. All around were naturally formed openings leading to deeper tunnels. The many paths of the cave system converged here, along with all its magic, pressing down on my skin with frenzied energy.

A thousand hands seemed to be on me all at once, spirits groping me everywhere from my hair to the seam of wet heat between my legs. Not the spirits that usually surrounded me. No, these were strangers; I got the distinct sense that they never had been human, perhaps barely existed at all. Yet they probed me with the wanton curiosity of mortals.

Thrumming fingers dipped into my pussy experimentally. My heart beat a wild tattoo as I slumped against a moss-covered boulder and moaned. My quaking legs spread of their own accord, letting the tongues of power undulate against every inch of me. The fingers shoved deeper, then impossibly *deeper* into me, stroking with such precision that my entire body gave out.

As I fell to the moss, I could have sworn I heard demonic growling in my ear. My nipples, tight and sensitive, yearned and throbbed as the spirits laved across them. I bowed on all fours and mewled as if in heat, my vision blurred with overwhelmed tears as I was entered from the back—everywhere. There was only plea-sure; something parted my lips and caressed my gums, my tongue, the back of my throat as I grunted hard. My unseen assailants left no opening unfilled.

Vaguely, I knew they were trying to distract me. Whether they were an extension of Hiberos or working with him, they were trying to keep me here.

He was *cheating*. Again. And such an aggressive attempt at slowing me down could only be seen as an act of dominance. That thought stoked the fire of rage in my heart as surely as it stoked my need.

With the rage, my orgasm came on all at once, building in pressure suddenly. I gasped and cried, "No, no, no!" not ready to have it ripped out of me—but it happened all the same. I screamed, raw and cracked, my eyes rolling back into the whiteness.

The spirits inside of me swelled, then disappeared with one last stab of pleasure, and I collapsed in a shivering, messy heap on the carpet of moss.

The ringing in my ears cut out abruptly when I heard it again: the clacking of pebbles, closer now, followed by the wicked, sonorous rumble of his half-purr half-bleat. Despite the weakness racking my limbs, I managed to push up. My stomach and thighs were soaked, the paint on my chest peeling somewhat. The perfume of ecstasy clung to me as I slunk forward on all fours, my shoulder blades high, hips swaying, ragged breath pouring from my mouth—more panther than hunter.

Finally, something rippled in the air behind me, and I threw a look over my shoulder. A pair of eyes glowed, their owner tucked just far enough into the darkness that I could barely see the outline of his bestial features. There was no trace of the smirk I expected. He was past that, panting and slavering just as I was.

"The wandering hands of ghosts." His voice slithered into the cavern and skimmed my tenderest flesh. He slithered in after it, as if to get a better look at me, and cooed. "But try as they might, they cannot taste the sweet, tart nectar dripping down your thighs. They cannot have your wreckage."

I certainly couldn't let him win now. Adrenaline shot into my legs near painfully, and I ducked into one of the tight squeezes, then through the tunnels once more. Breeze spurred me onward. When finally the underground became grass and sky again, I thought I was free—that, in the open, he had even less chance of catching me.

Wrong.

Before I quite registered it, the pound of hoofs rattled my world as he rushed me. With a surge of ferocity and a growl, finally, he overtook me. *Threw* himself at me, all his weight bringing us crashing down to the earth. In nearly the same moment, his fist was in my hair, tight to the scalp. His breath was hot and tattered and everywhere, teeth scraping my shoulder blades and the tendon where my neck met my shoulder. He pressed his lips to my flesh like simple contact wasn't enough, like he would only be sated if he consumed me flesh and bone. The strength he exerted over me was so powerful and sudden that I threw my head back and cried out with pleasure, thrusting back. In this moment, I wanted to be consumed by him. And if there was nothing left of me afterward, so be it.

Yet even in this position, pinned under him and wanting, I wrinkled my nose and snarled. "I let you catch me."

He may as well have shoved his root deep in me the way his chuckle made me clench and jump. "Then beg me to keep you before I cut you loose again."

A deep, resonant grunt made the curls at the side of my head waver, and next I knew, he was gripping me by the nape of the neck, my skin clutched in his large fist. I seized, and he used his leverage to move me freely. Pulled me back and positioned me under him roughly enough that my knees scraped the dirt. I hissed as I felt the skin open. No doubt little pinpricks of blood now mixed with the soil beneath us.

"I'd lie as quiet as a moss," he recited, voice husky. "And one time you'd rush upon me, darkly roaring, like a great black shadow with a sheeny stare to perce me rawly..."

Try as I might to wiggle against his strength, I could not move. "You cheated," I rasped, and bucked hard enough that the length of him slapped against me.

"You fell for it."

"After everything, you still choose to infuriate me."

"I could take you sweetly. I've done it before, and I'll do it again. But you aren't sweet," he said, shaking me slightly by the nape. He leaned and laid the muscled plane of his stomach across my back to huff directly into my ear. "You are a glorious fire raging through the forest, begging to be cooled. Here I am to cool you."

I felt anything but cooled as he braced a forearm across my chest and flipped me. The moment his hand left my nape, I fought against him, but he was ready, already crowding in and pinning my upper arms to my ribs. He pressed against me so hard that I had no choice but to wrap my thighs around his middle. Though I bucked this way and that, trying to wrestle myself on top, he stiffened and managed to hold fast.

"You don't own me." It wasn't strictly true—he held every part of me, the same way I held every part of him, and more than *safe*, in his orbit, I was *seen*. Still, the words made his eyes flash.

"No?" he rasped, canting his head. "You own me. I am yours. Yours to defile and dishonor and steal pleasure from."

My heart leapt in equal parts shock, awe at him, and intense, burning arousal. He spoke of this like I was ravishing *him* instead of the other way around. "What do you mean?"

"I've brought you to your knees," he said low. "If I asked, would you do the same to me?"

There was nothing but breath between us for several tense moments, our bodies tied in a knot. His eyes were round, almost innocent, sparkling like the starry sky above, and I was certain mine were the same. Clearly, I did not quite understand the significance of what he was asking me. Whatever this was, it was important to him.

"Speak plain," I whispered shakily.

"If I asked, would you take your fill of me, feigning no regard for my protests?"

I opened my mouth, but no words came out. Did he know what he was asking me? The pounding arousal between my legs—his and mine—might have shamed me if I had any shame left.

When I didn't answer, he said, "Ah, your hesitation is writ on your face. Forget my request."

But before he could duck in to suck at my pulse, I cupped his face and forced his gaze back to mine. For a breathless moment, we simply stared at one another. It had never occurred to me that he, too, might want to lose control. Be possessed. That he might want to surrender to *me*. That he might want to relish his absolute safety in *my* arms. Loving warmth exploded in my sternum at the thought.

"I'll try," I said at last. "But you aren't allowed to laugh at me if I muck it up."

His eyes were sparkling again. "Never, my brightness."

37

HIBEROS

My goddess, my brightness—mistress of every stroke of magic within me, mother of all my hope, mainspring of dignity and safety and love—threaded her fingers through my sideburns and pulled me in for a hard kiss.

We eased back into our rhythm. The chase had roused feelings I'd spent a thousand years trying to tamp down. Watching her collapse and lose herself in the spirits had made me yearn. Oh, to be cornered and stripped of my control. It was a desire I had never shared with anyone, not even Ashling.

But Mave understood. Of course she did. No being existed in this universe who understood me the way she did.

Her thighs tightened around my hips. Testing the waters, I shifted against her as if trying to wrench away—and pleasure wheeled through me when she clamped down with a grunt into my mouth. Her hands holding my jaw turned to one gripping my chin hard enough to bruise.

It came so naturally. Thrilling. This night, she was truly wild. It felt *good*. And the wetness sliding against my shaft told me she felt the same.

"Stop moving," she warned. Though I had her locked into a mean mating press, I may as well have been the one under her for how chastened her sharp golden eyes made me feel. "You still don't seem to understand, old goat." The nickname made my core clench in glorious indignation. "This new body is for me. You were made for my use tonight. Your cock is mine to ruin for others. Your divinity is mine to desecrate."

The shape of her eyes changed a bit—the subtle tilt of her brow—her way of asking if she was doing a good job. I sent encouragement through our bond.

And with my approval, she descended.

With a surge of strength, she twisted her thighs and flipped us so she was on top, crouching over me on her haunches and considering me. The calculated glint in her eyes was so predatory it took my breath away.

I ventured, "What are you going to do to me, my brightness?"

"I am going to take what I want. All I want." Licking her lips, she reached between her legs to pet my manhood from tip to base, coating it in my pre-cum. "And you can pretend you hate it, you can cry out for me to stop, but your body tells on you."

I growled and ground into nothingness, desperate for something to rub my cock against. She slammed her backside down on my hips, pinning them to the ground. "Stay still. You'll move if I say you can move."

Then she was climbing me, all the way up until her knees were planted on either side of my horns and her wet, silken pussy was inches from my nose. My mouth watered, my tongue burning to see if she tasted as heavenly as she smelled.

"Hope you aren't too attached to breathing," she remarked casually, and in the next moment, the whole of her weight was on my face.

I *couldn't* breathe. Her muscular thighs smothered me, and her knees kept me from moving my head. For a moment, instinctively, I bucked to relieve myself of the intense pressure. Every brush of my horns against her legs was so overstimulating I nearly wept. But she reached down to squeeze my wrist lightly.

It was Mave. Only Mave. My shoulders and neck relaxed, and I squeezed her wrist in return, signaling her to continue.

She eased back onto me and moaned as my tongue finally unfurled, prodding her entrance before exploring her hot, firm clit.

"See, my only?" she said in a tremulous whisper. "It feels good if you let it. You know," she added with a grin in her voice, "I always likened your old body's creaking to that of a chair. Now you really are one." And she reached back to pat the lowest plane of my abdomen. "Just furniture, aren't you? Meant to serve and look attractive."

I tried to inhale sharply, but of course I couldn't. I felt her fingertips brush my wrist uncertainly, but my heart burst with pride when, instead of squeezing me again, she sensed my urgent need and continued to roll her hips. She rutted against my tongue, every inch of her slick and tart and delicious. I guessed from the shift in her weight that she had thrown her head back, and the resonance of her moan told me her mouth hung open.

"Oh, gods," she gasped to the sky. "Mine, mine, mine."

She was like velvet against my tongue. I drank down every drop of sweet fluid, moaned, cleaned her with lewd sucking noises as she bounced and rocked on my face. Her clit and entrance both tightened and fluttered under my worship.

"Like that. Like that. Like that. It can't be so bad if you lick me so sweetly, can it?"

Meanwhile, my head spiraled, pleasure increasing as I became well and truly air-starved. Sparks burst in the darkness, but just as I was teetering on the edge of delirium, she lifted to let me breathe. Air squealed down my throat and into my spasming lungs. The darkness receded in time for me to see her expression go from mild concern to smugness.

Did she know how beautiful she was? I doubted it. The freckles dusting her cheeks shone through the streaky white paint on her face. The slight bump in her nose cast a little shadow. Her lashes, brown rather than red, fanned out in chunks with the salt of old tears. Her strong chin jutted out defiantly. And those new golden eyes cut to the heartwood of me. Enthralled, I couldn't help but reach out toward her round breasts, desperate to rub away some of the white-and-gold paint coating her skin.

She pushed my hands back. "All of a sudden you want to touch me? Are you daft?" she teased.

Honestly, I'd forgotten she was supposed to be brutalizing me. I licked my messy lips and whined, chastened. "Please, no more," I breathed. "I'm not strong enough."

That word—no—I think made the situation all the more real to her. She stroked a hand down my face, brows twitching. "I— Should I ... stop?"

"Oh, stars..." I huffed half-mad breaths up to the sky, barely able to keep my eyes focused on her for the pleasure flooding my body. I wished she'd go mad with me, be obscene and wild and inconsiderate—but, of course, that was a foolish wish, and this behavior, this very Mave behavior, was exactly what made her the only soul I wanted touching mine. "Let's strike a deal, eh? If I truly want you to stop, I'll say a word. Something I never would say otherwise, something that will get your attention. You choose."

She tilted her head in thought. Then—I didn't expect her to laugh, but she did, so genuine and beautiful. "When I played too rough as a child, Eytine used to shout 'Strategy!'"

My own grin hurt my face. "Strategy it is, then."

"And if your mouth is"—she cleared her throat—"occupied?"

"Then I'll tap the base of your spine four times, swiftly. But until then, show me no mercy."

And Mave heard me. She pounced on me all over again, smothering me with her thighs and pussy, bracing her hands against my sensitive horns without mercy or remorse as she rode my tongue. Her pace quickly became so quick and brutal that I could do nothing but lie there—like furniture, as she'd said—and let her use my mouth for her own pleasure. When the fingers of my right hand ventured over my hips, creeping toward the base of my cock, she forced through gritted teeth, "*Stay.*"

I nearly came there, from her grip and taste alone.

Breaths were shallow and far between. Soon, she was shuddering and bucking against me. *Yes, yes. Use me, my brightness.*

Think of nothing but your own pleasure, and how my body can give it to you.

She cried out to the moon and tightened her grip on my horns. The same thin, clear cum she'd blessed me with in her dream-scape squirted from her and dripped down my chin. My extended moan was muffled by all of her. *Oh, brightness, my brightness, yes!*

Her hands moved to my chest, where she braced herself for a moment, panting to catch her breath. Eventually, she slumped into me, all of her weight in a heap on my chest.

Good. I wanted her to crush me into the dirt, to feed the soil with my marrow.

She stayed there for stars know how long, recovering while my neglected root strained just inches from her core. It wasn't until I loosed a pitiful whimper—I couldn't help it—that she looked at me.

She looked at me. The way the entire universe shifted in that moment ... as though suddenly it all mattered. I swore to the stars I only existed when she looked at me. The Moon could only reflect the light of the Sun.

"Don't worry," she murmured, speaking against my lips. "I haven't forgotten about you." When I shivered hard against her, she gritted her teeth, and the voice that came out of her was so unholy, so far beyond human, that a frisson of fear raced up my spine. "Stop. Shaking."

My cock jumped in response, like I was some raring buck in his rut.

In the best way, we were losing ourselves tonight.

Slipping off me, she commanded me like I was her prisoner, like she had single-handedly conquered the fae and I was her spoils of war: "Spread your legs and put your hands under your backside."

With ragged breath, I obeyed, making my legs a V and pinning my hands beneath me. My eyes would not leave her. The way she stood over me, framed in moonlight, the paint on her thighs all but worn away from the juices of her own pleasure. She seemed to admire me the same way. A growl of appreciation came from deep in her throat, and I matched it with a subdued purr.

"This has changed." She knelt, using one finger to manipulate my cock. Although still the same size, shape, and thickness, it was now cherrywood-to-deep-blue with veins of fire opal. "I wonder if it'll still be as good?"

I nearly wept trying to stop myself from begging, pleading, promising her anything that I would be just as good and even better. Make her come every hour, be inside her every minute she was awake if she willed it. She wanted me to be furniture? I would be her throne, then, to bounce on or ignore as she pleased.

As if reading my thoughts, her gaze sharpened, and her lips curled into a smile. In one movement, she turned her back and sat astride me.

Her round ass, torturously close yet too far to kiss, was heavy on my rib cage. But something else, something above the small of her back, caught my eye. Something shocking and terrible and beautiful.

Scars. A matrix of scars, evidence of Gaius's whipping. They had healed over and disappeared when she took her fae form, and she'd been so upset to lose them. Her reminder. Her rejection of the Empire manifest. And now here they were again.

I smiled drunkenly. When this all was over, I would tell her the good news. But for now, they were my secret.

While I couldn't see what she was doing, she rolled back my foreskin and worked my cock with both hands, one on the shaft and one brushing the ridge of the tip. She spat, spread her saliva, and I was slick in her palms. All thought of scars and secrets left me as though my mind were oozing from my ears like honey. *That* was what she smelled of in this new form, I realized at last. Honey. Honey and a bonfire and the slightest hint of bread.

"Mave ... I can't— I can't. Stop. Stop this. Stop *me*."

She ignored me utterly. Even began to rock back and forth, using my abdominal muscles to stir the fire in her core. When, with a deep, thirsty moan, she leaned forward and took me into her mouth. Just past the tip, yet I nearly snatched my hands from under me to seize her thighs. Then she nibbled me, oh so gently, and ... *Mave. Fuck, my brightness.* My back arched, my jaw clenched, hot puffs of breath leaving me as the pressure in my shaft increased. She was nibbling me up and down with the gentlest nips and sucks, chasing the pulse. Each time I thought it could not get more unbearably sublime, somehow, I got harder.

Only when a tingling in my spine warned me did I manage to gasp out, "I'll come."

Mercifully, she pulled back, released her grip on me, and rested heavily on my lungs again. Her mane of curls, as deep a red as the rose, flicked as she threw a mean look over her shoulder.

"I'll come," I repeated apologetically.

"I heard you." She rocked harder on my middle, leaning back farther with one knee hitched, and I realized she had a hand between her legs. I wished I could see her playing with herself, but I imagined it: two slender fingers rolling the beautiful pink bud around and around, the flesh of her outermost lips tensing, her core shining under the moonlight. Her frame shook, breath frayed, as she brought a warm hand to the base of my shaft and lifted herself.

Yes, yes, yes. Closing my eyes tight, I whispered, "No! Not like that. Not inside. I can't. I won't. Do not take me into you. Not there, not your cunt, not like this..."

"Shh, hush." Either she'd lost herself in the scene, or she was too clever to hesitate even for a moment. "No crying. You know the rules. You're here to fill me, not whinge like a baby."

Oh, she was magnificent. She was so *bad*. And so good. Who would have thought straight-laced, black-and-white Mave would toe the blurred line with me like this?

This. *This* was paradise. Hang the Underland.

Then I was inside her, and the spiral turned dark. Warmth consumed me, her heat and tightness just one level below overwhelming. As she started moving, the level broke. My cockhead tapping her innermost wall. The way she deepened and gave as though forming around me. The shudder deep in her belly. I felt it all. Her cunt clenched around me, squeezing, fluttering, until her arousal gushed and I could move inside of her almost easily.

Regardless, already she was riding fast, and my hips were thrusting of their own accord to meet her. With her hands full of her own breasts, she threw her head back, her moans broken. The noise dragged me to the edge of madness. The pounding of my hips quickened—

And she reached down to strike my flank. "Uh!" It was half a warning, half a cry of pleasure. "You—you don't get to decide how I claim you," she said through heavy breaths. "Not until you admit this is what you need."

"I'm begging you," was all I could hiss. "Don't make me."

"Admit it, and I'll let you touch me. Admit you need me like I need you."

I threw my head back to groan at the unfairness, unable to stop writhing beneath her.

"Go on. I want to hear my throne admit it likes its new role in my court."

Oh, goddess. I spat out the words, if only because I feared what she might do if I emptied myself in her before she commanded it: "I need it. I can't have enough of it. Please, my brightness. I know neither of us can stop you from hurting me—but let me touch you, at least..."

I felt the beginnings of her own climax roll through her—the particular tightening of her insides, the unique hitch in her breath, the precise angle of her spine. She tipped her head back in ecstasy and breathed, "Touch me, touch me. Now, now."

In the next moment, I was digging my claws into her flank, helping her lift herself off of me only to slam back down again. The grove filled with the lewd noises of our union and the growls and gasps and moans pouring from our mouths. The paint on her sides and thighs melted off with our sweat. My cock split her—ravishing, ravished—pounding her insides like we might die if we slowed.

It rolled from her on a groan: "I can feel you in my *ribs*."

That tingling warning started again. But this time, I did nothing to allay it. It was time.

With a strangled cry, I felt it shoot through my center, through my penis—and then it was coming, the pressure finally releasing, the pulse overwhelming me. There was nothing but light and her, her, her.

She came within moments of feeling my warmth inside, her cunt taking over and milking me of every pump. We rocked together, completely wild, acting on feeling alone, our cries shattering the night.

Mave slumped against me, utterly limp, back arched with her ass in the air and her head down near my hocks. Her harsh breaths tickled the hide there. That sensation was what brought me back from the haze of my climax.

After a few moments of simply *breathing* and trying to remember myself, I shook my head. Blinked. Bleated a chuckle. Finally, sitting up slowly, I reached to encourage her to sit up, too —but she was as limp as boiled cabbage, moaning her protest.

She gave the same moan, louder and sharper, when I slid out of her.

"If you want me again, you need to give me a few minutes to recover, greedy thing."

Under the curtain of her hair, she lifted her elbow slightly, and peered at me through the gap formed by her underarm. Her golden eye was blazing in the shadow. Then she did something so out of character, something so carefree and utterly cute, that I couldn't help but laugh: she stuck the tip of her tongue out at me.

"Oh, my," I sighed, feigning exasperation. "Well, come on, then, naughty creature."

Eventually, I managed to negotiate her rubbery form into my arms, where I cradled her against my chest. She harumphed at first, then nuzzled in, getting comfortable. Her eyes closed, and a look of serenity crossed her face, one I didn't think I had ever seen on her before.

After a few minutes of breath and quiet, she said, "When I

made fun of you for being old ... er ... I never actually minded your creaking, I hope you know. You should know."

Out of habit, I rubbed the gnarled scar on my chest. "And you should know by now that you are the owner of my heart, one way or another. No matter in whose rib cage it lies, you are its sole ruler, and the only master who may move it, my rose—my brightness. Even the decay in Gaius's soul cannot erode that."

And it was true. No matter what happened next, even if we never tore my heart from that monster's chest, it would always belong to her. She had enough heart for both of us regardless.

At first, the thought made me smile; but at length, as I traced the patterns of the shooting stars above us, the notion turned darker. She was the sum of our light. If *what happened next* took her from me ... if I lost her ... it wasn't just my life that would end. Losing her now would make out of me a monster to rival Gaius. As soon as the cycle had been broken, it would start anew. As soon as the withering had gone, it would surely return. For as much as we'd needed to stop Gealach, I must admit that, in her position, I would be no better. I was no better. My moon would scorch the earth until there was nowhere the Aquilans could hide from me.

She watched my face—I could feel her gaze boring into me—and my troubles must be writ plainly upon it, because she reached up to touch my cheek, turning my attention to her. "You look miserable. What are you thinking about?"

"The coming battle," I answered honestly. For there was no doubt there would be one. The problem could not be solved the way we'd confronted Gealach; the Empire could not be reasoned with, and Gaius could not be healed of the rot inside him.

My gaze flicked to her face then. Since the moment the Horned One had imbued her with his spirit, her skin had taken on a radiant inner glow, but bringing up the battle quite literally dimmed her shine. Her eyes shifted from brilliant yellow topaz to her usual dark, stormy blue. But, never one to shy away from a difficult topic, she pursed her lips and nodded. "Yea. Reckon it'll be brutal."

I adored how resolute she remained, but the heartache and

exhaustion in her face broke me in a way I had not anticipated. This person was my one, and the thought that I could not protect her from the evils of the mortal world was so unbearable I nearly screamed to the heavens.

But ... perhaps there was something I could do yet. I searched the stars once more. Taking on all the memory and power of the Moon had granted me certain knowledge—magic and rituals arcane, archaic, even never before used. There was a life for us, one that would ensure I never had to worry about losing her again. One that would ensure she never relived the pain visited upon her in life.

It was terrible. It was selfish. It was cowardly. But I was always willing to be the "devil on her shoulder," to borrow a Dead World phrase.

She shifted against me, waiting for me to speak. I got the sense that she understood what I was thinking without my having to voice it.

"There is another choice," I said at last, freeing her from my arm and propping myself up on one elbow.

She lay in the grass with her hands folded over her paint-streaked stomach, peering at me furtively. She often gave me that look. I didn't think she knew it, but it was one of my favorites. I could not help but smile and lean in to give her a warm, lingering kiss.

She accepted it at first, leaning hungrily into me, before she came to her senses and prodded me away. "What are you talking about, what 'other choice?'"

I searched her again before gesturing to the sky. "We could leave," I said simply. "I will carve us a path through the stars and find us somewhere safe to rest. Forever, if you will it." Though her eyes widened, I forged on: "There are those out there like us, beings living in the Great Dark Beyond amid the planets. They have their own ways. Or if you'd prefer to avoid people entirely, we could sail into the heavens and go on forever."

"Is that truly a path you would walk?" she murmured.

"With you, for you, I would walk any path."

"Thousands—tens of thousands, maybe more—will die without us."

I lowered my chin. "Yes. That's true. They would die by my own hand if it would ensure your safety."

"Oh. I see." Mave sighed. She did not seem disgusted with me, or even disappointed; rather, she pulled me close, cradling my head against her chest as though I were a babe. "You're scared."

The words were so matter-of-fact, and my immediate reaction was to take offense. "I— Well ... yes." There was no use in dressing it up. I nuzzled her chest and inhaled her perfume, which sent shivers of euphoria through my limbs. "If after all of this I lost you, this time for good? Yes. I am scared of that."

"Hmph. I doubt it would be for good." Instead of elaborating, she ran her fingernails over my scalp. "But if in the coming battle I die, you must go on living."

The notion was so preposterous I snorted. "There is no me without you."

"Yes, there is," she insisted. "And I'm telling you now, I don't want—I never have wanted—you to kill for me. I want you to *live* for me. Not in the heavens but here. Watch after all I loved for me. Shepherd the people of Éire and make sure they're safe."

The cold hand of dread lay heavy at the base of my skull. Slowly, I closed my eyes and exhaled through my nose. They weren't the words I wanted to hear ... but I suppose they were the ones I should have expected. "The path through the stars is still open to you, my brightness."

Mave laughed a little. "I don't belong in the sky amongst gods, Hiberos. Domhan has always been where I belong. Here on this planet, in Éire, with my people. No amount of safety or godhood is worth leaving them."

She was glorious. She was fearless. She was breaking my heart.

"In that case," I said at length, propping myself up again, "you know what we must do. *When single shine the moon and sun.* It is time to take our last stand, do you agree?"

Now it was her turn to close her eyes and sigh. When she was ready, she nodded. "It won't be pretty."

"No," I agreed. "But that is what we're made for."

Her mouth twitched into a smile before she opened her eyes. They were brilliant gold again, as if the thought of our duty alone woke all the cosmic light inside of her. I felt my own magic stir in response. It was eager to mingle with hers. I was struck with the feeling that, when the time came, our power would tear us apart to join—we had no choice but to obey it if we wanted to survive the encounter.

"For now," she said with a yawn, "I want a nap. And then, who knows?"

A thrill ran through my abdomen, straight to my root. "Sleep, then, my brightness. Be ready for what I have in store for you."

And pray to the stars that it isn't our last night together.

38

MAVE

Drusilla felt knuckles nudging her shoulder, and in her heightened state, her consciousness called to me. I answered at once.

Yet when she turned her head, she found only Ryac crouched above her, elbows on his knees, eyes half-lidded. She hesitated to call the way he looked at her *affection*, but there was no trace of hunger or malevolence, which, for him, was close enough. They still had not spoken about him shoving his head between her thighs, and she doubted they ever would—especially as, mere hours from now, they'd part ways forever.

"Time to get movin'," he said, standing and offering her a hand up. Taking the height of her ears into account, she was almost taller than him, but he was unbothered. "One more push and you're home free."

Somewhere farther in the forest, one of his people whooped. Drusilla had seen neither hide nor hair of any of them, but they made their presence known; they'd been following all along, roving in a silent pack. How many of them, she didn't know. Not all twenty-four, or however many were left. Still, such loyalty. What hold Ryac must have on his moonless, for them to follow him into the clutches of the eagle and then back out at his whim. Once again, she marveled at the man's strangeness. He was like a faerie himself with his fickle and unpredictable ways. More than ever before, she questioned if this was some kind of convoluted trap.

Yet, her days in Sylvostum had been numbered anyway. By now, they had certainly noted her absence, all their suspicions of her confirmed. There was no going back.

"And where will you go after this?" Drusilla asked as she doused her modest fire.

Ryac stuck his thumbs in his waistband. "East. Co Ligea, I think. Not too far from Divlinn, perhaps north. There's another pack to the south we'd best not tangle with."

"No?"

"Uh-uh. We may worship the same god, but they are not friendly."

"And what of your packmembers back at Sylvostum?"

"They'll extract themselves soon if they haven't already. Hopefully, we didn't lose anyone. But my folk are slippery. No doubt you've noticed." He winked and picked around one of his canines with a fingernail. "One thing that can be said for Sergia is that without him, the quillies are falling apart."

Drusilla grunted. Perhaps it was Gaius's absence that had plunged the town into chaos. More likely, it was the blighted fae blood in their veins driving them all to madness.

With her bedroll and meager supplies packed up, and they headed onward once more. "And where'll you go?" Ryac asked at length. "Just going to stay in Cuanacht?"

"Perhaps. I haven't decided."

"Ah..." She felt him looking at her sidelong, studying her for a long time. Something she could not quite name hung in the air between them.

If Ryac was going to say something more, before he could, he slowed to a stop. His head flicked this way and that, and on his face was an expression Drusilla had never expected to see—

beneath a hefty measure of confusion, fear. She searched him again, calculating, and shifted her ears to try and pick up on what he heard.

Finally, she caught the sound: the distant snarling of a nasty fight, bodies hitting the ground. Then immediately afterward came the scent. Blood. Werewolf blood.

Someone was killing the moonless.

She wiggled her nose, trying to determine who, and though the wind wasn't quite right, she half-caught a familiar tang in the air. Almost as familiar as her own scent, although, whatever it was, it had ... changed, somehow. Stronger, deeper, burnt in a way that prevented her from recognizing it exactly. It couldn't be occulata speculatores; the notes weren't right, no leather oil, no poison, and even a squad of assassins could not take down a pack of Old-God-worshiping werewolves. Yet, if it were a dispatch of legionaries, they'd have heard them coming. Aquilan troops were not known for their subtlety.

Ryac's growl told her *he* knew exactly who it was. Drusilla side-eyed him for guidance. In the couple seconds she had looked away from him, he'd shifted into his wiry, lanky wolf form, his clothing shreds at his feet. The next moment, he was on all fours, bounding in the direction of the sound.

Was he out of his damned mind? Rushing *toward* the slaughter? Packs of any wolfen species were tight-knit, but she'd have thought he of all people—an anti-social creature driven by base instinct—would possess a stronger sense of self-preservation.

"Ryac!"

He tossed over his shoulder, "Leave!"

The uncharacteristic, urgent note in his voice made her heart roar like thunder in her chest. Licking her lips, Drusilla pulled her compass from the folds of her tunic, made sure she was still heading southwest, and began to run. As she did, she swiveled her ears back. Tried to pinpoint the source of the sound to make sure it wasn't coming any nearer. But she could no longer find it.

She did not stop running. The hair at her crest peaked, jolts of paranoia shooting up her spine as she leapt over roots and trod rough, blighted terrain. Every so often, she caught the moan of fomori, which the moonless had been keeping off their backs, but there was little she could do besides pray that it was one of the slower varieties.

Deadfall cracked loudly behind and to her right. In a flash, she wrenched her dagger from its holster.

A streak of white filled her periphery, and she readied to strike before recognizing Ryac. He was painted with blood, his hazy red eyes wild with the chase. Yet, with a sting of panic, she realized he was not the hunter but the *hunted*.

There was no time to ask what pursued him. She kept her eyes ahead, tracking deadfall that threatened to trip her and the trunks soaring past her. Soon, the forest's growth became less dense. They weren't far now from the valley that would lead her to the Éirins war camp. One more push—

With a sharp yelp of pain, the white streak beside her stalled abruptly and was ripped back from her vision.

No. Drusilla tried to get a glimpse of what had waylaid him— and clipped a tree with her shoulder. She was sent into a spin. Loose needles had her skidding across the forest floor, digging her claws into the nearest tree to keep from falling. As she did, she turned, panting, to regard Ryac.

There was nothing there. It was as though the trees had swallowed him up. But that scent ... blood and heat and *anger*, so much anger. Now that it was closer, she knew the smell.

She knew from whom it came. *She knew who hunted them.*

But how could he be here? And why did he smell so ... wrong?

Something glowed through the trees, licking the air like flame without fire. *Magic.* Red to gold magic lashing out from the man at its center. He was coming closer.

Drusilla swallowed, turned, and ran again. Yet even as she did, she knew there was no escape. If she were to reach the valley, then what? Then he'd be unimpeded by the forest, and she'd have no cover.

Not that the forest proved to be much an obstacle. Trees crunched behind her. His woeful cries of betrayal echoed off them. He'd spotted her, and now he was tearing the forest apart to get to her.

For over ten years, she'd assumed she would die by his hand eventually. She never could have guessed it would be like this.

For a minute or so, as she ran, all was quiet. Too quiet. Not even the fomori dared to make their presence known. All she could hear were her own panting breaths and the wind whistling in her ears.

Suddenly, there was a great crack like a lightning strike. A tree just paces in front of her began to twist, and then it was falling. With a yelp, she dug her claws into a nearby birch, stopping short to keep from being crushed and—

The trunk crashed at her feet and shook the earth.

It fell to reveal Gaius standing at the base.

He heaved, bare shoulders rising and falling as if, despite all the power radiating from him, merely breathing took great effort. Every inch of him seemed to bleed; crimson covered him so extensively that, at first glance, she thought he was flayed. Ram's horns wrought of pulsing magic spiraled from his curls. And in the center of his chest glowed a strange seed of red power, throbbing as with a heart beat, scarlet rivers flowing from it and into every vein on his body. In his left fist, he held Ryac—humanlike again, naked, and beaten half-conscious—by the nape like a naughty puppy.

"You." Gaius's voice ground and echoed like stone on stone. "All along, it was you."

He dropped Ryac, stepped over the trunk, and was mere feet away within seconds. Yet as he reached for Drusilla, his hands as blazing hot as suns on both sides of her face, it was not smugness that overtook him. He did not resort to calling her *mongrel* or threatening her with torture. Perhaps could not, the bizarre, unholy power paring him down to his most basic elements.

He wept. He gripped her by the throat and wept, hanging his head. "Why? I trusted you with my son. I loved you like family. *Why?*"

Drusilla stayed absolutely still, lips pulled tight, not daring to swallow the saliva pooling in her jaws. When he looked to her for an answer, she was mindful of his hand on her windpipe—a centimeter away from sudden death.

Behind Gaius, Ryac's pale form twitched just a bit, one shoulder lifting as if to push up from the ground.

She made her breathing more ragged and pressed one hand to Gaius's wrist. If she could manage to keep his attention... "It was a mistake, Gaius." Her voice was thin and low. "Can you forgive me?"

"You're asking for *forgiveness?*" he wheezed.

With her eyes alone, she indicated his full-to-bursting aura. "You were a legate before," she said slowly. "You are a god now. I will obey a god."

Gaius's eye was wide, pupil blown and starry, as if the word *god* slotted everything into its proper and logical place. Still, he held her inches from his face, shook his head, and asked, genuinely it seemed, "How? How can I?"

"That is what makes you a god, isn't it? The power to grant mercy. To grant mercy to some worthless lupercal."

Drusilla could sense the indignant reply on his tongue as he opened his mouth. As though he might refute her, tell her she wasn't worthless. But instead, he closed it.

Something new lit in his eye, tilted his brow—a singular self-awareness, and an unspoken, unspeakable sense of deprivation.

He stroked a thumb down the soft fur of her cheek. The first natural display of affection she'd ever witnessed from him.

And that was when Ryac struck.

Somewhere between picking himself up and lunging from the bracken, he'd shifted again. Now he was a snarling white blizzard, a whirlwind around Gaius, shredding and snapping and foaming. With a cry of surprise, Gaius's hold on Drusilla broke.

And she ran.

She did not look back. Even as she breached the treeline and tripped across the bleeding landscape, even when Ryac's attack fell silent, even as Gaius's miserable screams followed her, even

when she noticed with a gulch that the moon was *white*, not red—
she ran.

Ran. Ran. Ran. Ran until she saw rough palisades of the war
camp and the flying banners of Tuath Stag Gréine.

I JOLTED out of a trance to find myself standing on the beach of
black sand and diamonds. Something was coming, as surely as the
sunrise overtaking the horizon before me. With one eye, I watched
the sea turn yellow, and with the other, I saw through Faelon.

He hadn't been outside when the curse broke and the moon
returned to normal, but now he was gathered with the others—
wolfkerne, walking folk, fae, and rebel—looking up at it with awe.

A little node in the corner of his mind lit up. Me.

And, to my great surprise, he alerted to it.

*Auntie Mave! You're alive? Did you do this? Did you find
Hiberos? Did you fix the moon?*

Yea, I did, I replied. *You can hear me?*

*Mum, Orlaith, she told me about our connection. But ... I think
I already knew. Or, suspected. I always felt there was someone
there. You aren't angry, are you?*

No, no, it's fine. But are you okay? Is your mother safe?

He nodded, then, thinking I couldn't sense his answer, elabo-
rated. *Yes, but, please. What about my mother and father? Are they
okay? Do you know?*

I didn't know how to tell him about Gaius. I paused to find the
words. An icy shiver racked both our rib cages—and I shared in his
dread as he realized something bad must have happened.

A second later, I didn't have to tell him.

Gaius's roars shook the earth, the sky cracking like a whip.
Clouds roiled. Blackened.

What was that? A frisson of terror bolted up the boy's spine,
and he threw a look around the camp. Gasps and cries rose from
the crowd. He searched for Orlaith, who was almost always by his
side, but now he couldn't see her anywhere at all. The only person

who acknowledged him was the huge, woad-painted pig that usually followed Councilor Uaine everywhere. It had disappeared for a few days, but now it was back as if nothing had happened, and as panic rippled through the war camp, it squealed and hurried to hide behind Faelon. Very much in vain, given its wideness.

An archer on one of the palisades shouted to Muiri, who stood amongst her men, "There's something running toward the encampment. It's a wolf!"

I spoke into Faelon's mind. *It's Drusilla. Help her, quick.*

The boy launched into action, pushing his way to the front of the crowd, to Muiri. He didn't know how to get her attention besides grabbing her mail belt, and she looked down at him, her dark eyes cold and hard. It was obvious that many of the Éirins did not want him here, just as Ryac had said, but there was no time to dwell on it now. He had to save Drusilla.

"Please," he said, "it's not a wolf, it's a lupercal. My—" He hesitated, not wanting to say nursemaid. "My friend, Drusilla."

He did not expect Muiri's face to change when he said the name, yet her brow leavened, and she shouted for the archers to open the gate and let the she-wolf in.

Perhaps too late, someone said, "But what is she running from?"

Another roar shook the earth, and this time, Faelon recognized it. The timbre, the anger, the agony...

It was Father.

His heart wrenched and fluttered fearfully all at once. *Father. Mighty Ones, what's happened?*

The outermost gates groaned open, and Drusilla ran in. Clad in a traveling dress, she was a mess head to toe, her hood and cloak torn and caught with twigs, her fur ruffled, muzzle foaming, eyes wide and bloodshot. At once, she narrowed in on him. They ran, collided, clutching each other like it might be the last time they ever embraced.

Faelon couldn't stop shaking. "What happened?"

"I'm all right. I'm all right." She flicked her sharp yellow eyes at Muiri and Uaine, who had pulled up swiftly. "Something has happened. I was passing through Geatacoill, fleeing Sylvostum, and—" She shook her head, lips pulling back, nose crinkling. "The legate is possessed of some great and terrible power. He's ... changed. He has too much..."

"Too much what?"

"I don't know." Her ears pinned. "Where is Mave?"

A great hulking form stepped up beside Muiri and the counselor. Ferghal. He was still stuck in that bizarre in-between state, faoladh and man both, but the intensity seemed to have gone down, and he had his wits. "Mave left days ago to go try and find Hiberos."

"Hiberos? Of course she did, damned goat. Where did *Hiberos* go?"

"I dunno. She had a lead, and she were going to ask me to come help her, but that's all she said."

Faelon looked from one adult to the other as they argued, not sure how or when to say that the very person they were looking for was currently in his head. When there was finally a spare moment to say, "She's okay," he was shocked when Drusilla said it, too.

Their gazes met, his wide, hers knowing. How did she know that? Did she talk to her, too? There was so much he did not understand about fae. Could they all do that?

"Is he coming for us?" Muiri asked bluntly.

"He was chasing me. But I don't know."

The duskwarden growled. "Well, if he is, he's in for a hell of a surprise. I've got a pack of hungry wolves waiting to feast on him."

Faelon's heart leapt into his throat, pounding hard enough to make everything throb. What was going on? Somehow, he knew his father was sick, that he had done something so bad it was unspeakable, but...

Gaius had done so many awful things, to him and others—made *him* do awful things, and he knew they were awful—but every time he heard a cross word against him, an uncomfortable queasy feeling got in his stomach. Beyond that, the thought of him being in harm's way made Faelon ache in a way he did not understand.

The ground trembled again, and I could have sworn that Gaius sounded farther away. But I hadn't come this far by taking chances when it came to him.

If he wanted to hurt the people of this war camp, then he would have to go through me first.

I thought to Faelon, *I'm coming.*

Hiberos's warm hand on my shoulder shocked me out of my trance. My sight returned to both eyes; the strange, untouched sphere of the Otherworld came flooding back to me. I turned, grimacing.

Hiberos took me in with concern and all the heavens in his gaze. "What's happened?"

"Gaius is loose. It's time to go home."

"I see." His ears shifted, and I knew he was thinking about that path through the stars he said he would carve. "I won't offer you an escape again and incur your wrath, but it never hurts to remind you: Gaius is not your responsibility."

He was only trying to give me an out, so I couldn't be angry at him, but—"Unfortunately, he very much is. At this point, we are the only people who can stop him. Remember?" I tapped the gnarled scar on his chest. "It's your heart, and I am its master."

Though Hiberos's face shone with admiration, it was also the very picture of sadness. Nevertheless, he summoned his lunar scythe and, like the boline, used it to cut a tear in the Weave.

Magic not wholly unlike that of the Moon Gate whirled and spiraled within the rift. A moment later, the edge of Geatacoill lay on the other side, blurry, indistinct, and rippling slightly like the face of a lake. With a heavy sigh, I looked from the portal to him.

Our eyes met. He gave me a smile that could not be anything but rueful and stroked my new woven arm, squeezing the fingertips with his free hand. Keeping his promise, he spoke no words, but even if we were not godlings, I'd be able to read him. This was the last chance. This was our last opportunity to turn around, to give in, to follow that path through the stars—to leave everything behind and forget about it all. All the conflict and fear and endless, endless suffering. Everything human. Everything except for him. Us.

But he already knew my answer, so I could only give him a sorry smile in return. Escape was not salvation. Paradise did not wait across some divide.

Hand in hand, we stepped through the rift.

39

On the other side, neither Gaius nor Ryac were anywhere to be seen. The Mournful Palace had either sunk back into the earth or fallen, for it was not visible beyond the treetops. The first sunrise in a week painted the sky buttery yellows, dreamy periwinkles, and baby blues, broken up by lucent jade as Hiberos's moths circled us. The moon, a faint silver crescent, hung high above our heads in the dawn.

By the time we reached the war camp, it was full morning. Someone must have sensed us approaching, because the gatekeepers were ready, and opened for us without question.

When we entered, Faelon stood between Drusilla and Orlaith, waiting for us, his expression a mixture of sadness, fear, and heart-wrenching hope. The look in his eyes transported me back ten years, to Geatacoill, to that desperate sprint through the forest away from Gaius, when I'd pulled back the blanket protecting his infant face and seen a similar fear.

At such a young age. Mere *months* old.

Stars. My stomach tied in knots when I thought of how scared my nephew had been all his life. After we defeated Gaius, I would do anything to make sure he was never afraid like that ever again.

A fat pink blur darted out from behind Faelon and dashed,

squealing, into me. I knelt, narrowly avoiding a kneecapping, and let Conan crash into me with a "Oof!" followed by a song of furious grunts.

"I know, I know. Trust me, I didn't like leaving you behind, either. But look, I'm pink again. Like you." I chucked his flabby chin and summoned an acorn between my fingers.

He flapped his ears, gave me one last, hard look as if to say *Next time, I won't let you off so easy*, then slowly slurped the acorn into his mouth.

With Conan appeased, I straightened once more. The encampment was quiet, all stares, but I could not take my eyes from my family. Orlaith's posture was more relaxed than I'd seen it since my rebirth, and she wore moth clips in her new short hair. Beside her, an equally relaxed Erivon braced her shoulders. In that moment I saw them not as the fae queen and king I'd come to know but two people, flawed but striving, standing proudly with their son.

Taking us in, they shone with love and shock and reverence and, finally, as we approached, joy.

"You," Orlaith whispered. "You are the Moon and Sun. Gealach and the Horned One. You."

I bowed my head, frowning, and reached for Hiberos's hand again. This conversation might not be comfortable, but I felt I needed to get it out right up front. "Mother Moon said that she didn't expect me to be her ... heir, or whatever. I hope you aren't angry at me for stealing your birthright."

"Birthright?" Erivon looked from me to his wife. "I was not even aware this was a possibility."

"Mave," said my sister, a smile on her face despite the tightness in her throat. "Goodness. We never had ambitions to be gods. I think ... until recently"—she placed a hand on Faelon's shoulder —"we did not quite know what our ambition was."

I glanced at Hiberos. "We didn't ask to be gods either, yet here we are."

Erivon laughed. "Then you are the right choice. A king, or any leader, should be a servant and protector to their subjects. Those who yearn for power and acclaim rarely wield them correctly, or even to great effect. Those who feel they know best seldom listen to those who know better."

In my periphery, I saw Drusilla's ears pin. We inhaled at the same time, and I knew we both were thinking about Gaius.

"I don't know where he is," I said, "but he's not coming here, not yet."

"Anyway, we should leave before he does," Muiri said as she exited a nearby tent, her pouty lips in their perpetual frown. "One Aquilan with unchecked power and a mystical stimulant in his system is bad enough, but two-and-some legions hepped up on the shite?" She lifted her chin to address the crowd gathered near the gates. "It is time to abandon this front and fall back to Gallive."

"High King Alasdair will be expecting to meet us anyway," Uaine said, pointing at the sky. "He's meant to arrive at the bilé this morning. We might be able to catch him if we start moving now. Maybe Mave can ride ahead."

Hiberos chuckled. "I believe I can make myself useful here." And when he twirled the lunar scythe in his hand, it skimmed the weave visibly, catching it and making it shimmer but not quite tearing it open.

At this point, the majority of the camp, fae and human, had gravitated toward the commotion and looked on: Joa, her wife Eilliv, Manan, Paik, Menecon, Ferghal, a convalescing Oishin. Muiri surveyed the crowd for a few heavy seconds, then me, all of me, from the tips of my toes to the ends of my antlers. She sighed and...

I could see her breath. It fogged in front of her face, a misty cloud, as though the air around us was frigid.

Wait. No. Not a breath. It expanded outward and down in a pillar, and in moments, I could make out indistinct features floating within it. Soon, they sharpened, and I recognized the person standing before me.

It was Gwynedd.

I couldn't help but startle. The starry spirit smiled in reply, and Hiberos tilted his head, fascinated. Yet, when I opened my mouth to say his name, it occurred to me that no one else had turned to acknowledge him. He appeared only to us.

Muiri said something, but I missed it as I turned, taking in the camp. Lady above. The people watching us weren't just fae and human and werewolf—spirits stood amongst them, like blue stones bound in leather jewelry. Some I'd never seen before, some familiar faces without names, and some who made my heart clench when I recognized them. Tali, Eamon, the faintest outline of what must be my father, friends and cousins from Fraochgleann...

"Mave," Hiberos said, bringing my attention back to Muiri. Gwynedd still stood beside her, shimmering like the Great Dark Beyond. It made sense, I supposed, that a god could see spirits, but no doubt it would take me a good long while to get used to it.

Ruadan had been right all along. There were so many following me.

I only wished he were here, too.

"Sorry, what did you say?"

In the time I had been lost in the crowd, Hiberos had torn another rift in the Weave. On the other side sat Gallive, the abhan, and the black lough.

With one final glance around me, I squared my shoulders, took a deep breath, and asked, "Who's going with us to see the high king?"

Orlaith and Erivon urged Faelon forward first. The lad seemed unsure, glancing up the sky, in the direction of Geatacoill and Sylvostum ... then back to Orlaith for reassurance. Then me, and finally, Drusilla.

It was the she-wolf who took his hand in hers and promised, "I will be right there with you, Lucastos."

He exhaled shakily, rolled his shoulders. Held his breath like he was diving into water. And they jumped together and were gone. Uaine, Paik, and Conan followed close behind so they'd have someone to guide them through the city.

I stopped before the swirling portal, nodding to Orlaith and Muiri. "You two staying behind?"

"We should see to things here," Orlaith said softly. "We'll catch up."

"I'll go," said a voice behind them.

Muiri, Erivon, and Orlaith parted to reveal Solma, her usually proud shoulders slack, her gaze dulled, the silver-lined leaves of her hair limp and somewhat faded.

"You found him," she said, pointing her chin at Hiberos. Her tone and demeanor were completely desolate, but I did not understand at first.

"She found me," Hiberos said in confirmation.

Her nostrils flared as she sighed, but when she finally asked the question weighing her down, it was with exhaustion rather than fury. "Did you kill her?"

Poor Solma. No one was more loyal to Mother Moon.

"No. She chose to let go."

Her relief showed more in her body than her face, a great tension releasing, yet she was still etched with misery. Then, after a moment, her expression shuttered and turned to resignation. With her ears lowered, she knelt before me on both knees, narrowly focused on the dirt between us.

My power surged around her, uneasy—my honest reaction to realizing she was bowing before me. Not out of reverence but surrender. I wanted neither.

She spoke into my stunned silence. "Horned One, I swear my allegiance to you as the avatar of the Sun, and to you, Hiberos, as the new Moon. Take from me what you will. Punish me how you will. For how I spoke to you, I am at your mercy."

Her submission was genuine, but I knew Solma. Everything about her, now. She was doing this not because her convictions had changed but because she was accustomed to divine punishment. Manipulation, constantly being reminded that it was through the death of her father she lived. Conditioned to expect retaliation. Millennia of treading lightly around her fragile mother, goddess, lover, and wife all in one.

I did not need to look at Hiberos to understand his feelings on the subject—and I? I did not think twice before leaning forward, bracing Solma's arms, and helping her to her feet. Even in my godly form, she towered above me, a mighty bloodbriar hedge, her silver eyes clouded with grief, fear, torment.

Whatever she had said to me, I could not bear the thought of her still bound up and trapped by Gealach. I could not bear the idea that this power inside of me gave me power over her, and that I might wield it against her, even unintentionally. The thought was so painful and so counter to my own nature that I, for a moment, regretted stepping into this power altogether.

I squeezed her hand, bringing her eyes to meet mine. "Solma, I never wanted to—I never wanted to rule over you. Things may have changed, but there will be no punishment for you. Do you not see? I need you now more than ever. Holding this power inside of me, I need someone who will tell me *no*. Someone who will challenge me. I need you, as my commander."

Something passed between us then, a flicker of desire to understand and to be understood.

"I know that you're used to being asked to fall in lockstep with your gods," I continued, "but that is not what I want. That will never *be* what I want. We exist not to rule over you but to work with you and in you and for you. To put ourselves between our peoples and whatever forces may try to harm them. A relationship, not a tether."

Unexpectedly, Solma's face shifted, threatening to crumble.

"She loved us," she said, "I— Surely, it was more, we were more, we *meant* more. Surely, she loved us. Surely, there was more than just a thirst for obedience..."

For once, she spoke with very little authority. Like a child, she grasped for reassurance. So I took her hands in mine and squeezed hard. "She did love you, but despite being the moon goddess, despite all the power she had, and the hold she had over *you*, she was still ... human. D'you know what I mean? We all are. We are all that which makes humans imperfect and fallible and unique and evil and disgusting and loving and creative and kind, and capable of every wonderful and terrible thing that has ever been done to us and for us."

Beside me, Erivon spoke up, voice soft. "Parents are human, too."

With that, Solma broke. Finally, I saw something I never thought in a thousand years I would see. She wept, openly, ugly, bringing her hands to cover her eyes. "There was so much I wanted to say to her," she managed between gasps.

She needed to collapse, but she seemed incapable of letting go fully—so I pulled her into my arms and squeezed her until she went limp and quivered.

An awareness that was at once thrilling and terrifying bloomed in my chest. I was the Horned One. Orphaned, abandoned, neglected, the fae and Éirin both might regard me as their Lady, and how did one come to terms with that? What knowledge did I give, what did I keep, and why, and how?

How did a huntress from a provincial village, after claiming godhood, hold herself in herself?

·☽ ☽ ☽ ☾ ☾·

IF I HADN'T BEEN CONVINCED before, seeing the state of Gallive gave me the confidence that we'd done the right thing. When the withering hit the city, it had hit it hard. Doors were barred, windows boarded up. Those houses that had not been protected were ash now, cleansing fire started by King Tagh's men to purge the blight from the buildings. Refugees had flowed in from Sallach and greater Cuanacht, and only those who'd found a roof over their heads seemed to have made it out alive.

The people had banded together to help their neighbors, but there was only so much room, and folk lived on top of one another as it was. Piles of bodies clogged every close and mews, human and fomori alike, pale and naked and twisted such that you could barely discern one species from the other. The stench was otherworldly.

Solma and Menecon came through the portal and followed closely. Paik and Uaine were long gone. They must have already guided Drusilla and Faelon to the bilé—thank the stars, for the boy had already seen so much. To linger here ... I didn't even want to think of it.

Hiberos and I walked through the streets hand in hand, saying nothing as we watched citizens emerging from their homes for the first time in a week, their hard faces hollowed and their cold eyes ringed with shadow. They saw us and whispered, holding their children and loved ones close, none of them knowing if they should take up arms or cry with relief.

A tired people, too clever to hope for much. So it had been for centuries, even before the Shift.

In fact, as we passed the gathering masses, spirits began to appear next to their descendants—some new, some old, some ancient; some wearing leine and tartans, others in trainers and football jackets. A young punk woman in boots and a leather jacket linked arms with a work-wounded waif wrangling two toddlers. Not far on, a classroom of school children in their neat uniforms played jacks. Nobles, bogmen, musicians, laborers, and every combination; old, young, furious, tearful. They, too, watched with heavy stares. Knowing eyes.

We hadn't earned their loyalty yet. I had to imagine that, to many of them, it seemed there was no cure, no end to this pain. No salvation. We would have to prove otherwise through our actions.

I wouldn't have it any other way. Suffering may be in our inheritance, but fight was in our blood.

Even still, even with all this power, it was hard to convince myself there was anything I could do to fix what Mother Moon began. Like everything in Co Cuanacht, the De Siabair bilé was not untouched by the rot. Its bottommost leaves had withered to a sour yellow, and its roots were crawling with red and purple veins, still pulsing as though the tree was an appendage of some dreadful, ailing beast sleeping below ground.

All that. All that pain, all that work to stop the blood moon, and we still had not been able to reverse the withering. Only halt its progress.

Hiberos must have sensed the beginnings of my spiral, for he squeezed my hand as we entered the enormous ash. "We can reverse it. Only, it will take time. No one, grand gesture can undo harm like this. Remember that, my huntress."

"Right." I let out a slow breath. "Persistence."

He threw me a handsome smirk, winked, and wiggled our entwined fingers playfully.

As we followed the scents of humans to the great hall, I was surprised to see King Tagh awake and sitting in his throne. Like his bed, it was a tree grown into the proper shape, its branches and vines coiling round his arms and piercing his veins, sustaining him. I noted that his antlers had been sawn away to accommodate his frailty. He looked ill, but not nearly as terrible as he had the first time I saw him.

Sitting next to him, turned to face him in a high-backed chair, was a man I had never seen but whom, even without godly senses, I would recognize at first glance.

High King Alasdair alerted to our entrance and stood. Although he was no taller than one-seventy-five centimeters—why had we ever gone back to Imperial measurements?—his presence was much larger. He wore a mail coat, a long gambeson, and a tabard bearing red chevrons of Tuath Síol Ruairí. Hair that had once been brown but was now mostly gray framed a wide, bearded face with prominent brow- and cheekbones, and his heavy-lidded eyes were so blue they looked painful. Like all druids of his station, he had antlers, but rather than standing up they wrapped around his head like a crown.

As he descended the dais briskly toward us, he didn't exactly smile, but there was a certain light in his gaze. "Mave," he said like he knew me, then looked at Hiberos as though he wasn't beholding an ancient fae and aspect of the Moon itself. "And you must be Hiberos."

"I am."

We introduced both Solma and Menecon to the kings, but very few pleasantries were exchanged before Uaine arrived. Trotting behind him was Conan, pink belly jiggling, ears flapping. The high king looked at the pig and paused, perhaps trying to discern if this was a druid in disguise, a familiar, or merely a very smart, very nosy hog.

When he determined Conan was only civilized, not human, he turned the conversation back to me. "We have much to talk about. But I am quite restless, and we haven't much time. Come, I want to show you something."

With a respectful nod toward King Tagh, he motioned for his retainers to stay behind and exited the great hall.

Hiberos and I paid quick respects to the king before following him, Solma in tow. He led us down the lacquered white corridors, through an arcade of woven ash branches, and into a small, green courtyard or chamber open to the air. It resembled a hollow, as if we were nestled within a knot of the bilé.

In the center of the mossy patch, surrounded by wisps and heavy with the scent of magic, sat a large chunk of granite. I knew instinctively and with a shiver that this was a fragment of Lia Fáil. The Stone of Tara. A standing stone as ancient as the island itself, used for thousands of years to inaugurate the High King of Éire.

When High King Alasdair finally united the dissonant clans of Éire under his banner, he'd had the stone sundered into five parts, to be placed in each province: one in his bilé, one elsewhere in Ligea, one in Cuanacht, one in Muvane, and one in Tirconnell —to make sure there was never just one seat of power in Éire, as a show of good faith to the other kings. As we came closer to it, I saw that its face was engraved in four parts: a mound, a spear, a sword, and a cauldron.

Since the Shift, the Lia Fáil had served to not only coronate the king but to bind him to the land, to ensure he kept his oaths. The Weave resonated deeply with it, and it exuded all of the magic, memories, wishes, and intentions of all those who had used it for eons.

Alasdair approached the stone as though approaching an old friend, and finally, a real smile graced his face. He bent and touched the stone, and as he traced the etchings, the chamber itself seemed to growl low in greeting.

Not looking at us, Alasdair spoke as though he were speaking to the stone itself.

"When I was a boy, I had no hope that our land would ever be free from the Empire. Growing up on the borderlands between Divlinn and Westminia will do that to you. I hated everyone, including myself. But most especially, I hated my father. He lived in his memories ... could only soothe himself with liquor. He took what work he could, laying bricks for the quillies, but there was never enough to provide for the family—and that shame, it only made his troubles worse." He sighed hard through his nose. "Of course, when I was a lad, I didn't see it that way. I only ever saw him listless and mean while my equally listless, mean mother toiled to care for us. I despised him. Berated him. Then, one day, when Mother sent me to go fetch him from work, I saw something I could not believe.

"The bricklayers had risen up against the quillies. They were demanding a fair wage and protection from the Empire without citizenship. And who should be standing above them, orating like a king? My dad. The wastrel, the drunk, my mother's curse. Hopeful, loud, brave, and *keen* as a whip. *Smart.* Come to find out he had been the one to start their movement. My ordinary father. Like so many other fathers. Just a man. But not just. Righteous. Mythic.

"I thought, 'We have nothing, so why should *hope*—something so unreliable and foolish—why should that be any different?' But soon I realized that hope is not something you have. Hope is something that you make, and it can be given to others." He eased back on his haunches with another sigh. "So, rather than hating, rather than turning on the world in which I lived, rather than resigning myself to living in hell, no land, scoured by ignorance and want— rather than letting my memories hold me in their palm, I rose up. Took it upon myself to be the start. Flint struck against stone."

The Lia Fáil itself began to glow, and somehow, I knew the four other pieces were glowing, too, wherever they were kept. Still connected, still one, even across miles, even sundered apart.

"But the thing about fire," he said, with that unreadable

twinkle in his eye, "the thing about fire is that it needs to be fed. It can do so much, but it needs to be tended, needs fuel. That spark that started will soon be burned away and forgotten. The light only remains because of the thousands of other sparks, all making up the fire that little one started. It's only through nurturing that fire that you keep it burning." Finally, he looked at us. "When I was coronated by this stone, the land—the Lady herself, perhaps—granted me some insight into our country's past. I assume that you know more than even I do, now."

No words needed to be spoken. On an exhale, I let some of our shared knowledge flow into him, Hiberos and I two tributaries rushing to his sea. The lot of us were still a long while as the waters passed between us, not one way but both ways, mixing and changing.

At length, Alasdair rose to his feet, and he seemed younger than he had a moment ago. I wondered if the stone was giving him some vitality.

"I'm glad to have finally met you," he said, genuinely, for I could tell already that he did not say anything if he was not genuine. "I believe in your commitment. Alas, I pray you understand why I cannot relinquish any throne to you. No throne belongs to me." He inclined his head. "Gods you may be, and I will give you the respect you are due, but absolute power over this land is one thing I cannot give."

"And it is not what we want, either." I huffed a humorless laugh. "Stars feckin' save me. If I ever say I want to be queen, you have permission to lop my head off. All this sunlight and ... knowing ... is almost too much for my body to handle as it is."

He considered me for another long moment, then looked to Hiberos. "And you, faerie?"

With a grin, Hiberos twined our fingers and lifted our hands together. "High druid, the only thing I want in this universe is her, and my only ambition is to stay by her side. Your people are safe from me." Then, with renewed seriousness, he tipped his head, speaking only to me. "No matter what happens, I promise you, my brightness. They are safe with me."

Alasdair rested his palms casually on the pommel of the blade sheathed at his side. "Would you two be willing to give an oath to that effect? Not an oath to me, but to the land and its people."

I did not have to think about it; I may as well have already taken that oath. I nodded, and my nod passed through me, down my arm, and up into Hiberos like circulation. Where the flesh of our inner wrists kissed, my heart beat into him, giving him a pulse for the first time in many moons.

The high king nodded his approval. "In that case, step forward."

I lifted my foot—but stalled. A strange sense of foreboding crept over me, tingling in my sinuses like a sneeze. Something unpleasant tickled the back of my throat, and I caught a whiff of ... a whiff of *fresh* menstrual blood. Not quite the scent I had come to associate with the blight, but close enough that I froze.

Hiberos echoed my thought—"Something's coming"—and Solma growled, readying her spear.

In the next moment, a gentle tremor ran through the bilé, and not three meters from us, the moss withered to gray and split open.

40

All at once, sulfur and sea water joined the coppery scent of blood, a combination that stuck to the back of my throat and tickled my gag reflex. The thing standing before us was something halfway between a bride and a deep-sea creature: tall, slender, vaguely feminine, her jellyfish head and tendrils coming down like a veil around her. Her skin, translucent, insubstantial; her form, undulating as if still beneath the waves. The only spot of color on her was a diffused red glow in her head, which seemed to pulse with awareness as she acknowledged each one of us.

Whatever ran through her veins called to me. I knew without having to ask that this was a fomori, and an ancient one. More ancient than our war, more ancient than the Shift—one of the first to spring into existence when moonlight first touched sea foam.

The fomori stood waiting patiently, her glassy hands clasped in front of her. That was the most shocking thing of all.

Although he slowly unsheathed his sword, High King Alasdair's expression barely changed, and he never took his eyes off our new visitor.

Hiberos had to be the one to break the silence, his stance easing slightly. "Fomoire. One of the very first born."

With that acknowledgment, she dipped her head and finally

spoke, voice distant and many layered. "Sun and Moon, newly formed. This one is called Avelaval. This one made this one's way through the cracks of the earth, up from the depths, onto your shores, and finally here, at the behest of our mother."

So, she was not so much a leader of the fomori but a representative. At this very moment, many of them were probably watching us through her eyes. Although there was little passion in the voice, I felt a certain unspoken and ancient anger coming off it like cold off a tide—the anger of a first child, neglected and abandoned, struck servile in its hunger and resigned to its fate.

"Fomori," said Solma. "You are not like the others. Explain yourself." Her tone was controlled, but I heard the words for what they were: a last warning.

"Those others that you have met," Avelaval began, letting her arms waft by her sides in a passive, gentle gesture, "are wrought of violence and violation. Worms of snot. My type were the first born of love, beauty, curiosity, riverrun, a way, a lone, a last..."

I cut in before she could carry on. "So you do not claim your brethren?"

Her head bobbed slowly one way, then the other, then back again in perpetuity as she spoke. "We claim them. We are all fomoire. All cast out from our home. Moonless, mumbling. We all have watched from our empty holes as you light lanterns ... run cattle through flame ... feast and make merry. Glass eyes for an eye, gloss teeth for a tooth. We all have turned from the fae and from the humans, and all our types have waged war upon you, not the recently born alone."

Between the nonsense, she spoke the truth. I opened my mouth to ask a question, but the high king asked first.

"What are you doing here?" His face was calm as ever, but I noted the near-imperceptible shift in his posture, the hardening of his voice, the lowering of it in his throat, and the change in his eyes from a twinkle to flint. "For over a month, you have terrorized this country, eaten at the land. Spent the past week razing this city and killing my people. Explain, in precise language, why I should not cut you down where you stand."

Avelaval turned to me, and her head pulsed with light, as if she were passing a thought to me. But it did not feel like a thought. The sensation was indescribable. **You said you would let us back if we came. You and the manram promised.**

I recalled the goddess's words about taking care of the fomori, about giving them a chance to lift themselves out of darkness. Healing them, if they wished. If it weren't for pity, I would hold the same animosity toward them that Alasdair did. Perhaps I should anyway, given they had attacked, killed, maimed, and destroyed the innocent without question.

Forget my promise to Gealach. I should crush them. Should...

"They want to rejoin the world," I murmured, unable to look away from this strange, captivating, alien creature.

"Rejoin a society they betrayed?"

"The newborns did not ask to be created. They simply were, when the earth was rent and the tree was lost. Birth uncontrollable, accidental. They acted to appease Mother. Lunarised, luna*rinsed*. You were allowing people to hurt her, she said. The only way to stop the pain was to do exactly as she bid. Displace you. In the end, that was her error. But can we be un-born for obeying our mother? Are our makers and their makemade mates not meant to know everything, teach us everything?"

Avelaval drifted until she was looking straight down at the still-glowing stone, her voice still layered but turning deep and distinctly feminine. "Your stone. Let this one touch your stone. Let us take your oath beside fire's child and shadow's son. Like fae, we cannot break our word. We will work with the fae once again, and with the humans, if it means driving the earwigs out from our lands. Yes, you will need our help against the hungry heart-dog with the hellish heaven eye."

The king shook his head at the fomori, then looked at me. "And you, what do you think of this?"

"I think we need all the help we can get, frankly," I said, watching the fomori bob and sway, "and we have fought for eons. The goddess drove them underground because of their rebellion—

really, they and the fae don't have any legitimate quarrel with one another."

"The people will not approve of this," the king said darkly. "So many of their loved ones have died. So many were taken by the mist. We may win the battle, we may even drive out the Aquilans out, but is losing the faith of our people worth it?"

Hiberos hummed low. "There is no excusing all the death they caused, that is true. But surely Éirins of all people can understand why, in their pain, they surged forth—pressure, an infection finally being lanced. A way to reclaim their land, sanctioned by the very being that refused to acknowledge them for millennia. After so long in the darkness, can any of us say we would do better?"

I considered the fomori thoughtfully, and she looked back, swaying, patient, expectant. Again, something passed between us without word or thought; her head flashed again, and she answered my unspoken question.

Still, I swallowed, uncertain. "She says we don't need to let them in. They have their own sacred places. After so long in the darkness, like Hiberos said."

"Perhaps someday," she crooned, "we both will have healed enough to coexist. For now, all we ask is that you allow us to fight by your side, then allow us to return to our places in peace. Kisses to the antipodes. Perhaps someday..." she said again, distant and wistful.

After a thoughtful sigh, High King Alasdair gestured to the stone. "Fine. If you are ready, we will do it. The contract you make here will be binding forever. An oath to the land and the people. You cannot take it back. It will be physically, psychically, spiritually impossible."

He considered us again, perhaps warier. I wasn't surprised or even disappointed that a human, even a druid, needed time to process the bizarre, underlying bond I sensed—the symbiosis that needed to be reinstated, or reimagined. After all, human, fae, or fomori, we were all part of this land, part of each other, a circulatory system. Perhaps that had been the key all along. Éire was a body not functioning with all its organs.

"The three of you, and Commander Solma, too. Come and place your hands on the stone."

Solma stiffened. "Me?" She sounded so uncertain.

"You," the high king said. "You are part of this, too." Beyond that, he did not elaborate.

The others waited for me to step forward first, followed by Hiberos, then Avelaval and Solma. We placed our hands upon the stone, and it thrummed softly with each new touch. When Alasdair spoke, it was in a tongue that once would have been strange to me but that I now recognized as a very old dialect of Éirin, very similar to the lunar fae language. The meaning of the words flowed through all four of us like shared breath.

"Do you swear on your life and the lives of your generals, your lands, and all your people that you will do everything in your power to protect the people of Éire, especially our innocents?"

"I do."

"Do you vow to preserve the language and the lifeways of this land?"

"I do."

"And do you vow to, as long as it does not interfere with your other oaths, make this land and its people a refuge for the downtrodden and suppressed, whencever they come?"

"I do."

"Do you vow to keep these oaths as long as you shall live, afterwards into death, by whatever form you take, through whatever storms may come and whatever empires may rise?"

"I do."

With each oath, one of the four etchings on the face of the standing stone began to glow brighter, and when they all shone, Ogham I had not noticed carved upon the sides lit up in an arc, from the base to the top. From a wrinkle in the Weave, three daggers appeared, sticking out of from the top of the stone and shimmering a ghostly gold.

Alasdair was collected as ever, as if he had not just summoned celestial blades from a stone in the earth. "If you mean what you say, pull a dagger from the stone. This is the final step to bind your words."

Again, I stepped forward first, and wrapped my hand around the hilt of the first dagger. Hiberos came up behind me, his heat both familiar and overwhelming, and he lay his hand over mine, sealing our oaths together. The fomori trilled and wrapped her translucent fingers—which looked more like strands, really— around the blade next to ours. Finally, Solma set down her spear in order to take hold of hers.

"By Éire, I bind you to this land and its people as protectors. From this moment into eternity."

A surge of immense but understated power pulsed through the moss, against the soles of our feet, into the Lia Fáil, and, at last, into our hands. And as one, we pulled our blades.

The great tree itself tolled like a bell, and it was over.

We stood in silence, staring at the daggers in our hands. Physically, I didn't feel any different. I didn't even feel a greater connection to the land, yet a wash of supreme and divine *rightness* came over me. Whatever path I ever took, human, fae, ghost, or god, I was always supposed to arrive at this point, in one way or another.

Right here. In my land. Exactly where I was meant to be, doing exactly what I was born to do.

With a long, full-body sigh, Alasdair relaxed, as if he truly had not known until this very moment what our answers would be. "That is just the beginning. Making a promise and being able to keep it are two very different things."

"Yea, I'm well aware." My eyes were drawn to Hiberos's chest, to the brutal scar where the rivers met. "There's something you should know. The legate, Sergia, he holds within himself a power that is destroying him from the inside out. A part of Hiberos. He is not well. Losing his mind. Now's the time to strike."

The high king looked duly unimpressed. "Huh. I see. I ... suppose I'll leave my questions for later, but you'll have to explain to me why *now* is the time to strike. We've just been dealt a terrible blow. The land is in ruin, and as you said, the legate now harbors some ... unimaginable power within him. I find it difficult to believe that we aren't utterly unmatched, the way you've laid it out."

"I know things seem bleak, but trust me, if we hold back now, we'll only be waiting for Gaius to strike us first, and we'll wish we didn't wait." Here I motioned between Hiberos and I. "We can help. Before Gealach left this plane, she gave us something. A weapon."

"A weapon," he deadpanned.

"Knowledge." I looked to Hiberos, and he slipped his large, warm hand into mine, squeezing, then raising my fingers to kiss them. Although he said nothing aloud, I sensed his sentiments through our bond. *Tell him.*

"There is a prophecy that speaks of something, an ... event of some kind. A cosmic event that's supposed to end the 'war over land.' The Lady and the Horned One thought the prophecy was about them, how they'd defeat the Great Corruption. Then he died, and the prophecy couldn't be carried out without him. Rather than replace him, the Lady gave up hope and created the Underland, and the prophecy was never fulfilled. The event never happened. Now that there is a Sun and Moon of equal aspect again, the event *could* be triggered."

"And what does this ... 'event' ... do? In exact language, please."

"I wish I could tell you, but I can't. Since the god and goddess were never able to do it, it was a mystery to them, too."

"Does it reverse the withering? The damage the quillies have done?"

"No, most probably not. But what it produces will surely push them out of it. It would demonstrate our might—win us a battle, if nothing else." I spread my palms and shrugged. "The Aquilans are evil, not stupid. Even for countries they've annexed, if those countries show enough strength, they don't bother them too terribly. Albion has a whole standing army, for Lady's sake. It's easier for them to comply with the Empire, certainly, but the Empire is slow to sanction them or raise their taxes. More importantly, they don't try to erase their culture like they do ours."

Alasdair was thoughtful for a while, gazing at the Lia Fáil. "And this ... 'event' ... is it dangerous? Considering the oaths you took only just now..."

"Dangerous only to us," Hiberos said, "and to our enemies, of course."

The high king, again, contemplated this. Even knowing he was a druid and a brilliant leader, I had not expected him to be so thoughtful, but I suppose it made sense that the man who pulled all the warring kings together would be a man of equal parts passion and practicality, conviction and curiosity. "Well, then let us pray to the Lady we don't lose you, too."

I thought of what Gealach had said in the vault, about the Empire. *Oh, yes, and they always fall, my daughter.* When she spoke of the Great Corruption, it was with terror, hopelessness, grief. When she spoke of Aquila, the Sasanacha, the Normans, the Romans before them, she did not even use their names. They were that insignificant.

Renewed confidence surged in me. Though she may have been thinking on a cosmic scale, as yet, I did not. I'd see to it the Empire fell swiftly, at least on our shores. "I don't think the quillies have as much power as we have always been led to believe. The numbers, resources, perhaps, but power? It is all smoke and mirrors. They are hoping we won't notice—won't remember—how long our people have endured. By the Lady, if we cannot beat them, we will outlast them."

Avelaval made a noise not unlike a whale's call and drifted toward me, the glowing golden dagger now floating freely inside her body. "It is written: the manewanting human lioness with her dishorned discipular manram will lie down together publicly flank upon fleece. Yes, yes, and the fomoire will come at your call, fire-child. Simply think this one's name, and this one will appear."

With that, she spun around once, bobbed, and sank back into the gray moss. It turned pinkish, then emerald once more, as her scent was scrubbed from the air.

The high king wiped his nose, coughed quite elegantly at the back of his throat, and asked, "Do you really trust them?"

"I can't say I'm thrilled about it," I said. "But ... I made a promise to our mother. And you ought to know better than most that no empire was ever felled through division."

And felled it would be. We would reclaim the land they stole and defiled—and I would reclaim Hiberos's heart.

I looked forward to tearing it out of Gaius Helius Sergia's cold, empty rib cage.

THAT NIGHT and into the next morning, scouts-turned-seagulls flew over Westminia, Geatacoill, and the surrounding valleys. The majority came home. Those who did not were downed by snipers with senses so sharpened they could smell the magic above them.

The moment the scouts made landfall behind our line, which had been forced to fall back significantly, High King Alasdair called the coalition to order. We met in the war room of the De Siabair bilé, a chamber lined with sapphire velvets and lit by phosphorescent mushrooms. King Tagh was managing to stand with the aid of Uaine, as well as a crutch that wrapped organically around his arm to pump vitality into him.

Many spirits entered alongside High King Alasdair, long and recently dead both. They seemed to whisper amongst themselves, but I could only barely perceive the sound, like the murmur of a distant brook. The barest outline of mist lurking just within my peripheral vision stopped next to Solma, and I sensed the remnants of Gwynedd and my father.

I looked at the door, waiting for Ruadan to enter. Then I remembered he wasn't coming.

Alasdair cast his implausibly blue gaze around the room, then nodded to his current Gallowglass commander, who stood at the opposite end of the dragon-bone-accented table. Though technically ravishingly beautiful, the assassin was a cold, thin, pinched woman with over-slicked blond hair, and she spoke with no passion whatever.

"The Aquilans are looking strong," she said. "They drew inward early when the Gate exploded. Locked out the blight. Civilians aren't allowed to leave the city now. About the only thing out in that wasteland they're bothering to protect is their supply line from Westminia to Sylvostum. It an't much, but they're fed, and they will probably try to call upon auxiliary troops. Whether Westerus answers is another matter, but still. As long as that route remains unbroken, they're sitting in rather a ... well, perhaps not a *comfortable* position, but a sustainable one. Much more sustainable than our position would be, coming from the south."

King Manan asked, "How did their walls fare against the moonscorching?"

"Fort Alopex is starving and forsaken. Westeris Wall is a shambles. But Sylvostum fared well. Their artillery is intact, their armies are decently provisioned, and the land is a mess of feyiron thornwire."

"They'll be hard to crack," Ferghal grumbled, towering above us all now in his halfsies form.

High King Alasdair looked to me, and I nodded. It was my turn to fill them in about the fomori, their connection to the goddess, the Lady, and the land, and all we had discovered. "I've since parleyed with the goddess," I concluded, "and she no longer remains in this world. The fomori have agreed to ally with us until the Aquilans are driven from this land for good."

The reaction of the coalition at large was relief rather than indignation, and for that I was grateful—if surprised and a bit anxious, given it indicated unspeakable desperation and the direst circumstances.

King Lorbog—of course—asked, "What do they want in return? Do we have funds to pay them? Do they use money?"

"I think they want to be spared," I said. "I think what they want in return is ... forgiveness?"

"Gods below." He rubbed a hand through his beard. "Well, at

least it's not money. But what in the Lady's good name will we tell the people?"

"The truth," Alasdair said simply, quietly. "That every being born of this soil must stand to protect it. The truth is what they deserve. They will understand, and if they have questions, I can attest to their good faith and willingness to cooperate. So"—he leaned into the table and began moving markers across the antique map spread there—"uniting the Éirin forces westerly like this, in what remains of Geatacoill ... the Gallowglass running interference on the supply line in the east ... the fae sieging from the south, and..."

He straightened to ask me a question, then closed his mouth as the air filled with that intense, tidal scent. "At ease," he said when the Gallowglass and scouts reacted to the bloody chasm opening up beside me. Once again, Solma tensed up at my side.

The jellyfish fomori billowed out, her mass distinct but insubstantial, like the bilé had just spat out a clot of blood and mucus. The light in her head throbbed at me, then the high king, then scanned each of the horrified faces round the table. "You thought our name," she said with her multi-layered voice.

I tipped my head in her direction. "Can all fomori emerge from the earth like that?"

Her form pulsed gently as she processed the question. "Yes, Horned One. We live among the stone, within the soil, we pass through grass behush the bush to we travel the moyles and moyles through the Beneath and the seasilt and rush, and not along the surface of the land."

"All right ... erm ... good. Then nothing can keep you from coming from the north." Avelaval followed my finger as I traced it from the fae army pawn, north through Sylvostum, near the border of Co Tirconnell. "If your army rises here, then that makes *us* the hammer and the anvil. With their supplies cut off in the east and the Éirins slamming in from the west ... they'll crack like a walnut."

"Perhaps." Hiberos finally cut in, his ferociously warm chest pressed against my shoulder as he, too, leaned to wave his hand over the map. "But do not forget, the Aquilans have the better part of two legions at their disposal. If the Emperor agrees to send reinforcements, they will come from Tirconnell and Westminia. If they turn our plan against us, the fomori could easily be pinched between them in the north." He nodded to Avelaval drifting on my other side. "Immediately sacrificing our newfound allies would be foolhardy and evil."

I blew a red curl from my face. "Must you always temper my enthusiasm?"

Hiberos grinned and placed a heavy hand at the small of my back. "Save your violent intent for me, won't you, brightness?"

"Let's not forget their battle mages," Ferghal said, shuffling materiel to better visualize the diversity of the Aquilan troops. "And the fae blood turning them into rampaging monsters."

One of the scouts nodded. "Yea, it seems without whatever influence they were under with the blood moon, those beasts—the thornbloods, I think someone called them?—they've rejoined their legions. They're woven all throughout their forces now."

"And then there's that miasma. It didn't get all too far in Cernunnos when it detonated, and no doubt they have more of it … now would be the time to use it."

The high king said, "I've already briefed Manan and Tagh on this, but my Gallowglass have determined the effects of the miasma, at least in the imperial alchemists' trials. It blisters the skin like fire, chokes the lungs, and blinds all in one."

"How the hell are we supposed to fight against a miasma in the damned *air*?"

"The fomori do not need breath," said Avelaval, laying one hand against her chest. "Nor sight."

"The humans and fae will need to drum up something to protect the face…" Manan hummed thoughtfully. "We could manipulate its flow with wind? If we get our heads together, we can find a solution."

Solma inclined her head to signal she would be willing, but Menecon asked, "Whatever we create, will it be ready in time for the battle?"

From the doorway came another unexpected voice. "What about the moonless?"

The room turned to behold Drusilla, her ears flicking, eyes sharp. "The bloodwarden's band. They had a ... disagreement with the legate. They are who helped me escape. What became of them?"

A few members of the coalition put forth a motion to have her removed from the room, but the vote was dead in the water, and King Manan waved her forward.

As Drusilla approached the table, I nodded to the scout. "Go on and tell her. I trust her like I trust my right arm."

The scout eyed my woven prosthetic but nonetheless turned to answer Drusilla. "The white wolves? We only got glimpses of them, but they are there."

"He made Ryac an offer he couldn't refuse?" I suggested.

Drusilla's ears pinned. "Perhaps. There isn't much sense about that man. If he is still alive. But I suppose the truth will be revealed once you arrive."

"Right, so, they have the werewolves still. Greasy bastards." Ferghal placed a new pawn on the map, huffing and drawing back to assess his work. After a moment, he slapped his palms together and spread them as if to say *I've done all I can.* "That's the map, then."

And that was the map, then. Too much red, and not nearly enough blue, green, or gold.

I felt my entire being slump. It was turning out our chances were not as good as I had assumed.

41

In a week's time, the three armies—plus the Gallowglass in the east—were in place. In the valley south of Sylvostum, the fae faced the legion head on. In what remained of Geatacoill, the Éirins waited with their roots and bows and swords. To the north, I sensed the fomori rally, not yet rising from the earth but lying ready beneath the soil, waiting.

Even with two legions at his disposal, the quillies did not have our numbers, but their position was defensible. Between the thornbloods and the moonless, this would be a no-holds-barred, dirty battle. They would use everything at their disposal.

Including Gaius's crippling heartmagic.

I knew Sergia down to his core. But even if I didn't, his rage and desperation made itself known in other ways. The sky was orange like I'd only seen when Aiken Forest burned. Clouds as deep and dark a black as night rolled over the horizon to crown Sylvostum, and within those clouds, tongues and sparks and shards of shocking pinkish-red magic lashed and exploded.

I stood at the flap of one of the fae tents, unable to take my eyes off the spectacle. Hiberos joined me, slipping a warm hand across the small of my back before settling it on my waist, and waited for me to speak.

I tried to lean back into him for comfort, but nothing could quell the gurgling of my stomach. "How can he have this much influence over the land?"

"He harbors the heart of a god in his chest." He raised his free hand to the sky as if checking rain, though there was none. "Frankly, it would have been nice to know my heart held even a fraction of a power such as this. But I suppose it was in you all that time."

"Well, that would have been nice to know, wouldn't it?" I turned more fully to face him, clenching my jaw. "I'm bloody murderous we have all this knowledge yet don't know how to do what we need to do. We don't even know if it will work, or what will happen when we do it."

With his free hand, he cupped my throat, never taking his eyes from mine and rubbing my pulse point in a gentle circular motion. "I wish I could tell you. Know that I would."

"I know." I closed my eyes. "No more secrets."

"There are no more secrets between us," he reaffirmed, and placed a kiss on my forehead, smoothing my furrowed brow. His hand went from my pulse to my antlers, and a shiver racked me. It had never occurred to me that they could be *sensitive*. It made me blush, thinking of all the times I'd touched his horns without thought. I hadn't realized at the time how much restraint he'd displayed, not pushing me to the ground and fucking me senseless.

But the fight ahead and the doom it stirred within me loomed large over every other sensation, so I simply squeezed his wrist. "Why do I feel as though this battle will decide the war entirely? How can that be so?"

Hiberos shrugged one shoulder. "Every war has one last battle." He leaned in to murmur, "I know you feel that this conflict will never end. An understandable point of view. It's gone on like this for many thousands of years. There *is* an end."

"Is there, though? Or is this just part of the same old cycle?"

"You saw me in that vault. I have thought the same about Gealach and her natural law. And it was you, my rose, my brightness, who ended that nightmare." His voice was a whisper against my cheek now, his shoulder cocked to guard me from seeing the boiling sky. "There is an end. To everything, weal and woe. But..." He brushed his velvety nose against my temple. "If I am condemned to rush ever back to you, sad and weary, and sink and die down over your feet ... if we are locked into our orbits, predestined, predated ... if all my leaves drift from me once more ... if I must be stuck in a cycle, I am only glad for it to be with you."

I caught his lips in a kiss that did not last nearly long enough. He smelled of everything, beginning and end, and I felt that warm-milk-and-whiskey feeling once more.

Then I heard my name being called in a frenzied tone, and I broke from our embrace to see Joa sprinting toward me. She stopped just short of us, saluted hastily, and poured her message out in one long sentence: "The overhead Éirin scouts are saying the Aquilans have readied their siege engines, and they have something called siege breakers at the ready, and the legions are lining up and they're prepared, and they knew we were coming, and if we don't strike soon they'll send their first offensive wave, and they think it's going to be miasma, and I haven't even had time for tea—"

Hiberos spat out a laugh despite everything. "Joa! Slow down. One concern at a time, yes?"

She gulped a big lungful of breath.

"Did Commander Solma send you? What is it she wants to know?"

Joa saluted again. "Is there some way you can see what's going on behind the walls, more clearly? The commander wants to confirm what she's been told without running messengers back and forth."

"Hmm ... I could try this." Hiberos held a finger out, and one of his moths landed on the first knuckle. "The fidelity of its eyesight is nowhere near a bird's, but it may escape notice more easily. I've never sent one of them so far away from me, though."

He crooked his wrist to bring the moth closer to me, and with feather-light fingertips, I brushed its antennae. "What do you think, little one?" I asked. "Think you're up for the task?"

It effused a little puff of sparkling moth dust, and Hiberos's answering chuckle rumbled against my back and through my rib cage. "Off you go, then."

I watched the sky until the moth was nothing but a jade speck in the distance. Then it disappeared.

"Reckon I ought to try a bit of my own reconnaissance," I whispered, and Hiberos urged me to relax, wrapping me tight in his strong, warm, opalized arms.

"Go on. I will hold you against the riptide."

THE CHAMBERS WERE STILL A MESS. Nevidaea hadn't bothered picking anything up in ... the days ran together. Since the explosion that turned the moon red. Since that dreadful edifice had risen from the sundered earth. Only when it began falling apart, its spires and towers flaking off and crumbling like ash to the scarred earth below—only when the hideous blighted beasts retreated into the earth and left Sylvostum—had she finally shrunk away from the window.

But the merciful silence had not lasted long.

Something had come tearing into Sylvostum like Belos breaching the firmament in his rage to leave the earthly realm. The power and cries of fury cut the air—singing, a vibration. Gaius. Or whatever the blood moon had made him. She'd expected him to sweep through the town like an angel of death, to finally release her from bondage and into the cold, mad arms of Oblivion.

But he'd never come.

Was it all over, then? Was everyone back to normal?

Her hopes had been dashed when she peered out the window and saw that the city walls were swarmed by legionaries pumped with fae blood, their skin a shocking map of red rivers.

She'd turned her back to the window and sat against the wall beneath it, face hidden in her hands.

I should have gone when Ottavian offered. But she hadn't seen him for days. Had he been caught? Crucified?

Even if she were to leave, how could she leave knowing Lucastos was still out there, lost, maybe hurt? Mighty Ones, what had become of him? In the very core of her heart, she believed her child was still alive, but he could not be *safe*.

Now, Nevidaea felt her husband approach.

Or, whatever wore her husband's skin.

The walls, the floors, every stone her body touched hummed with the intensity of it; in the adjacent room, her birds fluttered restlessly, their feathers clutched close to their bodies as if they sensed the approach of a large predator. The dense wooden door muffled sharp orders, and she assumed the legionaries guarding her room were dismissed.

Then the door opened.

She expected to see him standing in all his glory, wearing his golden lorica, his red-and-purple frippery, perhaps even his helmet. But the creature that crossed her threshold was not an eminent commander.

The red veins snaking over his body, she had anticipated. The horns growing from his head, she had not. And he was naked, wearing only a loincloth. Yet through the blood soaking it and making it cling to his skin, she could hardly tell it was there. His extremities were wine-dark. But that was all she could discern before she turned her face away in sharp alarm, only able to bear looking at him obliquely.

In the center of his chest, glowing bright through muscle and viscera, was a throbbing ... something. It seemed too large for his rib cage. And while he swelled with its every beat, empowered by the magic flowing from it, he breathed heavily, and his limbs trembled as if he might collapse under his own weight.

This power, she could not name it. It was not of the Mighty Ones. It was something connected to this land—but so twisted it would be unrecognizable to either Éirin or Aquilan.

What have you done?

Nevidaea flattened herself against the wall, all breath, all sound trapped in her throat. Gaius's shoulders rose and fell with great effort. He took a few steps forward, every muscle swollen and straining, jumping, hypersensitive, too responsive to his commands. His shoulders and neck rippled and rankled like the skin of a cat. This tension looked especially painful.

"Gaius..." At last, she managed to force herself to speak to the monster lurking in her periphery. "You ... you're hurt. You're in pain. How..." After all he had done to her, it was the first thing she could think to say.

Dread and self-hatred made her shoulders creep up around her ears. She was pathetic. Pathetic. Even now, even after he had taken everything from her, all she could think to say was...

He took another step forward, leaving dark footprints in his wake. Skimmed a hand across her sheets on his way to grip one of the bedposts, streaking it with blood. He dripped. Drip, drip, drip —steadily onto the imported rug. At the tips of his curls quivered little droplets, and when he shook the hair from his forehead, they spattered against the walls, the bookshelves, *her*.

When they hit her cheek and burned her skin, she gasped. Wiped them hastily with her sleeve.

In response, he sneered.

Croaked.

"You ... are so ... weak."

His eyes were dark. So dark. Voids of hatred. There was no other way to describe them.

"You have given me nothing, yet you demand consideration. Respect. Look at all you've gained from clinging to me. And you don't deserve ... any of it. You ... are a parasite. You *all* are. You disgust me."

There was no emotion in his voice. No anger. Nothing.

She should be more terrified than ever. Yet as he tore the curtains from her bed, methodically and without effort, she was numb. Frozen to him. The feeling began at the crown of her head and swept downward through her body.

She didn't care anymore if he killed her. It did not matter how he looked at her, because it was far from the first time. It did not matter what he ruined, because she didn't own anything, not really. Not even herself.

She hugged her knees closer and looked down as he moved through the room, further taking it apart with all the passion of someone disassembling a chronodial.

For minutes or hours, it was as if he searched for something. Perhaps he did. Not in the room, but in her.

Whatever it was, he didn't find it. He looked at her for a long time, exhaled—

—and moved toward the adjoining room.

Toward her birds.

Something. *Changed.*

It would be far from the first time he'd taken a life. It would not even be the first time he destroyed one of her beloved pets. Yet something *changed* inside of her then. The numbness turned ice cold, then hot all at once, racing through her chest with such a fury that it launched her to her feet.

When she entered the menagerie, it was already a mess, cages upturned and feathers flying. Already, her prized violet budgerigar and her mate lay at his feet.

Four months. They'd been mated for four months and had finally lain good eggs.

Nevidaea tore her eyes from their broken bodies to watch Gaius wrangle a carrow. It screamed and tried to escape him with such a panic that it broke its wing.

"Why?" The voice that left her hardly sounded like her own. "Why are you doing this to me? I did everything you ever wanted of me. Even now, I'm right where you want me."

He looked at her with nothing in his face. "The pursuit of a free bird is more worthwhile than the pursuit of a caged one."

And he snapped the carrow's neck.

He doesn't want me.

He never wanted me.

I've wasted my life appeasing him. Them. All. Bearing me down. Dragging me out. Carrying me along. Father brother senator husband son and I kissed and I loved them and I said yes and opened myself and all because I thought I'd get something in return but they have nothing to give—and if they did...

If they did...

Hot,

wild

sanity

gripped her. Without thought, she picked up a discarded transport cage, swung it above her head, and brought it down on his shoulders with enough force that the strike rattled through her body.

If he made any noise of pain, she didn't hear it. He staggered forward, then wheeled round, staring at her in disbelief.

"I hate you!" she shrieked, shaking the cage above her head. Then her arm came down, limp at her side, her chest heaving.

For a long while, they simply stared at each other. When he'd first entered her chambers, she'd been afraid of the beast that wore his skin. But nothing wore him. This was him, in his truest form. In fact, this was the first time she'd seen him without his mask of perfection, of affected civility. Wax. A man of wax. Nothing but a porcelain shell.

For all that power, he still held nothing inside of him but infection and hatred—for everything, for himself.

Gaius spat a wad of blood, his tendons shivering. "You don't hate me," he rasped. "You need me. Without me, you are nothing."

Nevidaea raised the cage again, and punctuated each word of her next sentence by smashing it against the marble floors. "I don't need you!" She wiped spit from her mouth, her voice brittle, reedy, breaking. "If that makes me nothing, so be it! Let me be nothing. It's a fate preferable to being your wife."

His body radiated power. In one movement, he could snap her neck just as easily as he'd done the birds'. Yet something in him was coming apart. As surely as he had dismantled her room, she dismantled him. She didn't understand what or how, but she could not stop.

"Mighty Ones, I've done everything you have asked. I wept for you, bled for you. Raised a child not born of my womb. Never —not once—have I questioned you. I've let you defile me, deride me, debase me, without uttering a single word against you. I've done my hair how you said you like, worn the clothes that you said you like, run the household with your approval in mind. I stood by and pursed my lips while you slaughtered people—*children*—because I thought following your lead was worth it. That you could protect me. Protect us. Me and your son." With a blazing hot face, she shook the cage hard again. "You have given me *nothing*. Nothing but shame. All you've done, all I've let you do … to innocents. Innocents!" And she cast the gold-plated iron to the floor with a resounding clatter.

Gaius worked his jaw, eyes filled with murderous intent. "None of us are innocent—"

"It would be convenient for you if that were true, wouldn't it?"

"—certainly not the Éirins. For a century, they've stalked the borderlands, killing Aquilan civilians. They murder and neglect their own children, like Ryac. All throughout this conflict, they've employed dishonest, dishonorable tactics. Taken hostages, young people, tortured them."

She wanted to believe him. It would be easy. Familiar if not comfortable. But her gut turned in revulsion. If she could not trust his oaths, she certainly could not trust his words. "How *dare* you lie to me now."

"I am not lying," he rasped. "I have seen it with my own eyes. Murder. Cannibalism. Child sacrifice. *That* is the culture they are killing to preserve. It is the Empire alone who can stop them."

"The only person I've seen sacrifice a child is you! *Our* child!"

"*Our child* has been taken. By them. Kidnapped. Living in filth. Far from you or I, alone and lost in the care of barbarians."

Nevidaea's heart lurched, but she snapped, without hesitation, "If he is safe from you, then I owe those barbarians gratitude."

All at once, he was on her, his fists around her throat. Her vision dilated, flashed white, then blurred and blackened at the edges. Time seemed to stand as still as the breath in her lungs—swelling, building in pressure, but never moving forward.

This was the end.

She'd always known her death would come at his hands.

She thanked the Mighty Ones for two small mercies: that Lucastos was not here to witness it, and that she had not died vying for her husband's approval.

Just when it seemed oblivion was near—just when all feeling left her limbs, her only consciousness a small point of light at the back of her skull—a grating sound broke through the undulating blackness.

Without warning, the pressure on her throat eased. Her body hurt to the bones; she didn't notice that he'd borne her to the floor until her vision came back, slurry and swimming—and by then, he had strode to the door, leaving a trail of blood in his wake.

At the last moment, he stopped, then turned so his blazing red pupil was fixed on her. "I will finish with you later."

And as quickly as it had started, it was over. He was gone.

Slowly, the world came back. The light sharpened, hurting her eyes. Distant rumbling trundled through the valley. All around her, birds crowed and beat their wings frantically against their cages.

Nevidaea was still for a minute or more, thrilled and terrified to be alive.

Finally, she rolled over. Mousy brown hair, unbound now, clung to her sweaty face and got in her eyes. Her breath was brittle and shaky as a reed as she rose to her hands and knees, then, at last, swayed to her feet. There was pain, sharp. She winced. He must have sprained her ankle badly in their fall to the ground.

Out the window, the war machines rumbled closer.

Ottavian wasn't coming, she realized. Her chivalrous knight had been waylaid. She had to save herself.

She limped to the threshold of her bedroom, then paused, and turned to look at the birds still in their cages.

There was no time to save them. It was a shame. Leaving them behind would be the death of them, and these beautiful creatures, they were dearer to her than most any creature on earth. Many, she'd raised by hand from the moment of their hatching. She could open their cages, free them, but releasing them might kill them, too. They were exotic pets, not suited to this environment. They did not know how to find their own food.

Hobbling back, she threw the bolts of each cage and opened the hatches. Most of the birds, panicked though they were, shied away from their path to freedom. They huddled in the far corners, feathers tight, crests askew. The more vocal ones even scolded her.

What a shame.

She'd done all she could. They would either figure it out, or they would burn with the rest of the villa. And as much as the thought of the latter killed her, there was nothing for it. She had to leave. Over the threshold. Through the bedroom, limping past destruction and bloodstains.

At last, she faced the door.

It was locked; she knew it was locked. Every visitor locked it behind them. But there was nothing—literally nothing—she could do except try.

With a deep breath, she reached out and tested the handle.

It turned.

With nothing more than a push, the dense wooden door swung open. She stepped into the empty corridor beyond and looked down at the keyhole.

The light. She'd seen light through the hole, not because he took the key each time but because...

Because it had never been locked.

He'd been that certain of her obedience.

Relief flooded through her—along with pride, self-right-eousness, regret at so much lost time. Shame. A deluge so strong it almost bowled her over.

I only hoped those feelings would spur her to action.

Together, we left the unlocked room behind.

42

By the time the moth returned, it was already too late. The siege engines rolled forward, and on our mounts, we advanced alongside them. Any minute now, the battle would begin in earnest.

Perhaps it was the discovery that I could summon a horse of fire and sunlight, or perhaps it was the sounds of war flowing through me, but either way, I *felt* my godly aura awaken. It was a bizarre sensation—tingles all over, a rising but not overwhelming energy swelling my chest. My magic wove with Hiberos's as we moved in tandem, my horse and his panther, the battlefield bending around us as if it was dark and we were light, as if it was water and we were boulders.

The Aquilan archers waited on the parapets, and with my sharp sight, I saw their tension in stark detail: the muscles of their arms straining, the crimson throb and pulse of their stolen power. Some of them even displayed the signs of being—or *becoming*—thornbloods themselves. The crystal teeth, the blazing eyes, the shards poking through their sweat-slicked skin.

Centuriae emerged, orderly regiments of a hundred men each, with thornblood alphas filling the gaps. Even as their red, eagle-topped standards flagged, I had to ask myself ... if Gaius called for reinforcements, would the Emperor send anyone? Would Agorix Westerus even consider these beasts Aquilan?

Even if he did, we were fighting against something new. Something we did not understand. And no matter how large a force we had at our disposal, we could not prepare for an enemy we did not know.

This wouldn't just be a dirty fight. If we allowed the reins to slip through our fingers, this battle—this sole battle—would be our undoing.

I had been so assured of our victory.

Fae cavalry on their liveried harts stood at the fore, led by Erivon, who was magnificent in all-ebony armor. Orlaith flew down the line on her own mount, all silver, barking the men into rank. Shield-bearers and battle mages behind, archers at the back. Battering rams mounted on wheeled siege engines were pushed to the front line, flanked in a chevron by ballistas. The legionaries on the battlements of Sylvostum clustered like black birds in a rookery, their feathers ruffling and their beady eyes gleaming just the same.

On the front line, Solma galloped to us, messengers in tow. "Your orders?"

My eyes darted from the walls, across the valley, touching the very front line of the Éirin offensive in the west. Sylvostum was well-fortified and prepared, but with all three armies pressing them ... even if Gaius, in his madness, had had the foresight to request reserve troops...

Finally, I raised my eyes to the strange, sinister storm cloud above, unable to shake the feeling that something terrible was about to happen.

"We should all strike at once to weaken the defenses, spread them thin," I murmured. "Hit them hard to begin with, and then we can see about luring Gaius out to face us. Getting me and Hiberos to Gaius should be a top priority. The rest, I defer to you."

Solma began down the line again, shouting orders, directing her lieutenants to lead their troops left, right, when to hold, when to strike. Her messengers ducked behind the cavalry and sprinted west, while the fomori messenger sank into the ground like water and disappeared.

Thanks to Orlaith, the fae ranks were impeccable, tight at the front before fanning out. I cast another gaze over them. Slowly. Everything was perfect.

So what was this feeling of ... disappointment in my gut?

"This isn't right," I whispered.

Only Hiberos heard me, and he did not even question what I could mean. "What will make it right?"

Before I could even conceive of an answer, as if she sensed my distress rolling over the battlefield, Orlaith pulled up abreast of me. Her moony gaze scanned me up and down before locking with mine. "Funny," she remarked. "You are a god, but you've never looked more human."

And it all clicked into place.

It must have shown in my expression, because she quirked a snowy brow and, at length, murmured, "You all right? Hiberos won't need to dive back in and save you, will he?"

"The ... the fae are poised to lose everything if we're defeated. They have no land now. Not even a palace anymore," I said, throwing my head back toward where it once stood. "Nowhere else to go, no kingdom to occupy but this one. But they don't need me. They barely even know me."

She tried and failed to close herself. Her bottom lip twitched infinitesimally. "When you say that ... when you say 'they,' you really mean me. Don't you?"

I opened my mouth, but nothing came out. When I tried again, I managed, "Of course not. We follow each other. If we didn't, I would not be here now."

"But?"

My shoulders sank. "But ... the fae aren't who this war started with. It was you, Eytine—and me and the Éirins. I should be in the west, emerging from the trees. That is where I belong."

Orlaith stared at me for what might have been half a minute, the only sound between us the rumbling storm overhead. "Belong.

Right," she whispered, and after another yawning pause, "The fae aren't fighting someone else's battle anymore. *We* are not separate entities. I don't think we ever were. We don't belong apart, so we must belong together, no?"

"We've tried belonging together. One of us always runs away."

"There is nowhere to run now. Besides, most people don't know who they really are, or where they belong, until it is too late." She lifted her chin to the west. "Go. And go swiftly, with my wind behind you."

We exchanged one last look, all our grief and dissonance and love and unity laid bare.

Then I turned my mount west and drove it into a gallop. My blazing horse shot down the front line, the cloying wind in my hair, and in less than a second, I had overtaken and passed the sprinting messengers. Hiberos was only a few yards behind me. What remained of Geatacoill grew larger by the second.

I brought my mount to a trot as we wove through the outer stands of the forest's ancient oaks. The feeling of the place had changed, there was no doubt. The enchantment that had awoken and animated it was gone. The place felt deader, emptier than it had even when I'd thought it was a normal forest. Yet something remained still. Wounded, sleeping, heavy. Perhaps not consciousness, but if not that, I didn't know what to call it.

A spark.

If she still could be saved from the brink of destruction, there was only a chance for her if we won this battle. The Empire would harvest her, plow the earth, and forget she'd ever existed.

I surveyed the Éirin ranks as we approached. They weren't as orderly or as grand as those of the fae, but they were cleverly arranged, faoladh and warp-warriors creating a solid wall at the treeline, druids and archers cradled behind. The high king had added Divlinn's standing army to Manan and Tagh's forces, and I could have sworn every band of fianna I'd ever heard of were here with their horses and banners. Either Alasdair had pulled together the funds to hire them all, or they were here simply for honor.

Either way, I felt immediately at home. Not at ease—the

magical storm churning above and that persistent gut-dread prevented that—but at home.

The ranks rippled as they made way for me and Hiberos. I went straight for Alasdair, who rode a red hart, and Muiri, who sat astride the same black mare as when I met her. They acknowledged me, their eyes both equally piercing despite being on opposing ends of the color spectrum.

"Where is Manan?"

"With the druids," the high king answered. "Protected by the forest, in reserve."

I couldn't help but look at the sky again. I hated it, the way it bore down on us. "I think we could use them now, not later. A squad of ents wouldn't go amiss if we're trying to break through the city walls."

But he brushed me off. "Patience. Calm. If a time comes when we will benefit more from their capabilities of harm rather than healing, you have my word that I will call upon them."

By that time, Solma's messenger had arrived and relayed her plans. Muiri left us to disseminate the information to the various kings, mercenaries, and lieutenants.

"It seems we're starting this thing in earnest," Ferghal growled low, fully in wolf-shape now. He sniffed my ear deeply before bounding away to lead his wolfkernes.

The king tapped at his rein. "Forward!"

Locked into rank, as if truly one entity, the Éirin forces inched out of the forest. Hiberos and I inched along with them, keeping abreast of the high king. He must accept us as his equals, because he did not seem distracted.

As we emerged from Geatacoill, the Aquilans on the parapets bristled again. In no world could they not have realized we were there, but perhaps they had not understood just how many of us there were.

Shouts were thrown. The archers reached for their quivers and shifted, antsy.

We flowed out, taking our places as naturally as the boulders, the moss, and the roots they'd tried so desperately to flatten into arable land.

The sky roiled darker and snapped like a whip. Only the presence of spirits—a distinct breeze that blew directly through me, the scent of grave moss—tore my gaze away from it. I was not surprised to see them there, woven among their descendants as though they were a natural part of the crowd. They looked more solid than the wisps I'd seen whilst passing through Gallive. Almost as though they were really here. I swore they could have reached out and touched the living beside them: warriors in leine and chainmail, standing next to a man kitted out in a Brodie helmet, standing next to his brother wearing a flat cap and holding a rifle, standing next to a lad in a balaclava and beret, standing next to work-worn and wounded women with their sleeves rolled up. They flew a flag I would not have recognized mere days ago, torn and mended and rent and tattered and mended again. Their fifes played tunes long forgotten.

So much worn. So much forgotten.

It hit me then. I could give it back. Our songs, our stories, our language, customs considered ancient even centuries before the Shift. Inside me there was so much knowledge. Perhaps it had always been there, in the very grooves of my skin, in my veins and the roots of my teeth—withheld by circumstance. But no longer.

I could give it back.

And all these people ... they wouldn't have died in vain. Just as all those I'd loved and lost had not died in vain.

Then—

My eyes fell on a cart loaded with barrels and weapons, far back from the line, and with my newly sharpened vision, I noted a scrap of cloth peeking out from behind one of the barrels. I cocked my head. The fabric was a familiar red, and for some reason the shade seemed out of place...

"Would you like to give a speech?" Hiberos's voice sent a thrill up my spine.

His question caught me so off guard that I did a double take, doubting it was for me. He beheld me with the gravity of all the stars and planets in his gaze. He saw the spirits, too, yet he had eyes only for me. Beside him, High King Alasdair tilted his head, apparently curious to witness me address the front lines. We exchanged a long look. I wondered if he, too, saw what we saw.

I turned my horse and trotted along the line, letting magic carry my voice across the battlefield and into even our very deepest ranks.

Addressing both the living and the dead, I let the words flow.

"We have been fighting ... for so long. And the road has been so rocky. And it has made us ... hard, and tired. Times will continue to be trying..." It all came slowly at first, my throat thick, but somewhere along the way, I gained power and momentum. It rushed from me then.

"But what we do here today matters. Whatever the outcome, what we do today will ripple outward through time, into the past and future both. What we do today was foreseen by our ancestors and will be remembered by our children, and our children's children—memories in the body if not the mind. Stories told by negative space if not by words. Because death is not the end, my sisters and brothers."

I blinked back tears as I let my gaze slide from spirit to human to spirit again. "I promise you now, death is not the end. It is but one spoke of the wheel that is existence. *That* is a cycle that can never be broken—it is up to us, each individual, to decide how clean the waters be that carry them. If you could only see the centuries upon centuries of Éirin forebears standing next to you now. But feel them. *Feel* them."

The chins and shoulders of the warriors raised, swelled, as they breathed in the atmosphere.

"Axes will shatter," I cried, trotting back along the line. "Shields will break. The clover will run red. But the Éirins who come after will be able to hold their heads high, and to say that we fought to the bitter end. And make no mistake, come what may, there *will* be Éirins who come after us. As long as this land exists, in whatever form it takes, it will be ours, and we will belong to it. As long as this land exists, so will we."

Here I raised my sword, its blade shining, gossamer tongues of sunlight floating round it. "We will not yield!"

And I tugged my rein—

"We will not surrender!"

—galloping down the line with my sword outstretched so that it clanged against every cavalryman's blade, spear, and pike. The moment our steel touched—

"We will not go back again!"

—theirs sparked, enveloped in an enchantment of solar magic.

"Rise. Rise! For the ancestors. For those yet to come. For your kin standing beside you. *For Éire!*"

The Éirins raised their weapons and cried out, and the force of it shook the earth.

My heart had, not so long ago, been sent to the very depths of despair. But now, despite the unease, despite the storm, despite the war, the murder, the ever-hungering beast against which we fought, I'd never felt more pride in my people. Never felt more alive, the light and joy in my soul quite literally beaming through every pore.

The commanders took in hand their war horns and summoned that spine-chilling sound, the feary moans of mad gods. The high, melodic horns of the fae responded in kind. Finally, a bone-rattling female scream echoed afield north, and I knew it was the fomori signal.

The final go. No Underland. No coming back to life.

We were ready.

Before the reality could sink in, it began.

It all happened so fast. One moment, we were standing face to face with the walls; in the next, the Aquilans struck.

They shot first. Although there was no indication that they were about to do so, it was as if they moved as one, as if, without speaking, they all knew the orders of their commander.

The Éirins raised their shields, both physical and magical, and surged forward with an earth-shaking, sustained battle cry. The spirits moved with them, sliding through the ranks as wisps or sprinting beside their descendants or becoming one with the living to imbue them with vitality. As the rain of arrows crashed into us, without any thought or intent on my part, I summoned an orb of golden light in a radius around me. Hiberos did the same, his cool lunar bubble shielding those closest to us.

Men and horses fell, but the army was focused and hard as an arrowhead, crashing over the crest of the hill and closing in on the western wall. More centuriae had filed out in a panic. As the western gate was shut behind them, they fell to their knees, pikes extended from the cracks of their phalanx, waiting for the cavalry to break upon them.

To the south, Solma launched her screaming stars, which streaked into the air like a flame and exploded above our heads. A call to action. The fey army surged forward. Another rain of arrows came, and then another.

Catapults on the wall launched fireballs and clay jars, which, upon bursting, spread a red miasma through the crowd. The siege-breakers Joa had warned about. The fae were prepared with masks of enchanted glass, yet still, I expected them to break rank and run from the gas clouds. Some of them did. Some of them did not and fell despite their protection. But largely, the fae and their outsized elk, beasts of burden, held rank, driving the battering ram closer and closer. When the elk, finally starved of air, fell, people replaced them. And when a person fell, there was always someone waiting to take their place.

Sparks.

It was terrible. It was wonderful. It was heartbreaking. It filled me with hope.

We crashed into the waiting phalanx. Some horses were skewered, but there were not nearly enough Aquilan pikes at the ready. We smashed through the shield wall, into the thick of the quilly defensive. Cavalrymen swung their axes and trampled. Warp-warriors exploded with shield-and-blood magic, blasted their enemies apart. Archers on the hill haunted the treeline, raining steel down upon the parapets. The world was a haze of heat and blood and metal as I slashed one way with my sword, then the other, slicing clean through my foes like a hot knife through butter.

Thump.

The battering ram crashed against the southern entrance.

Thump.

Each one of its swings was punctuated by roars of effort and adrenaline from the army. All the while, more screaming stars, glaives, and moonshots.

Without warning, the sky flashed red, the clouds creeping outward. The earth trembled—or maybe it was just me—not from battle but from some unnatural, overwhelming power.

And then I heard him.

Gaius, his voice a hiss, sounding as though he was speaking just over my shoulder. "Hear me and despair. There is no hope for you. Any of you. The Mighty Ones answer the call of one of their own. It is too late to stop what's about to happen. You will not even live long enough to see it. This battle was over before it began."

I wasn't the only one to hear him; all around me, our combatants faltered, some even falling with the distraction. My heart leapt and lodged itself in my throat. He spoke only because he was scared of us—he wouldn't speak otherwise.

Using a push of godly magic, I elevated my voice above the slithering whisper: "Ignore him. He is nothing but a delusional, starving madman. We're scaring him! Keep pushing!"

"Forward," Alasdair cried from his hart, which reared up and kicked a thornblood brute in the face. "Don your masks."

He said it just in time. No sooner had most of the men pulled on their herb-soaked masks than shells of miasma made landfall, one by one.

A thornblood with glowing red claws pounced for me. I dodged at the last moment, running him through and bearing him to the ground. Mud and blood flew around us, painting my armor, skin, and hair.

Another rattling scream came from the north. The fomori had made it into the city and were no doubt wreaking destruction.

Suddenly, another, redder flash made me cast my eyes to the storm above. The sky snapped, an unholy growl rumbled through the battlefield.

And white filled my vision.

The world was nothing but searing, blinding light as I was blasted back.

Quick as a strike of lightning, something burned through my veins and was gone—and in the next fraction of a second, I hit the ground. Heather and stones caught against my armor and antlers. I flipped once and landed face first in a crater full of mud.

Ugh... Digging my claws into the blood-slicked soil, I dragged myself onto my hands and knees. Vision came back in blooms, then all at once. My thrown body had left a deep furrow in the battlefield, from where I'd been standing to where I was now, and along the way I'd lost my pelts, my bow, my sword—and my arm.

I looked from the brass mount at the end of my stump to the remains of my arm, twigs and bits of bone strewn in a trail. The cold of despair and the flame of fury tore through me. "Oh, for fuck's sake!"

But my next breath was one of relief, as each remnant glowed gold, shivered, and pulled itself together in a twinkle of sunshine. With a mere thought, I summoned the arm back to me. Good job it was a limb I'd already lost and not a new one.

I held my hand out for my bow next. It shuddered before skipping a little closer to me, but it did not come all the way.

Wait a minute. That isn't right.

And suddenly, rapidly, my limbs felt ... weaker. My neck strained holding up the massive rack of antlers atop my head. The golden flame filling my chest guttered.

Then I felt that quick, intense burning through my veins again, and when I looked down, I caught red rivers flashing under my skin. Every time they did, my power seemed to weaken further.

Gaius. He was drawing the godhood out of me, somehow, maybe through my fae blood but more probably with heartmagic.

Siphoning it, judging by the mass of the storm overhead and the growing intensity of the magical gales.

Taking it from me.

From *us*.

Oh, goddess, *Hiberos*.

An unbecoming grunt left my chest as I staggered to my feet. *Hiberos*. I cast about for him, eyes darting, frantic, panic gripping my spine and crushing my lungs. Even with his height, he was nowhere to be seen. Only flashes of his magic—big domes of glistening teal light—far afield in the southwest.

My feet carried me fleetly toward him, following a furrow not unlike my own. Bits of his hide, twigs and leaves, were left in his wake. He was alive, and well enough to be slinging spells, but still, the flame within me jumped; rage licked my heart. Take my power. Break my body. But never touch my people and never touch Hiberos.

Thump.

In the chaos, I'd nearly forgotten about the battering ram. Nearly forgotten that the inhuman power drinking from my veins had a source—a very real, fallible source that could be struck.

Mave.

The hairs at my nape stood on end. If any one thing could halt me in my pursuit of Hiberos, it was that voice.

A voice I didn't hear unless there was something I needed to know direly. Gwynedd.

I spun and saw him—just a glimpse. The faintest starry outline, so far removed from the physical realm that he could barely manifest even here, on a battlefield, where the veil was always thinnest. If that wasn't enough to make me turn back, he said one more word, a word that made me abandon Hiberos altogether.

Faelon.

Faelon. Faelon, who should be at Gallive, safe and sound in Drusilla's arms. Faelon, who should be resting assured that he would never have to suffer his father's whims again.

A pulse of lunar magic flowed down my and Hiberos's primal connection. It seemed to say, *Go. I can hold my own.*

Thump.

I followed the ghost of my druid-chief, my adoptive father, my guide. He was no more than a wisp, but even through the arcs of gore, snatches of miasma, and puffs of battle steam, now that I had seen him, it was as if I could see nothing else. We wove through the battle field, around legionaries bashing with their shields and Éirins thrusting with spears, around men killing and dying. Until finally Gwynedd led me to a roughshod wooden cart, once abandoned beyond the walls by the Aquilans, now overturned by fae bombardment, singed and still smoking.

The spirit disappeared in a mist, and right where he had disappeared, a scrap of red caught my eye. Fabric. The same fabric I'd seen...

Faelon had been here all along. Stowed away. He'd snuck out to battle.

"Fael—" I made to dart forward and push the cart off him, to reveal his hiding place and bear him away, back into the forest—

—but I was caught mid-lunge. Pain exploded and then tingled numb as something sank deep into my calf, scraping the very bone. I was slammed to my face, hair tumbling. Then, in one brutal movement, I was flipped and slammed on my back.

The world spun.

Thump.

My assailant leapt on me, pressing me into the riven grass with foam-frosted jaws snapping inches from my face. Before the world came into focus, all he was was a mass of white and glaring red. But I knew that smell.

Blood, wine, a working man's skin, and something almost human.

Ryac.

43

My vision cleared into sharp, painful clarity, and I had enough wherewithal to summon my sword to my hand. As the wolf snapped again for my face, I barred my blade against his neck. Yet my arms trembled with the effort it took to keep him off me, and—

Belatedly, I realize his scent had changed. There was a new note, adjacent to werewolf but not quite.

Fae.

With a renewed burst of energy and a roar, I flipped him off me. A slurry of thick, steaming saliva and blood flew as he was sent scrambling into a crater. Growling, whimpering, he struggled in the mud to point himself back at me, and while he did, I backed up to take him in. Beneath his white fur, every wiry muscle glowed a faint red. Gaius must have injected him. Around his neck sat a heavy collar and dangling chain of feyiron.

Other white streaks overtook the battlefield, each wearing the same collar and chain. The punishment for their disloyalty. Not wolves at all, now.

"Stop," I ground out. "Ryac. Can you hear me?"

As he dragged himself to his hind legs, his answer was a frayed howl backed by enough frenzy that it tossed my hair over my shoulders.

"If Gaius isn't controlling you, yield now," I said between harsh breaths. "Call off your pack, and I can guarantee you a return to Éirin society. You have my word."

Thump.

His entire form heaved with every pant, cloudy red eyes gleaming. Each tendon twitched. Jaws dripped. Claws twitched. His ears pinned back and up in anger, then down in turn. He was on the brink of striking again, yet something held him back.

"That's what you want, isn't it?" I rasped, one hand flung out, trying to keep his attention on my words. "I can make it happen. If you have free will, give up now, and come home."

Could I keep that promise? I had no idea. But I knew from watching him that, were he in his right mind, he'd have jumped at the deal.

Now? His lips pulled back, and his growl turned to a snarl, then another howl.

He was lost.

Behind me, something shuffled. Someone wept. I realized too late it was Faelon, still hidden.

Something *snorted*.

Thump.

Even as I registered it, the boy and the *fucking pig* darted from the overturned cart and sprinted toward the city walls.

I caught only a glimpse of them before Ryac's attention shifted, his predator's gaze fixed on the running target. He turned as if to give chase.

An opportunity. Hardly thinking, I pounced, and we fell into a heap of claws, teeth, and steel. This time, before I could hold him back with my sword, his sinewy forearm was pressed into my windpipe. I couldn't scream, couldn't breathe, and with the air knocked from me during the fall, my lungs spasmed.

A new scent joined the fray, along with a high-pitched yip. Someone dug into my other calf, my thigh. The moonless. The vibrations of their big paws against the earth shook through me. Glimpses of white fur painted my vision.

Their alpha had chased down prey. Now they were closing in.

The sky flashed again. Pain lanced my eyes and spit venom into my veins. A broken shout punched out of me. The plateau of godly power dipped again, and darkness closed in.

Just as I was about to fade, the sudden whine of a wolf sharpened my vision. Blood painted my face as the moonless were cut down. One by one. I slumped to the side and saw that Ryac alone was able to escape, scuttling back to Sylvostum with his tail between his legs.

By feeling alone, I knew who had saved me, the sensation of him near as familiar and natural to me as the set of my jaw and teeth. But for a moment, I was too weak even to look at him.

The ground thumped as he fell to one knee, turned me over, and all at once, blessedly, I was face to face with Hiberos.

He gathered me to his chest, and for a moment simply held me, his breathing more ragged than a god's should be. When he pulled back, searching me for injury, his cool magic rushed in to soothe the burn of my wounds ... and with him close, I felt a little bit of my overwhelming power return to me.

My taut body relaxed, and I almost wept with relief. Of course, if anything could mend me while Gaius tried to destroy me, it would be him. My Hiberos. My clever, beguiling Hiberos, whatever the moon had always meant and whatever a sun would always sing.

But the relief did not last long.

"Your hair," he whispered, and held it up to show me the strands of white beginning to eat the red away.

"Your hide," I said in turn, brushing my hands across his chest. Cords of him were turning back to oak before my eyes, the channels flowing outward from his heart losing their brilliance inch by inch.

Thump.

Gwynedd's spirit had drawn me far enough away from the battle that we would not be caught in crossfire, but apart from the crowd, there was a chance we'd be targeted as outliers. So, even in this isolated place, Hiberos dragged us behind overturned cart—and clearly did not know what to make of it when I struggled against him.

"Be still. Be still." Brow gnarled, he tipped my face one way, then the other, scrutinizing my pupils. "Why are you fighting? What's wrong?"

"Faelon. Faelon is here. Somehow, he found his way to the battlefield. He brought Conan? I ... I have to go after him. I have to find him before Ryac or, stars forbid, Gaius—"

Hiberos cut me off, waving his finger in front of my face. "Wait. Follow this. No, with your eyes, silly. Now is not the time to separate. Surely, you felt—" He lowered his finger and raked a hand through his raven waves. He, too, was beginning to gray. "When the... He can't be—"

"I think he is," I cut in. "He's harnessing the power of your heart to drain us. To ... become something like us, a bastardized version—"

"Then he is trying to be something he doesn't fully understand," he growled.

"Yes, but I don't think it's going to matter in the end. To him, to the Aquilans, power is power. Even if it will kill them."

Hiberos placed a hand over the scar on his chest, then mirrored it to rest over mine. "But when we stand together close like this... You feel it, do you not? It's as if—"

Again, I finished for him, nodding emphatically. "It's as if we're—what's the word?—*replenishing* each other's magic."

He nodded in agreement with my assessment, determination making his eyes glint. "That is something he doesn't have."

A strange, watery dread flowed from the crown of my head down my spine, and not a moment later, existence rumbled with a deep, rolling, envious growl. The sensation hissed through my bones.

With a jolt, an unseen force thrust Hiberos and I several meters back from one another.

It was as if Gaius could hear or sense us coming together, moving against him.

Could he?

Thump.

The painful whiteness eased from my vision, but I felt wounded—not outside, inside. On my mind, in my spine, the absence of something that had once flowed through me. With great confusion, I looked toward the battle and saw the Éirins, living and dead alike...

And suddenly I knew. Or rather, could not remember. I could not give a name to the flag they flew. I did not know what to call the strange weapons they were carrying. Did not understand the words of their battle cries. My body remembered remembering, but it was all gone. Siphoned from me. Stripped from me as surely as my strength had been.

I knew without a shadow of doubt who had taken it.

Just as he had taken everything. My innocence, my sister, my family, my village, my language, my very life. Now he was taking away the one thing tyrants were never supposed to be able to touch. My internal thoughts, beliefs, my cultural and hereditary memory. Knowledge of the oldest truths. Taking it not just from me but from everyone. And not only would he use it, he would *keep* it all. Out of our reach.

I had sacrificed my freedom. My nephew. My life. This...

I would not let him take this. And I especially would not let him take it for himself.

He had used his power to broadcast his intentions, to try and intimidate me. I paid him in kind. With a burst of energy, I threw my voice across the battlefield.

Unlike him, I did not wax poetic about godhood or my own pride or strength. The time for eloquence was far over. I simply told him what he needed to know.

"I AM COMING FOR YOU."

Thump.

With all the power of the sun behind me, I leapt, clearing

nearly a hundred yards and landing in the midst of the battle like a missile. My fire burned through the Aquilans, searing the flesh from their bones while at the same time mending the wounds of the Éirins—yet all shrank away from my power. From my blade I drew another, this one of pure fire, and wielded them in tandem, carving a niche for myself. When Hiberos joined me, all flashing opal and spinning scythe, I jumped back and summoned my bow instead, raining destruction with explosive arrows: upon the battlefield, onto the parapets of the city walls, and into the siege-breakers.

The Éirin archers followed my lead, targeting my targets. Between Hiberos and I, a path had been carved through the thorn-bloods and centuriae padding the walls. The fae moved their siege towers into place, three on the south flank and two on ours. Over the mud and blood flying through the air, I shouted, "Warp-warriors and faoladh into the towers!"

Warriors and wolfkernes piled into the siege towers, aflame with triumph as they climbed to the room at the top. Even as they were still piling on, militiamen braced themselves against the towers and pushed them toward the edge of the city walls.

As we neared, the legionaries' shouts rose in pitch, frenzied. Their arrows plinked uselessly off the back of the gangplank drawn closed at the top of the tower; any strike with swords was no more than a glancing blow, blades shattering against the strong fae alloy plating the tower. When finally they were close enough, Ferghal, first up the ladder, unlooped the gangplank's chain and let the winch fly.

Warp-warriors and faoladh burst forth across the gangplank. The top of the wall was chaos. Screaming stars and moonshot missiles exploded stone and sent shrapnel flying.

"We have to signal Solma to hold her fire for now, or she'll hit them."

"On it!"

The very last missile struck one of the ballistas mounted on the wall to my left. It came unseated, groaning, falling forward off the wall and taking screaming men with it. I fought through the fray closing in around the tower's base until I got a clear view of where the ballista had fallen. It had crashed partially against the wall itself and broke open a small gap.

For a moment, my heart lightened, thinking this might be a quicker way of getting fighters into the city. But no, unless we diverted efforts to open it, the crevice was too small to exploit. Far too small for a grown man to slip through.

Yet I watched, vision throbbing, as someone slipped through it regardless.

Not a man, though. A boy.

My boy.

Numbness.

Without pausing, I raced after my nephew.

Yet above, a precarious piece of debris was finally upended by the rush of warriors across the parapet. It landed with a crash, sinking firmly into the mud and completely obstructing the hole.

My hands were on it in a second, on the edges, pushing and prying with all my godly might to get it out. And it did budge—I did manage, with a groan, to leverage it out of the mud—but when I exposed the hole, it had partially collapsed. It was just barely too tight for me to pass through.

A panicked squeal to my left startled me. "Mother of—"

Never had I been so happy to see Conan. Painted in mud but alive.

I bounced on both feet like an excited toddler. "Yes! Yes! Conan! Follow him. Please, stars, follow him, make sure he's safe."

The hog glanced skeptically at the tiny hole, but he failed to escape me as I wrangled him over, flipped him on his side, and coated him in the slippery mud. Then, with a swift and mighty push, I slid him through like a lump of butter through a hot spud.

"Go!"

Conan leapt up and ran, squealing indignantly the whole way.

Sunlight glowed from my pores as I pushed and pressed and blasted with my fire, trying to get through after him, but there was nothing for it. There was too much pressure on the stones. And judging by the way the red-marbled storm clouds boiled above me, if I exerted much more power, Gaius would take it from me. The mere thought made me want to shriek with rage and tear out all my hair.

I'd have to fight my way back to the tower and make it over.

With ragged breaths, I returned to the battle—and was swamped. The quillies were drawn in like moths to a flame, overwhelming, a nuisance, slowing me down.

I'd told Conan to keep an eye on Faelon, but I could not leave him in the hands of a *pig*. Even as I fought against the swarm, I forced myself into the two-eyed seeing I'd been trying to perfect.

MOTHER. He was trying to find Nevidaea. Desperate to find her. Before confronting Gaius, she was his first concern.

No one stopped him. No one even noticed him. Legionaries and slaves rushed back and forth, hauling water, ammunition, equipment, balms, tar, wounded officers ... anything that could be moved was being moved. No one had time to acknowledge, let alone recognize, the legate's son.

Adopted son.

Kidnapped son.

Faelon's chest hurt, a sadness so deep, as he wove through the buildings and down cobbled streets he'd known since he was old enough to walk. Deeper into the city, the fomori were killing anything that moved, but he was quick, taking the byways to reach the villa. The villa that Nevidaea, I knew, had already left.

I pushed the thought into his mind: *No, not there. Look around you.*

Auntie?

But I couldn't fight and carry on with him at the same time. He glanced to one side, spotted a group of shambling fomori down the lane, and hesitated before ducking into a back alley staircase. If he was going to find anyone, he needed a weapon, because the streets were crawling with those monsters.

He picked the first building he saw, a barracks with a black-smith attached. The barracks were empty, but the coals in the stove were still burning low, the sheets and furniture a mess. Everyone had gotten ready in a hurry.

Still, with senses far sharper than most, he knew he was not alone. After a moment, straining hard to pick up any sound, a faint clanking came from the other room. Iron chains. A male voice cursing the Mighty Ones.

A prisoner, moonless, one of those thornblood monsters ... the blacksmith all corrupted by fae blood ... fomori? A million possi-bilities went through his mind, each more likely to hurt him than the last.

After another moment of hesitation, though, he approached on quiet feet. He pushed the door leading to the blacksmith's quarters, and light sliced in from the big window. He cringed against it. But when his vision focused, he registered the person at the far end of the room—chained to the wall by his wrists and ankles.

Ottavian.

The primus was badly beaten, stripped of anything but his tunic and trousers, and marked with a red cross on his chest.

Crucifixion. He'd been sentenced to crucifixion.

"Luca!" At once, Ottavian darted forward, nearly lunging for the boy and only coming up short because of the chains binding him.

With a cry, Faelon shrank back and reached for the short sword at his waist. Never had the primus spoken with such frenzy. Was he cursed, too? Going crazy just like the others?

But the man eased and fell to one knee. "It's me! It's me. It's all right." He spread his hands, wrists facing Faelon to show him his veins. His eyes were alight with fear, but his creased brow was soft with care. "It is truly me. It's all right."

It's all right, I confirmed.

With a breathless gasp, Faelon rushed into Ottavian's arms as if rushing into the arms of his very own father. Ottavian crushed the boy to his chest just the same, chains rattling. Their kinship was real. Outsiders within. The only sane Aquilans for miles.

"Thank Belos you're safe," the primus whispered, drawing the boy back. "Your mother has been worried sick."

A sting of fear—shot through with a delicate sliver of hope—penetrated both me and Faelon. "Mother! Where is she? He didn't..." Our vision was blurry with tears all at once. It was awful to acknowledge what Father might have done, but Faelon wasn't a child anymore. The harsh reality had to be faced. The harsh truths of what his father was capable of. "He didn't kill her, did he?"

"She was alive and well last I saw her. Or, as well as she could be." It was not the glowing reassurance he'd wanted, but it was truthful. "But what are you doing here? How..."

"I stowed away," the boy said. On cue, pig feet trapped across the barracks floorboards, and Conan bashed the door to the black-smith's room open with his dense head, sauntering in like he owned the place.

Ottavian stared. "What—"

"That's Conan," Faelon said.

"I know. But—"

"I needed to come here. Needed to find Mother. Needed answers from Father..." He trailed off, casting about the black-smith's room before picking up a hammer and chisel. With a bit of instruction from Ottavian, they broke the bindings on his wrists, then the primus took the chisel in hand to free himself of the fetters on his ankles.

"Son," he said as he shook off the last of them, "I fear your father is in no state to be answering your questions."

Faelon shook his head, squared his shoulders. "I *have* to speak to him. I must tell him about the natives, and my mother and father and aunt, how they've taken care of me. I'll tell the blood-warden, too. Ryac was wrong. About *everything*. They will take us back."

Even as he said it, I knew there was a shard of doubt lodged in his stomach, left there by the dirty looks and off-handed comments made by some of the Éirins. But still, he spoke the words. He wanted to believe them. That was important.

"Father needs to see what we are doing is *wrong*," he concluded decisively.

Ottavian's face was filled with pity. "I wish I could tell you your words could change the legate's mind, but ... he's ... different now. Even beyond what he was before, he's fallen. Mad." He clutched the boy's shoulder, led him to the window, and pointed to the sky. "That ... whatever *that* is, it is his doing. Whatever power he holds, it is beyond what any of us could have imagined. I don't even know if he would recognize you."

Faelon tried to keep his frame from shaking, but it was impossible. Still, he regarded the raging magic storm with a stiff upper lip. Cold resolve spread through his limbs. It was a sensation a child should never have to feel, and my heart burned with pride and regret both.

"I know," he whispered. "But I have to see him. I have to try."

No!

Despite the thought projected into his head, with a grimace, he repeated more quietly, "I have to."

"No!" My own scream brought my focus back to what lay in front of me.

There was no *trying*. Not with Gaius. He may have spared Faelon as a baby, when he was but a lump of clay to be molded, but now that he was a whole human with his own thoughts and feelings...

I had to get to him.

44

How many legionaries, thornbloods, and werewolves had fallen to my blades while I was tuned out, I had no idea. But I left them to my comrades, climbing the siege tower three rungs at a time. The gangplank at the top was askew, the Aquilans having tried to tear it off the tower, but I danced across in a flash.

My hair raged around my head as I tore through the enemy. They were thinning on the parapets, and the Éirins were slowly making their way down the wide steps leading upward, descending into the fortified city. But as always, the legionaries seemed endless—an inexorable, overpowered tide of red ebbing and flowing steadily. They were like automatons, trained to stand their ground no matter the cost or circumstance, and the stolen magic corrupting them made matters worse than ever before. Even with our numbers, we needed to strike them strategically.

Thump.

"Focus on opening the gates," I called to Ferghal, who I spotted on the perpendicular battlements. Without even a gesture from him, four faoladh shot across the parapets. No doubt the other two entrances would be barricaded like the south gate, but we must work at felling the barricades, letting in the masses of fomori. Spreading them thin.

A terrible uproar from the western battlefield made the hair at my nape bristle, but I could only focus on killing the man in front of me. One after the other.

Thump.

Soon, Hiberos was by my side, seamlessly resuming his slaughter. We were at the front line, trying to break through to the bottom of the steps now, and all the world was clashing swords, gurgles of death, the scent of adrenaline and viscera.

Between strikes, as a centurion and two other men were sliced in half by his lunar scythe, Hiberos called over their falling corpses, "The high king was struck down."

"*Fuck.*" A legionary came screaming at me, and I wrenched his shield aside with my false arm, grabbed his hair, then followed through by kneeing his skull concave. "Is he dead?"

"No. Or, he wasn't when he was borne away." A flash, a slice, an arc of blood, and another swath fell. Hiberos breathed hard, teeth bared, muscles rippling, hair clinging to his sweat-drenched clavicle. "But there's a reason emperors seldom lead from the front. Between that and this cloud growing above us"—with very little effort, he seized a thornblood and leveraged its weight to throw it over the parapet, into the city—"morale is waning."

Which meant we either had to end this quickly, or land a decisive blow.

Hiberos and I eased back slightly, letting a line of warp-warriors cover us as we looked to the sky together. Rose-red and snow-white strands both fluttered in my vision, faster and faster as the storm gales picked up. Every wind prickled like ... like *cosmic static*. It ate at the core of my power. The light of my soul.

"That," I said low. "I have to end that thing. But I have to go alone," I added as I turned. "I'll move quicker alone."

Thump.

He hesitated, glaring. Not because he doubted me. I understood. If our roles were reversed, I'd refuse to let him go alone. For an extended moment, he regarded me. Finally, he whispered, voice carrying only to me, "If you think you are ever alone, my brightness, you have not been listening when I speak to you. Go.

But do not for a moment think I've left your side. It does not matter where you run, or how far. If you are touching the heavens or earth, you are within my reach."

I blinked back tears—unexpected, ill-timed, troublesome tears. Then I was in his arms, pulling him to me for one fierce, selfish kiss. A wonder not keeping the stars apart but pulling them all into one dense, explosive mote. A kiss that renamed the planets. That made the silver thread between us moan like a harp string.

Then I was gone.

I followed the thornblood he'd thrown over the parapet and landed on its body with a crunch.

On my mad dash to the smithy I evaded Aquilans, dodging or blasting them back as I saw fit. The fomori covered me, swooping in on hideous, veiny wings or rising from the cobbles to ensnare those chasing me. With one eye, I watched the streets ahead of me; with the other, I searched through my connections.

Faelon, Ottavian, and Conan were searching for Nevidaea, trying their best to evade the fomori. Nevidaea had given up on trying to find a way out—all the ways out were blocked—and was hiding somewhere dark. And...

Wait.

And?

Drusilla's node at the periphery of my consciousness pulsed strangely, and when I switched to it, I was surprised enough to stop my sprint for a moment.

Oh, no.

She wasn't in Gallive. She was riding hard, had been for hours —hard enough that I didn't know if her horse would live to tell the tale. Trees with thick leaves rushed past her, offering glimpses of the wreckage of Geatacoill beyond. The horizon was a ferocious, boiling red, battle smoke spiraling into sky. She ran after that smoke with the same thought in her mind that I had.

Faelon.

She'd pieced it all together.

No, no, no.

Spy or not, Drusilla was a civilian. The last thing we needed in this stars-forsaken siege was another civilian in the line of fire.

But there was nothing I could do to tell her to turn back. When I tried to speak into her mind, I was met with an impenetrable wall. Either she didn't want to hear from me or her mind wouldn't allow it.

Bollocks. I had no choice but to continue toward Faelon and Ottavian.

Thump.

When finally I found them, they were both dressed in greatcloaks with the hoods pulled up, and were being accosted by a group of deep sea fomori with bulbs coiling from their foreheads. With a pulse of magical command, I called the fomori off and hurried over.

At my sudden appearance, Faelon jumped and stepped back; Ottavian raised a sword probably swiped from the smithy, his cloak falling back to reveal that he'd stolen a breastplate, too.

When Faelon saw it was me, he relaxed. Ottavian did not. The last time I'd seen him face to face, we'd parleyed outside of Bile Cernunnos.

"Where's Conan?" I asked, but before Faelon could reply, Ottavian cut us off.

"How dare you come here," he growled, swelling, fist tightening around his sword. "How dare you come to take him when you're laying siege to his very own home. How dare you come for him after harassing him and putting him in danger—"

"You know I'm only doing what I have to do," I returned sharply. "I always have."

"You *kidnapped* him."

"Ha! I was returning the favor, I guess."

"The Sergias did not *kidnap* him."

"What else do you call taking a child that isn't—"

"Here we go—"

"—*that isn't yours!*"

"What was Nevidaea supposed to do," Ottavian scoffed, "give him back? Let him live like a slave?"

"She could give him back to his real mother now."

"Mighty Ones!"

"Listen to yourself! Gaius did not *technically* kidnap him? No, he only *looted him off his mother's corpse.*"

"Stop *fighting!*" Faelon snapped. With his nose scrunched, he truly resembled the namesake that Eytine and Gaius had separately bestowed upon him—little wolf. "I feel as though that's all grownups want to do, is fight amongst themselves instead of helping. All I ever hear is people arguing about me, and I'm bloody sick of it!" He looked at me not with hatred but with conviction. "If you are going to help me rescue my mother, then you can stay with us. Otherwise, I don't need you around me now."

That stung as surely as it hurt to hear him still call Nevidaea *mother*, but I inclined my head and exhaled hard. "All right, fine. Okay. But if you're headed for the villa, she isn't there—not anymore." When fear filled his face, I clarified, "She escaped. She's squirreled away somewhere."

He glanced around the city, the worry in his expression undiminished. I could feel him think, *But she could be anywhere.*

Furtively, I glanced to the side, and found Nevidaea's sight in my periphery. She was still in that dark place. Sounds came through, faint and layered over the battle behind us: dripping, the squeak of tile under her bare feet as she pulled her knees to her chest.

Tile. The bathhouse. She'd probably chosen it because it was the only building with no traffic, somewhere Gaius would never think to look.

"She's in the bathhouse," I said, refocusing.

"How do you know that?" Ottavian demanded with no small amount of suspicion.

"It's a long story." Here I nodded at Faelon. "The connection we have. I have it with Drusilla and your mother, too."

"That thing you fed her," he said flatly.

"I— I wanted to keep an eye on you. Both of you." Blowing a curl from my face, I finally admitted, "For both your safety. Even though she's... I just— I couldn't ... I don't know."

Faelon's demeanor changed, softer in some subtle way I couldn't quite name.

I continued on through my teeth before either him or Ottavian could say anything more on the subject. "We should go to her. But once she's with you, you—"

THUMP.

I was cut off by a sudden explosion and wave of heat as the fae battering ram finally broke through the southern gates. Soon, the streets would be more dangerous than the battle field surrounding the city.

I grabbed Faelon's shoulder and urged us forward. "Come on."

We wove our way toward the bathhouse, Ottavian and I flanking Faelon. The lad stood upright, his eyes hard, mouth set in a determined line. I'd seen him frightened, concerned, confused, but I'd never seen him so resolute, and it stirred in me what seemed like every emotion at once.

We all had to grow up at some point and take charge of our destiny. I just wished I'd gotten to see him as a child. Hell, he was still a child, only barely eleven.

Finally, we reached the bathhouse and slipped inside, leaving the battle behind us. Dank, musty, and dark, it was nearly as unpleasant as it was during the day, when old Aquilan men walked around bare-arse naked. It was also empty, an odd thing for a bathhouse. Unnatural, liminal, in-between.

"Where is she?" Faelon whispered.

I squinted, trying to judge by the slant of the shadows, but there was no way to tell—the homogeny of imperial architecture did us no favors. So instead, I took a deep breath, then a risk.

"Nevidaea," I called. "You can come out now."

A little thrill passed from her brain to mine. Of fear, initially, then anger when she recognized my voice. *Mave*.

Then ... something new overtook her. Every negative emotion was washed away by a bizarre, floaty sort of wonderment. This was it. This was when it all ended. Finally. Mave was here to save her. All she had to do was stand and walk.

A woman possessed, she rose and left her hiding place. Crept down the hall. Drifted into the main bath area.

Between the columns separating us, the olive-green silk of her gown and the gold thread of her bird-wing mantle caught the light. Then she stood before us fully, pale, shadow-eyed, shaken.

She wasn't looking at her son like I thought she would. She was looking at me, her eyes as wide as if she were seeing me for the first time. Me. Mave. Not a threat, not a problem. An answer. A definitive answer.

I didn't know how to feel about that. Responsibility for her, on top of everything? But soon the moment passed, and she looked down at Faelon, who was already running for her.

She spread her arms. "Luca!"

He barreled into her but only allowed himself to be held for a moment before drawing away, bringing with him fistfuls of her skirt. "Mother, are you hurt? We almost went to the villa—"

Somehow, Nevidaea became paler. "Oh, thank all the Mighty Ones that you did not. Ottavian, my friend, I— But how did you know I..." Again she looked at me, seemed to work out another knot, and shook her head. "It doesn't matter now. I don't care if I ever know. Lucastos..."

When she leaned forward, he took her face in his hands, turning it this way and that. His tawny fingers stood out against her pallor—and lingered on her throat, where the skin faded from peach to purple like a watercolor of a sunset, the burst blood vessels embers of a bonfire at dusk. Subtly, her throat shifted as she drew in a breath and held it.

Faelon was quiet for a number of seconds, his hands hovering over the hand prints left by his father. "Mama, who did this?"

Her lips parted. But she said nothing.

As the silence stretched on without an answer, Faelon's very aura seemed to darken. Then he backed up and, in a movement very like Gaius, spun on his heel, knuckles white around the pommel of his short sword. His little jaw was tight, jowls tense, eyes aflame, and brow as stormy as the cloud above all our heads.

"Lucastos." Before he took even two full steps, his mother caught his arm.

He stopped to look over his shoulder. "I'm going to him, Mother."

"You can't!"

The boy started forward again, and this time, she snatched him with enough fervor that his body jerked. Protectiveness flared up my spine and through the shells of my ears, heating the tips. But I stayed put. This was between them.

Faelon grunted as he pulled against her, but she held him fast. "You cannot go to him, Lucastos, I don't want you to see him like he is, he'll hurt you, there is nothing— We have to—"

He managed to twist from her grip, his cloak swaying as he whipped round to face her. "Stop! Stop. Just *stop* it!"

His voice was raised. Forceful. Too grown up, on the edge of madness. To my great surprise, Nevidaea responded in kind, snapping, "I'm trying to *protect* you!"

"You think I don't know he might hurt me?" he shot back despite the way his hands shook. "That he might *kill* me? You think I haven't thought about it for, for months? You think that, that all that time he—when he was teaching me about war, I didn't realize I'd have to fight in one one day, and that I could die?" He threw a hand in my direction. "You think I didn't think of it, of, of dying, when we sacked the Éirins' tree? *Mors mihi lucrum*, it's the Sergia family motto! How am I supposed to *feel* about that? How am I supposed to carry on the same as before when I know my father wants to die, and that some day I'm supposed to die, too, and, and that I'm supposed to kill people that whole time, and *hurt* them—and have a wife and *hurt* her? How am I supposed to act when ... when I can't even be at my home or at my school without someone coming in and taking my blood from my arm, all so he can go and *hurt* the fae. Which, I'm *half* fae! What am I supposed to say to him, or think, or—or *anything*?"

"I don't know!" Despite her impassioned shouting, her face crumpled. "Luca ... when I married him ... it wasn't *like this*. You're too young—too young to know these things."

"Maybe! But I do, I know all of them. And I'm still telling you: I am going to see my father now, and if you try to stop me, I will run away." He looked at Ottavian and I, glaring, tense—not like a soldier but like a cornered lion. "Don't *any* of you try to stop me."

Neither Nevidaea or Ottavian knew what to say. No disciplined Aquilan boy would ever dare speak to his adults, his superiors, in this way; boys like that did not get into cadet academy. They could not be angry with him—couldn't be anything but ashamed, I reckoned—but they did not know how to respond, either.

As for me, despite the incredible danger Faelon was putting himself in, I couldn't help but consider him in a different light. I tilted my head, studying the determined set of his jaw. Never before had our souls felt so perfectly resonant. After all that, all the pain on my and Eytine's parts and all the meticulous sculpting on Gaius's...

I'd known then, in the glade that day. I'd said as much to Gaius, moments before he plunged his sword into my stomach. *Take him from me now. But you'll never take him from Éire.*

Finally, with a sigh, I broke the silence. "Well ... just because you have to confront him doesn't mean you have to do it alone. Promise me, though, that after you've done that, you'll leave with Drusilla. She's putting herself in harm's way to come get you."

The boy was shocked. He swallowed, but his voice was dry when he spoke. "I ... okay. Do you—do you know where my father is?"

"I don't have the same connection with him that I have with you."

Yet I thought back to the red thread he claimed connected us. He hadn't been fully wrong then, but he certainly wasn't wrong now. For better or worse, the heart in his chest connected the three of us. Him, Hiberos, and me.

If his plan was to hide from us, he would fail every time. And if necessary, we would hunt him to the ends of the earth.

But for now, I hardly needed to think about where I'd find

him. Because the string was tight and humming with not only Gaius's evil but the cool, silver touch of the Moon.

I didn't have to find him.

Hiberos already had.

45

HIBEROS

Minutes earlier

Mave was somewhere damp and dark, her pulse galloping like steed of flame. The gossamer silver thread between us was uncharacteristically taut. As the coalition offensive surged into the war district of Sylvostum, my hooves beat the cobbles in time.

She was strong, she was brilliant, she was brave. But she was mine, and I would not let her slip through my fingers.

I left the armies behind. They were holding their own, overtaking every corner of the city, slaughtering legionaries and blasting open gates as they went. Fire was exchanged between tree-cutters, fae arbalests, and a ballista seized by the Éirin army and turned inward against its masters.

I followed the feeling of the silver thread, cataloging every shift in her mood. There was bitter sadness, apprehension, dread, but also pride. Love. Almost certainly, she'd found Faelon. Yet, in the labyrinth of Sylvostum I could not quite work out where I might find her. Every turn I took, the thread seemed to tangle, forcing me to retrace my steps and untangle it—until, finally, I understood why.

Gaius.

I shoved down the rage. Rage was useless. No, when I found him and dismembered him joint by joint, it would be with pleasure and eminent precision.

A moon moth appeared seemingly from thin air and landed on the very tip of one of my horns, then in the next moment was off, wheeling merrily down the lane. It had found something. Wanted me to follow. And so I did, dutifully, sliding and side-stepping past fomori, fleeing civilians, fae, and militiamen.

It led me to the praetorium. The root—the breeding ground—of all these long years of discord.

Things had changed here. Drastically, frighteningly. All the stone had turned an improbable dark red shade with cracks of gold and little flecks of crimson glass. Vines burst from the ground to crawl along the walls and columns, and with them, dense, opaque crystals of scarlet obstructing the entry to the courtyard.

Another feeling, a hot, stinging, fiery feeling, throbbed in my chest.

Another thread.

Not silver but drenched in blood and apostasy and madness.

"Ah," I murmured. "So *there* you are."

Being inside of him was a strange sensation, one to which I was not the least bit accustomed. The inside of Mave was snug, secure, and steady as well-fitting armor. The inside of Gaius was sweltering, cramped, and erratically jagged, as though the body itself was dented, as though the shape of his soul buckled under the teeth of a great beast.

While I welcomed the full scope of physical sensation—and Gaius, as a study in ego, was somewhat fascinating—it was time to reclaim the errant organ and put it back where it ought to be. With its mistress.

I should resume my search for Mave, but... *I wonder...*

Swinging my scythe horizontally summoned a wave of lunar magic shifting from light teal to the deepest blue. As it fanned out like a swiping blade, it cracked the bloody crystals and sent them raining down, scattering across the scorched flagstones. The way opened almost too easily.

I took one step forward. The gales of the storm above and the sounds of battle faded, as though I'd stepped into the eye of a hurricane.

The palatial courtyard was a ruin. All the stone and marble here was the same as outside: darkest red, flecked with glass and shot through with deep gold brimstone. Pillars crumbled and leaned on their companions. Statues of Mighty Ones lay scattered, missing heads and limbs. The fountain in the center had been upended by the jagged crystals punching through the flagstones, revealing the well beneath it—clean Fraochgleann groundwater tamed into an Aquilan maiden's ewer and poured for the enjoyment of her masters. She was shattered against the ground just as surely as the rest of the stonework.

Beyond the courtyard, the praetorium's double doors were broken open, barely holding onto their hinges. In the gloom cast by the storm above, it was impossible to discern anything beyond. If Mave were here, she would probably beam her sunlight into it and flush out whatever evils lurked within. As it was, I did not care to announce my presence with a moonlit cantrip of my own.

As quietly as I could, I took another step in, holding my scythe at the ready across my body.

He was close.

And if the torture he'd inflicted upon me and the savagery of our last encounter was any indication, he was as thirsty for my blood as he was for Mave's.

Mave.

Though I yearned to plow forward, to call him out and demand a one-on-one battle, to duel him and to finally take vengeance for all the horror and heartache he'd brought her from the moment he'd entered her world—and then some, for everything his people did to her ancestors and land—facing him in such a way would be a blood-drenched madness of my own. Yet, although her discomfort alone would justify as slow and painful a death as I could give him, there was more than Mave's honor at stake.

There was my own pride.

I recalled that day at Cernunnos, during the siege, when his men had surrounded me. They had wrangled me like they would a beast, cornering me, catching my limbs with their whips and thick ropes, never giving me a moment to recover. With their comrades covering them, they had pierced me with feyiron nails. Weakened me. Lashed me to their horses and dragged me through the singed heather to their war camp.

The abominable mortality conveyed by even that little bit of feyiron in my hide was unlike anything I had ever felt. Even the enfeebling atmosphere of the Beneath was different. I had not known then what feyiron was—that was post-Shift lore, not kept by Guardians—but I had known I was dying.

Without her.

The cold hand of Death, raking her fingers across my hide with covetous hunger, and my soulbind was nowhere to be found. No beautiful lunar princess to watch me as I died.

For so long, I had been furious, *furious* at her for leaving, for dying the way she did. Then I understood. Then I felt how she felt all those eons ago. Then that singular loneliness was visiting me, and I realized fully and with explosive grief that I'd often thought of her death as something that had happened *to* me.

Not to her. To me.

But she was the victim. And, in a way, *my* victim—because, for all Death had done, at least it had been there when Mave died.

Relentlessly, endlessly, the Aquilans had tortured me. It might well have been that my captivity lasted only hours; I would not know, because it felt like an eternity.

Without her.

Even back then, Gaius had had a fascination with my heart, or lack thereof. Through the feyiron's burning chill, I was aware of him ordering his men to drag me from the pit where they held me. My body was spent, every ounce of willpower fed to the maw of this unknown destroyer; I was powerless to resist him as he cut me. As if he were a child dissecting a dead animal, with pitch-stained fingers he explored the cavity, and when that haunting mismatched gaze regarded me, it was like the feyiron: cold and hot all at once. Hungering, paralyzing.

Hard to believe he was merely a man. And I'd thought the *fae* had a great capacity for evil.

"Why do you not speak?" It was the only thing I clearly remembered him saying.

"Because I do not hear," I answered thinly. "Only a fool answers a fool according to his own folly. I answer only to *her*."

With a sort of needy, deprived anger I did not understand, he'd seized my jaw, his own clenched. "So, you surrender to me, then. I have the power to let you live or die."

"The only being who holds power over me is not here."

At the time, perhaps I'd thought I spoke of Gealach. Now if I understood anything, it was that, all along, I spoke of Mave.

Those things were still true. I answered only to her; she held power over me; I had spent too many centuries wrapped in my own pain, in the betrayals done unto me, when I should have stood firmly by her side. But for the injustice of being deprived of her, was I not entitled to my own small vengeance?

Gaelach was gone.

That left Gaius.

Let me at least taste what it is to wound you.

The thought brought an aching grin to my face and dredged a bestial purr from my chest.

The Moon, as it turned out, was a trickster god. Deceiver, impostor, shadow. The god of thieves, concealment, lore, and secrets, soulfasted to the Sun in a forbidden and long-forgotten ritual. Éirins for millennia to come would tell tales of his arch smile, his switchback legs, his erratic and frustrating behavior.

In over three thousand years, never had I felt more *myself* than in this moment.

I loved Mave. More than loved. She was my everything, lived within me, my sole and everlasting source of light. And she had changed me. *Freed* me. From myself, from Gealach.

But one could only overcome one's nature *so much.*

Surely, she'd find me before this strange dark triad we found ourselves in reached its inevitable conclusion.

A noise from the recesses of the courtyard made my ears prick up. Still grinning, I scanned my surroundings. Whatever stalked me, it wasn't Gaius, but it bore the mark of his ownership. I scented the air and realized I well knew that stench—

Realized too late. In the same moment, a white streak lunged from the shadows of the ruined courtyard. I pivoted, digging my hooves in and deflecting his blow with the shaft of my scythe. Ryac went flying, a disarray of limb and tail and chain.

As he scrambled to recover, his hazy crimson eyes were on me, his jaws dripping pinkish fluid. The feyiron collar he wore dug into his throat, and though he couldn't have been wearing it for more than four or five nights, the fur of his neck was rubbed away, his skin raw and bleeding.

I felt the same pity anyone would feel looking at a beaten dog. But with a bark, he pounced, so I defended myself. I dodged and swung, and when he dodged in turn, he only just barely evaded my glistening blade. The lunar power inside of it groaned to be released, but I was saving every inch for Gaius.

Ryac followed my every movement, snarling, his long neck moving almost like a snake's. Now he circled me with more calculated a glare.

I circled, too, observing him with much interest. "I wonder, is it the fae blood alone giving you this reaction to your collar, or is your kind close enough to us that it would sap your will regardless?"

My only response was gnashing teeth and the lather pouring from his mouth. Ryac had never been a scholar, but this was beyond the pale. The man could not speak—could barely comprehend anything not his master's order.

Once, manipulated by a pain unnameable, ravenous for something unattainable; now, he was gone. Rabid.

"You really ought to be ashamed, Gaius," I called with a playful lilt. "Sending a sick animal to fight a god in your stead.

How unlike you. It would be so unfortunate if, now you've attained all this power, you began acting like your superiors. Hiding behind marble walls like a *coward*."

The provocation had the desired effect. A great bolt of magic lashed from the storm cloud crowning Sylvostum and struck the flagstones with enough force to shatter them. Shards went flying; it was mere luck I shielded myself in time.

A wolf's pained yip told me Ryac hadn't been so lucky. When the dust cleared, the werewolf was slumped near a pillar, a mass of yellowed white fur.

The light just inside the praetorium shifted, and at last, Gaius appeared.

When last I'd seen him, his form had been rapidly deteriorating. Now I didn't know what to call the state of him. To begin with, he was flayed—not lacerated anymore but flayed. Without skin, his body was one unbroken, bright red shade, a high-gloss film of blood obscuring even the white of tendons. His steps were slow, deliberate, and the footprints left in his wake ate through the stone like acid. The only part of him that resembled flesh was the face, pale and untouched, but his hair was the same shade, no eyes, no teeth. Just red, and horns of bone for a crown. He wore not a stitch of clothing, but something floated round his head, almost like a halo...

No. Not a halo. When he turned his head to glance at Ryac's unmoving form, I understood. This creature Gaius had become—it had not one face but three. The secondary face on the left and the tertiary face on the right hovered a few inches from his head like porcelain masks. His curls, which I thought had turned white, were in reality molded, part of the masks. Each mask bore features exaggerated for theatre: the primary one was twisted in a glare I'd mistaken for Gaius's usual face; the second grinned in open-mouthed delight; and the third was utterly, completely devoid of emotion at all. Before my eyes, as he refocused on me, the masks shifted on a horizontal axis. Wrath was replaced by Apathy.

When Gaius spoke, it was loud enough that my ears flattened back. "Well. Here you are, without your keeper, again."

"And here you are without yours," I returned at a normal volume. "So, that makes us two cocks broken from our cages and raring for a fight. What savagery will we wreak upon each other?"

He spread his arms at his sides and summoned a shield of the same strange porcelain material making up his faces in his right hand, an antique spear in the left. They rippled with a subtle red light, like the faintest flame dancing over alcohol. "*Keeper*? If you mean the Emperor, you are an idiot. Emperors kneel to gods, not the other way around."

I observed him closely, the minute changes in his posture. "Is that what you are, a god?"

"I am the crusade. The fury, the fire honed, disciplined. I am the seat of warfare like ours, the kind that goes on for centuries. Enmity."

I couldn't help but laugh. Stars, even with unlimited power, he still did not know what he was. "Considering the Éirins have never tried to invade the Empire or wipe out their citizens, I would not consider *this*..." I gestured at the siege around us. "I would not consider *you* Enmity." Incredulously, I shook my head. "You still cannot let go of it, can you? Your desire for her to devote herself as fully to obsession and hatred as you have. Your desperation for her to be like you. Perhaps it is not the Emperor but my soulbind, my goddess, my brightness, who holds dominion over you."

A growl ripped through the courtyard, and with it, the sky roiled. I only just barely dodged a lance of draining power as it stabbed from the sky and punched into the flagstones.

Fool.

In the same fluid movement, I sprinted around the toppled fountain—and drove into Gaius from his flank. He was caught off guard, and we crashed against a pillar, dislodging it.

As Gaius staggered, Wrath was replaced with the grinning mask, Desire. "I see how you want it, *Moon*."

With the final word, he thrust us into combat.

The boom of the falling pillar overpowered our grunts and huffs as we met one another blow for blow, me raising my scythe to deflect lunges from his spear. Inch by inch, I backed him into the blackened bramble that had once been a lovely garden, and vaguely, I registered that Ryac's body was gone. It mattered little; it smelled as though he'd left.

Our fight tore to and fro like riptide. I knew he was holding back. So was I. We were sizing each other up, looking for weak points.

"Not even going to try?" I asked conversationally, throwing my head back to clear my streaky raven hair from my vision. "You wound me, O Enmity! Where is the crusade? The fury and fire?"

"I could say the same of you," he said coolly. "If you possessed the power of the moon, you could burn me from existence this instant. You are nothing but a symbol of divinity, with hardly any divine strength to wield in truth."

Again, I laughed, thrusting the head of my scythe toward his stomach. It squealed as it scraped against his shield instead. "Still just a silly human after all. Of course you would assume everyone desires to wield the full breadth of their cosmic power wherever they go. There's no subtlety about you. No complexity. No depth. No discipline. You lie to yourself."

Desire was replaced with Wrath, and I didn't think it was done consciously. "So nonchalant. So weak. Laughing and dancing about like a funny little satyr. Unserious. Unreliable. It's no wonder that her pulse races when she looks at me"—despite myself, my pulse jumped in turn—"that her eyes burn. I know she's driven to madness when we cross swords. In her deepest heart, she drips with need. No matter how many times she runs, she knows where she belongs. What she deserves. And after you're *dead*, that is where she will spend an eternity: in my sights, hunted."

"You know nothing about her."

"I know *everything*. Once I've borne her to her stomach—driven her face into the dirt and speared her on my cock and filled her with my seed—if she delights me, I'll even let her go. To be hunted another day."

Fury clouded my careful judgment. He could taunt me all he

wanted, but he would not speak an offensive word against my Mave. With a snarl, I slid back a step and swung my scythe the way it had been begging me to.

An arc of silken, starlit midnight sliced into him with sheer *ring*, dappling the courtyard with blood. But he was not deterred. On the contrary, he seemed metaphysically to latch on to the power and pull me in by it—and, overwhelmed by a horrific, earth-shattering rumble and an all-encompassing white light, I understood my mistake.

When my vision returned, I was across the courtyard, slumped against one of the vine-covered walls with the red blur of Enmity approaching briskly.

A meter from me, his pace slowed. He stabbed his spear at me, the tip a mere inch from piercing the knot of my throat.

Then his hands began to shake. And soon, he could hold neither his shield nor spear, and they clattered to the ground beside him.

In a surge of heat and desperate breath, he was upon me, on one knee between my thighs, clutching my throat and my face. Every word shook with hatred and longing and disgust and helpless, confused misery. "You are eating me away inside. Every throb. Every gush. Every cycle. Moving my blood. This fire, this furnace, this engine in my chest. You are destroying me. *It is agony.* Deep and hurting. I can feel you in my *ribs.*"

I longed to jump on him and snuff his voice out forever, but there was no energy left in my body. It was all inside of him, stoking his veins and muscles.

"There is only one way," he rasped. "Keep you close. Cool the fire. Cure the blood. Ease the blood. Eat the fire. Keep and eat and swallow and fuck and run and chase and rive and ruin. *You belong to me.* Both, both of you. Exist *for* me. Eternally."

Wrath turned to Desire, its eyes tipped up into gratified crescents, and he drew his arm back for his spear. For the strike that would end me forever.

There was a warm, amber flash.

For a moment, through my hazy vision and with Gaius

obscured by the light, I thought perhaps this was death. Perhaps instead of the cold, mad nothingness of the Beneath or the cotton-wool slumber of the Underland, I had reached the endless hunting fields of the old fae wilds.

Then the light faded to reveal Gaius, staggered—and the shaft of sunlight growing from his jugular. An arrow.

I followed its trajectory to its mistress. Her curls, whipping about her head. Her eyes of golden flame. Her gleaming antlers, squared shoulders, and fearless stance.

The silver string connecting us sang like bells.

I let my eyes close for a moment, felt my lips curve upward. "I told you, Gaius: 'the only being that holds power over me.' That includes my heart."

46

MAVE

I t wasn't until the thing looming over Hiberos turned that I understood it was Gaius. Whatever was left of him. The words spoken just before I loosed my arrow still slithered through my bones, fear calcifying to rage.

Forget the fact that Hiberos should not be here without me; Gaius was my quarry. I was the hunter now, and he the prey.

This ended here. Finally. Right where it all began.

I stepped into the eerie, quiet courtyard, bow gripped fiercely in my wood-and-bone hand. The power and volume of my voice made the stones ring. "Try to harm *my* Moon? Lay claim to *me*?"

I nocked a second arrow and sent it flying into the cold, white face of Apathy flanking that featureless crimson head. The arrow broke a hole through the cheek and sent a network of cracks spidering across one side, and Gaius buckled aside with a resounding grunt.

Footsteps filled the courtyard behind me. Faelon—with Nevi-daea and Ottavian in tow—stopped at my side and grabbed my wrist. "Careful!"

Our eyes met, but before I could say anything, a frail laugh shivered toward us, low and frayed and slithering about our ankles like a colony of eels. I watched the hair at Faelon's nape stand.

"Ah, little wolf, you have nothing to fear. It will take more than arrows."

The boy turned his gaze toward the war-torn remnant of his father. Through our connection, I felt him mustering all his courage and what remained of his love and admiration as he took a few steps forward. With a sharp gesture for Nevidaea and Ottavian to stay put, I followed him close as a shadow, ready to fire again at less than a second's notice.

"Father..." Faelon began in a whisper, carefully skirting the destroyed fountain. The bloody god-thing limped in a circle to face him. A thrill of disgust passed through me and the lad both when we beheld the ecstatic mask of Desire.

When Faelon said no more, Gaius gestured for him, sticky, wet threads draping from his outstretched arms. "Come now. Don't be afraid, Lucastos. Look, I've done it." To demonstrate, he spread his arms again, and the debris strewn about the courtyard rose off the flagstones. I braced myself to be pelted with them, but instead, the mess swirled around us slowly. The storm above our head followed suit, the black clouds turning into a ring rather than a mass. "I can make anything ours, little wolf."

"Father—" The boy choked back a gag. "Father, you ... you don't have any eyes. Or hair, or teeth. Or *skin*."

"We'll take this island, then the seat of the Empire itself. We'll be rehad and rehad." He crouched slightly like he was offering a very little child something very tempting. "Eldest son—no, prince —of the New Empire?"

I barely held my tongue. He already *was* a prince. He was Faelon, son of Eytine and Erivon. But this wasn't my fight. I'd defend him to my last breath if Gaius tried to lay a hand on him, but this decision was his.

Behind Gaius, carefully, Hiberos rose to his feet, the opalized veins across his hide a bit brighter now that I was in closer proximity to him. We locked eyes, and I nodded almost imperceptibly. *Hold for now.*

"Father..." After much hesitation, Faelon took another step forward, then another. Above us, lightning the same pinkish-red as amaranth flowers snapped through the sky and glowed deep within the ring of black clouds. "This is not ... right. You're scaring me."

Agitation colored Gaius's voice, no matter how he fought to keep it out. "I told you there is nothing to be scared of. I'm your father. Everything I do is for your own good. For the sake of *our* legacy, mine and yours. From the moment I first laid eyes on you, Lucastos, my every deed has been to secure your future."

The boy shook his head, swallowing hard, and though he faced away from me I heard the tears in his voice as he said, "No, Father. Not mine. The future *you* chose. But I know what future lies that way. *Mors mihi lucrum...*"

"*Death is my reward.*" Gaius tilted his head at the motto. Desire turned to cracked Apathy. "Is it not true? You would not be standing here before me if you were afraid of death. I taught you well."

Disappointment, anxiety, and exhaustion showed plainly in the set of Faelon's shoulders. "I'm here to keep you from hurting anyone else. Please, Father, just call off your troops. Meet with the kings. No one else has to die, on either side."

"You truly think that these barbarians will allow us to live in these lands in peace? They will drive us out, and that means killing every one of us, Lucastos. Whatever lies they've fed you, believe me, to yield, to show weakness, to retreat is not an option."

Faelon looked over his shoulder for my reassurance, so I bowed my head and said, "If he agrees to parley, no one else needs to die. You were right."

The red glaring through Apathy's cracks seemed to brighten. "*Mave.* Speak to me directly or do not speak at all."

"Everything I had to say to you has already been said. It's your son you have to answer to now. The son you stole and tried to twist to be just like you."

Those words seem to awaken something in Faelon, a thought he hadn't considered. He dug in the pockets of his cloak, withdrew something, and, as he closed the gap between himself and the bloody abomination, offered it out...

I tried to shadow him, but before I could see what he held, Gaius raised his arm. The glistening muscle swelled and bubbled, and the thick limb separated into two slender ones. It was with his new third arm that he conjured a volley of corrupted heartmagic so intense it blasted me back.

"No!" Faelon screamed.

"*Mave!*"

I lost my footing and was dashed against the rim of the well, barely able to keep my bow from falling in. Before I could recover, Gaius had me boxed in—with four arms, now, two on either side. The mask of Wrath was inches from my face. Unmarked. Unseeing. Inhuman.

Hard to believe this was the same commander, the one with the white cape and matching horse. Yet, it was. This wasn't some emergent godhead or new entity. This was Gaius, in command of himself. Madness had warped his ordinary cruelty for longer than he would ever admit.

Familiar ragged, putrid, blood-tinged breath hit my face. "I regret not taking the babe and killing you sooner."

"Father!"

"*Gaius!*"

He ignored Faelon, but Nevidaea's shout was enough to make him back off of me.

He moved rather too fluidly, as if minute by minute his body became more mutable, as if he bent his very own bones to his will. As I dragged myself to my feet, I saw that Hiberos and Faelon had been blocked from running to me by a shaft of boiling heartmagic, and similar shafts had risen everywhere the flagstones were significantly cracked.

When they shrank back into the earth, Hiberos was by my side at once, bracing my shoulders with his blazing hot chest pressed to my back. Burying his nose in my hair, he pulled me close, and our magic combined to send a cool balm spiraling through my battered body. For a moment, I gave myself over to the bliss.

Then Faelon caught my eye. He had sprinted to put himself between his mother and father.

My entire body went rigid. I broke away from Hiberos.

But there was little I could do. The geysers of flame shot upward again and caged me in. I shifted from foot to foot, looking for a way out before thinking, *To hell with it, I'll throw myself into the fire.* My indecision lasted no more than a fraction of a second.

Yet even as I leapt through the shafts of flame toward my nephew, I was already too late.

With a snarl, Gaius grabbed him by his forearms and tossed him aside. Far. Far enough that he hit one of the walls surrounding the praetorium.

The *snap* that echoed through the courtyard made me feel bloodless—icy-limbed, lightheaded. I forgot about Gaius. Nevidaea. Hiberos. Everything.

I ran. And I was running through Fraochgleann again, surrounded by fire yet chilled to the soul by a baby's distant cry. Someone may as well have taken a knife and twisted it into my heart for the pain bleeding me as I crashed to my knees by the boy's side.

He was alive, awake, and weeping softly. Three good signs. But judging by the way he cradled his arm, and the way his little leg was bent, he had not escaped unscathed.

"Faelon. It's all right. I'm here." I touched his freezing cheek. Ruby liquid had begun to rain from the heavens, leaving pink rivulets on his tawny skin.

When I looked back at Gaius and Nevidaea, they were both frozen, both staring at where their son had fallen.

Tears pricked my eyes but were immediately burned away by the flame coursing through me. I had nothing to say to either of them that had not already been said. All I could mutter was, "A pair of failures. Both. You both are bloody failures."

"Lucastos, my darling," Nevidaea croaked.

Gaius, on the other hand, swelled anew. Whatever regret had frozen him a moment ago was quashed, folded up and compartmentalized. "Let it be a lesson to learn from. No matter. Come here—I shall heal you."

But whatever little thread of hope, whatever longing for reconciliation had brought Faelon this far, had snapped. He shrank into himself and squeezed his eyes shut. Shivered as the rain pelted his rapidly paling face. "No," he whimpered. "Stay away from me..."

"What—?"

"I said *stay away from me!*" he repeated at the top of his lungs, and as a reflex it seemed, he snapped his jaws. I looked on with awe as his canines lengthened, his eyes changed, his round ears tapered. Long-buried heritage was coming to the surface. "Both of you! *Forever!* I hate you. I wish I had never been born. I wish I had never been born so you could never be my parents!"

Those words broke Nevidaea and Gaius both.

Perhaps it was Faelon that had kept Gaius clinging to the very last of his humanity, because before our eyes, the masks shattered, their shards raining down and sticking in his red-slicked torso. His four arms—three hands open, the bottom left clutching something tight—reached for us.

Nevidaea, though...

I would have expected her to break down crying. What mother wouldn't, facing the ultimate rejection from her only son? And for a few full moments, she did gape at Faelon. Disbelieving. Horror-struck.

Then she turned on Gaius.

With a ferocity rarely seen in humans let alone Aquilan women, she screamed. *Screamed.* Not words, just a howl, long and grating, filled with grief and hysteria and a rage suppressed for generations. Every chord of loathing and self-hatred tore into the unholy sound. Her body shook, every inch of it, hair and spittle flying, eyes wild, mad, unseeing. When the first scream ended, another one began, then another one.

She threw herself into Gaius, staggering them both back. Then she did it again, digging her nails into his gooey body and ripping. Veins and sinew came apart in her hands and yet still she pulled, snapping tendons, pulling out organs. He fought the onslaught, punched her with closed fists as well as scratching and shredding her in kind.

Hair and flesh were ripped away, bones cracked, one of her cheekbones caved in, yet she seemed not to feel it; his returning violence only drove her frenzy to a fever pitch. And before any of us knew it—before any of us could jump in and stop her—she'd driven him to the edge of the well.

Then she pounced on him, wrapped her thighs around his shoulders, and held on with all her might. He barked something in Aquilan, but the sound was smothered by her abdomen.

Over the cry of thunder and Gaius's muffled screams, I only barely caught her whisper to him. "You made me a monster. Now I free us both."

Though he gripped her clothing and smacked at her, it was too late. She leveraged her counterweight and sent them tumbling end over end, into the well.

"*Nevidaea!*" Ottavian sprinted forward. But there was nothing he could do.

As husband and wife plummeted into the earth, their screams mingled to the last, then were silenced with a distant splash.

The courtyard fell quiet.

It couldn't possibly be over.

It couldn't possibly be that easy.

Battle raged throughout the city, the commanders unaware of what had just occurred. Thunder growled overhead, but the lightning was gone. The sun leaked through the haze.

The world went on turning.

BESIDE ME, Faelon could do nothing but breathe rapidly. When I looked back at him, he was ashen, his gaze distant and his pupils blown. Despite his broken bones, he wasn't bleeding, but when I touched his chest, I sensed something wrong with his heart. His blood wasn't pumping as it should.

"Some— He's—" *Shock*, those remnants of the collective memories told me. *It's called shock.* "He's going into shock!"

My shout broke the spell. Ottavian and Hiberos both rushed to our sides. Ottavian's face was slack and hollow, his eyes the deepest pits of despair, yet still he rasped, "How do we treat it?"

"Help me get him on his back. Elevate his legs. Careful of the broken one. We should bundle him up as warmly as possible."

Ottavian threw his cloak into my arms, and while Hiberos settled the boy into the correct position, I folded him in the cotton wool, using my sunlight to warm him. "Faelon. Luca," I whispered, touching his chin with an over-warm hand. "Can you hear me?"

When he managed to focus on me, he looked nauseous and anxious but aware of his surroundings. A good sign in some ways, not so much in others. "Mama," he barely managed to squeak. "I ... I killed her."

I felt my entire face fall, and I cupped his cheeks in both hands. "No, li'l wolf, no. Don't you say that."

"She's gone, and it's my fault."

"It isn't." I kissed the crease between his brows and put our foreheads together. "Please, hold on. We need you here. You will see the sunshine again. You'll see a real Éirin summer."

I cradled him while he wailed. Apparently gods wept, too, for I could not hold back my own sorrow. For him, for the childhood he'd never have. For Nevidaea, all her pain and silence and effort and ultimate failure. For me, my sister, my people. For this land, for Geatacoill, pock-marked and maimed. All of it.

I was so tired of death. Aquilan, Éirin, it mattered not. So, so, so tired of death.

Commotion from beyond the praetorium walls drew my attention. The first thing to catch my eye was the way the cobbles beyond hiccuped and jumped as though alive, before fomori sprang from them. The leafy boughs of ents brushed the roof tiles as they stomped through the war district. Within moments, a crush of Éirins and fae crowded the praetorium gate, trying to see what was going on inside.

Ferghal, Solma, and other coalition members pushed to the fore and shouted orders, routing troops through the city proper. As the crowd dispersed, a familiar face clawed her way through, shorn hair mussed around her sweat-slicked seafoam face.

"Faelon!" Orlaith had Erivon in tow, and not far behind him, a group of aranfox healers. The fae king and queen fell to their knees next to their son, Orlaith across from me and Erivon by her side.

Hiberos had managed to work some magic on the boy; the aranfoxen stood by. "Hold him steady," Hiberos said, stripping bark off himself and handing it to me.

It rippled with magic in my hand, transforming into a stick of faewillow, which I stuck in the boy's mouth. "Go on, bite down, there's a lad."

Hiberos stretched and massaged his leg into a set position. The boy's scream of agony was only somewhat muffled by the stick. Orlaith's ears pinned; she was hopeless to know where to put her hands or what to say. Still, she did what she could, raking his curls away from his forehead and dabbing the sweat from his brow. "I'm here, little wolf. I'm here."

Watching them, my heart broke for her, for the boy, and for Nevidaea.

Once his arm was set, too, the healers bore him away on a litter, and after a harried embrace from my sister, they left me sitting on my knees. For a god, I certainly felt like a small, insignificant, unhelpful piece of shite. My shoulders slumped, head bowed. I combed my claws into my hairline and gripped at the roots, taking deep, even breaths.

None of it seemed real.

Perhaps I'd died in the labyrinth and this was all just an extended nightmare. Or maybe this was the hell Gaius had sworn he'd consign me to.

Then Hiberos settled in around me, his form heavy and warm and solid as ever. The ever-comforting scent of sun-warmed moss and blackberries, along with a new note of night-blooming jasmine, washed away the stench of blood and smoke and sulfur and damp wool. He cradled me, and I cradled him in return, our limbs tangled, our brows pressed together. His weakened soul drank from mine, but rather than drain my energy, he only augmented it; together, our spirits perpetuated, expanded, glowed like twin flames feeding a steady bonfire.

Gaius was dead. Our armies were plowing through Sylvostum. Sallach would soon be ours again.

Why, then, did I feel so uneasy?

"My brightness," Hiberos murmured in my ear, rubbing circles into the base of my spine.

I whispered, "What do I do now?"

No sooner had I uttered the words than the ground began to tremble.

At first, I looked toward the rooftops, thinking it was an ent passing us, but there were only birdlike fomori looking down upon the burning city. Still bracing each other, Hiberos and I stood, and turned toward the locus of the earthquake. The flagstones nearing the center of the courtyard shook so hard that debris around it jumped several feet in the air. The cosmic storm above roiled, rowling, and sparked. Pressure built. Finally, the trembling reached a crescendo—

And the well cracked in half.

The very earth split. Red liquid boiled to the surface. A huge object began to rise from it—round, dripping.

It wasn't until the object shifted that I realized it was a death's head coated in the same crimson film and crowned with the same horns as Gaius. Its pure white spine led to a crest of bone between its horns, some twisted facsimile of a cock's crown helmet. Eyeless, sopping, the thing clawed itself out of the muck as far as its torso, its hands bone-clawed and woven with bits of the battlefield: blood crystals, thornwire, stones and dead and broken scraps of artillery fragments. As it emerged, a gaping vertical slit opened in its chest, porcelain shards lining the gash like rows and rows of chipped teeth.

Then it wailed—whether with pain or anger could not be said —and the sound shook the city at its roots. I felt and heard infrastructure collapse below our feet. The back of the courtyard, where it wrapped around the praetorium proper, was swallowed into the earth.

"Ah," Hiberos said. "Whatever Gaius was trying to become ... there it is."

It wasn't Gaius—not quite. Or, not fully. He had been but a breeding ground for whatever this thing was. It had consumed him the same way it consumed the rest of the battlefield.

Hiberos and I readied our weapons at once. He rushed in head-on, swinging his scythe to rend the titan's fingers from its body. It was fast despite its size, but he was faster. Yet whenever he managed to slice something off, whatever substance made up the creature sank into the ground and was reincorporated; it simply grew the missing bits back, no matter how many times he cut them.

Meanwhile, as I loosed volley after volley of arrows, it simply absorbed them. When enough of them were inside, it used them as *armor*, even—moving spikes that could strike out at Hiberos or blanket its exposed muscle for protection. My arrows were made of sunlight, not steel, but even when I exploded them inside of its body, the blow was only pain. A temporary nuisance. It took but a moment to reconstitute a new arm or shoulder or jaw.

The earthquake had drawn the attention of others. Soon, our friends joined us. Ferghal shredded, Solma stabbed, Muiri climbed the spine to try and strike at its head. Manan and the druids called forth roots to bind its limbs, if only briefly. Some Aquilan soldiers even managed to fight against the corrupted blood in their veins, and under Ottavian's command joined us to turn their swords against this unholy abomination.

Yet no matter how many fighters joined our side, it mattered little. In fact, every time a man fell, he only served to feed the beast. Sometimes literally. It snatched soldiers up and threw them into its gaping heart-mouth with a voracious, persistent hunger. And minute by minute, it became visibly stronger, faster—it even managed to drag itself from the ground, towering twelve meters above the battlefield.

"Ferghal, Solma, Muiri!" I called their names between futile draws of my bow. "Pull out. You all need to pull out. *Now!*"

"Are you batty, kat?" Ferghal growled, ducking on all fours as the titan swiped its claws over his head. "Leave and let this thing eat you?"

"The more people that fight it, the worse it becomes. Look at it." We cried out in unison and were momentarily separated by an outsized stomping foot. "Go. Just *go!* And bar the gates behind you!"

Ferghal hesitated. I saw it in his face, the torture. The last time he left his commander behind, it had ended in tragedy. But, with a wolfen snarl, he withdrew and howled for his pack to follow. The armies extracted themselves by increments, evading the creature's grasping hands and ravenous mouth.

As they fled and sealed the praetorium, the titan wailed like a spoiled child left by its playmate, and moved to climb the walls. Considering it was only a head shorter than the roof, it would only take a few steps and a bit of effort. I fired another barrage of arrows, which sank into its spine and exploded, knocking it off the wall—but in no time, its writhing form reconstituted and clawed for freedom again.

"Hiberos!" I didn't take my eyes from the titan as it struggled for purchase on the pitted walls, but I threw my arm out to the Moon, and he came to me like a weapon summoned.

One way or the other, the end was near, and when it came, this time, I would be with him.

We braced each other's arms, panting hard, our wills as frayed and ragged as our breaths. But rather than go after the creature or watch in helpless awe, Hiberos grabbed my chin and forced me to look at him. "Mave, remember the prophecy."

In unison, we looked to the sky. The black storm clouds were moving in again, their lightning fingers grasping covetously, the ring closing and threatening to choke out the sunlight.

"When single shine the Moon and Sun," he said, and our gazes met.

"A conjunction. An eclipse." I tried to block out the chaos that reigned over the city as the bloody god escaped the courtyard and began wreaking havoc through Sylvostum. "But how do we—?"

"Do exactly what you feel," Hiberos rasped, pressing close until our chests were flush. "The same way deer know to migrate during the winter, or moths know to build their cocoon, or wolves know where to nest for pupping season. That is the correct way."

With a deep breath, I closed my eyes … and let my body take over.

Taking Tali's dagger from its place at my hip, I sliced my palm, letting it fill with blood. In unison, Hiberos and I raised our hands out and over in an arc, then rested them on each other's sternums. My blood sank into his hide.

All ambient noise stopped. The gales died. And a moment later, a shaft of pure teal light appeared behind him, stretching into sky until it disappeared within the clouds. Judging by the gold cast on the planes of his face, I could only guess a similar light stood behind me, bright as the sun. Our chests rose and fell in perfect sync, and slowly, images overcame me. Where Hiberos had been standing, I saw only runes, visions of past and future, people I knew but whom I could not name, squiggly lines connecting in perpetuity...

We pressed closer and closer until our hands were not on each other's sternums but wrapped around one another, palms pressed hard to the base of the skull and the base of the spine. Our lights combined turned green; our very shadows merged into one long skein of deep gray.

We braced hard against each other. And, as though they were celestial beasts of burden, we dragged the Sun and Moon into their yoke.

The land darkened and cooled, suddenly blanketed in twilight. Elk called. Wolves howled. Sheep brayed. Birds screeched. All the little animals hid in their dens. Above our heads, for just a moment of stillness, the eclipse was perfect: a crisp disk of black ringed with white fire.

Then, with a shock wave that flattened the buildings around us, the black crashed down in a pillar. The same white fire skated along its edge until everything, all the universe, was black and white and a low drone in my ears.

I watched from outside my body as my and Hiberos's flesh was seared away, then our bones. Nothing was left but the shaft of pure ink. It rippled like molten metal poured into a mold, and by inches was shaped into a figure not there a moment ago. It was humanlike, slender and nondescript in frame but with the build of a powerful fighter.

At first, it appeared as an opaque, pure black silhouette; then from its heart spread dolmen carvings, the spirals and arcs found etched on the most ancient of tombs. They glowed gold, brighter and brighter, until the body in its entirety flowed with the snaking lines. As the colossus unfurled and rose to its full height, the ink making up its surface was swept away, revealing moonstone plating.

In the next moment, my consciousness joined with it, with Hiberos. We loomed a good fifteen meters above Sylvostum. Up here, the gales were more powerful, the storm crashing around the head of our outsized construct, but such things were inconsequential.

In the distance, we spotted the bloody newborn god. The shock wave had only deterred it marginally; it crashed through the city, snatching up soldiers and materiel and leaving destruction in its wake. It grew and grew, climbing over the battlements into the valley beyond, ravenous for more.

When finally it turned and saw our colossus, the red titan of war grew in size, puffing up like a bear trying to intimidate a threat. A roar of warning made the sky itself tremble.

As one body—*At last*, whispered all of nature—Hiberos and I ran toward the valley. Toward our fate.

The titan wailed and staggered back, holding its arms out as if to halt us. But when we barreled into it, there was no stopping our momentum. We tore through the creature, strike after strike, our carvings singing with ecstasy.

Then we thrust our hands into its vertical maw, braced either side, and, with a roar, pulled outward.

Light spilled from our eyes. A thousand spirits' voices raised in chorus, a thousand hands long swallowed by the soil adding to our strength. The bloody god squealed and hissed and writhed and grasped at our wrists, but it was no use. Whatever vital red substance made it spurted and gushed—small jets at first, then huge gouts, and finally a geyser painting us both. The creature's bone claws scrabbled against our plating, trying to find any weakness in the carvings, but there was no seam, no edge, no juncture to exploit. We were nothing but protection, precision, passion.

And when we wrenched from its center the heart of the titan, feverishly, recklessly, wordlessly, eternally, breathlessly, desperately, tenderly *finally*, it was all over.

One last, wet wail shook the sky. Then the titan fell to its knees among the abandoned fae siege engines. Its rent body bled into the soil, worn away with every wave of power like a sandbar washed under the tide. Eventually, it was nothing more than a twitching puddle of goo strewn with metal and bone debris.

Soon, it would fade back into the earth and be gone forever.

We turned our back on the valley, the heart still clutched in our hand.

Pouring from the southern gates, standing on the battlements, and rushing out of the forested field hospitals, crowds as small as colonies of ants gathered to witness us. We approached in long strides. Turned our head one way, then the other. Then crouched, opening our right hand.

There lay Gaius, humanlike again, as naked, slick, and sticky as the minute he was born; broken, with Hiberos's heart glowing over his ribs. We laid him at the feet of the kings and commanders.

Then we straightened and tipped our head to the sky. The moon's shadow was just slightly off-center from the sun, and daylight had begun to warm the world once more. Our time had passed. We closed our eyes, giving ourselves over to the light ... and, with a sigh, shrank back into the ink and white fire.

The eclipse lifted. A breeze tickled curls against my cheek. When I opened my eyes, I stood in Hiberos's embrace, my head pressed to his clavicle.

We thought in unison, *Are we alive?*

Then we pulled back. In perfect tandem, we jumped and hissed in pain—and in perfect tandem, we looked down at our right palms. Where I'd cut myself, we both had identical wounds.

Again in time, we raised our heads, and the truth passed between us. We were connected now, physically, in a way neither of us had expected. When one suffered, the other would. Yet all I could feel was relief, joy, hope, pride. Love. For him, with him, within him.

We raised our hands and touched palms, simply basking in the simplicity and truth of the moment.

Then, a pathetic gurgle drew our gazes left and downward. Somehow, Gaius was still alive. Stirring.

I dropped my hand and approached, standing above him. The crowds around us looked on with the unnatural silence of pheasants hiding in the brush. He didn't seem conscious or lucid. His left hand held his father's spear, while his right was clutched tightly around something I could not see.

Right. Faelon had given him something. And all this time, he hadn't let go.

With a frown, I nudged his hand open.

A small wooden bird tumbled out.

47

It was strange. After the battle, the atmosphere of Sallach itself seemed to change. The storm cleared, the world warmed. Birds I swore I hadn't heard since before the burning of Fraochgleann called from the trees and bushes as I moved through what remained of Geatacoill.

It had been several hours since the wounded were borne away —Hiberos and I had taken our time helping Muiri, Solma, and Ferghal do a final sweep of Sylvostum to make sure it was clear of active hostiles. By the time we were finished, the moon was high in the sky.

The field hospitals were situated in the ashen clearing left by the briars. Barrel-topped wagons dotted the huge space, wanderer tinkers and sewists and cooks hard at work making the camp somewhat homely. Boughs of hastily druid-grown trees hung with the same floating lights that had once filled the library at Bile Cernunnos. In some places, tents had been erected, but mainly, the druids did their best work with nothing between them and the stars.

"Odd," Hiberos said as we passed a group. "The fact that whatever once animated Geatacoill is dead doesn't seem to phase them at all."

I smiled tiredly at him and the moths all about his head.

"Despite us being gods—apparently—the druids still have wisdom to teach us. Death is not the end but one path. One stage in the cycle. No?"

His ears shifted, and he slipped an arm around my waist. "Goddess, I love you. When you speak like that, you make me want to chase you through the woods until sun-up."

"As tempting as that sounds, my body is making smells I didn't even know I had. Bath, first."

Hiberos gave an open-mouthed scoff. "Have you considered that perhaps I want to enjoy the smells?"

"Trust me, you do not."

"Spoilsport."

One patch of clearing was especially crowded with healers and coalition members both. The Gallowglass guarded it in a tight ring of black leather armor, but between their heads, I spotted High King Alasdair propped up in a cot lined with moss, delegating to the other kings. I caught his piercing stare for just a moment, and earned a steady nod.

But he was not who I was looking for. I felt for the knots at the periphery of my consciousness. One of them was untangled, limp and unresponsive. The other two were pulsing with light, resonating off one another.

Reading my mind, Hiberos kissed me, leaving behind the taste of blackberries and the cool warmth of gin. "I will stay behind and speak with him. You go on."

My hand lingered in his even as I stepped away, our fingertips reluctant to part, but after another breath of his scent, I obeyed and followed the pull into the next patch of clearing.

This one was equal parts fae, Éirin, and Aquilan prisoners. The red-clad prisoners were the worst off of all, especially sickened now that their blood wasn't whipped up into frenzy. Judging by their pallor and lethargy, many of them would not live for much longer, and evidently this was a thought shared by most others, as Éirins and fae alike sat with them, making sure each had a blanket and a tot of whiskey at least. Among them, I spotted Paik lulling

Tatius into a sleep he probably would not wake up from; nearby, Menecon slipped a sheet over Thomasia's lifeless body. Though I scanned the crowds for any moonless, chiefly Ryac, I saw none.

Instead, I went to a plain canvas tent on the far end of the clearing and pulled the flap aside. On one half partially hidden by a sheet, Orlaith and Erivon slept on a bear rug in each other's arms, utterly dead to the world. On the other was a chair holding a similarly passed-out former primus using a fat, pink hog as a footrest. And next to that, a cot holding a battered—but very awake—eleven-year-old.

As I entered, Faelon perked up, cradling his arm in its sling.

"All right, sweetie," I whispered, crossing silently to come to his side. We both looked at Ottavian. "Damn, they're really out, eh?"

"Conan?"

"Ottavian."

"Oh. Yes. He needs it, so I didn't want to wake him."

With a fond smile, I wiped away a bit of mud hiding behind Faelon's ear. "Where's Drusilla?"

He leaned into my touch, swallowed the lump in his throat, and managed, "She stepped out to get me something to eat and left Ottavian in charge. But..." He looked down. "I don't think I can eat."

"If you can't eat, you can't eat." I knelt, folded his good hand into mine, and squeezed. Swiveling one ear toward the even breaths of the king and queen, I hesitated before asking, "Have they ... said anything to you?"

"Not really. I think they don't know what to do with me."

I huffed a dry laugh. "I know the feeling."

He reconsidered our fingers tangled together. "You aren't purple anymore."

"Yea, well, I didn't really like being purple to begin with. I do still have to deal with these pointy ears, though." A little light came back to his eyes, and I smirked. "Did you know your ears got pointy, too?"

"They did? When?" he asked, before realizing too late he maybe didn't want to know.

"When you were angry, and in a lot of pain." I tapped his cheek. "Your teeth got sharp, too."

His smile faded, and he was quiet for a time, thoughtful. "I don't really know what to make of it all. Fae ... Aquilan ... Éirin. And I don't know anymore what I'm proud of and what I want to forget." There was something more he wanted to say, something untold and festering, but if he was ever going to tell anyone, he would tell me. So I waited.

"What if I am just like him?" he whispered at last, searching my face. "What if, deep down, I can't escape it, and I end up just like him and everyone hates me?"

My shoulders slumped. My instinct was to tell him at once that he was nothing like Gaius, but I knew he wouldn't believe me —and I also wasn't a hundred percent sure it was the truth. His nature, of course, was kind and gentle, but sometimes I did see his father in him.

I folded my other hand over his. "Li'l wolf, people like that, bad ones that refuse to change ... they don't tend to ask themselves questions like that. They don't fear. They justify. Apart from that, you are kind and brave and like to care for others. You care about the difference between right and wrong. So you already have a clear advantage."

"But what about—" His entire demeanor changed, dark and numb. "My mother was kind and brave and liked to care for others, too. She still let father hurt me, and her, and so many other people. And Ottavian. He's kind. He's brave."

Unsure of how to answer, I searched his face, hating the confusion and despondency evident there.

The words came slowly, then flowed: "Kindness does not mean you're harmless, and bravery does not mean you're infallible. Nevidaea was afraid. Ottavian was lied to. You were hurt. People who live in fear and ignorance make terrible choices, and you grew up in a house filled with nothing but those things. But listen to me..." I lifted his chin. "You are not him. Not because you are perfect, or pure, or magically immune to evil and darkness. You are not him because you choose it. Every day. Even when it scares you. Every time you question yourself, every time you hesitate, every time you flinch from cruelty, *that* is you choosing a different road. That is you proving you are not like him. That you are unlimited."

Faelon sagged with grief, and I knew he was thinking of Nevidaea. "Mama. It isn't fair. It should not have been that way, she tried so hard..." On the last word, he choked, and tears overwhelmed him anew.

I swiped my thumbs across his fawn-brown cheeks and kissed his hair. Had she lived, she might have done a lot of good. But at the moment, that seemed less important than Faelon having his mother. "I know."

He searched my face desperately, trying to remain brave despite the sorrow racking him. "We could—could have lived somewhere new and taken care of whatever birds we wanted. But she ... left ...*me*."

Gently, I shushed him, combing my nails through his hair. "She chose. She made the choice she thought would be best for you. And in the end, it was what she did that gave us time to set your bones and put you on transport out of there. It might well be that what she did saved your life. I think if she knew that, she'd do it all over again."

He leaned into me, and I cradled him against my chest, rubbing tiny circles into his back. For a few minutes, he could do nothing but whimper like a frightened pup. The other adults in the tent finally stirred.

With a mighty sniffle, the lad whispered, "I don't know what to do now. I don't know where I fit."

"I think a lot of us feel that way right now. You aren't alone. Even so"—I pulled back to look at him earnestly—"you'll always have me and Drusilla, and..."

"And me," Orlaith said, replacing Ottavian in the chair without having to ask him to move. She brought with her the quilt she'd made for Faelon, which was now up to five squares, and laid it across his knees. "I am here. For both of you. No matter where you go or what you choose. *I* choose to keep us all together."

Tension I had not been aware of released, and I exhaled. *The rift shall close, the two made one.*

Watery outlines caressing the air around us caught my eye. Their features were not as clear as they'd been when tensions were high, but they lingered all the same. "And the spirits are here, too. For all of us. Gwynedd—you only knew him when you were a wee baby, but he loved you. My father. Fallen friends from the village you were born in. And all our ancestors. You're never alone, Faelon. No one is."

Saying the name out loud made all three of us pause in the same instant. After a moment's hesitation, I asked, "What name do you want to be called by, little wolf?"

He glanced furtively at Orlaith and gnawed his lip. "I ... I'unno. I'd have to think about it."

"You have all the time in the world." Tousling his hair, I finally rose to my feet. "But for now, rest."

"What about me?" Orlaith quipped, propping her feet up on the corpulent mound of painted pig flesh still lying in front of the chair.

"Yes, rest. Goddess's orders."

Below, Conan sighed and farted at the same time.

"And that goes double for you."

Orlaith and I exchanged a smirk as I turned away. But when I was halfway out of the tent, Faelon called me—"Auntie Mave?"—and I ducked back in.

"Yea?"

The boy swallowed thickly to ask, "Is my— Is ... Gaius ... dead?"

"No. He lived." Each word tolled like an iron bell in my chest. "He's being treated away from the field hospital."

"I think..." He hedged. "I think at some point, maybe, some-time in the future ... I'd want to speak to him."

My heart softened like butter. This poor, brilliant child, ever the white knight of mercy. "If that is what you want, then okay. I think I can arrange it."

THE MESS TENTS weren't that far away. Drusilla had been gone for too long.

Finding her was one thing, but I had not been able to slip into her vision since I'd caught that glimpse of her riding toward the city. I followed her scent and the warmth of her nearby consciousness until I was deep in the forest, properly hidden in dense shadow. When at last I peeped her bushy gray tail between two trunks, I crept forward on silent feet and crouched to watch closely.

She raised her muzzle to scent the air. If she picked up on my presence, she gave no indication; instead, she looked to the north. Watching. Waiting.

Soon, her whole body tensed, her crest standing on end, and with the next shift of the wind, I smelled him, too.

The lanky white werewolf appeared between two trees, his fur torn, flesh rubbed raw under the feyiron that still collared him. His jaws were dripping, but in the pupil of his hazy red eyes was a solid whiteness—therein lay the kind of madness seen only in men lost at sea, forced to drink salt water to slake their thirst. Somehow, he'd lived under the feyiron's tyranny for this long, but his time ran short. He limped, dragging his leg forward once. Twice. Then he collapsed in a heap at her feet with one long, weary moan.

For a beat, Drusilla was still. Then she produced a file from her skirts and knelt, sawing at the collar. She worked fast, merely pinning her ears against the terrible sound, and before long, I heard the metal break apart in her hands.

With a bit of precision and effort, she managed to ease it off his neck and cast it—both the collar and the chain attached to it—far away from him.

I thought he was dead, he was so still. But eventually, his chest rose and fell again. His wolf form receded. All that was left was the sweaty, disheveled exile beneath. From the freshness of the welts on his back, it was clear he'd been lashed quite badly, and his side was cut as from shrapnel.

I watched Drusilla trace the wounds with her eyes before moving her hand to lift his head slightly. "Ryac. Say something so I know you yet live."

He coughed, blood and bile and black clods of dirt spewing from his mouth and nose. When he finally looked up at her, on a shivering breath—"Hiya, a chara."

Drusilla shook her head and used a handkerchief to wipe his face. "I am not your friend. A life for a life. That is all this is." Ignoring the vulnerable, tender confusion on his face, she shoved a full sack into his arms. "Clothes and food. Take them and leave."

"My pack—"

"Your pack is all dead. The Éirins had to put even the survivors down in their misery. Now go."

Ryac froze, barely breathing, looking genuinely distressed. "But—but where ... where will I go?"

"Head east like you said you wanted to, but do not come back here."

His face—still bearing the nicks from her bite—scrunched as though he were trying to remember the details of a dream. I wondered if he was trying to recall my promise to him, and felt a flicker of pity.

Then his features slackened, and he set aside the sack, sitting up more fully. "But I want to go with you."

Her ears shifted. "I appreciate all you did for me, Ryac..."

"But?" And for once, he sounded not cheeky but broken, bleak, and desolate. Angry at himself for having ever thought this would end another way.

"But I am old enough to be your mother, and I am a lupercal, and I do not concern myself with the desires of men."

"You don't have to concern yourself with my desires." His voice was cracked, raspy, but not from the collar. "You don't ever have to think of me, or look at me, or speak to me. You don't even have to let me in where you stay. I'll sleep outside. Just let me be near you. All I want is to be near you."

Drusilla was silent. What did one say to that?

Finally, Ryac tucked his chin and muttered, "See? This is why you don't feed stray dogs. They always come back."

By the quirk in her posture and the slight, agitated movement in her tail, I could tell Drusilla was distressed, too. For anyone with a soul, it was disturbing to see a troubled, beaten animal beg for affection. Yet still she stood and backed up, poised to sink into the trees once more. She turned to leave, but at the last second stopped beside a trunk, looking back.

"Ryac," she said, "you can strive to be a man. A real man. I sincerely hope that, someday, you find someone—anyone—who treats you like one."

With that, she was gone.

Ryac stood frozen right where she had left him. Bedraggled. Bewitched. Bewildered. Bereft. Betrayed.

For about a minute, I stayed, trying to understand the slight shifts in his expression—but I left before Drusilla's scent could be lost on the wind.

Weaving through the bracken, I soon came abreast of her, and was only shadowing her for a few minutes before she cleared her throat.

"You realize I can feel you there, yes?"

Noiselessly, I slipped onto the trail beside her. She gave me a once-over, decided I looked okay, then refocused on the path ahead. Little by little, the hard-packed earth and dense roots were swallowed by ash. "And now it all reaches its end, no? Who could have thought the enslaved scullery maid would one day be the mistress of everything the light touches."

I smiled despite the tiredness of my bones. "You were the first to see greatness in me. That night in the attic, when I begged to know if you were a spy."

The angle of her ears changed, and I thought she was pleased.

"You said then our souls spoke the same language. Do you still think that?"

"I believe so, yes." For a bit, we walked in silence. "You know, I never had a mother—"

"Oh, Mave," she scoffed. "Please, pray, do not say another word. Already I am in my mid-fifties, and lupercal do not have a dazzling life-expectancy. And by Opia's forge, I am sick to death of being turned into someone's *mother*."

I laughed. "All right, all right, fair enough. I'll call you mo *chara*."

Her ears shifted again, and she gave me a hard sidelong stare. "You heard that, then?"

"Mm. You were searching for him. Why? Why save him? Just to repay your debt?"

"I dislike being indebted to anybody." Drusilla picked at a loose string on her sleeve. "A creature like that is destined to roam the earth in agony regardless, so it seemed almost cruel to subject him to any punishment. Perhaps that's reductive. Perhaps I've been charmed by a handsome face. Handsome in its own ... provincial, heavy-browed sort of way," she added quickly.

"Of course." At first, I grinned, but as we walked on and I thought more, my smile subdued. "I saw it, too. There's something there. Maybe you've given him a chance to finally turn his life around for the better."

She shrugged one shoulder. "Or maybe I've let a maniac cannibal loose on Co Ligea."

"If you did, I will surely be the first to hear about it. M'not stupid enough to think this protector business is over."

"No, you are not," she agreed mildly.

After a while of walking in silence, I asked, "What do you reckon will happen with Faelon?"

"Wherever he goes, I will stay with him for the time being. After that, who knows? I am free. The world is open to me."

As the sounds of the field hospital neared, we stopped and regarded each other for an extended moment, too aware of each other's feelings and frustrations and failures to let words spoil the perfect silence. Eventually, I coaxed a few lantern flies to land on her shoulders, and one on the tip of her snout.

"Love you," I said.

Drusilla quirked a brow and chuffed. "I love you, too."

48

Three moons later, Emperor Agorix Westerus landed at a modest port in the Sallach Delta, as it was determined Gallive and Divlinn were too dangerous. That was fine by me. I wanted him to see the work his men had done on our land—and how thoroughly we'd crushed them as thanks.

There was nowhere to meet but the ruins of the praetorium, the only building in Sylvostum not a shambles. In perfect condition, in fact. Hiberos said that it was its proximity to our shock wave that had somehow saved it. The construction and resisting vertical downward force, something called ... physics? It wasn't my thing; I let him deal with the lorekeeping. Thinking about how much we'd gained and then immediately lost, never to find again, would drive me mad. So I tried to appreciate what I still had.

Mainly, this was our island, this was far from our first war, and they'd have to send something stronger than Gaius to take it from us.

I intended to let the Emperor know as much.

When Hiberos and I finally showed our faces—after making Westerus wait an hour and a half, mind—the great hall was packed. Every member of the coalition was present, including the kings, queens, chieftains, and mercenary leaders who'd recently joined; some conversing, others deep in solemn thought. Solma, Menecon, and Erivon were there, too, though there was no Orlaith to be seen. High King Alasdair had donned his tabard, and you'd never know he was still badly injured for looking at him. He stood at the head of the room, in front of the large fireplace.

And nearby him, somehow isolated despite the number of people in the room, was Agorix Westerus.

I didn't know what I was expecting, but a rosy-cheeked, bearded man was not it. Average height and build, graying hair, unremarkable hazel eyes, and a slight overbite. He did not look evil or great, he was not handsome or ugly. Even his questionable facial hair choices made him look like someone's doddering uncle, not a calculating architect of genocide.

But he couldn't fool me. He wore a lion's pelt over one shoulder, no doubt hunted from the Suda. Pure gold accessories mined from the Saha, set with stolen jewels from the Sahel. His gaze darted from one end of the room to the other, filled with contempt.

As we strode into the hall, I heard him mutter, "Finally," under his breath. But he pressed his lips into a thin, safe line and took a few steps forward. "This is the 'Lord and Lady' we awaited, I presume?"

He spoke in Aquilan, despite knowing the probable majority of those present were not fluent. Solma widened her stance, trying to kill him with a look. A hot surge of adrenaline traveled from me into Hiberos, and with a wave of his hand, he charmed the entire room to speak only Éirin.

Westerus touched his throat and spluttered. "How dare you touch me with your magic? I was promised specifically that if I showed for negotiations, I could leave this place unharmed."

"I think you'll live if you have to speak our language for a short meeting," I said, approaching without even a glance at his retinue of bodyguards, adjutants, counselors, and servants. I spoke to him human to human, relishing in how it made him squirm.

"Short?" he scoffed. "Did you really think it wise to keep me waiting?"

"Honestly, I didn't think much of it." I nodded to the high king. "Do you mind?"

"By all means." He motioned for me to continue. It was nice to know I had his full confidence now.

With his blessing, I addressed Westerus. "Are you aware of the situation here, where an imperial veneficus inoculated the Seventh, Eighth, and Ninth Legions with untested fae blood?"

"I've been made aware of it," he said without emotion.

"That blood belonged to my sister, and my nephew. Gaius and his conspirators nearly killed them both. In addition to that, using this inoculation, Gaius led a strike force into the forbidden fae land. Doing that caused the destruction of the lunar faes' only home. But they are far from the only refugees he saddled us with. The Stag Gréine of Sallach, the legionaries of Fort Alopex, the civilians of Sylvostum ... all my responsibility now."

Westerus raised his chin. "Dispense with the soliloquizing, if you please, since you are so set on speaking to me freely. What do you want?"

"I want Tirconnell."

He was not surprised or offended; he merely deferred to one of his counselors, who squinted, calculating the figures in his head. "Impossible," the man said. "The farmland there sustains Westminia and much of southern Albion."

"That isn't really my problem, is it? The larger the empire, the more people you have to feed."

"The land would be of no use to you. The forests are gone, and the farmers are all transplants. Albionites, Umbrians."

I scoffed. "As much as I appreciate your concern, I reckon we'll find something to do with it. Listen. If you don't give it to us, we will take it. You may as well give it over freely, without bloodshed. You can tell everyone it's a stroke of political genius."

The room was silent. Westerus frowned. "I need time to think about it."

"No. I need an answer now."

He sighed with open exasperation, but after glancing around the room and doing his own sort of calculation, he said, "I cannot promise an overnight change ... and if you attack the settlers there without due cause or warning, the Empire will have no choice but to retaliate..." The tension stretched. "But very well, I will concede."

His counselors' adjutants began scribbling madly on their slates, already harried by the paperwork soon to come. I thought about asking for Westminia while I was on a roll, but one thing at a time. When I glanced back at Hiberos and caught his mischievous smirk, I knew we were thinking the same thing.

"Now, then, about the exchange of prisoners," said another of the counselors.

"You can have them all," I replied. "Provided they want to go with you. The inoculation Gaius forced on them has sickened them. They should see their mothers' faces before they die from his stupidity. In return, I expect all ours and our allies' back."

"Very well. It is done." The Emperor's words again caused a flurry of scribbling, murmuring, and frantic looks from his cohort. "As for Helius Sergia the Younger, my sources tell me he yet lives. Is that so?"

"It is so. He is being held at a secure location. But if you're going to ask for—"

Westerus waved a dismissive hand. "You can have him, and do what you will. There is no place in the Empire for trash like that. Let it not be said Sergia the Elder wasn't warned," he added with a sigh. "Logudoric mothers breed with bad blood."

I tilted my head. A pulse of reassurance, cool and soothing, flowed from Hiberos into me. "That's all I have to say." I nodded to High King Alasdair. "I give the floor back to you."

The assembly adjourned shortly after, the kings and Westerus withdrawing deeper into the praetorium to deal with minutiae and formal documents. Stepping into the courtyard, I was lost in my thoughts, now in large part shared with Hiberos. Had we done enough? Was this the beginning of the end of our island's strife, or was there more still to come? When the Emperor inevitably reneged on his promises, how would we answer? Exactly how much power did we truly have to wield?

A silent but solid presence beside me pulled me from my reverie, and I was surprised to see Muiri. Her truly enormous black eyes dazzled me every time we met. "You're not going in with the kings and queens?"

"Father's feeling well enough to take care of it today. He isn't dead yet."

The lot of us were quiet for a while, simply watching the other coalition members file out. At length, glancing at Hiberos, I said, "I wish there was something we could do for Tagh. There must be some healing magic..."

She cut me off. "Bodies fail. Death happens. No matter how much magic you use, we all live on borrowed time. Anyway, druids are stronger in the astral plane. I don't need to tell you that."

As if Gwynedd had heard her, a gentle wind caressed our faces, bringing with it the inexplicable scent of sun-warmed wheat. A deep breath of the unexpected perfume relaxed me body and soul. "Yea. Come to that..." I met her curious gaze. "Do you still have that periapt I gave you? The heart-shaped locket. Ruadan's soul trinket."

She nodded and, without missing a beat, withdrew it from a pouch at her waist. It was still as delicate and barely corporeal as the day he'd pulled it from his chest. "Obviously, I haven't had the time to send anyone to his daughter. I might not have the time for a while yet."

"Promise me, then, you'll at least send word to her? Or send someone else to fetch her?"

"I will do what I can. He won't be forgotten." Muiri lifted the locket and let it dangle from her fingers. In the mid-morning sun, it shimmered like something from a dream. When she tucked it back into her pouch, I thought that signaled the end of our conversation, but she spoke again. "I think I've been seeing him. His spirit, I mean, or ghost, or ... whatever. It must have something to do with the locket being in my possession."

I huffed a laugh. "Can't say I'm surprised. If druids are more comfortable on the astral plane, he's more comfortable on the spirit one."

"Why is that?"

"Maybe you can ask him when you find his daughter."

Muiri left soon after, and was immediately replaced by Ferghal, who had finally managed to get his wolf-shape under control. He was still as big, burly, and hairy as before, but he no longer suffered that monstrous in-between form.

"Well, kat," he said, thumping me on the back hard enough to make me cough. "You did fine work back there. Idya see his face? Moon's mercy. Fine work, if you ask me."

Uaine pulled up beside him, Conan in tow. "Agreed." My old friend reached across Ferghal to brace my wood-and-bone arm, his eyes filled with affection. "Once again, I am blessed to have you."

"I'm blessed to have you both, too." But I got a strange feeling, noticing how they glanced at one another. "What?"

"We, ah..." Ferghal scratched the back of his balding head. "We're going away for a while. Wanted to say goodbye before we did."

"Going away? The two of you?" I sniffed the air. "Are you two shagging?"

"No!" they cried in unison, leaping away from one another.

"No," Uaine repeated quickly. "Nothing like that. It's just that I helped him track down the band of walking people his mother came from, and I'm working currently on finding his father's clan, too. So, on his off time, he's been looking into something for me in return. My ... my twin." When I was too stunned to respond, he pressed on. "Mona used to tell me she thought faeries took him from where he was left at the edge of the forest. I always assumed she was just trying to make me feel better, but recently, I started to wonder..."

"And?"

"And we have a lead." Uaine gestured to Ferghal. "We're going together to find him."

"Éirin twins," I said quietly. "Alive and reunited. Imagine that."

I wished them luck, and with another odd glance at each other, they made their way. Conan watched them go before tapping forward, flap-eared, and sitting expectantly.

I quirked a brow. "Well, what are you waiting for, then?"

He grunted, eyes all asparkle.

"Oh, oh, I see." Laughing, I summoned a handful of acorns. "You've remembered I can do this at will. Now you'll never leave me alone."

I scattered them across the shattered courtyard, and he squealed, diving after them more like a leopard than an elderly hog.

The next person to approach was Solma. The leaves that made up her hair, once all red on top and all silver on bottom, were now mostly silver, and she leaned heavily into her spear whenever she got the chance. The real world was taking its toll on the fae, but I believed they could pull through and find themselves here, without turning into the vicious Seelie of the Courts or the untethered, feral Unseelie of the wilds.

Though she'd obviously approached for a reason, she did not seem to know what to say, so I put her out of her misery. "Commander. How are you feeling?"

"I will live," she said, and swung her gaze downward, avoiding me. "Hiberos, Mave ... my Lord and Lady ... there is something I have to say. Again. I was—"

Hiberos cut her off. "Solma."

The Guardian lifted her head, ears drooping, heavy-lidded silver eyes full of agony. Hiberos stepped forward and, letting his scythe hover on its own by his side, braced both hands on her wooden shoulders. I couldn't take my eyes off him; he was stunning, in form and aura, my perfect mate. My only.

"You and I were cut from the same god. We were alike in birth, in purpose, in body ... we even fell in love with the same princess." They both glanced at me, then back. "Your woes I have shared, your joys I have delighted in. Though we have disagreed, I have never *not* understood you." Here he held her farther at arm's length and shook her gently. "There is no need to speak the words aloud. It is unspoken. All is forgiven."

As if he had relieved her of a great physical weight, she seemed to stand taller. "Thank you ... brother. Long live the king and queen. Long live the Sun and Moon."

"And long live the Lunar Kingdom."

WHILE THE SKY was still dark, we arrived at the wreckage of Bile Cernunnos. The fomori lining the pathway into the sinkhole of followed us with their eyes, their heads turning in perfect unison as we descended.

The still-blighted land sloped downward in a wide, meandering spiral that led nearly a hundred feet into the earth. As the weeks had gone by, the bilé sank farther and farther until there was no differentiating its resting place from the Beneath itself. Carrion birds, both real and fomori facsimiles, scattered as we passed the lower boughs of the tree. The leaves had drifted from it. The charms, offerings, and ribbons hanging from the branches, once bestowed by its admirers from all around Éire, were decaying and unrecognizable.

It was hard to believe a withering like this could ever be reversed—and, frankly, we still were not certain it could be, not fully. That was one of the many reasons Hiberos and I were the only ones allowed down here. The kings and other druids were given some idea of the reality, but the common people did not yet need to know just how deep the rot had gone. How close it had come to destroying us from the inside out.

The common people, also, were under the impression that Gaius Helius Sergia was dead. As far as they were concerned, he'd perished after the battle.

Some truths were better left unsaid. Some truths were too horrible.

Standing before the great tree's entrance, where the moonwell had become a glittering black moat, I paused to gather myself.

Hiberos took a step ahead and turned in to me, bringing me face to face with his breathtakingly warm, handsome clavicle. I wanted to look up at him, but I could only take grounding breaths. In, out. In, out.

He canted his head. "It still bothers you that much," he observed quietly, without judgment.

"I know it's stupid," I muttered. "I just hate seeing it. I hate seeing *him*, and knowing that he's alive when so many better people are dead." My nostrils flared. "And I hate that he was right, that there's something connecting the three of us. He got what he wanted. Our red thread."

Hiberos chuckled and brought me close, brushing his nose against the shell of my ear. "Ah, yet it is but one thread. It is the only one he has, so of course he fixates upon it. But you, my brightness, have many others. As for our connection, he could not begin to understand it, not really. There are so many things he could never understand."

Looking into his eyes, being this close to him, brought me a comfort I never thought I would feel with anyone. Even the person I'd been closest to in the world, Eytine, I'd put on a brave face for her. With Hiberos, I felt my soul melted down to its most vulnerable and basic elements. The honesty of emotion, the bravery of expression, and the freedom of curiosity that normally only a child could feel, little they knew of the world. Now, to have the knowledge and responsibilities of a god and still to feel that when in his arms—and for him to see me both ways, through *both* eyes, and still worship me, protect me, believe me, balance me, *know* me … truly understand me down to my core, without either of us uttering a word...

That was freedom.

"You are my blessing," I said, seizing him by the sideburns and kissing him hard.

When we came up for air, the jasmine in his flower crown was blooming. "You are my light."

It was simple. It was true.

We turned toward the hulking corpse to which we were duty-bound, joined hands, and stepped inside.

The interior of the bíle, once lacquered oak, now resembled the inside of a womb: one large chamber only, pink, the surfaces not wood but porous, fluffy, pulsating tissue. In the center of the chamber sat what remained of Manan's old throne, and connected to it, a network of deep red roots—some fine, some thick, all traveling inward, into the body of the throne's occupant.

Gaius was dressed plainly from the waist down. His head was bowed, chin resting against his bare chest, where, nestled between the shadows of his lungs, slept a certain seedlike heart throbbing red through muscle and flesh. The tree drank of the magic trapped within him, siphoning it up and carrying it away, through its roots, into the soil.

Gaius himself had been the one to give me the idea, the final key to unlocking the secret. Though at the time I'd thought him addled, his theory rang true: *It was a map. Of my own veins. All the trees are connected.*

Bad blood had been Éire's bane; now it would be its salvation. An endless supply of fresh magic pumping through the bíle, across the land. A matrix of roots making up the Beneath. All connected. Rejuvenating, renewable energy flowing in its veins, bringing life back into the blighted wastes. All we had to do was visit him to augment his godly power with ours.

He did not look like he was in pain. In fact, he looked like he was sleeping, his cherubic curls carelessly tousled, dark lashes fanning across deep under-eye circles, perfectly symmetrical face slack. In all honesty, I wanted to believe he was as good as dead. But deep within me, the strange thread binding us hummed, and I knew that, on some level, he was aware of our presence.

"He was the one to destroy it all," I said over the soft hissing and creaking of the tree. "Now he'll be the one to heal it."

"It is what he deserves. He's finally made himself useful."

Yet I looked at Hiberos with regret heavy on me. "The heart should be in me, where it belongs."

"Agreed. But it is better this way. He could not hold that endless power within him, yet inside you, without his sickness fueling that 'engine' in his chest, the regeneration would go to waste."

I glanced at the scar on my right palm. Logically, I knew it mattered little. Hiberos's heart belonged to me in every way that mattered, our souls bound in our own, separate ritual.

At length, I sighed. "Let's wake him up."

It wasn't difficult. I let Hiberos handle it, since the thought of touching him made my skin crawl. All he need do was lift Gaius's chin, and the cursed monster opened his eyes.

Though his lids remained heavy and his gaze unfocused, he spoke in monotone, as though talking in his sleep. "You came back..."

"You'll stop being surprised eventually," Hiberos said in a conversational tone, checking some of the thinner roots before moving on to measuring the pressure of Gaius's blood. "How is the pain today?"

"Lonely," he moaned, "so lonely down here ... don't leave me..."

For the remainder of our visit, while Hiberos collected more overcharged blood for the druids' inoculations, that was all he repeated. "I'm lonely... Don't leave me..."

At last, our duty done, we joined hands again and started toward the exit.

Then Gaius spoke. Different words. His voice was still monotone, but there was an edge to it, a bit of bass and a seam of unspeakable fear and anger. "You will never be free of me..."

I turned and looked at him. He had managed to lean forward in the throne, his endless, hollow eye watching me beneath his thick lashes. Stars, the moment the land was healed, I would be so glad to be rid of him. But for now...

"No, Gaius. You will never be free of us."

The darkness closed behind me and Hiberos as we stepped back out, into the sunken place. Waiting for us was Avelaval, drifting gently, and she greeted us with the blinking light beneath her jellyfish veil. "Our Gealach, our Horned One. The hungry heartdog?"

"Taken care of for now," I replied.

She hummed distantly and swished her tendrils back and forth. "This one is glad to see you. This one comes bearing news of the fomoire."

"Oh?"

"Yes. It is time for us to go. You have everything in hand you need, and we must return to our sacred places. This one to this one's cold mad feary father, others to their rocks and stumps and bushes, others to their bricks and ladders and steel and plastick garbage heaps, others to their temples and labyrinths and cairns, others to their gardens and apple trees and whitespread wings, others to their graves and mire and moss, and others to their mead-owgrass and riverflags and bulrush and waterweed and fallen griefs of weeping willow."

Hiberos and I exchanged a look. My chest ached strangely. I had not expected the news of their departure to leave me feeling so ... sad. After all, the fomori had done little else besides try to kill me.

"Do you really have to go? If you want to rejoin the fae, surely, there must be something we can do."

"We must leave," she said. "If we stay, there will be strife. There is so much anger and hurt still inside of us all. We must go away, and cleanse ourselves, and you must stay away and do the same, Sun, Moon, humans, fae, and hungry heartdogs all."

My brow twitched with a wave of unexpected emotion. "So ... this is goodbye."

"Yes, Horned One. This is goodbye."

I swallowed, exchanged another look with Hiberos. "But ... the fae still don't know the whole truth about Mother Moon. They still think she was dead when the Guardians entombed her. How are we supposed to tell them?"

"Let them think it." She bobbed her head back and forth slowly. "Let the fomori shoulder that weight. Let Mother's suffering be our burden. It was not their mistake, and knowing will do them no good."

Surprisingly merciful for beings who were supposed to be enemies of the fae. Or perhaps they were just being practical.

As if reading my mind, Avelaval said, "It is an old pain. As old as mothers. A familiar pain. A quiet pain. Let it be ours. Our pain."

"All right," I whispered, closing my eyes a moment. First Gaius, now this. Was this what leaders did? Keep secrets from the people who were relying on them to make sound decisions?

For the thousandth time, I wondered why I had been chosen instead of Orlaith.

With one last farewell and a pulse of red, Avelaval sank into the ground and was gone. The other fomori followed suit, disappearing into root-bound walls and cracks and patches of blight.

The Beneath was quiet save for the whistle of phantom wind through naked branches.

·☽ ☽ ☻ ☾ ☾·

THE HORIZON WAS JUST TURNING orange by the time Hiberos and I hiked through the valley and to our special place, the hill and standing stone overlooking Aiken. It felt like a hundred years since we'd come up here together, and though we had only spent perhaps four days here, the impression those times left on my soul was much larger. We'd lain together in the grass, trading language, poetry, relearning each other's quirks and preferences.

"The last time I was here," I said, walking round the standing stone, "you were dead."

"The last time you were here," he countered, following me close like a stalking panther, "I was in your breast. Waiting for you to bring me back to life."

I walked quicker around the stone. "I spread your ashes."

He darted and caught me by the waist, nuzzling in close. "You are so good. Too good, my Mave. My good girl."

I snorted. "*Girl?* I am a *goddess.*"

"You may as well have been a goddess all along, as far as I am concerned."

"I would never call you a good *boy*."

Hiberos looked appalled. "Why not? I *am* a good boy."

We fell into giggles like a pair of children rather than all-powerful beings. Then he tried to tickle me, and I twisted his arm near to its breaking point.

"Agh! All right, all right, unhand me." When I did, he shook me off and rolled his shoulders.

"You actually are a very naughty boy," I muttered.

"I would not dare to refute that." With a purr and a flourish, he bowed, offering his hand. And when I took it, he pulled me back to the edge, and turned me toward the horizon. "Look, my brightness. Look upon your kingdom."

I let him direct me. Already, the sun was warming my face, waking the core of solar power within me. To think that I was the same Mave who had wondered what god's divine arrow was trained on me. Now I was the Hunt, the Horned One—but my sights were not trained on anything but the future. My arrows, keen and gold and always ready for service, were drawn not in my name but in the name of my people—all of them—and the land, inextricable from us.

Though I could not see it, over the horizon, the citizens of Sylvostum were waking up in the ruin of their city. By mid-morning, Éirin relief would be helping them put it back together, but for now, there was bread to make, children to dress, wool to weave, and sons and fathers to bury.

The world kept turning.

This was sovereign land. It was in my power to march the Sylvostians out of their homes today if I willed it, and let Westminia deal with them. Some of them might even deserve it. But that would not bring back the loved ones I had lost at Fraochgleann. That would not revive Geatacoill. It would only start another cycle, and in this land, there were already plenty cycles waiting to be broken.

There would be some plan. Some deal or initiative. The valley would grow wild and free once more.

Another day.

Things could never go back to the way they were.

I'd known that, but seeing and feeling it so plainly was like having a stone dropped into the waters of my soul and watching the ripples fade into nothingness.

Things could never go back to the way they were. There were some things in this life that, no matter how you reached for them, no matter how you yearned or wished, no matter the shape and depth of the negative space their absence left, they would never return. Sometimes, grasping for them only made them slip farther away.

I sighed into the sunrise. The stars melted like shards of ice as the sky turned a true, rich blue for the first time in so long. Warmth and light shone upon every inch of Éire.

Someday, the fomori would return. Someday, the fae would learn about Gealach. Someday, we would tell her story—the story of a woman who had lost everything, including herself, and still somehow managed to break free of the suffering entombing her.

We would tell her story. But for now, we told it through our own lives, all of us.

For now, we had to look to the future, not just of Éire and the humans living here but of the fae, too. For they were entwined, bound up like roots drinking of the same well.

Perhaps they always had been, like most things were. Now they touched, united as one. Now the river met the sea, and the blood of Éire flowed clear and everlasting.

EPILOGUE
MANY YEARS LATER

As the sun began its descent, casting our valleys and hills and holy trees in gold, the earth of Fraochgleann sang with excitement. All throughout the city, the air trembled with joy and anticipation, but the hub of Bealtaine was the town square.

The road to the town square was a feast of color and movement, paths flanked by torches and posts swathed in lilies and squill whose sleepy heads nodded in the breeze. On both sides, long tables groaned under the weight of roasted meat and overflowing cups. Fae and humans from all across Éire had arrived dressed in vibrant costumes, antlers, and crowns of flowers. Half-fae children squealed with delight as they chased young animals through the crowd, while nearby, adults danced and drummed and howled their delight.

The savory fragrances, the bright spectacles, the sounds of laughter...

Bealtaine night was so beautiful, and so wonderfully familiar.

The celebration carried on the same way every year, but knowing what came next didn't make it any less enjoyable. When the new night waxed, dusk would transform the festival. Crescent lanterns suspended on poles would cast a soft glow over the village. Under the watchful eyes of the stars, fire dancers would emerge to lead the procession up the hill. In their wake came warriors on horseback, each bearing the banner of an Éirin clan. These days, those ancient banners were joined by the purple-and-silver flag of the lunar fae.

At the night's heart, the Sun and Moon would rise to take their thrones. Ritual bonfires were lit on every hillside, until finally the last and largest bonfire at the top outshone them all, touching the heavens.

I turned this way and that in front of the mirror, brushing my dark red mane over my shoulders. The candlelight was almost too bright in here—because why not, all I did was make light—but turning my head full around was another thing. Finally, though, I got a good angle. With a little bit of Drusilla's help, my gown now fell just so, exposing the scars crisscrossing my back while still covering my shoulders.

Funny for a goddess to have insecurities. Hiberos would poke fun at me, and give my shoulders extra love bites as punishment.

The thought made me flush, so I hurried back to sit on my stool.

Prince Faelon Airgeadsnáithe, first of his name, stood behind me, very seriously focusing on the garland of flowers he was currently wrapping around my antlers. "Dammit," he muttered as he tore a petal, his voice uncommonly low even for the full-grown man he now was.

"Language." Drusilla's voice was raspier with age, but that, as well as the gray in her muzzle, belied her true nature. Still the same ever-sharp, over-clever woman as before.

I half-turned, motioned for the garland, and mended the petal with a tiny flash of light. Faelon and I smiled at one another. He had grown up to be so unbelievably handsome—tall, dark, and just broody enough—and my heart burst with pride whenever I saw him. His features were all the broad elegance of Erivon's face paired with Eytine's determined lines and forest green eyes.

"When I look into your eyes," I said softly, touching his cheek, "I see my sister."

He squeezed my hand. We'd talked many times before about

Eytine, and what parts of her lived on in Orlaith. At first, it made me feel like a traitor, as though I was implying Orlaith wasn't mother enough for her son. But, of course, Faelon understood, and he kept our discussions between us. He loved his mum, as he called her, but it would be senseless to pretend that he hadn't lost her, too. More than once. That thought made me draw the birds' wings mantle around his shoulders a bit tighter.

"Time," Drusilla said blandly, pulling thread through her embroidery.

My head snapped toward the chronodial, and I leapt from my seat. "Oh, hell."

If I was late, I would never, ever hear the end of it. Ever. Until the end of time. Probably literally.

I took one last look at my gown, not the unwieldy yellow dress of the May Queen but something simple and slender in burnt orange. Faelon threw my sheer shawl into my arms on my way past.

I was halfway out the door when he shouted, "Wait!" and darted after me.

Without question, I stilled. And with absolute precision, he placed Oishin's necklace on my collarbone and fastened it.

"There. That was close."

"Thanks, li'l wolf." I gave him a peck on the cheek, then fled the scene, picking up handmaidens along the way.

The maidens and I slipped through Fraochgleann and toward the hill, stealing through the night like village girls trying not to get caught visiting their sweethearts. As we approached, the hill was a white rapid of sound, the bonfire jumping high. The people were losing their sense waiting for the Sun and Moon to appear, so I sent the handmaidens up ahead of me to quell the frenzy at least a little. Although, truly, I just wanted a moment alone with him.

At the base of the hill, where shadow met moonlight and jade moths played, Hiberos awaited me.

As he turned, his horns caught the glow of the bonfire above, casting fractured light across his face. Half gold, half silver. All mine.

For a heartbeat, the world hushed. The drums, the howls, the drunken singing slipped away beneath the thunder of my heart.

"*Late*," he murmured, though his smile gave him away.

I sniffed. "Barely."

"Mm-hm. Always keeping me waiting."

"You waited a thousand years for me. What's a few minutes more?"

He stepped closer, and the moths fluttered about him as if they, too, were eager to join the celebration. "I have counted every second, my rose, my brightness."

"And I," I whispered, taking another step, "have wasted none."

"For once," he whispered back.

Our fingers met first, then our palms. The moment we touched, the valley inhaled, a great warm breath rolling through the hills. The bonfires above roared higher, answering me; the lanterns below brightened, answering him. Light and shadow and a thin silver thread twined into a braid that rose above the hilltop and slipped into the heavens.

Elemental.

"Ready?" he asked at last.

"For what?"

"For another year of being blamed for the weather," he dead-panned. "And," he added more tenderly, "for another year at my side."

I laughed, breathless. "Always, my only."

Together, we climbed the hill—goddess and god, stag and moth, May Queen and Green Man, hand in hand—toward the wild joy of this night, toward the people I loved so well, toward that which was rebuilt from blood and ruin and love.

And for the first time in all my lifetimes, it felt like coming home.

At last, the stars touched the moon.

THE END

READY FOR MORE?

After a lifetime of waiting, Eytine is convinced that the soulmate who haunts her dreams does not exist—that is, until the fae Moon King draws her into the forest. The ethereally seductive Erivon reveals that not only is Eytine his soul's mate—she is the reincarnation of his once-immortal queen.

Sign up for my newsletter and read BRIDE OF THE MOON KING, an exclusive short story, for free:

https://islaelrick.com/newsletter/

ATTRIBUTIONS

Works quoted in this novel:

- "[i carry your heart with me (i carry it in]" by E.E. Cummings
- "Táim sínte ar do thuama" ("From the Cold Sod That's O'er You," aka "I Am Stretched on Your Grave") by Anonymous, translation collected by E. Walsh
- *Finnegans Wake* by James Joyce
- "The Night Visiting Song," a traditional ballad

ABOUT THE AUTHOR

Isla Elrick lives in beautiful Central Maine with her partner and their two pitbulls. As a D&D, video game, and history nerd, folklore and fantasy have always played a huge role in her life. She firmly believes that unabashedly cheesy, profound love is made all the better when paired with the darkest despair and horror, and her love of angst and the macabre mixes in her slow-burn, Gothic-inspired romances. Plus, monsters are hot. (We guess her parents shouldn't have introduced her to The Phantom of the Opera at the tender age of eight).

www.ingramcontent.com/pod-product-compliance
Lightning Source LLC
Chambersburg PA
CBHW022346020726
47500CB00002B/152